NICHOLAS RAVEN

AND THE

WIZARDS' WEB

VOLUME 1

~ PROLOGUE AND CHAPTERS 1 - 39 ~

THOMAS J. PRESTOPNIK

Visit Thomas J. Prestopnik's website at **www.TomPresto.com**.

Cover Artist: Kelly McGrogan
Cover Layout: Ryan McGrogan
Maps: Thomas J. Prestopnik

Nicholas Raven and the Wizards' Web - Volume 1
ISBN-13: 978-1511432337
ISBN-10: 1511432330

Library of Congress Control Number: 2015905654
CreateSpace Independent Publishing Platform
North Charleston, SC

Printed in the United States of America

For every reader in search
of an exciting adventure.
I hope you find one
inside these pages.

CONTENTS

PART ONE
TROUBLE IN KANESBURY

PART TWO
THE ROAD NORTH

PART THREE
MACHINATIONS

PART FOUR
PRELUDE TO WAR

MAPS

Map One
The Lands of Laparia

Map Two
The Kingdom of Arrondale

Map Three
The County of Litchfield

Map Four
The Village of Kanesbury

Each map follows twice.
First as a two-page spread, and then on a single page.

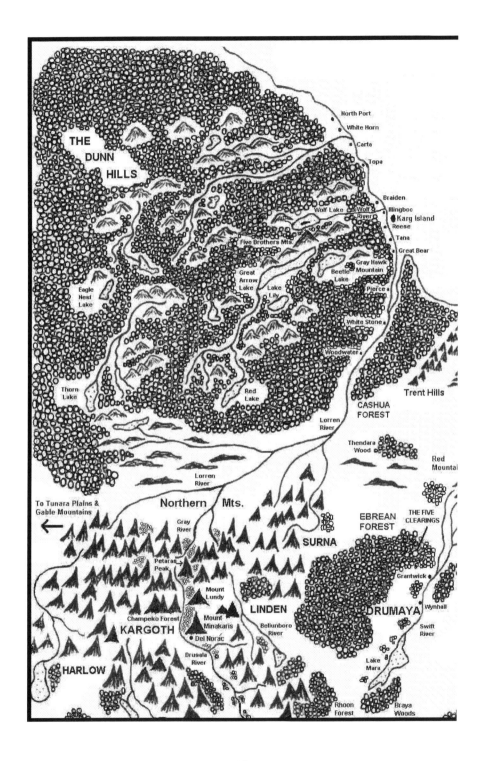

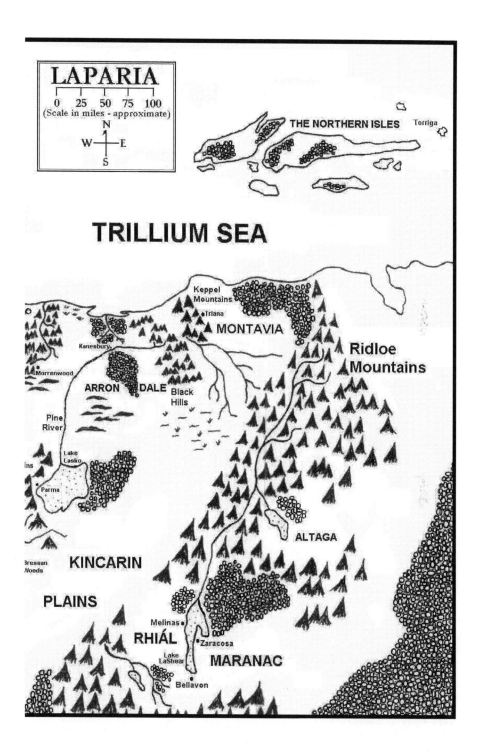

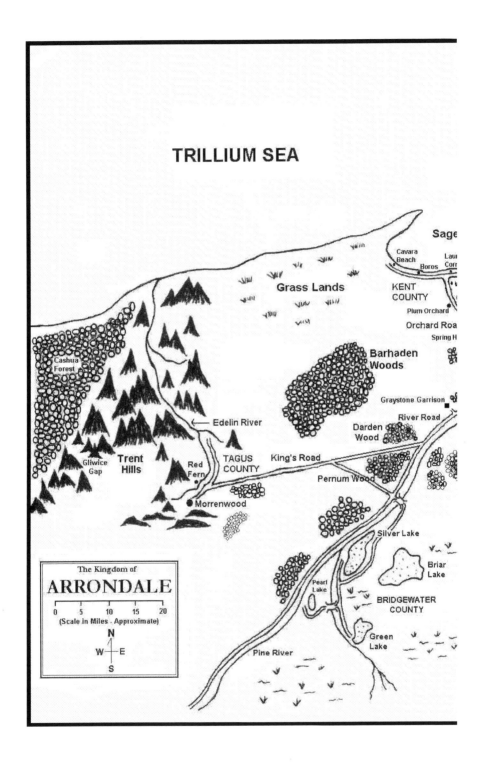

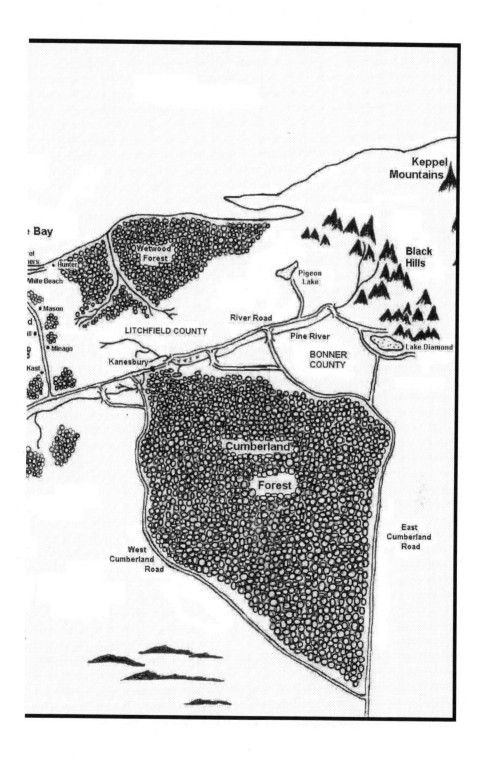

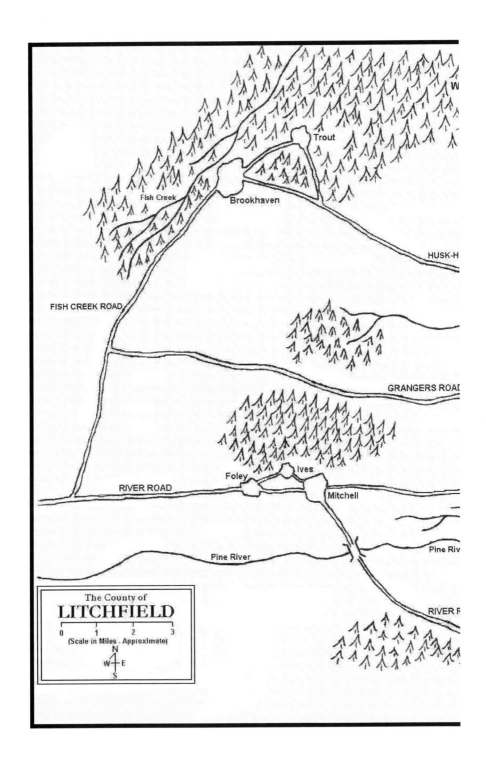

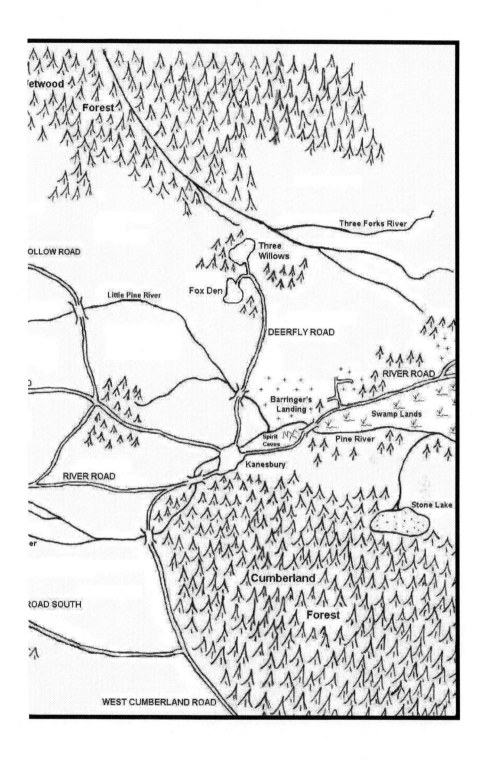

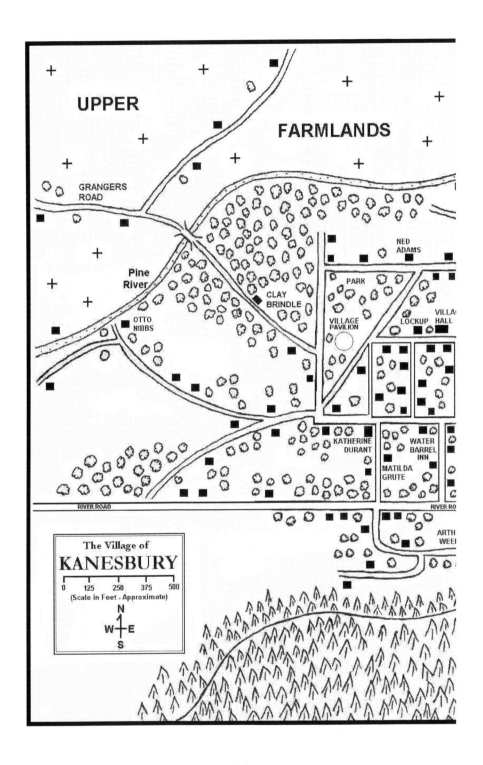

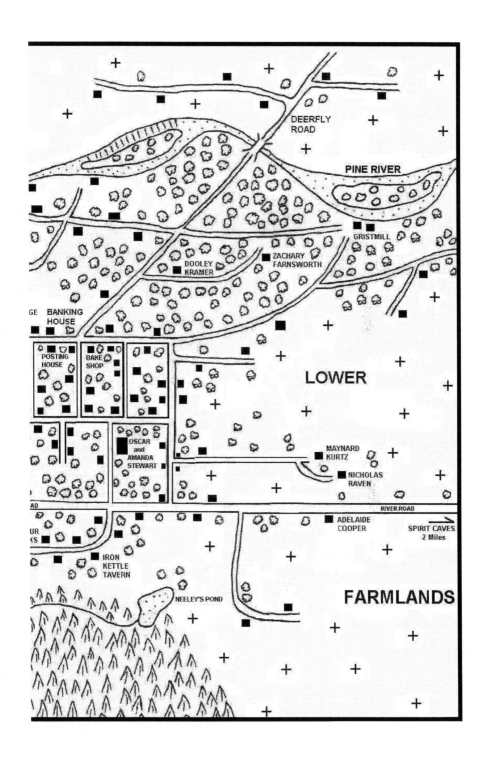

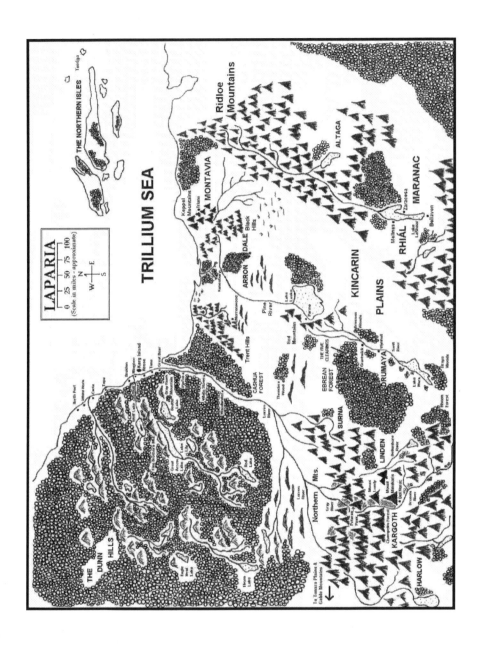

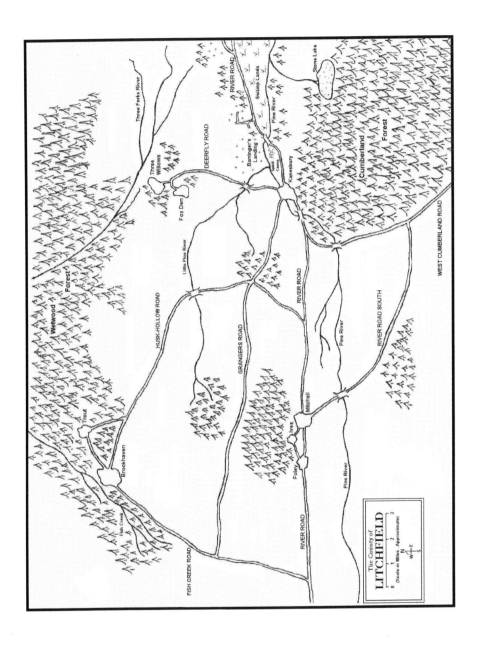

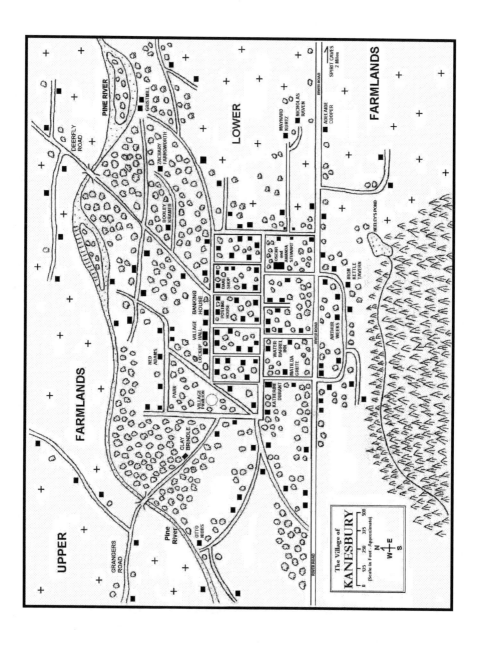

FOREWORD

This novel has been nearly forty years in the making. The first nugget of a story idea, as best I can remember, came to me in autumn 1978 at age fifteen as I walked home from high school one evening down a wooded hilly path with two schoolmates. Though no plot or themes occurred to me then, I recall stars and moonlight through the bony tree branches and the sweet scent of decaying leaves and soil. I observed grassy tracts of land just beyond the woods, imagining a secret gathering of people out there. An army perhaps? A conclave of spies? I don't remember fleshing out the scene much more at the time, but I decided that that evocative setting would be included somewhere in this epic fantasy I would one day write. I can't pinpoint a specific scene now in my completed novel that resulted from that walk through the woods above my small city in central New York State, but it ignited something in my imagination and remains my earliest recollection of starting to plan this particular story.

But even with that, *Nicholas Raven and the Wizards' Web* wouldn't have come to fruition were it not for an earlier discovery I had made in 1975, forty years ago this spring. Then, I had learned about and read J. R. R. Tolkien's *The Lord of the Rings* and *The Hobbit*, in that order, and became hooked on the books and amazed by the vast scope of their plot, characters and geography. I had read them several times through over those next few years with much enjoyment and soon after decided that I wanted to write my own epic tale someday. And while I experimented with various story forms and genres back then, including a first attempt at a fantasy novel which only made it to seven chapters, it wasn't until autumn 1978 when I began collecting the snippets of plotlines, settings and characters that would slowly form the foundation of Nicholas Raven's story.

Beginning in April 2011, I began posting monthly updates on my website about various aspects of writing this book, but here I will just highlight the stages of its creation. My first outline, handwritten in a spiral notebook, was completed in July 1988 over the preceding ten year period which covered most of my high school days and continued on a few years after graduating college. A slightly revised second draft was finished in September 1988. I was twenty-five at the time, and though happy with the outline, I knew that I wasn't ready to write the story yet. First, I wanted to hone my writing skills, convinced that if I had attempted this novel back then that I would end up with a poorly executed version. Second, I wasn't intellectually or emotionally ready to handle such a huge task, reasoning that I needed to face a few more years of life's rigors to mature and get in the proper frame of mind. In retrospect, it was a wise decision.

Though the story was always in my thoughts as I wrote other books, it wasn't until almost eleven years later that I finally felt ready to tackle this project so dear to my heart. I began writing Chapter 1 in June 1999 but quickly moved away from the keyboard to draw four maps for the story, knowing I would need them to properly maneuver my way around the lands I had created. I also took a little time to again revise my outline between June 1999 and February 2000. It wasn't until March 2000 that I fully jumped back into the writing process, and over the next eight years I had completed the prologue and the first twenty chapters (Parts One and Two), finishing that chunk of the book in late January 2008. It was a very slow writing pace, however, because during that time I also revised and self-published two previously written children's novels and then wrote two more. This was my Endora trilogy fantasy series (*The Timedoor*, *The Sword and the Crown* and *The Saving Light*) and *Gabriel's Journey*.

Guessing that I'd be old and decrepit by the time I finished the book if I continued at this pace, I decided that I would devote 2009, 2010 and part of 2011 entirely to its completion, figuring that it would be more than enough time to reach the end of the first draft. But for the rest of 2008, I promised myself that I would first write my Christmas novella, *A Christmas Castle*, an idea I had begun planning in January 2000 and was eager to start. And so I did. It wasn't until the end of January 2009, after once more revising parts of my outline, that I again continued writing *Nicholas Raven and the Wizards' Web*, eager to begin Chapter 21 after a one year respite.

I remember sitting down at my desk early on that gray, late January morning, ready to write Chapter 21, the first chapter in Part Three of the book. At that time, the outline was divided into eighty chapters, so there were sixty more to complete, a mountainous task, to say the least. Looking at the project as a whole, a small part of me briefly wondered how I could ever reach the end. So I just dived into it, typing one word at a time, completing one sentence at a time and eventually piling one paragraph on top of another. And as one month dissolved into the next and each chapter fell into place, a little over two years passed by. Spring 2011 had finally arrived, the time I had first estimated when the book would be completed. But I was nowhere near finished with it, reaching only to the end of Part Eight.

The total chapter count had now passed eighty and would continually change and eventually reach 120 after the last draft of the outline was completed and other, longer chapters were split into two (and in one instance, split into three) for a better story presentation. From early May to mid September of 2011, I wrote what were then Chapters 79 through 85, finishing another section, Part Nine. My next task, writing Part Ten, proved to be the most challenging and grueling part of completing this novel.

At the time, Part Ten comprised eight chapters (86 though 93), a section which brought most of my characters and plotlines to a conclusion before things were to be wrapped up in Part Eleven. But what I had outlined on paper, which had so far survived several revisions, was far different from what I would eventually write over the following year. My original version of the story's conclusion, imagined over thirty years ago, was not going to make the cut. So I tinkered with the outline once again–big time.

The fourth draft of my outline is filled with tiny, handwritten paragraphs to replace much of what I wrote for Part Ten (which itself was eventually split into Parts Ten and Eleven). My notes from decades ago presented a more perfunctory ending to the main story and didn't incorporate the newer themes I had developed. Also, now that my geography was established, I had to make a few changes to get some of my characters to where they were supposed to be in a logical way. This proved to be a good thing as I was able to eliminate one unnecessarily complicated chapter when I reworked the story, but other, better scenes were also introduced.

So September 2011 through September 2012, including about another month afterward for editing, was both writing heaven and hell for me–creatively stimulating when the new and improved ideas fell into place, yet a mentally agonizing process at times to build the pathway to those new ideas. Nearly every day I was imagining my maps and where my characters were going and what they needed to do, revising ideas along the way and taking a few unexpected turns. It was an exhausting year of writing, yet rewarding as well since I believe the time and pains I had taken to improve the story has paid off. On my website posts (Update #18 - September 25, 2012), I wrote that Part Ten of this book turned out to be 498 pages long before my first edit of this section, took a year and a week to write, and contained five more chapters than originally planned. I still get worn out thinking about that year of writing but am very happy with the result. I hope that whoever reads this book will have an enjoyable and memorable experience as well.

Finally, I would like to thank a few people who helped me as I wrote and prepared this book for publication. To my sister-in-law, Jan, who read the first edited draft while continually sending me notes regarding plot, characters, grammar and the like over many months of reading, offering far more than a general overview of the book for which I had asked; to my nephew, Nathan, for reading the same draft and sending me a detailed critique and a list of helpful suggestions; to my niece, Kelly, for drawing many draft cover sketches and the lovely web and moon artwork for each volume and for refining my original ideas; to my nephew, Ryan, for formatting all three cover layouts, finding the perfect typeface to go along with the story and creating the beautiful background colors and cover effects; to my mom, for offering words of encouragement as we talked about the book from time to time over coffee at her kitchen table, and to my dad, who I believe was with us there in spirit; to Professor J. R. R. Tolkien, whose words and wonderful stories inspired this writer forty years ago; to family members and friends who have kindly inquired about the progress of this book over these many years; and to God above for giving me the ability, patience and perseverance to fulfill this lifelong dream. My unending and heartfelt thanks to all.

Thomas J. Prestopnik
June 6, 2015

NICHOLAS RAVEN

AND THE

WIZARDS' WEB

VOLUME 1

~ PROLOGUE AND CHAPTERS 1 - 39 ~

PROLOGUE

Fifty years ago...

They'll forever regret the day I return.

The wizard Vellan pulled the wolf skin cloak tightly about his shoulders as he trudged through the desolate brush lands. Bitter winds of New Autumn chilled him to the bone despite the blinding sunlight that stabbed through breaks in the ashen clouds. The Gable Mountain Range lay three days behind in the west. Vellan prided himself that he hadn't once glanced back in the direction where his foolish and faithless companions still resided. Yet his black thoughts contemplated a day far in the future when he would again stare them down from the sacred hilltop of Ulán with vengeance and crushing might at his side. A day he would proudly show his fellow wizards what they could have achieved had they abandoned their fear, timidity and lack of vision and stood by his side. A day he would finally destroy them.

In time. All in good time.

Vellan clutched an oak staff, pounding it on the hard grassy ground with each step. A clear crystal globe the size of his fist was mounted on top, reflecting the blood red color of falling leaves. The wizard's staff was his most prized possession, something he had owned for just over half of his twenty-eight years. How joyful he had been to receive it on his thirteenth birthday, indicating that he was accepted into the wizards' order to begin his training. He had proudly used the staff ever since during his many travels abroad. So let the others disagree with his views now, expelling him from their order and driving him out of the valley. What did *they* know? But they would never get his staff back. Vellan had refused to turn it over when they banished him. And though his training in the magic arts was still not finished, he knew he could teach himself what little remained. He didn't need further instruction from the other wizards, convinced he was well beyond their skills and parochial mindset. Why, he could teach *them*! And he vowed to one day take the magic arts to such lofty levels that they could never imagine.

Blind fools! They have the world at their hands yet refuse to grasp it.

Vellan sighed wearily, caressing his whiskered face. He had grown tired of revisiting the arguments which had churned endlessly in his mind these last three days. He walked faster, his heavy cloak swaying behind him, his long black hair blowing in the breeze. Though he had wandered many miles from home in a valley tucked among the Gable Mountains where his fellow wizards resided, he only now approached the true end of their realm. The Mang River snaking just ahead through the brush lands marked the eastern border of the lands where he had spent nearly his entire life.

He squatted down at the water's edge and took a cold drink. The briskly flowing river narrowed and was less deep a few miles to the north. He would hike a little longer and cross at that point where he would bid a final goodbye to his old life with each step across the water. Beyond the Mang River were the Tunara Plains, stretches of barren land he must also cross before reaching Laparia, his ultimate destination. Somewhere in that populated region he would seek shelter and privacy while pondering what to do with his life. But where to ultimately settle? Vellan already had an idea.

The young wizard took one more drink, refilled his water skin, and then moved on. The few miles hike north along the river's edge proved swift and uneventful. He found a spot to cross near a straggly grove of birch trees as the sun sank low in the west and the clouds gradually parted. A haunting orange glow painted the surrounding rocks and grassy shore. He draped the bottom of his cloak over his left arm and stepped one foot into the shallow river. The dirt washed off his boot and muddied the water. When he took his next step, his oak staff sliced through the water and hit the sandy river bottom. Vellan now stood completely outside the wizards' realm.

He shuddered as he saw it happen—a final insult from the other wizards. The clear crystal globe on his oak staff slowly dulled in color, turning ashen gray and then totally black. Vellan's dark eyes widened in horror as his heart filled with rage. He ran shouting across the river, the cold water splashing about him like liquid fire. He raced up the opposite shore, twirling about and stumbling as if in a mad delirium, kicking stones and thrashing at the dry stalks of grass.

"No! No! They can't do this to me!"

Vellan raised his staff with both hands and cried out to the skies, his face twisted in agony. He grabbed the bottom of the staff and lurched toward a nearby boulder half buried in the ground. He smashed the top of the staff against the rock with all his might, shattering the blackened crystal and splintering the upper portion of the wood. He heaved the staff to the ground as he bounded about in rage for several more moments until finally collapsing to his knees near the rock. The young wizard buried his face in his quivering hands, his eyes dry and stinging, and every breath a painful chore.

Vellan remained there unmoving for nearly an hour, feeling a kinship to the rock and soil until the sun dipped below the western horizon and the first few stars speckled the darkening skies in the east. And though the breezes had calmed, the cold night air eventually forced him to his feet. It was time to move on. His numbed mind and heart could sort through the horrid details later. He felt weak as he wrapped his wolf skin cloak tightly about him. With mixed feelings, he retrieved the remains of his staff and continued his lonely walk eastward, his banishment and humiliation now complete.

PART ONE
TROUBLE IN KANESBURY

CHAPTER 1

Plans Made

Nicholas Raven walked briskly along the village streets of Kanesbury, convinced he had at last discovered the answer to his problem. Now he couldn't wait to tell the world.

The sweet smell of wood smoke peppered the crisp autumn air as a mischievous breeze sent leaves swishing across the hard dirt road. He lifted his jacket collar up over the back of his neck, blowing a few puffs of air into his hands to warm them. He had been craving some adventure and purpose in his life and now knew where to find it, yet he wondered how Maynard and Adelaide would take the news. But this was something he needed to do. All of his nineteen years had been spent in Kanesbury, the last few of them helping out on Maynard Kurtz's farm and working as a bookkeeper at the local gristmill. Now it was time to get out, he decided, or else he would surely die of boredom.

Kanesbury, a tiny community in the kingdom of Arrondale, was nestled on the northern tip of the Cumberland Forest. Morning sunlight dappled the ground as it sliced through clusters of red and orange leaves clinging precariously to the multitude of trees protectively lining its streets. As Nicholas neared the bake shop, two men with weather-beaten faces were digging a hole in front of the establishment. The scent of fresh bread and pastries wafted through the air. He stopped to watch, raking his fingers through a head of light brown hair. A load of long wooden posts rested on the back of a horse-drawn cart. Preparations were underway for the Harvest Festival in five days.

"We still got half the village to outfit with these posts," Arlo Brewer told Nicholas. "Ask your boss for the day off so you can help us," he joked, one thumb wrapped around his suspenders. "You know how fussy Mayor Nibbs is about his festival torches. Wants 'em just right for the celebration."

"You men are doing a fine job, as usual. I'm just here for a slice of pumpkin bread on my way to work," Nicholas said, examining the posts. "They look taller this year."

"Mayor Nibbs ordered the torches half an arm's length longer," the other man replied, puffing on a pipe. "Drew Chance caught his straw hat on fire as he walked by one last year, remember? But he is a tall chap." Zeb Walker spat into the hole. "Only a drunken stilt-walker will be in danger this year," he added, bursting out laughing.

Nicholas looked forward to the Harvest Festival, the annual three-day holiday held throughout the village. Most communities observed the tradition during the month of New Autumn. Villages throughout Arrondale set aside the first three days of the second full week to revel day and night. He planned to meet with friends at the Water Barrel Inn that first evening to share a mug of ale and kick off the festivities. He hoped Katherine Durant might accompany him to the village dance on the final night if he could first work up the courage to invite her.

During those three days, Kanesbury would be inundated with traveling craftsmen and acrobats, soothsayers and conjurers, all looking for a free meal or a few tossed coins for their efforts. The locals loved the entertainment as visitors would wander through the evening streets lit by the giant torches. Crowds of wide-eyed children and chattering adults would play games of chance and gobble down outdoor cooking at its finest. For three autumn evenings the village would appear magical under the stars, a perfect place to live. Nicholas was saddened, realizing that he would soon be leaving it behind.

He said nothing of his plans to Ned Adams, his employer, while working at his desk that morning. Nicholas performed the bookkeeping for Ned at the stone gristmill perched upon the banks of the Pine River. With the last flour shipments of the season being readied for delivery to other parts of the kingdom, Ned's mind was juggling enough details at the moment. Nicholas' news could wait for a less hectic moment. Besides, he thought it best that Maynard, who was like a father to him, should learn of his plans first. The young man decided to tell him sometime after dinner, unsure how he would receive the news.

Maynard Kurtz wandered out of the sagging barn beside his house later that evening. The horses were secure for the night. He glanced up at a rich blue sky as the first stars of twilight blinked on. The setting sun painted streaks of purple and orange across the western horizon. Neither the Bear Moon nor the Fox Moon was out tonight.

As he walked under a towering oak near the corner of his house, Nicholas sauntered across the grass behind him. "I see you've mended that break in the pasture fence. I had planned to fix it tomorrow."

Maynard turned around. "Hello, Nicholas. So Ned finally let you out to enjoy some fresh air?" Nicholas resided in a small cottage in back of Maynard's house as a portion of his salary for working part-time on the farm. "I had time to repair the fence this morning. How're things at the mill?"

"Busy as usual readying the final shipments before winter. Ned's bouncing around like a fish out of water."

Maynard grinned as he signaled for Nicholas to follow him to the front porch. Maynard sat his large frame down on the top step, pushing his long silvery-black hair behind his shoulders. He was fifty-four, widowed, and the respected head of Kanesbury's five-member village council. Nicholas stood on the ground adjacent to the steps, leaning an arm on the railing. His green eyes darted anxiously about.

"I'm simmering some stew over the fire. Join me for supper, Nicholas?"

"Thanks, Maynard. I will." He rolled his boot over a fallen acorn, knowing it wouldn't be easy breaking his news. A part of him felt selfish for wanting to leave the farm, especially after all that Maynard had done for him. Maynard Kurtz was more than just an employer–he was a friend. And on crisp autumn nights like this, when crickets were alive in the fields and dusky twilight framed the trees and houses as silhouettes against a blazing horizon, Nicholas couldn't envision a better place to live.

"You've been awfully quiet these last few–"

"Maynard, there's something I need to tell you," Nicholas said at the same time.

Maynard smiled, leaning back on the steps and stretching his legs. "You first. I sensed you've had something on your mind lately."

Nicholas nodded and sat on the bottom step, staring guiltily at the ground. "I've been growing restless here, Maynard, I guess. Not just on the farm though. Kanesbury in general. Thinking maybe I should– Well, just thinking that..." He cleared his throat.

"Thinking that life's passing you by while you're cooped up like a chicken in this little village?" Maynard raised an eyebrow as Nicholas looked up at him.

"Something like that. How'd you know?"

"Understandable for a man your age. You feel that the world is waiting for you to conquer it. Yet here you are at nineteen, helping me harvest my fields and keeping track of every sack of flour Ned Adams has stored inside his warehouse." Maynard sat up and rested his hands on his knees. "Doesn't feel fair at your age."

"I want to make something of my life, Maynard, not that I don't appreciate living here. I understand that the jobs both you and Ned do are important," he added, a hint of an apology in his voice.

"You needn't justify your feelings to me, Nicholas. I was your age once. I had my own dreams." Maynard glanced up at the starry sky. "Some came true, others didn't. I even invented new dreams along the way. Marrying Tessa was the best one of all."

"So you didn't mind staying here when you were my age?"

"Sure I did–at times. What boy doesn't dream about going off on an exciting journey? Seeing strange new places or being a hero. But most men tend to settle down once the right woman comes along and the years go by. They make the best of a new life together. Few men are destined to be world travelers, Nicholas. Or heroes."

"I'm not looking to be a hero. I was only hoping for a bit of adventure. Maybe just a little excitement until I do settle down."

Maynard chuckled understandingly. "I know. So tell me what you have in mind. More schooling in one of the larger cities? Maybe start your own business? That might impress Katherine Durant."

Nicholas looked up. "*What*?"

"I've seen how you look at her in the village." Maynard grinned. "And on more than one occasion lately you've found an excuse to go to the Stewarts' household in hopes that she might be working there, or so I've heard."

"Don't believe everything you hear," he replied with a guilty smile, quickly changing the subject. "But more book learning isn't exactly my plan, or starting a business either." Nicholas stood and climbed a few steps closer to Maynard, speaking softly as if revealing a long-held secret. "I was thinking about traveling to Morrenwood to join up with the King's Guard. What do you think?"

"*Hmmm*," he said, stroking his chin. "I didn't expect that answer." He looked directly at Nicholas. "That would surely impress Katherine."

"Be serious!" He playfully punched Maynard in the arm. "What do you think? Your opinion means a lot to me."

"Well, I appreciate that you value my musings so much," he replied. "And though I could dispense enough advice to fill up Neeley's Pond, the final decision is yours alone. What you think deep inside your heart is what you'll ultimately do."

"A hint of an opinion from you would be nice though."

Maynard nodded. "What position do you see yourself holding in King Justin's army? A guard in the Blue Citadel? Maybe work yourself up to an advisory post? Or do you just want to be a grunt soldier going out on maneuvers throughout Arrondale?"

"To be honest, I'm not sure," Nicholas admitted. "I remember when the King's soldiers passed through two months ago to register new recruits. Five more had signed on. I knew two of them. When they all marched off for Morrenwood three weeks later, I felt they were doing something special. Made my life here seem kind of dull."

"They might wish they were back here again if Arrondale ever gets involved in the war down south. You've heard the talk."

"Who hasn't?"

"War isn't a glamorous adventure, Nicholas, though it may appear so to a pair of impressionable eyes far away from the fighting."

Nicholas walked on the porch and sat on the edge of a railing. "I'm not eager to fight in a war I don't know much about. But there must be other jobs a soldier is trained for. There must be something else out there in the world for me!"

"I'm sure there is." Maynard stood and stretched an ache out of his shoulder. "And we'll discuss it over a bowl of stew. Now let's go inside before my dinner boils away."

Nicholas nodded and followed him inside, closing the front door to keep out the chilly night air.

Adelaide Cooper joined in the debate two nights later while seated around the dinner table in Maynard's kitchen. Adelaide lived directly across River Road from his farm and felt it was her duty to keep an eye on Maynard and Nicholas in a motherly sort of way, though neither really minded her well-intentioned intrusions on most occasions.

"Bad times are on their way," Adelaide said between sips from a mug of hot spiced cider. "I can feel it in my bones." She patted Nicholas' arm uneasily, capturing his gaze with her steel blue eyes. Adelaide was several years older than Maynard, but her short, thin frame topped with curls of gray belied the fiery spirit inside her. "What makes you want to traipse about the countryside all the way to the capital? Doesn't the King have enough soldiers? And during autumn besides? I'm frozen to my toes thinking about it!"

Nicholas took her hand and gently kissed it. "You're worrying yourself to pieces, Adelaide. I haven't even packed my traveling gear yet."

"Then you've chosen a day to leave?"

"Not yet, though definitely sometime before winter if I don't change my mind. I still have to finish my duties at the gristmill and here on the farm," he said.

Adelaide pleaded with Maynard to talk some sense into the boy. "In case you haven't heard, there's a war down south. What if you join the King's Guard and then get tangled up in all that fighting and killing?" The war between the kingdoms of Rhiál and Maranac in the southeast corner of Laparia had been raging for several months. "Joining the army now is just asking for trouble, Nicholas. Why do you think King Justin has been raising recruits? He plans to step his toe into that conflict!"

Maynard dished out another helping of fried potatoes, onions and mushrooms onto his plate before refilling his mug with cold water from a wooden pitcher. "I went through those same arguments with Nicholas over the last two days, Adelaide. But to be honest with you, a small part of me envies him."

"Now don't you get any silly notions into your head, Maynard Kurtz. One daydreaming fool at this table is enough." Adelaide glanced at Nicholas. "Don't take that too personally, dear. I just don't think you're thinking with a clear head. With any luck it'll pass by morning."

Adelaide attacked the food on her plate as Maynard and Nicholas exchanged amused glances. Low candles in the center of the table cast a warm glow on their features. Nicholas observed the tightness in Adelaide's face, distressed to see her worry. He thought it best to change the subject.

"I'll grab a few pieces of wood outside," he said, standing up. "The fire's getting low and the pile by the hearth is almost gone."

"Okay," Maynard said, watching him walk out the front door into the blackness of night. He looked up at Adelaide over a forkful of greens. Her eyes slowly met his as shadows flickered on the walls. "He's a young man now, Adelaide."

"I know."

"He's got to follow his own path in life."

"I know that too, Maynard. But why such a dangerous path?" She sighed as she set her fork on the pine table top. "I'm not his mother, but I worry about him so. After the way his father was killed, I... Well, I just don't want the same thing happening to Nicholas. Especially in some far off war."

Maynard gently touched her hand. "I understand, Adelaide. I do. Nicholas always did have a restless nature about him. Maybe not knowing his father had something to do with it."

"Then I suppose it isn't fair to blame him if he really wants to leave Kanesbury," she said with a sigh. "But I don't have to like it!"

An hour later, Nicholas walked Adelaide down the porch steps as Maynard bid them goodnight and closed his door. Crickets chirped sluggishly in the fields under the cold stars. Nicholas carried an oil lamp to guide their way across the grass, its circle of yellow light swaying back and forth along the ground as they approached his cottage in back of the house. Adelaide took her oil lamp back.

"Sure you don't want me to walk you to your front gate, Adelaide?" he asked. "It's especially dark tonight."

"Nonsense. I may be an old woman, but I'm still an able one." She gently squeezed his arm. "Now go get some sleep and I'll see you soon."

"Goodnight," Nicholas said. He watched her walk through a patch of scraggly grass toward River Road before heading inside.

Adelaide crossed the dirt road and swung open a low wooden gate in front of her house. She walked past a tall hedge before climbing up the front porch steps. A cool breeze whistled over the tops of the dried grass stalks dotting the lonely countryside. She hung the oil lamp on a small hook and sat down on a rocking chair and stared into the inky darkness. With thoughts of Nicholas swimming in her head, she wondered if sleep would find her tonight. She folded her arms and rocked back and forth and soon nodded off.

Over an hour later, Adelaide awakened with a start when she heard a noise, or thought she did–a whisper of voices across the road near the storage shed behind Nicholas' cottage. She stood and extinguished the oil lamp, straining her eyes and ears into the night though hearing nothing but the rustle of hedge leaves. She chided herself for imagining things, then grabbed the cooling lamp from its hook and went inside.

Nicholas raced to the home of Oscar and Amanda Stewart after work the next evening, guessing that Katherine Durant would be there. He knew that if he didn't ask her to the dance soon, he might be too late, if he wasn't already. He cut across their side lawn and scurried through a grove of white birch trees, noting through the branches the crescent Fox Moon hanging low in the west. The kitchen windows in back of the stone estate glowed with warm yellow light. People dressed in white cooking smocks were visible through the panes, bustling about the kitchen preparing for an annual party the Stewarts held on the first night of the Harvest Festival.

Nicholas noted that the kitchen door had been left ajar to let some of the heat escape. He edged up close and peeked inside.

Clamoring voices competed with the clattering of kettles and the chopping of knives on butcher blocks. Bundles of pungent herbs hung from nails in the rafters. A blazing pyramid of oak wood crackled in a stone fireplace against the far wall. Katherine Durant stood at one of the island counters in the middle of the room kneading bread dough, her long brown hair hidden underneath a smock. She smiled upon seeing Nicholas and beckoned him to step inside, wiping away a dab of flour on her cheek. Katherine, almost two years younger than Nicholas, was employed part-time on the house staff for Amanda Stewart and was also the niece of Mayor Otto Nibbs.

"You're two days early for the party, Nicholas. Or are you here to lend a hand?" she playfully asked. "I'm not sure if Oscar is home at the moment, but I can ask someone to check."

"Not necessary," he replied. "I'm not here on mill business. And I think my kitchen services would be more hindrance than help if I lent a hand, Katherine. I'll fix you dinner sometime and prove it," he said with a grin. "What are you making?"

"Apple-walnut bread. Mrs. Stewart wants ten loaves baked for the party. That's in addition to the ten loaves of blackberry-carrot bread that I'll bake tomorrow. She does like to feed her guests."

Even while covered in flour in a steamy kitchen, and up to her wrists in bread dough, Nicholas thought Katherine looked as pretty as ever. They had been acquaintances for a time as Nicholas had talked to her here on occasion when delivering paperwork from the gristmill on Ned Adams' behalf.

"So what brings you here tonight?" Katherine asked as she dumped out some freshly diced apples and chopped walnuts from a wooden bowl and worked them into the bread dough with her slender fingers. She was one of several people whom the Stewarts employed, though she felt less like a servant and more of a family member since her mother and Amanda Stewart were close friends.

Nicholas' heart beat rapidly as he worked up his nerve. "Well, I was wondering if you might be—"

"Nicholas Raven!" A stern voice shot across the room like a crack of thunder. Katherine and Nicholas turned to see Amanda Stewart step into the kitchen through the archway of an adjoining hall. The tall, sturdy woman looked at Nicholas with a questioning eye. "You're not distracting my prize bread baker, are you?"

"I wouldn't want to be accused of that, Mrs. Stewart," Nicholas said with a hint of mirth.

"Good. And as long as you're here, I wish to direct you and your two strong arms downstairs. Lewis needs assistance carrying some blocks of ice up from the cellar. The ice boxes in the pantry need replenishing. The bottoms are all cleaned out, ready to fill."

"I'll be happy to help, ma'am."

"Thank you." Amanda offered a faint smile before raising the wick in an oil lamp attached to the wall near the archway. She then proceeded to inspect the work of her staff.

Nicholas glanced at Katherine, taking a deep breath to steady his nerves. "Say, before I'm banished to the ice cellar, I was just wondering if you had plans to, uh…" He stared briefly at the floor and looked up. "Would you be interested in going to the pavilion dance with me on the last night of the Festival? That is, unless Lewis or somebody else has already invited you."

"He hasn't–yet. And that would be wonderful," she replied. "I'd love to go!"

Nicholas grinned, feeling more at ease. "That was easy. I think we'll have a good time there."

Katherine shaped the bread dough into a neatly rounded pile before slicing it into four equal parts to form into loaves. She stopped working and looked up at Nicholas with her rich brown eyes. "I do want to go with you, though I'm ashamed to say that I've been avoiding Lewis of late. I think he wanted to ask me." Lewis Ames was a gangly youth of seventeen, sporting a mop of black hair in a perpetually tangled mess. Katherine thought his clothes always looked ill-fitting on his lanky frame. "I believe he has a terrible crush on me, Nicholas, but I don't want to break his heart."

"That's sweet of you, Katherine, but I don't think a *no* from you will crush him," he said, not quite believing his own words.

"Well, now that I have plans, I can stop avoiding him," she said. "In the meantime, I've heard some news concerning you, Nicholas. Word is about the streets that you're planning to join up with the King's Guard in Morrenwood."

"How'd you find out already?"

"You didn't expect to keep a secret in this village, did you?"

"I suppose not, but I did plan to let others know in time."

"Well, when you take me to the dance, I'll expect a full account of your plans." Katherine tapped a finger to his chest. "I want to hear what kind of hot water you plan to get yourself into."

Amanda again called to Nicholas from near the fireplace. "When I asked you to assist Lewis, Mr. Raven, I did mean today." She gently touched her silvery hair. "Before all my food spoils in this wilting heat, if you would."

"I'm on my way, Mrs. Stewart." He smiled at Katherine and whispered to her. "I'll explain everything later. I promise."

"You'd better," she said as Nicholas hurried into the pantry and down the cellar steps.

Nicholas left Amanda Stewart's home through the front door half an hour later. Two oil burning lampposts marking the entrance to the estate blazed warmly in the waning light. He made his way down the tree-lined street to River Road. Dusky twilight painted objects in gray shades as a thin breeze rustled leaves on the trees. Nicholas barely recognized the figure walking up the road toward him until they were only steps apart.

"Well if it isn't Ned Adams' right-hand man! What is our boss gonna do without you keeping the books for him all neat and proper?" Dooley Kramer offered a crooked smile, letting a white puff of breath escape that smelled distinctly of ale.

"Just coming back from the Iron Kettle, Dooley?"

"Getting an early start on celebrating the Festival, Nicholas." Dooley raised a bony index finger. "Just downed a quick one, is all."

Dooley Kramer worked as a laborer in the gristmill and was a dozen years older than Nicholas. His weathered coat smelled of pipe smoke and his eyes were fixed dark and glassy in his thin, triangular head. Uncombed dirty blond hair grew down to his shoulders, and two day's growth of beard covered his face.

"I just learned at the Iron Kettle that you're leaving these parts, Nicholas. Is that true news I'm hearing?"

"If your friends at the tavern are saying so, then it must be," he replied with a roll of his eyes. "Have they picked out my replacement at the mill?"

Dooley slapped him good-naturedly on the arm. "Those boys aren't that sharp! But who knows, maybe Ned will see it in his heart to promote *me* to bookkeeper. I'm good at figuring numbers in addition to all the grub work he pays me for."

"That'd be a step up for sure," Nicholas said, knowing very well that Dooley would be the last person chosen to replace him.

"It would be a step up for a fellow like me. But I know my place in the world, so no sense in getting my hopes up." Dooley clasped his hands on Nicholas's shoulders and shook him. "*Ahh!* But you are going places, boy! Off to fight with the King's soldiers. Good for you!" He fumbled with Nicholas's collar in an attempt to straighten it, then grabbed onto the ends of his open jacket. He wrapped a finger around one of Nicholas' middle buttons and pulled the material taut. "Make sure to always look your best when those higher-ups inspect you. Yes, sir, that's some good advice. Say, exactly when are you leaving Kanesbury?"

"Not right away," Nicholas said, taking a step back, confident that Dooley had had more than one mug of ale at the Iron Kettle.

"We'll sure miss you when the time comes."

"I appreciate that. But I do have to get going, Dooley. There's still work to be done at home. Good talking to you."

"Understood." Dooley scratched his head and offered a handshake. "See you on the job in the morning then, Nicholas."

"Bright and early," he said with an uneasy smile. "Goodnight, Dooley."

"And goodnight to you, sir!" he replied as Nicholas continued walking down the road into the gloomy twilight. Dooley Kramer kept a watchful eye on him until Nicholas turned left around the corner and disappeared onto River Road.

Dooley looked around, alone on the silent street. The light from the lampposts on the Stewarts' property glowed warmly in the distance through the wavering tree branches. He rubbed his chin and squatted down, running his hand over the cold dirt ground. He grunted with satisfaction when his fingers touched a small round object, grasping it instantly like a spider catching a fly. He stood and examined the button he had secretly pulled off of Nicholas's jacket, grinning as he pocketed his catch.

Adelaide sat on her front porch in the evening shadows as Nicholas walked by a short time later. She rocked in her chair with a heavy shawl draped over her shoulders, observing the starry sky. Nicholas walked through her front gate and stood at the bottom step.

"Maynard is right," she said matter-of-factly. "You have to find your own life, no matter how much it upsets this old lady."

Nicholas smiled. "You're not that old, Adelaide."

"You are sweet." She slowly got to her feet. "Have to check on my kettle of soup. Had supper yet?"

"I had a bite when I visited Katherine at the Stewarts' home. Not hungry now."

"Well I am, so I'll politely excuse myself, Nicholas. Say hello to Maynard for me. I'm sure I'll see you both during the Festival."

"No doubt. Good night, Adelaide," he said as he passed through the gate.

"Good night, dear," she replied, retreating indoors to eat a supper of bread and soup by the light of a single candle. In spite of her earlier words, she still was deeply troubled that Nicholas planned to leave the village, possibly walking into unimaginable peril. Several hours later in the deep of night, Adelaide once again sat in her rocking chair on the front porch to clear her troubled mind. A lazy chorus of crickets played in the fields and a haunting breeze glided down the road, disturbing the dried grass and weeds.

She again heard voices somewhere in the blackness of the field across the road. She sat up and remained still, noting distinct whispers and a flicker of light near the shed behind Nicholas' cottage. She wondered if Nicholas or Maynard might be out, but the hour was so late. And since the farmhouse and the cottage windows were as black as pitch, she assumed both men were probably asleep by now. When Adelaide noticed the flicker of light a second time, she hurried inside to light an oil lamp, threw on a coat and went back outdoors, walking across River Road into the grass.

As she neared the shed, Adelaide could distinguish two separate voices within. Yellow light outlined the door frame of the low windowless building. Adelaide cautiously stepped closer to the entrance, pausing every few seconds to listen. There was movement inside, but little talking now. She couldn't stand the suspense any longer and placed a hand on the knob, swinging the door open.

Shadows leaped on the walls as she held up the lamp in the cramped, dimly lit room. A man setting down a sack of flour spun around and faced Adelaide, his eyes wide like saucers.

"Dooley Kramer!" she whispered. "What are you doing here?" An oil lamp rested on the ground near his feet.

"Well, I'm..." He swallowed hard and looked to one corner of the shed.

Adelaide glanced in that direction as well, the lamp casting a sickly glow over a few bales of hay. Standing there was a tall man in a long leather coat, his stern face glaring at Dooley.

"Is that you, Zachary Farnsworth?" She shook her head. "I don't understand. Why are you both here? I'd better wake Nicholas."

"Don't do that!" Farnsworth warned in a gruff whisper.

Adelaide took a step backward when she caught a glimpse of a steel blade that he slowly removed from his coat pocket. *"Oh dear..."* She saw Dooley glance at Farnsworth for silent advice, watching as both their faces tightened in sinister resolve. She accidentally dropped her oil lamp as she ran out of the shed and across the black grassy field toward her house, too terrified to scream. The pounding in her head drowned out the sound of heavy footfalls swiftly closing in.

CHAPTER 2

A Trap is Sprung

The Harvest Festival began two days later. Throughout the morning and early afternoon, people milled about in the streets and yards of Kanesbury, attending small parties and luncheons to kick off the three-day event. Residents from farms and small communities outside the village slowly trickled in during the day. By mid-afternoon, wandering musicians, magicians and acrobats had arrived to display their talents. Colorfully costumed stilt-walkers strolled through the streets like nimble giants pulled out of some fantastic dream. Musicians deftly played their fiddles, flutes and hand drums on street corners and under the park pavilion, drawing those who gathered to watch and listen into spontaneous dance. And up and down the busiest streets, magicians made stones and fruit and even a cawing crow disappear before applauding onlookers.

As twilight settled in under clear, crisp skies, one by one the oil lampposts in town were lit, casting a warm flickering glow over smiling faces and bony tree branches. But only when the festival torches planted around the village had been ignited did the celebration officially begin. Cheers and hollers echoed in the autumn air as the torches cast off colorful light and engulfing warmth, assuring all that somehow the brief days and long nights that lay in the winter months ahead would not be so bad.

Nicholas stepped out of his front door shortly after sunset on his way to meet some friends at the Water Barrel Inn. A brilliant crescent Fox Moon hung high in the west. As he walked past the farmhouse, Maynard stepped out onto the porch and called to him.

"Don't mean to keep you from your fun, Nicholas, but have you seen Adelaide today?" Maynard gripped the railing. "I had promised to walk over to the park with her this evening, but I haven't seen her today or yesterday. She's not in her house either."

Nicholas shrugged. "I last talked to her two nights ago. Maybe she's helping the other ladies set up food tables at the pavilion."

"Or Amanda Stewart is talking her ear off someplace."

"Most likely," Nicholas said, anxious to get going.

"Well, I'm sure I'll find her. You go and have a good time."

"Okay, Maynard. If I run into Adelaide, I'll let her know you're looking for her."

"Thanks," he said, waving him on his way.

Nicholas hurried down the road into the village, feeling alive and lighthearted. The brisk air and sweet smell of wood smoke filled him with an energy that made him believe he could conquer any obstacle that life threw in his path. After a dizzying week of work at the gristmill, he was especially eager to unwind at the inn with friends over a game of triple dice and some ale. With any luck, he hoped to run into Katherine at the Stewarts' party later on and spend some time with her, too.

Ned Adams, Nicholas' employer at the gristmill, swam frantically through the crowded streets with Constable Clay Brindle at his side. Ned was a thin man with thinning hair. His hands gesticulated wildly as he explained his predicament to the constable.

"It was Dooley Kramer who told me, Clay. *Dooley Kramer*, if you can believe that!" Ned tried to keep pace with Constable Brindle who walked at a furious clip despite having two stout legs that were forced to carry a paunchy upper body. "I never knew Dooley to be such a conscientious worker."

Clay Brindle carried a torch in one hand. He removed a handkerchief from his coat pocket with the other and patted away beads of sweat dotting his forehead. "Now just take a breath, Ned, and settle down. Tell me the facts again–slowly this time."

"All right, Clay. As I stated earlier, Dooley came to me and said he'd been walking along the river like he does most nights. When he passed the gristmill, he thought one of the side doors was slightly ajar and he examined it. Sure enough, the door was open. The wood was splintered around the lock as if somebody broke into the place."

They turned onto the main business street in the village, now jammed with revelers and entertainers. Lively strains from a fiddle and the soft beats of a hand drum filled the night air. Several villagers weaved through the street carrying torches that blazed in various colors, the result of a whimsical magician's trick. Flames of plum, silver, emerald green and scarlet cast gentle hues on the delighted expressions of passersby. Clay Brindle and Ned Adams maneuvered though the boisterous crowds until they began to thin out where the road to the gristmill curved northeast. From there it led directly to the mill situated on the banks of the Pine River, its waterwheel hidden in the darkness.

"What happened after Dooley spotted the open door, Ned?"

"He checked inside. Dooley said he lit one of the oil lamps and looked around the place. That's when he discovered–"

"–the missing flour sacks?"

"Yes!" Ned replied bitterly. He kicked a small stone up the dark dirt road illuminated by the torch held aloft by Constable Brindle. Lethargic chirps of crickets in an adjacent farm field replaced the jovial voices back in the center of the village. "Dooley was inspecting the orders that were ready for shipping when he saw some spilled flour on the floor. When he looked closer, he discovered some of the original sacks had been replaced with ones filled with leaves and pinecones to make it look like a full order. Can you believe it? The thief must have accidentally ripped a sack when removing it."

"That's positively rotten," the constable muttered.

"Dooley found parts of other shipments missing, too."

Constable Brindle picked up his pace, his arms pumping back and forth in sync with his legs. The torch waved wildly in the air. "Is Dooley at the mill now?"

"Yes. He's examining the books, trying to determine precisely what's missing." Ned scratched his brow and frowned. "These are the last shipments before winter. Who would do such a thing?"

When they entered the main storage building at the gristmill, Dooley Kramer was busily poring over the account books. Light from an oil lamp bathed his hunched figure and frazzled hair in an eerie yellow glow. He sat at Nicholas' desk and glanced up when Ned and Constable Brindle walked into the room.

"Thanks again for all your help, Dooley. Find anything?" Ned asked.

Dooley tilted his head slightly, raising a single eye in Ned's direction. "After counting what's left in the orders that were disturbed, and comparing that to the numbers marked in the books here, I've figured there are twenty sacks of flour missing."

"Twenty!"

"Yes. And I'm sad to say that I packed those very shipments just two days ago with Arthur Weeks."

Constable Brindle waved the torch. "Show us."

Dooley led them to a corner of the storage area. Flour sacks were piled chest high in several rows. He set his oil lamp down on one of them. "I saw flour spilled on the floorboards," he said, pointing. "The thief must've torn one of the sacks. And notice the replacement sack filled with pinecones in this one order."

The constable raised his torch, nosing his way between Ned and Dooley for a closer look. "This is the work of a clever one, that's for certain. Deviously clever."

"I want that scoundrel thrown in your lockup and left to rot!" Ned spastically waved a finger in front of Clay's nose. "That's just for starters!"

"Take a breath, Ned, and quit trying to poke my eye out!" The constable brushed past him. "Let me examine the area in peace."

"You might want to look in your office," Dooley suggested to Ned. "I noticed some items in there scattered all over the floor."

Ned rushed to the office as Constable Brindle continued snooping around. "More light, Dooley."

"Right away!" Dooley lit another oil lamp and hurried over to the constable.

"Thanks," Clay said, hanging it from a nail in the wall, creating more flittering shadows in that area. He knelt down on a knee and swept his fingers through the pile of spilled flour, cold to the touch. He next examined the sack of pinecones and scowled when something caught his eye. The constable directed his gaze to a patch of floor just beyond the spill. He reached down and grabbed a tiny object laying there, rolled it through his fingers and then slipped it inside his vest pocket just as Ned stormed out of his office.

"That miscreant looted my private office, too! I had a leather pouch filled with silver half-pieces locked inside my strongbox. They're gone! Someone pried the box open and stole the pouch." Ned's oil lamp shook like a storm-tossed ship at sea as he flailed his arms. "You find this hooligan at once, Clay! Deputize the entire village if you have to. I'll be first in line to volunteer."

Constable Brindle hung Ned's oil lamp on another nail and motioned for him to sit down before addressing Dooley. "You said Arthur Weeks helped you fill these orders?"

"Yes, sir. We both put in extra hours this week. Arthur worked more than me, cleaning up the place at the end of the day. He likes earning the extra pay before things slow up for winter. He locked up a couple of times, being the last one here. Mr. Adams will attest to that."

Ned nodded, rubbing his chin. "They both did some fine work this week. Our busy season, you know. Arthur worked well into dark on a couple of nights recently."

"Did he say anything that might indicate he'd pull a stunt like this?" the constable asked Dooley.

"No, sir! Not in the least." Dooley grinned. "You know Arthur. He minds his business pretty much. Does what he's told. Doing extra clean-up work for pay is one thing, but a scheme like this, well... That would just be too much work to interest him."

"Still, I'd like to have a word with him," Constable Brindle said. "Know where I might find him?"

"Probably plopped down on a chair at the Iron Kettle right now, celebrating. That's his usual haunt."

Ned agreed that they should seek him out at once. "Yet I find it hard to imagine Arthur having anything to do with these matters," he added. "Truth is, I find it difficult to believe that any of my workers would stoop to such treachery. Something's rotten here, I tell you. Like a basket of forgotten fish, something's very rotten!"

The Iron Kettle Tavern sat slumped on the south side of River Road like a tired, wet dog. Several layers of dried mossy growth blanketed its sagging roof. Firelight from within peeked through an assortment of cracked and dirty windows. Inside, pipe smoke drifted to the ceiling like gray and white snakes hovering over the chatter of drinkers, gamblers and braggarts. Oil lamps hung from low rafters over crowded pine tables as a roaring blaze in the corner fireplace viciously sputtered and snapped.

Constable Brindle and Ned Adams stepped inside and drifted through the packed room, soon spotting Arthur Weeks turning away from the bar with a freshly filled mug of ale. He wore a brown water-stained coat and quickly gulped from his drink when he saw the two men approach.

"Arthur, we need to talk to you," the constable said, wiping his brow. "But it's awfully warm in here. Step outside for a minute?"

"Sure," Arthur said, suspiciously eyeing Ned Adams.

When they stood outside the front door, Arthur questioned them with a twitch of his pointed nose. "What's going on? I come here to get away from the serious faces you two are wearing." He attempted a laugh.

"Clay needs to ask you a few questions, Arthur, about some goings-on at the gristmill."

"All right." Arthur Weeks downed another mouthful of ale.

Constable Brindle explained about the robbery at the mill, noting the surprise etched on Arthur's narrow face. "Since Dooley mentioned that you helped pack those orders, and that you also stayed late on a few nights recently to clean up, well, is there anything you might be able to tell us about the missing items?"

"Yesterday was the final workday of the week," Ned added, "so the robbery probably happened last night after you locked up."

"Whenever it happened, just know that I had nothing to do with it," Arthur said. "I put flour sacks on those piles, not pinecones. Just because I was the last one to leave the mill on some nights doesn't mean I was up to anything crooked."

"No one's accusing you, Arthur. We're just trying to piece together events. Any information you can supply would be helpful," the constable said reassuringly. "On those nights you worked late, did you see anything unusual or notice anyone hanging around the area? Perhaps someone walked by who you normally didn't see near the mill."

Arthur Weeks stared at the constable's torch that had been set against a nearby rock. The flames sputtered in the cold night air. He shook his head before looking up to speak. "It's usually pretty quiet up there after work hours. I didn't see anyone in the area that– Well, I didn't see any strangers hanging about. That's the honest truth."

"Whoever robbed me probably broke in during the dead of night," Ned mumbled dejectedly. "I just can't believe this could happen." He stepped away from the others and looked up at the starry sky.

Clay Brindle patted Arthur on the shoulder and smiled a quick thank you. "Okay then. We'll figure it out somehow," he said, picking up the torch. "Let's head back to the mill, Ned, and look around some more."

"All right."

Arthur Weeks quickly drained the last of his mug as Constable Brindle and Ned started to walk away. He watched them uneasily for a moment, took a deep breath and then called to them. "Wait! There is one thing I just remembered." The two men turned around and hurried back. "Something that might be a bit unusual."

"What, Arthur? What'd you see?" Ned asked.

"Well, I'm kind of reluctant to say as I don't want to get in any trouble. After all, Mr. Adams, you gave me instructions that I was to lock up the mill doors after cleaning the store room on those evenings I stayed late."

"I understand, Arthur. Just tell me and the constable what's on your mind. I promise you won't get into any trouble."

"I appreciate that," he said apprehensively as he looked into his empty mug. "I think I could use a bit more ale first to settle my stomach, if you don't mind. It'll help me to tell my story."

"Of course, of course!" Ned Adams pushed Arthur back into the tavern and signaled to an exasperated Clay Brindle to follow. Clay set the torch down and accompanied them inside.

After Arthur refilled his mug at the crowded bar and promptly gulped down a third of it, he was prepared to resume his story. The trio remained inside, cramped into a corner of the room beneath a mounted deer's head whose black eyes seemed to watch their every move. The trio soon became the object of curiosity of many in the tavern who quietly speculated what business the constable and Ned Adams could possibly have there.

"Like I said outside, I didn't see any strangers around the mill after closing up, but I did see someone I know stop by a couple of times. I hesitate to say who because I don't want to get anyone in trouble," Arthur said.

"We'll determine who'll get in trouble and who won't," the constable replied. "Now enough stalling, Arthur. If you have something to say, spit it out!"

Several people eavesdropping nearby were emboldened by the constable's outburst and stopped pretending they weren't listening. Many circled around the men for a better take on the story to the obvious annoyance of Constable Brindle. He exhaled slowly through his clenched teeth and glared at Arthur Weeks.

Arthur stared back at all the curious eyes fixed on him and took one more gulp of his drink. "It was Nicholas Raven. He stopped by the mill on a couple nights just before I closed up. He told me he had to catch up on the bookkeeping."

Ned Adams tightened his face. "I don't understand. Nicholas worked extra hours himself on many nights. The books were always kept up-to-date. Even during our busy times, every ledger entry was checked and double checked."

"That's what I always thought, too," Arthur said. "But I'm just a laborer. If Nicholas said he had other work to do, who was I to say otherwise?"

Constable Brindle wiped his brow again. "How long did Nicholas stay when he stopped by those few times?"

"Difficult to answer," Arthur replied. "You see, this is what I had hoped to avoid saying, not wanting to get me or Nicholas in trouble." He rubbed a finger behind his ear. "I don't know how long Nicholas stayed at the mill because, well, he was still there after I went home." He looked at Ned with remorse. "I'm sorry, Mr. Adams, but Nicholas insisted that I leave when I finished my work. Even though I was under your orders to lock up the storage building when I was done cleaning, Nicholas told me not to. He promised that he'd do it after he finished up. I told him I'd be more than happy to wait, but Nicholas wouldn't hear of it. Told me he might be there several hours working on the books. And since he had more authority, what was I to do? So I went home after he assured me that I wouldn't get in any trouble." His eyes connected with Constable Brindle's. "But seeing you standing here in front of me, I guess that's not to be."

Ned told Arthur not to worry. "Telling the truth is best. I appreciate it. There's just one other thing I need to know."

"What's that?"

"When did Nicholas last stop by the mill while you were working late?"

"That would be last night, sir."

"The night of the robbery," Ned whispered.

"Yes, Mr. Adams. Nicholas seemed..." Arthur hesitated as the eyes in the crowd bore down on him. "Well, Nicholas seemed particularly anxious to get rid of me then."

"Why do you say that?" a voice in the crowd asked.

Constable Brindle spun around. "Leave the investigating to me, Bob Hawkins! I think I'm qualified to handle matters here."

"Are you saying that Nicholas stole something?" someone else asked, struggling through the tightly packed crowd of onlookers in hopes of getting a better view.

"Yes!" a third voice answered. "Open your ears."

"Quiet, all of you!" the constable ordered.

"Nicholas stole some sacks of flour!" another added.

Soon accusations and speculation rolled through the tavern like ripples on a pond. Several people pawed at Arthur for more information as the constable tried to keep them back. Ned also mentioned that part of the stolen shipment had been scheduled for delivery down south in Bridgewater County. That only intensified the bitter reaction since Bridgewater County had suffered heavy flooding early last summer, making its residents more dependent on provisions from other regions.

"A lot of people down there depend on those supplies," Bob Hawkins said. "And you're telling me Nicholas Raven stole them?"

"We haven't accused anybody!" Clay snapped. "So don't you boys start."

"Looks like he's a thief to me," someone said to murmurs of agreement.

At Ned's urging, it was decided to pay Nicholas a visit to get his side of the story. But despite Constable Brindle's order that no one should follow them, several men filed out of the Iron Kettle Tavern anyway like a colony of ants. They paraded behind the constable and Ned Adams with oil lamps swaying and torches held aloft, their calls for justice punctuating the autumn air like a deep and steady drumbeat.

The Iron Kettle was left quieter and less crowded moments later. But drinks still poured forth from the bar and the chatter of patrons continued to fill the air. As the flames jumped and snapped in the corner fireplace, a man sat alone at a nearby table, hidden in the smoky shadows. He sipped his drink and drummed his fingers over the table top, leaning back in his chair after witnessing the unfolding events. He sipped his drink again. A hint of a satisfied smile spread over the face of Zachary Farnsworth.

They marched in a pack along River Road. Constable Brindle and Ned Adams led the way. Soon they neared Adelaide Cooper's house on their right, bathed in darkness behind the wooden gate and hedges. The constable and Ned turned off the road at that point and headed straight for Nicholas' cottage. A wavering line of torch and oil lamp light followed them over the grassy field. Constable Brindle rapped his chubby knuckles against the front door. The windows were dark.

"Nicholas, you in there? It's Clay Brindle. I need to talk to you." His words evaporated under the chilly night stars with only the field crickets responding.

"He's not home," someone in the crowd softly remarked.

"I can see that as plain as the night against my nose!" Constable Brindle sputtered.

Ned pointed to the farmhouse. "I see a light in Maynard's back window."

"We'll visit him shortly." The constable raised his torch and looked around, noticing the shed behind the cottage. "Let's look in there first."

He and Ned approached the shed with a few men shadowing them. Several others drifted off to different parts of the property, bathing the area in a flickering orange and yellow glow. Dried grass and leaves crunched underfoot.

Ned glanced at the constable with flames reflecting in his wide eyes. "Do you think we should snoop around here without Nicholas? I only wanted you to question him."

"This is a legal matter, Ned. As village constable, I have the right and responsibility to investigate wherever my suspicions lead." He placed his fingers on the doorknob, ready to push open the door, when a figure came running toward them through the darkness.

"What's going on here? What are these people doing on my property?" Maynard Kurtz stepped into the light, slightly out of breath. "Clay, why are you sneaking onto my land in the middle of the night?"

Constable Brindle quickly explained matters as Maynard furrowed his brow in disbelief. "I understand how you feel, Maynard, but rest assured that no one is accusing Nicholas of anything yet."

"I should hope not! Nicholas is not a thief and you know it."

"Where is he now? I want to speak to him."

"He went to the Water Barrel Inn." Maynard eyed the uneasy faces surrounding him, unable to fathom why they would accuse Nicholas of such a dreadful deed. "He'll be happy to answer any questions you put to him, Clay. You too, Ned."

Ned tried to smile. "It's nothing personal, Maynard. I just need to find my missing goods and money. I have orders to fill. You can understand that."

"I do." He glanced at Constable Brindle. "But before you leave, Clay, there's another matter I need to ask you about."

"Can't it wait, Maynard?"

"It's Adelaide. She's nowhere to be found. Have any of you seen her lately? Nicholas talked to her two nights ago, but neither of us has seen her since."

"Maybe she helped set up for the festivities with the other ladies," Clay suggested.

"Nicholas said as much. I was supposed to meet her tonight. It's not like Adelaide to miss an appointment."

The constable shrugged, though noting Maynard's apprehension. "If any of us see Adelaide, we'll let you know."

"All right. Maybe I'm worried about nothing," he replied before indicating for the constable to proceed with his search.

Clay pushed the shed door open and stepped inside, holding the torch aloft. The pungent smell of dried straw soaked the air. He gasped as Ned and Maynard followed him in. A few of the other men craned their necks to get a peek through the doorway. Piled on the dirt floor among a few sheaves of straw, empty bushels and several farming implements were the twenty sacks of flour stolen from Ned's storehouse.

"I can't believe my eyes!" Ned whispered. "Nicholas Raven, of all people."

Clay walked among the stolen goods, touching a few of the sacks to make sure they weren't merely an illusion. He looked at Maynard and shook his head. "I'm sorry about this, but I do have to find that boy right away."

Maynard stared dumbfounded at the stolen items. "Bring Nicholas back here first, Clay. Give him a chance to explain."

"You have my word."

Ned gently grabbed Clay's arm holding the torch and directed the light toward one of the straw sheaves. A bit of leather cord stuck out. Ned tugged at it and removed a small cloth pouch hidden inside. He emptied the contents into his hand.

"The silver half-pieces stolen from my office." After counting them, Ned carefully replaced the coins in the pouch and closed it. "All accounted for. That's one bit of good news anyway." He set the pouch on the bundle of straw.

The constable motioned for everyone to leave the shed and closed the door as he stepped outside. The group stood impatiently in the chilly night air waiting for Constable Brindle to speak. He stood in silent thought for a moment, rubbing a hand over his face.

"All right. Here's what we'll do." He pointed to three of the men that had followed him from the tavern. "You three stand guard until Ned and I come back with Nicholas. Nobody goes inside, you hear?" Constable Brindle scanned the faces in the crowd until he saw Arthur Weeks hiding in the background. "I want you to accompany us, Arthur."

"*Me*? Are you sure?"

"Of course I'm sure! You're my prime witness so far. We'll talk to Nicholas and get his side of the story and then return here to show him the evidence. Maynard, you're welcome to tag along. The rest of you boys ought to go back to where you came from. This is a legal matter, not a parade."

"I'll wait here," Maynard said.

"We're going with you," Bob Hawkins added. "I don't want to miss this."

Constable Brindle raised a finger, nearly poking Bob in the chin. "I don't want you interfering with my investigation! Mark my words, I'll toss you in the lockup if you do. So just keep your distance." With that warning, Clay Brindle and Ned Adams left for the Water Barrel Inn. Arthur Weeks followed with his head held low, talking softly to himself.

The Water Barrel Inn was larger and brighter than the Iron Kettle, and just as crowded on the first night of the Harvest Festival. The bottom half of the building was constructed of chiseled stone blocks, with knotty pine planks running vertically above. The walls were strewn with animal pelts, wood carvings and fresh pine clippings. A man with a beard tended to a fireplace, adding pieces of wood to the wildly snapping flames.

Nicholas sat at a table with several friends, drinking ale, devouring roasted chicken and laughing at the stories told by one another. He wasn't aware that Constable Brindle had entered the inn until he felt a heavy hand press down on his shoulder. Nicholas turned around and instantly noted the distress in Clay's dark eyes. When he saw Ned Adams and Arthur Weeks standing behind the constable, both as somber as mourners, he set down his drink and stood.

"What brings you here, Clay?"

"You do, Nicholas."

"Is everything all right?"

"I need to have a word with you. It's rather important. I..." Constable Brindle then noticed the front of Nicholas' jacket and his heart immediately sank. He looked the young man straight in the eyes as if searching for any other explanation than the one he now believed was only too true.

"I'll be happy to talk," Nicholas said. "But why the grim face?"

Bob Hawkins yelled from the back of the crowd. "He's here to arrest you, thief!"

Constable Brindle stormed through the crowd and grabbed Bob by the collar. "Now just shut your mouth or I'll arrest you for interfering in my investigation! What did I tell you earlier?"

"All right! All right! I won't say another word." Bob Hawkins shook his head nervously, as if waiting for the constable's fist to strike. Constable Brindle released him and marched back over to Nicholas. The inn was deathly silent.

Nicholas slowly shook his head, wild disbelief in his eyes. "What's he talking about, Clay?"

"We don't have to discuss this in here, Nicholas. Let's go outside."

"No. I have nothing to hide." He pointed to Bob Hawkins. "And what did he mean about you arresting me?"

"There's been an incident at the gristmill, Nicholas. Goods were stolen. Some of Ned's money, too."

Nicholas shot a glance at his boss. "Is that true, Ned?"

"Yes, Nicholas. Someone robbed the place last night." Murmurs of excitement and contempt swept through the crowd. "And, uh... Well, I better let Clay do the explaining."

"I wish somebody would!"

"Calm down, Nicholas." Constable Brindle pulled out a handkerchief and dabbed it across his forehead. "I need to talk to you because we found the stolen goods. They were piled inside the shed behind your cottage. The money, too."

"*What*? That's impossible!"

"He's telling the truth." Ned walked up to Nicholas. "I just can't believe in my heart that you'd do such a thing, Nicholas, but we found twenty flour sacks inside your shed. And a small pouch of coins I kept locked in my office."

"I never took those items. Is this some sick joke?"

The constable shook his head. "We were up to the gristmill earlier. Dooley Kramer discovered the missing goods. Then after we questioned Arthur Weeks, well, things started to fall in place."

Nicholas felt his heart racing as the room grew unbearably hot. He shot a glance at Arthur Weeks who tried to hide behind a few of the men in the crowd. His thin facial features were framed between long straight locks of black hair. Nicholas addressed the constable again. "What did Arthur say? I don't understand his connection to this?"

Constable Brindle patiently explained how Arthur had testified about Nicholas returning to the gristmill late last night. "According to him, you were the last person there last night and on several other nights as well. He claimed you had to catch up on your bookkeeping."

"That's ridiculous! The books were up-to-date. I wasn't at the gristmill last night. I had no reason to be."

Clay turned to Arthur Weeks who meekly squeezed through the crowd to face Nicholas. "What'd you tell me earlier, Arthur, when Ned and I questioned you outside the Iron Kettle?"

"Well," he whispered after swallowing hard. "I said I stayed late at the gristmill to clean up last night, just like Mr. Adams asked me to. We've been so busy lately." Arthur stared in Nicholas' direction but couldn't look him in the eyes. "Before I left, well, Nicholas showed up. He told me to leave early so he could do his bookkeeping."

"That's a lie! I never talked to you last night, Arthur."

"Yes, you did."

"I wasn't at the gristmill last night!"

"That's about how I remember it," Arthur mumbled, slipping back into the crowd.

Nicholas held out his hands in stunned disbelief. "Clay, he's lying!"

"We'll get to the bottom of it," Constable Brindle promised. "But you still have to explain about the items found in your shed."

"I want to see them," Nicholas demanded.

"I'll take you there shortly. I have a few men guarding it now. But there's still one other piece of evidence I need to show you. I've kept it secret until now."

Ned Adams threw an inquisitive glance at the constable. "What are you talking about, Clay? What evidence?"

"Something I found on the floor at the gristmill. You were inside your office at the time, Ned." Constable Brindle reached inside his vest pocket and removed a small object. "I discovered this near some spilled flour close to one of the orders that had been broken into. It's a button. My guess is that the thief accidentally popped it off his jacket. Probably caught it on the stack of flour sacks in his hurry to leave." The constable held up the plain brown button for all to see. The crowd looked at it with greedy eyes.

"Who does it belong to?" someone asked.

"Shortly after I walked in here, I noticed Nicholas' jacket when he stood up. The color of the material matches the color of the button. It's hard to see if you're not specifically looking for it."

Nicholas glanced down at the several buttons along the right side of his jacket. One was missing near the center. Nicholas snapped his head up, his eyes locking onto Clay Brindle's skeptical gaze. "I never noticed that one was missing."

The constable held the button he had found next to one on Nicholas' jacket. "An exact match."

"He *is* the thief!" a patron in back whispered.

"Constable Brindle did some fine work," a second voice added.

Ned Adams looked unkindly at Nicholas, stunned by the turn of events. He looked him dead in the eyes, prepared to unload the mixed emotions churning like a storm inside him, but then simply turned and walked away.

As the crowd grew more vocal, Constable Brindle decided it best to get Nicholas out of the inn and over to the shed right away. The cool evening air calmed the crowd as they departed, though the constable was annoyed that the group of men now following him had grown larger. A line of oil lamp and torch light again snaked along River Road, accompanied by the shuffling of feet and bitter whispers of condemnation.

When they reached the shed, Maynard ran up to Nicholas, a mix of horror and sympathy etched upon his face. "Clay said you're responsible for–"

"I didn't do anything wrong," Nicholas assured him, placing his hands on Maynard's shoulders. "I don't know what's going on, but you've got to believe me."

"I believe you, Nicholas. You know I do."

Clay Brindle ordered the shed door opened and several oil lamps placed within. Nicholas was invited to look inside and see the evidence for himself. His heart raced when he saw the piled sacks of flour. Ned's pouch of silver half-pieces sat on top of a straw bundle. Nicholas backed out of the shed, shaking his head.

"We found this just before we tracked you down at the Water Barrel," Constable Brindle said. "Can you explain how those goods found their way here, Nicholas?"

"No, I can't," he softly said.

"And can you tell me why the button from your jacket was sitting on the floor near the orders that had been ransacked?"

"I can't explain that either, Clay." His words sounded heavy and lifeless. "I only can say that I didn't commit this crime."

Clay Brindle sighed, throwing a glance at Maynard and Ned. Neither uttered a word. Arthur Weeks stood back in the shadows. The chirping crickets in the rustling grass and the sputtering torch flames were the only sounds audible for the next few moments. The constable rubbed his neck and then looked at Nicholas.

"There's a lot to sort through, Nicholas. We'll have to go over it detail by detail to get to the truth. You say you're innocent, and you're allowed that privilege, but..." Clay kicked the toe of his boot into the dirt. "Since there's conflicting testimony and all the evidence points to you, I'll have to take you to the lockup."

Before Nicholas could speak, Maynard protested. "Clay, you can't do this!"

"I'm sorry, Maynard, but legally I have no choice."

"Then I'm coming with you."

"That's fine."

Nicholas held up a hand, appreciating Maynard's concern but not wanting to upset him. "It's all right, Maynard. The constable is just doing what he has to." He turned to Ned Adams with a pained expression. "I wish I could prove I'm innocent, Ned."

"I wish you could, too."

The constable tapped Ned on the arm. "I'll need a list of everything that was stolen before you can take the goods back to the gristmill. Just in case there's a trial."

"I understand."

"You can do that now while I take Nicholas to the lockup or wait until morning."

"I'll start now, if it's okay with you, Maynard."

"Fine," he muttered.

"I'll send someone to fetch Dooley Kramer so he can bring back a horse and cart."

The constable nodded. "All right." He turned to Nicholas, clearing his throat. "I'll need to keep your jacket, too, Nicholas, after we get to the village hall. Also for evidence." He tried to sound as gentle as he could with his next few words. "I guess we better get moving now. It's time."

With those words, Nicholas realized the magnitude of the trouble he was about to face. With those simple words, all his new-found dreams of travel and adventure disintegrated before his eyes like piles of sand upon a wave-tossed shoreline. The unfairness of it all tied his stomach in knots. The lies of Arthur Weeks enraged him until his head hurt. The slow walk to the lockup with Constable Brindle would end everything he had longed for. What would his friends think of him now? What would Katherine think? His world was falling apart.

"Can I grab another jacket, Clay, since you plan to take the one I'm wearing?"

"Sure, Nicholas," he said, cracking a kindly smile. "I'll let you do that."

Nicholas nodded in gratitude and walked away from the shed, making his way around the side of the cottage as the other men followed. He rounded the corner to the front, recalling sitting on Maynard's porch steps only five days ago and discussing his future plans. That rush of excitement had now turned into a dull ache in the pit of his stomach. Events of someone else's design had changed everything and he was helpless to fight back. Or was he? Nicholas decided then and there that he couldn't let them win. He *wouldn't* let them win, whoever they were.

As Nicholas approached the front door of the cottage, he slowly reached for the handle while taking a deep breath. Suddenly, he dashed over the grass alongside Maynard's farmhouse to the opposite end, running furiously into the field just beyond. He ran as fast as he could in the thick shadows, scrambling in one direction and then another, hoping to make his way north into the wooded area along the Pine River.

"Nicholas! You come back here!" the constable bellowed as he made a futile effort to chase after the young man. He flailed his arms, ordering the others to pursue at once. They shot past Constable

Brindle like a pack of hungry wolves in search of fleeing prey, fanning out into the dark field with oil lamps and torches blazing among the dry crackling grass. Their earsplitting shouts shattered the peaceful night.

CHAPTER 3

The Awakening

A heavy fist hammered the tabletop, rattling three glass tumblers and an empty gin bottle. A trio of men, seated in a dark corner of the Iron Kettle Tavern that same evening, gawked at each other in stunned silence. A blaze crackled in the fireplace in an adjacent corner. The din of competing conversations from other patrons filled the smoky air.

"Something's seriously wrong here," one of the men whispered. "*Dead* wrong." He gravely observed his two companions, shifting his eyes left, then right, in a rigid line. "We're out of gin!" he finally burst out laughing, his mouth crammed full of widely spaced teeth, one of which was missing on the bottom.

"That's a good one, Gill! We can't celebrate the Harvest Festival properly with an empty bottle in front of us. I'll get another one." George Bane tried to stand up, his puffy cheeks as red as apples and his eyes most surely to match in the morning. He plopped back down in his chair. "Give me a moment first."

"You're soused," Gill Meddy said. "Nearly pickled, I'd say. Good thing you don't have a wife 'cause she'd lock you out of the house tonight for sure."

"Yours *will*!" George said, dropping his head to the table in a fit of laughter.

"Stick your face in a feedbag and shut up about it!"

George Bane looked up, rubbing his unshaven face. "Then you get up off those spindly legs, Gill, and buy the next bottle if you're so sober."

"Didn't I buy the last one?"

"I thought I did. Did I?"

The third member of the group calmly stood and indicated to George and Gill not to bother themselves. He grabbed the empty gin bottle and offered a thin smile. "It'll be my pleasure to buy the next one," he said, even though he had purchased the first one as well. "Sit back and relax until I return."

"Much obliged," Gill said, while George nodded with a glazed look in his eyes.

The third man walked to the tavern counter and paid for another bottle of gin. Mune stood chest-high to most of the men in the room. He had a slightly stocky build, topped with a head of short, thinning black hair and a well-trimmed goatee. His smiled displayed an abundant set of white teeth under piercing sea gray eyes.

When Mune returned to the table, he uncorked the gin bottle and refilled the three tumblers. George Bane and Gill Meddy, a couple of local farmhands, greedily drank from their glasses, pleased they had met this stranger passing through Kanesbury. It wasn't unusual for outsiders to visit the village during the Harvest Festival, and the two men were more than happy to be the recipients of this particular outsider's generosity.

Mune sat down and took a sip of his drink, leaning back in his chair to continue listening to the wild and fanciful yarns that George and Gill spun in their friendly competition. He was quick to refill their glasses when needed.

"Remember that time, Gill, when... That time when–probably fifteen years ago–when, uh, whatever-his-name dared me to climb that dead pine tree?" George slapped the table. "I can't believe I really did that!"

"He did!" Gill excitedly assured Mune. "It was the deadest, driest pine tree ever, standing right in the middle of this field, see? The rotting tree had been dead for years and that was the summer we had nearly no rain besides. The tree was drier than kindling."

"Not a needle left on it!" George said. "Some of the thinner branches snapped off if you just looked at them."

"You don't say." Mune's eyes widened in feigned fascination.

George gleefully pointed to himself. "And I climbed it! That guy who dared me–I still can't think of his name, but he doesn't live around here anymore–had to pay me two copper half-pieces on that bet. What a fool!"

"And the best part," Gill added, slurping down another mouthful of gin, "was that the tree fell down in a storm not a week later! Now isn't that a good story? Isn't it?"

"Most certainly," Mune said as George and Gill doubled over in convulsions of drunken laughter. He pretended to take another sip of his drink before casually lowering his glass to the side of his chair. With George and Gill not paying attention, Mune emptied most of the glass, carefully pouring the gin through a crack in the floor planks. He had executed this procedure several times during the evening, not allowing even a single drop to hit the floorboards during this latest attempt. When George and Gill recovered, Mune was already refilling the three tumblers.

"My, but you men certainly have had some exciting times in your youth," he said. "Little seems to bother us during those carefree years. It's our advancing age that makes us more cautious in our choices, don't you think?"

"Yeah, I guess," Gill mumbled, offering a shrug.

"Still, I do enjoy a challenge now and then to make me feel alive. A risky gamble or a wild dare is just the right spice sometimes!" Mune raised his glass, a wicked grin painted across his face. "To taking chances!"

George and Gill lifted their glasses with unsteady arms to join in the toast, downing the gin in a single gulp. Mune quickly refilled their empty tumblers and then sat back and stared at the two men, both now teetering on the edge of awareness. Their eyes darted like flies, their heads bobbing like driftwood on an ocean. Suddenly, Mune set his glass down with a thump and cleared his throat.

"You've inspired me, gentlemen! Your stories of joyous youth have awakened in me memories of my own adolescence."

Gill rubbed a finger across his nose. "Sorry, sir. We didn't mean to."

"That's a good thing!" he said, pulling out a small cloth pouch from the inside pocket of his coat. "So in keeping with the spirit of the moment, I wish to propose a dare." He tossed the pouch onto the center of the table, where it landed with a metallic thud. George Bane and Gill Meddy stared at the object, tongue-tied, then glanced at Mune, their eyes focused on his mischievous grin.

"What did you have in mind?" George asked.

"I recall you mentioning earlier in the evening that there are some caves just east of the village."

"The Spirit Caves," George said. "Less than two miles out along River Road. But I don't remember mentioning those tonight." With one elbow firmly planted on the table, George rested his tired head in the palm of his hand.

"Yes, the Spirit Caves. That was the name." Mune slowly untied the cloth pouch and gently poured out some of its contents. A stream of silver and copper half-pieces glinted in the dim light. "I could swear that one of you spoke about those caves tonight."

Gill's eyes popped open. "We easily *could* have! Now that I think about it, George or I probably did say something about them. Don't you think, George?"

"Guess so..." George mumbled, enthralled by the clinking coins. There was enough money in that pouch to equal two months of his salary as a farmhand. The corners of his lips turned upward like thorn points. "What kind of dare do you propose, Mr. Mune?"

Mune had them hooked and he knew it. He picked up one of the silver half-pieces and rubbed it between his fingers. "I hear that those caves are haunted. Is it true?"

"Don't know if they're haunted exactly, but I recall hearing strange stories as a boy. Some creatures were supposed to have been trapped inside, if you can believe that." George watched as the coin gently somersaulted between Mune's fingers, the light of the tavern gleaming dully off it. "We can tell you about those caves if you like."

"Perhaps on the way over."

"On the way–*over*?" Gill Meddy clutched the glass tumbler. "You want us to go to those caves? *Now*?"

"Considering your condition, walking along the main road would take us less than an hour to arrive," Mune said. "Besides, the air is refreshing tonight. A perfect time for a walk. You can fill me in on the details surrounding the legend of these so-called Spirit Caves on the way over and then decide if you wish to accept my challenge."

"Which is? You haven't actually told us yet," George said.

"Gentlemen, my dare is a simple one," he replied as he dropped the coins into the pouch one by one, each metallic clink luring his companions closer to his web. "Whichever of you spends the longest time inside the caves will receive the entire contents of this pouch." Mune pushed the full bag of coins in front of them. "If you both stay in there, let's say for two full hours, then can you split the money evenly. In either case, the payoff is substantial. Hardly much of an effort for two such daring men."

George looked askance at his challenger. "What's the catch? Sounds too easy. Doesn't it to you, Gill?"

"Yeah, I suppose..." he said while longingly starring at the pouch of coins.

"No catch," Mune assured them. "Just the thrill of the dare. Unless those stories you regaled me with earlier were simply tall tales from two men who really have nothing to show for their lives up to this point."

George slapped the gin-splattered table. "I really did climb that dead pine tree! Probably no more than thirteen years old when I did it. We weren't telling no tall tales, were we, Gill."

"No. Mostly."

Mune shrugged. "Well all that matters is the here and now. Your desire for another victory is what counts. So you may either accept my dare, and we'll set off for the Spirit Caves at once, or simply refuse and there'll be no hard feelings. We'll remain friends and finish up this bottle of gin."

Gill sat back in his chair, combing his hands through his hair as a gush of air shot out through his puffed cheeks. As tempting as the offer was, Gill had a deathly fear of enclosed spaces, especially haunted caves in the deep of night. The thought chilled him. All the liquor in the world couldn't prepare him for that stunt. George, however, stared at the bag of coins, his dizzy head already contemplating how to spend the cash. All it would take was spending a few hours in a dark cave. How difficult was that?

"I'll pass on your offer," Gill said sadly.

NICHOLAS RAVEN AND THE WIZARDS' WEB - VOLUME 1

"We'll do it!" George blurted out at the same time before shooting a poisonous glance at Gill. "What do you mean you'll pass?"

"Just what I said, George. I have no hankering to go exploring dark caves in the middle of the night. You know I don't take well to being locked up in little spaces. Besides, I got my lovely wife to think about."

"As if she'd miss you for a night!"

"Maybe..." Gill trailed off, helping himself to more gin.

Mune locked eyes with George. "Now's your chance to double the reward. Do you go it alone, sir, or will your fears get the best of you, too?"

"I'm no coward!" George said, refilling his glass and drinking it down in a single swallow. He grinned bitterly at his challenger and slammed the glass on the table. "I'll show you, Mr. Mune. Let's go!" He stood on a pair of wobbly legs and managed to slide behind Gill to get out of the corner, slapping him on the shoulders as he passed by. "See you in the morning, friend. Maybe have an egg breakfast with you at the eatery. My treat!"

Gill nodded gloomily as Mune plucked the pouch of coins off the table, watching through bleary red eyes as he and George exited the tavern.

They walked east along River Road, with Mune balancing a torch in one hand while holding up a staggering George Bane in the other. A cool breeze blew at their backs, carrying George's gin-marinated babblings across barren farm fields and through nearby woods. Mune patiently endured his stale breath and flailing limbs, though several times wanted to abandon the drunken mess on the side of the road and be done with him. That meant, however, completing the assigned task ahead himself, and Mune refused to do it no matter who gave the orders, so he continued on. Far above, a large crow circled, gliding over the shifting air currents, its sleek black wings blending invisibly with the sky.

"How 'bout we stop for another drink!" George blurted out deliriously.

Mune rolled his eyes. "Yes, it's been a whole twenty minutes since you've had your last drop."

"Are we going to meet with those ghostly fellows?" George asked, tugging at Mune's collar.

"Stop choking me! *Who*?"

"Those creatures in the Spirit Caves."

"That's just a ridiculous legend you heard as a child, my friend. I assure you, nothing lives in those caves."

"Glad to hear you say that, *umm*... What's your name again?"

"George Bane." Mune paused for a moment to prop up his rubbery burden.

"Oh, that's right. I..." George thought for a moment before snorting with laughter. "No, that's *my* name!" He playfully slapped Mune on the face. "You're trying to trick me, but I know who I am. What I really wanted was... Uh, can't remember what I wanted, but I think I could use a nap."

"Just a little farther, George, and you'll have a bagful of money for your troubles. Tomorrow you can take all the naps you want. How would you like that?"

George rubbed his eyes and sniffed. "That's an awful nice gesture, mister."

"Indeed it is, George. Indeed it is."

Mune hustled George along the remainder of the way, encountering no other soul during their travels. Freshly fallen leaves cluttered sections of the dirt road, rustling like harsh whispers as the men swished through them. Their awkward steps over the vast countryside were illuminated only by the glow from the single torch. Occasionally light from a distant farmhouse was visible over blackened fields or peeked through a grove of trees, seeming to blink as they passed silently by.

At last the caves appeared in view, looming off to the left like yawning stone faces chiseled into the cliffs. A handful of tall pines stood scattered about, their boughs bobbing in cool currents like the arms of slender giants. Thick grass and weeds, now dry, brittle and lifeless, littered the base of the rocky formation. On the opposite side of the road, directly across from the caves, stood the dilapidated remains of a two-room wooden guardhouse. An army of weeds and saplings had slowly consumed it over the years. Mune hastily studied the caves from the road while trying to keep George Bane on his feet.

"Time to see exactly what you're made of, George. Your tales of derring-do have come home to roost. Do you have what it takes to live up to them?" He shook George by the shoulders to boost his confidence. "Or are you merely a drunken fraud like your friend?"

"Gill's not here?" George asked, craning his neck for a look.

"We left that mess back at the tavern. All the money goes to you–after you fulfill the terms of my dare."

George gazed at Mune, his face wrinkled as if he had just awakened from a deep sleep. "Dare? What dare? Why are we here?"

"Apparently you put away too much gin into that fat head of yours, my dear friend." Mune held up the pouch of coins in the torchlight so that George could see it. "Remember our bet? Don't go to sleep on me now." He hastily poured a few coins into George's hands. "Take these with you into the cave to boost your confidence."

"I can have these?"

"Sure! Sure! And to earn the rest, all you have to do is walk far into those caves for an hour or two and you'll be golden." Mune planted the torch into George's hand. "Take this to find your way around. Oh, and I have another little incentive for you. My good-luck piece!" He reached into a pocket and removed a small glass sphere slightly larger than an acorn. It glowed with a bluish-white color in the fire light, capturing George's fascinated attention.

"That's such a beautiful, uh–*what is it*?"

"An old bauble I like to carry around," Mune said, massaging his whiskers. "Here. Take it." He handed the sphere to George, watching his eyes pop open.

"I couldn't!"

"Please do. It'll bring you good luck when you're inside the caves. Guaranteed to drive away any fears you bring along."

"That'd be a good thing," George mumbled, still unsteady on his feet.

Mune sported a toothy grin. "Yes, it truly would. So are you ready?"

George snapped to attention, a dimwitted smile pasted on his face. "I believe I am. Just point me in the right direction!"

"My pleasure," Mune whispered.

He gingerly led George across the road to the small patch of land in front of the caves. The scent of pine needles soaked the air.

After stomping a path though the weeds, they approached one of the openings in the cliffs. Inside it appeared darker than the night.

"I'll wait for you out here," Mune said, backing off.

George stood like a child before the mouth of the cave, eerily lit in the glow of the torch. He glanced at Mune. "You want me to go in here?"

"Yes! Yes! That's the dare." Mune hastily removed the pouch of coins and held it up, shaking the bag so the silver and copper half-pieces jingled. "This is the reward that awaits you. Now in you go!"

George scratched his swimming head, a part of him wondering if this wasn't some weary and complicated dream. "Well, all right then. If that's what I'm supposed to do." He took a deep breath and placed a foot inside the cave, ducking slightly as he stepped through the entrance before disappearing within. Mune darted across the road at that point, hiding behind the corner of the abandoned guardhouse. High above, a black crow descended in a graceful spiral, quietly landing on top of the cliffs.

George Bane held the torch aloft, its flame softly dancing and projecting wild shadows against the stone walls. The cave was cold and dry with hardly enough room to stand. George inched along through the narrow passage with unsteady steps, catching himself on the wall now and then to keep from falling. The gin that had turned his legs into rubber now played tricks with his mind, making the walls transform into nothingness before suddenly reappearing as solid rock. He clutched tightly onto the glass sphere that Mune had given him, telling himself everything would be all right. The bluish-white color of the sphere seemed to intensify.

"What am I doing here?" he whispered. "George Bane, you're a fool!"

After several minutes, the narrow passage opened into a larger section where the air felt cooler. He stood to his full height. The light of the torch illuminated bleak surroundings, a depressing blandness that made him uneasy. He yearned to turn around and race home, but the lure of the money sang to him during brief moments of lucid thought, pushing him onward.

This section of the cave branched out in several directions. George picked the easiest passage to maneuver through and moved on. Twenty minutes later he began to wonder how far he should go. Had Mune given him any specific instructions? Though moving was preferable to standing in one spot, he thought it best to retrace his steps and find the entrance. He could wait near the opening until Mune signaled his time was up, then exit this horrible place, collect his prize and leave.

When he turned around, the sides of the cave appeared wavy. The smoke from the torch smelled acrid. George felt sick to his stomach but kept shuffling forward. At one point he forgot where he was and why he was here, but it came back to him after turning into another passage. Though difficult to tell one section of the cave from the next, he thought this area looked especially unfamiliar. Had he taken a wrong turn? He stepped cautiously forward, hoping to spot a recognizable landmark. The air felt damp now. Steady plops of dripping water echoed along the walls. The gurgle of an underground stream was audible. He tried to think where he had made a wrong turn but couldn't concentrate as a sense of dizziness overwhelmed him. His heart pounded. He thought he could hear the blood pumping through his veins.

George nearly tripped over a scattering of large rocks littering the floor and maneuvered around them. The air felt particularly colder in this section. An icy shiver shot up his spine. He realized he was lost, so he stopped and turned full circle to get a fix on his surroundings. The torch illuminated a vast cavern strewn with rocks half his size, many covered with dried lichen that resembled pale, peeling skin. Pointed stone formations extended down from the ceiling like sharp teeth. George thought he heard a whisper, but reasoned it away as the wind calling through fissures in the rock. Then he heard it again.

"Is that you, Mr. Mune? Trying to sneak in here and scare me back outside?" He looked this way and that, waving the torch in front of him like a sword. Beads of sweat dotted his forehead. "A bet is a bet. I'm not leaving a minute before I can collect my winnings! You hear?"

He heard the noises again. Definitely whispers–sharp, hushed tones that filled the air like the buzz of insects. He backed into a wall and almost dropped the torch. "Show yourself!" He slashed the air with the torch, trying to beat away an invisible enemy. "Get out of here!"

He then felt a burning sensation in the palm of his other hand. George quickly unclenched his fingers around the glass sphere that was now warm to the touch and glowed nearly as bright as the torch. Soon it was so hot to hold that he threw it across the chamber where it struck the opposite wall and shattered.

"Some good-luck piece that is! Trying to hurt me with it?" he cried. "Where are you, Mune? I know it's you in here. I know it. Show your shifty self!"

Slowly and ghost-like, a faint blue mist rose from the shards of scattered glass, spreading over the cave floor like low fog on a marsh. The blue swirls wrapped around George's ankles and encircled the rocks, lapping against them like waves on a lakeshore. He watched in terrified fascination, unable to move.

Then the whispers started again. Louder, sharper, faster. George heard strange words or fragments of sentences, none of which made any sense. *Awake! Conquer!* Someone was speaking, someone within the mist, a disembodied voice giving orders and explaining events from the past. But who were the words for? *Arise! Go forth!* Who were the words from? *Glory! Revenge! Vellan!*

George's chest tightened when he saw faces appear within the rocks on the ground. Vague outlines of grim, terrible features emerged on one end of each rock as the blue mist washed over them. Deep, dark eyes set in weary countenances stared out helplessly into the blackness. Years of dirt and lichen slowly disintegrated off the rocks, revealing bulky, roughly hewn shapes beneath. George stood paralyzed, unaware of how long he had been watching, as if staring at both life and death at its origin. Then the whispers stopped and he noticed movement along the floor. The blue mist swirled and eddied, enveloping the rocks even higher. He trembled, slowly realizing that these objects were never rocks to begin with.

A shadow darted across the wall. George found his wits again and spun around, looking every which way, quivering. "Who's there? I know someone's there," he said in a thin voice. "Just stay where you are!"

More shadows, thin and fleeting. Movements through the cave, silent and swift. The blue mist churned like the edge of a maddening storm cloud as George bolted. He stumbled across the invisible floor, tripping over his own missteps. Where were the rocks? Most of them were now gone. Still the mist billowed, now nearly up to his waist. George knew he had to pick a path and get out. He shifted directions, unsure of which way to go as the roiling blue mist prevented him from seeing an arm's length in front. He slashed the torch through the air, gritting his teeth, afraid of what he couldn't see. But something definitely lived in the mist. Shadows. Movement. More shadows.

Suddenly, something jumped up in front of him from underneath the fog, barely chest high. All he saw over his frantic screams were wild eyes glaring at him, teeth and scars and a flaring nose under a tangle of dark hair, and tattered, dirty brown coverings. George stumbled backward and dropped his torch which extinguished at once. He screamed again while scrambling along on his knees and searching for an exit. The creature flew by, knocking him in the shoulder. George heard the patter of footfalls throughout the caves, heard the grunts and whispers of the fleeing shapes as he scrambled to his feet. He felt for an opening in the darkness, found one and started to run, not knowing which direction he was heading in, feeling in front of him in the inky blackness, his heart pounding, his head swimming, a wall suddenly finding his body and slamming against it. George Bane saw white fire in his mind as his hands clutched his head, unaware of the warm blood trickling off his forehead, unaware of the voices and the movement receding in the mist, unaware of anything more as he collapsed and succumbed to the darkness.

CHAPTER 4

A Wizard and His Apprentice

They slipped quietly out of the caves, one by one, like shadows in the night. Mune watched from a safe distance across the road, peeking around the corner of the old guardhouse. After a twenty-year slumber, the creatures had finally been awakened, and he had no desire to be the first person in their path. They possessed the fury of a lightning strike and the cunning of crows, and now they were loose again in this region of Laparia. Mune wondered what it would lead to, recalling the stories he had heard regarding their sentence to an eternal sleep. But the few details he knew were sketchy at best. Much had happened twenty years ago, and even greater events had transpired before then. Now a thread from the past was unraveling at this moment outside the tiny village of Kanesbury, one strand of many in an intricately woven history of which he could only guess.

The Mang River lay far west of the Northern Mountains and the Tunara Plains, snaking north and south like a silvery strip of thin ribbon. Several days' journey west beyond the Mang stood the Gable Mountain range, a labyrinth of sharp peaks scraping the clouds and casting ebony shadows, at whose base lay winding valleys and bulging woodlands known to few outside the region. Exactly when in time the first wizards had arrived there, or from where they had originated, was known only to them, but their society flourished for countless years. The wizards perfected the magic arts and raised families undisturbed in their forest, valley and mountain homes.

As part of their training, the wizards traveled periodically into other regions of the world for a year or two after their twentieth birthday to observe the ways of others. Yet as generations passed, the outside world flourished and spread across Laparia while the wizards in the Gable Mountains grew fewer because of their self-imposed isolation. Though their lifespan surpassed that of common men, the wizards were not immortal, knowing deep in their hearts that their race would one day fade away like mist at sunrise.

Nearly sixty years ago, a day after his twentieth birthday, the wizard Vellan set out on his first journey to the outside world. He studied the history, arts and sciences of other realms, enthralled by their rich and varied cultures. What fascinated him most was that one individual, a king, whether wisely or corruptly, could rule an entire population or launch a great army. It was a concept foreign to him among the order and harmony that existed naturally in the Gable Mountains. Yet a part of him, however much he tried to deny it, also viewed segments of his society as tedious and stunted.

Vellan returned home after nearly two and a half years abroad, welcomed back with a ceremony atop the sacred hilltop of Ulán, the place where he had received his wizard's staff at the age of thirteen. After regaling his fellow wizards with tales of the outside world, he dutifully returned to honing his craft. But memories of the freedom and excitement he experienced during his travels–the equivalent of which he never found at home–would envelope him upon observing a starry night sky though snow-covered pines or inhaling the sweet scent of wood smoke on a crisp autumn breeze. He yearned for something more beyond the study of magic.

Vellan married a year later, quelling his longings for the outside world through devotion to his wife, Audriana, and to his studies. He again felt at home and at peace in the Gable Mountains. But after another year had passed, a fellow wizard returned from his first journey abroad, recounting stories of wonder and excitement. Once again, Vellan yearned for a life other than his own.

Half a year later, shortly after his twenty-fifth birthday, he abruptly left Audriana to explore the world again, causing much consternation in the community. While common for a wizard to travel several times to the outside, usually ten to twelve years would pass between trips. But neither Vellan's wife nor the other wizards could change his mind, and so he departed on a cold and misty morning.

Vellan was particularly fond of the Northern Mountains of Laparia and spent much time there practicing his craft. With each passing day, he grew more enamored with a life of freedom and vitality he thought sadly lacking in the Gable Mountains. And though the wizard knew he must eventually go home, this time he eagerly looked forward to it.

He made his return three years later, though his welcome was subdued. He was again allowed to discuss his travels upon the hilltop of Ulán, though many were less than enthusiastic to listen. But this time Vellan offered more than bland accounts of his journey. He instead presented a plan for reorganizing their society.

"Why be contained within the boundaries of the Gable Mountains? We must awaken ourselves from this living death and expand our influence, or we shall wither away," he warned them. "And since the world of men craves our influence and wisdom, what better way to help ourselves than by helping them? The outside world needs our order imposed upon them!"

For weeks Vellan tried to convert other wizards to his side, but only succeeded in chipping away the tranquil foundation of their home. When his methods bordered on deceit and violence, a council of the oldest wizards assembled. On the hilltop of Ulán, he was expelled from the wizards' order and forever banished. Vellan, disgraced, vowed revenge as he turned his back on the other wizards and his wife. He left the Gable Mountains in his twenty-eighth year, crossing the Mang River that marked the eastern border of the wizards' realm. As he stepped into the water, the globe on his oak staff turned black, punctuating his expulsion, the color mirroring the darkness in his soul. He smashed the staff against a boulder in his rage, shattering the globe before he collapsed in sorrow.

He later settled down in a sparsely populated section of the Northern Mountains along the Drusala River which he named Kargoth. Isolated for the next ten years, Vellan feverishly devoted himself to perfecting his magic. His powers grew immensely and he cast a spell upon the water. The scattered populations in the river valley either moved away in fear or exhibited a strange devotion to the man in the mountains. Many eagerly volunteered into his service after drinking from the river.

His most monumental achievement was set loose upon the world five years later after spending weeks at a time holed away in secret caves perfecting the spells of his twisted craft. The Enâri emerged from the caves under a blood red sky at twilight, taking their first breaths of the mountain air. Vellan's creations were short burly creatures with fierce eyes and firm jaws. Made from the rock and soil, and infused with the magic of the black arts, he fashioned a horde of these beings to do the bidding that his human followers were either too timid or too weak to perform.

The young wizard first instructed his new race to build a stronghold in and around Mount Minakaris along the upper half of the Drusala River. The Enâri worked day and night for three years building the fortress just north of the city of Del Norác. Vellan continued to create more of his creatures, forming a vast army with unwavering devotion.

As the years passed, the wizard's influence encroached upon the other three mountain nations. With an unlimited supply of labor, Vellan mined vast amounts of iron, coal and silver and established trade relations with his fearful neighbors, cementing agreements on his terms after demonstrations of swift but violent incursions into selected villages, with promises of wholesale slaughter should those in charge reject his overtures. But the terror generated from a few burning crop fields, or a scattering of families whose murdered corpses were riddled with arrows, was usually more than enough to crush a population's spirit and earn its grudging loyalty. Vellan's powerful army eventually gave him total sway over those neighboring governments and their economies, allowing him to mold them into dependent satellites of Kargoth.

As his power and influence grew, Vellan constantly brooded over the humiliation he had suffered at the hands of his fellow wizards twenty-three years earlier. Now he was ready to strike back at their home in the Gable Mountains. He first planned a full-scale conquest of Laparia, intending to achieve as an individual what he had once desired for the entire wizard community–control. After befriending or conquering these realms, he imagined marching his expanded forces of Enâri and loyal men to the Gable Mountains to show the wizards what they could have attained if they had only listened to him. Then in the next moment, he planned to crush the wizards' realm out of existence in one brilliant stroke.

Vellan knew he would need help in this endeavor and took on an apprentice. Caldurian lived in the Red Mountains in central Laparia and had become acquainted with Vellan during his earlier travels, often assisting the wizard. Vellan trained Caldurian for five years as he himself had been taught. The young man possessed an amazing aptitude in magic and quickly grew in strength and power.

In time, Caldurian was sent out to forge alliances with other kingdoms. But except for the rulers of the Northern Isles on the Trillium Sea, no one wanted any relationship with Kargoth, having learned from other wandering wizards about Vellan's betrayal in the Gable Mountains. For two years Caldurian tried to make diplomatic headway, but was shunned at nearly every turn.

Not wanting to fail Vellan, Caldurian embarked a year later on a second journey to Arrondale, accompanied by five hundred Enâri creatures, and Xavier, an eagle who served as his dutiful messenger and spy. They arrived in the capital city of Morrenwood where he pleaded his case with King Justin and his advisors. But the answer was the same as a year ago—no.

In a rash attempt to change the King's mind, Caldurian recruited Madeline, a nursemaid to the King's granddaughter, Princess Megan. Madeline agreed to arrange for the kidnapping of the infant so Caldurian could use the child to bargain for King Justin's loyalty to Vellan. The plot was foiled and Caldurian fled with Xavier and the Enâri. Madeline escaped with them, leading the wizard to a temporary refuge with a relative while the Enâri hid in the nearby woods. Eventually they were forced to flee east, hiding out in the Cumberland Forest to rethink their strategy.

The village of Kanesbury lay at the top of the Cumberland Forest. On occasion, Caldurian or Madeline would discreetly venture into the village for supplies or information. By chance one day, Caldurian learned that the village mayor, Otto Nibbs, was a second cousin to King Justin. He saw in this fact one last, desperate opportunity to convince the King of an alliance with Vellan. He arranged for secret talks with Otto Nibbs, promising him riches and power if he could persuade King Justin into an alliance with Kargoth. While Otto pretended to consider Caldurian's offer, he sent word to Morrenwood informing the King of the wizard's whereabouts.

Caldurian grew suspicious of Otto's stalling, realizing he had been played for a fool. In a fit of rage, he unloosed the Enâri on Kanesbury. They terrorized the village, ransacking and burning buildings. Several men were wounded in the conflict, including Jack Raven, a local farmer who was leading his wife to safety. Alice Raven was days away from having their first child. Jack died of his wounds a few days after King Justin's troops arrived. He never saw his son, Nicholas, who was born a week later.

The Enâri creatures fled the village as the soldiers pursued them, taking refuge in caves less than two miles east of Kanesbury. King Justin's soldiers guarded the cave entrances, trapping the Enâri inside. Caldurian, Madeline and Xavier were apprehended soon after. Caldurian was distraught when captured and his powers were temporarily weakened.

Accompanying King Justin was Frist, a wizard who had made multiple journeys to Laparia from the Gable Mountains to monitor Vellan's growing dominance. Frist had traveled to Kanesbury with the King when learning about Caldurian's attack. With few options, Frist cast a sleeping spell over the Enâri while they hid inside the caves, admitting that it was the most he could do without risking further bloodshed. Though a powerful wizard, Frist didn't possess the capability to turn Vellan's creatures to his will or to destroy them, at least not at the present time. He suggested a plan to safeguard the village should the creatures ever awaken from their slumber.

Frist instructed a local blacksmith to construct a small iron box with a locking lid and key. The wizard took the box, which fit into the palms of his hands, and was driven out to the caves that afternoon with King Justin and Mayor Otto Nibbs. A large contingent of villagers went as well and observed in silence. Caldurian, Madeline and Xavier, under heavy guard, were also forced to watch.

Frist stepped inside one of the caves, set the iron box on the ground and opened it. He scooped up a handful of soil and poured it into the box while whispering strange words. For over two hours he cast his spell, uttering words in a strange tongue as his face tightened in pain. Finally, he pointed at the box and the cover fell shut with a deathly thud. Frist placed the key inside the lock and turned it before collapsing to the ground in exhaustion.

He emerged an hour later at sunset, pale and shaking. He presented the iron box and key to King Justin, explaining that he had created an embryonic spirit within that would slowly grow in strength and power, hopefully one day able to destroy the Enâri horde should it be released. That day, however, would be years away since the spirit needed time to develop and effectively rival Vellan's power living within the Enâri. As a precaution, Frist cast a second spell over the iron box and key which allowed that key alone to unlock it. No other force, no matter how great, would be able to pry the lid open. Frist, nearly sapped of all his strength, climbed into a carriage and asked to be taken to a secluded spot in the woods where he slept for three uninterrupted days.

King Justin relinquished the box and key to Mayor Nibbs, telling him to keep them close at hand. But as Otto accepted the items, the eagle Xavier broke free and swooped past the mayor, seizing the key in its talons and flying out of sight. Despite that setback, Otto still possessed the iron box–soon dubbed the Spirit Box by the locals–and deemed his village safe. A manned guardhouse was built across the road from the caves–similarly named the Spirit Caves–as an added precaution. But after several years and fading memories, it was abandoned and slowly decayed.

King Justin eventually released Caldurian and Madeline, instructing them to warn Vellan not to interfere in Arrondale again. They were escorted to the southern border, taunted by the jeers of the citizens of Kanesbury along the way, many whom demanded the wizard's arrest, and some even his death. While passing through Kanesbury on the first leg of their journey south, Caldurian heard the mournful cries of Xavier in a nearby field where the bird lay injured under a shade tree. Wounds were visible on the back of its head and behind its left leg. Caldurian tended to the eagle and brought him along on their march, his hatred of the people of Kanesbury growing.

Earlier that day, after Xavier had escaped with the key, he took refuge in a field near Kanesbury, resting in the shade of an oak tree. The bird examined the key in its beak, unaware of a ten-year-old boy exploring close by. The boy spotted the eagle and crawled toward it through the tall grass while clutching two stones. The dark eyes set in the boy's pointed face locked onto the bird, desiring its catch. His wind-tossed hair was as light and brittle as the grass. With the eagle's back to him, the boy slowly stood, imagining the trajectory of one of the stones before hurling it through the air, striking the back of the bird's head, stunning it and dislodging the key from its beak. Xavier wobbled a few uncertain steps when a second stone struck it behind the left leg. Its wings flapped explosively as it dizzily fluttered away, leaving the key on the ground.

Buoyant with victory, the boy raced under the tree and spotted the key in the grass, grabbing it with his sweaty fingers. At home he found a strong piece of twine and strung it through the key, tying the two ends together. He looped it over his neck, keeping the key hidden underneath his shirt. Dooley Kramer revealed this treasure to no one during his youth, and many years would pass before another finally learned of his secret.

Caldurian, Madeline and the wounded Xavier were released at the southern border of Arrondale. They first journeyed to the Red Mountains where Caldurian had been raised. Along the shores of Lake Lasko, Xavier died. The loss of his messenger and confidant saddened and enraged the wizard. He vowed revenge against the people of Kanesbury, particularly Mayor Otto Nibbs, for the humiliation and torment they had caused him.

He and Madeline continued to Kargoth, during which time Caldurian took her on as his apprentice, teaching her the wizard's craft as Vellan had taught him. When they reached his stronghold in Mount Minakaris and explained their failings, Vellan exploded in anger. The disintegration of his plans and the loss of an Enâri company incensed him to no end.

Vellan retreated to the darkest recesses of his fortress, feeling powerless and drained of vengeful thoughts. But over the years, time slowly returned his emotions to what they once were–base, vindictive and arrogant. He again plotted how to exact his revenge on his fellow wizards, envisioning a more direct way to go about it.

For a second time twenty years later, the wizard of Kargoth set his plans in motion, once more sending out Caldurian as his primary accomplice. He vowed to gain the allegiance of other realms in Laparia, only this time not through diplomacy but rather at the point of a sword. And Caldurian, out in the world on another mission for Vellan, saw a perfect opportunity to exact a bit of revenge against those who had humiliated him years ago. And it would all begin during the Harvest Festival in the tiny village of Kanesbury.

Mune watched in amazement from behind the guardhouse as the Enâri escaped from the caves. They marched north to an area called Barringer's Landing just as their creator's disembodied voice in the blue mist had instructed. They were told of the events of the last twenty years as they were revived, including the details of their imprisonment. That only filled the Enâri with rage and strengthened their loyalty to Vellan.

Mune grinned wickedly. Everything was going according to plan just as Caldurian said it would, and he was eager to report this good news. He would meet with the wizard before dawn on the edge of the Cumberland Forest to receive his new orders.

Mune observed as the last of the Enâri exited the caves and then heard the flapping wings of a large black crow. Gavin had been perched on the rocks above the caves and now took to flight. He served as a messenger for Caldurian's team and would follow the Enâri north to make sure they arrived at their destination and then make his report. Satisfied that all was in order, Mune trudged exhaustedly back to Kanesbury in the chilly night air.

Gavin, in the meantime, watched the Enâri from the air on their northern trek to Barringer's Landing, a tract of uncultivated farmland containing several abandoned barns. They were to assemble there to await Caldurian's return and final instructions. The Enâri scrambled around or over the Spirit Caves to the north side and then trudged across a shallow section of the Pine River. The sounds of splashing water accompanying their raucous conversations were cloaked in the night's inky blackness.

Gavin watched with a sharp eye as their shadowy forms crossed the river and traversed the gently sloping hills beyond. The wind slapped their faces as they shot through fields of dried grass. For the first time in twenty years the Enâri tasted freedom, and in their hearts each of them vowed never to let down Vellan again. Except for one.

Gliding on a high current of warm air, Gavin noticed that one of the Enâri was lagging behind. His running stride slowly turned into an easy gait, then an aimless walk that separated him from his companions. The crow swooped to a lower altitude and clearly saw a confused and troubled look on the creature's face. Maybe a forced twenty-year sleep had taken its toll on some. Gavin flew toward him, alighting on a nearby thorn bush and cawing several times.

The Enâr stopped, easily understanding Gavin's language, one of the many traits Vellan had instilled in his creation. He looked up, his eyes empty, his mouth half open as if trying to form words that wouldn't take shape. He staggered closer to the crow.

"Are you hurting?" Gavin asked.

The creature nodded and plopped down in the grass, holding his head in his hands. Gavin flitted over and landed on a tuft of weeds, stretching his glossy wings before folding them snugly. The creature mouthed a few inaudible words.

"I don't understand," the bird said. It bobbed along the ground and jumped on the creature's left arm. "Speak louder. What do you want to tell me?"

The Enâr, whose name was Jagga, raised a weary eye to the crow. It exhaled slowly through his teeth and then suddenly grabbed the bird by both legs with his right hand. Gavin flapped up a storm trying to escape, but Jagga held on tightly as he jumped to his feet, keeping the bird at arm's length.

"Let me go, trickster! When Caldurian hears of this outrage, you'll be punished. When Vellan hears of it, you'll be turned into the stone and dirt you were made from!"

"You value yourself too highly, crow." Jagga had a new life about him. His strength and stamina were evident in his gravelly voice. "Neither Caldurian nor Vellan would value your life over mine." He squeezed the bird's legs tighter. "And if you wish to keep yours, you'll answer my questions."

Gavin flapped his wings again, but Jagga held on firmly, so the crow relented. "What do you want?"

"Information." Jagga walked slowly through the cool dark field. A breeze rustled his tangled hair. "I need to know about the threat."

"What threat?"

"The threat to the Enâri, to our very existence." Jagga's cold eyes bore down on the crow. "Vellan told us every detail about our imprisonment when he spoke to us from the blue mist. I learned how we were forced to sleep for twenty years by the cruel hand of the wizard Frist. I know about the spirit that has been growing inside an iron box for the same length of time, and of the existence of a single key that can release it and destroy the Enâri." Jagga shook his fist in the air, causing Gavin to squeak in discomfort. "I know the bumbling tactics of Caldurian got us into this mess, but I'll never understand why Vellan sent some of us away under his command. Caldurian is a failure. But Vellan willed it, so I complied. But not anymore. I have my freedom, and I intend to keep it."

"Be off then! Let me go, beast! I won't mention this incident to my superiors."

Jagga snarled. "I don't trust you any more than Caldurian, crow, and would gladly crush you in my fist if I didn't need you."

"And I would carry you high into the air by my talons had I the strength and drop you onto a pile of sharp rocks to end your miserable existence!"

"But that fantasy is not to be. Answer my questions and I might think about letting you live. Fly off to that fool Caldurian afterward and tell him your tale of woe."

"Be quick about it! What information do you seek, Enâr?"

"First, who ventured into the caves and released us?"

"Some local from the nearby village. Mune conned him into delivering a device into the caves, a device created by Vellan to release you from your sleep."

"Who is Mune?"

Gavin craned his neck and snapped his beak. "An associate of Caldurian. He does much of his dirty work, strictly for profit."

"A coward," Jagga said. "He hadn't the courage to enter the caves himself and face our awakening."

"Caldurian only told Mune what to do, not how to do it. And since the Enâri are indeed awake, you ought to be thankful. The job was handled successfully."

"Apparently Caldurian's only success." Jagga glared at the crow. "What are his plans now? Vellan didn't reveal that when waking us."

"I don't know the details of Caldurian's latest orders. But he will meet with you on Barringer's Landing a day after he finishes some other business in Kanesbury."

Jagga recalled the name of that small village from twenty years ago. "That is where our troubles began. What business does Caldurian have there now?"

"I'm not at liberty to say."

Jagga shook his fist several times, jarring the bird. "Well, crow, you had better say before I squeeze the life out of you!"

"Caldurian would lose confidence in me if I betrayed his trust!"

Jagga squeezed harder as Gavin struggled. "For the last time, what is Caldurian's business in Kanesbury?"

Gavin couldn't tolerate the searing pain in his legs any longer. "*He's found the key! He's found the key!*" The bird's wings flapped wildly. "Caldurian is going to meet with someone who has the key to the Spirit Box."

Jagga loosened his grip slightly as his eyes widened. "Who?"

"I can't say!"

Jagga placed his other hand around the bird's neck and gazed into its eyes. "Unless you want to die, crow, you better tell me every detail about that key. If any other words come out of your mouth next except those, don't expect to ever utter another. Hear?"

Gavin's heart pounded. He quickly told Jagga everything he wanted to know. "Caldurian is supposed to meet with the man tomorrow evening."

"What's his name again?"

"Farnsworth. Zachary Farnsworth."

"And you're sure he has the key?"

"Yes, I told you he does!"

"How did Farnsworth come to possess it?"

"He's friends with the person who found it years ago–Dooley Kramer."

"You're telling me the truth, crow?"

"Yes! I swear it!"

Jagga lessened his grip as he contemplated what to do. Possessing the key would guarantee his safety, and part of him believed that Caldurian wanted to retrieve the key for the same reason–to protect the Enâri. But Jagga distrusted Caldurian as much as the people who imprisoned him, wondering if Caldurian would use the key to force their continued cooperation in Vellan's absence. But Caldurian would also need the Spirit Box to do so. Did he possess that already, and if not, who did? Jagga's mind raced along several lines of reasoning at once, wondering who in the world controlled his existence. *He* wanted control. *He* needed to ensure his safety, desiring nothing more than to live in freedom, a servant to no one. Jagga realized that he must locate Zachary Farnsworth or Dooley Kramer before Caldurian did. It was his best chance for success.

As those thoughts ricocheted through his mind, Jagga inadvertently loosened his grip just enough for Gavin to escape with a powerful flap of his wings. The crow shrieked, taking a peck at Jagga's forehead before flying out of reach on a nearby shrub.

"You're in for it now, traitor! I'll report you to Mune before the sun rises. He'll let Caldurian know about your treachery."

"You do that!" Jagga scowled. He made a half-hearted grab for the bird, but Gavin was mindful of his intentions and shot high into the air.

"You'll never catch me twice, Enâr!"

"I should have wrung your neck when I had the chance. Now be gone! I have plans of my own," he said, running off in the opposite direction of his companions.

Gavin watched him from above as he raced west along the Pine River toward Kanesbury, wondering what mischief he would cause in the village. He then flew off to Barringer's Landing to check on the progress of the others, knowing that Caldurian would be angry once news of this defection reached his ears.

CHAPTER 5

The Party

Zachary Farnsworth dipped his hands into a ceramic washbasin of cold water and splashed some over his face. He patted his eyes dry with a towel while staring at himself in a wall mirror, appearing refreshed despite the weariness deep in his bones. He dabbed the water away and straightened his collar, looking forward to the party now underway at the Stewart estate. After extinguishing an oil lamp on a shelf, he stepped into the hallway.

A light breeze drifted in through an open side window. Farnsworth slipped on a vest in front of a standing mirror, fastening each brass button as he contemplated who would attend tonight's party. He managed the local banking house for Horace Ulm and thus secured an invitation from Amanda Stewart. He hoped one day to buy the bank from Horace should he ever pass on, but with his employer's constitution still intact into his late fifties, he didn't foresee himself as a prominent business leader in the village any time soon. He believed that tonight's invitation resulted solely as a courtesy to Horace. But Zachary Farnsworth was confident he would soon imprint his mark upon Kanesbury, and then Amanda Stewart and her ilk would have to show him the respect he deserved.

In time. All in good time.

As he put on his evening coat, he heard a swish of leaves outside the window. As his was the second of two houses on this dead-end lane, he rarely had individuals pass by his property. Farnsworth adjusted his shirt cuffs as he stepped out onto the front porch to investigate. The night was cold and black. The aroma of decaying leaves and wood smoke wafted through the air. Several pine and maple trees surrounding the property engulfed the house in an extra blanket of shadow.

An oil lamp's swaying cone of light was visible a short distance down the road. The figure of Dooley Kramer soon emerged into view, plowing through mounds of fallen leaves. Farnsworth waited impatiently on the porch until Dooley was in earshot.

"Bored with the village festivities?" he asked with a smirk.

"There've been some wild ones tonight." Dooley grinned as he set the lamp on the bottom step, running a hand through his disorderly mop of hair. "I wanted to tell you how things turned out. Couldn't find you at the Iron Kettle."

"I came back to dress for the party. Have to look my best for the ladies, you understand."

"Yeah, I understand." Dooley grunted. "Understand that I'm not allowed in any of those uppity gatherings."

"One of these days you'll have the status and wherewithal to celebrate like me. In the meantime, we have to stick to our plan. But you may get some public recognition tonight nonetheless."

Dooley looked up skeptically before spitting in the dirt. "*Meaning?*"

"Meaning, I'll corner Ned Adams at the party and subtly sing your praises. You were, after all, instrumental in helping discover who stole the flour and money from the gristmill. Once word floats around the village, your reputation might rise a notch or two. Ned will have reason to consider you for Nicholas' job."

"Really think so?"

"Of course! You have a good head on your shoulders, Dooley, when you apply yourself." Farnsworth momentarily stepped back into the hall, extinguished an oil lamp near the mirror and closed the door, throwing the house into darkness.

Dooley whispered. "Is *she* inside yet?" Farnsworth nodded. "What are we going to do with her?"

"I'm working on a plan, but we'll deal with that later." He met Dooley at the bottom of the porch stairs and indicated for him to walk along. "What is the word on Nicholas Raven? Is he enjoying the inside of the constable's lockup?"

"Not exactly," he said. "Ned Adams sent for me a short time ago. Wanted me to drive a cart to Nicholas' shed so I could take the items back to the warehouse. When I arrived, he said that Nicholas had run off after being arrested. Bolted through the field like a jackrabbit. Can you believe it?"

Farnsworth halted. "Where is he now?"

"Constable Brindle sent some men after him, but the last I heard is that Nicholas disappeared. No one's seen him around Kanesbury. Constable's still looking."

"No matter," Farnsworth said as he continued walking. "Nicholas is out of the way whether he sits in the lockup or flees to another county. That's what Caldurian wanted and that's what we delivered."

"I still don't understand," Dooley said, swishing through the leaves. "Why does that wizard want Nicholas Raven out of the way?"

"I don't question his reasons. I do what I'm told. It's part of our deal."

They neared Dooley's house a short distance down the road. Small and overgrown with dried weeds from summer, with a cracked window on the second floor, the wood and stone property looked as unkempt as Dooley Kramer himself.

"There's something else I don't understand, Zachary."

Farnsworth exhaled with obvious frustration. "What?"

"If Caldurian wanted us to get Nicholas out of his way, and Nicholas was already planning to join up with the King's Guard, then why did we go through all the trouble of framing him for robbery? Plus now we've got Adelaide in your cellar to deal with."

Farnsworth sighed wearily. "If Nicholas left to join the King's Guard, my dense friend, then you'd never have had a chance at getting his old job. Do you honestly think that Ned Adams would let you assume Nicholas' duties if he had simply left for the capital as planned?"

"I'm not stupid, you know! I could do his job."

"No one is saying you couldn't, Dooley. But we had to give Ned a compelling reason to hire you. So now that you've *discovered* the break-in at the mill and figured out what was missing by poring through the ledgers, why, Ned Adams must be thinking that maybe you've got more potential than you've been letting on. And if he's not thinking that, I'll make certain he does tonight at the party."

"The one I'm not invited to."

"Don't sulk. Anyway, if you take over Nicholas' duties, you'll be required to make deliveries directly to the storage cellars in the Blue Citadel. We'll sweeten our end of the deal by handing Caldurian a potential spy in Morrenwood, namely you."

"*Me*! Why me? And what does he need a spy there for?"

"Why *you*? Because no one would expect a lout like you to be capable of spying. And as I told you earlier, I don't question Caldurian's reasons, but his spies are everywhere. So why not hand him an extra one as a bonus? That can only improve our worth in his eyes." Farnsworth pointed a finger at Dooley. "Do as you're ordered and everything will fall into place. The details aren't important. I don't even know all the details. These wizard folk work in strange ways. But if we play along and don't cross him, we'll be feasting like vultures in this village before you know it."

Dooley grunted and spat on the ground again. The pine trees creaked in the gentle wind under a field of fiery stars. The sickly glow of the lamp light outlined the sour discontentment on his face.

"Sounds good when you say it, but there's still another part of the bargain I don't like. Not one bit, I tell you!"

Farnsworth understood what Dooley implied. "But that is the key to our reward!" he insisted. "Tomorrow night is the night. I'll meet with Caldurian as planned to fulfill our end of the bargain, and then we'll be sliding steady on ice afterward."

"I just don't want to fall through the ice," Dooley said. "And how do we know Caldurian will keep his word? I don't want to give that wizard my key!"

Farnsworth grabbed Dooley by the collar with one hand, staring him down with a vicious gaze. "Don't foil my plans, you hear? We've plotted this carefully for months and we're close to the finish. I won't tolerate any slip ups!" He shoved Dooley aside, breathing heavily.

"I was only saying–"

"I don't want to hear it, Dooley! We're giving Caldurian the key and that's final. Imagine what he'd do to us if we went back on our word."

"Suppose he does anyway? I don't trust him. It's my key and I want it back! Let's not hand it over until we see more of our reward."

Farnsworth walked in circles and shook his head. Some days he thought his alliance with Dooley Kramer wasn't worth the aggravation. "We agreed that I was to be entrusted with the key, right?"

Dooley clenched his teeth. "*You* agreed!"

"In case you're forgetting, I can easily inform Caldurian exactly how you found that key twenty years ago."

"Shut your face!" Dooley kicked some leaves and trudged to his front door.

"Think how furious Caldurian would be if he discovered the truth about a mischievous little boy pelting his eagle with rocks until he nearly killed the bird."

"Stop it!"

"Then stealing the key from the bird and running away as it lay dying in a field, bleeding under the hot sun."

"Shut up, Zachary, or I'll knock you one!"

"What do you say about such a story, Dooley? How long do you think Caldurian would allow you to live after hearing that?"

Dooley stood with his back to Farnsworth, his lungs burning and his throat bitter. He cursed the day he ever told Farnsworth about his treasure. He tightly gripped the handle of his oil lamp and imagined smacking it across the side of Farnsworth's skull, but simply stood there instead, knowing that his neighbor was calling the shots.

"Go to your stupid party! But if things turn out wrong…"

"Everything will turn out perfectly, Dooley." He shrugged as Dooley continued to stand with his back to him. "Well, what more can I say? I'll talk to you tomorrow. Get a good night's sleep. We'll have plenty to do in the days to follow."

Farnsworth continued down the road until he disappeared out of view. Dooley breathed erratically and stomped on the ground before shuffling to his front door and pounding his fist into the frame. But after a few moments, he glanced in the direction that Farnsworth had taken, the road disappearing into blackness. He looked the opposite way toward Farnsworth's house, thought for a moment, and then hurried through the leaves back up the road, determined to retake control of the situation.

The party was in full swing at the Stewart estate when Farnsworth arrived. Many business owners, as well as Mayor Otto Nibbs and the five village council members, milled about the bright and spacious rooms. Wine, ale and traditional Harvest berry punch flowed freely throughout the evening. A wide assortment of foods and desserts filled several tables. Plates heaping with roasted turkey, beef and ham were surrounded by raw and boiled vegetables. Blackened trout steamed with the scent of lemon and rosemary. Bowls of salted potatoes floating in melted butter nudged for room with wedges of cheese and platters of ripened fruit. Loaves of sliced breads–apple-walnut, blackberry-carrot and frosted cinnamon–took up another table entirely, accompanied by wooden vessels of freshly whipped butter and assorted spiced cream spreads. Trays of colorful hors d'oeuvres floated about the rooms upon the steady hands of the house staff. Framed against the large windows in one room were four musicians, dutifully playing stringed instruments and flutes, sending soothing sounds wafting through the air to the approving ears of Amanda Stewart.

Farnsworth quickly discovered that he wouldn't have to broach the subject of the gristmill robbery. The names of Nicholas Raven and Dooley Kramer were on the lips of all the party guests. When encountering Ned Adams near a fireplace, who explained that he had only stopped by to make an appearance since he was too upset to enjoy himself for an entire evening, Farnsworth subtly suggested that perhaps Dooley would make an apt replacement during Nicholas' absence.

"My thought precisely, Zachary, though I intend to give Dooley a trial run first." Ned drank from his glass of ale. "I've underestimated Dooley. He can be quite conscientious when he puts his mind to it. I was mightily impressed with the man as he helped out during the robbery tonight, though he should consider taking a brush more often to that unruly mop on his head."

Farnsworth chuckled. "He has a few good traits inside him. More responsibility might make a model citizen out of Dooley yet."

"The book work at the mill is nearly complete for the year. All that's left are some large deliveries out of county. I think I'll let

Dooley handle those in Nicholas' stead. If he has no problems, then perhaps I might train him in the bookkeeping over the winter lull."

"A fine idea, Ned." Farnsworth helped himself to a slice of dessert bread at a nearby table. "And who can blame you for watching out for your interests? You have to act quickly to put the situation in order. If Dooley can help, so much the better." He took a bite of the bread, savoring each morsel. "By the way, any word on Nicholas yet? I heard he fled before he was arrested."

"It's true." Ned looked despondently into his drink. "I still can't get over what happened. I never anticipated that he'd... I mean, Nicholas of all people! He's been such a fine worker to all the sudden–" He looked up, his eyes red with anxiety. "I probably shouldn't have come here tonight. I'll give my regrets to Amanda and Oscar and head home. I'm feeling tired. Excuse me, Zachary."

"I understand."

Ned Adams set his glass down and drifted through the talkative crowd. Farnsworth watched him depart, devouring the rest of his bread with inexpressive bliss.

Katherine Durant entered the busy kitchen carrying two empty bowls and a platter, depositing them near the sink for Lewis Ames to wash. Her hair fell limply in the humid air and her feet were stone heavy. Lewis was up to his elbows in soapy water and eyed Katherine with an infatuated grin.

"I hope I don't come off sounding crude or impolite, Katherine, but..."

She tried not to smirk or sound haughty. "Yes, Lewis?"

He scratched his forehead, leaving a line of soap suds above his eyebrow. "I was wondering if... Well, seeing that Nicholas won't be accompanying you to the dance the day after tomorrow, do you think that–?" Katherine sighed and slumped her shoulders as Lewis spoke. He immediately knew her answer. "Oh, I see."

She was about to enter the pantry, then turned to Lewis. "That's a very sweet offer, and thank you. But to tell the truth, I just don't feel much like celebrating the Festival after what happened to Nicholas tonight. And I particularly don't feel like dancing. I'd go home now except that I promised Amanda to stay and help."

"I understand. I shouldn't have asked." Lewis went back to scrubbing a large copper pot.

She managed to smile and patted him on the shoulder. "I'm going to find something to eat and go outside for a few minutes. I need a break."

"Okay."

Katherine walked into the pantry and stared at the ice boxes, realizing she wasn't quite that hungry. All she really wanted was some time alone away from the boisterous guests. Anxiety about Nicholas' situation jumbled her emotions. She had no idea where he was, and listening to the assorted rumors at the party, she wondered if he would ever return to Kanesbury. Until she had a chance to speak with Maynard Kurtz or Constable Brindle, she knew her mind could not rest.

"*Down here*," a voice whispered.

Katherine spun around and looked into the kitchen through the doorway. The staff went methodically about its business, cooking, preparing and washing in the synchronous perfection which Amanda Stewart demanded. She shrugged the voice off to her imagination and prepared to leave, but it called out once more and she turned around.

"*Downstairs. In the ice cellar.*"

The door to the ice cellar was slightly ajar. Katherine cautiously opened it, allowing light from the pantry to fall upon a dark figure sitting a few steps below. A finger was placed over its lips, indicating for her to be quiet.

Katherine's spirit rose as she mouthed Nicholas' name. She grabbed a candle from a nearby shelf, lit it from a burning oil lamp, and then descended the stairs into the ice cellar with Nicholas leading the way. They took refuge in a far corner near a stack of ice chunks covered in straw.

"What are you doing here, Nicholas? How'd you get away? I've heard so many rumors tonight, I don't know who or what to believe." Katherine wedged the candle between two squares of ice and hugged him, feeling protected by the cold shadows surrounding them. "I'm so glad you're all right. Or are you? Are you safe? What's going to happen? Can I help?"

"Calm down," Nicholas said, grinning for the first time in many lonely hours. "You're chattering like a squirrel."

"Sorry, but I'm so relieved to see you." Her eyes sparkled in the candlelight. "How long have you been hiding here?"

"About an hour. After I ran away from Constable Brindle, I stayed in the woods along the river and followed it nearly to your Uncle Otto's house on the other side of the village. But not knowing what to do next, I circled back this way and slipped in through the cellar door behind the house. I figured with all the people here, news of what happened tonight should be plentiful. I was hoping to see you, explain my side of the story and get some information." Nicholas rubbed his arms for warmth. "What I'd give to be upstairs by a fireplace."

"Let me sneak a bite down for you to eat. That'll warm you up. Then you can tell me what's going on. The gossip around town is as thick as summer flies."

"I wish I knew what was going on, Katherine." The candle illuminated the despair etched upon his face. "I haven't a clue."

Katherine hurried upstairs and hastily threw together a turkey sandwich which she brought to Nicholas along with an apple and a cup of Harvest berry punch. They sat on the floor. "You probably think there's no reason to celebrate, but the punch is especially good this year. It'll give you energy."

"I do feel drained." Nicholas attacked his sandwich and washed it down with some punch. His head cleared and he felt calm and secure with Katherine by his side.

"So what happened?" she asked. "Tell me about the robbery."

"Apparently I'm a thief," he said sarcastically. "The shed in back of my cottage was filled with sacks of flour and a small pouch of money, all of it stolen from Ned's gristmill. And I'm the one they're blaming." He took another bite of the sandwich. "Of course, if I didn't know I was innocent, I'd think I was guilty myself. The evidence looked very incriminating."

"You have no idea how those items ended up there?"

"No. But they must have been placed there no more than three days ago. That's the last time I recall going into the shed. Most of the things I need to work on the farm are in Maynard's barn."

"Maynard had no knowledge of this either?"

"He was as stunned as I was," Nicholas said. "I thought of going back to his house, but I'm sure Clay or his men are waiting there for me. I don't know what to do."

"Well don't think about turning yourself in, Nicholas. You're not guilty and you'd be forced to sit in one of the constable's cells until he gets to the bottom of this mess." Katherine raised an eyebrow. "*If* he gets to the bottom. I like Clay Brindle, but he does take his time about some matters. Why did they suspect you?"

Nicholas polished off the remainder of the sandwich and punch, wiping his mouth with a coat sleeve. "It was that spindly Arthur Weeks. He accused me of going back to the mill at night while he was cleaning up." His face tightened. "Arthur said I ordered him to go home because I needed to finish the bookkeeping. He places me at the mill alone at night, insinuating that I was the likely suspect. Said it right to the constable's face. I'd like to grab a handful of that liar's greasy black hair and sail him right off a cliff!"

Katherine grinned. "That's quite an image."

"I'm serious, Katherine." But he couldn't keep a straight face either and laughed softly with her.

"Not too loud, Nicholas. Someone might hear us."

"With that racket upstairs? I doubt it." He bit the apple and thought for a moment. "There's still something I can't figure out. Constable Brindle said he found a button from my coat on the floor near one of the orders that had been broken into." He showed Katherine the spot on his jacket where the button once had been. "Though it definitely is my button, I have no idea how it got there."

Katherine looked reassuringly at her friend. "Someone's behind it, Nicholas. But if you can't figure it out now, the constable or Maynard eventually will. Give them time."

"I suppose I have to." He raised a questioning eye. "Do you think I'm doing the right thing? Running away like this? Maybe I should turn myself in until they discover the truth. Part of me feels like a coward for hiding out."

"You're feeling conflicting emotions right now, Nicholas. I can't tell you what to do, but I'll support whatever decision you make." She stood. "But take a day to think about it first. A good night's sleep will clear your mind. Decide in the morning."

"That's assuming I get any sleep. Maybe I'll sneak back to Maynard's place in a few hours. I don't think Clay or his men will keep watch all night. I could get a few hours of rest in the barn."

Katherine patted his shoulder. "I have to go back upstairs. Stay as long as you like. All the ice boxes are filled, so no one should be back down here tonight. I'll bring you more food before you leave."

"Thanks, Katherine." He tried to smile. "I guess this throws our dance plans right down the well."

"We'd draw a lot of attention arriving at the pavilion arm in arm, wouldn't we?"

Nicholas nodded with a smile, trying to make light of the situation. But inside he was churning with bitterness and confusion. His plans of the last few days were crumbling to bits before his eyes and he knew of no way to stop it.

CHAPTER 6

A Thief in the Night

Night deepened as the skies clouded over several hours later. Jagga hid in a grove of maple trees across the road from Dooley Kramer's house. A short time earlier, the Enâri creature had accosted an inebriated local as he wandered along a deserted street, demanding the location of Dooley's home in exchange for his life. Now, Jagga patiently waited for the right moment to strike, planning to sneak into Dooley's house, surprise him and grab the key. A man with a mop of tangled, dirty blond hair had entered the house a short while ago. Jagga assumed that he was Dooley and waited. A dull light glowed behind two shuttered windows. The street lay deathly quiet. Jagga held his ground a few more minutes to make sure no one else was around. When he was about to dash across the road, he noticed a tall thin man swishing through the leaves and heading directly for the house. Jagga growled under his breath as the man knocked on the door. A moment later Dooley answered and let him inside, so Jagga waited impatiently and observed.

Moments later the front door reopened. "Wait for me inside," Dooley said over his shoulder as he exited his house. "It'll be easier if I talk to Zachary myself."

A voice called from within. "But maybe I should–"

"Arthur, let me handle this!" Dooley slammed the door shut, and with an oil lamp in hand, trudged up the road to Zachary

Farnsworth's house. Jagga's watchful eyes followed him for a moment before the Enâr stealthily tracked him from along the edge of the woods.

Dooley stepped onto the front porch. After a tentative knock, the door flew open. The lamp light illuminated Farnsworth's twisted face. He grabbed Dooley's arm and hauled him inside, slamming the door shut. Jagga watched curiously from the trees and then hurried around to the side of the house where he spotted an open window. He clearly heard the voices of two men inside and squatted beneath the window to listen.

"Where is it?" Farnsworth shouted. "I know you took it, Dooley! Tell me before I bust your head open!"

Dooley whimpered like a dog. "So I took it, okay? I came back here after you went to the party and found it."

"You *found* it? Why, you broke into my house, you little rat!"

"The key was mine! I want to decide when we hand it over. *If* we hand it over."

Farnsworth held his seething temper in check. "If I don't have that key in my hand when Caldurian arrives tomorrow night, we'll both be finished. That was part of the deal. Do you understand what I'm saying, Dooley?"

"I never agreed to any of this. You talked to that wizard behind my back."

"Are you dense?"

"Don't talk to me like that! Maybe *you're* dense. I say we keep the key until after we get everything we want. Consider it insurance."

There was a crash of glass as Farnsworth flung aside a decanter of wine with his arm. "See how upset you've made me, Dooley. Now where is that key?"

"Back at my house where it belongs, and you're not touching it. I'm tired of you always stepping on me. It's always your way, your idea. Well, enough, Zachary! Things haven't gone so smooth with you in charge," he spouted, his voice quavering. "You still got that old lady locked in your cellar which is a crimp in our plans if ever there was one. And Arthur Weeks is at my house this very minute demanding to get paid for his part. That's why I'm here. He wants his money!"

"Tell that beanpole he'll have to wait a while longer. He'll be paid by the end of the week."

"He'd better. If you cross him, Arthur says he'll go straight to Clay Brindle and tell him how he lied about Nicholas. Then we'll all be sitting in the lockup. And that key you're harping about won't get us out of there!"

"You're an annoying pest if there ever was one!" Farnsworth lashed out. "Why couldn't you just leave matters in my hands?"

As Farnsworth continued his tirade against Dooley, Jagga decided he had heard enough from outside the window. Having discovered the location of the key, he quietly slipped away from the house as the two men argued on and scurried back down the road to Dooley's residence, determined to secure his freedom.

Jagga stealthily approached and peered inside Dooley's kitchen window. There at a table, jittery and white as a ghost, sat Arthur Weeks, mumbling to himself as he drummed his fingers on the table top. An oil lamp and a few lit candles illuminated the room. Jagga stepped aside, his back to the house, and glanced up through the trees to consider his options. There wouldn't be much time to act since Dooley might return at any moment, possibly with Farnsworth in tow. He clenched his fists and walked to the front door.

He turned the knob and quietly entered. The glow of light from the kitchen was visible in the darkened hallway. Jagga took each step carefully, conscious of the tiniest squeak in the pine floorboards. He was used to living in caves and woods and among open spaces. The confined living quarters of men seemed stifling and prison-like. Suddenly his knee slammed into a small table hidden in the shadows, sending a slew of objects clattering to the floor.

"Is that you, Dooley?" Arthur called from the kitchen.

Jagga stood still, the element of surprise now gone. He wondered if he should bolt. A light from the kitchen grew brighter as Arthur approached carrying an oil lamp.

"I didn't think you'd be back so soon. Was Zachary reasonable about my demand?" He held up the lamp and the light hit Jagga's stony, scarred face. "He'd better be or–" Arthur's jaw dropped when confronting the vacant stare of the short, burly Enâr bathed in the sickly light. He stood frozen, the lamp shaking in his extended arm. "*Oh...*" Arthur Weeks swallowed hard. "You're not

Dooley," he nervously said as if trying to mollify a snarling dog blocking his path. "You should leave." Arthur flinched as Jagga glared at him, his heart pounding as the stranger stepped forward. "Or I could leave."

Arthur suddenly pivoted on his heel and ran back to the kitchen as Jagga pursued in a flash. He screamed as the Enâr trapped him in the room and lunged at him. A crash of plates and the overturning of wooden chairs ensued as the two fought. The candles extinguished one by one as they were knocked down.

"Where's the key?" Jagga demanded when he grabbed Arthur by the collar.

"Let me go! I don't know what you're talking about!" Arthur Weeks struggled like a fish on a hook and then slammed a fist into Jagga's ear, causing him to release his hold. Arthur dove under the table to the other side of the room. "What are you?"

Jagga howled in pain as he got to his feet, holding the sore side of his head while sending a chair crashing into the wall with his free hand. Arthur made a move toward the doorway, but the Enâr blocked his way, trapping him in a corner.

"Tell me where the key is! I know you're in league with the other two. Tell me!"

"I don't know what you're talking about! I don't know anything about a key!"

"I think you do." Jagga grasped an object he spied on a countertop and slowly approached a terrified Arthur Weeks.

"Stay away!" he said. "Whatever you're looking for, I don't have it. Dooley Kramer lives here, not me." His face perspired profusely. The long black locks on the side of his head stuck to his cheeks like wet grass clippings. Arthur pressed his body against the wall in a futile effort to break it down as he watched the Enâr step closer. "Please stay away..." The wildly fluttering flame inside the oil lamp softly reflected off the metal knife Jagga clutched in his hand.

"I'm not leaving without that key," he muttered as he closed in on his target. "And I'm going to find it, one way or another."

Dooley sauntered back to his house twenty minutes later through a swirl of autumn leaves. He had survived his confrontation with Farnsworth who reluctantly agreed to let him hold onto the key for the time being. He also promised to pay off Arthur Weeks within two days. Dooley breathed in the vigorous night air, feeling full of himself for having stood up to Farnsworth. He had plans to go places and to make his mark in the village, too, and tonight went a long way toward boosting his confidence. He could only imagine better things to come.

Then he turned the knob on the front door. The light from his oil lamp illuminated the hallway. Dooley scowled when noticing the hall stand knocked over and a bevy of items strewn across the floor. He scratched his head.

"Arthur! What'd you do while I was away? Clean up this mess." He gently moved a few things aside with the toe of his boot. "I leave for a few minutes and look what happens," he muttered. "Arthur, get out here!"

Disturbing silence filled the rooms. Dooley looked up, raising his lamp which cast flickering shadows. "Arthur?" He stepped over the spilled items and headed to the kitchen. "You still here?"

He poked his head into the room and his chest tightened. The kitchen had been torn apart. The table and chairs overturned. One window smashed. Dishes and food canisters thrown across the floor. Arthur's oil lamp sat on a counter beneath a cupboard that had been ransacked, its doors wide open. Dooley shuddered and raced across the room, desperately searching for a wooden salt box he had stored in that cupboard. It was gone. He surveyed the floor and then spotted the salt box which had been thrown against the wall to his left. The hinged lid was open and a spray of salt dusted the floor. He grabbed the box but already knew the worst in his heart. Farnsworth would kill him for sure. This couldn't be happening. Someone had stolen the key from its hiding place.

"I'm dead!" he whispered as he got to his feet. "Dead."

Dooley's hand trembled as he tried to hold the lamp steady. His exhilaration of just minutes ago came crashing down, leaving a knot in the pit of his stomach. He stepped back, shaking his head. How could he fix this? He then bumped into an overturned chair, spun around and saw him. Sprawled on the floor behind the table lay Arthur Weeks, his eyes open as he gazed up at the ceiling, dead to the world. His body had been hidden from view when Dooley first entered the room. He stared at him for several minutes, unable to take his eyes off the knife wound in Arthur's chest.

Dooley cautiously knelt on one knee by the body, gently holding the oil lamp near Arthur's face. He prodded the corpse's arm with a finger to make certain he was dead before turning away and taking a deep breath. The scent of blood sickened him. He got to his feet and stumbled around the kitchen wreckage, holding his head and mumbling.

"Who did this, Arthur? Who did this? I need that key back!" Dooley kicked a metal canister across the room and glared at the dead body again. "Who did this to you, Arthur? Tell me! I need to find that key or Farnsworth will kill me next!"

Arthur kept his gaze fixed on the ceiling as Dooley rambled about, whimpering and cursing his bad luck. All seemed lost. His plans were decaying and either Farnsworth, Caldurian or Constable Brindle would make him regret this day for the rest of his life. There was little he could do to salvage the situation though he tried to think of something as he ran around like a madman. He howled at his ill fortune, kicking the walls and punching the air with his fist. In a spasm of rage he ran out of the house screaming, not even aware of the words he was shouting.

"Murder!" he screamed into the night, twirling in circles on the road, sending up a shower of leaves that glowed in the light from the lamp he still clutched in his hand. "Murder! Murder! There's a killer loose in Kanesbury!"

Farnsworth soon came running down the road toward Dooley's house with a glowing lamp in hand, stunned at the sight of his crazed neighbor in convulsive fits in the road.

"What's the matter with you, Dooley? It's the middle of the night!"

"Someone help!" he cried, unaware of Farnsworth's presence.

Farnsworth yanked him by the arm, snapping his body to a sudden halt. "Shut up, you fool! What's going on?"

He stared at Farnsworth with a vacant expression. "It wasn't my fault, Zachary. It wasn't. I didn't steal it, and I certainly didn't kill him. I didn't!"

"What are you jabbering about? Are you drunk?"

"No, but I will be before the sun rises!" Dooley suddenly broke down in a fit of laughter, dropping his oil lamp. He bent over, his hands on his knees, laughing uncontrollably until he started coughing and sobbing. "Arthur's dead!" he said. "He's lying on my kitchen floor and I don't know what to do about it."

"*Dead? How?*"

"Someone killed him," he said, pointing to the house.

Farnsworth dashed inside for a look and felt his blood turn cold. He had never seen a murdered man and the sight sickened him. He returned to the street and saw Dooley sitting in the middle of the road. Before he could say anything, he paused to listen. Voices approached from the main section of the village.

"People are coming, Dooley! Quick! Tell me what happened."

Dooley looked up and sighed. "The key is gone. Whoever did this stole it."

"*What?* Besides Caldurian, who else knew we had it? Did you tell anyone?"

"No! I swear!"

The voices grew louder. A mob was heading their way.

"We can't let anyone know about the robbery! Do you hear me?" Farnsworth grabbed Dooley by the collar and lifted him to his feet. "DO YOU HEAR ME?" he said, shaking him violently.

"Yes, yes! But what do we do?"

"Let me think a minute! Let me think!" He rubbed his face with one hand, looking left, looking right, and then glared at Dooley. "I've got an idea. I know who committed this murder."

"You do?"

"Not really! But as soon as the constable gets here–because I'm sure he's with that crowd–you're going to tell him exactly what I'm about to tell you."

"Which is?"

"First things first," Farnsworth said, clenching his fist. He slugged Dooley square in the jaw, sending him sailing across the road and stumbling over a tree root. Dooley wiped away some blood from his lip as Farnsworth helped him up.

"What'd you hit me for?"

"I didn't hit you," Farnsworth said. "Nicholas Raven did!"

"*Huh?*"

"Shut up and listen!" he ordered. "You tell everyone that Nicholas Raven broke into your house tonight while Arthur Weeks was visiting you. Nicholas tried to attack Arthur, so you intervened. Nicholas then punched you, and by the time you got up, Arthur had already been stabbed and was dying. Got that so far?"

"Yeah... I think."

"Then you and Nicholas fought in the house, causing all the mess, but he pushed you down and fled before you could stop him. That's when you screamed for help."

"But why would Nicholas come here?"

"For revenge, you idiot! He wanted to get back at Arthur for accusing him of being at the gristmill on the night of the robbery."

"Oh."

"And whatever you do, don't mention a thing about the key. Got it? This was simply revenge and murder, not robbery."

"Okay. And what are you going to say?"

"Nothing, because I can't be seen with you," Farnsworth said. "I'll wander down here after the others arrive, saying I heard a commotion. Now I've got to leave!" he insisted, rushing up the street toward his house. "And stick to the story!"

A few moments later, a crowd of people turned the corner and hurried toward Dooley's house, their path through the deep night lit with a host of torches and oil lamps that illuminated the trees with a demonic orange glow as if they were on fire. Dooley swallowed hard, awaiting their arrival with dizzying thoughts.

With a trembling hand, Katherine shook Nicholas' shoulder. "Wake up! You have to get out of here right away." She held a flickering candle in her other hand which cast ghostly shadows in the ice cellar.

"*Huh?*" Nicholas opened his eyes, momentarily forgetting where he was. "Katherine? What's the matter?"

"You have to leave, Nicholas. Now! You're not safe here."

He sat up in the cold gloom and stretched, his head swimming with uneasy sleep. He only now realized the toll that exhaustion had taken on his body. "How long have I been out? I only wanted to close my eyes for a minute. I was so tired."

"You've been asleep for a couple of hours. And as much as I hate to send you away, Nicholas, I'm afraid I must for your own sake."

He noted the fear in Katherine's eyes and the strain in her voice. "Why? What's the matter?"

She knelt in front of him, the candle unsteady in her quivering hand. "Word is all over town, Nicholas. There's been a murder about half an hour ago inside Dooley Kramer's house."

A sickening chill shot up his back. "Dooley Kramer is dead? I can't believe it."

"Dooley wasn't murdered, Nicholas. Arthur Weeks was. He was stabbed while visiting with Dooley. At least that's the latest rumor floating around upstairs." Katherine brushed some hair out of her eyes. "There's a search party looking everywhere in the village for the culprit."

Nicholas couldn't believe what he was hearing as he tried to shake the last bits of sleep out of his head. "Who did it, Katherine? Who killed Arthur?"

She gently touched his hand. "You, Nicholas. They think you did it."

"*Me!*" He jumped to his feet. "Why, I've been down here for hours. How could I have killed him?"

"You couldn't have," she said. "I know so, but Dooley claims that you attacked Arthur in revenge for implicating you in the gristmill robbery."

Nicholas rubbed a hand over his eyes. "I seem to be getting all sorts of crimes blamed on me tonight. What a Harvest Festival this turned out to be."

Katherine explained the details of what she had heard while Nicholas listened in stunned silence. A few hours ago he thought his world had come crashing down upon him, sending him to the lowest point possible. And now this. Could it get any worse?

He paced uneasily after Katherine finished and then leaned his arms on a stack of ice, burying his head between them. He remained silent for a few moments as Katherine looked on. "Why is this happening to me? I only wanted a little adventure in my life, not–*this*." He turned to Katherine. "A while ago I could have strangled Arthur Weeks for lying about me, but now he's dead. And now Dooley is lying about me too, accusing me of the murder.

What's going on?" he asked, almost pleading with Katherine to provide him with the truth that neither one could possibly know.

"I wish I had an answer, Nicholas, but I don't. I'm as puzzled as you are."

He looked about in the swirl of shadows, trying to collect his thoughts. "I was thinking about turning myself in, figuring that Constable Brindle would find out who really robbed the gristmill. That would be the right thing to do, Katherine. But now…"

Katherine set the candle down and grabbed Nicholas by the shoulders. "But now we're talking about murder. We both know you're innocent, Nicholas, but proving it is another thing. Someone is framing you, and Dooley and Arthur are involved."

"Arthur's dead now."

"Exactly. And I don't want you to be next!" She held Nicholas's face and looked directly into his eyes. "Forget about what you should do, Nicholas, and think about your life. I don't want you to end up a corpse like Arthur Weeks. You may not be able to think straight right now, but I can. Let me think for you."

He nodded. Katherine took his hands and they both knelt in the shadows. "I think you should leave Kanesbury," she whispered. "For your own good." Nicholas was about to protest, but she placed a finger to his lips. "I know you think you're running away, but I'm trying to save your life."

"I appreciate it, but–"

"Nicholas, given some time, Constable Brindle and Maynard will get to the bottom of this mess. Trust me. Both of them think so much of you, and neither in his heart can really believe that you murdered a man. Give them time."

"Running will just make me look guilty."

"Yet if you stay and turn yourself in, there'll be demonstrations and confusion. You'll be convicted just because you're an easy target," she said. "But more importantly, the real killer is still out there. What if he comes after you next? With you out of the way, things will calm down so a proper investigation can be conducted."

"I don't know…" Nicholas sat on the floor, his back against a block of ice. "Where would I go?"

"Morrenwood. You were planning to join the King's Guard. Then again," she reconsidered, "the search party might think that too and scout along the main roads."

"That dream has kind of lost its appeal for me."

"Then take the back roads and disappear elsewhere for a while. But don't tell me where," she advised. "I wouldn't want to accidentally let it slip."

Nicholas smiled with deep appreciation. "Thanks for helping me, Katherine. You've always been so kind whenever I've seen you, though I know you're like that with everyone."

"Nearly everyone," she joked.

"And even though we've just been friends for a while, I thought perhaps one day..." He looked upon her as a cold sadness weighed upon his heart, wondering if their budding friendship could have ever blossomed into something greater if he had been given a little more time. He tried to smile. "Well, I sure was looking forward to that dance at the pavilion."

"So was I, Nicholas." She returned a smile and stood, offering her hands to him. He got to his feet. "Now promise me you'll leave the village tonight."

"I promise," he said, nodding dejectedly. "But I still have mixed feelings."

"How could you not? But trust me on this. I'll get word to Maynard and Constable Brindle tomorrow that you're okay. I'll tell them that you were here at the time of the murder. It'll help in the investigation."

"No! You can't do that, Katherine. Now you must promise me that you won't say a word," he frantically pleaded. "Let the constable investigate on his own to start."

"But why, Nicholas? My testimony will help prove you're not guilty."

"It will help, but until Clay discovers more solid evidence, the real killer is still out there, as you said." Nicholas was filled with unease. "If word gets out that you can prove my innocence, then you're in danger, too. You could end up just like Arthur Weeks."

"Nicholas, I won't keep your innocence a secret."

"Katherine, please! If you don't give me your word that you'll say nothing, then I'll turn myself in right now. I won't put anyone else in danger, especially you."

Katherine was torn between seeing justice served and Nicholas' stubborn concern for her, but she finally relented and promised to say nothing to Constable Brindle. "I'll do as you ask, but only because I couldn't bear to see you in prison."

"Thank you. Now I'll rest easier on the road."

Katherine smiled. "At least I can help you out there. I have something for you." She took the candle and walked over to the cellar stairs, grabbing a small tied bundle on the bottom step.

"What's that?"

"Some items you'll need for your journey. I put them together as soon as I heard about the murder." Katherine untied a thin rope wrapped around a rolled up blanket. Inside was a cloth sack. "I've prepared some food for you. You can't starve, after all. There's dried meat inside, along with some biscuits, cheese and fruit."

"Do the Stewarts know that you're robbing them?" he lightly asked.

"With all the party food upstairs, I could have given you a week's supply and nobody would notice."

"Thanks." He took the items and retied them as before.

"I'd give you an oil lamp, but I think you'll be better off without it. Tonight the darkness will be your friend."

"Nowhere near as good a friend as you've been, Katherine." Nicholas hugged her goodbye, not wanting to let go. The sweet warmth of her body would soon be followed by the bitter cold of the dark outdoors, and he was now reluctant to tread the unknown paths that awaited him. What once offered adventure and wonder suddenly seemed bleak and disheartening. He didn't want to leave but knew he had no choice.

"I'll never forget your help, Katherine. And please keep an eye on Maynard when you can."

"I promise. And if you get settled somewhere, send me a post so I'll know how to reach you about the investigation."

"If I'm able to. Just don't let anyone know–for your own safety."

"You keep safe too, until you can finally return."

Nicholas shrugged. "I can't even imagine that day right now," he said, hugging her one last time. "But I'll try."

A few minutes later, he quietly slipped out the back cellar door and up a set of stone steps leading to the shadowy lawn behind the estate, giving Katherine a final goodbye glance before weaving among the shrubbery and trees. The Fox Moon had already set, providing him a secure cover of darkness.

Throughout the village, the laughter of revelers and the shouts of search parties peppered the crisp autumn air. Katherine whispered farewell as Nicholas darted across the lawn and disappeared into a thicket of trees. She was unable to see precisely where he exited the property, wondering where his journey would ultimately take him. As the cool air chilled her, she reluctantly stepped back inside the ice cellar and closed the door on the tumultuous night, uncertain if they would ever see each other again.

CHAPTER 7

Two Meetings

After witnessing the release of the Enâri from the Spirit Caves, Mune walked back to Kanesbury, flushed with satisfaction that his task had gone off without a hitch. Caldurian would certainly congratulate him at their dawn meeting for a job well done, or so he hoped. Though the wizard trusted and confided in him, Mune had rarely known him to impart the slightest hint of friendship, let alone crack a joke or offer a pleasant smile. He found Caldurian wanting in the social graces, unable to imagine sitting next to him in a tavern, each hoisting a mug of ale while picking at a plate of roasted venison. But since Caldurian paid him well for his services, and the adventures throughout Laparia were exhilarating, he had remained loyal to the sullen and mysterious wizard for many years.

Mune passed through Kanesbury in the darkness, staying on River Road until he neared a wooden bridge less than a mile beyond the village's western border. The cold waters of the Pine River flowed beneath. Perched on a railing was the messenger crow Gavin, as black as the night itself. Mune was expecting him as he stepped onto the bridge, his boot steps echoing along the wooden planks. He stopped in the center and extended an arm. Gavin fluttered his wings and hopped off the railing, perching on Mune's forearm.

"Punctual as usual, Gavin. A credit to your feathered race." He removed a handful of berries for Gavin to feed on. The bird cawed, bobbing its head while feasting before again alighting on the railing when finished. Mune leaned over the bridge and watched the swift, silent water below, a hundred stars reflecting on its mirror-like surface. "Can I assume that our Enâri friends made it safely to Barringer's Landing?"

"Friends?" Gavin sputtered. "They are an uncivilized bunch. Made from dirt and rock, which says volumes about their character."

Mune grinned. "I agree. The Enâri are an uncouth lot, yet useful to our cause. But they must be particularly irritable after a forced twenty-year sleep inside those cold caves," he said with a chuckle.

"And how! The Enâri proceeded noisily to their assigned spot to await Caldurian's arrival. Several arguments and fist fights broke out immediately to see who would be in charge of which company." Gavin tapped his beak on the railing. "But I let them have at each other and flew off. My task was to see if they arrived safely– which they did–so I left. Let them pummel each another if that's how they wish to amuse themselves!"

"Still, job well done. Caldurian will be pleased," Mune said. "Anything else to report before I meet with him?"

The crow flapped its wings apprehensively and walked along the railing closer to Mune. "There was one minor hitch which I'm certain will not please Caldurian."

He raised a suspicious eye. "Oh?"

"Apparently one of the Enâri took off on his own, a particularly thuggish and ill-mannered individual. Bad enough that he deceived me, but he nearly killed me, too! We're supposed to be on the same side, after all. I don't deserve that kind of treatment!"

Gavin flapped his wings again and scratched his talons into the wood as Mune tried calming the crow so it would finish the story. Eventually the bird recounted his run-in with Jagga, the creature's knowledge of the key, and how it had forced Gavin to reveal Caldurian's plan to retrieve the key from Zachary Farnsworth. "That slug had me clamped in his fingers, threatening to squeeze the life out of me. If I hadn't told him all I knew, I'd be a dead crow right now. A dead messenger! And let me tell you, dead messengers aren't useful to anyone! You can tell that to Caldurian when you see him."

Mune fed more berries to the crow to settle it down, though the bird remained bouncy and skittish for some time. Mune sighed and thought for a moment, wondering what he'd tell Caldurian and fearing how the wizard might react.

"If we're lucky," he said, "that Enâr may have only talked a good game, gotten the information he wanted from you, and simply fled. He might be miles away by now."

"I saw a fire in that creature's eyes. He was determined to obtain the key by any method. His loyalty was to himself alone."

Mune tugged at his goatee. "Then let us assume the worst. Suppose he does manage to find this Farnsworth fellow and steal the key. What then? He still flees, keeping the key safe or destroying it, but in either case preserving his existence." He nodded as he thought aloud. "That's precisely what Caldurian wants in the end–to keep the Enâri safe. Maybe this isn't a disaster after all."

"I hope you're right. Caldurian likes things done his way. Any deviation in the wizard's plan is sure to upset him, no matter the outcome."

"True. But that's my problem now. You'd best be off, Gavin, until you're needed again. I'll tell Caldurian that you did your usual best."

"I would be much obliged, Mune." With that, he emitted a mournful caw and flew away, his wings flapping softly in the chilly pre-dawn air.

Mune could only see the bird for a moment before darkness fully engulfed it. He walked across the bridge and continued along River Road for several minutes until it forked. The River Road portion continued to the west while the West Cumberland Road curved south. As instructed, Mune headed south for a quarter mile and then stepped off the road and entered the Cumberland Forest to his left. He expected to find Caldurian some two hundred paces into the darkened woods.

The tallest pines creaked mournfully in a breeze that gently rocked them. Mune swished his way through rotted undergrowth and fallen leaves, wishing he still possessed the torch he had taken to the Spirit Caves. But as that had burned out hours ago, he counted off his paces, guiding himself as best he could through the pre-dawn gloom. He was tired and hungry, eagerly looking forward to the end of this task. On top of that, his feet were sore as the soles of his boots had begun to wear away after the many miles of travel these past few weeks. He suddenly stopped, detecting a flicker of light a short distance ahead behind a cluster of trees. Mune inched closer, not daring to call out Caldurian's name, though certain no one else was in the vicinity.

A few steps closer and he saw a warm, blazing campfire partially blocked from view by three large tree trunks. Mune hurried toward the light, anticipating a bit of breakfast perhaps, but found no one there. The crackling fire was well stoked, emitting waves of warmth which felt soothing after the constant slap of cold night air. A pile of dried twigs and smaller branches lay nearby. Two short logs had been placed in front of the blaze to be used as seats, yet not a soul was in sight.

"Now where is he?" muttered Mune, looking around. "Just like a wizard. Keep us regulars waiting despite the fact that we've been up all night doing his dirty work." He glanced farther into the woods with his back to the fire, but couldn't see anything except tree trunks and darkness. He shrugged.

"You are well compensated for all of that *dirty work*," a voice softly replied.

Mune spun around. On one of the logs in front of the fire sat Caldurian, wrapped in the folds of a heavy black cloak with a hood draped over his head. He turned toward Mune, acknowledging him with a glint from one eye peeking out beneath the hood.

"Where'd you–?" Mune walked toward the fire and scratched his head. "I wish you wouldn't pop out of thin air like that, Caldurian. Scares the blazes out of me."

"I prefer to see whom I'm meeting with before anyone sees me in case an uninvited guest happens to tag along."

"Other than me, what fool would be up and about at this dreadful hour? Present company excepted, of course," he quickly added with an awkward smile.

"Have a seat, Mune. You're obviously tired."

"Thank you." He sat on the log next to Caldurian, extending his feet and warming his hands by the fire. "You don't know how good this feels. After dealing with two drunken yokels half the night, and those crazed Enâri cooped up for twenty years–not to mention the dramatics of that hysterical Gavin–why, I'm just about ready to curl up in a ball somewhere and sleep for a week myself."

"But then you would miss all the fun," Caldurian said ominously. "And we have so much work still to do." He removed his hood, revealing a thin face that harbored a pair of dark, brooding eyes. Long locks of iron gray hair flowed over his hunched shoulders and a short beard of matching color was trimmed to a point. "Why, we've taken only the first few steps in our quest."

"Understood. Though might I ask what precisely *my* next steps are in this grand scheme?" He chuckled. "I don't know how many more miles these boots can take."

"They are looking a tad threadbare," the wizard remarked before removing a parchment envelope from a pocket hidden inside the folds of his cloak and handing it to him. It had been sealed with a blot of red wax. "The details of your mission are inside. You can familiarize yourself with them on your own time. You'll be heading north to the grasslands on the shores of the Trillium Sea. There you will meet with my contact from the Northern Isles."

"That ought to be interesting," he snickered. "The Islanders are about as refined a bunch as the Enâri."

"Their reputation as a militant people is often exaggerated, but they've been loyal allies to Vellan over the years and are a necessary component of our plan. You will meet with Commander Uta. Show him every courtesy."

"Of course."

"I'd talk to Uta myself, but other matters need my attention."

"Even wizards can't be everywhere at once. Don't worry. I won't let you down."

"I know you won't, Mune. Nonetheless, you'll have company on your mission. Seven nights from tonight you'll contact an old acquaintance of ours–Madeline. Again, details of where and when are in the letter."

"Madeline? So how is the old girl? I haven't crossed paths with her in nearly two years," he said with a mixture of delight and apprehension. "It'll be a treat to work with her again–for the most part. She can be a bit, well, *focused*, don't you think? Madeline never quite learned how to relax and enjoy a mission."

"Madeline is my apprentice and one of my most trusted associates, Mune. Even more so than you, no offense intended."

"None taken."

"She has done all I have asked of her and more. And if I must say a bit boastfully, her mastery of the magic arts under my instruction over the years has been a source of unending pride." Caldurian casually waved a hand in front of the fire, causing the flames to leap and spark like an excited pup. "I dare say that when my time has passed, Madeline might well exceed the heights I have attained."

Mune shifted uncomfortably in his seat. "Perhaps, but I think all that training has gone to her head. She has a much stonier personality than when I first met her. Madeline wouldn't know how to slow down if Vellan himself cast a relaxation spell upon her."

"Sort of like me?"

"Yes, well... *No!* I mean, all of you wizards are– Well, everything is so grave and serious with your type all the time. Noses always stuck in a spell book. Most things a life-and-death matter." Mune unbuttoned his coat, suddenly feeling rather hot. "Not meaning to criticize, but..."

Caldurian silenced him with a raised hand. "Quit while you're ahead, Mune."

"Good idea."

"We wizards can get easily riled. Were you anybody else, you'd have been transformed into a stick of wood by now, sputtering on this fire for uttering such words." He raised his lips in the slightest of smiles. "But since you're sitting here, still thinking and breathing, I'd take it as an indication that your service to me in the past, like Madeline's, has been much appreciated."

"Understood," he said with a nod. "Enough said."

Caldurian tossed a few more twigs on the fire, letting loose a volcano of sparks that rose to the blackened treetops on a ribbon of gray smoke. "And now, Mune, to your report. I trust that events went well?"

"Swimmingly."

"Splendid. So the Enâri were released with no trouble, Gavin made sure they headed directly to Barringer's Landing, and–exactly how do two drunken yokels fit into the picture?"

Mune whistled a few notes before he looked uneasily at Caldurian. "Let me modify that. Perhaps *nearly* swimmingly?" He quickly explained the goings-on in Kanesbury that evening–his hoodwinking of George Bane into entering the Spirit Caves, the awakening and escape of the Enâri creatures, and Gavin's report on the bridge regarding the stray Enâri creature and his possible search for the key.

Caldurian remained silent as he digested the news. Mune wished that the wizard would either lash out in anger or accept matters at once and deal with them. But watching Caldurian sit stoically, running every detail over and over in his mind, unnerved him mightily. On top of that, hunger and lack of sleep began to gnaw at him. Mune wanted this meeting to end quickly so that he could eat, rest and be on his way to meet Madeline. He hated disappointing Caldurian even when the bad tidings weren't his fault.

The wizard finally perked up, poking a stick into the glowing embers. "This adds a complication to my plans," he said quietly. "I never anticipated disloyalty among the Enâri assigned to me, even a rebellion of one."

"I suppose being held prisoner for twenty years was bound to set at least one of them off," Mune said, trying to be supportive.

"Maybe I tried too hard to believe that their allegiance to Vellan would transfer to me over time," he continued, almost speaking to himself. "Vellan created the Enâri race, after all. Why should I expect their devotion? I have not earned it yet."

Mune gazed uncomfortably at Caldurian, clearing his throat. "I was wondering..."

The wizard turned to him, his old self again. "Yes, Mune, a job well done despite the last minute difficulty Gavin had reported. Not your fault. Now, you were wondering?"

"Yes. As I see it, whichever Enâr broke away looking for the key, won't the same objective be met? Won't Vellan's creatures be safe in the end whether you or the Enâr retrieve the key?"

"One would think so, wouldn't one," Caldurian fumed, his caustic gaze bearing down on Mune. "But saving them isn't the entire objective. The Enâri must be commanded. If even one of them runs off, believing he has the ability to control his fate, imagine what would happen if another were infected with that same wild sentiment. Then another and another. There would be chaos in the ranks!" He studied the ground and sighed. "Vellan created them, so naturally they show him total allegiance. Besides, he would never destroy his own work. But with the threat created by the wizard

Frist, why, the Enâri's very existence could conceivably be threatened by anyone."

Mune glanced sideways. "Even you?"

Caldurian returned an impenetrable gaze. "I will look after Vellan's creatures and use them as needed. But I must have their total cooperation. If holding their fate in my hands by possessing the key would help to achieve that end, well then..."

Mune scratched his head. "Just out of curiosity, how many of the Enâri did Vellan release into your care?"

"Five hundred strong. That was twenty years ago in order to aid my efforts in persuading King Justin into an alliance with Vellan." He flashed a bitter smile. "And you know what a success that turned out to be. An unmitigated disaster right outside the borders of that pitiful village of Kanesbury!" His eyes burned with seething rage. "But I will get even for the humiliation those people caused me. That bumpkin of a mayor, Otto Nibbs, will have no idea. And one traitorous Enâr will not spoil my plans! I will have my revenge." Caldurian remained lost in his own world until he noticed Mune staring curiously at him. "Was there something else you wanted to know?"

"One thing," he inquired, raising a finger. "How many Enâri did Vellan create?"

Caldurian thought for a moment. "I couldn't begin to imagine. Tens of thousands perhaps? It was thirty-five years ago when the first of their race saw the light of day. Vellan has steadily expanded their numbers over time, improving the stock, replacing those that eventually die out. But the Enâri have vastly grown. Vellan has put much of his strength and power into their kind. They are like his children, his legacy, who will live on after he is gone–if such a day is imaginable."

"Interesting," Mune said. "Yet melancholy, too. But if that key were to unlock the Spirit Box–wherever that is–and release the spirit created by Frist..." He cast an inquiring eye at Caldurian. "What would happen to the Enâri living in Kargoth?"

Caldurian stroked his beard. "The five hundred troops with me, I suppose, would be destroyed in short order. Frist was a very powerful wizard, once equal to Vellan. However, I am reluctant to speculate what effect it would have on Vellan's troops closer to home. Remember, that spirit has been incubating for twenty years, growing and multiplying in strength unfathomable. I don't suspect that even Frist imagined his counter-creation would exist untouched for so long a period." He raised an eyebrow. "Are you asking, Mune, if that spirit has the potency to extend itself far across Laparia? Wondering, perhaps, if it could engulf the Enâri everywhere in its phantom tendrils and obliterate the race entirely?"

He swallowed hard. "I guess."

"Well," he whispered with a gleam in his eyes, "your guess is as good as mine."

The wizard abruptly ended the discussion as the first thin strains of gray dawn stretched across the treetops. He invited Mune to remain by the fire as long as he wanted, though he would now leave to prepare for his meeting with Zachary Farnsworth later that evening. The wizard needed some time alone to think and disappeared deeper into the woods, but not before pointing his fingers and whispering a brief spell at a clump of dried leaves near the fire. Suddenly the leaves rematerialized into a nest of clean straw upon which rested a round loaf of bread, a chunk of dried meat, a wedge of cheese, a filled water skin–and a shiny new pair of leather boots. Mune beamed with delight and turned to thank Caldurian, but the wizard had silently vanished into the encroaching dawn.

CHAPTER 8

A Key to a Plan

The second day of the Harvest Festival offered a mix of subdued celebration, endless rumor and wild speculation. Nicholas Raven's escape, coupled with the murder of Arthur Weeks and the robbery at the gristmill, was more than enough to keep the village abuzz for weeks. But it soon came to light that Adelaide Cooper had disappeared and not a soul had a clue to her whereabouts. Constable Brindle vowed to find Adelaide, wondering if there might be a connection between her going missing and the other strange events of the previous night.

And when everyone thought that affairs couldn't get any more peculiar, several relatives and friends of George Bane reported him missing, too. Constable Brindle's eyes bulged and his face went scarlet at the news. He couldn't tolerate his villagers fleeing, disappearing or being murdered directly under his nose, especially during the Festival. More than once that day he wiped his sweaty forehead and spat on the ground in disgust.

Gill Meddy, wanting no blame for any of the goings-on yesterday, tried to shrug off one of the worst hangovers he had ever experienced and ventured discreetly to the Spirit Caves later that morning. Though vaguely recalling the particulars of their conversation at the Iron Kettle Tavern last night, Gill was certain that many people saw him drinking there with George Bane. And who was that other gentleman from out of town lavishing them with drinks all night? *Dune*? *Mune*? *Rune*? Gill couldn't recall but blamed the stranger for his predicament anyway. He needed to find George, reasoning that if he didn't, he might be named as a suspect in his disappearance. Should that happen, he feared that accusing fingers might also point to him regarding the other scandals brewing in the village.

To his relief, Gill found George fast asleep just inside one of the cave openings. He roused the man from his slumber and helped him into the daylight. George's forehead was caked with blood and puffed with bruises. His clothes were dirty and torn. His eyes held a look of speechless terror which remained for many weeks. He mumbled something about ghosts and demons and a chilling blue fog, but could recall nothing more from his strange journey through the Spirit Caves. He had roused himself awake several hours earlier and stumbled blindly through the caves until he reached daylight. He collapsed in joy and slept again for several hours until Gill woke him.

On their way back to Kanesbury, Gill didn't ask George for any more particulars about being inside the cave. That was just as well since George Bane had no intention of speaking about them. And when anyone asked where he had been, he would only say that he had had a bit too much to drink during the Festival and wandered into the woods to sleep it off. He apologized for adding to the village's troubles. Constable Brindle happily accepted his explanation and crossed one headache off his list. Gill and George promised each other to forget that they had ever met the stranger in the Iron Kettle, shaking hands on it later over a lunch of soup, bread and milk.

Caldurian emerged from the woods along Neeley's Pond shortly before midnight and slipped unnoticed into Kanesbury, keeping clear of any late-night revelers. The crescent Fox and Bear moons had already set. Dressed in his black cloak with the hood draped over his head, the wizard walked swiftly and silently along dark streets and through patches of woods to the home of Zachary Farnsworth, a walking staff his only company. He extended a hand through his sleeve, rapping his bony knuckles upon the wooden door. A few moments later the door cracked open. Farnsworth peered out suspiciously, his face aglow from a lit candle he held.

"As I'm probably the only guest you were expecting at this hour, I suggest you stop staring like a curious cat and let me in," Caldurian whispered.

Farnsworth quickly obliged and opened the door. Flickering candlelight illuminated Caldurian's icy features as he swept past his host in silence, removing his hood. Farnsworth's heart pounded as he closed the door, wondering if he would ever see the light of day.

He led the wizard to a small den in back of the house. Red and orange flames crackled in a fireplace, casting fitful shadows against the walls. Heavy drapery covered the only window in the room. Farnsworth set the candle on a small table, indicating for Caldurian to sit on one of the two chairs in front of the fireplace. The wizard did so, leaning his staff on the side of the mantel.

"Shall I light more candles?" Farnsworth nervously asked. "It may be too dark for your liking."

"On the contrary. Some business is best handled in the shadows."

"Very good then. A drink perhaps? Some tea or wine? Maybe ale? I have a cask of fresh–"

Caldurian raised a hand. "No beverages are required, nor food of any kind, Mr. Farnsworth. I am here only to talk, not to be waited upon. So if you would..." The wizard pointed to the empty seat opposite him.

Farnsworth nodded. "Uh, right then." He sat uncomfortably in the chair, arrow straight with hands upon his knees. He tried not to stare directly into Caldurian's eyes, several times awkwardly shifting his gaze. The firelight cast a coppery glow over the wizard's face, making it appear both kindly and sinister at once. Farnsworth had forgotten how intimidating the man could be.

"Shall we get to business then? I believe you have something for me." Caldurian held out a hand, ready to take possession of the key to the Spirit Box.

"Yes, well about that..." Farnsworth nervously cleared his throat. "Uh, might we discuss the subject for a moment?"

"Discuss? What is there to discuss? This matter was settled months ago."

"Oh, I agree, sir. But one must allow for, well, unexpected circumstances."

"*Unexpected*?" Caldurian folded his fingers into a fist and slowly retracted his arm. "Unexpected, you say?" He glanced at the fire, rubbing his chin before leaning back in his chair and studying Farnsworth's vacant expression. "Explain yourself–and be quick! I have a timetable to keep. I won't tolerate incompetence or deception for an instant."

"Deception? I assure you, Caldurian, that no one is trying to deceive you. Don't think such a thing!"

"So then you have the key with you?"

He exhaled deeply. "Well, not exactly, sir."

"Then incompetence must be your strongpoint," the wizard coolly replied.

"No! No! Why, I had the key just last night. Honest, I did."

"Where is it now?"

Farnsworth swallowed. "Stolen."

"Stolen? You expect me to believe that?" Caldurian sat on the edge of the chair, his eyes burrowing into Farnsworth like hot coals. "You've had the key in your possession for five years, and now, one night before you're to turn it over to me, it gets stolen? You expect me to believe that?" He jumped out of his chair with hands raised high, hovering over Farnsworth like a hungry vulture. "What kind of chicanery is this? Nobody dares to outsmart the wizard Caldurian!"

"Believe me, I'm not!" Farnsworth wailed, balled up in the chair while shielding his face. "Just please don't kill me! I swear I didn't take your key! I swear it on my life!"

Caldurian stood still over his trembling host, and then like a bird landing, he buried his arms into the folds of his cloak and sat back down. A few seconds passed before Farnsworth showed his face. He wiped away tears and sweat while quivering uncontrollably.

"While I still have my anger in check, Mr. Farnsworth, perhaps you'd better explain what happened."

"I'd like to very much, sir," he hoarsely mumbled. "You see, since I was to be out last evening at one of the local celebrations, I decided to leave the key with my accomplice, Dooley Kramer, for safekeeping," he lied, bitterly recalling how Dooley had swiped the key from him the night before. "You remember Dooley, don't you?

Anyway, while I'll was out, Dooley was home visiting a friend. Arthur Weeks–that was the man's name," he said, rushing his words. "But when Dooley went outside to get some firewood, there was an attack inside the house and… Well, Dooley heard a scream and went back in." Farnsworth leaned forward as if pleading with Caldurian to believe him. He explained how Arthur Weeks had been killed and the key stolen. "Dooley got beat up himself at the end, but it was dark and he couldn't see who slugged him. By the time I arrived, Dooley was wandering dazed in the street. We figured that Nicholas Raven was the culprit, the guy you wanted us to get out of town. So that's what we told everybody. We don't know how the thief found out about the key, assuming it was Nicholas, since only Dooley and I knew about it." He wiped his brow again. "But don't worry! We never mentioned a word about it to the constable or anyone. Everyone believes that Nicholas killed Arthur out of revenge."

"And you expect me to believe this convoluted tale?" the wizard asked.

"I swear it's the truth!"

"Why would Nicholas steal the key if he knew nothing about it? And even if he did know where it was, why would he want it?"

"I can't explain that, sir."

"You can't?" Caldurian smirked. "Well, maybe I can."

Farnsworth strained to look interested, all the while wondering if Caldurian believed him. He didn't know who really stole the key, but he prayed that the wizard believed it was someone other than himself or Dooley. Otherwise both of them would surely be joining Arthur Weeks in short order.

"You know who took it?" Farnsworth asked, his face pale despite the golden tint of firelight.

"I have a good idea, but I wanted to reassure myself that it wasn't simply you trying to con me out of more than I'm already giving you."

"No, sir! Definitely not." He relaxed just a little. "So if Nicholas didn't kill Arthur Weeks and take the key, then who did?"

"I suspect it was one of the Enâri. A renegade attempting to take matters into his own hands."

Farnsworth squinted in bewilderment. "One of the *what*?"

Caldurian sighed. "Is your memory so inadequate that you can't recall the name from twenty years ago? Yesterday you held the key to their very existence in your hand, only to foolishly lose it."

"Are you referring to those beings trapped inside the Spirit Caves? Of course I remember them," he said. "I just never knew they had such a fancy name. Most folks here called them ruffians or invaders. No one gives them a thought nowadays."

"Well, in Kargoth and places more sophisticated, they are referred to as the Enâri race. You might well remember it."

"Why's that?"

Caldurian stared into the fire, studying the snapping flames in their hypnotic dance. "Because they've been reawakened, prepared to fulfill Vellan's orders." The wizard turned his head, pinning down Farnsworth with a venomous gaze. "The glory days are back, my friend. Old players are ready to finish a game that most won't suspect is again underway."

Farnsworth felt a chill run through him. "You mean to tell me that those devilish creatures are out and about?"

"As of last night. They have been freed from their sleeping spell and now await my arrival at Barringer's Landing."

"Why, they caused a wagonful of trouble in Kanesbury twenty years back. Do you plan to unleash them here again?"

"I will put the Enâri to other uses far from here," the wizard said. "They will assist in Vellan's grand scheme. However, my own designs for Kanesbury will be handled much more subtly at first."

"I hope so. Those Enâri nearly wrecked the village last time. I don't want any of that now. I plan to make something of myself here and want the village left in one piece. We had a deal, remember?"

"I'll uphold my end of the bargain as long as you do the same. Though you're not off to an auspicious start by losing that key."

Farnsworth stood and added another log to the fire. "I'm sorry, but that was unanticipated. But I've done everything else you asked for, and a little extra." He returned to his seat. "Nicholas Raven is gone, just like you wanted. You won't have to worry about him showing up here any time soon," he said with a chuckle.

"Glad to hear it."

"If I might ask, why was it so important to get rid of that kid in the first place? How does he fit into your plans?"

The wizard held up a finger. "If you needed to know, then I would have told you."

"I'm only curious. What has Nicholas ever done to you?"

Caldurian smiled grimly. "I've never met the man nor laid eyes on him. In fact, the only thing I know about Nicholas Raven is that he resides on Maynard Kurtz' property, and that's all that really concerns me." The wizard noted that his answer only raised more questions of the man sitting opposite him. "Put your curiosity in check, Mr. Farnsworth. My business is my own. We may have a deal but we are definitely not partners. I am in charge and don't forget it. I will tell you what you need to know and when you need to know it. Do I make myself clear?"

"Perfectly," he softly said.

"Good. Now on to other matters. Do you have any information about the location of the Spirit Box that Otto Nibbs took possession of twenty years ago?"

"I'm afraid not, sir," he said with a sigh. "On three occasions Dooley and I broke into the mayor's home while he was away. We searched each room several times over, being careful not to disturb anything. No luck. It is definitely not in his house."

"Too bad," Caldurian said, massaging his temple. "Perhaps it's hidden elsewhere in the village or maybe Otto passed it along to King Justin over the years."

"Why would he do that?"

"Lots of reasons," he replied, recalling how the wizard Frist had created the iron box over which he had cast a spell preventing it from being opened by any force other than a single, magic key. "As the years passed and the box remained closed, leaders in Morrenwood may have realized what a powerful weapon they would possess should the key eventually turn up. No doubt King Justin's network of spies has made him aware of the growth of the Enâri race in Kargoth. What a blow to Vellan it would be if his creation was destroyed." He pounded his fist on the arm of the chair as his face tightened. "I detest this uncertainty! Now I have neither the key nor the box. Without at least one of them, I can't assure the survival of the Enâri. Without them both, I can't control the Enâri." He paused a moment, his shoulders slumping. "Still, I must forge ahead without that luxury. Perhaps the Enâr who betrayed me has already disposed of the key so that no one will ever find it. That most likely was his intention. I'll just have to live with it. Now, was there something else you wanted to tell me, Mr. Farnsworth?"

"Yes!" he said, trumpeting an encouraging note. "Since you wanted me to get rid of Nicholas Raven, I put some extra thought into the process, hoping to take full advantage of the situation."

"*Meaning*?" he asked, teetering on the brink of impatience.

"Meaning that I didn't merely get rid of him. Instead, I replaced him," Farnsworth said with a satisfied grin.

He quickly explained how he and Dooley had framed Nicholas for robbing Ned Adams' gristmill and told of Nicholas' subsequent flight from the constable. He purposely left out how they had kidnapped Adelaide Cooper, an inconvenient witness to the frame, who was now bound and gagged in his cellar. Should the wizard ever find out, Farnsworth feared that Caldurian would further question his competence in handling matters. He told the wizard that the unexpected murder of Arthur Weeks, now also blamed on Nicholas, probably sent him fleeing out of the county with a reputation beyond repair. He assured Caldurian that Nicholas Raven would never be heard from again.

"So at a party last night, I cornered Ned Adams and shrewdly suggested that he consider Dooley Kramer as Nicholas' replacement, considering all that Dooley had done to assist in *discovering* the thief. Well, Ned was quite taken with my idea, I'll tell you. He gave me many warm words of praise."

Caldurian folded his arms and sighed. "This helps me *how*?"

"Dooley's immediate duties will be to finish making any final deliveries before winter sets in, including a large shipment of flour to Morrenwood." He flashed a scheming grin colored coppery-gold by the flames. "A large part of the shipment goes directly to the storage cellars in the Blue Citadel. Would you turn your back on an extra set of eyes and ears in the enemy's camp?"

"That depends if the eyes and ears are attached to somebody with a brain in full working order."

Farnsworth took the wizard's comment in stride, detecting the slightest hint of satisfaction on the man's face. He knew he had scored a minor victory with this bit of handiwork, hoping to make up for some of the inconvenience he had caused by losing the key. At least Caldurian would leave here on a positive note.

"Your associate may come in handy. I'll get word to you if I need his services," Caldurian said. "But I will definitely need your assistance again, Mr. Farnsworth."

"Certainly, sir. What can I do?"

"Shortly after I meet with the Enâri, we will head north to the shores above the Keppel Mountains. I have a meeting planned there with allies from the Northern Isles."

"You're tangled up with the Islanders?"

"Don't look so shocked. They may have a militant streak, but they're just the kind of people Vellan requires to complete his task. I most likely will borrow a few of those troops to assist with my own work here."

Farnsworth didn't like the sound of that. He knew the wizard had less-than-honorable intentions for Kanesbury, particularly Otto Nibbs, and was willing to let him have his way with the village as long as he and Dooley were rewarded in the end. But to bring in soldiers from the Northern Isles? Did Caldurian want to ruin the village before he could get his hands on it? Before he could worm his way into a position of power and make a name for himself? That was the point, after all, of spending four laborious years in an effort to contact the wizard through a complicated web of intermediaries. Farnsworth had wanted to make a deal in exchange for the key, to find out what it was worth to the wizard to get his hands on it. He didn't want his prize damaged before he could collect. He had put too much work into this.

Farnsworth recalled a day almost five years ago when he happened to spot Dooley Kramer sitting alone on his front step, lost in thought. Dooley was fingering a metal object attached to a length of twine that he always kept around his neck. Farnsworth believed the piece of metal looked like a key and was about to inquire as he walked by, startling him from his daydream. Dooley quickly concealed the object down the front of his shirt, refusing to say what it was before finally bolting indoors.

Farnsworth, however, had his suspicions. While he had never been a close friend with his neighbor, thinking Dooley slovenly and uncultured, he always acted civilly toward him. But ever since the incident on the front step, he had made it a point to engage Dooley in conversation whenever they met, though never mentioning the object hanging around his neck.

After cultivating a friendship of sorts and earning his trust over the months, Farnsworth invited Dooley for drinks one evening at the Iron Kettle Tavern, refusing to let him pay for even one mug of ale. Hours later, after several downed mugs and a half bottle of gin to boot, Dooley was freely babbling about his life's story in a corner table away from other curious ears. Farnsworth easily broached the subject of his hidden possession later that night and was entertained with a tale from Dooley's childhood about an eagle, a scheming young boy and a magic iron key.

The next day when sobered up, Dooley realized with horror that Zachary Farnsworth knew everything. It wasn't long afterward that Farnsworth suggested they team up and take advantage of the opportunity that had been hanging around his neck for fifteen years. Dooley agreed, realizing he had no choice, especially with subtle reminders from Farnsworth warning him how much trouble he could land in if village leaders, or even officials to the King, should ever find out that he possessed the key to the Spirit Box. Dooley wondered how anyone could find out, unless Farnsworth himself informed them. But he never pushed the point and agreed to Farnsworth's idea of seeking out the wizard Caldurian if at all possible, the one person who might bargain generously for the key.

So after many wrong turns, dead ends and leads that went cold, Farnsworth finally made contact with the first of many intermediaries and negotiated an initial meeting with Caldurian four years after learning that Dooley possessed the key. Farnsworth and Dooley concocted a tale about how Dooley had obtained the key, telling the wizard that he had won it from a stranger while gambling in a tavern. Dooley feared that if Caldurian ever found out he had injured his eagle as a child in order to steal the key, then he would be as good as dead. Farnsworth often reminded him of that fact.

Now, a year later after their first meeting, Zachary Farnsworth again sat face to face with Caldurian in the dead of night in his own home. What further machinations this wizard had planned, he couldn't begin to guess.

"Exactly what kind of additional help do you need from me, sir? And how do those Northern Islanders fit into the picture?"

"Don't let them rattle you," Caldurian assured him. "After I meet with them above the Keppel Mountains regarding Vellan's instructions, I shall have a private meeting with an individual who is sailing over on one of their ships."

"Who's that?"

"You'll find out soon enough," he said cryptically. "Arileez is his name. He lived alone on one of the smaller, uninhabited islands and has agreed to assist me. You will find him a most intriguing fellow."

"He's coming *here*?" Farnsworth uttered with a sense of foreboding.

"Yes. You will answer any questions Arileez has–in explicit detail, mind you–about Kanesbury and its people."

"Why?"

"That you will find out as necessary."

Farnsworth nodded anxiously. "When and where am I to meet this Arileez fellow?"

A snake-like smile spread across the wizard's face. "He'll find you in his own time and manner. Rest assured."

"If only I could," he thought a short time later after Caldurian had departed and he replayed the wizard's troubling words in his mind. Farnsworth remained on edge all night, frantically wondering what trials he would yet have to endure before finally getting his due.

Caldurian arrived at Barringer's Landing at dawn as a ribbon of pale yellow light stretched across the eastern horizon. Patches of thin grass and thorny brush squeezed out of the barren soil north of the Spirit Caves. Several abandoned barns and dilapidated fencing stood as silhouettes, a testament to failed attempts over the years to cultivate the unyielding tract of land. This served as an ideal location for a temporary camp for the wizard's small army.

Caldurian flung open a set of barn doors as the morning unveiled its ashen face. A feathery mist lay on the ground. Inside, the remains of several campfires sputtered and cooled on the dirt floor, surrounded by dozens of sleeping bodies. The Enâri had sprawled out wherever space was available, either on the floor or in the upper lofts.

The wizard shook his head in amused disbelief. "Twenty years of sleep, and what do they do?" he muttered.

He walked over to the Enâr closest to the doorway who was snoring near a small fire. Caldurian recognized the creature as Gwyn, one who had served as the wizard's aide during their travels twenty years ago. Apparently Gwyn was still acknowledged as the ranking Enâr among the group. Caldurian was pleased since he had served admirably in the past.

The wizard nudged Gwyn gently with his foot, causing him to jump instantly to his feet in a defensive stance while wielding a dagger in the chilly morning air. He looked wildly around as his eyes adjusted to the faint morning light.

"Return that knife to its sheath, Gwyn. I've had too few hours sleep last night and am hardly in any condition to fight."

Gwyn blinked rapidly, eyeing the wizard framed against the milky dawn outside the door. He loosened his grip on the knife. "Is that really you, Caldurian? Has our leader returned?" he asked in a gravelly voice typical of the Enâri. Two rows of large crooked teeth attempted a smile, and for a brief moment Gwyn's stony face, framed by tangles of long dark hair, seemed a bit less frightful than usual.

"Your leader has indeed returned, though your true master still resides in his stronghold in Kargoth," Caldurian said. "However, Vellan has one more task for you to perform before you'll have the privilege of returning to serve at his side."

"I understand," Gwyn replied, sheathing his knife. "We are ready to serve Vellan. You need only tell us how."

Caldurian directed him to awake the Enâri sleeping in two other barns nearby and gather them into this one building which was the largest. Gwyn dispatched a few scouts and several minutes later the barn was packed solid with Enâri. Most stood, though some sat in the lofts or perched on the rafters, all anxious to hear the wizard.

"We'll hike north of the Keppel Mountains to meet with our allies from the Northern Isles. Together, we'll march boldly into the tiny kingdom of Montavia and establish a foothold for Vellan in the northeast," he explained. "Twenty years ago he attempted to impose order on Laparia through diplomacy with disastrous results. This time Vellan will strike a blow with a force and fury that cannot be repelled. He will have his way with your help."

Several Enâri eagerly asked for details about the impending conquest of Montavia and of Vellan's intentions afterward. As good as it felt to be free from the Spirit Caves, it was even more exhilarating to again have a purpose by serving their true leader.

"Vellan already dominates the Northern Mountains. And he's had his fingers in the war between Rhiál and Maranac in the southeast, secretly manipulating events. Matters should come to a boil in those parts soon enough," Caldurian said. "So, my friends, we are the next rock in the foundation. We will establish ourselves in Montavia with aid from the Northern Isles. I don't expect much resistance. Montavia is a rural, peaceful kingdom. I think it boasts of more livestock than people," he scoffed. "The capital of Triana will fall like autumn leaves."

"And then?" an Enâr asked from deep in the crowd.

Caldurian smiled. "Then we complete by force what we had failed to do twenty years ago by word. We hit Morrenwood from three directions like lightning bolts!" He slapped his hands sharply. "And when King Justin's capital crumbles like a house of straw, the kingdom of Arrondale will fall in line with nary a whimper. Then all of Laparia will be in Vellan's control!"

The Enâri pounded their fists on the cold ground and wildly cheered, creating a brief uproar that chased the sleep from their heads. "This time we will prevail!" one shouted out.

"I have no doubt," the wizard said. "No doubt whatsoever."

Caldurian noted, even after all this time, how eager they still were to please Vellan out of sheer devotion. He also wanted to please the wizard of Kargoth with a rousing success, though realized that his loyalty had not aged as well as the Enâri's over the passing years. He suspected it would never reach such levels again.

They remained on Barringer's Landing until dusk. Caldurian met privately with Gwyn and a few other higher ranking Enâri to plan their journey to the Keppel Mountains. He calculated a five or six day march. The Enâri could easily hunt the food they needed, though Vellan created them to endure harsh conditions for days at a time with limited food and water. Caldurian did, however, transform piles of dried hay in one of the barns into heavy cloaks, one for each Enâr to combat the cold autumn nights.

His last piece of business before they departed concerned the missing member of their troop. In a brief discussion with Gwyn, Caldurian learned that the Enâr who had fled was named Jagga.

"After we escaped from the caves and arrived here, I counted to make sure everyone had made it safely back," he said. "Of the five hundred, only one was missing. I dispatched scouts to look for him, but they returned empty handed. We searched the fields the next morning but were equally unsuccessful."

"Jagga wasn't lost or injured," Caldurian said. "He deserted your ranks in an effort to satisfy his own selfish desires." The wizard explained how Jagga had tricked Gavin into revealing the whereabouts of the key. "And since the key was stolen, I can only assume that Jagga was the one who had murdered to get it. But where he is now..." Caldurian shrugged. "Perhaps he'll dispose of the key to protect all the Enâri or find his way back to Vellan and let him destroy it. But in either case, none of our enemies have it."

"Still, I brand Jagga a traitor now that I know what became of him," Gwyn said bitterly. "He violated his pact with this group. I would kill him were he here now!"

"I don't doubt that you would. But vengeance at its proper time," the wizard said with longing. "Savor the thought for now."

Just after sunset, after Gwyn had ordered the Enâri in line, Caldurian started them on their trek to the Black Hills and beyond. The crisp twilight air heightened their senses. The Fox Moon, nearly at first quarter, cast a gentle light from high above to guide them. Only a few miles west in Kanesbury, the third night of the Harvest Festival had commenced.

CHAPTER 9

A Change in Direction

Nicholas hiked northwest along Grangers Road into hilly farmland with only thoughts of Katherine keeping him company. After leaving the security of Amanda Stewart's ice cellar almost two hours ago, he had weaved his way through the village in secret, hiding in shadows or taking refuge among trees, careful to avoid any festival revelers. He stayed away from River Road altogether, certain it would be the first place that Constable Brindle and his men would patrol.

After placing a few miles between himself and Kanesbury, Nicholas felt chilled and fatigued, yet believed he was safe from pursuit. But the need for rest badgered him, so he stepped off Grangers Road and plopped down in a grassy field to recuperate while contemplating all that had happened in the village–the robbery at the gristmill, his attempted arrest and escape, and the chilling murder of Arthur Weeks. Surreal images swirled in his mind like an endless bad dream.

But he couldn't deal with the situation logically and tried to block it out. He tossed the blanket roll Katherine had provided him on the ground and lay down, resting his head upon it. He gazed at the stars, brilliant gems that hypnotically soothed him and slowly washed the strain and exhaustion out of his limbs. He smiled, his eyes fixed on one constellation as if sensing its slow westward arc across the sky. He felt as if he was moving too, floating away to a place far from all the troubles that plagued him. As the stars grew unfocused, he chuckled and felt a cool wind sweep across his face and exhaled deeply as both eyelids closed and merciful sleep took hold.

They were chasing him. Voices barked at Nicholas from behind, ordering him to stop. Thundering horses galloped closer and closer. No escape in sight. He ran as fast as he could, lungs burning, heart pounding. He could hardly see in the darkness, tripping over branches, scattering frosty leaves. Cold wind slapped his face. They had him cornered like a wild animal. Trapped!

Nicholas sat up with a jolt, his head swimming with the remnants of an exhausting dream. Only the icy darkness surrounded him. How long had he been asleep? He glanced at the stars and noticed that a few of the constellations he had been observing were now sinking behind the western horizon. He realized he had slept for several hours and that it must be past midnight.

He slowly stood, grabbed the blanket roll and continued along Grangers Road. Still cold and drowsy, he knew he should either build a fire or find shelter and get some proper sleep for the remainder of the night. He would quickly wear himself down otherwise at this grueling pace with no chance of arriving in Morrenwood or elsewhere in good health and spirits. He then wondered exactly where he was intending to go. His feet were moving, but he felt like he was walking in place.

A short time later he spotted a farmhouse with a barn set in back of the property. A string of large oak trees dotted the area, reminding him of Maynard's farm. He couldn't imagine what his friend must be thinking now, wondering if Maynard felt saddened, betrayed or disappointed. The idea of turning himself in again invaded his thoughts.

Nicholas hurried to the barn and slipped in through a side door. Three horses and a few head of cattle slept noisily in their stalls. He floundered in the darkness until he stumbled across a large pile of hay in one corner away from the animals and the main doors. Without a second thought, he dropped into the tangy smelling pile, untied the rolled-up blanket and draped it over his shivering body. He fell asleep in an instant.

A pair of round, leafy green eyes stared unblinking at him when he awoke. Beams of morning sunlight shot in through a side window, illuminating the freckled face of a young girl not more than thirteen. She watched Nicholas with a mix of curiosity and infatuation. He sat up startled, a piece of hay stuck in his hair.

"My mom says you can have breakfast with us if you'd like," the girl said matter-of-factly. "We're having eggs and fried beef. Do you like eggs and fried beef?"

"Uh, sure..." Nicholas plucked the hay out of his hair, looking askance at the girl. "You're, um–*who*?"

"My name's Holly Nellis. I live on this farm, mister. I found you this morning when I went to visit Elly. One of the cows over there," she said, pointing in the opposite direction. "I always preferred Gretchen–for the cow's name, of course!–but my dad chose Elly. Said the face reminded him of his father's cousin Elly," she said, punctuated by a fruity chuckle. "Anyway, Mom checked you out, mister, after I told her I found you. She decided not to poke you with a pitch fork. Mom let you sleep on instead because she thought you looked honest. I agreed."

"Thanks," he said, still half dazed. "Is it all right if I get up?"

"Sure. Eggs are frying in the pan."

"That's just fine, Holly," he replied, believing he should bolt as soon as he stepped outside the barn. He was still near Kanesbury and word of his escape may have reached this farmhouse. But since Mrs. Nellis hadn't wakened him earlier at the point of a pitchfork, he assumed his presence hadn't aroused any suspicion on her part. And a hot breakfast right now sounded too good to pass up, so he decided to chance it and stay. "By the way, Holly, my name is Nicholas."

He stood and rolled up the blanket, retying it around the sack of food Katherine had given him. Holly watched and grinned as if fascinated with a new pet she had been given for her birthday. Nicholas smiled back.

"You're sure your mother invited me inside?" he asked a few moments later as she walked with him to the house. A sweet smell of wood smoke issued from the chimney as a swirl of autumn leaves settled along a stone path leading to the porch. Nicholas set his blanket roll on the bottom step. "I'd appreciate a meal right now, but the last thing I want to do is intrude."

142

NICHOLAS RAVEN AND THE WIZARDS' WEB - VOLUME 1

"You should have thought of that before sleeping in our barn," Holly joked. "Besides, you know my name now, so I'm not a stranger. Mom and Dad always allow passersby a drink at the well if they need one. Sometimes they'll give them a slice of bread and dried beef to send them on their way."

"That's very kind of your parents. They must be nice people. I guess I picked the right barn to settle in," he said as they ambled up the porch steps.

"I guess you did."

A flood of warm kitchen air greeted them, peppered with the scent of frying eggs and sizzling slices of beef. Holly's mother ushered Nicholas to a seat at the table as if he were her visiting son. Mr. Nellis, still at his seat eating breakfast, eyed him stonily for a moment until satisfied that the stranger seemed a good fit for his table, then smiled and extended a hand to shake. Before Nicholas could utter a few words of thanks, Mrs. Nellis set a plate of fried eggs and beef in front of him, accompanied by slices of buttered bread, a wooden pitcher of milk and a mug of hot spiced cider. In moments, the four of them were eating and talking as if Nicholas had sat down there for breakfast every day.

"That's an honorable thing, wanting to join up with the King's Guard. You should be proud of yourself."

"Thanks, Mr. Nellis, but like I said, I'm still contemplating the matter."

Nicholas felt uncomfortable talking about the details of his life in light of recent events, but knew he had to tell his hosts something to explain his presence. But the longer he enjoyed their generosity and friendship, the easier it was to let slip details about who he was and where he had come from. But a part of him didn't care. It felt wonderful to be included again after experiencing the harsh life of an outcast last night.

"I'd like to pay for your hospitality, Mr. Nellis. I have a little money with me," he said. "Or maybe I could chop firewood instead."

"Nonsense. Sally and I are more than happy to offer up our barn to someone on a cold night. Why, if old Elly didn't mind having you sleep in there, why should we?" he said, erupting in laughter.

"Russell, you are a wit!" his wife said, placing a hand to her mouth to suppress a fit of giggles. "Nicholas, pay no mind to him. He's a teaser, that one."

"Sam's just like Dad," Holly said to Nicholas, poking an elbow in his side. "Always quick with a joke."

"Who's Sam?"

"Sam's our son, Nicholas. About your age. He's usually up by now tending to chores, but we're letting him sleep late today," Mrs. Nellis explained. "On account of the Harvest Festival. He and some friends were out celebrating late last night."

"*Oh?*" Nicholas said, his throat tightening as he swallowed a piece of bread. "Where did they celebrate?"

Mr. Nellis slurped from his mug of cider before greedily attacking the beef on his plate with a knife and fork. "Living out here in the middle of nowhere, Sam and his buddies usually tramp down through the fields into Mitchell, Ives or Foley to see what those villages have going on."

"Last year they went to all three villages!" Mrs. Nellis said with wide-eyed amazement. "In one night! Imagine that. Boys, you know."

"That's great," Nicholas said, at ease again as he picked up his fork. "Hope they had a good time."

"No doubt. But this year," Mr. Nellis continued between mouthfuls, "the boys hiked into Kanesbury for a change of pace. Wanted to see how you people celebrate."

Nicholas turned a shade paler, nearly dropping his fork. "Oh really."

"I suppose when Sam wakes up, you two can compare stories," Mrs. Nellis suggested. "Now wouldn't it be funny as fish, Russell, if Sam and Nicholas ran into each other last night? And now here he is, having breakfast in our very own house." She grinned at Nicholas. "Isn't that a funny thought?"

He nodded awkwardly while chewing on some bread. "I guess..."

"Nicholas, why'd you leave your village last night?" Holly piped up. "I mean, with all the celebrating going on, why leave then of all times? What's another day or two?"

"Oh, eat your eggs, Holly, and don't pry into the man's business," her father said, turning his attention to Nicholas while pointing a fork in the air. "Now who's farm did you say you worked on, Nicholas? I conduct some business in Kanesbury on occasion."

"I don't believe I mentioned it," he uncomfortably replied.

"I remember an Albert Hardy. Think that was his name," Mr. Nellis thoughtfully muttered, scratching an ear. "You know him?"

"More cider, Nicholas?" Mrs. Nellis asked simultaneously, taking his mug before he could reply.

"No," he responded to both questions at once.

"I believe his name was Hardy," Mr. Nellis said to himself. "Let me think..."

"One more mug of hot cider on a chilly morning will do you good," said Mrs. Nellis, hustling off to the wood stove and ladling out more of the drink from a steaming kettle. "Oh, I think I hear Sam skittering around upstairs," she added, handing the mug back to Nicholas. "I'll fetch another setting so you two can talk at the table. Holly, dear, pull another slice of beef out of the salt barrel and toss it on the frying pan."

"Sure, Mom," she said, bouncing up from the table.

"Now, Nicholas," Mr. Nellis began, "if you'd like to stay here for a while and–"

"You know, there's something I need to do!" Nicholas blurted out, standing abruptly and knocking the table with his knee, trying desperately to think of an excuse to leave before Sam came downstairs. "Outside, there's uh..."

"Say no more," Mr. Nellis added. "The privy's just out back."

"*That's* it!" Nicholas said, grateful for an excuse as he hurried out backward through the front door. "Thanks."

Holly grinned. Just at that moment, her brother Sam bounded into the kitchen, grabbing a slice of bread off the table and shoving half of it into his mouth. He washed it down with a cup of milk.

"Not even a *good morning* first, Sam? We have a breakfast guest," his mother hastily explained. "Some manners please?"

"Sorry," he said in muffled words. He playfully punched his sister in the arm before sitting at the table and looking around. "Who's here?"

"Sam, don't be a gnat!" said Holly as she returned to the table rubbing her arm.

"Don't pick on your sister!" Mr. Nellis wiped a slice of bread through a river of egg yolk on his plate and devoured it.

"If she didn't look like a toad's first cousin, I wouldn't have to," Sam joked.

"Gee, let me set some time aside later to laugh at that one," Holly said dryly. She stuck out her tongue at her brother.

"Sam, behave," Mrs. Nellis said as she hastily prepared him breakfast. "Did you have a nice time with your friends?"

"Yeah, Ma. But you wouldn't believe what happened last night in Kanesbury." He stood to get some cider. "There was a murder in the village," he said, dipping a mug into the kettle and scooping out some of the hot drink.

Mrs. Nellis put a hand to her hip. "A murder? Sam, don't take cider that way, you'll drip all over! Are you serious?"

Sam nodded enthusiastically. "It happened a few streets away from the main celebration." He retook his seat. "Who knows, but I may have passed right by the murderer during the night!" he gushed as if it were something to be proud of. "Never had that kind of excitement down in the three villages."

"Well, Sam, I don't think the Kanesbury village council planned such an activity to coincide with the Harvest Festival," his mother said with a disgusted smirk.

"Who got killed?" Mr. Nellis asked. "What happened?"

His son explained the details he had collected by word of mouth the previous night, describing a foiled robbery, an escaped criminal and a dastardly murder. Mr. and Mrs. Nellis had never heard of Arthur Weeks when Sam mentioned the victim's name. "I'm not sure who the guy was exactly. I couldn't get every scrap of information. Too much commotion. Search parties throughout the village all night. Really exciting!"

"*Oh dear...*" Mrs. Nellis shook her head, turning the eggs over in the frying pan and pinching some black pepper in a dish to sprinkle over them. The thinly sliced beef sizzled in its juices.

"Who killed him?" Holly asked eagerly.

"Some guy," Sam said.

"Holly, I don't think you should be listening to this talk," Mrs. Nellis cautioned.

"*Aw,* Mom!"

"Leave the girl alone," Mr. Nellis said, his plate now cleaned.

"The murderer worked with the guy he killed, from what I gathered," Sam added.

"Really?" Mrs. Nellis said, fascinated. She transferred the eggs and beef to a plate.

Holly sighed loudly, rolling her eyes. "So who did it, Sam?"

"Holly!"

"Sally, let the girl be."

"No one you'd know," Sam said, teasing his sister.

"Dad, make him tell me!"

"Sam, don't annoy your sister."

"I'm not!"

Mrs. Nellis was walking over with the plate. "Breakfast on the way, Sam. More bread?"

"So who was he?" Mr. Nellis snapped.

"Yeah, Sam, who was he?" echoed Holly.

"No more bread, Ma." Sam gulped his cider, setting the mug down with a thump before turning with a sigh and glaring at Holly. "The guy's name is Nicholas Raven, as if it makes any difference to you!"

Sam's plate dropped from Mrs. Nellis' hand and crashed to the floor. She stood paralyzed, her son's breakfast scattered at her feet. Russell Nellis leaned back in his chair, the kitchen walls spinning in front of his eyes. Sam blinked in confusion as Holly jumped out of her chair and pressed her nose to the front window, searching the landscape.

"What's going on?" Sam asked, observing everyone's surprise while scratching his neck.

"Nicholas never planned to use the privy," Holly said, her head buried in the curtains. "His blanket roll is missing off the porch steps." She turned and faced her bewildered family. "He's gone!"

Nicholas ran along Grangers Road, distancing himself from the Nellis household until he felt safe to walk again. He imagined with horror the expressions on Russell and Sally's faces should their son ever mention the name Nicholas Raven in connection with a murder. He felt awful for running out after the hospitality that the Nellis family had shown him, but he knew he had no choice. He wondered if they might contact the authorities in Kanesbury, tipping off Constable Brindle as to his whereabouts, or worse yet, come after him on their own. He occupied himself with these uncomfortable thoughts for the next half hour, constantly craning his neck to look back and pausing to listen for the rumble of galloping horses.

But after an hour had passed without meeting anyone other than a scattering of farmhands tending to their chores, Nicholas again felt safe. He unbuttoned his coat as the rising sun gently beat down. The tranquil countryside refreshed him, offering only the sounds of a passing breeze, some chattering blue jays and an occasional lowing cow, quite opposite the bedlam he pictured now overwhelming Kanesbury. He quickened his pace.

Not wanting to stray too far to the northwest, he left Grangers Road twenty minutes later and headed for an expanse of woods to his left. He figured he could spend most of the day concealed among the trees while working his way south. Nicholas planned to emerge from his wooded refuge before dusk and hike through the fields to River Road and walk the rest of the way to the village of Mitchell to see what fate awaited him.

When safely in the woods after noontime, Nicholas sat down against a tree to rest. He devoured some of the bread and meat Katherine had provided and drank ice cold water from a stream. The warmth and light of the open air didn't reach into the dampness of the shadowy woods and he soon felt chilled again. He turned up his collar and buttoned his coat, feeling the spot where one button was missing.

He recalled when Constable Brindle held up the piece of incriminating evidence in the Water Barrel Inn for all to see, condemning Nicholas on the spot in the eyes of many. He racked his mind to figure out how that button had ended up near the pile of spilled flour. He knew Arthur Weeks had lied about him being at the gristmill on the night of the robbery and wondered if he might have planted the button there himself. But how? He imagined Arthur sneaking into his work area while he was temporarily away from his desk, ripping a button from his jacket before slinking away unnoticed. He couldn't think of any other explanation.

But Nicholas wanted not to think about it. It made him too angry and he pushed the wicked affair out of his mind. Still having plenty of time to reach River Road before dusk, he decided to catch a nap. Finding a bed of leaves and undergrowth deeper inside the woods, he wrapped his blanket over him, lay down and fell asleep.

When he opened his eyes, Nicholas spotted a ray of orange sun slipping in through the trees, bathing a pile of freshly fallen leaves in a crimson fire. He stretched sleepily as if waking up on a day off from work until realizing that the sun shot in low from the west. He had slept away the entire afternoon.

Nicholas hurriedly collected his things and shuffled through the leaves and twigs to the edge of the trees. A rich blue sky blanketed a field of grass and brushwood painted gold by the fading sun. Accounting for uneven terrain, he estimated it would take forty minutes to reach River Road. He started at once, tramping south through shadows as a starry twilight descended.

A rural landscape of farmhouses, apple orchards and pasture fences was transformed into a sprawling silhouette pasted against a ribbon of light along the southwest horizon. The crescent Fox Moon lounged lazily on high. The invigorating air of the open road mingled with the spicy scent of decaying grass and wildflowers upon acres of rich farm soil. He breathed it in to clear his head. When he finally reached River Road, he felt momentarily at peace.

Nicholas hurried along west, now less than a mile from the village of Mitchell. Approaching its eastern border, he spotted an array of campfires scattered ahead in a field on the right side of the road. Moving closer, he saw a cluster of tents had been pitched in the grass. He heard voices and noted shadowy figures moving around the flames. Nicholas slowed as he neared the encampment when a dark figure suddenly jumped out of the shadows into the middle of the road, blocking his path.

"Who dare passes by unannounced?"

Nicholas froze. His heart pounded when he saw a glint of moonlight reflecting off a dagger pointed directly at him. "I'm Nicholas Raven from Kanesbury," he said, eyeing the knife as if it were a snake ready to strike. "Who are you?"

"I'll tell you," a second voice disgustedly said. A man rushed toward them from near the campfires. "He's a fool of a soldier who's going to be rationed to one meal a day if our captain catches him harassing the locals." The second man pushed the other away from Nicholas. "Get back to you tent, Earl! Battle might find you soon enough."

"Oh, I was just having a little fun," Earl muttered before shuffling off to the campsite. "You're always so serious, Hal."

Hal shook his head apologetically. He was only a few years older than Nicholas though appeared much more mature for his age. "Sorry about Earl's misplaced enthusiasm. He's an antsy sort. Desires to be in the thick of danger even if he has to conjure it up himself."

Nicholas straightened his collar. "A long hike in the hills might calm him down."

"Good idea."

Nicholas shook Hal's hand in thanks and then pointed to the tents. "Why are you people camped out here?"

Hal led Nicholas to one of the fires and offered him some dried venison, biscuits and water. He made a few introductions to others nearby. "We're soldiers from Montavia. Two hundred of us, all volunteers, passing through Arrondale with the permission of King Justin. Some of us are to train with his soldiers at Graystone Garrison less than twenty miles west of here. The rest will march to Morrenwood for instruction. But if need arises, we'll ride into battle together should the war in the south take a turn for the worse."

"How long have you been on the march?" Nicholas asked with envy, wistfully recalling his desire to join the King's Guard.

"About seven days."

"Seven? I didn't see you in Kanesbury. This road passes through my village."

"We didn't use River Road until now," Hal informed him. "Our captain led us from Montavia through jagged mountains, over windswept hills and across rivers and streams. All part of our training. Using roads would be, well, too easy."

"Right now a day's march along a dirt road would suit me just fine," one of the others joked. "I expected more adventure than sore muscles when I volunteered." His companions laughed.

"You'll have your wish shortly," Hal said. "There's less than two day's journey before the remainder of us reach King's Road. The captain told me we'll march directly to the capital from there. Soon we'll unite with our fellow countrymen abroad in service to our great King Rowan."

Nicholas appeared surprised. "Others from Montavia are training in Morrenwood?"

Hal nodded. "Ours is a small kingdom, tucked safely between the Keppel and Ridloe Mountains. But we're not naïve. The stench of war in the air from the south is unlike any Laparia has known. Many hands are involved in it, some unseen. And should it spread this way... Well, Montavia must protect itself at any cost."

"Still, why train with Arrondale's army?"

"Though King Rowan keeps his own guard, Montavia has avoided war for most of its history," he explained. "To better prepare ourselves, King Rowan requested of King Justin that our troops be allowed to train with his, to which your monarch readily agreed."

Nicholas warmed his hands over the crackling flames as a thin trail of smoke twisted up to the sky. The faces of the weary soldiers were dappled with flickering firelight. "A few men from my village volunteered to join the King's Guard. I was considering it myself," he said, staring into the blaze. "Who knows, we may still meet again in the capital."

"You're on your way there now?" one of the men asked.

"I'm traveling in that direction, but taking my time about it," he said. "I have a few things to think over first. Personal matters."

Hal offered an encouraging smile. "I believe you'd make a worthy soldier."

Nicholas took a bite of food, tossing an awkward glance his way. "Thanks for the vote of confidence, but my interest in joining wasn't entirely patriotic. I was looking for a bit of adventure, too."

Hal shrugged. "Nothing new with young men your age."

"And other than a few generalities, I don't know much about the war between Rhiál and Maranac," he added. "I guess that doesn't say much for one so eager to join the King's Guard."

Hal understood his mixed feelings. "Many young men, when enlisting, see only a grand adventure instead of cold reality. That doesn't mean their intentions aren't true. I'd wager most men in this camp joined out of a desire to see other parts of Laparia, thinking they'd have a fine time. There's nothing wrong with that." He added a few sticks to the fire. "And some of them may yet see other lands before the end–only for what the world really is, and at its worst."

"But why all the fighting?" Nicholas asked. "Who started the war?" Others admitted that they were unclear on the particulars, too.

"That part of the south has been a troubled region for years," Hal said. "And though others are more educated on its history, I can fill you in on recent events."

"Please do," Nicholas said, anticipating a rousing tale.

"Rhiál and present day Maranac were each half of the once united kingdom of Maranac that split apart decades ago. I don't know all the reasons why," he said, "but the two kingdoms managed to live in peace. That is, until the events earlier this year."

"What happened?" he asked.

"King Hamil of Maranac was assassinated, and his only child, Melinda, disappeared at the same time. Many believe she is dead. Hamil's older brother, Drogin, who had been passed over for the throne when his father died, is now king. He resented not ascending to the throne before his younger brother, so he waged war against Rhiál, determined to reunite the two realms by force."

"But why would Arrondale and Montavia get involved? How does that war affect our two kingdoms?"

Hal stood, glancing at the stars now out in their full brilliance. "Rhiál has requested help in its fight, not being strong enough to withstand Maranac alone," he explained. "More importantly, word is out that King Drogin blames agents from Rhiál, in league with Arrondale, for the assassination of his brother. He wants revenge."

"That's ridiculous!" Nicholas said. "King Justin is an honorable man. He would never condone such doings."

"Most would agree, but war has been waged. And should King Drogin succeed, who knows what misery and misfortune he might send our way. If he falsely blames Arrondale for the assassination of King Hamil, he may use that excuse to launch a war against your kingdom, and in time, perhaps Montavia. If diplomacy can't prevent that, then we must be prepared to fight."

Nicholas shook his head, again feeling his imagined military adventure quickly losing its luster. A trip to Morrenwood held little appeal at the moment, but a return home offered even less. His mind wrestled with the dilemma as the campfire snapped and sputtered in the chilly night air.

Nicholas was given some blankets and allowed to share one of the tents to spend the night. But before sleep found him, he remained around the fire past midnight with several of the soldiers, listening to stories of their journey and exploits. Yet despite an unadventurous start to their mission, most of the men envisioned a future filled with exciting and dangerous escapades. Most had never traveled far beyond their hometowns and boldly speculated about what Laparia had to offer. Nicholas again felt the romance of unexplored roads and wide open spaces tugging at his heart.

But in the first glimmer of gray dawn, the lofty dreams of the previous night had been reduced to cold, vague memories as tents were rolled up and backpacks slung reluctantly over shoulders in the damp autumn air. Soon the two hundred weary soldiers from Montavia crossed River Road into another field and headed south toward the Pine River. They silently vanished into an eddying mist that cloaked the ground, leaving Nicholas alone again on the road with his thoughts and dreams in a tangle.

CHAPTER 10

On King's Road

Nicholas spent a few hours that morning rambling about the village of Mitchell. The residents there, as in Kanesbury, were enjoying the final day of their Harvest Festival. But the pleasant aromas of outdoor cooking and the cheerful din of the crowds did little to dispel his melancholy. What he wouldn't give to be home enjoying the last night of the Festival instead of being branded an outcast. He left the village by noon, feeling as sad and alone as when he had departed Kanesbury.

A short time later, he walked through the village of Foley about a mile to the west. He stopped for lunch in a tavern on the main road. The laughter and camaraderie of other patrons reminded him of the many good times he had enjoyed at the Water Barrel Inn. But instead of cheering him, the memories tormented him as he sat alone off to one side of the room. He ate his meal quickly, paid the bill and departed.

He took shelter in some woods that night, building a small fire to keep warm and devouring the last scraps of food Katherine had supplied him. While eating, he contemplated the last few days of his life, staring moodily into the flames, not quite sure what to do or where to go. The next day found him back on the road, discouraged and wandering aimlessly through other tiny communities on his way to Morrenwood. He politely declined offers for a ride from anyone passing by on a horse and wagon, preferring the solitude of his walk.

He spent the night in an abandoned barn as heavy rains fell, battering the roof relentlessly well past daybreak. He found little sleep during those hours, hounded by tiring and fitful dreams. He took to the road later the next morning, exhausted and miserable. The damp air smelled of rotting hay, and huge mud puddles challenged his every step. Low drifting clouds appeared as tattered sails on a ship, threatening more rain. The charm and adventure of the open road wore thin as each hour passed.

River Road had begun curving southwest when he reached the intersection with King's Road. He roughly estimated that it was forty miles to Morrenwood, recalling colorful maps he had studied as a boy in Maynard's house. River Road, however, continued south for over a hundred miles to Arrondale's border and beyond. Nicholas had never stepped foot outside the kingdom and considered traveling south to see what that part of the world had to offer. But he quickly dismissed the notion, knowing he couldn't run away forever. Whether joining the King's Guard or not, he wanted to finish his journey to the capital if only to clear his mind. Rambling about the countryside was not a long-term option. Standing at a fork in the road, he tucked his blanket roll under his arm and headed west.

Stretches of pine woodland lay a stone's throw away on either side of King's Road during those first few miles, the Darden Wood towering to the north and the Pernum Wood to the south. Since it was nearing sunset, Nicholas decided to soon settle down for the night. He walked another half hour as fresh breezes swept along the road, breaking up clouds and clearing the sky. He watched the sun dip behind a string of rolling hills in the west, tinting the skyline strawberry-red. As twilight faded, a field of stars ignited like glowing embers. The Fox Moon, just past first quarter, loomed high in the east. Lingering just above the western horizon hung the larger Bear Moon, now only a sliver of a crescent.

Nicholas yawned as he turned off the road to his right. He headed for the Darden Wood as the trees on that side appeared closer. He hoped to find a dry spot to build a fire, lie down and sleep for hours. He had fled Kanesbury four nights ago and every muscle in his body ached. He was sure he had lost a little weight since then and quite certain he could use a hot bath and a change of clothes.

He approached the woods through a short expanse of dried grass and weeds. The towering pines reached for the crystalline stars above which he gazed at for several moments, comforted by their steadfast security. He strolled blithely toward the woods, still looking upward in amazement when he suddenly stumbled over a gopher hole. Nicholas fell, crashing his elbow hard into the ground. He flopped onto his back, muttering in pain as he massaged his injury. He chided himself for being so clumsy and then laughed as he imagined himself dancing with Katherine with the same poise and grace.

He sat and rested for a moment, his ego bruised more than his elbow, when he noticed a flicker of light inside the woods. Nicholas strained his eyes for a better look, wondering if he was imagining things before slowly getting to his feet. But he had only taken a couple of steps when the world suddenly tipped sideways again. He felt his feet kicked out from underneath him and stumbled to the ground a second time, his elbow again slamming into the cold dirt. When he turned and looked up, a dark figure loomed over him with a large stone clutched in its fist poised precariously above his head.

"If you're planning to rob me, I have very little money," Nicholas said, wincing. His elbow burned with pain.

The hooded figure wavered slightly, still holding the stone above Nicholas. "I am not a thief!" The voice was that of a young woman. She removed her hood with one hand, revealing waves of hair that cascaded down her shoulders. The moonlight cast a soft glow upon her troubled eyes. "And I'm not here to hurt you, though I can't assume the same about you, sir."

"Oh, so that kick to my legs from behind was just a friendly welcome?"

"I needed to get the advantage before you attacked my camp," she replied. "Tell me—do you work with Samuel? Did he send you to find me?"

Nicholas sat up on his good elbow, causing the woman to raise the stone in her defense. "Look, I'm not here to rob you or to find you," he said amiably. "Nobody sent me. And as for this Samuel fellow—never heard of him." He raised an eyebrow. "That rock aimed at my head is really starting to annoy me. Could you lower it please?"

"I could, but I won't, at least not yet." Her voice wavered. "First explain why you were heading toward my shelter."

"I didn't know anyone was in these woods," he said. "I'm just looking for a place to spend the night. I didn't even see your campfire until after I, um..."

"Inspected the ground for bugs?" she said lightly, cracking a thin smile. "Not the most sure-footed gentleman in the ballroom, are you."

"Hey, that was a big gopher hole. And that second trip from you was totally unnecessary," he said. "Couldn't you see I was already injured?"

The woman looked at him askance, still uncertain of his intentions. "I'm sorry if I hurt you." She lowered the rock just a bit yet still kept a cautious eye upon him. "You seem a friendly enough sort, but there are plenty of trees on the opposite side of the road. Perhaps the Pernum Wood might be more to your liking."

"Are you serious?" Nicholas said, carefully standing up as the woman took a defensive step backward, the stone still raised in front of her. He rubbed his sore elbow and scowled. "You attacked me, remember? And you want *me* to leave?" He sighed, shaking his head with mild annoyance yet attuned to the distrust and fear still evident in the woman's demeanor. "Look, miss, I'm not going to cause you any trouble, but I'm certainly not going to trudge all the way back to those other woods because you say so."

"A gentleman would."

"Maybe a gentleman without an elbow burning with pain." Nicholas shook his head, not wishing to sound combative or sarcastic. "Look, you stay by your fire and I'll keep to the edge of the trees over there, well out of your way," he said, pointing west. "I just want some sleep. Goodnight." He leaned down and grabbed his blanket roll and shuffled off toward the distant trees as the young woman watched him depart with an icy stare, still clutching the stone.

When Nicholas reached the woods at a spot he thought was an appropriate distance away, he gathered some twigs and dried weeds and tried to start a fire. With his sore elbow still bothering him, he had difficulty generating a flame, finally getting a small blaze going that sputtered and snapped as some of the kindling was still damp. But the fire didn't last long, producing more smoke than heat, and he soon gave up trying to stoke the blaze. Being too tired to search for drier fuel, he finally lay down on the ground bundled in his hooded coat and blanket, hoping sleep would soon take him.

Something moved in the shadows. When Nicholas opened his eyes, the beginnings of a dream scattered from his mind. A sound had awakened him–a snapping twig? The crunch of dried leaves? He was shivering in the night chill. Then he noticed her figure standing nearby among the trees, the smoke from his dead fire swirling in front of her.

"What's wrong?" he asked, sitting up, not sure how long he had been sleeping. He rubbed a hand through his hair, still a bit bleary-eyed.

"If you'd like, you may sit by my fire and keep warm," the young woman said.

"No rock?" Nicholas replied with a faint smile, noting that she had approached unarmed.

"No flames?" she responded dryly, indicating the charred twigs with a turn of her head. "Being downwind of you, all I could smell was damp smoke for the last half hour. I couldn't sleep."

"Sorry."

She beckoned him with a wave of her hand. "Follow me. I could inspect your sore elbow if you'd like."

"Thanks."

She gazed curiously at the weary stranger. "Do you have a name?"

"Nicholas," he said, standing up while still wrapped in the blanket. "And you?"

"One thing at a time," she replied guardedly while leading him back to her section of the woods. "Let's tend to that injury first."

A short time later, Nicholas was savoring a sweet apple in front of a warm fire. The soreness in his elbow subsided as the evening chill left his weary limbs. He noticed the woman throwing several glances his way as if still not convinced that he meant her no harm. They were about the same age, and in the glow of the firelight he noticed how pretty she looked. A pair of dark brown eyes matched the color of her hair. He thought he noted a slight resemblance to Katherine but kept that to himself.

"Thanks again for the apple. My food supplies have dwindled down to nothing," he said.

"I'm happy to share with someone in need." She nervously tended to the fire. "If I may ask, why are you out alone in these parts without food or a horse?"

"I might ask the same of you."

"I still have food."

Nicholas smiled. "You've got me there. But if you must know, I was heading to Morrenwood. Thinking about it anyway."

"Morrenwood?" She glanced uneasily his way. "What's in the capital city?" she asked, feigning a casual air.

"I was considering joining up–" Nicholas caught himself, wondering if he should reveal any of his personal life to a stranger in light of recent events. But as he was about forty miles away from Kanesbury and no authority had yet found him, he decided that maybe it was safe to open up a little to this woman who had just demonstrated a bit of kindness despite her earlier behavior. "I was thinking about possibly signing on with the King's Guard–in spite of my recent failed attempt to build a campfire."

"I'm impressed. That's a noble calling." She added a few sticks to the blaze and then tightened her cloak around her. "But why did you say *possibly*?"

"There are other complications I'm not eager to talk about. Some things back home still need tending to and, well... Maybe I should go back there."

"And where is home?"

Nicholas was reluctant to answer as another wave of distrust swept over him alongside the memories of his escape. But sensing no deceit on her part, he decided to take the extra step and gain a bit more of her trust and perhaps make an ally, if only for one night. "I'm from Kanesbury, a small village to the east."

"I've heard of that," she said, seeming to relax a bit. "So you left home before first attending to these unfinished matters? You must have been in a hurry."

He shrugged. "Like I said, it's complicated. I really don't want to discuss it."

"Understood."

"Not that I'm being rude or ungrateful for your hospitality–excluding that kick in the legs," he quickly added. The woman tried not to smile. "By the way, what's your story? And your name?"

She thought for a moment, her chin resting gently upon her folded fingers as she studied the flickering flames. "You may call me Megan. And I'm on my way to visit a relative in Kent County."

"That's quite a hike north. Where in the county does your relative live?"

"My great aunt Castella resides in a seaside village called Boros on Sage Bay. I've been told it's quite lovely there."

"And you decided to go to Boros all alone?"

Megan looked directly into his eyes. "That is also a complicated matter, Nicholas. I'll spare you the details."

"I'd love details. A good story would suit me right now even if it's only about your aunt. I've been bored silly the last few days."

"She's my *great* aunt. But don't expect me to provide details of my personal life just to ease your boredom, Nicholas. After all, I'm not a wandering storyteller."

"Only trying to make pleasant conversation. And maybe I could help you since you said it's a complicated matter."

"That assumes I *need* help."

"We all could use a little," he replied, again sensing her prickly attitude returning. "You're stuck here alone in the woods and I'm just wondering why. And who was that Samuel fellow you mentioned earlier?"

"If you needed to know, I would have told you. Besides, you didn't want me interrogating you earlier, so now I'm asking the same favor as pleasantly as I can–please mind your own business."

Nicholas leaned back, his mouth slightly agape as the snapping flames sent a flurry of sparks skyward. "Sorry, Megan. I didn't mean to offend." He took a last bite from the apple and tossed the core into the woods. "Maybe I'll visit the folks over at the next campfire. I hear they're planning to sing songs later on."

"How amusing." Megan combed her fingers through her hair during a few moments of icy silence before gently gazing at Nicholas. "Look, I'm sorry for being brusque. It was uncalled for. But I just don't feel comfortable going into detail about..."

"Yeah, I understand. Complications. I have them too, Megan, and I shouldn't have pushed you."

160

"Perhaps we should tell each other ghost stories instead."

"I heard a few scary ones growing up."

"Or you could tell me more about your village," she suggested. "And your family. Just the general details, mind you. Leave out any of the complicated parts."

"Agreed," he said with a pleasant chuckle. "But promise not to fall asleep if you get bored. Kanesbury isn't the center of excitement in the kingdom."

"Don't be too harsh about your hometown. The busiest and most fascinating places in the world can at times have all the charm of a dreary prison," she said. "Or so I'd imagine," she quickly added.

"I suppose. But Kanesbury is a nice enough place. Plenty of good people living there. I just needed to get out and see something new. Bored, I guess." Nicholas stood to stretch his legs and escape the heat of the fire. "I imagine you don't think my reasons for joining the King's Guard are so noble now."

"It's not my place to judge. But at least you're considering offering your services to King Justin despite the reason. That's more than most men would do."

"But the closer I get to Morrenwood, the more doubts I have. I don't like to have other matters hanging over my head."

"What did your family think about you leaving home?"

Nicholas sat by the fire again, quiet for a few moments as he thought about Maynard and Adelaide, the only real family he could claim. He vaguely recalled how his mother looked, and any memories of his father were the result of other people describing the man to him over the years.

"Well, my good friend Maynard supported my decision to join up with the King's Guard if it was what I really wanted. That was before my other problems snowballed. He and his wife, Tessa, raised me as their own since I was ten." He glanced at Megan with a smile, happy to tell her about Maynard. "He always gave me the best advice yet allowed me the freedom to find my own way. The same with Tessa." Nicholas stared into the fire, recalling past sorrows. "She was really sick with fever about two years ago and passed away. That nearly devastated Maynard. He's better now. Strong inside, just like the huge oak tree planted near his house."

"He sounds like a good, honest man," Megan said. "I hope I'm not being intrusive–and tell me if I am–but what happened to your real parents?"

Nicholas warmed his hands by the fire and spoke to the flames. "It's all right to ask. I don't mind talking about them. My father, Jack, died shortly before I was born, so all I really know about him was from what others told me. He was thrown from a horse during a bad storm one night away from home. Took some serious injuries. And, well, that's what happened."

"I'm sorry. It's too bad you never got to know him. All sons should have a father to raise them." She hooked a finger to move some hair out of her eyes. "And all daughters a mother."

"It would have been nice. And though I don't remember, I'm told my mother never really recovered from the shock of losing him. Her name was Alice," he softly said. Embers glowed deep red within the fire as the flames cast wavering shadows over the lower pine boughs. Gray smoke meandered lazily through the bending branches. "She died when I was five. Sickness also, like Tessa. Maybe from a broken heart, too. Anyway, her older brother and his wife raised me, reluctantly, until I was ten. They lived on a farm outside the village. Neither were the best farmers nor parents," he admitted with a laugh. "Everyone knew it. They had three children of their own which were three more than they should ever have had in the first place."

"Nicholas, you make them sound awful!"

"They were in a world of their own and I was just another mouth to feed. One of my teachers during winter lessons suspected as much and took me under her wing. She was very kind, offering me extra help to read and write, or a hot meal at home now and then. She and her husband weren't able to bear children and liked having me around. They even paid me for doing odd jobs on their farm when lessons weren't in session."

Megan smiled. "Maynard and Tessa?"

He nodded. "In time they offered to raise me as their own, which my aunt, uncle and I readily agreed to. So I'd been living on the farm ever since."

"Quite an interesting childhood, Nicholas."

"But since we haven't compared it to yours yet, it may be as dull as dry mud. Does your family know you're hiding out here in the middle of nowhere?" he asked. "Running away perhaps? I wonder if your great aunt Castella really exists at all," he said with mock suspicion. "Or maybe there's more intrigue to your story than you're willing to admit." He grinned but quickly turned serious when realizing that Megan was less than amused with his banter. "Hey, I'm only joking, Megan. Don't look so sour."

"I am not sour!" she said with a sharp edge to her voice. "Just tired. Perhaps we should put aside these irksome inquiries about each other's families and get some sleep. I've had a long day."

"Sure." Nicholas scolded himself, realizing he had stepped over the line. He knew Megan had no intention of continuing their discussion any further that night. "I'm not tired. If it's all right, I'll just sit here awhile."

"Suit yourself. Stay by the fire the entire night if you'd like, but I'll be leaving at first light." Megan retrieved a blanket roll from the shadows and spread it across some soft pine cuttings she had gathered earlier. She lay down and faced the fire, covering herself with her cloak. "I have more food you're welcome to share with me at daybreak."

"Appreciate it."

She closed her eyes. "Good night, Nicholas."

He gazed at Megan, feeling protective all of the sudden while wondering who this woman really was and how she had ended up here. "I'll tend to the fire. Good night."

Nicholas watched as the flames delicately illuminated her face. Though Megan looked at peace, he could discern a trace of apprehension etched in her features. Despite his growing curiosity, she deftly guarded the details of her personal life which he decided were none of his business. And since he wasn't eager to tell of his woes, he knew he shouldn't expect others to do the same. Yet it would be nice to unload his thoughts and get another perspective. Perhaps if he dared to open up first? But that would be impossible since Megan was leaving in the morning and traveling in the opposite direction.

Nicholas again debated the wisdom of joining King Justin's guard. Running away wouldn't solve his problems, yet he still needed time to figure out what to do. And he missed Katherine and Maynard, wanting so much to talk with them to determine what really happened back home, knowing he couldn't solve the matter by himself.

He added a few more sticks to the fire, finally settling down for the night an hour later. He needed sleep desperately despite what he had said earlier and lay down on a bed of dried undergrowth, wrapping himself tightly in his blanket. He hoped their dual complications might be easier to deal with in the light of morning.

They awoke simultaneously an hour after sunrise with the cold gray ashes of the campfire between them. Slivers of sunlight slipped into the woods and a sapphire blue sky hung above the treetops. Crisp autumn air slowly washed the remains of last night's sleep from their heads.

Nicholas yawned as he sat up, stretching a kink out of his back. "I don't suppose the innkeeper set out any hot spiced cider or darlaroot tea."

Megan smirked. "Would you like that with your eggs and biscuits, or before?"

"Give me a moment to decide," he said, sitting with his knees bent and the blanket wrapped around him. He shivered as a morning chill shot through him.

"Don't take too long," she replied, fumbling through a small sack of food. "The kitchen closes soon."

"I'm famous for snap decisions after a full night's sleep," he said, pausing a moment. "And I've just decided something important." Megan turned around clutching an apple she had retrieved from the sack. "I'm going back home."

"Oh?" she said, trying not to sound surprised. "So there'll be no mighty adventure with the King's Guard in your future?"

Nicholas caught the apple Megan tossed to him. "Maybe some day, but right now I have to get back to Kanesbury. Like it or not, there are some matters I can't escape nor should ever have run away from in the first place."

Megan offered an encouraging smile. "Those dastardly complications. They plague us all, don't they?"

"Life would be dull without them."

"What exactly will you do once you get home?"

"Still working on that part," he added, taking a bite of the apple. "I need more time to think through the details." He took a second bite. "But I was figuring, Megan, while I'm doing all this lofty thinking, maybe I could keep you company on the road as we'd both be going in the same direction for a while. If it's all right with you, of course. I don't mean to impose my charming and delightful company on someone unasked for," he added with a wink.

Megan removed a bread roll from the sack and sat down next to Nicholas. She ripped the roll in two and handed him half. "It just so happens that I've been sorely lacking any charming and delightful company of late," she said, playfully jabbing him in the side. "It's tough to come by on the road."

"Isn't it though?"

"Just don't expect a fabulous culinary experience like this at every meal, okay?"

"No more than twice a day, tops."

"Only on the condition that you promise to scrounge up all the firewood."

"As long as you don't tell me how to *build* the fire."

"Agreed," she replied, extending her hand as Nicholas shook it with a smile.

END OF PART ONE

PART TWO
THE ROAD NORTH

CHAPTER 11

A Brief Visit

On their first day of traveling together, Nicholas and Megan walked leisurely along River Road, passing through a tiny hamlet now and then, and stopping only long enough to eat or chat with the locals for the latest news. They kept their conversation to a few topics, aware of each other's skittishness when broaching personal matters.

Nicholas, though, grew weary of hiding his problems and was tempted to tell Megan about the strange events in Kanesbury. But second thoughts cautioned him and he held his tongue. How could he tell her that he was an accused murderer and thief despite the falseness of the charges? Since she had no more proof of his innocence than did Constable Brindle, Nicholas feared she might run away if he told her.

He wondered at the same time about her life story. Could it be any worse than his? He seriously doubted that since Megan seemed too decent a woman to have wronged anybody. Yet that didn't stop him from speculating about what she was hiding.

At noon the following day, they reached the intersection of River and Orchard roads, the former which continued east while the latter stretched north into Kent County on the shores of the Trillium Sea. When Nicholas had first passed this spot on his way to

Morrenwood, he hadn't cared a whit where Orchard Road might lead. Now his plans had changed.

"I'm going with you," he told Megan matter-of-factly before she could fashion a few words to mark their departure.

"Excuse me?"

"I said I'm going with you. I mean, I'll go with you–all the way to Boros–if you don't mind some company. Just to see that you get safely to your great aunt's house." Nicholas smiled awkwardly as he tugged at his jacket collar. "I've got plenty of time on my hands."

Megan raised a skeptical eyebrow. "Not eager to rush home and face those unappetizing complications? How bad can they be?"

He dug his boot into the dirt under the warm autumn sun. A flock of blackbirds chirped monotonously in a nearby grove of elm trees. "Pretty bad," he muttered, looking at the ground. "So I spend a few more days mulling things over up north. *Then* I'll go home." He looked desperately at Megan. "What's wrong with that?"

She smiled and shook her head. "Nothing at all. Some people are forced on the run, others just run away. In the end, they all need the same thing."

"What's that?"

"Time and understanding." Megan smiled, indicating the road north. "Come on, Nicholas. I'd love some company."

They walked for a couple of miles, stopping once to drink from a cold spring flowing along a shady embankment. Though it was the first month of the autumn season, the afternoon felt unusually warm. Nicholas and Megan enjoyed their brief respite under the falling leaves of some sugar maples. Patches of cobalt blue sky winked through the upper branches.

The road inclined steeply at one point and they paused to catch their breaths near the top. They were rewarded with a spectacular view of the changing foliage for miles ahead. Acres of maple, elm and birch trees covered the hilly area below near the village of Kast, bathing its nestled homes in shocking splashes of tangerine, crimson and gold. Tall pines scattered among the woods accentuated the bursting collage with somber stripes of dusky green.

"Isn't it beautiful, Nicholas?" Megan placed her hands to her face, absorbing the incredible sight.

"I never tire of it," he said.

"I've never seen such a stunning display!" she added, wide-eyed and smiling like a child just given a new toy. "There are mostly pine trees around the mountains near Morrenwood–which are very nice, don't get me wrong. But this view is amazing!" she burst out, not realizing the words she had just spoken.

"You're from Morrenwood?"

"*What*?" She turned to Nicholas, half paying attention. "What'd you say?"

"You're from Morrenwood, Megan? From what you just said, I assume you must live in the capital city."

Her smile disappeared in a heartbeat. She lowered her hands, distractedly smoothing out the light brown peasant dress she wore. Her cloak lay draped over one arm. "Did I say Morrenwood?"

"You did."

"Well, I... I've passed through that part of the kingdom once. That's what I meant. It's so different from this area," she said rigidly.

"If you are from Morrenwood, that's okay," he said kindly.

"I may be or I may not," she excitedly uttered. "It doesn't matter to you, does it? Why even ask about something so trivial?" She flopped her heavy cloak onto her other arm and marched ahead without looking back. "Let's get going. Can't chatter away all afternoon. Only a few hours of daylight left."

Nicholas smirked as Megan marched down the dirt road, raising small puffs of dust with each foot stomp. "Right behind you," he replied, studying his companion with deepening curiosity.

They ate a brief lunch in the village of Kast which consisted of the remaining food items Megan carried with her–two red apples, a stale bread roll, a tiny wedge of goat cheese and one slice of dried salted beef. Each savored the remaining scraps, washing them down with water from a stream on the outskirts of the village. Megan refilled a water skin she carried with her and then each took a few moments to wash their hands and faces. They sat on the stream bank afterward and soaked their feet in the crisp water. Miles of road weariness flowed out of their tired limbs, and the gurgling water rushing over mossy stones nearly lulled them to sleep. But within the hour, they took to the road again, refreshed and eager to forge ahead a few more miles before twilight.

Nicholas wrestled with a thought before speaking. "I'm curious about something."

"About what?"

"If you had expected to travel all the way to Boros–from wherever you call home–well, you didn't exactly calculate your supply of provisions properly, did you."

"I now have a second mouth to feed," she retorted.

"Good point," he said. "But even taking that into consideration, you still didn't plan very well. Unless you have money with you or decide to beg from the locals."

Megan shot a sarcastic glance his way. "I had planned to steal what I needed, if you must know."

"Don't get upset. We'll have plenty to eat until we get there. I've got some money. I was only curious."

"About what?" Megan stopped in her tracks and faced him, her arms akimbo. "What is your point, Nicholas? So I'm not an expert at arranging trips on the open road. Do you want to berate me for that?"

"No."

"Though I noticed that your meager supplies ran out long before mine did."

"But my trip was spur-of-the-moment," he said. "I was lucky to have what few provisions I did. But you had a destination in mind, so I was wondering why you didn't fully prepare."

Megan sighed disgustedly. "Still waiting to hear your point."

"My point is... Well, I guess there really isn't a point. I'm just worried for you, Megan. I keep thinking about that person you mentioned earlier–Samuel? Is he after you? Are you on the run from him and had to leave in a hurry?"

"You don't give up, do you, Nicholas. Didn't we agree not to pry into each other's personal business?"

"Yes, but if you're in trouble I'd like to help."

"You're walking to Boros with me. Isn't that enough?"

"You know what I mean."

Megan draped the cloak over her shoulders. The warm afternoon air had cooled slightly as the sun began its westward descent. "No, I *don't* know what you mean. You may be in trouble, too, Nicholas, and I'm not allowed to know why. But just because you're more than eager to assist, I'm supposed to break down like a helpless maiden and tell you my sob story? I'm not a little lost girl. I can take care of myself!"

"Didn't say you couldn't."

Megan walked ahead and then quickly turned around, waving a finger at Nicholas. "You men in my life are all alike, thinking that I need to– I mean, thinking that we women need to be kept out of harm's way whenever trouble comes bounding along. Well, I'm quite sick and tired of that type of thinking!" she snapped. "I don't like to flee at the first whiff of adversity. I'm not a coward."

"Oh, and I suppose I am. Is that what you're implying?"

"I'm implying nothing, Nicholas."

"Admit it. You think I should have stayed home and faced my problems head on. Say what you really mean."

"I don't want to say anything! Are you always this exasperating?" She whirled around and stormed up the road, wrapping the folds of her cloak tightly about her waist.

Nicholas glared at the sky and gritted his teeth before going after her. "Slow down! This isn't a race."

"Keep up! I want this trip over with as soon as possible."

"So do I!" he muttered, matching pace with her brisk steps.

"Then go home. No one's stopping you. I'll find the way to Boros on my own."

"There, you said it again! *Go home.* So you *do* think I was wrong for running away from my problems."

Megan stopped and spun around, nearly colliding with Nicholas who steamed forward like a mad bull. He faced her fiery eyes and the tip of her index finger again pointed at him with a vengeance.

"I'm not accusing you of anything, Nicholas. Do you understand? I can't and won't judge your decision because I know none of the facts." She grabbed the edges of his unbuttoned jacket and held him tightly in place. "Maybe you're babbling on about these feelings because you're wondering if you did the right thing. Did you ever consider that? And you can struggle all you want with the guilt or regret. That's okay. I suspect things look bleak for you," she said, trying to be a bit gentler, but her frustrations were already close to boiling. "But just please don't take your problems out on me!" She shook him while clutching the folds of his jacket. "I've got enough to endure in my own life!"

She released Nicholas, straightening out his jacket and realizing she may have been a bit overly dramatic. Megan raised her eyes in a silent apology and then hurriedly continued up the road as Nicholas stared at her with a stunned and crooked smirk plastered across his face.

"We'll both get over our troubles one of these days, I promise you. It's only a matter of time before–" Megan then realized that Nicholas hadn't been following her. She turned around and saw him frozen in his stance, glassy-eyed and mouth agape, and trudged back to him. "What's the matter? Look, I'm sorry if I came across a bit too strong a moment ago. I can sometimes be–"

Nicholas remained lost in thought, holding the folds of his jacket and slowly rubbing his thumb along the right side where the brown button was missing. He looked up at Megan as if aware of her presence for the first time.

"Are you feeling all right?" she asked. "Are you ill?"

Nicholas softly spoke two words. *"Dooley Kramer."*

Megan shook her head. "I don't understand. Who is Dooley Kramer?"

"An important piece of the puzzle." Nicholas offered an encouraging smile, putting her at ease. "I worked with Dooley back in Kanesbury. We were both employed in Ned Adams' gristmill. Dooley is one of the laborers. I do the bookkeeping for Ned."

"But why are you thinking about him now?"

"Because I just now realized that he helped to turn my life upside down." He smiled again. "Thank you, Megan."

"For what?"

"For shaking some sense into me."

"You're welcome, I think," she said, still in the dark. "And though I'm not quite sure what you mean, I apologize if I was too loud about it."

"Perhaps just a *little* bit loud, ma'am," another person said as he rattled up alongside them in an open wagon, gently pulling on the reins to halt his two horses. "I heard your voice way down the road near the last farmhouse I passed. Is there a problem here?" he asked with an air of suspicion, clutching a wooden cudgel that lay next to him on the seat that he carried on the road for protection.

Nicholas and Megan hadn't noticed the stranger approaching. He sat straight as a board, puffing a pipe and sporting a short, brown beard. Atop his head rested a sun-washed hat, whose floppy, tattered brim shaded a pair of chocolate colored eyes.

"We're just having a friendly argument, sir," Nicholas assured him. "More or less."

Megan blushed. "I was voicing a minor difference of opinion with my friend. I hope we didn't disturb you."

"Not likely," he said, releasing his grip on the cudgel, momentarily convinced that the young lady was not in any danger. "I have two sons who play and argue from sunup to sunset. I'm used to it." He exhaled a stream of pipe smoke which twisted in the air like rope. "Where're you two headed, if I might ask?"

"North," Megan replied. "To Boros."

"That's quite a hike on foot. Lose your horses?"

"Never had any to start with," Nicholas said with a sheepish grin. "This journey was a little spur-of-the-moment for both of us."

"I see," the man said, eyeing them more closely. Though he suspected that the couple's circumstances were a bit peculiar, they seemed kind and decent enough on the surface. And as he prided himself on being a good judge of character, he decided to follow his instincts. "Need a lift? I'm going as far as Minago which will cut a few miles off your journey."

"Much appreciated," Nicholas replied, realizing that darkness was only hours away and their food supply was nonexistent. He eyed Megan to see if she was agreeable.

"That's a very kind offer and we accept," she told him.

"Then climb on board up front," he told Megan with a pleasant smile before glancing at Nicholas. "You sit in back."

"Much obliged," he softly said as he walked to the back and climbed on, sitting on the edge of the cart with his legs dangling over the side. Several empty wooden crates were piled behind him, and a few bruised apples rolled around as the cart rumbled steadily along.

"My name's Joe Marsh. And you?"

They introduced themselves, happy to have new company on the road despite Mr. Marsh's somewhat gruff exterior. But as the cart rattled on and they listened to his stories about running an apple orchard and selling his produce up and down Orchard Road, Nicholas and Megan were quickly enthralled by his stories and sense of humor, and for a time forgot about their own troubles as they peppered him with questions about his life and family in Minago.

When Mr. Marsh asked Megan about her great aunt Castella and the reason for her trip to Boros, he received only a few perfunctory replies, sensing reluctance on her part to open up about the matter. He shot a brief glance at Nicholas in back who returned a bewildered shrug, guessing that Nicholas had had as much success as he in prying any information from her. But Megan's evasiveness prompted a fatherly concern for the young woman in Mr. Marsh rather than suspicion, so he gradually changed the subject and talked about his own family again as the miles rolled away beneath them.

"You two are in luck," he later said as they drew closer to Minago and the daylight had began to wane. "My older son, Leo, is heading north up the line tomorrow to make more apple deliveries. Boros is his last stop. I'd bet he'd love some company."

Before Megan and Nicholas could even say they'd consider his kind proposal, Mr. Marsh had invited the two home for dinner, saying there was plenty of space for them to spend the night so that they could leave first thing in the morning with Leo. After he mentioned that his wife was preparing a turkey stew and baking fresh apple bread for the evening meal, Megan quickly accepted when seeing Nicholas eagerly nodding his approval. Mr. Marsh was delighted as his horses trotted home.

Joe Marsh and his wife, Annabelle, lived outside the village of Minago on a small farm and apple orchard where they raised sweet yellow corn, a few milking cows, juicy red Corlian apples and two sons, Leo and Henry. They soon passed through the village ablaze in autumn colors as the setting sun washed over tree-lined streets. People hurried about on last minute errands before the shops closed. Joe turned onto a road heading east out of the village, passing over a covered bridge. The rhythmic clip clop of the horses' hooves over wooden planks played in sync with the rush of icy stream waters below. He waved at a driver on a passing wagon loaded with sheaves of freshly cut hay for delivery in the village, then turned into a small farm another half mile up the road. Joe Marsh reined his horses to a stop under a weeping willow tree next to the main barn, glad to be home. He jumped off the cart and extended a hand to help Megan step down.

"This is a lovely place," she said, admiring the property.

A house of chiseled stone blocks sat off to the left, with trails of gray smoke rising from its chimney. The main barn, painted apple red, rested on a foundation of the same stone. Behind the building was an apple orchard, its trees still bursting with fruit, and a corn field whose brown stalks had already been harvested yet still needed to be cut down and burned. An assortment of pine trees and sugar maples, together with the large weeping willow, guarded the place like unsleeping sentries.

"Belle and I have lived here for over twenty years, and neither of us could imagine a better place," Mr. Marsh said with pride. "I'll take you inside to meet her first, and then you two can wash up if you'd like."

"Appreciate it," Nicholas said, walking around from the back of the cart.

At that instant, a pair of raucous voices bellowed in the near distance, growing louder and stronger every second, charging along the right side of the barn. Suddenly, two people tore around the corner as fast as rabbits and shot in front of the building, one chasing the other, arms flailing and boots pounding, howling like wounded animals, until the first one slipped and the second one tripped, and then both went sailing though a lake of a mud puddle left over from the rain a few days earlier.

Megan turned her head to avoid the splash as Nicholas looked on in amusement. Mr. Marsh removed his hat and sighed, flicking a dab of mud off the brim and placing it back on his head. The two figures stood up, spitting and dripping mud from head to toe. Then the first one slapped his hand against the willow tree before both plodded over a patch of grass toward Mr. Marsh.

"Megan and Nicholas," he said dryly. "I'd like you to meet– *my sons*, Leo and Henry. Though at the moment I can't tell which is which."

"Nice to meet you," Leo, the taller one, said. He scraped away globs of mud around his eyes, grinning awkwardly. "My kid brother said he could beat me in a race from the last fencepost on the orchard to this willow tree out front. I won."

"Are you sure about that?" Megan asked, trying not to laugh.

"I'm not sure these two have half a brain between them," their father muttered. "I'll save the introductions for later after you two wash off in the stream," he indicated to his sons. "Your mother will disown you if you step one foot in the house like that."

"Yes, father," they said simultaneously before sheepishly shuffling off to the stream behind the barn. Leo glanced back while on his way, happily noting that Megan was watching him depart in spite of his muddy coating.

Two hours later they were all seated around the kitchen table, thoroughly stuffed with turkey stew, roasted corn on the cob and hot apple bread with butter. Earlier, Mrs. Marsh insisted that Nicholas and Megan let her soak their travel-stained garments for a few hours while they washed up, supplying Nicholas with a spare set of clothes from Leo and providing Megan with some of her own.

"I'll hang everything next to the fire. They'll be dry by morning," she insisted.

Megan had also talked about her journey to Boros to visit her great aunt, though offered no details about where she was traveling from. Nicholas said that he was from Kanesbury and provided only sparse details of his life. But neither Mr. Marsh nor his wife pressed either one for more specifics, believing they would open up to them more if they were not pushed. And when offered transportation again, Nicholas and Megan agreed to drive up north with Leo the next day as he made his deliveries.

"My orchard is famous for its Corlian apples," Mr. Marsh boasted. "You won't find a sweeter or crisper variety in this region. You can take my word for it."

"And don't dare challenge him on that point either," Leo said with a wink, looking Megan's way. "Father is the self-proclaimed apple king around here."

"That's something you should be proud of," she said. "Having a king for a relative is quite an honor."

"Oh, we're all proud of Joe," Mrs. Marsh added. "He sells apples up and down the line to a string of bake shops and restaurants. Many of our customers have been with us since the orchard first started producing."

Mr. Marsh retrieved his pipe on the fireplace mantel, lit it, and rejoined the others at the table, blowing a string of bluish-gray smoke rings that drifted lazily toward the ceiling. Megan chuckled in delight and blushed when noticing Leo gazing at her. He had just turned twenty, tall with black hair and an amiable smile, and much more presentable without a coating of mud splashed across his face. He hoped one day to save enough money to buy a few acres of land and start his own orchard, cultivating an entirely new variety of apple.

"Father taught me so much about the business–planting, grafting, selling and what not–that I feel I could outgrow half the orchards in this area!" He gushed with enthusiasm as he chattered on about his future ambitions. "I have great plans." Megan was deeply impressed and told him so.

"Just so long as you don't put me out of business," his father joked. "I'm not ready to retire yet."

"You'll never retire, Joe. You wouldn't know how," Belle quipped. "You've got apple cider in your veins!"

Shortly afterward, while Megan helped Mrs. Marsh clear the table and wash the dinner plates, Nicholas walked to the barn with Mr. Marsh, Leo and Henry to finish loading a wagon with apple crates for tomorrow's run. The sun had dipped below the horizon, producing a frosty nip in the air. The crescent Bear Moon, larger and higher in the west tonight, aimed its pointed tips at the gibbous Fox Moon farther across the sky and lounging above the eastern horizon. The men worked under the duo's silvery glow, lighting only one oil lamp to finish their work in the barn.

The crates filled the larger of two wagons Mr. Marsh owned, stacked four layers high and secured with successive bands of rope. A large canvas tarp was spread over the back of the wagon and likewise secured. While Henry and his father attended to this last detail, Leo found a chance to take Nicholas aside and question him about a matter he had been agonizing over all through dinner.

"After you travel to Boros with Megan, what were you planning to do? Find a job there?"

"Doubtful," Nicholas said. "I'll probably head back home to Kanesbury. There are some matters I need to attend to that I didn't want to mention at dinner."

"I see. So then you and Megan aren't courting or engaged or anything along those lines, are you?" he asked hopefully.

"Oh, nothing like that," Nicholas said. "Megan and I just met by chance on the road." He eyed Leo with a suspicious grin. "Why? Has she already snared you with her charms?"

"I *am* taken by her." Leo scuffed the sole of his boot over the ground. "I couldn't stop gazing at her at dinner. I think she took notice of me, too. At least I hope she did. She smiled a couple of times. Did you happen to see? Were those smiles directed at me?"

Nicholas bit his lower lip to keep from smirking, but assured Leo that Megan may have been taken with his demeanor. "Except for that bit in the mud puddle. I don't suspect that that's the best way to attract a woman."

"No, I suppose not," he admitted with a laugh.

"She is a pretty thing," Nicholas added, "but very secretive about her background. Something's bothering Megan, but I don't know what. I suspect she's in trouble."

"Trouble? What do you mean?"

Nicholas shrugged. "Megan wouldn't give me any hints, and when I tried to press her for specifics… Well, I suggest you don't try right away either, Leo."

"I'll keep that in mind."

Mr. Marsh interrupted their discussion after he and Henry finished securing the tarp. As all was now ready for the morning journey, the barn doors were closed for the night and the quartet marched back into the house. Mrs. Marsh provided everyone with a mug of hot spiced cider in front of a roaring blaze. They sat and talked late into the evening as the crescent Bear Moon slid quietly below the western horizon, leaving the Fox Moon as the lone guardian in the night sky.

CHAPTER 12

A Conversation Among Friends

Leo hitched a team of two horses to the apple wagon and rolled it out of the barn at sunrise. The morning light brushed the stringy branches of the willow with a golden hue as wisps of white fog crept along the ground like slinking cats. A stream behind the barn gurgled icy and swift, washing over tufts of lanky grass leaning over the bank's edge.

He estimated that his deliveries would take two days, with an additional half day for the return trip. Today he would travel to the villages of Spring Hill, Mason and Plum Orchard, make his required stops, and then spend the night in Plum Orchard as darkness settled in. Tomorrow Leo planned deliveries to White Birch, Laurel Corners and finally Boros, after which he'd backtrack to White Birch and call it a night. His third day on the road would be a swift return home, making only a couple of brief stops to pick up some supplies that his father needed on the farm. All in all, Leo enjoyed the apple run, as he called it, which he made a few times during the growing season. As this was the last run of the year though, he was glad to have Megan and Nicholas along for company. The autumn daylight grew less and less each swiftly passing day, and traveling the roads alone now was usually a bleak affair.

They ate a large breakfast at Mrs. Marsh's insistence before loading the wagon with food supplies and other traveling provisions.

Leo crammed these as best he could in what little space remained alongside the sweet smelling apple crates.

"Now, Megan, if you're ever in our parts again, don't think twice about dropping by. You'll always have a place at our table," Mrs. Marsh said.

"I appreciate that very much."

"You too, Nicholas. I expect to see you on your way back to Kanesbury, whenever that will be."

"I'll be knocking on your door one day soon," he promised.

Henry and Mr. Marsh also said their goodbyes, and soon Leo, Megan and Nicholas rode off the property as the morning sun inched above the trees in back of the house. As they disappeared up the road, Henry scrambled to the barn to begin his daily chores. Mr. Marsh, puffing on a pipe, wrapped an arm around his wife and walked with her back to the house, both expecting to see their son again in about two and a half days, though it was not to be. Neither parent could have imagined the fate that awaited him or his newfound companions.

The first leg of the journey proved uneventful. Nicholas, Megan and Leo chatted amiably during the few miles to Spring Hill, stopping along the way when passing a stream or pond to allow the horses to drink. As Orchard Road had several peaks and valleys, and the wagon was heavily loaded with apple crates, they made slow time starting out. But the landscape, soaked with sun and autumn colors, provided for an enjoyable ride. A bitter breeze plagued them part of the morning, so Megan sat between Nicholas and Leo, bundled in her cloak, its hood draped snugly over her head until she warmed up.

Spring Hill boasted twice the number of residents as Minago, and they were out among the streets in full force when Leo entered the village. Shops were doing a brisk business, and in the center of town, farmers hawked the last of the produce from their harvest in the open markets. Winter loomed on the calendar's horizon and people were stocking their larders in anticipation of the blustery white days to follow.

Leo brought the wagon to a stop by the side door of one bake shop to deliver the first of his orders in the village. He removed a sheet of folded parchment from inside his jacket, scanning over a list of names and numbers.

"Something smells good," Nicholas said, breathing in the air around the shop. He jumped off the wagon and offered Megan a hand to help her down. A small sign fastened to a wooden door read EDNA'S BAKE SHOP–ALL DELIVERIES THROUGH HERE, PLEASE. "Perhaps we ought to try a little of Edna's cooking," he suggested, imagining the array of breads and pastries inside.

"We haven't been on the road that long," Megan said.

"But everything smells so delicious!"

Leo chuckled as he scanned his list, then refolded it and placed it back in his pocket. "I learned early on that, as tempting as it might be, I can't afford to eat at each place I make a delivery. I've neither the time nor money to do so."

Nicholas frowned. "That's not the answer I wanted to hear."

"Seven crates for Edna," he said as he untied the tarp over the wagon. Nicholas assisted him. "However, many of the owners on my route always insist that I help myself to a sample of their baked goods before I leave. Once I got a whole rhubarb pie."

Nicholas perked up. "And Edna?"

Leo nodded with a grin. "She's awfully generous. Glazed cinnamon and walnut rolls are her specialty." He grabbed a crate of apples, hoisted it on a shoulder and headed inside the bake shop.

Nicholas took another one and winked at Megan. "I'm glad we took Mr. Marsh's offer for a ride," he said, following Leo inside.

"You and your *stomach*," she replied with a smirk.

They departed thirty minutes later, each savoring a slice of Edna's black currant bread with butter. The first batch of glazed cinnamon and walnut rolls had already sold out. Leo placed the money for the order inside a small leather pouch securely tied to his belt, then directed the horses to a restaurant several blocks away, the second of four deliveries in Spring Hill. After that, it would be back on to Orchard Road to the tiny village of Mason where he had only two deliveries.

The village of Plum Orchard would be their final stop for the day, at which point the supply of apples would be half gone. The horses usually acted more good-naturedly at that point as each shipment lessened their burden crate by crate.

"Tell me more about this apple orchard you're so eager to start," Megan asked Leo on their way to Mason before noontime. She gently patted the back of his hand as he guided the horses. "I think it's fascinating."

"I could go on for hours more–"

"Please don't!" Nicholas jested.

"–but I'm getting bored talking only about myself," Leo said. "What about you, Megan? What have you been doing with your life? You haven't said much about that."

Nicholas turned his head slightly, challenging Megan with a *how-are-you-going-to-avoid-his-questions-too?* kind of stare. He surmised that Megan was as infatuated with Leo as he was with her, noting the way she hung onto his every word. He was curious to watch how she would avoid Leo's inquiries into her personal affairs despite her fondness toward him.

"There's really not much to tell," she said.

"This relative of yours in Boros–what's her name again?"

"Castella Birchwood. My great aunt Castella. She would be, let's see... My grandmother's sister–on my mother's side." Megan casually observed the countryside rolling past. "It's been so many years since I've seen her, Leo. I wonder if Aunt Castella will recognize me."

"You've got too pretty a face to forget."

She bowed her head coyly, glancing at Leo as he dutifully guided the team of horses along the bumpy dirt road. Nicholas shook his head and sighed.

"Now, Leo, don't try to work those boyish charms on me," she playfully warned.

"At least not while I'm present," Nicholas said under his breath, at which point Megan lightly jabbed him with her elbow.

"I'll behave myself," Leo promised. "Still, I'm curious why you're visiting Aunt Castella if you haven't seen her in such a long time. Does she know you're on your way?"

"She does," Megan said uncomfortably. "Leo, I wonder if–"

"How did you contact her? And why are you traveling alone?" Leo kept his eyes focused on the road as he fired his questions at Megan, though he could sense the scowl forming on her face. "My parents were too polite to ask you, but I tend to be a bit more direct. I mean, it is odd that you're being so tight-lipped about who you are and where you're from, especially after my family provided you with meals, a place to sleep and a ride to Boros. I'm just wondering, is all."

Megan folded her arms as she sat back in her seat, fuming. "Excuse me, Leo Marsh, but I didn't know I was required to answer every question posed to me just because you were wondering. I had always assumed good deeds were performed out of genuine kindness, not in an effort to extract information from the recipient of such."

"I'm not interrogating you, Megan." Leo glanced at her apologetically.

"Sure sounds like it to me. Did Nicholas put you up to this?"

"Don't drag me into your argument, Megan! I've had my turn with you and learned a valuable lesson. *Mind my own business!*"

"How amusing."

"It's true," he said. "Leo, keep the conversation strictly about the weather or your apple crop and you'll be okay. Otherwise, speak at your own peril."

Megan turned to Nicholas, her lips pressed angrily in a thin line. "As if you've been so candid? I don't recall you being any different than me, Nicholas. Just as secretive! Just as evasive! What exactly are all those troubles at home? And who's that Dooley Kramer character you mentioned to me yesterday just as Leo's father showed up? Don't think I forgot about that, but notice that I didn't harass you to talk about him either." She tugged on Leo's jacket sleeve. "If you're so curious about people, why don't you question Nicholas about the details of his life? That seems only fair, Leo. He's got as much to hide as you apparently think I do."

"At least he told me what village he lives in, Megan. Other than your name and hair color, I really know nothing about you–and I would like to know more."

Megan folded her arms again. "Maybe that's all you'll ever get to know about me!"

Nicholas chuckled. "Her hair *is* a lovely shade of brown."

Megan seethed for a moment before gathering up the folds of her cloak. She suddenly stood up as the wagon rolled along. "Stop this rickety thing at once! I'm not going to subject myself to this humiliation a moment longer."

"Sit down, Megan, before you fall over!" Leo warned.

"No, I will not!" She shook Leo's shoulder, causing the wagon to veer off its straight line. "Let me off at once!"

Nicholas tried to pull Megan back into her seat, but she clung onto Leo and distracted him from driving so that he had no choice but to rein in the horses to a stop. He directed the team to the side of the road and then tossed the reins down with a flash of anger, glaring at Megan.

"Don't you dare give me that offended look, Leo, because I can top it without even trying!" Megan stood and waved him aside. "Now please get out of my way."

"Fine!"

Leo jumped off the wagon and Megan followed, refusing a helping hand. Nicholas muttered in disgust and joined the others on the road.

"*Megan...*" Nicholas gently placed a hand on her shoulder, which she rebuffed with a sharp twist of her body.

"I don't want to hear any excuses from you either, Nicholas. You and Leo have both acted boorishly. You've turned out to be nothing but a couple of ill-mannered bumpkins, I'm sorry to say." She stormed up the road. "Now if you please, leave me alone!"

Nicholas and Leo looked at each other and shrugged. "Think we stepped over the line?" Leo asked.

"Leaped over is apparently more like it." Nicholas indicated for Leo to start the wagon moving again while he ran to catch up with Megan. Confronting the fiery indignation of this woman for the moment made his problems back home seem almost inviting. He raced up to her.

"I told you to leave me alone," she said without looking back as she heard him approach.

"We're not going to. Leo and I owe you an apology."

"Fine. Apology accepted." Megan marched along the left side of the road, brushing against waist-high stems of grass long gone to seed. Several large oak trees dotted the landscape. "Now turn around and run along home to Kanesbury." She heard the rattle of Leo's apple wagon as he slowly neared. "And *he* can drive right past me because I no longer need a ride to Boros."

"Megan, you're throwing this whole situation out of proportion. We realize you're upset and we're sorry, but can't we talk this through?" Nicholas pleaded.

186

"Please, Megan," Leo said gently from the wagon as he pulled up alongside them and halted. "Let's stop for lunch and discuss this. There's a road that turns off to the right up ahead. That'll take us into Mason where we can have a bite to eat. You can tell us why you're so upset."

Megan turned to face them and raised her arms, ready to scream. "Don't you two understand? There is no need to discuss anything. My life is not open to discussion, but for some reason you two cannot get that obvious point through your thick skulls! Therefore, I chose to continue to Boros on my own. Thank you and good day."

She hurried up the road, her cloak weaving from side to side. Nicholas and Leo watched her for a moment, tongue-tied, uncertain how to salvage the crumbling situation.

"What do we do now?" Leo asked. "We can't let her leave like this. I don't want her to leave. You've got to do something!"

"Like what?"

"I don't know. You've known her longer than I have. Say something! Anything to get her back."

Nicholas shrugged, his thoughts reeling as Megan grew smaller in the distance while Leo's beseeching gaze bore down upon him. What could he do to make her stay? What could he say that would remedy an already overly confused situation? He and Leo had each put a foot in their mouths enough times to set Megan off, so why risk any further damage? Nicholas then realized that if the situation was so grim, one more idiotic comment wouldn't make any difference. But what could he say that wouldn't sound phony, stupid or self-serving to draw her back? What words of friendship would turn her around? What did she want or need to hear?

Nicholas slowly took a deep breath as he walked a few steps beyond the wagon, his eyes fixed on Megan. He exhaled sharply as the autumn sun gently massaged his neck and decided to risk it, calling out to her.

"Just so you can't say I never opened up to you, Megan. About those complications of mine..." He uneasily cleared his throat. "Well, how does murder and robbery sound to you? I'm wanted back home for both, if it matters to you anymore."

He glanced up at Leo and shrugged, indicating that that was the best he could do. Leo, however, sat arrow straight and wide-eyed, wondering exactly who he had been giving a ride to these last few hours.

"So, Nicholas, uh, *that's* what you came up with to say?" Leo said guardedly.

"Yep," he replied matter-of-factly. "And it's all true, by the way." Leo flinched. "The accusations," Nicholas quickly added. "Not the deeds."

Leo swallowed. "*Oh...* Good to hear."

Nicholas grinned, then returned his gaze to Megan and immediately went slack-jawed. The cry of a blue jay peppered the air as she slowly walked back toward him.

"I don't make it a habit to associate with murderers and thieves," she softly said as she faced Nicholas.

"Me either," Leo added.

"Luckily for both of you I'm neither of those things. But there are a lot of people back home convinced otherwise. So you can see why I wasn't eager to let people in on my little secret."

"I understand now," Megan said, gently touching him on the shoulder. "By the way, those are pretty good complications. I suppose there must be a terrific story behind them."

"And I suppose you'll want to hear it."

"Every detail." Megan glanced up at Leo, offering a contrite smile. He extended his hand and helped her back onto the wagon, smiling back as her face brushed past his. "Nicholas, you can tell us your tale on the way to Mason if you're so inclined."

He agreed and climbed onto the wagon from the opposite side, at which point Leo snapped the reins and the trio once again rattled along the dirt road into the next village.

By the time they reached Mason, Nicholas had recounted everything that happened to him in Kanesbury on the first night of the Harvest Festival. Only seven days had passed since he ran away from Constable Brindle, though it seemed like a lifetime ago. And despite being in the dark about why people were conspiring against him, Nicholas finally had an inkling about who those individuals might be.

"I knew from the start that that lanky Arthur Weeks was somehow connected to my troubles. He lied right to my face!" Nicholas sputtered with disgust.

"How does that Dooley Kramer fellow fit into all of this?" Megan asked. "When you first mentioned his name to me yesterday, you looked mesmerized."

Nicholas recalled how Megan had grabbed the edges of his jacket when she was upset with him. That minor action had opened his eyes. "Constable Brindle discovered a button from my jacket near one of the orders that had been stolen from, but I had no idea how it could have ended up there." He showed Megan and Leo the spot on his jacket missing a button.

"So how *did* it get there?" Leo asked.

"I couldn't figure it out until Megan grabbed my jacket yesterday and shook me."

"Everyone needs to vent their frustrations now and then," she joked.

"Good thing you did, because it reminded me of something that happened two nights before the Festival." Nicholas told them of his encounter with Dooley after having left Amanda Stewart's home. "Dooley was drunk, pretending to straighten out my jacket. At the time I only noticed his stinking breath and just wanted to get away."

"You think he ripped off a button and placed it in the gristmill?" Leo asked.

"That's the only logical explanation. And he works with Arthur. Apparently those two were hatching some plot or other."

"Trying to get your job?" Megan speculated.

"Possibly, but neither are qualified for it. And that seems like an awfully lot of trouble to go through for a job that doesn't pay much more than those two already earn."

Leo smirked. "Dooley Kramer sounds like a model citizen."

Nicholas stroked his chin with a puzzled glint in his eyes. "That's the funny thing about it, Leo. Dooley can be a slacker sometimes, and you don't have to twist his arm for him to indulge in the ale. But he was never a serious troublemaker. Either was Arthur. I find it hard to believe that those two cooked up this scheme on their own." He sighed. "Then Arthur is murdered in the middle of the night and I get blamed. But I know I didn't kill him, so who did?"

"Dooley?" Leo suggested.

"They were in on the plan together," Megan said. "It doesn't make sense."

"Unless Dooley was only using Arthur to help him frame Nicholas before killing him and blaming it on Nicholas." Leo smiled proudly. "Makes sense now, *huh?*"

Nicholas shook his head. "Except that I still don't know what Dooley was after. A robbery *and* murder? I find it difficult to believe that those two hatched up such a plot on their own. Others must be in on it. But who? And why?"

"You'll never find the answers while hiding out here. You must go home and confront your accusers head on," Leo advised.

"I know you're right, but I need time to think, Leo. That's why I agreed to go with Megan to Boros first–to buy time. And to build up my nerve. I'll probably be tossed in the lockup the moment I step foot in Kanesbury."

"But going back home might prove to some people that you're not guilty," said Megan. "That should count for something. And now that you can finger Dooley Kramer as a suspect, that'll give the authorities another angle to investigate."

"I suppose so," he said, sounding encouraged. "I have to admit that talking to you two about my problems has taken a heavy weight off my shoulders. The world doesn't look so bleak."

"It helps to speak with friends," Megan said.

"Wise words for anyone," Leo added, gently patting her on the knee.

Leo made quick work of his two apple deliveries in Mason, so they had time to stop for lunch at a small restaurant in the village. The cool, dark interior glowed with candles fastened on the stone walls. A steaming tureen of soup and wooden bowls and spoons were set on their table. They also shared a small loaf of warm pumpkin bread which was served sliced and buttered. For half an hour the trio enjoyed a simple meal in the quiet of the shadowy establishment, temporarily setting aside the problems of the road.

"Leo, do you ever get sick of eating apples?" Megan asked at one point. "Being around them constantly, you must get bored at times about their look or taste, don't you?"

"Never, Megan," he said without hesitation. "Apples are my livelihood, so I never take them for granted. Besides, how can I get bored with something I care so much about?" he added with a hint of a smile while staring directly into her rich brown eyes.

She felt herself blush, glad that the room was painted in dim shadows. Nicholas quietly groaned as he ate his soup.

"Your flirting on the apple wagon is bad enough, you two," he teased. "But please, not while I'm eating my lunch!"

Megan and Leo tried to conceal their embarrassment before the three started to chuckle as they finished their meal. A few of the other patrons cast curious stares until the laughter settled down in the usually quiet place. Soon all eyes shifted back to their own tables. Except for one pair.

But the three young travelers seemed blissfully unaware of their surroundings at the moment. Unaware of the gentle flickering of the candles as traces of a cool autumn breeze slipped in through cracks in the wooden window shutters. Unaware of the clattering of crockery pots and metal utensils being washed in the back kitchen in tubs of hot soapy water. Unaware of the scrutinizing set of eyes watching them from a corner table, studying their faces, especially the young woman's, and wondering how these three came to be here.

The lone gentleman seated at that table quickly finished his meal and walked up to the front of the restaurant to pay his bill. He grabbed his coat and hat dangling on one of the wall pegs near the entrance, put them on, and then took a last furtive glance at Nicholas, Megan and Leo as he slipped out the door, a hastily designed scheme brewing in his mind. His current plans were taking him south, but backtracking north might well be worth the short delay. He must grab the opportunities when they appeared, and a grand one had just fallen into his lap.

The man hurried to his horse tied to a nearby post and removed a pipe and a pouch of tobacco from his saddlebag. As his thoughts raced, he filled his pipe, lit it, and returned the pouch to the bag. He took a few puffs, exhaling a bluish-gray smoke that wreathed the air with a pungent scent of cloves. He affectionately scratched the horse behind its ears as he untied it, feeding the animal half a raw carrot he kept in his pocket. He then climbed on his steed and headed north at a steady clip.

He knew his former contact would still be in the village of Plum Orchard since she had other business to attend to there. He only hoped she would appreciate the time and effort he was putting into this spur-of-the-moment endeavor and reward him appropriately. After all, that's what mattered to him most–the money, not the politics. He took a few more draws on his pipe as he galloped along the dirt road. The wind scraped his face as he greedily calculated what he could earn from this latest deal.

CHAPTER 13

The Plum Orchard Inn

Leo crossed off the name of another satisfied customer on his list. Corlian apples were especially popular when the last shipment of the year rolled around, and this had been his third of four deliveries in the village of Plum Orchard. He then drove to the Plum Orchard Inn, the final stop of the day. The inn was the largest lodging house in the vicinity and the most popular with travelers journeying up and down the dusty expanse of Orchard Road. He and his companions would dine and spend the night there before continuing with the second leg of his marketing route in the morning.

The wagon rolled up to the inn as a cool and windless twilight settled upon the countryside. The Plum Orchard Inn was nestled among a grove of white birch and maple trees. The two-story rectangular building, painted gold like summer wheat and freshly trimmed in white, stood with its back facing north. A glass encased candle highlighted each of the freshly washed windows, greeting the approaching night with a genial glow. Behind the inn were the horse stables and a storage barn, and close by, a pond fed by a bubbling spring from the surrounding hills.

In front near a stone walkway leading to the main door stood a white sign attached between a pair of wooden posts. Two flickering oil lamps hung from extended hooks on either side to illuminate the hand-carved wording.

PLUM ORCHARD INN
lodging, fine dining & spirits
Ron and Mabel Knott, proprietors
~ Established in 721 ~

As Leo pulled the wagon around to a side door, the faces of many patrons were visible through the windows as they enjoyed their meals in the first floor dining rooms. Megan looked on in wonder.

"What a lovely place!" she said. "The grounds are neat and clean, and the building is aglow." Her white breath dissipated in the chilly air. "I'll bet it's toasty warm inside."

"We'll have you sitting by a blazing fire in no time, Megan." Leo brought the wagon to a halt and jumped down to unload the last order. Nicholas joined him.

As they removed the tarp covering the apple crates, the side door leading to the cellar storerooms opened. Out stepped Ron Knott carrying an oil lamp, ducking so as not to hit his head on the doorway. He smiled broadly under a reddish-brown mustache which matched the color of the thick mop of hair on his head. He hung the lamp on a hook near the door and extended a hand to Leo.

"I saw you driving by, so I came down to let you in myself. All the other help is occupied elsewhere. We're busier than bees tonight."

"I hope you can squeeze in two additional visitors, Ron. I brought some unexpected company along."

"Mabel and I always have room for friends of the Marsh family."

Ron and Mabel Knott, who were about the same age as Leo's parents, had become acquainted with Leo and his family over the years. Several times during the apple growing season, Leo and his father would choose the Plum Orchard Inn as their overnight stop along their marketing route to the north until it eventually became a three-or-four-times-a-year tradition. Once a season during the warm summer months, Mrs. Marsh would take Leo's place on the trip just to enjoy a night away from home at the Plum Orchard Inn with her husband. The Marshes and the Knotts had become friends ever since.

Leo introduced Ron to Nicholas and then to Megan, who still sat upon the wagon wrapped snugly in her cloak. "You and your wife run a charming place," she said. "I can't wait to see the inside."

"As soon as I help the boys unload these apples, I'll give you the grand tour."

"I'd prefer dinner first," Leo jested as he handed each of his helpers a crate of apples.

"Mabel's already seeing to that," Ron assured him as he led Nicholas into the cellar. "And she can't wait to get her hands on these Corlians. The last shipment is nearly gone and she has plenty of pies still to bake."

After unloading the apples, Leo and Nicholas refastened the tarp over the remaining crates, totaling about half a wagon. Ron's youngest son, Fred, showed up and his father instructed him to drive the cart to the storage barn for the night before taking the horses to the stables.

"Give the team a good drink from the stream before you feed them."

"I will, Father," the fourteen-year-old said as he eagerly hopped onto the seat of the wagon. His favorite chore around the inn was taking care of the horses, especially when he could ride them.

"I'll stop in and check on the pair later," Leo said as Fred offered a wave goodbye.

"Let's get you folks inside and out of this chill," Ron said.

He removed the oil lamp from the hook and closed the cellar door, leading the trio around to the front of the inn as the evening deepened and the stars bloomed. The Fox and Bear moons cast faint silvery shadows through the surrounding trees, but a scattering of clouds drifting in from the west eclipsed them from time to time. Ron opened the front door and ushered his guests inside. The warmth, aromas and soft music briefly slipped out across the front lawn and walkway until the door was shut and cold silence again ensued.

Across the road in a field, hidden behind a clump of short scraggly trees, a man watched intently as the four individuals entered the Plum Orchard Inn. His eyes shifted left and right as he deeply inhaled from a pipe, pondering his options. The subtle smoky scent of cloves nuzzled the dry tree branches above.

"It's so good to see you again, Leo!" Mabel Knott hugged him like a bear. "But then I always say that, don't I. Still, it's true. And who are your friends?"

Leo introduced Megan and Nicholas who each received a similar hug from Mabel Knott. She seemed like a favorite aunt they had known for years, wrapped up in her tattered red shawl with a smile popping out on her face with amusing regularity. A thick braid of dirty-blond hair trailed halfway down her back, and large blueberry colored eyes glistened in the candlelight from the entryway.

"Just make sure you say an extra special hello to your folks when you get back home, Leo. I won't see either one of them until next apple season," she instructed.

"I'll do so first thing I get back," he promised.

"Now let's get you three settled with some supper right quick. I'm sure you're nearly starved after being on the road all day. I'll let you eat in the back dining room tonight. It's quieter in there."

After hanging their coats on some pegs near the door, Mabel led the trio down the front hallway which branched off into several rooms. Ron returned to the kitchen. The main dining room was through the first doorway on the left, now filled with the light chatter of dinner guests and soft strains of music. A young lady played a flute while sitting on a cushioned stool near a large crackling fireplace. She wore her long black hair wrapped in a kerchief of autumn colors, playing her haunting notes as if unaware that anyone else was listening. A smaller dining room connected through a corner door.

Off the right side of the main hallway was a large common room. A long table lined with wax-dripping candles ran down the center of the room. Several wooden benches and chairs were arranged around the walls. A stone fireplace against one side blazed and crackled as red and orange flames greedily consumed huge chunks of maple wood cut last summer. The smell of freshly poured ale drifted among the shadows and quiet conversation.

The kitchens were located in back and also in part of the cellar. A narrow staircase in front of the hallway led up to the overnight rooms on the second floor.

Mabel escorted her guests through the main dining area into the back room, stopping now and then to briefly say hello to other diners or simply offer them a wave and a smile. She loved her inn and adored most of the people who patronized it, finding her greatest happiness in life making them happy to be there.

"Sit down and I'll send Elaine in with some bread, butter and tea right away," she promised. "Dinner won't be far behind. I took the liberty of planning the meal for you as I knew you'd be hungry."

"Thanks, Mrs. Knott," Nicholas said, immediately catching a reproving eye from both Mabel and Leo.

"We'll have none of that around here," Mabel said in a mock reprimand. "*Mrs. Knott*, indeed! It's *Mabel* to my customers, and Mabel only. Understand?"

"Perfectly, Mabel," he replied, trying to keep a straight face.

"Very well," she said, scurrying out of the room. "I'll be back to check on you soon, rest assured." Then she was gone.

"Now there's a darling woman or I've never met one," Megan said.

Leo grinned. "Just never call her Mrs. Knott. I learned that lesson years ago. But she is a sweetheart."

A few moments later Elaine, Ron and Mabel's sixteen-year-old daughter, hurried in carrying a tray laden with a teapot, three cups, a basket of sliced and steaming bread, three plates and knives, and a bowl of butter, all of which she unloaded upon the table with swiftness and grace.

"Nice to see you again, Leo," she said, flashing him a smile before introducing herself to Nicholas and Megan. "By the way, how's your brother doing these days? I haven't seen him since he stopped by with your father on the first trip of the season."

"Henry's a pest like always," he joked.

"Now, Leo, don't pick on your brother. He's a dear."

"And you're smitten with him, Elaine. Shall I relay that information to Henry?"

"*Ohhh...!*" She playfully slapped Leo's arm. "Dinner will be here shortly. Enjoy the tea." Elaine held the tray under her arm like a book and slipped blushing out of the room.

They sampled the bread and tea, finishing up just as dinner was served. Elaine returned to clear away some of the dishes as her mother bustled into the room behind her. Mabel set down a small platter of roasted pork slices on a bed of greens surrounded by a mix of glazed carrots and broccoli. A bowl of apple-cinnamon relish, a plate of biscuits and a wedge of cheese accompanied the main course, topped off with a metal pitcher of cold raspberry-mint juice. Their hosts soon left them to enjoy the hot food in peace.

The back dining room held four other tables, two of which were occupied. A small stone fireplace gently crackled and warmed the air. The few windows looking out to the front and west were trimmed with rust colored drapes and a glass encased candle on the center of each sill.

"I must say, Nicholas, that our meals have vastly improved since we met Leo's father on the road." Megan savored each bite.

"A bit of dry bread and cheese, or maybe an apple–no offense, Leo–gets tiresome after a while," Nicholas said. "Especially on a cold night along a lonely road."

"No offense taken," he replied.

"Though I can't quite remember my aunt Castella," Megan continued, "I'm sure she'll also provide you both with a delicious meal before you leave. For all the trouble..."

Her words trailed off as she dabbed at her food, ignoring the bits of small talk between Nicholas and Leo. For the first time since she had met him, she realized that she wouldn't see Leo again after tomorrow. He would return home, as would Nicholas, and she would remain stuck in Boros along the cold seashore in autumn. She couldn't imagine a more dismal fate and wondered if Leo would soon forget her. She liked him very much and wanted to see more of him, but there were too many complications, she thought, borrowing Nicholas' word. She chided herself for getting attached to these people because she knew they could not possibly be a part of her life.

The hungry diners each tried a piece of dessert cake later upon Mabel's recommendation, though Megan merely nibbled at hers. Nicholas and Leo noticed that she had grown unusually quiet as the evening progressed and asked her if she was feeling all right.

"I'm very tired," she explained, setting her fork down and pushing aside the plate. "All the traveling these past few days has finally caught up with me. Perhaps I'll retire early if you don't mind. I'm really quite sleepy now."

"Sure, Megan. We can't have you nodding off tomorrow in the middle of a conversation with Aunt Castella," Nicholas said. "You better get some rest."

"Wait here while I find Mabel to arrange a room for you," Leo said as he excused himself from the table and exited the room.

Nicholas watched Megan while he finished his cake, studying her careworn face. "Are you sure you're feeling well? You don't look your usual chipper self."

"I'm okay, Nicholas. You worry about me too much."

"That's been my job lately. I could stay in Boros for a few days until you get settled in if you'd like. Keep you company. Though I'm sure you'd prefer Leo's company instead, but he has a business to help run."

Megan smirked, but the melancholy look in her eyes betrayed her true feelings. "I would like him to stay, but after all, we've only just met. I'm behaving like a schoolgirl with a crush, yet..."

"How long will you remain in Boros?"

"I'm not sure." She propped an elbow on the table and rested her head glumly on the palm of her hand. "I'm not sure of much these days, Nicholas. Too many things are happening at once. Too many people to worry about who are worrying about *me*. Sometimes I wished I lived far away in a tiny hillside village with nothing to do except feed chickens and bake bread."

Nicholas laughed. "You don't look like a feed-the-chickens kind of woman, Megan. I see you destined for greater things."

"I appreciate the sentiment, but right now chickens don't look so bad."

Nicholas pulled his chair closer to the table and leaned in. He stared at her for a moment, his concern and friendship apparent. "Tell me what's going on," he whispered. "I'll be happy to listen. Won't even offer a comment or a word of advice. You can trust me."

Megan breathed deeply and folded her hands. She so wanted to confide in somebody and had begun to trust Nicholas after he had opened up to her, realizing that a new perspective on her situation might help clear up matters. But trust was a fragile thing, and maybe it would be better to arrive in Boros with her secrets intact. It was a dizzying debate raging in her head and wearing her out until Megan came to a snap decision.

"Nicholas, this may sound hard to believe, but–"

"Your room is all set, Megan." Leo sauntered over to the table. "Mabel placed you in the last room on the west side. Nicholas and I will be across the hall."

"Thanks, Leo," she said, her words clouded with a tinge of disappointment.

"We'll draw straws, Nicholas," he added. "Short one gets the floor."

"So long as the winner buys the first round of ale in the common room," he said. Leo quickly agreed.

"Well, you boys stay up as late as you like." Megan yawned. "I'm going to sleep now. I can barely keep my eyes open."

"Suit yourself, though the ale is especially good here," Leo remarked.

After leaving the dining area, they bumped into Elaine in the main hallway who escorted Megan to her room on the second floor. Nicholas and Leo walked into the common room, ordered two mugs of ale and took a seat on one of the side benches near the fireplace. The room was shadowy and still, save for the popping sparks from the fire and the muted talk of several conversations. The air was awash with the sharp scents of wood smoke, ale and various dried meats and cheeses available for patrons on a side counter. Bunches of fresh pine clippings and dried goldenrod hung from the walls.

"I was thinking that maybe I should stay in Boros a few days to keep an eye on Megan," Nicholas said between sips of his drink. "I mentioned it to her while you were arranging for the rooms."

"Are you going to?"

"If she wants me to, though when I suggested that she'd probably rather have you staying there, Megan admitted how much she cares for you." He noted Leo's smile in the dim light. "Maybe you can visit her in Boros once or twice before winter sets in."

"I plan to. I only wish I knew what was bothering her."

Nicholas stretched his legs and glanced at the flames dancing in the fireplace. "She was about to tell me but stopped when you came back. She wants to open up, but I think she's scared of something. I can't imagine what."

"Women are tough to figure out," Leo said, downing part of his drink. "But I'm willing to spend some extra time trying to figure out this particular one. She caught my eye the first time I saw her after climbing out of that mud puddle."

"I think Megan would be pleased to hear that," Nicholas said.

The glass encased candle on the sill at the end of the upstairs hall gently flickered, casting a circular reflection that bobbed upon the ceiling. Elaine, carrying another lit candle in a pewter holder, guided Megan down the gloomy passage.

"Thank you for your help, Elaine," she said as she stopped at the door to her room. "I'll sleep like a bear in winter tonight."

"There's a basin of fresh water in the room, and I lit the oil lamp on your bedside table. Should you need anything else during the night, just give a holler," she softly said. "And Mother insists that you and your friends join her and Father for breakfast tomorrow before you leave. So come prepared to the table with an appetite."

Megan smiled with amusement. "Mabel is too kind, but tell her I look forward to it. Goodnight, Elaine," she said as she slipped inside her room and closed the door.

"Good night."

Elaine walked down the hallway, followed by her shadow gliding silently across the wall. The second floor was quiet except for the occasional murmur of voices drifting up the staircase from the main dining room. She passed by several other doors and then walked down the stairs, not noticing that the third door from Megan's room had been opened just a crack, an eye of its occupant peering through, having studiously watched the two women just a moment earlier.

Now that Elaine had left, he opened the door wider and craned his neck into the hallway. A lock of his straggly hair fell over one eye and his clothes were infused with the scent of pipe smoke. The guest, who had checked in less than an hour ago and went straight to his room, noted precisely which room Megan had entered. He stepped back inside his room and quietly closed the door.

A few minutes later he emerged again after scanning the hallway for other guests. Not a soul was in sight. Dressed in a coat and hat, he cautiously walked to Megan's room carrying a square parchment envelope sealed with wax. After a last furtive glance down the hallway, he slipped the envelope under Megan's door, knocked lightly upon it, and then hurried through the corridor and down the stairs. No one was present in the entryway at the bottom of the steps, so he left the inn through the front door and raced around toward the back stables under the cloudy cover of night.

A few minutes earlier, Nicholas and Leo were finishing up their first round of ale in the common room. Several more patrons had drifted in from the dining area as the evening meals concluded. A few of them enjoyed a nightcap of wine while others preferred some leisurely conversation and a pipe in front of the fire.

"My compliments to the innkeepers," Nicholas said. "The quality drink they serve is unusually good."

"Ron keeps an impressive store of ale and wine casks in his cellar," Leo informed him. "He received a particularly good shipment of ale all the way from Drumaya last year that my father and I sampled. But he wasn't able to get any this year as I found out over the summer. Limited supply, and the cost nearly doubled." Leo frowned. "In addition to the ale, I hear there's turmoil brewing near Drumaya as well."

"Rumblings of war are spreading all over Laparia lately," Nicholas said. "We can be thankful for a brief respite here with the Knotts. My, but those two seem perpetually busy, don't they? Though apparently enjoying every minute of it."

Leo nodded. "Ron and Mabel even brew batches of plum wine to serve at the inn when the mood strikes them. So whether it's cooking meals, greeting guests or stabling horses, the Plum Orchard Inn is their life. They had *better* enjoy it!" he said, polishing off the last of his drink. He handed his mug to Nicholas. "And speaking of horses, I'm going to check on mine and make sure Fred has the apple wagon secured for the night."

"All right. I'll get us another round."

"I'll meet you back here shortly," Leo said, leaving the shadows of the common room.

Megan glanced around her tiny room dimly lit by a single oil lamp, its low flame flickering on a nightstand next to the bed. A pair of heavy drapes had been untied so that they covered the room's only window. A maple dresser stood against the wall near the door, on top of which had been placed a filled water basin, several washcloths, a tiny mirror and two unlit candles. The small fireplace opposite the foot of the bed contained a few cold burnt logs. Two wooden chairs sat at an angle on either side.

Megan prepared to turn up the oil lamp and decided she preferred the low light instead. It better matched her grim mood. She sat down in one of the chairs and stared at the opposite wall, not really tired. She just couldn't face Nicholas and Leo for the rest of the evening, knowing they'd be having a good time while she was miserable inside. With luck, she hoped she would soon grow tired and put an end to this dreary evening. Constant thoughts about arriving in Boros tomorrow, and then losing Leo shortly after, tormented her like a disturbing dream. All she could do was accept the fact that there was nothing she could do to alter the situation. She despised the constant disruptions in her life lately because of larger concerns over which she had no control. Would they ever end? Would they ever leave her alone?

A knock at the door startled Megan. She stood, shaking the sullen thoughts from her mind. She opened the door and glanced up and down the deserted hallway, wondering if she had imagined hearing the knock. When closing the door, she noticed a small envelope lying on the floor. She picked it up, sat on the edge of the bed and adjusted the wick of the oil lamp for additional light.

The parchment envelope was sealed with candle drippings without a trace of handwriting visible on the front or back. Megan couldn't imagine who would send her a note in this manner, or why. She broke the seal and removed a folded piece of cream colored paper and began to read.

Megan, meet me behind the stables as soon as you can. It's very important that I speak to you at once. Tell no one. Leo

She read the note a second time, her heart racing. What could Leo want that he had to tell her in so secretive a manner? She wondered, almost hoped, that he was having similar feelings to her own. Maybe Leo was thinking about a future for them together somewhere, somehow. Maybe there was a chance to find happiness in this world. Then Megan realized that she was thinking like an excited child and tried to calm down. They had just met, after all. She would speak to Leo first before jumping to any conclusions. She slipped the note back inside the envelope, extinguished the bedside lamp and quietly left her room.

Downstairs, she removed her cloak from one of the pegs near the main entrance and slipped it on to brave the chilly night. She was about to leave the inn when Ron Knott called to her from behind.

"I thought you'd already retired for the night," he said pleasantly. He carried a tray of dirty dishes from the dining room on his way to the back kitchen. "I hope your accommodations are satisfactory."

"Oh, they're quite lovely, Ron," Megan said as she walked over to him. "I just need some fresh air. Not as tired as I thought I was. Please don't let me keep you from your chores."

"No bother," he said, displaying a grin under his bushy mustache. "My chores around here never end." He set the tray down on a bench along the wall. "However, I wouldn't be a proper host if I didn't watch out for the safety of my customers."

Ron opened a door alongside the staircase and removed an oil lamp. He lifted its glass globe and lit the wick using a candle burning on a window sill near the door. He handed the lamp to Megan who smiled with appreciation.

"How very sweet of you. You're spoiling me too much on my short stay."

"I wouldn't want you stumbling in the dark. I'd never forgive myself," he said. "And my dear Mabel would crown me for sure if anything happened to you."

"Thank you."

"I could fetch Fred if you'd like some company. Most folks stay indoors after darkness this time of year."

"Really, I'll be fine, Ron." Megan slowly inched her way to the door. "I'd prefer a bit of solitude actually. So thank you again, and I'll see you and your wife tomorrow at the breakfast table."

"Looking forward to it," he said, picking up the tray of dishes. "And when you're finished outdoors, set the lamp on the floor near this bench so I'll know that you made it back safely inside for the night."

"I will," she promised. "Good night."

"Good night," Ron said as he drifted down the hallway and disappeared into the kitchen. Megan, with the oil lamp in hand, wrapped her cloak tightly about her and stepped out of the Plum Orchard Inn into the crisp autumn air.

The sky was as dark as a crow's wing. A thick blanket of clouds had drifted in from the west, blotting out the stars and the two moons. Megan walked along the stone path, stopping by the front sign bathed in yellow light. Ron and Mabel Knott were such good hosts and fine people, she thought, just like Leo's parents. She hated running away from others and wished she had stood her ground back home and stayed there. But it was all for her own good, they had told her, so she promised to go to Boros where Aunt Castella would be awaiting her arrival. But what good was safety if she was miserable all the time? She took several deep breaths of the night air and turned around, strolling across the lawn toward the side of the inn.

The main storage barn stood off to the right behind the Plum Orchard Inn, with the horse stables on the left. A large oak tree grew in the wide space between them. Megan could hear the gentle babbling of a creek that flowed behind the pair of buildings. She slowly walked in the direction of the stables, guided by the ring of light cast on the ground. The spicy sweetness of freshly fallen leaves peppered the air. She tried to imagine what Leo could want as she moved along the right side of the stables and turned the corner, stepping behind them.

With the inn out of sight, everything was now bathed in inky blackness. The stream gurgled louder and the rustling of the trees sounded dry and desolate. Megan held up the lamp, its pale light stretching over the ground and the knotty planks of the stable wall.

"Leo," she whispered, seeing no one around. She stepped cautiously along the back wall. Each snap of a twig or crunch of a leaf echoed loudly in the night air. "*Leo?* It's Megan. Where are you?" No reply except from the water and the wind as she continued to the other end of the building. "Leo," she repeated more loudly. "If you have something to say, I'd wish you come here and say it. We could have met in the common room. It would have been much easier." She turned the corner at the far end of the stables. "Not to mention warmer and–"

Suddenly, Megan felt a hand press against her mouth from behind. An arm flung roughly across her waist pulled her backward into the body of a man, taller than she, who dragged her across the grass away from the stables. Megan dropped the oil lamp and tried to scream. Her right arm was locked behind her attacker's arm, but her left arm was still free. She desperately pulled at the hand covering her mouth, but the man's grip only tightened. Megan dug her heels into the ground to slow him down, but to no avail. His clothes reeked with the smell of stale tobacco smoke. The scent of cloves nearly overwhelmed her. That scent. That familiar scent...

"*Megan?*" Leo appeared around the corner in back of the stables where Megan had first shown up. He held an oil lamp aloft thinking he had heard her call out his name just a moment ago, but wondered how it could be since she had already gone to sleep. Leo had been inside the stables checking on his horses when he heard the voice. He scanned the darkness behind the stables, but as no one was there, he guessed he must have imagined the voice.

But just as he turned around to head back to the inn, a woman screamed. He shot along behind the building like wildfire and rounded the opposite corner, accidentally kicking an oil lamp that had been cast on the ground. He vaguely saw two people struggling near the banks of the stream and hurried toward them.

"*Megan?*" His heart pounded as he scrambled over unfamiliar terrain.

"Help me, Leo!"

Megan had bit into the palm of her attacker's hand a moment earlier, causing him to move it so she could scream for help. The man now saw Leo charging at him in a circle of light, not having calculated for such a complication in his plan. With only an instant to think, he shoved Megan to the ground and barreled headfirst at Leo and tackled him to the weedy soil. Leo was momentarily stunned as his back slammed against the ground and his oil lamp went flying, unable to see the face of his attacker in the gloomy night. But as his heart raced, Leo instinctively shoved the palm of his right hand up as hard as he could and slammed it against the man's chin, causing him to groan in pain as his head was flung backward and he toppled sideways. Leo immediately turned over and scrambled to his feet, somewhat dazed and preparing to hurl himself at the shadowy figure. But he heard the stranger gasping and saw his hands flailing near his neck as the man struggled to stand. Leo was momentarily disoriented about what was happening as his head swirled with confusion.

"Let go!" the man struggled to say, trying to catch a full breath. He managed to get to his feet while purposely pushing his body backward.

Leo then realized that Megan had pounced upon the stranger from behind and grabbed his shirt and coat collars, pulling at them as tightly as she could while he thrashed about for air. But Leo's brief feeling of pride for Megan's actions quickly turned to horror when both she and the man tumbled backward and fell into the grass. Megan screamed as the assailant rolled off of her. He sprinted to the stream, jumping across several rocks in the water before vanishing into the blackness across the field to where his horse awaited.

"Come back!" Leo cried out angrily, ready to chase after him in the pitch darkness as his mind and heart raced with fevered disregard for his own safety. Then his concern shifted to Megan and he ran to her as she stood up in the nearby grass.

"*Leo!*"

"Are you all right?" he said, wrapping his arms tightly about her quivering frame as she buried her head in his shoulder. He gently held her face in his hands and gazed into her troubled eyes. "Who was that?" he asked, glancing over the stream, a part of him still wanting to chase after the man but knowing he dare not leave Megan alone.

"I don't know," she replied, her thoughts in a whirl as her heart beat wildly. She hugged Leo again, not wanting to let go. "I just want to go inside."

"All right," he whispered, rubbing her back as he held her, wondering who the stranger might be and why Megan was out here in the middle of the night. Leo hoped she would finally explain her mysterious behavior to him and Nicholas later on, but right now he simply held her trembling body. There would be time enough later for answers.

CHAPTER 14

Secrets Revealed

A dozen men scoured the grounds around the Plum Orchard Inn with oil lamps in hand, but discovered no sign of Megan's assailant. He had vanished like a whisper in the cold night. Ron Knott, devastated that such an incident had occurred at his establishment, recruited his son, some of the inn staff and a few guests to join in the search. He hurried along the side of the inn to the front steps and met Nicholas who was heading indoors.

"Not a trace of the brute," Ron said, his words laced with bitterness. "Nothing like this has ever happened here before. It just tears me to pieces!"

"It's not your fault," Nicholas said.

"I shouldn't have let Megan walk out into the night unaccompanied." He rubbed a hand through his hair as puffs of white breath floated to the blackened sky. "What was I thinking?" Nicholas slapped a consoling hand on his shoulder as they walked inside.

A blanket of warm air greeted them in the hallway. A steady clip of hushed but excited chatter issued from the common room. Mabel poked her head out of the main dining room when the front door opened and signaled for Nicholas and Ron to follow. Megan and Leo were seated at a table near the fireplace, both looking pale and weary from their ordeal. Elaine brought in a kettle of hot tea and a tray of mugs and then slipped out of the room now empty of dinner guests. Mabel looked at her husband inquisitively. Ron shook his head.

"No luck, I'm afraid. We looked everywhere. The others are still outside."

"He took off like a jack rabbit," Leo said, holding Megan's hand across the table.

"I'm sure he won't trouble us again," she said. "Not with so many people keeping watch."

"Rest assured, young lady. I'm going to have two men patrolling outside until the crack of dawn. We'll work in two-hour shifts," Ron said, volunteering for the midnight hour. "Even a squirrel won't get near this inn without us knowing about it."

"I appreciate your efforts, but..."

He raised a hand. "Not another word, Megan. I handle things here at the inn, and that will be that."

She smiled a sincere thank you.

"Now you're certain you have no idea who that man was?" Mabel asked Megan as she sat down at the table.

"Not the slightest," she replied, staring at the note he had slipped under the door. She had asked Elaine to retrieve it from her room earlier. "Yet there was something oddly familiar about him, though I can't put my finger on it."

"I'd like to put my fist on him!" Leo muttered.

Mabel gently patted his hand before addressing Megan. "You take all the time you need to think about it, dear. There were several people who dropped in tonight just for a meal or drinks in the common room, and then left. Perhaps one of them sneaked upstairs unnoticed and slipped the note under your door."

"But why?" Leo asked.

"Sure I can't fix you a bite to eat, Megan? The staff is still cleaning up in the kitchen."

"No thank you, Mabel. You and your husband have done more than enough. All I really need is a good night's sleep. I'll think better in the morning."

"That's a good idea," Nicholas said. "Leo and I will be right across the hall, so you needn't worry about anything."

"And the inn doors will be bolted tight and patrols outside," Ron added. "You couldn't be any safer if you wanted to be."

Megan took her leave of the Knotts as Nicholas and Leo accompanied her upstairs. Ron sat at the table opposite his wife after everyone had left. He stretched his legs, exhausted and bleary-eyed. Mabel shrugged with bewilderment.

"Now what that was all about, I couldn't begin to tell you," she said. "Megan didn't say too much while you were outdoors, and Leo seemed just as perplexed when I spoke to him alone a few moments earlier." She poured them each some tea. "He is fond of the girl but admitted that she's a bit of a mystery. I hope he knows what he's getting himself into."

Ron picked up the cup she had slid across the table. "I don't think he does, dear," he said, taking a drink. "And that's what intrigues him the most, I'm afraid."

Two candles flickered on the maple dresser as a gentle breeze rattled the window panes. Nicholas adjusted the oil lamp on the night stand, casting away shadows that lurked in the corners. Megan and Leo sat in the chairs on either side of the fireplace as a small blaze crackled, warming the room. Nicholas took a seat on the foot of the bed. He and Leo stared at Megan with a mix of intrigue and skepticism, saying nothing for several moments.

"Why are you two gawking at me like I have a mouse perched on my head?" she asked with a sigh. "You boys can go now. No need to stay and hold my hand as if I were a scared child. I'm all right."

"We'll be the judge of that," Leo said. "Besides, you can't get rid of us that easily."

"What are you talking about?"

Nicholas leaned forward. "Megan, you can get away with shrouding the facts in front of Mabel and Ron, but Leo and I deserve the truth now. You owe us that much. What's going on? Who was that man behind the stables? Was it that Samuel fellow?"

Leo sat up. "Who's Samuel?"

"It wasn't Samuel," she explained with coolness in her voice. "Samuel would never harm me."

"Who's Samuel?" Leo echoed.

"Someone who Megan told me was after her," Nicholas said. "She mentioned his name after we first met but never told me anymore about him."

"Because you didn't need to know anymore."

"He wasn't an old suitor, was he?" Leo asked curiously. "Or perhaps a current one?"

Megan bowed her head with frustration and amusement. "Samuel is old enough to be my father, Leo. You have nothing to worry about."

"I was just curious."

Nicholas stood up, his impatience growing. "So who left you the note then?"

"I can honestly say I don't know, Nicholas. I truly don't. You must believe me."

"We do," Leo said. "You might not know who was after you, but you must surely know why, Megan. Someone went to a lot of trouble to lure you alone outdoors."

Nicholas agreed. "If you're in some kind of danger, we want to help. All you have to do is trust us."

Megan stood and walked to the curtained window, caressing the thick drapery with her fingers, her back to her friends. How she hated to deceive them yet wanted nothing more than to tell them everything that instant. She turned and faced her companions.

"It's difficult to open up."

"No it's not," Nicholas said. "I told you my story."

"But you wouldn't believe me if I told you mine."

"Try us," Leo said. "Besides, I like stories. Just sit down and speak. We won't even interrupt."

"If it were only that simple..." Megan sighed again and returned to her chair. Nicholas sat back on the bed.

"You're not a thief or a murderer, are you?" he joked, pleased to see that she returned a faint smile. "So it can't be worse than my predicament."

"My problems are more, shall I say—*family oriented*?"

"Who doesn't have family problems?" Leo asked. "I love mine dearly, but sometimes..." He raised his eyes and the trio laughed, melting the tension in the room.

Megan leaned forward, elbows on knees, resting her chin on top of her folded hands. "My family has been very protective of me lately," she said softly. "Father worries about me all the time, especially since my mother died a few years back. But Grandfather is even worse."

"He lives at home with you?"

She nodded. "We have a big household. An extended family arrangement. And though I love them all dearly, it's hard sometimes to find a moment of privacy."

"So you ran away to live with your great aunt Castella in Boros," Nicholas surmised. "However," he said with a smirk, "that wouldn't explain your mysterious and intriguing behavior."

"Make fun of me if you must, but if you had a grandfather like mine, Nicholas, you'd understand," she said. "And I didn't run away to Boros. This was an arranged visit–secretly arranged–which, regretfully, I agreed to."

"He's just teasing, Megan," Leo said. "We're really interested in what you have to say. Tell us about your grandfather. Does he run things around your house in spite of your father's wishes?"

"You might say that," she said, leaning back in her chair. "Grandfather has a dynamic personality. But don't misunderstand me. He's a very sweet and dear man, but he has a lot on his mind lately. Things are happening. And all of that has spilled over in his concern for me."

"What things are happening?" Nicholas asked. "And where are they happening? You're not making much sense."

"At least tell us where you live," Leo said. "What harm is there in that?"

"Fine. I'm from Morrenwood," she replied, glancing at Nicholas. "And you needn't gloat, thank you. You correctly guessed that fact after we had first met."

"And the world isn't crashing down because you told us," he said. "See, it's easy to confide in your friends."

"I suppose you're right," she replied, taking a deep breath and relaxing.

"What does your grandfather do for a living that your life is in such a whirlwind?" Leo asked.

"Well, he's…"

Megan paused, finding it difficult to look Leo in the eyes. But when noting the genuine concern upon the faces of her two companions, her hesitation to confide in them was lessened. She stood and walked toward the door, knitting her fingers together. Her mind raced with a dozen concerns but she finally decided to trust their budding friendship and turned around. Leo and Nicholas remained in their seats with eyes fixed upon her.

"What does Grandfather do, you ask? Why, he's…"

Leo craned forward in his seat. "*Yes?*"

"He's just the…"

"The *what*?" Nicholas gently asked.

"…the *King*." Megan nervously hooked a finger through her hair and cleared her throat. "Of Arrondale. *That* King."

A piece of wood popped in the fireplace, sending up a shower of sparks. Leo and Nicholas glanced at each other, expressionless, and then looked curiously at Megan as if they had misheard her.

"No really, Megan, what does your grandfather do?" Leo repeated. "You can tell us."

"I just did," she calmly said, walking briskly back to her chair. She spun around and plopped down in the seat. "My grandfather is King Justin of Arrondale. I presume you've both heard of him."

"We've heard of him," Nicholas said, trying to keep a straight face. "But I thought his daughter always rode around on a white horse with a jeweled saddle."

He burst out in a short laugh and Leo couldn't help but join in. But when they caught an icy gaze from Megan, they both composed themselves immediately.

"Are you two juveniles just about finished?"

Leo grinned, stretching his legs and resting his hands behind his head. "Nice joke, Megan. But if you don't want to tell us what your grandfather does, that's okay."

"Though I am curious as to what your father does," Nicholas quipped. "Does he get to be in charge of the Blue Citadel when your grandfather takes a holiday?"

Nicholas and Leo again broke out in a fit of laughter as Megan watched them with a scowl upon her face until they quieted down.

"My father, I'll have you know, is Prince Gregory, son of the King and heir to the throne of Arrondale."

Nicholas smirked. "Oh, and so that would make you a…?"

"A princess," she muttered under her breath.

Leo glanced at the ceiling and whistled a few doubtful notes before addressing Megan. "Why are you telling us this? I don't understand."

"Because it's true," she said, unclasping a small chain around her neck. "Because you wanted me to be honest, so..." She handed the chain to Leo. "I'm being honest."

Leo sat on the edge of his chair as he examined it. A small silver medallion was attached to the fine gold chain. Etched on the front was an image of the Blue Citadel guarded by majestic pine trees with mountains and a winding river in the background. On the reverse lay a field of tall grass through which a horse galloped under two rising full moons. A sword was engraved on either side of the picture. Leo studied the stunning images and then handed the medallion to Nicholas.

"It's beautiful, Megan. I've never seen such accomplished engraving before," he said with a slight tremor in his voice. Nicholas nodded in agreement.

"The front is my grandfather's residence in Morrenwood. The Trent Hills and the Edelin River are pictured in the background. On the reverse is my family's crest, a stallion running freely through a field of tall grass as the Fox and Bear moons, both full, rise in the east. Swords frame the picture on either side."

"Two rising full moons are a sign of good fortune," Leo said.

"I was fortunate to have you around earlier," she replied, looking at him with gratitude.

Nicholas handed the medallion back to her. "It's really nice," he said as she fastened it around her neck and placed it out of sight.

"All of us of the royal bloodline wear one of these. A craftsman was commissioned to engrave one on the day of my birth." Megan looked at Leo and Nicholas who both leaned forward with mixed feelings. "We treasure them but never wear them openly."

"*Oh...*" Leo said.

"You can imagine why I was so secretive about my identity. It's not something one would just blurt out under the circumstances." Megan leaned back in her chair and noticed that Nicholas and Leo still looked at each other with a hint of skepticism. "You both do believe me, don't you? I wouldn't reveal this information to people I don't trust."

"Sure we... I mean..." Leo swallowed hard. "It's just ..."

Nicholas rescued him. "What he's trying to say is that it's just so much to absorb." Leo nodded uneasily. "It's not everyday we meet a princess, especially one traveling alone on the road."

"Or on foot," Leo added.

"And so far away from home," Nicholas said.

Megan folded her arms and fumed. "So you don't believe me? Just say so!"

"Megan, we–"

"What about the medallion? Isn't that proof enough?"

Leo stood and rested a hand on Megan's shoulder. "It's definitely a point in your favor. But you must admit that a story like yours, uh..." He looked at Nicholas for support.

"Needs a bit more proof, is all," Nicholas said. "If either Leo or I claimed we were a prince, well, I can imagine your reaction."

"I would believe you," she whispered with difficulty. Megan looked up at Leo, patting his hand that rested on her shoulder. "All right, who am I kidding? I wouldn't believe you for an instant. But I am telling the truth. I'll just have to do a better job at convincing you. My great aunt Castella will vouch for me when you meet her."

"Okay," Nicholas said, hoping to change the subject.

"And we promise to get you to her safely," Leo added. "Unless you'd rather have us take you back home to Morrenwood."

"No, Boros will be fine. After much arguing and sulking, I relented and gave Grandfather my word that I would go there, so I shall keep my word as a princess of Arrondale should. However, I didn't promise that I would *stay* there, but we shall see."

"Why did your grandfather send you to Boros alone?" Nicholas asked. "That doesn't make sense if you are who you say you are."

Megan sighed. "He didn't send me alone, silly. One of his trusted guides accompanied me."

"Samuel?"

"Yes. We left Morrenwood unannounced, staying off the main roads. He was to take me to Boros for safekeeping," she groused. "As if I were some precious piece of artwork to be stored away until a storm passed. How humiliating! But I finally agreed to go just to shut everyone up. Oh, how exasperating the last few weeks have been! Everyone talking into my ear at once. *Megan, you shouldn't stay around here–times are dangerous. Megan, Caldurian is on the loose again. Remember what happened to you when you were an infant?* Like I would remember that? How ridiculous! Can't I just live my life like a normal person for a change? That's why I ran away from Samuel the first chance that presented itself. I couldn't stand being under anyone's control anymore. I know it was probably childish of me to flee, but I decided to walk to Boros alone to keep my promise with no one to tell me what to do on the way. Well, except for you two on occasion. But that's another story. Grandfather will be furious with me, no doubt, but I don't care. I'm not a little girl anymore!" She glanced at the fire, her cheeks flushed scarlet as she calmed down. "So, do you think we should throw on more wood?"

Leo grabbed a few pieces of dried maple piled on the side and carefully set them in the fireplace. The flames revived and warmed the room. He noticed the gentle glow on Megan's face and thought she looked so beautiful, princess or not. She was speaking freely now and he took that as a sign of her trust. He sat down, flashing a quick smile her way for support.

Nicholas rubbed his hands together as if about to indulge in a grand feast. "Now you really have me intrigued, Megan. Tell me how you ran away from this Samuel fellow. And why were you going to Boros? What danger were you fleeing?"

"It's a long story, Nicholas."

"We have all night."

Leo agreed as much but remained silent.

"Very well," she said, turning her chair more toward the fire to ward off a chill. She stretched out her hands to warm them, glancing at Leo and returning his smile. She stared into the dancing flames while speaking, soothed by their hypnotic rhythm. "I was almost kidnapped from the Citadel when I was an infant," she said matter-of-factly. "That's when much of this trouble started."

"Kidnapped!" Leo angled his chair to better face her. "Are you serious?"

"Oh yes, I had quite an exciting infancy, so I've recently learned," she replied with bitter amusement. "Apparently a woman named Madeline, one of my nursemaids then, was involved in the plot twenty years ago."

Nicholas shrugged. "Why would someone want to kidnap you, Megan?"

"I'm a princess, remember?" she said sarcastically. "You have to believe that part of my story for this part to make sense."

"Okay then."

"Anyway, there was a wizard named Caldurian–"

"I've heard of him!" Nicholas said.

"–who had recruited my nursemaid to kidnap me. It was all done in an effort to force my grandfather into an alliance with that tyrant, Vellan, in the Northern Mountains."

Leo scratched his head. "I've heard of Vellan. Most everyone has. But I don't recall ever hearing about that other wizard."

"Caldurian is an apprentice to Vellan," Nicholas said.

"And just how do you know that?" Leo asked.

"Local history. Caldurian caused a bit of a ruckus in Kanesbury just before I was born. I've heard stories about him growing up, though some of them seemed more fantastic than real."

"A *bit* of a ruckus?" Megan waved a cautionary finger at Nicholas. "Take my word for it. Those stories you heard were most definitely true. Over the last few months I've been well versed in the turbulent politics of the past and present by my grandfather and his advisors. Matters are bubbling just under the surface in Laparia right now. Alliances are shifting. Wars are breaking out. And there are reports that Caldurian is again on the loose in Arrondale. But what he's up to, nobody can say with certainty."

"That's why you were sent to Boros?" Leo asked. "In case this Caldurian came after you again?"

"Apparently so. To keep me safe like a vase of precious crystal. Tucked away in boring Boros under Samuel's protection until the current troubles are resolved–whenever that'll be." Megan slumped in her chair, twirling a lock of hair around her finger. "Sometimes it's rotten having to be me."

The room was silent, save for the crackling flames. Nicholas thought about his earlier desire to join up with the King's Guard, wondering where in Laparia he might have been marched off to had he sworn an oath to serve. Megan's words sobered him up and made him reexamine his reasons for wanting to leave home. He revised his picture of the world, now seeing himself as the smallest of fish in a vast sea of sharks. He wondered what difference, if any, he would have made by going to Morrenwood merely in a quest for adventure.

Leo chuckled. "I'll bet Samuel will be in a fix for losing you. Might he be out of a job when he returns to Morrenwood?"

"I'll explain the situation to my grandfather the next time I see him. Samuel will be fine, though I imagine he's still out in the wild looking for me. We left Morrenwood one night dressed in simple clothing, riding in a horse-drawn cart off the main roads in order not to draw attention." Megan recalled that dreary evening with resentment, having felt like a criminal being transported to a prison far away. "But we hit a terrible rut in the road and a wheel was badly damaged. So we loaded our supplies on the horse and walked. What a treat that was."

"When did you sneak off on your own?"

"Not until that first evening after we had met Carmella."

"Who's she?" Nicholas asked.

"She is someone whose likes I have never met, even in Morrenwood," Megan explained in amusement. "Here we are, walking along a muddy road, miserable and tired, when we come upon this colorful shack on wheels off to one side. Two horses are grazing in the grass nearby, and hovering over a small fire behind the wagon is Carmella, even more colorfully dressed than her living quarters. She offered us food and endless talk about her unfinished training in the magic arts." Megan doubled up in laughter. "I shouldn't act like this because Carmella was such a dear woman to us. But talk about eccentric! She certainly fit the bill."

"How does she fit in the story?" Leo asked.

"Carmella told us that her previous driver had abandoned her after only a few days on the road, thus she was stranded for a time. A person of her station, she claimed, should not have to drive herself, though I'm not exactly sure of what station she imagines herself a part."

"Maybe she talked her driver to the brink of insanity," Nicholas playfully suggested.

Megan couldn't disagree. "Anyway, Samuel promised to drive her if she would allow us passage to Boros. Carmella agreed, having always wanted to explore that part of the kingdom. So we loaded our supplies into her cramped living quarters, hitched up her two horses and tethered our steed to the back, and off we went. And what a sight we were."

"So you escaped that night?" Leo said.

"Yes. After everyone was asleep, I slipped away into the woods and headed east. I had had enough of Samuel's overbearing protection and Carmella's endless chatter about her magic spells, her evil cousin, Liney, and her orange hands."

"*Orange hands?*"

Megan couldn't help but laugh at Nicholas' comment. "Apparently Carmella's cousin turned her hands a lovely shade of pumpkin during their last encounter many years ago. I don't think they get along too well. Carmella had been trying to track down Liney to remove the spell when her driver abruptly left. Since she was going in the same direction as we were, Samuel agreed to take over the reins and be her driver," she said. "But I just had to get away from everybody in the end before I burst! And so I did."

"Only to meet up with two farmers," Leo quipped. "Do you think you're much better off with us for company?"

"I'll let you know."

"Perhaps your grandfather was right to keep you protected," Nicholas said. "Whoever slipped that letter under your door must have known who you were."

"So you believe my story?"

He nodded. "I had my doubts at first, but…" Leo kept silent, contemplating all that Megan had told them. "It's possible that Caldurian hired someone to kidnap you again, trying to finish what he couldn't accomplish twenty years ago."

"But why kidnap me now? For what purpose?"

"Because you're the King's granddaughter," Leo said. "And I apologize for speaking bluntly, but you're probably still seen as a valuable bargaining piece to the enemy."

Megan sighed, wishing for a moment she were home even if it was amid the chaos that seemed a permanent fixture of life in Morrenwood. "You're right, you know. Maybe I should have stayed with Samuel. None of this would be happening now. Maybe Grandfather knows more than I care to admit." She stood and looked at Nicholas and Leo with a vacant stare. "Maybe I should go to sleep now. I suddenly feel very tired. I am so not looking forward to the rest of my journey, wherever it takes me."

Nicholas stood and headed toward the door. "Try not to think of that now, Megan. Just get a good night's rest and we'll see what the morning has in store."

"You sound like my father," she said with a smirk. "And any words of wisdom from you, Leo, before I retire?"

Leo, who had quietly followed Nicholas to the door, shook his head. "No." He looked clumsily at his feet. "We could all use some sleep now, so I'll just say goodnight."

"All right..." Megan spoke hesitantly, sensing a sudden chill in Leo's demeanor.

As Nicholas opened the door and stepped out of the room, she tugged at Leo's shirt sleeve. He reluctantly turned and faced her questioning eyes. Nicholas, sensing that she wanted to talk to him alone, walked across the hallway and entered their room. Megan signaled for Leo to stay as she closed the door.

"Can we talk for a moment?" she asked.

Leo nodded. "Sure. What's the matter?"

"Apparently *you*. At least that's the impression I've gotten in the last few moments. Is something bothering you?"

"What do you mean?"

"You're awfully distant all of the sudden. Sullen almost." Megan gently took his hand in hers. "What's bothering you, Leo?"

"Nothing's bothering me, exactly. Just tired, I guess."

"*Exactly*? What's that supposed to mean? Tell me what's on your mind." She detected uncertainty in his eyes and perhaps a hint of sadness. "Are you still not sure I'm whom I claim to be?"

"No. Now I very much believe you, Megan. After listening to your story, I have no doubts." He pulled his hand away from hers. "You're definitely a princess from Morrenwood."

"I'm pleased that you believe me."

Leo nodded. "*Great...*"

Megan looked at him askance. "And what's *that* supposed to mean?"

He shrugged dejectedly. "It means that you're a princess and I'm just..."

"Yes?"

He offered a pleasant smile. "I'm just an apple grower from Minago. Probably not the kind of company you're used to keeping."

"I know lots of different people, Leo. What's your point?"

Leo spoke to the floor. "My point is that I should take you to Boros, say my goodbyes and get on with business." He looked up, gazing longingly into her eyes. "I've been imagining things that just can't be, now that…"

"Now that what?"

"Now that you're *you* and I'm *me*." He shook his head. "I'm very fond of you, Megan, but we hardly know each other. Soon you'll be living with your great aunt and I'll be miles away. But *who* we are, well, that's an even greater distance between us."

Megan scowled. "Are you saying I'm not good enough for you, Leo?"

"No! I was thinking just the opposite. I may sound confident–or almost boastful–when talking about my passion for the apple business and my future dreams. But after learning who you are, those aspirations have somewhat diminished in my mind."

"Oh, so I suppose you're implying that I'm some royal-snob-of-a-princess with her fussy nose stuck in the clouds who wouldn't dare be caught dead in public next to this apple grower. Is that it?"

Leo squirmed, leaning uncomfortably against the dresser. "Well, yeah, something like that. I mean–NO! Not the royal fussy nose part. I never thought *that*! Just the last part about you not wanting to be spotted–even *dead*–next to me. That's sort of what I was thinking."

Megan glared at Leo, nearly making him flinch. Then her features softened like a spread of grass after a warm spring rain. "Well, Leo Marsh, I'll have you know that I was definitely not thinking any such things." She kissed him on the cheek. "And don't you either. In the short time I've known you, you have far surpassed many of the people I've encountered in the political corridors in Morrenwood in both intelligence and demeanor. Believe me when I say that it's *who* you are that matters, not *what* you are."

"I appreciate that," he softly said, taking a step back and fishing for the door knob.

"I think you have fine dreams, Leo," she said with admiration. "And a part of me envies you for that as at times I feel like I'm drifting through life with no dreams of my own to anchor me to a purpose."

Leo nodded, feeling that the Megan he had first met was again standing beside him. "That's very kind to say. But I'm sure you'll find your own dream to pursue someday."

"I truly hope so."

Leo stared at her, suddenly at a loss for words. "Uh, should I go now? I'd rather end on a positive note and not make any more brilliant remarks tonight."

Megan smiled. "I think you should."

"Okay. Just make sure you lock your door."

"I will. And thanks for caring, Leo. We'll talk in the morning."

"Sure then. We'll talk." He opened the door and took a few clumsy steps backward into the hallway. "In the morning."

He slowly closed the door, wearing a slight grin, and watched Megan until she disappeared. He heard the click of her door lock as she turned the key. The hallway was now painted in gray shadows. Leo exhaled deeply as his heart raced, wondering who this young woman really was. A half dozen thoughts ricocheted in his head, about her, about them, and he felt confused and elated at the same time. And terribly worried.

"Did that conversation just really happen?" he asked Nicholas a few moments later as they sat in front of the fire in their room. "Megan *did* say she was a princess, right? I didn't imagine that."

"Neither of us did. She said it. And after listening to her story, I believe her. Though seeing that medallion sure helped."

"I believe her, too. And she's not stuffy like I imagined a real princess might be," he remarked. "Not out of touch with the commoners, I'm happy to say."

"Particularly your average apple farmer?" Nicholas said.

Leo nodded. "I had my doubts for a moment, but she put my mind at ease. It's too bad the common room is closed. I'd like a mug of ale right now. What a night this has been."

They talked for over an hour about the latest turn in their fortunes and where tomorrow might find them. Both sensed that exciting and perhaps difficult times were in store, each agreeing that keeping watch over Megan was their top priority. Leo yawned, feeling the rigors of the day finally catching up with him. He peeked out the door into the hallway, now quiet and deserted. No light issued from beneath Megan's door. She was probably sound asleep.

"I'll take the floor," Leo said, grabbing a rolled-up feather mattress and two extra blankets that Elaine had left in the room. "I know Ron and the others will do a fine job watching over the inn, but I prefer to keep my own watch. Wake me at dawn, Nicholas."

"Sure. But where are you going?"

"Not too far."

Leo stepped into the hallway and unrolled the feather mattress in front of Megan's door. He lay down on it and covered himself with the blankets. "I'd like to see anyone try to get past me tonight," he whispered, pointing a thumb over his shoulder to indicate the door. "And don't tell her about any of this, okay?"

"Your secret's safe with me. Goodnight."

"Night," Leo said as Nicholas closed the door, leaving him on the floor in silent darkness. He curled up on the thin mattress, sensing Megan's presence behind the door. In the vagaries and wild thoughts of half-sleep, Leo felt certain he would do anything to protect her, including forfeiting his own life. At this moment, Megan was worth the world to him, though he had only met her a short time ago. He couldn't wait for the days ahead to unfold, imagining their life together wherever it might lead. Then a deep sleep took hold of him, as rich as sweet wood smoke wafting through the autumn pines.

Nicholas rolled out of bed at first light and slipped into his boots. He yawned, raking a hand through his tangled hair and then opened the door to wake Leo. As he stepped into the hallway, Megan's door opened. Both immediately glanced at the floor where Leo lay sound asleep at her feet. They looked at each other in silence. Megan smiled in the dim light and raised a finger to her lips, shaking her head. Nicholas understood. She stepped back inside her room and quietly closed the door. Moments later, Nicholas nudged Leo's shoulder with his foot. He stirred like a bear in mid-winter.

"Wake up, you lazy doormat. Time to head out."

Leo looked up as if not quite sure where he was, his eyelids refusing to open all the way. "*Uh huh... I know... Apples...*" He twisted the knots out of his back as he rose to his feet, scooping up the blankets and mattress roll in his arms. "Got to deliver the apples. But it's still so dark," he mumbled.

THOMAS J. PRESTOPNIK

Suddenly the rattle of Megan's door lock sounded. Leo, now realizing where he was, charged past Nicholas into the room just as her door opened. He then spun around and looked back out the doorway alongside Nicholas as Megan stepped into the hallway.

"Good morning, boys!" she said in a chipper voice. "I'm glad to see you both awake and ready to go."

"Looking forward to a hearty breakfast," Nicholas said.

"Sleep well?" she asked, eyeing Leo who still clutched a bundle of blankets.

"I slept like someone who…" Leo nodded and yawned. "Yeah, I did…"

"Great! I'll meet you two downstairs for breakfast," she said, walking by with a playful wave of her fingers.

Nicholas and Leo smiled until she left the hallway, and then Leo leaned against the door frame and slumped to the floor.

"I slept like someone who slept on a pile of rocks!" he muttered, massaging his neck.

"That's the price of romance," Nicholas said with a chuckle as he offered his friend a helping hand up off the floor.

The trio ate a quick breakfast in the main dining room before most of the other guests had risen. Ron stopped in briefly and happily reported that there were no other incidents while they had slept. He told them that the Plum Orchard Inn was as quiet as a passing cloud during the night.

Later, Leo retrieved his wagon from the storage barn, still half-filled with apple crates for delivery. He fed and watered his team and then waited for Megan and Nicholas in front of the inn, savoring the crisp morning air. His friends hurried out the front door moments later with Ron and Mabel. Megan, the hood of her cloak draped over her head to fend off the morning chill, carried a bundle of food that Mabel had prepared for the rest of their journey.

"There's still a long road ahead. I want the three of you well fed," Mabel insisted.

"And apparently well groomed, too," Megan said, quickly rubbing the back of her fingers over Leo's smooth face as he helped her onto the wagon. "You and Nicholas were beginning to look the tiniest bit–*unkempt*–shall I say?"

"Ron was kind enough to provide each of us a shaving blade this morning," Nicholas said as he hopped up onto the wagon. "We're traveling with a lady, after all. Must look our best."

Leo turned his head and smiled knowingly at Megan, then gathered the reins to begin their journey.

"There is one other thing," Ron said in a low voice. "Something about last night. Mabel just informed me while you were getting ready."

"What?" Megan asked, her suspicions rising.

"We believe we know who tried to kidnap you," Mabel said. "A man had paid for a room for the night shortly after you arrived, but there was no sign of him this morning. The fireplace in his room hadn't been used nor his bed slept in. He was only three doors down the hall from you." She described the man as best she could remember, but her description provided no help.

"Do you know his name?" Leo asked.

"He signed the register as J. Oaks."

"I'm not familiar with that name," Megan said.

"Probably made up," Ron guessed. "Someone planning such a dishonorable act would most certainly wish to remain anonymous."

"Most likely," Megan agreed. "Oh well, I can't do anything about it now, and I refuse to worry about the matter for another moment. Besides, Leo has deliveries to make. We had best move on."

"If we stay on schedule, I'll pass by this way tomorrow afternoon," Leo said. "I'll stop in for lunch and let you know how we fared up north."

"You'd better," Mabel said. "I'll have some ale and a plate of peppered beef and biscuits waiting."

After Ron and Mabel bestowed a few words of caution and many wishes for a safe journey, Leo snapped the reins and the horses clopped away from the Plum Orchard Inn. The trio first planned to head north to White Birch as a dazzle of color and sunshine from a brisk autumn morning stretched across the countryside. The Knotts waved goodbye to their guests and then sat on the front porch steps for a few moments and watched them fade into the distance.

The curtains in a second floor window of the inn were briefly moved aside as another guest also watched the departing wagon with great interest. She watched curiously as Nicholas, Leo and the young woman wrapped warmly in a cloak rolled away, contemplating what next to do about them.

CHAPTER 15

Table Talk

Mune arrived at the Plum Orchard Inn that evening as the sun dipped below the western horizon. Starry twilight cloaked the candle-lit building in subtle shades of indigo. He was exhausted as his horse clomped the last few steps toward the inn, but he knew a warm meal and a bit of ale would thoroughly revive him. If not that, then a conversation with *her* most certainly would.

Mune paid for an overnight room and Elaine escorted him to his door along the back hallway. "I'm meeting a friend for dinner this evening," he said. "Is there a place where we can dine in private?"

"Most of the guests are eating in the common room tonight," she replied, "so the main dining room isn't crowded. But I could set a table in the back if you'd like extra privacy. No one will be in there."

"If it's not a bother," he said with a smile.

"Think nothing of it," she pleasantly replied. "Your table will be ready in ten minutes."

Mune took her hand in his and gently patted it. "In that case, my dear, I'll be down in twenty. My friend will arrive when the mood strikes her."

Elaine smiled perfunctorily before heading down the hallway. Mune returned a smile and watched her disappear around the corner. With his hand on the doorknob, he thought about the dinner meeting ahead. He sighed and entered his room.

Mune poured himself a cup of tea from the pot Elaine had left on the table and then slathered butter over a steaming biscuit he split in two. He greedily ate this and a second one as he waited for his accomplice. The crackling fire nearby and murmur of guests from the main dining room nearly lulled him to sleep. He had traveled many miles lately, carrying out Caldurian's orders at the oddest hours. Now one of his biggest tasks lay ahead and the anticipation kept him awake most nights as he imagined the fruits of his success. But the dread of failure lurked behind every enticing vision, thus nights of restful sleep became a rarity of late.

Mune bowed his head as he gently rubbed above his eyebrows. He felt a light headache coming on and the steam rising from his teacup soothed his weary eyes. What he'd give to sleep past dawn for once. Such a luxury was worth more than the silver and copper half-pieces he had used to bribe that drunken local from Kanesbury to enter the Spirit Caves. He chuckled. Oh, the people he'd meet in this business.

He looked up. There she stood, staring down at him like a vulture with an appetite. Mune hadn't heard her glide into the room and nearly knocked over his teacup in surprise. She hovered for a moment, then pulled out a chair opposite Mune and sat down.

"Your face is as hard as granite. Careful so you don't crack under pressure."

"A pleasant evening to you too, Madeline. Have two years gone by that quickly?"

Madeline smiled slyly and poured herself some tea, sitting arrow straight. A single candle burned on the table near the teapot. She gazed at it momentarily and the flame extinguished.

"It's too bright in here," she said. "I prefer the hush and solitude of shadows when discussing business."

Mune smirked. "Caldurian has rubbed off on you, I see. No walks in the cheery sunshine with you folks." Madeline crinkled her brow ever so slightly. "Sorry. Just trying to lighten matters."

"Not on my time, please."

"Of course." He pointed to the plate of hot biscuits. "Have one? Or shall we order our dinner instead?"

Soon they were dining on roasted chicken, glazed apple rings and herb potatoes. Mune ate heartily amid the small talk while Madeline, as was her habit, tasted little of her food, preferring to drink tea for her main course. Her watery green eyes watched in fascination as Mune consumed his meal with gusto. He shot a glance at the woman studying him–willowy and not much taller than himself, with a shock of flaming red hair wrapped under a black silk kerchief with gold embroidery.

"What?" he asked with a full mouth. "I'm hungry."

"I can see that." Madeline gently set her teacup down. "So what news does Caldurian send this way?"

Mune rested his hands on the table, a knife and fork wedged in each, scanning the empty room suspiciously. He leaned forward, swallowing his food, and whispered. "We're going to take the Citadel." Madeline raised an eyebrow as he nodded vigorously. "It's all in his letter," he said, indicating his coat pocket with the tip of the fork. "We'll have help from the Northern Isles, of course," he added, taking another bite of chicken. "We're to meet with a Commander Uta to hash out the details. It'll be quite an adventure."

"So Vellan wants a foothold right on King Justin's doorstep," she mused with delight. "How many troops will the Isles provide us for this ambitious endeavor? Taking the capital city will not be accomplished merely because we wish it."

Mune shook his head and sipped his tea. "You misunderstood me, Madeline. We're not after the *city* of Morrenwood–at least not yet. We simply want the Blue Citadel itself." He glanced warily around the room again and lowered his voice further. "Caldurian has something planned for there. Something big. But he provided few details so far."

"Caldurian never reveals his secrets–or Vellan's–all at once," she said with a hint of admiration. "Shrewd, yet exasperating at the same time." She detected a faint smile growing on Mune's face. "Why that look, if I may ask?"

"You may," he gleefully replied. "It just gives me a modicum of pleasure to know that not even you, Madeline, the closest friend Caldurian has–excluding Vellan, of course–are trusted with all of his innermost thoughts." Mune pursed his lips. "*Hmmm*, then again, I'm not even sure Vellan knows all the machinations that go on inside Caldurian's head. He is a cagey one."

Madeline tightened the woolen shawl draped over her shoulders as she subtly glared at her companion. "Caldurian, however, did teach me a spell to shrink toads down to the size of an ant. And I'm very good at it."

Mune grinned. "Well, enough said on that subject then." He attacked more of his food as Madeline sipped her tea. "Have you ever met him, by the way?" he added as an afterthought. "Vellan, I mean. I've never had the pleasure, if that's the appropriate word. Caldurian's mentioned him little, though rumors about Vellan are as legion as the stars."

"I've had the fortune to meet him on a few occasions, though mostly in Caldurian's presence. Vellan is a rather reclusive sort and values his privacy."

Mune nodded as he stabbed a potato wedge. "I suppose all that plotting and scheming have something to do with it. One probably needs a lot of alone time to plan so much mischief and destruction." He popped the potato into his mouth. "Such sustained malevolence demands focus, after all. It must drive one insane after a while. Just glad I'm only implementing the plans." Another potato quickly followed. "Overworked now as it is. Devising all this strategy would be the death of me!"

Madeline's gaze was as dry as sand. "Where did Caldurian ever find you?" She poured herself some more tea. "And why?"

"Because, my dear, I do my job, I do it right, and I keep my complaints to a minimum. That is worth a fortune these days." Mune was steeped in self-satisfaction. "Good help is hard to find, so when you find it…" He looked up. "Where is that girl? I could stand some ale right now."

Elaine cleared the table after their meal and brought Mune a pitcher of the inn's finest ale. After leaving another pot of tea for Madeline and a plate of dessert bread, she left them alone again to the quiet shadows of the back room. Mune filled his mug and drained half of it immediately before grabbing a slice of bread.

"Shall I assume, Madeline, that we're leaving first thing in the morning?"

"Day begins at dawn, Mune, so why shouldn't we?"

He sighed. "Just once I would like to get out of bed *after* the sun rises."

"You're in the wrong line of work if you wish that."

"I know. But one day I'll be wealthy enough to rise just in time for my midday meal. I mean, why go through all this work if I can't enjoy the fruits of my labor?"

"There is still much to do, so I suggest you forgo your self-indulgent daydreams. Caldurian is probably on the border of Montavia as we speak, ready to perform his next task in Vellan's plan. We must do our part, too."

"And we will. But you're just so focused all the time on what's next at hand. I need a little levity and a bit of ale now and then to keep my interest from waning." He winked. "Shouldn't we enjoy implementing this grand scheme of ours?"

"Joke if you like, but we have to be prepared. Events are moving quickly. Things are happening." She took a slow sip from her cup, keeping an eye on her dinner guest. "*Unexpected* things."

Mune looked at her askance. "What have you heard?"

"There's going to be a war council in Morrenwood. King Justin has summoned other leaders in the region and requested that they send emissaries to attend. My contact in the Blue Citadel gave me this information only a few nights ago when I met with him east of the Barhaden Woods."

"This isn't a good development." Mune stroked his goatee. "King Justin has been reluctant to step into the fray in the south, despite raising an army. And he tolerates Kargoth's grip on the nations in the Northern Mountains because Vellan hasn't extended his grasp north into Arrondale yet. Would he call a council just to assess the situation? Or does he have other plans in mind?"

"I think he wants to go on the offensive," she said. "For too long King Justin has been safe within his borders as smaller and weaker realms have felt Vellan's sting. I believe he's getting uncomfortable now, realizing it's only a matter of time until he's drawn into the mix. That's why we can't rest, even for a moment."

Mune poured himself more ale. "Can he get the support he needs from abroad?"

Madeline offered a grim smile. "Oh, I think King Justin would go it alone if he had no other choice."

"But where would he strike? Down south seems the only likely option," he speculated. "If he can't help Rhiál achieve victory against Maranac, how could he directly challenge Vellan in

231

Kargoth?" He grabbed another piece of bread. "Will your contact be able to worm himself into that council somehow? What a whirl of words that will be!"

"No."

Mune lifted the bread to his mouth and froze. "*Excuse me?*"

"I no longer have a contact there. His situation was–compromised."

He flopped the slice of dessert bread onto his plate. "Well a fine time for that to happen. For twenty years you've been able to mine him for information, and now…?"

"Everyone outlives his usefulness eventually," she said with surprisingly little regret. "But there is a bright spot."

"Enlighten me."

"My contact is still in my employ, and at this very moment he is tracking a valuable quarry." Madeline smiled knowingly as she folded her arms around her small frame. "What we first thought was a loss has turned into a substantial gain. I can now erase a twenty-year-old blot in my service to Caldurian."

Mune spread his hands and sighed. "Okay, now you've lost me, Madeline. You're apparently delighted by some turn of events, but I haven't a clue. Will you make me privy to your little secret?"

"Of course," she said, amused by his befuddled expression. "I just enjoy the fact that I can rib you so easily. I haven't had the pleasure in two years."

"Then by all means enjoy it," he replied, picking up the piece of bread and ripping a bite out of it. "And to think I was under the impression that you were a humorless stick-in-the-mud. Now what's going on?"

"My dear Mune, fortune smiles upon us today. We have an opportunity to advance our campaign against King Justin with very little work on our part."

"I'm intrigued. Especially the part about very little work."

"I knew that would please you," she replied, leaning forward and lowering her voice. "Guess who left the inn very early this morning?"

"Guessing games? That's so unlike you, but I'll indulge your brush with whimsy. *Hmmm*, was it Vellan?"

Madeline poured herself more tea and sampled a slice of bread. "You're as amusing as a thorn patch." She briefly dipped a small corner of the bread into her tea before eating it. "Princess Megan herself had spent the night here, believe it or not."

Mune wrinkled his brow in doubt. "The King's granddaughter was *here*? She spent the night in this inn?" He indicated Madeline's cup with an inquisitive glance. "What exactly is in that tea?"

"I'm neither mad nor intoxicated, Mune. Princess Megan of Arrondale was really here, accompanied by two young men in a wagon stacked with apple crates."

"And that added fact is supposed to make your story more credible?"

"I am so tempted right now to try out that shrinking spell," she muttered.

Mune relented and sat back in the chair, nursing his mug of ale. "All right, Madeline, give me the details. I'll shut up and listen. How do you know it was Princess Megan? You haven't seen her since you tried to kidnap her as an infant."

"But my contact has. The princess has grown up right under his nose. And he saw her only yesterday in a small restaurant in the village of Mason and overheard she was heading this way." Madeline sensed his growing doubt. "Let me back up several days. That should help you keep track of events."

"I'd appreciate it," Mune said, taking a gulp of his drink.

"My contact, unfortunately, was a little bit over zealous after learning about the upcoming war council. He worked in the kitchens but had a few duties in other parts of the Citadel. But he had asked one question too many of people he shouldn't have, he told me, and began to arouse a few suspicions." Madeline sighed. "And it didn't help that he was spotted in a restricted corridor near the meeting chamber, trying to assess the layout for his report to me."

"What happened to him?"

"He felt he had no choice, so he fled before anyone could question or detain him." She smirked. "He told me he wasn't that disappointed to be leaving anyway. Working in the Blue Citadel all these years had lost its charm. And despite earning a little extra on the side as my informant, he felt there were more lucrative opportunities for his services throughout Laparia now that Vellan had sufficiently stirred things up."

"You learned all this just a few days ago?"

"Yes. We had arranged to meet east of the Barhaden Woods. I was on my way here to Plum Orchard, so after our meeting, he accompanied me to the inn and then left two mornings ago. He was heading east to the Ridloe Mountains and planned to follow them south to find his fortune in the war."

"I don't mind instigating war," Mune said, "but I prefer to keep my distance once all that nasty fighting breaks out. It's not healthy." He stretched his legs and rested his hands behind his head. "So about your contact, how did he–say, what is his name, by the way? Since he's out of the Citadel now, there's no need to keep it a secret anymore."

"I never like to divulge information if I don't have to, but I suppose it doesn't matter now. His name is Dell Hawks."

Mune shrugged. "But how did he ever bump into the princess? He just *left* the Citadel. Isn't that where Princess Megan is supposed to be?"

"One would think. But Dell claims he saw her yesterday afternoon in the village of Mason and overheard that she was on her way to the village of Plum Orchard."

"With those two apple sellers," he said skeptically.

"I can only tell you what I saw through my window. So he rushed back here, knowing that I would still be around, and tried to arrange her abduction last night. But…"

"No luck?"

"No. One of Megan's companions rescued her before Dell could carry her off. But he is heading north to track them down. We'll find her yet."

Mune sat up, hungry for more bread. "See, a money-making opportunity falls at Dell's feet even before he gets a whiff of war in the south. Now that's luck! Though I still can't comprehend why the King's granddaughter is out here in the middle of nowhere with two locals. It doesn't make sense. Does she have a twin?"

"No."

"And you definitely saw her?"

"I saw a woman in a cloak leaving here this morning accompanied by two men. Her face was concealed by a hood, but who else could it be?"

"Well that's proof enough," Mune muttered sarcastically, receiving a fiery glare from Madeline. "And your Mr. Hawks never gleaned any information about the princess going abroad while he was still employed in the Citadel?"

Madeline sat back, her hands folded on her lap. "Again, no. He was only a kitchen worker. His access was limited."

Mune grinned. "*You* were only a nursemaid twenty years ago, but look at you now. You're rubbing shoulders with some pretty important figures." He poured the last of the ale from the pitcher into his mug. "Now that we have the time, tell me what happened when you first tried to snatch the infant princess. What went wrong?"

Madeline drew her lips into a tight line, recalling those days so long ago. She hadn't minded being one of a handful of nursemaids employed in the Blue Citadel, helping to care for the children of royalty. It was a satisfying job in its way, yet deep inside she had yearned for something more out of life. Something exciting. Princess Megan had been the newest addition to the bloodline, and her mother had been in frail health shortly after her birth. One of Madeline's duties then was to take the child outdoors to the courtyards for fresh air on particular days. It was while walking through the labyrinth of corridors one afternoon that she had first laid eyes on Caldurian, a young, ambitious wizard of twenty-six. He was being escorted to meet with envoys of the King, and as Madeline brushed past him in the hallway with the baby in her arms, she couldn't help but be entranced by his dark eyes which pierced into the deepest recesses of her soul in that brief instant. As she exited the gloomy corridor into the warm sunshine, her heart beat wildly and her limbs shook. Words and images flooded her mind, revealing a world of grandeur and possibility beyond the Citadel. Madeline couldn't comprehend what had happened to her in those moments, but she knew she wanted to meet that mysterious gentleman.

Caldurian found her instead. After a series of meetings with some of the King's representatives, the wizard was allowed to wander in the courtyards while King Justin pondered his offer of an alliance with Vellan. Caldurian spotted Madeline late in the afternoon talking with two of her fellow nursemaids near one of the garden fountains. A mere glance from him was enough to lure her away. She followed him behind a row of hedges. They sat on a stone bench away from any distractions. Madeline hardly said a word at first, but Caldurian sensed that they had much in common and was instantly attracted to her.

"You are thinking, '*Why does he want to speak with me?*'" Caldurian said, observing Madeline out of the corners of his eyes. She sat on the edge of the bench, looking forward, the tips of her toes barely touching the ground. "And are you wondering what value you might bring to this relationship?"

Madeline nodded a few times, bravely glancing up at Caldurian, taken in by his amiable smile, his long dark hair and a vibrant sense of purpose.

The wizard gently tapped his boot upon the cobblestone pavement. "I would answer that I see much potential in you."

"Madeline," she whispered after a nervous pause. "My name is Madeline."

"And mine is Caldurian. I am a wizard."

"Yes, I already knew that–both your name and your livelihood. Word spreads around the Citadel like wildfire when somebody important arrives."

He grunted. "Well, I shall shortly know how important King Justin finds me. I fear not very."

"What is it that you seek here?"

"An alliance between Arrondale and Kargoth. My leader, Vellan, has placed his utmost trust in me to convince King Justin that such an alliance would be advantageous."

"To Vellan? Or to the King?"

Caldurian laughed, noting that the young woman seemed less ill at ease. He stood and faced her. "How many years have you seen, Madeline? Nineteen? Perhaps twenty?"

"Twenty and a half."

"Well, twenty and a half suits you nicely. You are quite lovely and charming if I may say so without seeming too forward," he said, eager to get to know her further. He took a step back and studied her for a moment. "Tell me, what is it you want out of life right now? Speak quickly! Do not think!"

"I want to know the world!" she blurted out, slowly looking up mystified at Caldurian. "Tell me please–what does that mean?"

The wizard smiled. "It means that you could put your talents to better use elsewhere than inside a nursery in Morrenwood. I sensed you had potential the instant I laid eyes on you."

"I thought I had heard you talking to me inside my mind as you passed by. Was I imagining it?"

Caldurian smiled again and sat back down. "See, you proved me right."

"That I have potential?" Madeline nervously ran her fingers through her head of blazing red hair. "Potential for *what*?"

Caldurian turned to her. "To know the world, of course. And I would be delighted to teach you."

Mune waved a hand in front of Madeline's face. "Hello! Your thoughts are a thousand miles away. Did you hear me?"

"I heard you," she replied dryly.

"So tell me what went wrong with the kidnapping?"

"Bad luck."

Mune sat forward, leaned his elbows on the table and nodded. "*Meaning…?*"

"Meaning, I learned a valuable lesson–that you should always prepare in excruciating detail." She noted the empty pitcher of ale. "And never take your job lightly."

Mune rolled his eyes. "I never have. I just prefer to find entertaining ways to *do* my job. But don't change subjects. What happened?"

"Caldurian never told you this story?"

"No. Our conversations are never quite this social. He's usually very sober, serious and stupendously dull." He pointed a cautionary finger at Madeline. "Don't you risk becoming like that. Tell me everything!"

"There's not much left to tell. Caldurian's negotiations with King Justin were bearing no fruit. I met the wizard the following morning and he told me as much. He planned to leave that evening after his final session, believing that King Justin and his representatives were being diplomatic, merely going through the motions but never having any intentions to align themselves with Vellan. He seemed resigned to that fate, yet I sensed a tinge of desperation in his voice," she said. "Caldurian didn't want to fail Vellan a second time, and when I told him I had to return to my nursemaid duties, he suddenly went silent, deep in thought. I could see the strain in his face as he whispered to himself. Then his eyes opened wide and he looked at me, having discovered another option. What's more, I knew that I would now be involved in his activities."

"That's when he planned to kidnap the princess?"

A thin smile formed on Madeline's face. "That's when he planned that I would kidnap the princess. He would use the infant as a bargaining tool to gain King Justin's allegiance. I also believed that it would be a test of my loyalty to Caldurian should I wish to join forces with him."

Mune grinned in admiration. "What a gutsy maneuver on his part. Forgive me for being blunt, but how did your plan fall apart?"

She tapped a fingernail against her teacup. "We didn't have you as part of our team, Mune, otherwise the endeavor would have been an astounding success."

"A pity I didn't know you two back them. Now out with it. What happened?"

"I employed the assistance of one of the kitchen workers, a gangly sort who was quite smitten with me at the time. He had a knack for pilfering a loaf of bread or a wedge of fine cheese from the kitchens and would brag to me about selling the items to the villagers. So I knew he might be inclined to help me–"

"–pilfer a princess?"

"Precisely. Dell Hawks was easily influenced with a smile and a kiss back then."

Mune leaned back in his chair, thoroughly enjoying Madeline's account. "Dell Hawks, you say. My, but you two have quite a history."

"Anyway, I met with him on my afternoon rounds in the courtyard. I had the child with me and we chatted on some rocks under a birch tree. He was smoking that awful smelling pipe of his as he was fond of doing. I think he believed it impressed me. The princess took a fancy to him, as I had hoped. Couldn't have her crying through the Citadel corridors as he carried her away. At least that was the theory."

Madeline recounted how she had explained Caldurian's plan to Dell, emphasizing that no harm would come to the child and that a handsome profit awaited them both. He quickly offered his services.

"We decided to make our move at twilight. Caldurian would be out of the Citadel by then and I would be on duty. Megan's parents usually spent some time in one of the gardens with her at this part of the evening before Prince Gregory would go off to consult with his father on matters of the day. One of the other attendants would then assist his wife on a short walk thereafter to help her regain her strength while I carried the infant to the nursery to await her mother's return." Madeline helped herself to another piece of dessert bread. "Only this time I took a detour."

"To where?"

"To the cellar kitchens. More precisely, to one of the storage rooms nearby. Dell said he would leave a large wicker basket inside the room farthest from the main kitchen as it was usually vacant. There I would place the bundled infant inside, then set a false bottom over her and fill the basket with a few loaves of bread and some vegetables. Dell was to meet me there and take the basket outdoors through a side door and deliver it to Caldurian's party as they waited to depart. He would claim it was compliments of the head kitchen attendant for use on their journey. Caldurian and company were to ride out through the main gates as darkness fell without suspicion. That was the plan."

She slowly raised her tea cup and took a long sip as Mune drummed his fingers on the table. "Oh, quite teasing, Madeline, and get on with it. What happened to throw your fine plan into chaos?"

She set her cup down and folded her arms. "Dell Hawks never showed up. He was sent on an errand and could not worm his way out of it, so he later told me. I waited for him for several minutes, already quite late for the nursery. I was expected there and knew people would soon come looking for me, realizing I was now compromised and would be interrogated should I be found. So not wanting to connect our plans to the kitchens, and possibly to Dell himself, I hurriedly carried the infant to another corridor and left her there, knowing she would be found unharmed. I then bolted out of the Citadel through another cellar exit and found Caldurian's contingent readying their horses and wagons to depart. He could see by my eyes in the moonlight that the plan had collapsed, yet had me climb into one of the wagons and hide under some blankets just before he departed. We passed through the main gates before the incident had been discovered. I boiled in silent rage at my failure. Caldurian forgave me, pleased that I had pledged my life in his service. We took refuge with a relative of mine in nearby Red Fern and..." Madeline sighed regretfully, nodding her head. "Well, that's a whole other story."

"Oh? What happened in Red Fern?" Mune asked, bubbling with curiosity.

"I'd rather not talk about it and spoil this lovely meal," she coolly replied. "Anyway, Caldurian and I later learned that we were suspected in the attempted kidnapping and eventually fled east to the Cumberland Forest. Fortunately, Dell Hawks had never been implicated."

"And thus he remained your spy for these past twenty years. How wonderfully convenient."

"And how utterly inconvenient it is that he can no longer spy for us on the eve of the war council." Madeline sighed. "Still, if he can track down Princess Megan and rectify our mistake from twenty years ago..."

"That would be quite a gift for Caldurian, wouldn't it? Quite a bargaining piece." Mune glanced curiously at Madeline. "But if your Mr. Hawks does kidnap the princess, what will we do with her?"

"I've given that some thought. We'll leave her in the capable hands of the Northern Islanders. They could hold her prisoner on one of their ships until she is needed. She'll be safe with them," she said confidently. "No chance for someone to rescue her or to even know she is there."

"That'll work for me," Mune said, downing the last of his drink. "Now if you don't mind, I'll excuse myself for the night. I have to send word to *him*, and then I'd like to get a full night's sleep before we're off in the morning."

Madeline shooed him away with a flick of her hand. "Enjoy your evening as you wish. I'll finish my tea here with the fire and quiet. I need to think. But be prepared to depart at sunrise. We have much to do."

"As you wish," he replied, standing up and pushing in his chair. "It's been enjoyable catching up on old times, Madeline. It really has. We should do it more often." He nodded as he walked out of the room, leaving his accomplice alone in the shadows, nursing her cup of hot tea.

Shortly afterward, Mune stood under the trees behind the Plum Orchard Inn, whispering details about the upcoming war council to the crow perched upon his arm. Gavin attentively listened as Mune spoke in the chilly night air, his white breath quickly dissipating in the light of the Fox Moon now nearly full and climbing high in the eastern sky. The crescent Bear Moon sank low in the west behind some nearby maples.

Moments later, Gavin flew off to relay the latest information to Caldurian. The wizard now stood miles away above the Black Hills on the shores of the Trillium Sea, greeting a ship from the Northern Isles. Mune strolled back to the inn to retire for the night, exhausted, yet satisfied with the day's accomplishments.

CHAPTER 16

Spies on the Bridge

Nicholas closed his eyes and deeply inhaled the cold sea air as the wagon rattled on through the narrow streets of Boros. The tiny fishing village was a collection of stone and wood houses and shops bunched snugly together like a cluster of grapes along the shores of Sage Bay. Leo had completed his apple deliveries for the day, first in White Birch and Laurel Corners, and now finally in Boros. Nicholas felt a sense of relief that Megan would soon be safe inside the home of her great aunt. Megan sat silently between them, her eyes closed and head gently resting on Leo's shoulder as the horses contentedly clip clopped through the first hints of gauzy twilight.

"Is that the place?" Leo asked, pointing to a gray stone house near the end of a winding street. A candle burned in each of the downstairs windows and a wreath of dried goldenrod and corn husks adorned the wooden door.

Megan looked up. "Yes. Samuel had given me explicit directions as a precaution in case we ever became separated."

Nicholas grinned. "Bet he never expected you to separate yourself from his side."

"I wouldn't be much of a princess if I couldn't take care of myself."

Leo nervously cleared his throat. "Just to be safe, it might be best if we didn't mention the word *princess* while we're in public."

"Point well taken," she said with amusement. "I'll just pretend to be plain common folk like you two boys. Any pointers?"

"Sure. Eat with your fingers and wipe your mouth on your shirt sleeve," Nicholas said with a smirk.

"I'll keep that in mind," she replied, enjoying the salty breeze as it brushed across her face. Sea gulls cried mournfully above the shoreline as the few remaining rays of orange sunlight pierced through a grove of tall pines in the west.

Great Aunt Castella Birchwood opened the door and gazed uneasily at the trio gathered on her front step. A slight breeze rustled the gray curls hanging down her forehead. She tightened a green and gold checkered shawl around her thin shoulders as she suspiciously glanced beyond her visitors at a tiny wooden bridge farther down the cobblestone street now absent of any pedestrians. She bit her lower lip before returning her focus to Megan, Nicholas and Leo.

"It's been nine years since I last laid eyes on my niece's daughter, but I can tell at a glance, Megan, that you are indeed her," Castella said, suspiciously eyeing her companions. "But who are these two? And where is Samuel?"

"These are my friends, Aunt Castella. Very good friends," she replied, vaguely recalling the last time she had seen her great aunt at her mother's funeral. Megan was eleven at that horrible time, young enough not to comprehend why her life had been turned upside down, yet old enough to forever remember the stinging pain of those sorrowful months. "Samuel isn't here with us. It's a long story."

"I see. Then you'd better tell me all about it at once. I'm not getting any younger," she said, flashing a dry smile.

After directing Leo to a patch of land on the left side of the house where he tied up his horses, Castella invited everybody into the house. She glanced once more at the wooden bridge before closing the door and locking it with a large key.

They were seated at the kitchen table in short order as Castella scurried about the room, hanging a kettle of water over the stone fireplace for hot tea and preparing a plate of honey biscuits, apple slices and cheese. Megan insisted on helping, but Castella wouldn't hear of it.

"I'm seventy years old and then some, and not much good at chopping firewood or cleaning out the horse stall anymore. I let my housekeeper, Ivy, do that. But I can lay out a snack for my guests to enjoy," she said, stoking the flames of the fire and tossing on another piece of wood. She sat down at the table after everything had been served, her skin pale in the candlelight. "Now bring me up to date on your journey and I'll fill you in on what's been troubling me."

"What are you talking about?" Megan asked. "Is something wrong?"

Aunt Castella raised a finger. "You first, please."

Nicholas nodded. "Tell your aunt everything that happened, Meg."

"For you own safety," Leo agreed.

"I should understand then that these boys know who you are?" Castella asked.

"Nicholas and Leo know I'm King Justin's granddaughter," Megan said. "I couldn't hide that secret forever."

"Not from us or from someone else." Leo swiped an apple slice from the plate and bite into it. "She was nearly kidnapped at the Plum Orchard Inn."

"*What?*"

"Leo! Don't blurt it out. You'll scare my aunt to death."

"Tell me what happened!"

"She has to know, Meg. We can't keep secrets," he said, chomping on the fruit. "Not bad. Red Hills Creek variety?"

"Yes. The shops were out of Corlians," Castella said, eyeing Leo curiously upon his question. "But what about this kidnapping?"

"Out of Corlians? Well, that shouldn't be a problem anymore," he said with a pleased smile. "In fact–"

"Don't get him started!" Nicholas pleaded while slicing off a piece of cheese and stuffing it between two halves of a biscuit. "Enough apple talk," he pleaded. "Let Megan tell the story."

"I wish one of you would," Castella said. "I grow uneasy when I hear the word kidnapping, especially when it pertains to my great niece. Now, Megan, what happened? And don't worry about scaring me. I'm too old to get scared–but not impatient. So talk!"

Megan quickly related the events from the previous night at the inn, informing Aunt Castella how she had run away from Samuel and Carmella and eventually met Nicholas and Leo. Castella was grateful that they had accompanied her to Boros, shuddering to think where her great niece might be now had she been on her own.

"Your father will be furious," Castella predicted. "And as for your grandfather..."

"I wouldn't blame them," Meg admitted, "but I'd probably be in less trouble if I had just remained in Morrenwood. I was supposed to be protected here in Boros, tucked safely and anonymously out of the way from the danger of the times."

"But somebody found your trail, so now what do we do?" Nicholas asked.

"How about posting a message to your grandfather?" Leo said. "He can send a troop of his best soldiers here to take you back home."

"Don't be silly, Leo. I don't intend to have the King or even the local authorities waste their time looking after me." Megan sipped her tea, gazing stubbornly across her cup. "Besides, we gave that man at the inn the slip. He probably ran off for good. I don't think we have anything to worry about now."

"If only that were so," Castella gravely whispered. "I had a feeling something wasn't right even before you arrived. Your story confirms my suspicions. You are in danger, Megan, and there isn't time to let others worry about your safety. *We* have to."

"What are you talking about, Aunt Castella?"

"What danger?" Leo asked.

"I'm afraid whoever's been following you now knows you're here," she said ominously, her steely green eyes gazing over the teapot as she refreshed her drink.

Nicholas leaned back in his chair, wondering if they had been followed from the inn. They had talked freely enough in public on several occasions and someone could have been listening. "How do you know this, Castella? Who knows we're here?"

"I don't know who, but someone is definitely on your trail." She sipped her tea with a trembling hand. Though it had been years since she had seen her great niece, she felt close to Megan and protective nonetheless. "Earlier this morning there was a knock on my door. Ivy was out in the back garden harvesting the last of the carrots, so I answered the call. A young man had stopped by with a delivery of fresh fish. I told him he had the wrong address but he seemed perplexed. After I told him my name, he realized his mistake and left. I watched him leave, assuming he'd try another house nearby, but he went straight to the wooden bridge near the end of the street and spoke to another man who was fishing in the stream running below. I thought that that was odd."

"Why?" Leo asked.

"Because that stream is thick with weeds. Nobody ever fishes there especially since the docks are just a stone's throw away." Castella sighed as if stating the obvious. "Anyway, the man who had mistakenly stopped here talked to the second man on the bridge for a few moments and then left him there alone to continue fishing."

Nicholas shrugged. "And that indicates what?"

"First it indicates that the chap knows nothing about catching a fish for dinner," she replied with an amused grunt, putting Megan momentarily at ease. "But he stayed there for over an hour. I peeked through the curtains every so often, noting that he occasionally glanced this way as if furtively studying the house. Later, the first man stopped by again and switched places with the fellow who was fishing. Now *this* man pretended to fish after the other one had left. My curiosity was eerily piqued. I had Ivy take a look when she came inside, and after another hour or so, the second man returned and switched places with the first. When it happened a third time, I grew deeply concerned. I knew my house was being watched…" Aunt Castella glanced at Megan with apprehension. "…and I knew *you* were on your way to my doorstep."

Leo jumped up. "Nicholas and I can run down there right now and confront those two characters. Just give us each a heavy walking stick if you have some handy. We'll take care of them."

"My brave protectors," Megan said with a smile.

"Now don't be foolhardy, Leo. Besides, they aren't there anymore," Castella calmly stated. "I noticed they were gone when you knocked on my door. The bridge was empty. They must have seen you arrive and sprinted off, fishing pole and all."

"Now they know you're here," Nicholas whispered to Megan.

"But where did they go?" Leo wondered aloud.

Aunt Castella rubbed her thin hands together. "More importantly, who did they tell?"

"Oh, enough already!" Megan complained. "There's a cloud of mystery and alarm hanging over this room as thick as yesterday's

246

churned butter. I won't have it. I won't make myself a prisoner to our wild imaginations."

"Being nearly kidnapped last night was not our imaginations," Leo said. "You have to take your safety seriously, Meg. And if you won't, we will."

"He's right," Castella agreed. "When your grandfather sent word to me weeks ago about your pending arrival, I thought you'd be safe and anonymous here in the middle of nowhere. But we were both wrong. He only wanted to keep you safe in case danger–or even war itself–spread to the capital city. But danger tracked you to our little village of Boros nonetheless."

"What are you saying, Aunt Castella?"

"Your secret is out, my dear girl, and I can't guarantee your safety inside the walls of my modest abode. I do apologize," she said, folding her hands upon the table. "Now that you've been spotted, it seems that your journey here has been for naught. Therefore, perhaps it is wisest that you should flee elsewhere, or even return to Morrenwood."

"*Humph!*" Megan slumped back in her chair and glared at Nicholas and Leo. "And I suppose you two agree? Cart the little girl back to the Blue Citadel where she can start all over. Move her around like she's merely a crate of apples, completely ignoring the fact that this crate of produce has had just about enough of fleeing and hiding and being looked after! If I had ignored everyone else and stayed home in the first place, then none of this would be happening!" She stood and slammed her tea cup on the table. "If someone wants to kidnap me, let them try. Now please excuse me for a moment."

She breezed past the table and disappeared into the adjoining room. Nicholas and Leo glanced at each other, feigning expressions of fright before turning to Castella.

"Maybe we should talk to her about this later," Leo said softly. "Give her a few moments to calm down first."

"*Several* moments," Nicholas suggested.

Castella stood and started to clean off the table. "Things will work themselves out. In the meantime, the pile on the hearth is low, Nicholas. Could you go out back and bring in more wood?"

"Sure will."

"And, Leo, perhaps a bit of handholding in the other room might be in order," she added. "I'll join you shortly with another pot of tea."

"Maybe I should leave her alone a little longer," he said with unease. "Just to be on the safe side."

"Good luck however you handle it," Nicholas remarked with a chuckle as he slipped out the back door.

The shadows were thick behind the house when Nicholas stepped outside. He took a deep breath of the cool evening air that danced with a scent of fresh pine and sea water. Wisps of purple and gray clouds drifted above the distant trees in the deepening twilight. A long pile of chopped wood had been neatly stacked several yards away in some tall grass. A few crickets lazily chirped. He wandered over but suddenly stopped when seeing a dark figure stooping over the far end of the stack. His heart raced, fearing that one of the men Castella had spotted on the bridge was lurking about, perhaps waiting to ambush Megan during the night. He looked around, but finding nothing to arm himself with, he raced to the closer end of the pile and grabbed a piece of firewood, raising it in the air like a club.

"I don't think you'll find the fishing all that great back here," he muttered as he approached the individual, a scowl creeping across his face. "Now don't try anything foolish and you won't get hurt." The stranger, holding an armful of logs, slowly turned toward Nicholas and stared at him in the gloom.

"Exactly why would I go fishing in a grassy field?" a voice curiously asked, noting the weapon in Nicholas' hand. "You're not planning to hit me with that, are you?" Nicholas flinched when hearing a young woman speak and quickly lowered his arm. "Because if you're not, be a gentleman and help carry some of this into the house. Castella likes a full pile by the hearth when she wakes up in the morning."

"Uh, sure..." he said, flushed with embarrassment as he tossed the piece of wood aside. Nicholas was grateful that they were somewhat hidden in shadow, hoping he didn't look as ridiculous as he felt. "Sorry, but I thought you were someone else." He extended his arms and indicated for the woman to give him the firewood.

"Someone you wanted to hit with a stick?" she said, slightly amused.

"Not exactly." Nicholas shrugged as she added a few more pieces to the pile in his overloaded arms so that he had to steady it with his chin.

"That should do," she said, leading the way back to the house. "And you are...?"

"Nicholas Raven. I arrived here a while ago with Megan," he said. "You must be Castella's housekeeper. Ivy, is it?"

"Ivy Brooks. But I only work here a few days each week," she replied while opening the back door to let Nicholas step into the now empty kitchen.

He knelt down on one knee and deposited the firewood near the stone hearth as Ivy closed the door and locked it. Nicholas stood up just as she turned around, seeing her face clearly in the light for the first time. He was immediately taken with her soft smile and gentle light brown eyes that matched the flow of hair upon her shoulders. Ivy wore a light beige blouse with a gray and white house skirt that draped down to her ankles, just covering the tips of a pair of scuffed black boots. He stared at her for a moment, gawking slightly and at a loss for words.

Ivy blushed amid a growing smile. "I don't have a dirt smudge on my face, do I? I'd been working out in the garden earlier."

"No. You look fine," he said. "No smudge. But even if you had one, you'd still look–fine." He took a clumsy step backward, bumping into the wood pile he had just set down, believing his words at the moment were as ungraceful as his feet.

"Careful there."

"I'm all right," he said, placing one hand on the mantel and trying to smile confidently. "And so are you. Still no smudge."

Ivy grinned affectionately. "Thanks for clarifying that. Unfortunately, I think I smudged you when I handed off that pile out back." She walked up to him and quickly ran her thumb over a small speck of dirt on his chin. "Castella would never let me hear the end of it if she knew I was putting one of her houseguests to work."

"I don't mind," Nicholas said as he and Ivy briefly looked into each other's eyes. The soft touch of her hand upon his face made him briefly forgot all the confusing trouble that had plagued him over the last several days. And though they had only met,

Nicholas instantly felt an easy and comforting bond in her presence. He couldn't help but smile.

"There. You look like your old self again, Nicholas."

"I'll assume that's a good thing. I've been on the road for days and feel dog tired. Hope I don't look it," he said.

"Not at all," she replied as Castella walked into the room.

"Oh, there you are, Ivy. I thought you had gotten lost in the darkness," she said as she squeezed between the couple to check on the tea kettle heating over the fire. "I see you've met this fine young gentleman. Megan is in the other room with one Leo Marsh. I'll introduce you to them shortly. Then we can discuss our plan."

Ivy looked at her guardedly. "So they both know about Megan's identity?"

"Oh, yes. Her secret is out."

Nicholas shifted a perplexed gaze between Ivy and Castella. "*Plan*? What are you two talking about? What plan?"

"Water's ready," Castella said, sighing as she lifted the heavy metal teapot with a small towel wrapped around its handle. "Ivy, can you get five cups ready on a tray so we can serve in the other room?"

"Who has a plan?" Nicholas asked as Ivy and Castella bustled about the room to ready the tea. "Is this about protecting Megan?"

"Of course, dear. And you and Leo have done a fine job so far," Castella explained as she poured the water. "But Ivy and I have been plotting ever since we realized that something rotten was afoot with those men fishing on the bridge. We'll tell you all about it when you join us in the sitting room," she replied with a grandmotherly sort of smile. "More biscuits with your tea?"

They gathered in the room just off the kitchen. After making a round of introductions, Castella had her guests quickly bring her housekeeper up to date on their adventures along the road and at the Plum Orchard Inn. Megan even told Ivy about the attempted kidnapping by her nursemaid nearly twenty years ago. Ivy quietly sipped her tea as she listened. Thick velvety drapes covered the windows to keep out the encroaching darkness. A small fireplace and several candles scattered about the room cast a gentle glow upon their faces. When Nicholas finished telling the remainder of the story, bringing Ivy up to the point when they knocked on the front door, Castella smiled and nodded, setting her teacup down on a small wooden stand beside her chair.

"Good. Now that we all know what's happened, we have to prepare for what's to come," she calmly said as she glanced at her great niece. "Megan, you have to leave."

"But I just got here!"

Castella smiled. "I don't intend for you to leave this instant, dear, nor am I going to send you off to Morrenwood tomorrow. This departure I have planned is just a short term measure to protect you while you're in Boros."

Leo sat next to Megan and instinctively placed his hand upon hers. "Where do you want to send her?"

"I'm sending her nowhere," Castella said as Ivy walked to the front door. She removed Megan's cloak from one of the wooden pegs on the wall. "You and Nicholas will be *taking* her somewhere."

"We will?" Nicholas asked with an uneasy edge to his voice. "*Where?*"

Ivy held up the long dark blue cloak and glanced at Megan. "May I?"

"Certainly," she replied, not sure what Ivy had in mind.

Ivy slipped Megan's cloak upon her shoulders and draped the hood over her head, spinning playfully around as everybody watched with a mixture of wonderment and curiosity. "This will do just fine. Just fine indeed," she said as she removed the hood, revealing a soft yet confident smile. "And you'll be leaving midmorning tomorrow."

Everyone spent a restless night under Aunt Castella's roof, unable to sleep in the first hours of darkness and then plagued by bouts of fitful dreams before the first gray light of dawn arrived. Nicholas and Leo each insisted on sleeping in a chair, one by the front entrance and the other near the back kitchen door, just as a precaution. Megan told Leo that all the fuss was an overreaction, though she was touched by his gallantry. Ivy was also charmed with Nicholas' protective stance and told him as much shortly after she found him sound asleep in the kitchen early the following morning, his head tilted sideways against the back door with a few blankets draped over him. She gently nudged him awake, greeting him with a smile.

"The sun will be up soon," she whispered in the morning chill. "I'll get a fire going and fix a light breakfast. Then I have to leave."

Nicholas sat up straight, massaging the aches out of his sore neck. "Where are you going at this hour, Ivy?" He tried to fight off the remnants of sleep still tugging at the edges of his mind as he ran a hand through his tangled mop of hair.

"Did you forget our plan already? I'll leave for the market as I usually do most mornings when I'm here. Later, you, Megan and Leo will meet me at my uncle's candle shop near the shore." She added a few pieces of kindling and dry straw to the fireplace. "Do you remember the directions?"

Nicholas nodded as he tossed off the blankets and knelt next to Ivy on the hearth, grabbing two fire stones by the wood pile. "I shouldn't have let it burn out during the night, but I guess I needed sleep." He sharply hit one stone across the top of the other as he held them near the straw until a series of sparks erupted, quickly igniting the fuel. Soon the kindling burned and crackled and he slowly added larger pieces of wood to the flames.

"After hearing those stories about your travels, I probably shouldn't have wakened you so soon," Ivy said, staring at Nicholas as the orange and yellow glow of firelight reflected off his face.

"I don't mind. It's kind of nice being up this early when it's so quiet," he replied as he gazed into the fire. "A bit of calm before the hectic day ahead."

"Not too hectic, I hope," she said as they both stood up. A moment later Ivy handed him an empty tea kettle. "Now take this outside and fill it from the water barrel while I slice some bread. We can enjoy a few quiet moments and some cinnamon tea before the others awake, if you have no objection."

Nicholas smiled as he lightly drummed his fingers against the metal container. "That's worth losing a bit of sleep over," he said as he headed out the back door, eager to get to know Ivy a little better.

A while later after everyone was awake, Ivy left Aunt Castella's house and ventured into the silent streets. The sun was peeking over the eastern shoreline as the nearly full Fox Moon prepared to hide below the western horizon. Several hours afterward, the call of seagulls and the clatter of horse-drawn carts filled the crowded dirt and cobblestone roads of Boros, now fully awake to another day. Aunt Castella said goodbye to her great niece outside the front door. Megan wrapped herself in her cloak, and as Ivy had requested, she draped the hood over her head. Nicholas and Leo stood on either side, determined to protect Megan as they leisurely walked to the candle shop according to Ivy's instructions.

"I'll expect you back before afternoon," Castella said. "Hot soup will be waiting."

"See you then," Megan replied with a wave before locking her arm around Leo's.

Aunt Castella leaned against the open door for support as she watched the trio saunter down the sun-drenched road as if they hadn't a care in the world. "Oh, I truly hope so," she whispered to herself, glancing warily at the wooden bridge in the distance, though seeing neither of the two fishermen from the previous evening. "I truly hope so."

CHAPTER 17

The Switch

Nicholas, Megan and Leo wandered through the cool sunny streets for nearly two hours, stopping occasionally to peer through the window of a local bakery or examine the fresh silvery offerings at a fish market. A brief stroll along one of the wooden piers was also in order. Several boats had drifted out as the rising sun sparkled brilliantly off a line of waves lapping gently onto shore. Farther inland along a short stretch of sand, fishermen were busy with repairs to their boats and netting while others warmed themselves around a bonfire near wooden fishing huts that dotted the shoreline, enjoying a break with hot tea or cider. They knew days like this would be fewer and fewer as an icy winter drew near, silently preparing for the dark and lonely times ahead.

"As much as I enjoy this tour of Boros, I think we should go to the candle shop now," Megan said. "My feet are hurting."

Nicholas nodded. "I guess we've made our presence known to anyone who might be watching us."

"Okay," Leo said, gently tightening his arm around Megan's. "But a part of me is still uncomfortable with this plan. I feel as if…"

She sensed his concern. "What's the matter, Leo?"

"I feel as if we're abandoning you, Meg. I don't like it."

She turned and looked into his eyes, her smile instantly putting him at ease. "Don't worry," she said. "This is not the last time you'll see me. I promise."

Leo smiled as a cool wind cut through the air. "A princess would never break a promise to one of her subjects, would she?"

"Not this particular one."

Nicholas cleared his throat to get their attention, signaling for them to follow him. "I think the candle shop is along the next lane."

"Lead the way," Megan said, taking Leo's hand. "Let's get this silly scheme underway."

The streets grew narrower in this section of town and some of the roads still hadn't been paved with cobblestone. Many of the stone and wood shops, whitewashed earlier in the spring, sported a dull sheen after enduring months of mischievous breezes laced with a salty sea spray. The fourth building down the next street was a candle shop. The low stone structure, wedged between a potter's store on the left and a tailor shop on the right, contained two windows with brown shutters and a single stone step leading to a narrow wooden door. As Nicholas opened the door for his friends, several strings of tiny sea shells attached on the inside gently resonated and announced their presence. Megan removed her hood, happy to be inside where it was warmer. Two other customers quietly examined the merchandise.

A man of about fifty with a mop of black hair matted down on his head looked up from the back of the room, his gray shirt splattered with bits of dried wax. "Ah," he said with a smile, raising a finger. "With you in a moment. Just stringing up some wicks for my wife to start dipping." He softly called over his shoulder. "Nell, we have visitors."

A moment later a rosy-cheeked woman peeked out through a curtained doorway, her dark hair tied up with a blue and white striped kerchief. She approached the trio, smiling. "Good morning. Here to check on that *special order*?" she asked cheerfully as she smoothed the wrinkles out of her apron.

"Uh, yes," Leo said hesitantly. "Is it ready?"

"Nearly. Follow me." Nell glanced at her husband. "Aubrey, we'll be in the back. Keep an eye out here."

"Always do, my dear," he replied, slicing up chunks of beeswax for melting as his wife and the three visitors disappeared behind the curtain.

The back room was almost twice the size of the front, lined with shelves stuffed with wooden boxes of wax blocks, wick rolls and dye powders. A single window allowed in the early noontime light that splashed across several work tables. Nicholas' heart leapt when he saw Ivy standing near the window, the sun's glow gently highlighting her soft fair skin. When she smiled, he couldn't conceal a boyish grin.

"Well, fellow conspirators, so far, so good," Ivy quietly said, quickly introducing everyone to her Aunt Nell. "Uncle Aubrey will keep watch for us out front."

"Ivy already explained everything to us," Nell said, offering a slight curtsey to Megan. "Pleased to meet you. Though forgive me for not using your proper title." She glanced at the doorway and whispered. "Never know who might be listening."

Megan blushed, slightly embarrassed. "Thank you for your kindness and assistance, Nell. But please, think of me only as another customer. No need to treat me differently from anybody else who walks into your shop."

"Oh, I could never do that!" she said, nervously fidgeting her fingers.

"Leo and I will give you some lessons," Nicholas joked, approaching Ivy.

"I'm sure you boys would," Megan replied, glancing at Leo as if expecting a wisecrack in response.

"I'm not saying a word," he replied. "Not a single word."

"Wise policy," she said lightly. Megan then addressed Ivy with a mix of anxiety and appreciation for what she was about to do. "Are you sure you want to go through with this? Part of me thinks we're making a big fuss over nothing."

"I'm happy to do it," she said.

"We must, dear," Nell added, shaking her head. "After what Ivy told me, I'm convinced beyond a doubt that you need our protection. Our family will be honored to be in your service."

Nell indicated to Megan that she should remove her cloak. Megan reluctantly did so, handing it to Ivy to again try on as she had done in the sitting room the night before. Ivy draped the heavy, dark blue material over her shoulders, set the hood upon her light brown hair and wrapped the folds about her.

"No one will be the wiser," Ivy playfully whispered. "And we're nearly the same height, too, Meg. If any individuals are keeping an eye on your movements though the village, they'll have no reason to doubt that it is you walking back to Castella's house. Use mine until I can get this back to you," she said, pointing to a light brown cloak hanging on a wall peg near the doorway. She flipped the hood off her head and smiled. "This plan will be flawless."

"Rest assured, I won't take my eyes off of you for a moment," Nicholas said, feeling overly protective of Ivy.

"And what about Meg?" Leo asked. Uneasiness crept over him when he realized that he would have to leave her alone.

"She'll stay here with us until nightfall," Nell explained. "Then Aubrey and I will take her home when we close up shop. You needn't worry, Leo. Megan will be safe. In a day or two we can arrange transportation to get her out of Boros under the cover of darkness and back home where she belongs."

"It *sounds* like a good plan," he said, still not fully convinced. He hated having Megan out of his sight and hoped she felt the same way about him.

Ivy noted the worry etched upon his face. "She will be safe, Leo. Trust us."

"Maybe we're overlooking the obvious," Nicholas jumped in, hoping to put Leo and Megan at ease. "We don't need to arrange other transportation. If Leo and I depart from Aunt Castella's in the morning and leave Boros, then whoever is chasing after Meg will believe she has remained here." He glanced at Nell. "If your husband will take her to the next village east of here during the night, we can pick her up there tomorrow."

"Laurel Corners," Ivy said. "My folks live there. Megan could stay with them until you arrive."

"We'll take you back to my parents' home from there," Leo confidently told her. "You can remain there until we figure out how to get you back to Morrenwood."

Megan sighed. "I'm starting to feel like a piece of luggage again."

"But a well-protected piece of luggage," Nicholas joked.

A short time later, after Leo said goodbye to Megan in private, he returned to the front room where Nicholas and Ivy awaited. He appeared sad and distant, wondering if Megan could ever truly be a part of his life.

Suddenly Megan peeked through the curtain, signaling for Ivy. She hurried into the back room, wondering what Megan could want. Nicholas and Leo patiently waited until Ivy returned a few moments later, finally ready to leave.

"What was that all about?" Nicholas asked.

"She forgot to tell me something," Ivy whispered while adjusting her cloak. "Best not to talk about it here. Ready?"

Leo thanked Nell and Aubrey for all of their help and was assured that Megan would be waiting for them in Laurel Corners the following morning. After Ivy donned the cloak hood once again, she, Nicholas and Leo stepped out of the candle shop into the cool afternoon, prepared to visit more stores along the lane in order to cement their illusion into the minds of any who might be watching.

A couple hours later, after they had enjoyed some shopping and a supper of stew and bread in an out-of-the-way establishment, Ivy decided it was time to return home. They stepped outside into the approaching twilight. "Castella will be more than worried by now. And if anyone was spying on us from a distance, I'm sure they're convinced it is Megan who is still walking with you two boys. My face and hair are well concealed in the folds of this hood."

"Both of which are too pretty to be hidden," Nicholas said as he awkwardly fished out a small wrapped package inside his coat. He handed it to Ivy.

"What's this?" she asked.

"A little something I picked up in one of the shops while you weren't looking," he said. "Consider it a thank you gift for all the help you've given us."

"That's not necessary." She untied the string around the white cloth wrapping, revealing a small gauzy scarf tinted with the colors of autumn. "Oh, how lovely, Nicholas! Thank you."

"I wanted you to have it."

Ivy smiled. "I'll think about you every time I use it to tie up my hair."

"Or when you wipe away a dab of dirt on your cheek from bringing in the firewood," he playfully suggested.

"Very funny."

Nicholas took her arm in his as the gray shadows deepened. Orange sunlight splashed the cobblestone road and the sides of a string of tired shops. Lighted candles had been placed in several windows of nearby homes, and a few outdoor oil lamps along some of the wider streets were being lit. Above the gentle waves washing upon the shore of Sage Bay, seagulls cried in their restless flight.

After several minutes had passed, Nicholas couldn't help but notice the uneasy silence that had gripped Leo since they left the candle shop. Ivy observed his anxious state as well and tenderly squeezed his hand. "She'll be safe, Leo. Uncle Aubrey will not let Megan out of his sight."

Leo tried to smile as they turned a corner down a quiet lane dotted with a few trees and some low shrubbery. "My mind tells me that that's true," he said as some people passed them by in the opposite direction. Shadows thickened as the sound of horse hooves echoed in the distance. "But my heart is having a more difficult time accepting it."

"You only have to get through this one night," Nicholas said.

Suddenly Leo had an idea. "Maybe I should return later tonight and help Aubrey escort Meg to Laurel Corners," he eagerly suggested.

"Let's keep to our plan," Ivy cautioned.

"I agree," Nicholas said as they ambled past a string of small stone houses, many with their windows darkened. A glimpse of the distant water could be seen in the small openings between the buildings. Two figures, cloaked in the shadows, followed them from behind, though they kept their distance. "We'll only draw suspicion if you leave Castella's house in the middle of the night."

"I suppose you're right." Leo glanced up at the sky as the Bear Moon, nearly at first quarter, drifted westward. The full Fox Moon had not yet risen in the east. When he looked up the street again, he noticed that two people had just turned the corner into the lane and headed in their direction. "And I suppose it's going to be a very long night, too."

"You'll survive," Nicholas said lightly, trying to cheer his friend though empathizing with his plight.

He glanced at Ivy, happily noticing that she was looking his way. She squeezed Nicholas' arm and he felt an unspoken bond between them grow suddenly stronger. He looked forward to knowing Ivy better, yet wondered what might become of this budding relationship if he departed in the morning. Ever since leaving Kanesbury nine days ago, his life had been a constant whirlwind. He wondered if he was merely hanging on, allowing himself to be swept away by events and emotions to avoid facing his troubles back home. Or did the people he recently met really mean something to him, especially Ivy? Walking beside her, he felt an undeniable sense of joy and knew that it must be so.

Before he could think more about it, Nicholas realized that the two people approaching them had suddenly quickened their step. He felt unnerved and instinctively glanced behind him. Leo did likewise. The two other figures who were tailing them also moved faster now, stalking the trio like a pair of hungry wolves. Nicholas grabbed Ivy's hand, his heart beating wildly as he silently vowed to protect her with his very life.

"What's happening?" she breathlessly asked.

Leo pointed to their right, indicating a narrow lane that opened up ahead. Nicholas nodded, knowing they'd have just enough time to turn onto that street before any of their pursuers in front or behind could reach them.

"*Now!*" Nicholas whispered, tightening his grip on Ivy's hand as Leo kept watch over her from the opposite side.

They hurried around the corner and down a deserted side street which was fully engulfed in the evening gloom. Lit candles in some of the windows provided the only light to guide them. The echo of distant footsteps filled the air like the buzz of annoying insects, growing louder as they sped down a cobblestone path.

"Turn left up ahead," Leo said, hoping the next street might be busier and provide them a means of escape or assistance. He craned his neck back, seeing the devilish glint of firelight reflect off the eyes of their four pursuers.

"Just a few more steps!" Nicholas whispered to Ivy, his mind clear and sharp as it suppressed bitter anger below the surface. He felt a surge of confidence that they would gain the upper hand as soon as they cleared this lane and bolted onto the wider street ahead.

Then a harsh turn of events overwhelmed them.

Four more shadowy figures emerged from around the corner up ahead and barreled toward Nicholas, Ivy and Leo with terrifying silence, barely allowing them time enough to stop. They knew that a retreat in the opposite direction was impossible just as the swarm of hunters crashed over them like a giant wave.

Nicholas heard Ivy frantically scream as he was dragged to the ground, feeling the cold press of cobblestone to his face. He grabbed someone by the leg, pulling him down as he scrambled to his feet, catching Leo out of the corners of his eyes being pushed against a stone wall. Nicholas lunged forward to help his friend, jumping on the back of one of their attackers and pulling him to the ground. As Nicholas rolled on his back, the candlelight in a nearby window reflected off the face of a man standing nearby who calmly observed the four men who were fighting Nicholas and Leo. His thin eyebrows and sunken cheeks made him appear cold and calculating. Nicholas sprang to his feet just as another man stumbled backward over him after being pushed by Leo, causing Nicholas to fall down on one knee and wince.

"*Sorry!*" Leo called out just as two more men lunged at him and dragged him farther down the middle of the street. Their attackers seemed less intent on harming them than merely delaying them.

Nicholas rushed to help Leo before the two men on the ground could interfere. But a moment later they were on top of him again, dragging Nicholas down as he struggled to keep his stance. He could still see that fifth man hanging off in the distance, patiently watching. Then his foot was kicked out from under him. Nicholas plummeted to the road, wondering where the last three men had gone to when he heard another muffled scream in the distance. It was Ivy. In the cold pit of his stomach, he knew the horrid answer. Those last three men were whisking her away.

"They've got Megan!" Nicholas shouted, having wits enough not to mention Ivy's name as a fierce anger boiled inside him.

He yanked his arm away from one of his attackers and thrust a fist into the man's jaw. A burst of searing pain shot up Nicholas' arm as the man groaned, rolling onto his side. Nicholas jabbed an elbow in the other man's chest and jumped to his feet, stepping over the injured bodies before rushing to Leo's aid. But before he could help his friend, Nicholas was slammed in his side and shoved against the corner of a stone house, falling to the ground as his shoulder burned with white-hot pain. He looked up in a semi-daze, recognizing the man who had pushed him. The stranger's vacant observing eyes looked upon him for an instant before he sprinted off, signaling for the other four to follow. The two men on the ground jumped up and trailed their leader down the street. Leo's two attackers saw their companions flee and shoved Leo to the ground before following them to the end of the lane. All disappeared around the corner. Leo struggled to his feet and hurried over to check on Nicholas who held onto his shoulder in obvious pain.

"You okay?" Leo asked, breathing heavily.

"Still alive," he said, his head feeling on fire. After Leo offered him a hand up, Nicholas glanced down the street. The five men had disappeared. He looked down the other end of the lane and indicated for Leo to follow. "They took Ivy this way! The other three men took Ivy this way," he said with desperation, his voice cracking.

"Let's go!" Leo said, sprinting down the cobblestones.

He and Nicholas emerged onto the next street which was nearly as quiet as the previous one though better illuminated with a few oil lamps. A handful of pedestrians walked along in the distance.

"Split up!" Nicholas said, on the verge of panic. He raced in one direction while waving wildly for Leo to go the opposite way.

Nicholas glanced between the houses and shops as he sprinted past, scanning the faces of passersby and listening for the sound of Ivy's voice. But no call was forthcoming. He stopped several individuals on the next street, frantically asking if they had seen a young woman in a cloak with three men. But none had, and so he stumbled forward though the deepening gloom with his tortured thoughts, stopping now and then to look and listen, retracing his steps or wandering in circles. He knew that every passing second was sending Ivy further and further into some unimaginable doom. Soon he couldn't think straight and found it a struggle to breathe. A cold night breeze glided off the sea waves and brushed across his face, drying a teardrop that had streamed down his cheek.

Leo found Nicholas a half hour later wandering aimlessly along a side street, quiet and grim. Both had retraced their steps several times and had even searched along the main road near the sea, all to no avail. There was no sign of Ivy or any of the eight men who had attacked them. Nicholas felt as if she had disappeared from the face of Laparia altogether.

"She's gone..." he finally muttered, his heart beating painfully and his eyes filled with wild fear, not expecting Leo to provide the slightest bit of good news. "What do we do now?" he asked as full darkness descended, making him feel like a tiny speck in a vast and turbulent ocean. "What do we do *now*?"

CHAPTER 18

Visitors from the North

Ivy opened her eyes in darkness, not aware of how many hours she had been sleeping. She heard a mournful breeze whistling through cracks in the door and thought she detected the sound of waves along the seashore, wondering if she might still be in Boros. She sat up with a struggle, her hands tied behind her back, her feet tightly bound. A pungent scent of wild herbs and stale vegetables lingered in the air. Just where had those three men taken her? And what had happened to Nicholas and Leo?

Moments later she heard voices, whispered bits of conversation as someone removed a wooden bar outside the door. Slowly it opened, allowing a cool breeze to sweep inside the abandoned root cellar. Pale light from an oil lamp cast shadows upon the walls and low ceiling as two figures approached. Both were short in stature, though one, a woman, appeared thinner and more elegant. The other, a slightly stocky man who carried the lamp, seemed less concerned with his appearance.

He walked toward Ivy and held the light close to her. A sickly yellow glow emanated through a series of vertical scores cut into the copper plates surrounding the flame. The man briefly examined her face and signaled for the woman to take a look.

"Here she is," he said matter-of-factly. "What do you think?"

The woman advanced, wrapped in a dark cloak lined with fox fur. She leaned forward, studying Ivy's features with a pair of inquisitive eyes set beneath locks of flaming red hair wrapped in a black silk kerchief with stitching of fine gold.

"So this is who they delivered to me," Madeline said, more to herself than to the others. "And after all this time…"

"Who are you?" Ivy asked defiantly. "And where am I?"

"We are outside the village of Cavara Beach, about five miles west of Boros," she said. "And as for who I am–"

"Release me at once! I don't care who you are."

"Such anger in your voice," Madeline calmly said, standing back while massaging her chin and remembering events from twenty years ago. "It's been such a long time since we last met. I thought you'd be happy to see me again."

Mune, holding the oil lamp, stepped back and chuckled. "That was quite humorous coming from your lips. Why, you've nearly cracked a joke," he said with delight. Madeline looked at him askance. Even in the pre-dawn gloom, Mune could see in her eyes that she wasn't in the mood for his banter. "Sorry…"

"What do you want with me?" Ivy said, struggling to get up. "I demand an answer!"

Madeline held up a hand to calm her. "And you shall have one, Megan. Trust me."

Ivy felt her heart beating rapidly, realizing that these people thought she was Princess Megan. She was both pleased and terrified at the same time. They truly believed that she was King Justin's granddaughter, at least in the shadows of this root cellar. But since the woman said she hadn't seen her in some time, Ivy felt a growing confidence about getting away with the charade. She then wondered if other associates in her kidnappers' circle might know more information about the princess, including what she looks like. Ivy's confidence waned. Perhaps she would be discovered in short order. Perhaps the switch wasn't such a good idea after all.

"Why do you call me by that name?" she asked, believing that by denying Megan's identity she might fully convince her captors that she was the princess. "My name is Ivy."

Madeline smiled in the pale light. "Of course it is, my dear. My name is Madeline, by the way. And though you probably won't remember me, I used to be your nursemaid when you were an infant."

"What are you talking about?" she scoffed, recalling that Megan had mentioned Madeline's name in Castella's house. "My mother tended to me while I grew up on our farm, as she did with all my brothers and sisters. She couldn't afford to hire a nursemaid even if she had wanted to."

Madeline smirked. "Nice try. But your deception will not fool me, Megan. I know who you are. You cannot hide your true identity. Dell Hawks, my old associate inside the Citadel, knows who you are. He had been following you and those two farmhands for a few days. He hired the men who kidnapped you in Boros."

Ivy sighed. "Well you've kidnapped the wrong person, so please release me. If you'd like, get that Dell Hawks fellow to come back and identify me."

"Sorry, but he's off to war in the south," she replied. "More lucrative opportunities down there. Your kidnapping was only a spur-of-the-moment operation."

"I am not this Princess Megan you speak of."

Mune glanced at Madeline, slightly unnerved. "Do we have the right girl?"

She grimaced. "Of course we do, Mune! She's just posturing, hoping to convince us otherwise."

"I'm telling the truth!" Ivy insisted. "I'm not a princess. What a preposterous story."

"Of course you're not," Madeline replied. "And I suppose you've never been to Morrenwood either? Nor looked upon the Blue Citadel framed against the majestic pines and the Trent Hills?"

"Never," Ivy said, her voice emitting the slightest quiver.

Madeline intently studied the girl's face, searching for the truth. "If you're suffering from a bout of amnesia, then I believe you, my dear. But there is more than one way to discover your identity."

"I don't know what you mean," Ivy replied, averting her eyes from Madeline's penetrating gaze.

"Perhaps *this* will refresh your memory." She bent down and gently lifted Ivy's cloak, pushing it back from her shoulders to reveal the collar of her blouse and the scarf Nicholas had given to her.

"What are you doing? Leave me alone! Though we are of the same age, I am not Megan," she insisted. "You have to believe me!"

"My dear girl, I never mentioned the age of the princess," Madeline said. "But thanks for the added confirmation."

Madeline hooked a finger behind Ivy's neck and felt the touch of cool metal. Mune watched in fascination as the lamp flickered. A moment later, she lifted a gold chain up over Ivy's head. Attached to it was a silver medallion that she removed from her prisoner. Mune brought the light closer so they could examine the find.

"What is it?" he asked, eager to see the treasure.

"Proof," Madeline said, eyeing the etching of the Citadel and a winding river among the pine trees and mountains. She flipped the piece over and smiled as the image of a galloping horse under two rising full moons stared back at her.

"It's quite stunning," Mune said, glancing at Ivy. "Too bad the rising full moons aren't bringing you any good fortune today."

Madeline smirked. "All members of the royal bloodline receive one on the day of their birth."

"I– I found it on the roadside," Ivy said, not sounding particularly convincing. "I'll sell it to you!"

"Enough said." Madeline gently draped the medallion back over Ivy's head. "A princess of Arrondale shouldn't be parted from such a beautiful heirloom, *hmmm*?"

Ivy scowled and turned her head.

"So she's a princess after all," Mune said, calculating her use and value in his mind. "Now what do we do with her?"

"We load her onto the wagon and continue our journey. It'll be a long and miserable ride over some uncomfortable terrain, so let's get going."

"Can't wait," he grumbled.

"Where are you taking me?" Ivy demanded to know, locking gazes with Madeline. "You will not get away with this. I have very powerful friends."

"As do we. In fact, we're on our way to meet some of our friends visiting from the north," she said, taking the oil lamp from Mune so he could untie Ivy's feet and assist her out the door. "I know you'll be pleased to make their acquaintance."

They departed in the windy darkness before dawn, rattling away on a small covered wagon drawn by a pair of horses and guided by the light of two oil lamps affixed to the front. Ivy remained tied up in the wagon, lying on the floorboards, her head resting upon the folds of an old blanket. She felt satisfied that she had convinced Madeline and Mune that she was Princess Megan, but the ramifications of her actions were only beginning to sink in. What would be her fate now that the King's enemies believed they had his granddaughter captive? A sense of impending doom slowly encroached upon her.

At last the main road out of Cavara Beach came to an end. From there they would travel over hard-packed dirt paths where they could find them, providing that a sudden rain storm wouldn't clog up the way with mud and cause them a severe delay. The horses trotted north toward the edge of the Trillium Sea and then headed west along the grasslands, a harsh unpopulated region of the kingdom. Thin stretches of stone and sand beaches bordered a boundless field of tall brittle grass, all plagued by cold winds and gray skies for many months of the year.

For nearly two and a half days the trio slogged onward, seeking out hardened paths parallel to the beaches or sometimes through the grass itself where the snarling vegetation grew particularly low and unobstructing to the wagon wheels. Madeline occasionally ordered a stop to rest the horses or to partake in a brief meal from some of the food supplies packed for the trip. Late into the first night, Mune built a small fire to sleep by, though only for a few hours since the wood supply they carried was limited and finding a piece of driftwood along shore was a rarity. Well before dawn had broken, they joylessly journeyed on in the chilly darkness under thick gray clouds as the peaks of the Trent Hills grew in the distant west.

Ivy was allowed to travel with her wrists tied in front of her since Madeline didn't fear an escape attempt while in this desolate terrain. Ivy, however, knew that she wouldn't survive the elements if she ever tried to flee. But maybe someone would rescue her, she thought, blindly hoping that Nicholas and Leo would miraculously pick up her trail. But how could they, she depressingly wondered, feeling they would have located her by now if they were ever going to. Ivy touched the scarf Nicholas bought for her in Boros. She had tied it around her neck, feeling a connection to him as her fingers caressed the fine material. Then an idea struck her, though she admitted to herself that it was just a fanciful dream. She untied the small knot in the scarf and removed it, holding it near the back opening in the cart so that the material fluttered in the passing breeze.

"Nicholas..." she whispered, releasing the scarf. It sailed down the road, twisting in a salty current of air until finally landing against the tall stalks of grass along the edge of the stony shore. Though Ivy convinced herself that it would be impossible, she imagined Nicholas one day finding the scarf and returning it to her. That tiny glimmer of hope sustained her for only a short while.

As the journey continued, Ivy again grew despondent with the blandness of the unchanging scenery and the stubborn secretiveness of Madeline and Mune. Neither proved very talkative during this trip, and with the constant sea breezes taunting them, she was unable to hear the bits of conversation that passed between them while they guided the horses along their weary way. She felt that she may as well have been alone.

The second day of traveling mirrored the first–cold, gray and monotonous. A bit of sunshine peeked out on the third day, and by late afternoon the clouds had broken. As the sun dipped in the west at twilight's approach, the line of clouds above the distant Trent Hills took on subtle shades of purple and orange along their wispy edges. The Bear Moon, just beyond first quarter, climbed high in the east, while the Fox Moon, a few days past full, had not yet risen. Ivy detected the subtle glow of the larger moon through the light fabric covering the wagon, wondering if Nicholas and Leo were gazing upon it as they looked for her outdoors. Had Uncle Aubrey and Aunt Nell joined in the search as well? Was anybody concerned with her whereabouts? Such notions drifted about in her mind, though Ivy repeatedly told herself that someone must be looking. She made herself believe this as the bitter sea breezes battered the covered cart.

As the sun descended behind the blackened peaks, Ivy detected voices in the distance. She sat up and looked out the front opening, noticing Mune was pointing toward the water. She couldn't see anything in the gloomy distance upon the sea from this vantage point, though she noted a glow of firelight up ahead as the wagon began to slow.

"Where are we?" she asked.

Madeline glanced back. "Our friends are here. Right on time."

Mune reined the horses to a halt, jumped off the wagon and offered a hand to assist Madeline down. He quickly ran around to the back and helped Ivy disembark.

"Now behave, princess, and there'll be no trouble," Mune whispered, taking her by the arm and leading her around the wagon. "Folk from the Northern Isles are rumored to be a quarrelsome, ill-tempered lot—and those are their good qualities. So mind yourself."

"I'll behave as I wish," she muttered.

"No. You'll behave as you're told," Madeline said, pointing a finger at her as she and Mune approached the others. The horses restlessly stomped in place, eager to run through the tall grass. "I have an important meeting with Commander Uta, and if you wish to complicate it, then you'll suffer the consequences. Understood?"

Ivy saw a ruthless fire burning in Madeline's eyes and knew that the woman would not hesitate for a second to harm her if she should interfere with her plans. She took a slow breath and muttered a single word. "Understood."

"Good. We know each other's mind, so let's meet our hosts," she said. "Don't give me cause to bind your hands behind you."

Madeline trudged toward a few small round tents in the distance. Unending waves of tall grass reaching shoulder high to most men bordered the area to their left. The glow of a large bonfire danced upon the grass stalks and the coarse tent material, both undulating in the breezes off the water. Mune and Ivy followed Madeline, observing several tall men wandering about, some engrossed in conversation while a few kept watch in the shadowy perimeter. A shower of sparks flew into the air as someone tossed a piece of wood upon the fire, causing Ivy to glance up at the mini burst of fireworks. That's when she noticed a large ominous hulk floating upon the water in the deepening gloom. Anchored just offshore was the large wooden ship that had carried these men from the Northern Isles, its three tall masts standing bare against a charcoal sky like tall and lanky skeletal remains.

"So Caldurian sends his favorite underling to deal with me," a gruff voice called out. "As if I don't deserve the wizard's full attention for my part in his grand schemes."

Madeline sighed as she approached the man. "Caldurian has his hands full in Montavia, so don't whine, Commander Uta. It doesn't become you."

"I suppose not," he replied, removing the hood of his long brown coat. The tall man seemed to loom over Madeline and Mune, grinning through several days' growth of beard as the wind tossed his thick tangles of unkempt hair. He smoked a pipe and a sword hung lifelessly at his side.

"This is Mune, by the way," she added, pointing a thumb behind her shoulder. "My associate."

"Thanks for that eloquent introduction," he uttered, fingering his coat collar.

"Can we speak in private?" Madeline asked.

"Near the first fire," Uta said, indicating an area beyond the tents. "Lok! Burlu!" he called out. "Join us." The commander glanced at Madeline. "*My* associates." He stared curiously at Ivy, noting her hands tied in front. "Who is this girl? A prisoner?"

"A possible bargaining tool," Madeline said. "I'll explain shortly."

"Do so."

Mune uncomfortably cleared his throat. "Yes, about her. Is there a place we can confine her for the moment? I don't think she should be privy to our discussion."

Commander Uta nodded. "There's an empty tent that'll do. Kalik!" he shouted.

A soldier ran up and nodded at Uta. "Sir?"

"Put this woman inside one of the tents," he ordered, grabbing Ivy by the arm.

Ivy tried to yank herself away, glaring at the man. "Do you mind, sir? I'll have you know–"

He leaned in, nose to nose with her, his tightening grip and bitter breath causing her to wince. "What I mind are unnecessary words uttered by annoying young women. I don't know you. I don't want to know you. But that one has brought you along for some reason," he said, indicating Madeline. "So until I get all the facts, do as you're told and keep your words to yourself. Do I make sense?"

Ivy nodded, swallowing hard. "Yes."

"Good." He handed her off to Kalik. "Stand guard outside the tent. No one approaches or talks to her. If anyone does, he'll be hanging by his wrists over the side of the ship. Understood?"

"Completely, sir." The man swiftly led Ivy away through a throng of soldiers loitering about the stony beach, all wondering who the young woman was and where she had come from.

"Follow me," Uta said to Madeline and Mune, hiking swiftly to the first bonfire nearest to shore and away from the taller grass. Two other men, similarly dressed as Uta, hurriedly caught up and followed. As they gathered near the fire, Uta introduced the two men as Lok and Burlu, two captains under his command. Lok, nearly the same age as Uta, had a subdued eagerness in his dark eyes set within a wind-burned face underneath some straggly, thinning hair. A small scar ran across his left cheek just near the earlobe.

"Captain Burlu is heading farther west to Karg Island to oversee our activities on the Lorren River," Uta said, introducing the younger of the two captains who merely nodded in reply. "He will replace the current administrator there."

"Though he may already be dead from boredom," Lok commented with a snicker.

Commander Uta sighed wearily. "Captain Lok will accompany me and the others on our primary mission."

"Glad I have that to look forward to," Lok replied, his words laced with sarcasm. He ground a small stone into the dirt with the toe of his boot. "I may have been cheated out of a command, but at least I won't get stuck being a bureaucrat like you, eh, Burlu?"

"Be thankful it *isn't* you," Commander Uta said, throwing a sharp stare at his scowling captain.

Mune sensed a bit of tension between Uta and Lok and hoped to diffuse it with a question. "Commander, what is the nature of your operation on the Lorren River?" he asked, sitting down on a rock near the fire.

"The Northern Isles are providing soldiers and supplies up the Lorren on rafts into Kargoth. Our tribute to Vellan," he said with a roll of his eyes. "We shall see what dividends it pays us in the future. We coordinate everything from Karg Island, a small desolate patch we've confiscated just off shore."

"More like a prison," Lok muttered. "See how wonderfully you're rewarded, Burlu, for all of your years of service to the Isles. A job behind a desk!"

Uta grabbed Lok, clamping his fingers tightly about his shoulder. "Your unsubtle jokes are starting to annoy me," he said. "It is not my fault that you were passed over to command this mission, Lok. Maybe it's a result of the poor attitude you constantly carry around. Just be thankful you are still part of the mission." The commander glared at his captain before releasing him. "Now on with business."

"Yes, let's," Madeline said, a hint of boredom in her tone. "Save your petty squabbles for another time. We're here to discuss the job Caldurian hired you for."

"What are the particulars?" Uta asked.

"We need you to lead one hundred of your finest soldiers–in secret–down through the Trent Hills for an attack on King Justin's residence in Morrenwood," she said.

"The Blue Citadel?" Commander Uta burst out laughing. "As much as I take pride in the fighting ability of my men, one hundred soldiers will not take and hold the Citadel. That idea is sheer lunacy. Caldurian's plan, no doubt. It's no wonder he failed miserably in his attempt to take Arrondale twenty years ago. A clever wizard he may be, but a military tactician he is not."

Madeline closed her eyes for a moment before stepping away and ripping out several pieces of grass nearby. She twirled them up into a compact ball as she returned, the moisture magically dissipating from the vegetation as she did so. "The aggressive nature of a soldier from the Northern Isles may be legend, Commander Uta, but as I stand here, I realize that you and your ilk lack one important quality–imagination."

Suddenly the ball of grass was enveloped in a deep reddish-orange glow and then burst into a controlled flame. Madeline lifted her open palm and whispered a few words, sending the fiery mass sailing through the air with a shrieking whistle. The burning sphere landed near the water, rolling for several yards until it was finally extinguished by a gentle wave lapping upon the shore.

"Impressive..." Uta whispered.

"I would be more impressed if you had faith in our plan," she replied. "We don't need you to take the Blue Citadel for keeps. This will be a quick raid with a specific purpose, the full details to be provided when appropriate."

Uta grimly smiled. "You have me intrigued, Madeline. What can you tell me now?"

"I can tell you that Caldurian will more than make up for his past errors in judgment. We will take the kingdom of Arrondale in the end," she assured him.

"And how do my troops engineer the beginning of this strategy?" Uta questioned, still a bit of a skeptic.

"You must lead them through the Trent Hills, traveling only at night," Mune said, leaning back to stretch his legs. "You must remain invisible. Let the wilderness conceal you until you are called upon. We'll provide the details about where to take your men, and there you'll remain holed up until called upon."

Uta scowled as he rubbed his whiskers. "For how long?"

"Until we are ready for you," Madeline said flatly.

"I need time to gather my men and prepare."

"You shall be well compensated," she said. "Is there a problem?"

"Yes, Uta, is there a problem?" Captain Lok asked pointedly. "Can you handle the situation?"

Uta snarled at Lok and raised a fist, but held his punch before turning to Madeline. "I must first sail to Karg Island to finish my business there and get men and supplies–"

"Yes, yes!" Mune said, standing up and warming his hands by the fire. "We didn't expect you to leave this very minute. We just need you and your men in place before the end of autumn. That'll give you several weeks to work out the details. Caldurian must finish his work in Montavia first."

"Very good then," he replied. "You'll have what you wish."

Captain Lok grunted. "So we needn't worry about the success of our mission, Uta, now that you have time to get all those pesky details in order." He casually picked the dirt out from under a fingernail. "Unless, of course, you would prefer to stay on Karg Island in Burlu's place and let me lead this mission in your stead. I'll be happy to command it while you attend to those less nerve-racking tasks on the Lorren River."

Commander Uta smiled bitterly in the glow of the firelight, having had enough of Lok's incessant whining. "Thanks for the suggestion, but I'm afraid you won't be able to take my place on this mission, Lok, since there's been a change in plans."

"A change?" he asked. "What are you talking about?"

"Since you presume to know much about the administrative duties on Karg Island, I'm sending you there instead of Burlu," he told him with calm satisfaction. "Burlu will instead accompany me through the Trent Hills."

Lok started to laugh, believing that Uta was attempting a joke, though not entirely sure. "Your sense of humor is not as sharp as your sword, Uta."

"Perhaps not, but I wasn't trying to be humorous." He rubbed his whiskers. "I've grown weary of your constant complaining and disrespect, Lok, and should have left you back on the Isles. Well, now you will have your own island to command."

Lok sputtered. "You can't do that to me! I'm a captain. I deserve this mission."

"Burlu is a captain also, and has sense enough to keep his mouth shut and not embarrass me," Uta said. "But more importantly, I am commander, and my authority outranks you both. So you'll do as I say unless you'd rather spend the rest of your time here locked up in the cargo hold. Your choice!"

Lok silently fumed as the fire highlighted the tight furrows on his brow. He glared at Burlu who merely returned the slightest trace of a smile. "Why, I should–"

"–save your argument for another time!" Madeline said with an icy stare. "We have more issues to discuss." Lok glared at her and went silent. "Good. Now before we hash out the details of the raid, Uta, we need to talk about the girl."

"Who is she?" he asked, glancing at the tent near the grass where she was being held. "What's she got to do with all this?"

Mune chuckled. "That girl, my dear commander, is King Justin's granddaughter, Princess Megan."

Uta shook his head doubtfully. "You speak nonsense."

"He speaks the truth," Madeline said. "She is the princess. How we obtained her is not important, but she may come in handy should our mission be compromised."

"I will not fail in the mission!" he snapped, feeling insulted.

"Most likely not," Madeline replied. "But we can use the girl as part of a backup plan just in case."

"All we need is a place to keep her out of the way for a time," Mune said. "And unharmed. Your ship perhaps?"

"Fine," he agreed. "But I can go one better. I know the perfect place to hide the princess," Commander Uta said, glancing at Lok with a snake-like grin. "Captain Lok, this is your lucky day."

Lok looked up, still stinging from being booted off the mission. "*Oh?*"

"Not only are you gaining the exciting administrative duties on Karg Island," he said with boundless glee, "but you are hereby promoted to a newly created position most suited for your talents."

"And what position is that?" he hesitantly asked.

"Royal babysitter," Uta replied. "And don't foul it up!"

CHAPTER 19

Fifty Copper Pieces

Nicholas and Leo returned to Aunt Castella's house later that evening. Both were dazed by the turn of events as if caught in a bad dream from which they could not wake, yet they vowed to continue searching for Ivy all night. Nicholas apologized profusely, blaming himself for the devastating turn of events.

"If only we had headed home sooner or had taken a different route," he said, his face pale with worry. "But there were so many of them against us."

Castella saw the fear and heartbreak in his eyes, assuring him that they would find her. "The fault is not yours, Nicholas. Ivy and I dreamed up this plan," she said, touching her trembling fingers to her lips as she shook her head in dismay. She admitted they had made a terrible mistake. "We must get word to Ivy's aunt and uncle. They should be at home with Megan by now. They live close to the candle shop. And Ivy's parents need to know what happened, too. They're in Laurel Corners."

"We'll take care of the particulars," Leo promised, noting that Nicholas' thoughts seemed miles away at the moment. "We'll send word back as soon as we can."

"All right," she said with a quiver in her voice, offering to fix them a quick bite to eat. But as hungry as Nicholas and Leo were, they declined. Time was their enemy. Castella bid a teary-eyed farewell, hugging each of them as if they were her sons. She locked the door when they departed, wrapping her shawl about her shoulders as she wandered through the cold and empty rooms late into the night.

Nicholas explained to Aunt Nell and Uncle Aubrey what had happened a short time later. The color immediately drained from their faces as they sat around the table in the couple's kitchen. Megan was just as horrified, angry that she had allowed herself to take part in such a dangerous escapade.

"That's it!" she said. "I will no longer hide. It was selfish of me to agree to this ridiculous plan, and now Ivy is paying the price!"

"We'll find her," Leo said.

"You had better!" she angrily replied, instantly regretting her tone when she saw Leo recoil, appearing hurt. "I'm sorry. I didn't mean to react like that. It wasn't your fault. It's just that…" Megan shook her head and sighed. "It's just that so many lives have been turned upside down lately and it's all because of others' concern for my safety. Well, it ends now."

Leo placed a comforting hand on her shoulder. "It's all right. We've all been through a rough patch lately, but we'll find her. Still, I'd feel better if you stayed here for the night."

"Whoever kidnapped Ivy already believes she is me," Megan said. "I secretly gave her my royal medallion in the back room of the candle shop, so I don't imagine I'm in any danger at the moment." She noted the apprehension in Leo's eyes. "But for your peace of mind, I'll remain here until daylight."

Leo smiled. "It'd make me feel a whole lot better."

"And I'll feel better when we nab the scoundrels who did this," Aubrey said, repeatedly pounding a fist into his other hand. He promised to help Nicholas and Leo after he contacted his two sons. One he would send to Laurel Corners to inform Ivy's parents of the situation while the other would join him in the search. He promised to round up some of his other friends and the local authorities to help, too. If they had no success by midnight, they agreed to return here to figure out their next course of action.

"We're operating on the assumption that Ivy is still in Boros," Nicholas said, hoping with all his heart that it was true. "But what if they transported her out of the village? What do we do then? She could be anywhere."

No one knew how to answer his concern, though everyone feared that that possibility might have to be faced. Leo tapped Nicholas on the shoulder, wanting to divert his thoughts to the immediate search. "We'll figure it out," he said, heading to the front door. "But we best get going now."

"All right," he replied as he stepped outside into the autumn darkness, putting on a brave face though his confidence steadily waned. He felt cold and helpless, wondering if they were just going through the motions for the sake of doing something. Where would they even begin to look?

The Fox Moon, just shy of full, had since risen in the east, combining its light with the nearly first quarter Bear Moon hanging in the western sky. The extra illumination along the streets and shore provided Nicholas and Leo with a burst of added hope, though it faded quickly as they checked inside a string of empty fishing huts along the beach and received a series of shrugs and blank stares from passersby whom they had questioned.

"This is getting us nowhere!" Nicholas sputtered. "She could be anywhere in Kent County by now." They stood on a dirt road near the bay as a series of gentle waves lapped upon the shoreline. He glanced at Leo, feeling frightened and empty. "Tell me what we should do."

Leo was at a loss for words. He, too, wondered if their efforts were in vain but didn't reveal his thoughts to Nicholas. When he struggled to find some words of encouragement, an unexpected voice called to them in the darkness.

"Apparently your search isn't going well," a man said, walking toward them through the shadows along the dirt road. "I've been following you for some time."

"Who are you?" Nicholas asked, staring suspiciously at the individual dressed in a dark coat with stringy hair down to his shoulders. When the stranger stepped into the full moonlight, revealing his thin eyebrows and sunken cheeks, Nicholas' jaw dropped and his eyes grew wide with anger. He leaped at the man, grabbing the folds of his coat and shaking him. "Where is she!" he shouted as a stunned Leo looked on. "What'd you do to her?"

Leo pulled him away from the stranger as the man tried to break free. "What are you doing, Nicholas?"

"It's *him*, Leo!"

"Who?" he asked, holding Nicholas back. "What are you talking about?"

"He's one of the men who attacked us on the street earlier! I caught a glimpse of his face in the candlelight." Nicholas broke free of Leo's grip and lunged at the man once again, tackling him to the ground. "Where'd you take–Megan!" he shouted, his thoughts racing and his face as hot as fire. "Tell me now or I'll beat it out of you!"

"Hold it!" Leo said, grabbing Nicholas' clenched fist as he raised it in the air. "Let's question him first."

"Yes! Listen to your friend!" the man said, gasping for breath. "I have information about your friend. I can tell you where she is."

Nicholas released the man and stood up, signaling to Leo that he was sufficiently calmed down. Leo nodded and stepped back.

"Tell us your name," Leo said.

"You can call me Sims."

"You know where Megan is?" Nicholas bluntly added.

"Yes," he said, still catching his breath.

"And you'll tell us?"

"Yes," he repeated, standing up and brushing himself off. He stared at Nicholas and Leo as his eyes narrowed. "For a price."

Nicholas' face tightened. He clenched a fist at his side. "What'd you say?"

"Yeah, I don't think we heard you correctly," Leo added, his anger rising.

The stranger, brimming with smugness, smiled. "You both heard me. You'll get the information for a price." He raised a hand as Nicholas and Leo simultaneously stepped forward. "I know you could both attack me right now and beat me to near death–and I suppose I couldn't blame you. And I don't have my hired hands with me either. They've been paid off and dispersed."

"So you're at a disadvantage," Nicholas said.

"Not entirely," Sims replied. "I have the information you seek and time is fast running out."

"What do you mean?" Leo asked, glancing at Nicholas whose eyes welled with concern.

The man tucked his hands into his coat pockets to keep warm. "Though your friend is safe for the moment, she's not in the area. Your search of Boros is in vain."

"Tell us where you took her," Nicholas implored.

"Three of the men I hired transported her to an arranged location due west, though she will only remain there for a short while," he said. "Sometime before dawn she'll be picked up and taken away, though what her ultimate destination is, I cannot say."

"I suppose you're the one who planted the two spies on the bridge near Castella's house?" Nicholas asked.

"Of course. I had to keep an eye on my quarry, after all."

Leo fumed. "Why'd you kidnap Megan?"

"I was simply hired to do a job," he explained, recalling how Dell Hawks had recruited him the previous night in a local seedy tavern, paying him an advance of five silver half-pieces. "My employer has since paid me the balance for a job well done before fleeing south for more lucrative opportunities where the war rages."

"I hope a sword finds him swiftly," Nicholas said, restraining himself from attacking the man again.

"I don't understand," Leo said. "If the man hired you to kidnap our friend, then why did he head south without her?"

Sims chuckled. "He didn't have the girl kidnapped for himself, but for two other individuals. I don't know all the particulars of why he did so–nor wanted to, frankly–but I do know where your friend is being taken. And since my employer is no longer in the vicinity, I find that I have another lucrative opportunity before me."

Nicholas shook his head with disgust. "You think you're going to make money at both ends of your sick deal?"

"Why not?" he asked. "Though I'm certain you two don't have the financial means of that other gentleman, I'll wager you should be able to scrape up, say–forty copper pieces in a hurry? Your dear friend is worth that at least, right?"

Before Nicholas could lunge at the man, Leo stepped in front of his friend to calm him down. "This is no time to lose your temper."

"Wise policy," Sims remarked.

Then Leo spun around and plunged a fist into the man's gut, causing him to buckle to his knees. "Allow me instead."

"Leo!" Nicholas said in stunned amazement. He then addressed Sims who was bent over in agony. "You sure about those forty copper pieces?"

The man took several deep and difficult breaths while slowly getting to his feet, eyeing Leo and Nicholas with contempt. Then a snake-like smile spread across his face. "You got off a nice hit–and maybe I deserved it–but you won't get a second chance. More importantly though, I'm not easily intimidated. I still have the information you need, but now it'll cost you *fifty* copper pieces. And the miles between you and your friend are increasing. So care to make it sixty, or are you ready to deal?"

Nicholas and Leo both realized they had little bargaining power, and as precious time was running out, they agreed to Sims' demand. And though Nicholas at first objected, Leo insisted that he would use some of the money from his apple sales to cover the fifty copper pieces.

"We'll reimburse my parents the first chance we get," he said.

"*Fine...*" Nicholas agreed, slowly steaming as he glared at the man who held Ivy's fate in his hands. "Let's get this over with."

Leo explained to Sims that he first had to return to Castella's house to retrieve the money and get his two horses for the journey. The man agreed.

"Hurry back. I'll only wait here a short while," he said. "And remember, if you bring the authorities with you, you'll never see your friend again."

"We won't," Leo promised before hurrying off into the darkness with Nicholas. "I have a *better* plan," he whispered when they were out of the man's earshot. As they stood underneath an oil lamp on a deserted street corner, Leo quickly told Nicholas what they each had to do, sending him off to find Aubrey and his two sons while he returned to Castella's house. "Hurry back here as soon as possible so we can make the deal with Sims."

"All right," Nicholas said, sprinting down a cobblestone lane. "Hurry back yourself!"

"I plan to," he replied, disappearing into the darkness in the opposite direction.

A cool breeze rolled off the bay a short time later, brushing through a patch of tall dry grass along the dirt road. Nicholas and Leo emerged from the nearby shadows atop the two horses that once pulled Leo's apple cart. Stabs of moonlight revealed the subdued satisfaction upon Sims' face when he greeted them. Leo clutched a tiny cloth pouch and tossed it to him. The man caught it, nodding when he heard the muffled jingle of coins inside. He untied the leather drawstrings, poured a few of the copper pieces into his palm and counted them before briefly peering inside the pouch.

"Seems to be fifty pieces here," he said. "I'll trust you and won't count the rest."

"Oh, so that makes you an honorable thief and kidnapper?" Leo muttered.

"Where's Megan!" Nicholas demanded as he and Leo dismounted. "Tell us now."

Sims looked around to make certain they were alone. "Your lady friend was taken to an abandoned farm just outside the village of Cavara Beach," he said, giving them specific directions. "She's inside an old root cellar on the property. But like I said, the two individuals who paid for her kidnapping are supposed to retrieve her sometime before dawn. They're probably on their way there now. I was told they have a schedule to keep."

"Where are they taking her?" Leo asked. "Why do they want her?"

Sims pocketed the money and shrugged. "Those answers are beyond my knowledge, gentlemen. You wanted to know where she was taken and I told you. Our deal is completed."

Nicholas took a quick step toward Sims, tempted to grab him by the collar a second time, but restrained himself. The horses restlessly bobbed their heads in the cool autumn air. "You know nothing else? How could you not?"

Sims sighed and shook his head. "Look, I was only hired to grab the girl and transport her to a designated location. Nothing more, nothing less." He noted Nicholas' clenched fist, and wanting to end this transaction on a painless note, he relented a bit. "My employer did mention something about a waiting ship when we chatted, so I assume whoever arrives at the root cellar to get the girl will probably travel close to shore. But I can't tell you anything more because I *know* nothing more. Your best bet is to find the farmhouse before the others get there first. You have no other option."

Leo agreed and glanced at Nicholas, his expression indicating that they had garnered as much information as they were going to get. Now it was time to leave.

"Spend that money fast," Nicholas warned as he and Leo climbed back on their horses. "Because if we ever see your face again…"

"I think he gets the point," Leo said, gathering the reins as he stared down at Sims. "Now let's get out of here." He and Nicholas quickly trotted away as Sims looked on and chuckled.

"Fine work," he whispered to himself, patting the pouch of coins in his coat pocket.

He swiftly headed back into town to grab a bite to eat in a tavern and plan his journey south the following morning, anticipating better opportunities abroad. But as he turned a corner onto a narrow dirt lane a few minutes later, he thought he saw a dark shape dart though the shadows up ahead. He paused for a moment and spun around, sensing that someone was following him. Another figure slowly emerged into the moonlight filtering down in the lane directly in front of him.

"Now just where are you off to in such a hurry, Mr. Sims?" a deep voice asked.

Sims grunted. "As if it's any of your business? And how do you know my name?" He pulled out a dagger that glinted in the pale moonlight. "I don't think you want to get in my way, old man."

"Oh, but I think I do," Uncle Aubrey replied with a throaty chuckle. "And so do they," he added, pointing ahead.

Sims glanced over his shoulder as Aubrey's two sons stepped into the light, each holding a large walking stick that they emphatically pounded once onto the ground. At the same time, Uncle Aubrey pulled out a large knife from underneath his coat, casually picking off bits of wax stuck to the blade.

"I believe you have some money that belongs to a friend of ours," he softly said. "Fifty copper pieces? The three of us are hoping that you'll return it without incident so we can all go home in peace. I'm looking forward to a slice of mince pie my wife baked and don't want to keep her waiting."

Sims glared at Aubrey and his sons, his shoulders slumped in defeat. He slowly returned the knife to its sheath, muttering under his breath in the bitter night air as he reluctantly fished the pouch of copper pieces out of his coat pocket. He tossed the bag to Aubrey, listening as his money disappeared and knowing he must do the same before the next rising sun.

CHAPTER 20

The Grasslands

Nicholas and Leo hurried to Castella's house after leaving Sims. They grabbed a few provisions for their journey to Cavara Beach, hoping that Ivy would be there when they arrived at the farmhouse. Aunt Castella insisted that they eat first, so Nicholas and Leo sat down at the kitchen table for some soup, cheese and bread.

"Neither of you boys will be of any use if you don't keep up your strength," she said. "I've made up a sack with some dried beef, a few apples and several biscuits. That'll sustain you to the next village and back. And there are two filled water skins, too."

"Thanks, Castella," Nicholas said. "With any luck we'll have Ivy back here by noontime tomorrow."

"May it be so," she softly replied as she joined them at the table. She sipped from a cup of hot tea, steeped with worry. "I don't think sleep will find me tonight."

"Rest if you can. You need to keep up your strength as well," Leo reminded her, finishing his soup. "Now we must be off. It's past midnight and the Bear Moon has already set. We only have the Fox to guide us now."

"It's nearly full, so there'll be plenty of light unless the clouds roll in," she said. "But be careful regardless. The night roads can be treacherous."

NICHOLAS RAVEN AND THE WIZARDS' WEB - VOLUME 1

"We will," Nicholas said, putting on his coat and hugging her goodbye. Shortly after, he and Leo were on their horses in the cool night, heading for the main road.

"Be safe," Castella whispered as she watched them disappear into the gloom from her front doorstep. Moments later she went back inside to take refuge from the darkness, closing the door as she wistfully wondered where the warm sweet days of summer had gone.

The main road to the village of Cavara Beach proved to be a cold, dark and bumpy stretch, overrun in parts with dried grass, deep ruts and sharp stones. Low scraggly bushes encroached upon the sides, tinted shades of deathly gray in the moonlight. Nicholas and Leo progressed slowly on horseback, riding carefully so their steeds wouldn't injure themselves along the narrow course.

"Not the best maintained road in the county, is it," Nicholas muttered.

"I haven't made an apple delivery this way in two years," Leo said. "A lot of people have moved east to Boros and Laurel Corners where the fishing and farming are better. There might not be a village of Cavara Beach in ten years."

"Let's just hope Ivy is there now," he said as a cool wind off the water brushed against his face. Despite the risk, he urged his horse onward a little bit faster.

When they finally reached the village, it lay in a state of gloomy sleep. Windows were shuttered as a few flaming oil lamps in the narrow streets flickered and sputtered in the breeze. They passed silently along the main road and headed into the countryside, looking for the third turnoff to the right. Sims had instructed them that that would be their first turn. When a few clouds drifted in from the west and dimmed the moonlight, Nicholas feared they would be too late. They had already lost precious time on their way to the village and were now mired in the murky maze of undefined roads and footpaths that were difficult to navigate.

"Are you sure we're going the right way?" Nicholas asked a while later after making two more turns, scratching his head as he looked about. The two had paused a moment to survey the landscape after wandering about aimlessly for an hour as the Fox Moon drifted westward.

"Sure we are," Leo said halfheartedly. "At least I think so. Maybe we made a wrong turn that last road back."

"Or maybe Sims lied to us." Nicholas climbed off his horse, trying to keep his frayed nerves in check. He grabbed the reins and walked along the dirt path to stretch his legs as Leo followed.

"Let's go on for a bit longer," he said. "If we don't see what looks like an abandoned farmhouse soon, then we know we're on the wrong path."

Nicholas nodded, not in the mood for words. When the moonlight peeked out of the clouds a half hour later, highlighting a desolate expanse of grassy fields and dark water in the distance–but no sign of any farmhouse–Leo glumly concluded that they were heading in the wrong direction. Nicholas agreed and they turned around, backtracking to their last turnoff to determine where their path went awry. They continued along the previous road for about a half mile until they reached a turn onto another road they had passed earlier.

"Should we try this one?" Nicholas asked, noting that it was a left turn from where they had originally approached. "I know Sims said this next turn was also to the right, but maybe he misspoke or we misunderstood."

"Or he sent us on a lost cause," Leo remarked, quickly shaking the thought out of his head. "Can't start thinking like that or we'll get nowhere. Come on. Let's go."

Leo snapped the reins lightly and his horse trotted along the road. Nicholas followed, mustering up what he thought were the last traces of hope within him as the Fox Moon dipped in the west.

Several minutes later they noted a small farmhouse in the distance, though when they passed by it, they smelled smoke drifting from the chimney and moved onward. Another mile down the road Nicholas pointed out a second farmhouse, this one also clearly not abandoned. They trotted by in dismal silence, neither wanting to say that they may have been deceived by Sims as they trudged through the dreary predawn veil slowly settling over the landscape. A nagging weariness tormented them. They each battled a lack of sleep and wondered how much longer they could continue without rest. Leo was about to say as much when he noted a dilapidated barn slouched in the field to his right, a gaping hole punched into its roof.

"Look!" he said, pointing it out.

Nicholas glanced up, shaking the sluggishness out of his head. A one-story house of wood and clay bricks off to one side of the barn appeared to be in even worse shape. "That has to be it!"

They hurried down the road and crossed some tall grass that had taken over the property. When they neared the house, its shutterless windows yawned in the darkness. They jumped off their horses and scouted around while the two animals grazed. The Fox Moon slowly sank behind the tips of the Trent Hills in the distant west as a hint of gray tinged the edge of the eastern horizon. Dawn would break within the hour.

Nicholas raced along one side of the house while Leo ran the opposite way around the barn. The smell of decaying grass and damp soil permeated the air. They met up on the back side of the barn, shrugging their shoulders as they frantically craned their necks in the gloom. Then Nicholas spotted a low roof near the edge of the field camouflaged by clumps of tall grass and thorn bushes.

"A root cellar!" he exclaimed, racing to the front of the structure as Leo followed. He stopped suddenly when he saw that a low door at the entrance had been left ajar, a black silence oozing out. He threw a worried glance at Leo before hurrying down a few stone steps and slowly opening the door, ducking his head as he stepped inside. Though very little gray light seeped within, he immediately realized that the tiny enclosure was empty. He sighed and stepped backward, leaning against the wall.

Leo walked inside, stooping so as not to bump his head on the low ceiling. He wondered how late they had arrived since Ivy left.

"*If* she had been here," Nicholas said despondently. "Is this the right place? And if it is, Ivy could be anywhere right now."

"It has to be." Leo sniffed the air, noting a familiar scent. "Smells like somebody burned a candle in here. Maybe an oil lamp."

"She *was* here!" Nicholas said excitedly, standing up quickly and bumping his head on a wooden beam. "*Ow!*" he muttered, rubbing out the pain though he couldn't help but laugh at himself.

Leo grinned and yawned at the same time. "No doubt she was. But if we don't rest, Nicholas, we're never going to find her. The sun will be up shortly. Let's sleep for a couple hours and then get our bearings. Whoever kidnapped Ivy will have to rest, too. And since they don't know they're being followed, maybe they won't be in a hurry."

Nicholas was about to protest but realized Leo was correct. His eyelids were heavy and his thoughts in disarray. So they agreed to grab a quick nap on the east side of the barn, knowing the rising sun would jar them awake. They plopped down in the tall grass, bundled in their hooded coats, and promptly fell asleep near the horses. As the Fox Moon disappeared behind the Trent Hills, a light mist formed upon the dirt roads and fields, swirling about in a gentle breeze, momentarily safe in the lingering night.

Nicholas felt the warm touch of light upon his face as he slowly opened his eyes, the pungent scent of grass and soil dancing in the breeze. He stretched, feeling rested, and then sat up, his heart suddenly racing when he noticed the sun blazing behind a thin layer of gray clouds. How long had he slept? It must have been several hours past sunrise, he calculated as he shook Leo awake.

"Get up! We overslept."

"*Huh?*" He struggled to sit up, scratching his head. "*What?*" He noticed the sun climbing high in the eastern sky. "Oh…"

A few minutes later they were standing on the main road, eating some dried beef and bread as they surveyed the landscape. The western end of Sage Bay was only a short distance to the east, its gentle waves tipped with the subdued morning light. The shoreline of the Trillium Sea lay about five miles to their north, its rich dark waters hugging a slate gray horizon. A vast expanse of grasslands stretched westward like a sea of brittle stalks swaying in unison wherever the capricious winds commanded it. Nicholas wondered where they should go next.

"I can't imagine these roads go much farther west," Leo said. "There's nothing in that direction except tall grass. And Sims mentioned hearing something about a waiting ship. So whoever abducted Ivy must be traveling along shore."

Nicholas agreed as he took another bite of his cold breakfast. "We'll head north for the shoreline and follow it west. If a ship's waiting somewhere, we shouldn't miss it."

"Assuming it hasn't sailed off."

Nicholas didn't want to ponder such a thought. He walked over to the horses, ready to begin the next leg of their journey.

The clouds thickened as they reached the seashore. Nicholas' spirits fell when he gazed upon the somber stretch of water and the unreachable horizon. If Ivy were already on a ship, where would she go? The Northern Isles were the closest place out on the water, nearly two hundred miles away. With an aching heart, he wondered how he would ever find her.

They trudged westward along the shoreline through the gloom and desolation. The wall of tall grass to their left stood like a legion of silent sentries. Nicholas and Leo rode their horses as often as possible, walking alongside them when the terrain turned too stony or soft from recent rains. They spotted impressions of horse hooves and wagon wheels on the ground from time to time which encouraged them as they set out. Meals and rest stops were brief, though they paused to sleep from time to time.

As darkness descended, they attempted to make a small fire using the tall grass as fuel, though it wasn't dry enough to do so. In the end, they took shelter within the grass to escape the ceaseless breezes off the Trillium Sea, sleeping for a few hours near the horses. When they awoke, the full Fox Moon was still high in the clouded sky, its gauzy light enough to guide them through the night as they marched onward in sluggish silence.

Chances of finding Ivy briefly increased when Nicholas spotted the remains of a small campfire the next morning. The damp smell of cold ash enlivened his spirits and urged him and Leo on at a faster clip. Their need for food and sleep diminished over the next several hours as they made steady progress.

"We must be gaining on them," Nicholas said, hoping that speaking the words would make them come true.

"We are," Leo replied, encouraging his friend despite the miles of rugged shoreline ahead.

They continued onward for several hours, enduring the bland and chilly surroundings. Pangs of doubt again crept into both their minds, forcing them to wonder if they were merely chasing an illusion. If Ivy was already on the sea, each additional mile of their journey would make such a bitter outcome all the more heartbreaking. And if they didn't find her soon, when would they admit to themselves that their efforts had failed?

After following a gentle curve along the shoreline, Nicholas noted a flash of familiar color in the gray light which purged such gloomy thoughts from his mind. He jumped off his horse and scrambled to the edge of the grasslands. Leo slowed his steed and trotted over toward him.

"What's the matter, Nicholas?"

"Nothing's the matter," he said, reaching to the ground. "Luck's finally joined us in the search!" He grinned, clasping Ivy's scarf in his hand and joyously holding it up. "She's left us a sign. We're on the right track."

"Then let's not stop to celebrate," Leo said. "Get back on your horse."

They urged themselves forward through the slogging hours of the dreary afternoon, finding no more signs from Ivy as the air cooled and the clouds drifted slowly overhead like a mass of gray mountains. Occasional hoof prints or wheel tracks offered the only hint that they were still on the correct course. Nicholas sighed as they journeyed into another night, wondering if Ivy and her captors were traveling just as fast as he and Leo were as he watched the distant tips of the Trent Hills fade into darkness.

After another brief meal and a few more hours of sleep, they moved on underneath a canopy of clouds. The Fox Moon, now past full, had risen in the east, and the larger Bear Moon, still a few days from full, lingered higher in the west. Both glowing orbs cast their gentle light above the cloud cover, guiding the travelers cautiously along the water's edge. But after a few hours had passed, the Bear Moon set in the west. And before the break of dawn, the Fox Moon also deserted the night sky, dipping behind the distant mountains as the landscape succumbed to darkness. Sleep again called to Nicholas and Leo, so they took shelter in the grass and slept for a few hours until the lemony face of the sun again graced the eastern sky.

After they had traveled a few hours in the morning, Leo finally spoke the words he had been thinking during the night. The horses trotted on at a slower clip, noticeably more tired than when they had begun their journey.

"This is our third day of traveling," he said flatly, his eyes ahead on the terrain. A few breaks in the clouds allowed a splash of sunshine upon the dark water and the waves of grass. "We're getting low on food, and the horses are–"

"I know what you're going to say, Leo. *How much longer can we go on?*" Nicholas pushed off the hood of his coat as a cool breeze brushed through his hair. "I was thinking that, too."

"The Trent Hills are nearly upon us, and we're quite a ways from Boros. I never expected us to go this far," Leo admitted. "I never expected we would have to."

"Me either." Nicholas gazed up at the struggling sun trying to find its way out of the clouds. "Ivy may already be on that ship Sims talked about, but I don't want to think it or believe it."

"I know."

He glanced at his friend, wanting advice and direction. As much as he had endured since fleeing Kanesbury, Nicholas had never once felt the guilt and anguish that now tormented him as he reluctantly entertained thoughts of abandoning their search. Maybe it was a task too big for them to handle alone. He said as much to Leo, feeling awful for putting such thoughts into words.

"Let's give it until morning," Leo said. "If we don't find Ivy, well, maybe we can come back again better prepared."

"But if she was taken to the Northern Isles, we're sunk. I can't imagine what might happen to her there."

A chill ran through Leo when he heard the despair in Nicholas' voice. He didn't know what to do, but maybe others would.

"We do have one arrow left in our quiver," he said. Nicholas glanced at him with questioning eyes. "Our friendship with a princess. Maybe Megan can convince her grandfather to launch a rescue effort." He immediately saw the doubt scrawled upon Nicholas' face. "It's just a thought."

"I'm sure one of the last things on the King of Arrondale's mind is the problems of two commoners like us," he replied with a grim laugh. "He'd boot us out of the Citadel for sure, not that we'd even get a chance to see him in the first place."

"I suppose you're right. The lack of sleep is getting to me."

"Me too." Nicholas loosened his grip on the reins, wanting so much to plop down in the grass and sleep the day away. But they continued on in bouts of silence as the day slowly progressed and the clouds began to break, neither knowing, yet dreading, what decision the morning would bring.

They stopped at noontime for a brief meal and then treated themselves to an apple each that Castella had provided. Leo took two additional pieces of the fruit and fed them to the horses who were much appreciative of the juicy, sweet snack. After a short rest, they faced the drudgery of the bleak seaside terrain once again. For two hours they progressed in subdued silence, each wondering where tomorrow would find them. The grass to their left stood particularly tall, swaying in unison along a stretch of shore less rocky than usual. The Trent Hills rose gracefully against a slate gray sky less than ten miles away in the west.

A few more hours passed as twilight gently enveloped the shoreline and the clouds began to break. The sun prepared to dip behind the mountains as the Bear Moon climbed high in the east. Nicholas was lost in thought, his eyes to the ground ahead of him. Leo glanced out across the sea in the last light. A repetitive string of small waves washed hypnotically onto shore. As he took a deep breath of salty air to clear his mind, he thought he noticed an object upon the water several miles down shore. He gently reined his horse to a halt and gazed unblinkingly at the spot not far off the water's edge. Then he saw a flash of light upon the shoreline in the same vicinity. When Nicholas finally realized that he was riding alone, he turned around and saw Leo sitting statue-like upon his horse.

"Why'd you stop?" He turned his horse and sauntered over to him. "See something?"

"Take a look," Leo said, pointing. "Way down shore just off the water's edge. Looks like a ship. And I see firelight, too." He glanced at Nicholas. "Somebody has come ashore." Upon closer scrutiny, Nicholas arrived at the same conclusion, suggesting they bolt the remaining miles to rescue Ivy. "Not so fast," Leo cautioned. "We don't know how many are down there or what kind of armaments they carry."

"I know," he said, coming to his senses. "I'm talking faster than I can think. We have to approach in secret. And on foot."

Leo agreed. "The sun will set shortly, so we'll have the cover of night. I suggest we ride along as close to the grass as we can for another mile or two, then abandon our horses. We'll trek the final mile or so through the grass so we won't be spotted and then wait for full darkness."

Nicholas took a deep breath, now wide awake as his heart beat steadily. "And then?"

"Then we make our move," Leo replied. "But don't ask me what that is just yet."

Swiftly and steadily they traveled nearly two miles along the grass as the sun slipped behind the mountains. The darkness deepened as the smell of wood smoke drifted from the west. They finally dismounted and led their horses into the tall grass.

"Stay here," Leo said, petting his steed before he removed two more apples from the food bag, one for each horse. "We'll be back soon. Wish us luck."

"And if luck fails, a sharp dagger is a good substitute," Nicholas said, unpacking a small knife still in its sheath that Castella had packed away in a blanket roll tied to his saddle. He attached the knife to his belt, his heart pounding and his senses sharp, determined to fight anyone who might get in his way. "I'm certain Castella tucked one away for you, too."

"She did," he replied, finding his own knife and arming himself. "Now let's see who we're dealing with." Leo indicated that they should hike westward through the grass, keeping inside the vegetation until they determined how many people were on shore.

The last mile proved difficult. The deepening darkness concealed them and the constant sea breeze muffled any sounds they made rustling through the brittle grass. They felt as if they were fighting their way through a dense forest. As they moved parallel to the shore, they monitored the bright flames of the bonfires through the grass to keep them on track. When at last arriving near the encampment, the two plopped down to rest.

"I counted five tents," Leo said, gazing through the grass and studying the glow of firelight dancing off the sides of the round structures. "Almost as many bonfires, too."

Nicholas inched closer for a better view. "Doesn't look like a whole lot of people," he whispered. "Less than twenty." He noticed a few men bundled up in coarse, long brown coats, some wandering along the shore while others warmed themselves near the fires.

"Maybe others are on board the ship," Leo said. "Or in the tents."

"We have to get near the edge of the grass to really see what's going on. The tents are obstructing our view."

Leo agreed, pointing west. "All right. We'll continue forward. Then we'll veer right toward the shore and away from the bonfires. It's darker there and we'll get a more direct view."

Nicholas led the way, circling around to the far side of the encampment. Several minutes later they were able to crawl up to the edge of the grass line, now looking east and concealed in complete darkness except for splashes of moonlight that occasionally peeked out of the still breaking clouds. From this vantage point they clearly saw a ship resting upon the water. Three rowboats had been pulled onto shore. Five round tents were pitched in a line along the edge of the grass, and the roar of four crackling bonfires saturated the cool night air. Gathered around the largest fire nearest the water were five individuals, three similarly dressed as the other men walking along shore, the tallest of them unshaven and smoking a pipe. As he seemed to be doing all the talking, Nicholas and Leo assumed he was in charge. What intrigued them most were the other two people near the fire, one, a thin yet formidable looking woman and the other a short man with a goatee. All were immersed in deep discussion.

Leo nudged Nicholas and pointed to an area beyond the last tent. There stood a small covered cart, and the two horses that pulled it now roamed freely near the grass.

"Those two shorter people by the fire must be the ones who took Ivy from the root cellar," he said, recalling what Sims had told them.

"But where is *she?*" Nicholas muttered, clutching a handful of grass. He studied the area like a hawk, hoping for a glimpse of Ivy. Most of the soldiers were standing by the fires, either eating or engaged in conversation, while a few others roamed about on patrol. But there was no sign of Ivy. One man stood alone near the middle tent, pacing near the entrance in apparent boredom. Nicholas sighed, wondering if Ivy might already be on the ship, when it suddenly hit him. He pointed to the man.

Leo shrugged. "What about him?" he whispered.

"He's the only person on shore near one of the tents," Nicholas said. "Nobody is anywhere near the other ones. Why?"

Leo grinned. "He's guarding Ivy!"

"Has to be!" Nicholas wanted to rush to her at once.

Leo calmed him down, telling Nicholas that they had to approach the rescue logically. If Ivy was inside the tent, how would they get her out? And if she wasn't, what would be their next step? Nicholas thought for a moment, realizing that it would be impossible to sneak past the man guarding the entrance since he was in plain view of everyone else on shore. Slowly a smile crept across his face.

"Maynard always told me there was more than one way to shoe a horse," he said, quickly explaining his idea to Leo. "Stay here and keep watch while I go to work. If there's any trouble, let me know."

"Be careful," he said as Nicholas scrambled through the grass, making his way back behind the line of tents.

Nicholas stayed hidden in the grass until he was directly behind the center tent and then slowly crawled toward it, concealed in shadows. When he poked his head through the stalks into the open air, the back wall of the tent was only an arm's length away. He carefully touched the coarse material, feeling along the bottom seam. It was tight to the ground and Nicholas knew he wouldn't be able to lift it to look inside. He traced his fingers along the seam in both directions, hearing the muffled voices of those upon shore. Though he was well concealed if he remained behind the tent, he felt as if he were being watched. Then he found it.

To his left, a wooden stake had been driven into the hard ground. A short length of rope attached to the bottom of the tent was fastened to it. Another stake was to his right. Nicholas removed his dagger, carefully cutting through the two pieces of rope, certain the sea breezes and crackling bonfires would muffle any noise he might make. But in his mind, every sinew of rope he cut seemed to snap like a twig, alerting the enemy of his presence. In a short time though, he severed both ropes and carefully raised the bottom of the tenting. It would lift only high enough to allow Nicholas to slide beneath it while lying on his back. He did so, holding his breath as he sneaked inside.

A faint light flickered upon the cold dirt as Nicholas peered within. Bundles of animal pelts had been tossed about, and a single wooden support pole anchored into the dirt rose to a vented ceiling. A few lit candles, each attached to a metal holder fastened to the pole, shed a gentle glow upon the sides of the tent. He turned his head to get a better view of one section when he suddenly felt a hand placed across his mouth from the opposite side. He reflexively grabbed at the individual's wrist, his eyelids snapping wide open. But an instant later he loosened his grip, grinning underneath the hand that touched his lips.

"*Shhh*," Ivy whispered, smiling at her rescuer. "And don't get up. I'm not sure if the light in here is strong enough to reflect our shadows upon the side of the tent."

"I didn't notice *your* shadow," he softly said. "The light from the bonfires is much brighter and there's a little moonlight, so I think it's safe. But I'll stay down here anyway." He smiled again, captivated by Ivy's composure during such a difficult time. "How are you feeling? Are you hurt? Are you hungry? Are you ready to leave?"

She gently caressed her fingertips across his cheek. "I'm not hurt or hungry, Nicholas, but I'm definitely ready to leave. I tried to get out the back way after I untied myself, but couldn't lift the stakes out of the ground."

Ivy beamed joyfully in the candlelight knowing that Nicholas had come after her. How he had found her and what obstacles he had overcome to do so, she couldn't imagine. He could tell her all about it another time when they were free, but right now she savored the moment, feeling so close to this young man she had met only four evenings ago, believing he would have gone to the ends of the world to save her.

"If you follow me out the back, we can meet up with Leo and take our leave," he said. "No time to say goodbye to your gracious hosts though. Who are they?"

"The woman is named Madeline, apparently that nursemaid to Megan when she was an infant. The other is a gentleman called Mune," she explained. "They believe I'm Princess Megan. I learned I'm supposed to be taken to an island under the guard of a man named Captain Tarosius Lok. The last place in the world I want to visit is the Northern Isles." She revealed the silver medallion Megan had lent her. "This little trinket helped to convince them. Luckily Megan had the foresight to lend it to me at the candle shop or who knows what kind of trouble I'd be in otherwise."

"You're still in a bind until I get you out of here," Nicholas said, signaling for Ivy to quietly follow him out the back of the tent. "Let's find Leo and the horses."

"Where is he?" she asked as Nicholas disappeared underneath the tent.

"Keeping watch. Hurry now!"

Leo diligently gazed through the thick stalks of grass after Nicholas had disappeared, keeping watch over the soldiers upon shore. He tallied their numbers, feeling particularly pleased with his and Nicholas' ingenuity. But when a man near the farthest bonfire raised a hand in the air, apparently signaling to another soldier farther down shore to the east, Leo stopped counting. Moments later the second soldier approached, rushing toward the bonfire. Leo assumed he had been patrolling the shoreline. The man spoke a few words as something large followed close behind him in the darkness. Leo's heart nearly skipped a beat when the soldier held up his hand, clutching two pair of reins in his fingers. Leo gulped hard. Their horses had been discovered.

Nicholas savored the warmth of Ivy's hand in his as they treaded silently through the grass. For a moment he felt invincible, having rescued a woman he was falling in love with though he had only known her for a short time. All the problems of the last several days seemed insignificant as they faded in his mind.

They moved directly south of the tent to conceal themselves well within the grass, then veered right in an arc to meet up with Leo. Nicholas glanced at Ivy, and though they were cloaked in shadows, he could see through the filtered light of the gibbous Bear Moon that she was smiling back at him. He was about to whisper to her when several frantic shouts from the shoreline chilled the blood in his veins.

"What was that?" Ivy said as Nicholas' grip tightened.

"Hurry!" he replied, picking up the pace through the tangles of grass. "I think they know you're missing."

"That was certainly fast!"

Earlier, when Commander Uta had ordered two of his soldiers to patrol the shoreline in each direction, the man scouting east spotted two horses grazing freely in the grass less than two miles down the shore. Discovering no sign of their owners, he coaxed the horses out of hiding and led them back to the encampment to alert the others. When Uta ordered a search of the area, the guard in front of Ivy's tent checked on her at once, discovering her escape.

"You fools!" Madeline muttered when peering inside the tent. Mune nudged past her and lifted up the back section, glaring at Commander Uta. The soldier who had been guarding the tent dropped to his knees and felt underneath the opening, discovering the frayed ropes.

"Somebody cut them from outside," he sheepishly said.

"Obviously," Madeline said, seething. "They've fled into the grass. Uta, order your men to find them."

Commander Uta signaled one of his men to coordinate the search at once as he, Madeline and Mune exited the tent. He turned to Madeline, his face hardened with concern. "Who could have done this? Spies of the King?"

She shook her head. "I don't know. But if your presence is discovered in these parts, commander, Caldurian's plan may be compromised. You must leave now. Mune and I will go with you."

"You will?"

"We *will*?" Mune added, his face contorting at the unappealing thought.

"Just until he can set us safely ashore somewhere else," she explained. "None of us can risk being discovered here, Mune, so don't make such a to-do about it."

At that moment, a half dozen soldiers sped past them and disappeared into the tall grass like wild animals in search of prey. A few of them carried flaming sticks of wood pulled from the bonfire.

"We need more light," Uta said. "This could take hours! Maybe we should leave without the girl."

"No!" Madeline protested. "I went to too much trouble to get her." She brushed past Mune and Commander Uta, marching toward the edge of the grass. "I'll provide the extra light."

Nicholas and Ivy nearly collided with Leo amid the grass. He had scrambled to find them moments after he saw the soldier walking along shore with their horses. The three of them squatted low in the vegetation as Leo hastily explained what he had witnessed.

"You slipped out of the tent just in time," he said.

"But now what?" Ivy whispered.

"We burrow deeper into the grass and then veer east," Nicholas said. "We'll head back north to the shore when it's safe, though we may have to spend a few hours hiding in this mess."

Leo nodded. "All right. That'll have to do. I think—"

Suddenly there was a jumble of frantic voices. Flashes of light flickered through the grass to their left and right. The rustle of dried grass stalks grew deafening. The search had begun.

With heads bent, the trio waded through the forest of tall grass in a straight line south away from shore. Sporadic voices, cold and harsh, punctuated the inky blackness. Wherever there was a flash of light, they turned in the opposite direction, trying to stay in a southerly direction. Nicholas recalled the night he was pursued through a farm field by Constable Brindle's men for a crime he didn't commit. A flood of horrible memories washed over him. Though he had once craved some adventure in his life, he was certain that this wasn't what he had in mind.

"How are you holding up?" he asked Ivy, clutching her hand.

"I'm all right," she said, feeling as if she were trudging through a nightmare. "But I'll never look at a walk through tall grass the same way again."

"I promise you a long leisurely stroll in the sunshine if we get though this," he told her.

But before Ivy could respond, a ball of light whistled past them just a few yards to their left, illuminating the tops of the swaying stalks. The mysterious object glowed for a moment in the distance before being silently swallowed up in the vegetation.

Leo stopped and spun around, facing an equally perplexed Nicholas and Ivy. "What in Laparia was that?"

"I haven't a clue," Nicholas muttered, scanning the skies.

Suddenly another burning orb sailed directly overhead, swift as a bird as it cast a swath of light upon them. Nicholas could better judge the distance this time and realized the fiery object was but an arm's length above their heads. A third orb streaked by to their right, skimming the tops of the grass like a stone skipping across a pond.

"What are they?" Ivy said, a tremor in her voice. She held tightly onto Nicholas' arm.

Before anyone could hazard a guess, two more burning spheres soared directly above, one higher than the other. Their red-orange glow splashed a warm yet terrifying light upon them until both flaming projectiles disappeared with a swoosh into the grass. Nicholas, Leo and Ivy remained still, their breathing slow and heavy as the Bear Moon drifted toward the west through the remaining remnants of clouds.

"I see them!" a voice shouted from the shore.

"So do I!" called another man from somewhere in the grass to their left.

"What do we do now?" Ivy asked as the sound of hands and feet thrashing through the vegetation angrily filled the air. The soldiers from the Northern Isles were closing in on both sides.

"We separate!" Leo said, hastily formulating a plan. "We push south a few more yards, then I'll head east. You and Ivy curve west. We have to confuse them. We'll meet up on shore at dawn."

Their pursuers grew nearer as another burning ball of grass flew overhead, momentarily casting aside the night. Nicholas gave Leo a reassuring nod.

"Good luck!"

"You too!"

Leo plowed through the grass with Nicholas and Ivy following hand in hand, all stooping as low as possible. Moments later, Leo veered to his left in silence. Nicholas and Ivy drifted right, hoping they had bought themselves a little time. But less than a minute later, a ruckus of frustrated shouts erupted as the two pursuing groups of soldiers converged.

"Spread out, circle around, then start to close in!" their leader shouted as he held aloft a blazing torch that fluttered in the sea breeze. He sent half the men southeast, the other half southwest. "They can't go much farther!"

Amid the snap and rustle of the tall grass, another display of burning lights sailed overhead like a shower of meteors. Leo glanced up, covering his eyes to shield them from the glare. He was hoping Nicholas and Ivy were safe when he caught a glimpse of torchlight a few yards away. He stopped. His heart raced. He was certain he hadn't been spotted and crouched down low, waiting for the light to pass. Slowly the glow of the torch drifted off to his left. He hurriedly stood up, pivoted on his foot, and headed in a northerly direction, guessing he was now outside the circle of his pursuers.

Then he crashed into a black barrier and was pushed backward into the grass.

"I found one!" a voice shouted. The soldier, who had earlier extinguished his torch, jumped upon Leo before he could get back on his feet.

Commander Uta's voice sailed across the grasslands from shore. "Find the girl and get back to the ship!"

Leo and the solider struggled on the ground before finally separating and getting to their feet. Leo suddenly remembered the dagger Aunt Castella had given him and pulled it out, its silvery edge glinting in the sporadic moonlight.

"Step back!" he warned between gulps of cool, salty air.

But the moonlight wasn't bright enough for Leo to see the soldier's blackened torch rising through the air. It smashed against his wrist, knocking the dagger into the grass. Leo yelled out in pain, grabbing his wrist to his chest, yet he had just enough wits to glance at the solider and see a second blow sailing his way. He spun around and avoided a hard whack to his arm, but got tangled in a clump of grass and nearly toppled over. He looked up a second too late as he caught his balance, only long enough to see the wooden torch come crashing through the air. Leo didn't feel where the blow landed nor could smell the pungent grass against his nostrils when his body fell to the ground like a sack of flour. Silence and darkness swiftly overwhelmed him.

"I still hear them," Ivy whispered as she and Nicholas slogged through the grass that seemed to grow taller and closer together as they burrowed deeper inside.

"I'll get you out of this," he promised. "Trust me."

"I do trust you," she said, squeezing his hand.

Nicholas was about to tell her that he had recovered her scarf when one of the soldiers called out. A moment later, Leo's yell tore through the darkness. Nicholas' heart went cold.

"What could've happened?" Ivy said with a gasp, her hand covering her mouth. She imagined the worst, wondering what misery had befallen Leo in his attempt to save her. "We have to go back and help him!"

Nicholas wanted to do so immediately as bitter anger welled up inside him. But logic told him that he must keep Ivy out of danger by continuing to run. Turning back would only result in their capture since some of the other soldiers had surely zeroed in on Leo's location by now. But the debate became irrelevant when the rustle of grass grew louder nearby.

Nicholas and Ivy stopped. Someone with a torch swiftly approached from the right. Nicholas pointed, planning to flee in a line perpendicular to the soldier's path. But before he and Ivy took another step, a second soldier without a torch advanced from the opposite direction. Then a third one closed in from the very route Nicholas had planned to move. He glanced at Ivy. They were being surrounded.

The flicker of two more torches suddenly appeared through the stalks in the distance. More footsteps, muffled whispers and the crunch of dried grass. Nicholas guessed that the glow of the flaming orbs must have given away their location. They had to make a run for it now before it was too late. He looked at Ivy, caressing the side of her face, knowing by the steely look in her eyes that she was ready to make a final dash.

They never got the chance. Nicholas was suddenly tackled to the ground as someone pounced at his legs from behind, unaware that a soldier had been stealthily crawling through the grass toward him.

"Nicholas!" Ivy screamed. But before she could reach him, a pair of arms grabbed her from behind, taking her breath away. A cold, calloused hand covered her mouth as she was pulled through the grass and darkness. Another pair of arms grabbed her by the legs. Ivy felt as if she were floating recklessly through the night as the tall grass fronds brushed against her face and shoulders.

Nicholas rolled over and attempted to jump to his feet upon hearing Ivy's harrowing cry, but found himself gasping for breath after a hard kneecap landed squarely in his gut. He collapsed in the grass, unable to breathe for several moments as the frenzied shuffle of footsteps echoed in his ears. The soldiers were fleeing back to shore, back to the ship, and taking Ivy with them.

Nicholas flopped over on his side, feeling momentarily paralyzed as he tried to inhale a few agonizing lungfuls of air. Though he hadn't been hit in the head, his skull felt on fire. He wondered if Leo was in any better shape. Slowly he was able to breathe again as the spicy bitter scent of the grass revived him. He struggled to his knees, straightened his back and deeply exhaled, certain that none of his ribs were broken. As he slowly stood, he again heard Ivy's frantic cry pierce through the bitter breeze. It sent a chill up his spine and made him forget his injuries. He raced through the grass as fast as he could, swatting the stalks out of his way as he headed for the shoreline.

The bonfires blazed as Nicholas broke through the edge of the grass and raced to the water, the horror of the situation now starkly displayed before him. Two of the three rowboats were already out on the Trillium Sea, being swiftly paddled to the anchored ship. On the water's edge, two burly soldiers sloshed through the gentle waves, pushing the third rowboat away from shore before climbing into the boat with the final group. In unison, a half dozen paddles, three on each side, were dipped into the water. The rowboat started to pull away.

Nicholas saw Ivy struggling in the back of that last boat, unable to free herself from the two men who held her down. "Nicholas!" she cried in a last desperate bid for help.

"I'm coming!" he shouted, unsheathing his dagger as he sprinted toward the boat still in the shallows.

As soon as his feet hit the water, Nicholas leapt into the air in an attempt to jump into the rowboat, not thinking how he would single-handedly fight off eight soldiers. But as his foot landed on the tip of the vessel, now slick with seawater, the man closest to him raised a wooden oar and rammed it squarely into his chest. Nicholas' arms flailed upon impact and he slipped off the edge, crashing backward onto shore. His head pounded the hard ground as the dagger flew out of his fingers, landing with a dull clank against a stone embedded in the dirt.

He thought he heard Ivy's cry drifting vaguely through the night as he stared up at the dizzying array of stars peering down through the tattered clouds. He thought he felt the push of water against the soles of his boots as a cool breeze swept across his face. The string of bonfires crackled in the distance and the smell of wood smoke drifted lazily across shore. Then Nicholas closed his eyes, his frantic thoughts and blurred vision finally succumbing to despair and utter darkness.

END OF PART TWO

PART THREE
MACHINATIONS

CHAPTER 21

The Umarikaya

Caldurian had marched northeast through dying fields and across bubbling streams since leaving Barringer's Landing six evenings ago. Four hundred and ninety-nine Enâri creatures dutifully followed in his steps. What mischief the traitor Jagga was up to since he had fled and stolen the key, he couldn't begin to guess. That hitch in the operation was now entirely out of his hands.

The wizard and his troops rested as necessary under crisp moonlit skies or beneath the eaves of sweet pine, steadily making their way to the shores of the Trillium Sea to a point directly north of the Black Hills. There, Caldurian expected to see a ship from the Northern Isles anchored offshore if Commander Jarrin kept to their schedule. Several other ships were to land farther eastward along shore above the nearby Keppel Mountains, preparing for the invasion of the kingdom of Montavia as Vellan had instructed. But first Caldurian had business of his own, anticipating a visit with someone onboard Jarrin's ship. He tugged at the point of an iron gray beard as the folds of his black cloak swished through the brittle grass. The wizard smirked, hoping his special guest hadn't intimidated the commander and his crew too much.

At sunset, he heard waves lapping against the pebbly beaches of the sea, the stretch of water appearing like an inky wasteland. He and his reawakened soldiers eagerly approached the shoreline where a ship from the Northern Isles stood silhouetted upon the water against the darkening horizon. Large bonfires crackled on shore and several men from the Isles milled about the flames to keep warm. The nearly full Fox Moon rose in the east while the crescent Bear Moon, two days from first quarter, lingered high in the western sky.

"Now we can rest awhile, Gwyn. Our ship is here." Caldurian glanced down at the ranking Enâr who served as his aide, its firm jaw and dark eyes framed by a tangle of dirty hair that hung over its bulky, cloaked shoulders.

"We Enâri can do the work of ten shiploads of the Islanders," Gwyn said in a gravelly voice. "But we will work with them if we must."

"We'll need every ally to enact Vellan's wishes," the wizard replied as they approached the fires. Several Island soldiers looked on with suspicion. "But rest assured, Gwyn, you and your kind are closest to Vellan's heart. Your safety is all that matters to him. He will be delighted to welcome you back to Kargoth when our task here is over. It was a harrowing twenty year absence, but that will make your victory sweeter. Always keep that in mind."

"I will," he replied, trudging ahead as he knew Vellan would wish.

A moment later, a tall, unshaven man with a crew cut weaved through the soldiers and bonfires and approached Caldurian. He wore a long, weather-stained brown coat and black boots. Firelight reflected off the sword hanging from his side. He looked at the wizard and then glanced at Gwyn with curiosity in his dark, untrusting eyes, never having seen his kind before. The remaining Enâri soldiers stood silently behind their leader.

"Good to see you again, Caldurian, as well as your—*friends*." Commander Jarrin nodded at the wizard. "This will be an interesting alliance."

Caldurian smiled. "There'll be interesting times ahead for everyone if we just keep our wits about us and our priorities straight. I trust your journey from the Islands proceeded smoothly?"

Jarrin nodded. "*He* is with us. He drank the potion you gave me, then kept to himself during the entire voyage." With a tilt of his head, the commander indicated the bonfire farthest down the shore. "That most curious individual awaits your audience." He leaned in and spoke softly to the wizard. "He gives me the shivers."

310

Caldurian nodded in the chilly breeze, placing the hood of his cloak over his head. Twilight deepened as the sun disappeared in the west. "You are not used to his presence, Jarrin. He is a force to be reckoned with, a power unlike any other. Did it test your nerves when you retrieved him from his island prison?"

"He is here, isn't he? I don't wish to discuss the details of my voyage."

"Noted. And I'm sorry to have separated you from the other ships, but you have been well compensated," Caldurian replied. "Now excuse me, commander. I must speak with Arileez. Later we'll discuss our plans for Montavia." He turned to Gwyn. "You and the others rest now. It's been a grueling trek. Show Commander Jarrin every courtesy."

"As you wish," Gwyn replied with a grunt, crinkling his face as he stared back at the towering shipman. Caldurian departed, walking swiftly down the stony shore to the last bonfire where Arileez waited.

The bonfire popped, spitting a shower of sparks high into the air as Caldurian approached. Arileez, the passenger from the Northern Isles, stood bathed in an erratic mix of light and shadow. He gazed upon the wizard with lifeless eyes beneath a hood partially concealing a skeletal countenance framed with straggling stands of white hair. His frayed cloak and coverings made of animal skins and woven fibers hung upon him like tattered sails wrapped about a ship's mast after a bruising storm. A constant whoosh of waves battered the shoreline behind him.

"Thank you for joining us on the mainland," Caldurian said, greeting Arileez with a slight nod. "I appreciate your assistance."

"I appreciate that my curse has been lifted. Still, I will expect my due in time." He spoke softly, his voice gruff yet laced with a delicate shrill as if a wolf and seagull were communicating with one voice. "Now, how am I to do your bidding? When last we spoke, you had not provided many details, only possibilities of a new life for me."

"And you shall have it," Caldurian said with conviction. "You could rule the kingdom of Montavia if you wish, or occupy any of a handful of other thrones in Laparia. Or perhaps you'd like to carve out a new place where you can call the air, land and water all your own? The possibilities are endless."

Arileez appeared to laugh. "As a prisoner on my island for many years, I've become used to a life of solitude, so I'll carefully choose my reward. But it can wait until after I earn the gratitude of you and Vellan."

"You already have that, Arileez. Your assistance will go a long way toward helping us both achieve our goals."

"So, wizard, what am I to do?"

Caldurian looked sideways, noting that the soldiers upon shore kept their distance out of fear and intimidation, yet still they couldn't help but fix their gazes upon him and the strange passenger from the Isles. He knew no one could hear their conversation, but Caldurian didn't like to take chances when revealing any plans.

"Let's walk," he said, motioning for Arileez to follow him down the shoreline. "I have two jobs for you to complete–one at my behest and one from Vellan. The first is not far from here. You will be meeting with a gentleman named Zachary Farnsworth in the village of Kanesbury."

Arileez nodded as they walked away from the firelight. "And my second assignment?"

Caldurian grinned, contemplating the elaborate web of Vellan's design. "*That* will be a feat unparalleled. In one bold stroke, we will achieve much, Arileez. So very much."

"I will help as I can as a sign of my thanks. It was fortunate that you found me stranded on my island two years ago," he said, his words sprinkled with indebtedness. "It will be good to put my powers to use other than for my own entertainment. That dreariness had dragged on for too long."

"I can't imagine how the years wore away at your spirit and sanity. The anger you harbor toward your captors must have multiplied over time. It is a cruel fate that I would wish on no one," Caldurian said, staring at the stony ground.

"Well, I might wish it on some, though I can't imagine that any of my tormentors still live," Arileez replied distantly. "My fate was sealed many years ago."

"As you had often told me."

"Yet through our conversations, I can almost taste the feeling of liberation that revenge upon the descendants of my captors will bring to me. I will fight with Vellan," he proudly said, "who, like me, was terribly aggrieved."

"You speak the truth," Caldurian replied, "and I'm pleased to play a part in correcting these injustices."

"So I thank you again." Arileez filled his lungs with fresh sea air as he imagined the possibilities that awaited. "It was chance that brought you to me, and I will take advantage of that fortunate circumstance."

"Yes, happy chance. Where would we be without it?" he softly said, raising an eyebrow beneath his hood while recalling the moment when he had first heard about this mysterious sorcerer secluded on a deserted island off the eastern reaches of the Northern Isles.

Three years ago, Caldurian had journeyed to the Isles on one of his many missions for Vellan, carefully laying plans for the current conquest of Laparia. While meeting with Commander Uta on board a vessel to discuss future troop and supply shipments to Kargoth, the commander wondered if Vellan would ever again grace the Northern Isles with his presence like he had years ago.

"He's become a recluse," Uta said with a laugh. "He sends you to do his dirty work while he hides out in his mountain. Soon he'll be a mere memory or a figment of people's imaginations, just like the sorcerer of Torriga."

"Who is that you speak of?" Caldurian asked, his curiosity piqued as he gazed over the ship's side. "And where is Torriga?"

Commander Uta explained that Torriga was a tiny deserted island off the eastern shore of the largest island in the archipelago nation of the Northern Isles. Legend on the Isles told of a sorcerer who lived alone on Torriga, whose power was so great and deadly that only a few had ever mustered the courage to venture onto the island, yet never returned. Uta could offer Caldurian no information beyond the local legend, admitting that it was probably all untrue. When Caldurian returned to Kargoth two months later, he mentioned the conversation to Vellan in his mountain abode, wondering if the wizard had ever heard of such a sorcerer in his travels years ago.

Vellan spoke in the gloom while sitting on a cushioned wooden chair inside one of his upper chambers, the shadows cast from a small, round fire pit dancing upon the walls. His splintered wizard's staff leaned against the side of the chair like a silent advisor.

"*Sorcerer?*" Vellan whispered. "That island sorcerer is descended from the Valley of the Wizards just like me, but is so much more powerful in certain ways. Oh, so much more." He turned to his travel-weary apprentice, his dark eyes reflecting the red and yellow flames. "I believe he is the Umarikaya."

Caldurian shrugged. "I don't understand. What is that?"

"A tale from childhood. A fiction," Vellan said, "to keep us children from misbehaving."

"Please, tell me more," he asked, clearly intrigued.

Vellan explained the tale of the Umarikaya that he and other children were told whenever they would get in trouble for being particularly mischievous or deceitful. The Umarikaya, a terribly wicked wizard, had been sent to a faraway island as a child to live out his life in seclusion as punishment for disobeying his parents, with a powerful spell cast upon the island so he could never escape.

"If any of us children ever acted too irresponsibly, we were told that we would be sent to live with the Umarikaya until we learned to behave," he said with a grim smile. "And that threat would keep young impressionable boys and girls in line until they were old enough to know it was simply a myth passed down from generations that parents used in childrearing." Vellan leaned back in his chair. "Or so I once thought."

"What do you mean? You're not saying that..."

"That the legend is true? Perhaps. Or maybe the legend of the Umarikaya grew out of real events." Vellan told Caldurian about his first voyages to the Northern Isles when he was in his early twenties. "The Isles are a structured society, to put it kindly, which is part of the reason I admired that nation. It encouraged a discipline from its people which the Valley of the Wizards lacked. Years later while on another voyage around the Isles, my ship passed a nondescript island in the east far off the main island. I thought nothing of it at first and the ship never came close to approaching it, yet something propelled me to stare at that dot of a landmass as it drifted by in the distance. I thought that I sensed something, *felt* something, in the vicinity. Some magic perhaps?"

Caldurian leaned forward, entranced. "What did you find?"

"I asked the ship's commander to tell me the name of the island and about its history. He was hesitant at first, waiting until the island had drifted out of sight before mentioning its name–Torriga. He had told me it brought ill fortune to sailors to speak of the island while it was in view. But later on shore, the commander explained the legend of an evil sorcerer who had been living on that island for countless years, and how any who had ever ventured there would never return. I thanked him for the information and asked how I could arrange transport to the island as soon as possible."

Ten days later, Vellan drifted toward the island, having paid a local sailor an exorbitant amount of silver to take him to Torriga. The ship was anchored well offshore and Vellan took a rowboat alone to the island as no one else had the nerve to accompany him. When he approached the rocky beach, waves of fear, anxiety and nausea overwhelmed him until he regained control of his emotions. But before he had even stepped foot on the island, he knew the place was overwhelmed with wizards' magic. He sensed it in the air, land, water and vegetative growth, yet knew the magic wasn't native to this location. A terrifying anxiety gnawed at Vellan and he would not stay long on shore. He quickly filled a small pouch with a handful of beach sand and a few stones and rowed back to the ship, seeing no living thing upon the island. As soon as he boarded the ship, he ordered the commander to set sail back to the main island at once.

"After I closely studied and tested the sand and stones, I knew that the legend of the Umarikaya was a reality," Vellan said. "The magic present in the beach items was of a magnitude that even surprised me. The spells cast on that island must have been created by several wizards many years before I was born."

"What kind of spell was it?" Caldurian asked.

"A confinement spell, but unlike any I had ever encountered in my training. Some powerful wizards had been at work on Torriga."

Caldurian was still a bit confused, gazing at his teacher in the shadows for a fuller explanation. "Why is this sorcerer, this wizard, on the island at all? Surely the children's story of the Umarikaya is not a true one. What parents would send a disobedient child away forever, imprisoning him by magic on a faraway island? It doesn't make sense."

"The story is merely a fable, but it was based on grains of truth from the past," Vellan said. "When I returned to the Valley of the Wizards after my first travels abroad, I spoke extensively with many of the oldest wizards who had not yet departed on their final journeys, learning as much as I could about the origins of the Umarikaya. I also researched the most ancient texts in our libraries until I pieced together as best I could the truth behind the legend." He rose and walked toward the fire pit, a circle of polished flat stones that reflected firelight like glass sheets. He stood with his back to Caldurian, a silhouette against the snapping flames. "There *was* an adolescent imprisoned on Torriga. And though I could not discover an exact date of his confinement, I suspect it happened well over a hundred years ago."

"But why? What parents would do such a thing?"

"Not the parents," he said flatly, staring into the fire. "The young wizard was condemned by society, or at least by its most powerful leaders. You see, some were afraid of him, of Arileez. That was the boy's name."

Caldurian listened intently in the gloomy confines of the upper chamber. "What did he do?"

Vellan turned and again took a seat. "It is not what Arileez did, it was what he *could* do–or eventually *might* do. He was quite an unusual wizard with a strange power, a gift actually, not present in any other wizard, at least not in any that I have known or heard about during my lifetime in the Valley."

"What was this gift?"

Vellan smiled. "I will tell you, but first we must discuss the details of your next mission. I need for you to return to Torriga and make contact with Arileez. Find him. Befriend him. Gain his trust."

"What?"

"Fear not, Caldurian. I won't send you back this instant," he replied. "We have several other duties to attend to first before we launch our assault on Laparia. But sometime next year you need to make another voyage to Torriga and seek out Arileez and coax him to our side. Promise him whatever he desires. I suspect he will be bitter and angry at the world. You must stoke those emotions to gain his loyalty. He could be a most valuable asset to our cause."

Caldurian sighed, rubbing a hand through his beard. "I suspect what Arileez would want most is freedom. How can we get him off the island through such a powerful confinement spell?"

Vellan chuckled bitterly. "Oh, it is a powerful spell all right, to most ordinary wizards. I, however, am a few notches above ordinary and am not embarrassed to admit it. That is part of the reason that I was banished from the Valley of the Wizards. And I've had many years to develop a counter spell to the one cast on the island. I will provide you with a potion that he must drink in order to pass through the spell and leave the island. Releasing Arileez will not be a problem." He glanced sharply at Caldurian. "Only don't let him know that. When you contact Arileez and gain his allegiance, promise that you'll do everything you can to free him. Tell Arileez that you know of a powerful wizard who might be able to break the spell if given time to study it."

"*You.*"

"Of course. Encourage his allegiance to me until he willingly offers us his services for his freedom. But you must also insist that you will help him escape regardless of any repayment on his part. It would be the charitable thing to do, after all," he added with a hint of sarcasm.

Caldurian snickered. "I understand. Still, I must ask you something, Vellan. If you have already developed a counter spell, why haven't you returned to Torriga and released Arileez years ago?"

"Because I know the extent of his powers, my apprentice. Who knows what would happen if I released such a force on a whim? Would he be a friend or an enemy? An asset or a challenge?"

"I see."

Vellan leaned back in his seat. "But now I see a place for Arileez in my plans. He can play an important role and bring me such an advantage as I had not known before. But we must carefully cultivate him, Caldurian. I am yet about three years away from releasing the Enâri still asleep in the caves outside Kanesbury. That will mark the beginning of my return to prominence. So later next year you must seek out Arileez. That will give us plenty of time to introduce him to our cause and flame the embers of his own discontent to use to our advantage. Can you do this?"

"Of course, my wizard. Your apprentice will dutifully serve however needed," he replied as the nearby flames grasped at the wavering shadows. "Your will is my own. I will seek out the Umarikaya and then one day deliver your potion to him. And that is all it will take to free him?"

"Oh, it will free him all right. And a little bit more."

Caldurian furrowed his brow. "*Meaning?*"

"I will save the particulars for another time," Vellan replied. "All that matters now is that this strategic move will repay our efforts a hundredfold. It is all starting to fall into place at last."

Caldurian nodded perfunctorily, wondering what kind of peril he had just volunteered to confront on that deserted island. He laughed to himself, knowing that this wouldn't be a task that he could blithely reassign to Madeline or Mune. He would have to do the legwork on this one himself, no matter what the personal costs. If he were lucky, perhaps something good might come of it in the end. He looked up at Vellan, noting the reflection of firelight in his eyes.

"Pardon me for asking again, but what is so special about this Arileez?"

The Fox and Bear moons looked on as Caldurian provided Arileez with the details of his dual assignments, one from himself and the other from Vellan. When he finished, Caldurian looked across the Trillium Sea to the distant horizon.

"Welcome back to the real world, Arileez. This taste of freedom that Vellan has provided is a mere sampling of the marvels you will attain because of your allegiance to our cause. I know you won't disappoint."

"Indeed I won't," he replied, gazing at the horizon as well, unable to see the Northern Isles just beyond for the first time in over a hundred years. Arileez felt empty and anxious at once. "I must be off now," he said as he and Caldurian walked back toward the bonfires and the bevy of curious soldiers.

"Make sure to tell Zachary Farnsworth to be patient," Caldurian said with a stern edge to his voice. "He is too eager to reap his reward before it's ripe. Not the ideal person to work with, but sometimes we cannot choose our associates. I'll make time and find my way back to Kanesbury by the end of next month. Good luck."

Arileez nodded and walked away from the fires, disappearing into the distant shadows. Everyone on the beach watched with a sense of relief when the stranger finally departed. Caldurian then searched for Gwyn and Commander Jarrin to discuss the impending invasion of Montavia.

Caldurian marched with the Enâri for a few more hours during the night before stopping to rest, staying close to the shoreline. Commander Jarrin and his men had departed earlier, sailing eastward to rendezvous with the other ships in the invasion force now anchored above the Keppel Mountains. The wizard and the Enâri troops would meet them there to launch the attack that was set to begin at dawn four days from tomorrow.

Later the next morning as their march resumed, Caldurian detected a faint, familiar sound rolling upon the sea breezes. A tiny black spot high in the sky descended toward the wizard from the west. As he searched the skies, he noted the familiar shape of the messenger crow, Gavin, swiftly approaching. He landed on Caldurian's extended arm, warily keeping both eyes on the mass of Enâri creatures marching obediently along.

"What news from the west?" Caldurian asked, sensing the crow's uneasiness. "Mune had told me about your encounter with Jagga. I don't think you need to worry about a similar scare with any of these others."

"Still, I shall stay close to you while delivering my message," the bird replied. "I need only one lesson in Enâri brutality to remember it well. But I am here on business."

"What is it?" the wizard asked with curiosity.

"I have a savory bit indeed. King Justin is planning a war council which is set to begin nineteen days from today, the tenth day of Mid Autumn."

"How did you come across this information?"

"I talked with Mune last night at the Plum Orchard Inn," he said. "He received the message from Madeline, whose contact in the Blue Citadel informed her so."

"Ah, the always useful Dell Hawks."

Gavin cawed as if amused by the comment. "Not useful anymore," the crow said, explaining how Dell's services as a spy had been compromised. "He is now heading south to make his fortune off the war between Rhiál and Maranac."

"Unfortunate. A set of eyes and ears at the war council would help us immensely. Still, I can't cover every spot in Laparia no matter how much Vellan would like it so. I guess we'll have to..." He slowly tilted his head, suddenly struck by a thought.

"What is it, Caldurian?"

"Perhaps this goes against my better judgment, but we may be able to place someone inside the Citadel. Whether he can wiggle his way in to eavesdrop on the council is a whole other matter." He brought his arm closer to his face, speaking softly to Gavin. "I need you to deliver a message to Zachary Farnsworth in Kanesbury. He said he could deliver me a spy inside King Justin's residence in Morrenwood, so let me put him to the test. Maybe he can repay me for bungling the business with the key."

"I'll find him at once," the crow said after Caldurian relayed his instructions.

"Though I would have preferred Madeline's informant. That will be a loss. But as long as the meeting with Commander Uta proceeds, things should go fine. Madeline and Mune are preparing one half of Vellan's latest maneuver. I sent the other half on his way yesterday," he said, referring to Arileez. "After the Umarikaya performs his task for me in Kanesbury, Madeline can have his services to enact Vellan's plan. But it should all work out in the end." He stared into Gavin's coal black eyes, seeking confirmation from the crow to calm his worries. "At least I hope it will."

CHAPTER 22

The Road to Triana

Eleven ships from the Northern Isles were anchored offshore when Caldurian and the Enâri arrived a day and a half later. The vessels, pasted against a slate gray sky, were crammed with troops, supplies and weapons for the battle ahead. Knives and swords had been sharpened, bows tightly strung and quivers filled with arrows, and spears and shields made ready. Scores of soldiers had already set up camp away from shore, delivered from the Isles days ago on one of the ships' many voyages. A cluster of tents dotted the northern foothills of the Keppel Mountains like mushrooms after a rain. Lines of rowboats were beached lifelessly upon shore as crackling bonfires burned brightly in the late afternoon gloom. Caldurian was pleased with the sight, confident that victory over Montavia would be swift and with little bloodshed. When the rural population was faced with such an overwhelming force, the wizard foresaw little resistance. The capital city of Triana would soon be under his control.

He instructed Gwyn to find food and quarters for the Enâri while he sought out Commander Jarrin. A short time later the wizard found him inside one of the larger tents, huddled with the other ship captains while preparing their battle plans. A map of Montavia was spread out across a small table, illuminated with several candles as a salty breeze rustled the brittle grass outside. Caldurian greeted the men with a cool nod. All were dressed in long, heavy brown sea coats similar to Commander Jarrin's, their faces careworn by bitter winds and a lack of sound sleep.

"We're reviewing the final placement of troops," the commander told Caldurian, inviting him to squeeze through the group and view the map. "Triana is located near the eastern edge of the Keppel Mountains, less than a two day march south. The bulk of our forces will be directed there. I don't expect King Rowan will put up much of a fight when he sees our numbers."

"I don't think so either," Caldurian agreed. "It is an aging population in Montavia. Many of the younger families have found a better life in Arrondale or down south. And since war has never come to this tiny kingdom in recent history, preparations against it have never been one of Montavia's top priorities. It will easily fall."

"And when this war is over, Montavia will make a nice plot of land for the Northern Isles to seize," one of the others joked. "We need space to stretch our arms and legs!" A stern glance from the wizard cut short any laughter from the rest.

"Know that Vellan is looking out for the interests of the Isles. Your nation will be repaid for your many years of assistance to Kargoth," he explained. "But first things first." The wizard addressed Commander Jarrin, scanning the map. "What of the larger villages?"

"There are six we need to secure. A company of two hundred men to each will keep the populations in line." He pointed out a few small fishing villages on the map many miles farther east down shore. "We dispatched a few dozen troops to scout out the roads around these villages as a precaution. Should anyone travel this way and spot our ships, we'll prevent them from getting word to Triana."

"Well done, commander. Will you be ready to march tomorrow morning?"

"Yes, at the break of dawn. On the second morning after that, we'll begin our assault."

"And did you bring the supplies for the Enâri as I requested?"

Commander Jarrin eyed one of his captains, a bald man with a trimmed black beard, who addressed Caldurian. "We have weapons on my ship and fighting raiment for your Enâri troops, sir. The armory smithies have fashioned swords and clubs suitable for their height. There are also crates of leather jerkins, boots, headgear and the like similar to our own, though everything has been tailored to your specifications."

"Good. Make arrangements with Gwyn to have the items unloaded and distributed." The wizard glanced at Jarrin. "Now, commander, if there is an empty tent, I would appreciate some much needed rest. I'll see you before dawn."

"As you wish." He instructed the same captain to escort Caldurian to his tent before attending to the battle needs of the Enâri. When the wizard disappeared through the flap, an unnerving tension dissolved at once. Jarrin caressed his whiskers and breathed a slight sigh of relief, happy not to have Caldurian's watchful gaze upon him. He returned to the map and finished speaking to the others, eager to start and finish this mission as quickly as possible.

Caldurian emerged from his tent well before sunrise. Thin clouds drifted overhead, casting a gauzy veil over the gibbous Fox Moon sinking in the west. The damp, breezy air smelled of the sea as it teased the snapping flames of the bonfires along the shoreline. Fire tenders patrolled the area in watchful silence.

Soon the graying campgrounds shook off the night as both the Enâri and the troops from the Northern Isles awoke. Breakfasts were cold and sparse, and provisions and weapons were swiftly packed. Some soldiers remained on shore with the ships, but the bulk of the men marched south under Commander Jarrin's orders. The Enâri dutifully followed Gwyn. But every last soldier knew that Caldurian was ultimately in charge and that his word was never to be challenged. Montavia would fall by his design.

The skies cleared to deep blue by late morning as the sun drifted across the sky. The dry, grassy terrain was littered with the fallen leaves of autumn. Gurgling brooks meandering down from the Keppel Mountains to their right were crisp, cold and noisy. The sea breezes had disappeared as they passed through spindly woodland and stretches of wide fields ripe with the scent of rich soil and decaying weeds.

The troops veered eastward and the sun-tipped mountains retreated slightly in the distance. The first sighting of any major road occurred near twilight. The dirt highway ran north to south and the company followed it for almost a mile, at which point another road branched off to the southeast. Commander Jarrin halted and consulted with Caldurian. Here some of the companies would break off and proceed to the larger villages outside the capital. Jarrin, after studying a map, appointed three of his captains to the task.

"This road branches off just beyond that second hill, leading to the different villages. Surround and infiltrate from all sides, killing only if you have to. We want to occupy Montavia, not destroy it. Let the locals go about their business, but round up the village leaders and bring them to the capital city."

Shortly after, three companies totaling six hundred soldiers and their supply wagons disappeared into the dim light and distant pines. Commander Jarrin signaled for the remaining Island and Enâri troops to continue south down the main road until nightfall.

"I'm pleased with our progress, commander. May we be as fortunate the day after tomorrow," the wizard said.

Jarrin nodded. "I wish so, too, though it is awfully quiet in these parts. The distant mountains loom over us as if spying, and the still air bothers me. I miss the salty breeze off the Trillium and the crash of waves against my ship." He glanced up at the starry sky. "After we take this kingdom, I will request a command back on the Isles. I would be too restless to remain in these lands permanently."

"I, too, am restless," Caldurian admitted, fingering an amber colored glass vial sealed with a wooden stopper hidden inside his cloak pocket. "Though unlike you, I am restless for a change in my circumstances. But until that time, we march. Now if you'll excuse me, I must talk to Gwyn. Halt the troops for the night at your discretion."

"As you wish," he said, a stream of air slowly escaping between his pursed lips after the wizard had left.

The final leg of the journey commenced the following dawn. Two hours into the march, Commander Jarrin released three more companies onto other roads to make for the remaining large villages. About five hundred troops from the Isles, in addition to the band of Enâri fighters, were now left for the assault on the capital city. By early afternoon they were less than a two hour march from Triana.

He halted the advancing column which stretched out like a brown snake weaving its way among the grass, rocks and trees. The bright sunshine offered little relief from a persistent chill saturating the air.

"We'll head into the wilderness and take cover now as we make our way toward the capital," he told Caldurian and his captains. "We'll halt about three miles from the city's edge before breaking up to surround the perimeter. We attack at dawn." He eyed Gwyn who stood dutifully at the wizard's side. "Your Enâri troops will make the initial assault of King Rowan's compound. I and the remaining hundred of my soldiers will follow. Understood?"

Gwyn snarled under his breath, tugging at the snug collar of his leather jerkin. "Don't fret, commander. My troops will do as they're told. Worry about your own."

"It is my job to worry about everyone, Enar. Now let us slip into the trees and move on," he said, wading through a patch of goldenrod spread out before a distant wilderness of maple, oak, elm and pine. "With luck, this time tomorrow we'll be feasting on King Rowan's store of venison and ale."

Before the first gray light of dawn touched the slumbering sky, Commander Jarrin guided his remaining one hundred troops and the Enâri soldiers the final three miles to the capital city. His other troops had departed last evening to take their positions around various parts of the city, waiting for the signal to move in. The commander emerged from nearby hilly woodlands, greeted by a few slumbering farmhouses of stone, sod and wood.

Triana was the largest city in Montavia, having spread outward in a lazy circle as its population grew. Thin columns of blue-gray chimney smoke drifted above log and thatch rooftops into the awakening sky. Candlelight flickered from home windows of the earliest risers. Soon barn doors were opened, forge furnaces stoked and bread dough on bakeshop tables vigorously kneaded.

King Rowan's residence, affectionately dubbed Red Lodge by the locals, occupied the center of Triana near the Gestina River which flowed down from the Keppel Mountains. The long main building with a series of gabled rooftops rose three stories high, its base built from the redstone quarried in the mountains coupled with solid oak posts and beams harvested from nearby forests. Several smaller structures, including storehouses, additional residences, horse stables and a garrison, were laid out in the vicinity, all surrounded by a thick outer wall of stone rising the height of two grown men. The main gate faced south, with several smaller gates built around the perimeter. A series of oil lamps hung at various spots above the wall burned steadily throughout the night year round. Sentries guarded each gate, which were barred every evening, and patrols walked along the top of the wall from sundown to sunrise.

Before Triana's residents had taken to the frosty streets, Commander Jarrin funneled his men into the city, leading them swiftly to Red Lodge along hard, rutted dirt roads past strings of houses and shops. Caldurian, Gwyn and the other Enâri closely followed. Vellan's stone and soil creations were especially eager to avenge their forced twenty-year sleep on anyone. The pale light from the Fox Moon, three days past full, dipped toward the mountains in the west, casting a dull sheen across the rooftops and sky.

The trek to the center of town went uninterrupted until the inebriated ramblings of a man stumbling out of the shadows caught their attention. The stranger, who had just awoken moments ago in a pile of hay after a night of merriment in a local pub, looked up at the approaching soldiers from the Northern Isles pouring into his city. He rubbed his eyes and stood frozen in place, wondering if he were imagining the surreal scene of invading troops scattered before him. But the man hadn't a moment to raise a hand or open his mouth to question his senses. He instantly fell backward, landing on the road like a sack of dirt, an arrow sticking out of his chest. His opened eyes gazed lifelessly at the shimmering morning stars drifting overhead.

Caldurian nodded in approval at the soldier who had fired the arrow upon his command. The troops then silently moved on to the center of town, arriving at King Rowan's residence a few minutes later. Red Lodge lay still under the freshening gray sky, the sputtering oil lamps the only sound carried on a slight breeze. They kept watch from a safe distance, hidden in the shadows of nearby buildings and trees, making sure the way was clear. With a raised hand, Commander Jarrin dispersed his troops to each entrance of the outer wall. Gwyn, likewise, signaled for the Enâri to take their

NICHOLAS RAVEN AND THE WIZARDS' WEB - VOLUME 1

positions at even intervals around the wall, each of his soldiers armed with a length of rope tied to a metal hook, preparing to fling it over the stone wall.

Caldurian and Jarrin, who had remained back in the shadows with a handful of soldiers, glanced at one another. After Jarrin nodded, affirming his readiness, the wizard placed his hands over the tip of an arrow one of the soldiers had at the ready and whispered several words that none could understand. Soon the arrow tip glowed blue and burst into a ghostly flame. In one sweeping move, the soldier raised the bow and aimed at the sky, launching the burning arrow high into the air directly above the center of the Red Lodge compound. The signal was sent. The invasion of Triana was at hand.

"What was that?" a voice on the wall called out in the gloom. "Did you–"

But a moment later he was silenced by another arrow, as were all of King Rowan's men who patrolled atop the wall, each targeted by Commander Jarrin's best archers. Their bodies fell over the wall to the shock of any guards standing below inside near the gates. At that instant, the Enâri troops hurled metal hooks over the wall and scrambled up the ropes, climbing in seconds to the top of the wall like insects. Nearly five hundred of Vellan's mountain creatures now surrounded Red Lodge from the top of the wall before jumping into the courtyard just as a warning bell clanged repeatedly in the darkness. The raid was no longer a secret.

A clash of swords echoed in the darkness as another half dozen blue flaming arrows sailed overhead, all descending upon one particular storehouse inside the compound. In seconds, flames burst from within the building, spitting out from windows and the rooftop as panicked shouts of alarm rippled behind the walls. Caldurian listened closely as the sword fighting intensified, a few screams and muffled words punctuating the moment. As the first hints of dawn intensified, the wizard smiled, hearing the one sound he had been eagerly anticipating. The main gates had been unbarred by the Enâri from within and flung wide open. He imagined the same thing happening at all the lesser gates as the sounds and voices of the fighting suddenly magnified.

Seconds later, soldiers from the Northern Isles charged inside the compound while the Enâri overwhelmed their outnumbered opponents near the wall. Commander Jarrin's troops bolted toward

Red Lodge as a slew of King Rowan's guards scrambled down the wide front steps. Swords were drawn and the fighting commenced at once, but most of the royal guard was quickly defeated by the tidal wave of Island men and a stampede of Enâri who joined the clash as the fighting near the gates diminished. The remaining members of the King's Guard retreated inside and tried to bar the main entrance, but the sheer weight of Jarrin's men slamming against the thick wooden doors like an avalanche of boulders was no match for the opposition. The doors burst wide open and the invaders spread through the royal quarters like wildfire.

Outside, Caldurian passed through the main gates in triumph with Gwyn and Jarrin at his side as the sky brightened in the east. The long, wide courtyard dotted with trees, shrubbery and gardens contained a sea of Enâri soldiers. Many had made their way into the smaller buildings, fighting whoever opposed them. The garrison had long since been emptied while the fire in one of the storehouses continued to burn. Slain bodies of Montavian soldiers lay about, their spilt blood slowly reddening in the growing light. A few of the Enâri had been killed, though their lifeless corpses were devoid of any bloodshed and their eyes had turned the color of dark stone.

"At last a success I can report to Vellan!" Caldurian said as he marched up the front steps of Red Lodge, the first distant cries from within the city reaching his ears.

"The alliance between Kargoth and the Northern Isles has succeeded beyond my expectations," Commander Jarrin pleasantly admitted.

"You had doubts?" the wizard remarked as they entered the building, walking down the main hall illuminated by oil lamps attached to wooden pillars decorated with garlands of autumn leaves and berries. "Surely they are erased at this point. Don't you agree, Gwyn?"

"Absolutely!" the Enâr replied with a satisfied grunt, thrilled with the taste of victory after a long, tiresome confinement in the Spirit Caves. "I had no doubts."

"Well, the doubts are behind me now," Jarrin said. "Now let's see what lies ahead instead, shall we?"

"Indeed we shall," the wizard remarked lightheartedly. "And the first item on our list is an appointment with King Rowan."

The clash of swords resonated throughout Red Lodge as the first rays of sunlight seeped in through the southeast windows. Most of the royal guard had been killed or taken prisoner within the hour, though a few skirmishes still raged in some of the rooms. Enâri guards were posted throughout the building, including near the kitchens and offices, instructing all workers to continue performing their jobs. The flash of a sword blade or the threat of a wooden club kept the civilians in line.

Havla, one of Jarrin's soldiers with a mop of long, stringy hair, had located King Rowan who was now engaged in a battle on the second floor and protected by a stalwart group of his guardsmen. Caldurian instructed Havla to lead the way there at once, and soon they were rushing down a wide hallway whose walls were carved with elaborate woodworking bedecked with tapestries and flickering light. Throaty shouts and the striking of metal against metal were audible inside a room at the end of the corridor. A dead soldier from the Northern Isles lay sprawled upon the ground near the doorway.

"Hurry!" Commander Jarrin cried, drawing a sword.

A moment later, he and Havla burst into the room with Caldurian and Gwyn close behind. Several dead bodies were scattered near a stone fireplace, the wooden floor stained with blood. Two of King Rowan's soldiers were ushering a man out of the room through a second doorway in back as Jarrin entered. The soldiers immediately closed ranks in front of the man whose fierce brown eyes matched the color of his short hair. He wore a silver waistcoat over a black, gray and white checkered tunic, brown boots and trousers. A sword in his ornate scabbard hung lifelessly at his side.

"We'll hold off the intruders!" one of the guards shouted to the man. "You must leave now."

"Nonsense! I'll fight to save my house to the end," King Rowan cried, urging the guards on.

The two men sprang forward with swords drawn, fighting Commander Jarrin and Havla. Moments later, one of the guards was struck dead by Jarrin. Havla was seriously wounded shortly after, earning a swift death. The King then drew his sword, glaring wildly at Caldurian and Gwyn as he advanced. Gwyn unsheathed a sword, preparing to rush forward, when the wizard held him back.

"Not necessary," he softly said, glancing at the Enâr who looked up at him in puzzlement. But when King Rowan advanced in a fiery rage, Caldurian raised an arm and extended his fingers, causing the sword to fly out of the King's hand. The wizard pulled out a dagger at his side an instant later and flung it at King Rowan, sending him collapsing to the floor upon his back. The second guardsman fell dead at the same moment as Commander Jarrin pulled his reddened blade from the man's body.

The King stared at the rafters, feeling dizzy as he listened to his pounding heart. He turned his head, noting the dagger handle sticking out of his shoulder. Blood had begun to cake on his checkered tunic. The wizard advanced toward him with slow, deliberate steps that cast dull echoes off the high ceiling.

"Will you kill me now, scoundrel?" King Rowan said with contempt.

Caldurian looked down. "If I had wanted you dead, I would have pierced your heart. After all, my aim is impeccable." He reached down and pulled out the knife, causing the King to wince. The wizard placed a hand over King Rowan's wound and the pain temporarily subsided. "Still, I'd have your court physician examine that wound if I were you. We'll talk afterward."

The late morning sun slipped through a window in the King's upper study. Outside, the Gestina River sparkled in the distance as the remaining leaves from a thicket of white birch trees fluttered onto the flowing water. King Rowan gingerly slipped on a dark blue waistcoat over a clean gray tunic, both of which had been supplied to him after his physician attended to his wound. The King sat down in a chair in front of a large pine table that served as a desk. Caldurian had allowed the physician to be brought in after King Rowan was confined to his upper study. Two soldiers from the Northern Isles stood guard outside the door.

A few moments later, the wizard walked into the room accompanied by a woman wearing a beige dress with decorative embroidery and a blue woolen shawl wrapped around her shoulders. She was in her mid-thirties, her long blond hair set in a thick braid. As soon as the woman saw King Rowan, she rushed to his side.

"Are you all right, Father? I had feared the worst," she said, a slight tremor in her voice as she took his hand.

"I'm quite fine thanks to Elwood," he replied, indicating his physician with a slight turn of the head. He then glanced at Caldurian. "Thank you for allowing my daughter-in-law to visit me. I didn't want her to worry."

"Vilna may stay here as long as you cooperate," Caldurian said before gazing at the young woman. "I'm sorry to hear that Prince Kendrick is no longer with you. I heard of his passing a few years ago when I was on the Isles. An accident, was it? A rockslide?"

Vilna scoffed at him with an icy glance. "You care not a whit for my dead husband, wizard, so why pretend?"

"Vilna, please," King Rowan whispered, patting her hand.

"I'm sorry, Father, but I will not pretend to be civil with this invader. Let him lock me up in a garrison cell if he must."

"Perhaps not yet," the wizard replied dryly.

"We will cooperate," the King promised. "But the death of my son is a family matter, so allow us to keep it such. Do not upset my daughter-in-law any further."

"My apologies." Caldurian pointed to a fireplace in the corner of the room. Suddenly the low flames ignited with a roar, the rush of warm air swaying a set of thick red drapes adorning the adjacent window. "That's better. It's damp in here."

"Some hot soup would do His Majesty a world of good," Elwood piped up, glancing cautiously at the wizard. "Just a suggestion."

"Then make it happen, physician. Alert the kitchen to your request and have them bring lunch for all of us. I could do with a bit of soup myself."

"As you wish," he replied, nervously raking his fingers through a head of gray, straw-textured hair before fishing through a leather medicine bag that rarely left his side. Elwood removed a glass vial containing a coarse, dark powder and handed it to King Rowan. "And if it would please you, sir, sprinkle a bit of this ground rasaweed in your tea before bed over the next few nights. But just a bit, mind you, as it is quite potent. It will help you to get a deep, recuperative sleep which is most necessary after your injury."

"It *doesn't* please me, Elwood," the King gruffly replied, grabbing the vial and slapping it down on the desk. "But I would like some soup."

"Of course," he said with a nod before hurrying out the door.

"He performs his duties admirably, though is a bit tiring to be around," Caldurian quipped a moment later. "Like a busy child that has to be constantly watched."

"Elwood has been in my service for years. He's earned my respect and admiration countless times," King Rowan said. "But now that he is gone, I will speak freely. Surely you're not here just to pass idle chatter with my daughter-in-law and me, are you?"

"You could have endured a worse fate," Caldurian said, "had Vellan himself invaded your domain. So be thankful for that bit of fortune. But what's wrong with some conversation? And speaking of children, where are yours?" the wizard remarked, focusing his gaze upon Vilna. "Where are the heirs to the throne of Montavia?"

Vilna scowled with disdain, countering his potent stare for a moment before glancing at King Rowan for solace. The King sighed, addressing Caldurian.

"Brendan and William have been in Arrondale for six weeks. They insisted on accompanying some of my troops who've been traveling in rotations to train in Morrenwood with King Justin's finest," he explained. "Arrondale has a far superior military, and I am not ashamed to say that I welcomed their training and knowledge. My men have enjoyed visiting our neighbor to the west and returning as superior soldiers."

"I must admit that you faced our initial invasion with a much heartier resistance than I had expected," the wizard replied.

"You beat us in numbers only," Vilna said. "Were we more evenly matched, the Island men and Vellan's pitiful creations would not have stood a chance."

"Perhaps."

King Rowan's face tightened as he took a deep breath. "Know this, Caldurian. When word gets out of Montavia about your attack–and trust me, it will–reinforcements will arrive and drive you and your host out of here. And my two grandsons and the remaining Montavian troops still training in Arrondale will be leading the charge. Mark my words!" The King leaned back in his chair, his dark mood somewhat lessened. "No matter how many of your troops infest my lands, you cannot guard every house and road and woodland in the kingdom. Patriots young and old will sneak through your nets and plan a resistance. Your stay here is temporary."

Caldurian nodded as he paced about the room, briefly admiring a painting of the nearby countryside. "That's one way to look at it. Yet more men from the Northern Isles will eventually pour onto your shores, and Vellan is most certainly going to march additional columns of Enâri this way, transforming Montavia into something you will not recognize." He turned and faced King Rowan. "That is another way to look at it, sir. And if you were a realist, you would admit that that is Montavia's fate. But deep in your heart, I think there's a part of you that has already admitted it, that has accepted defeat. It's just a matter of time until your mind accepts the same truth."

King Rowan grunted. "Your words may dishearten the souls of others, but I am not easily discouraged. Montavia has suffered a grave defeat, but my nation is not dead yet. Help will soon arrive–" A knock on the door interrupted him. Three individuals from the kitchens entered, carrying trays of food and a pitcher of cold milk for the King's lunch. "–and arrive when least expected. No, Caldurian, the people of Montavia will not give up so easily! Word of this outrage will reach King Justin's ear in Morrenwood and the resounding reply will crush you." The King looked at Vilna who returned a steely, yet barely perceptible smile.

"We shall see," Caldurian said. "But at the first sign of any revolt, my response will be swift and deadly. Your garrison cells will be filled up with more than just your soldiers. That is why I am having the leaders of your largest villages brought here tomorrow. You will demand the cooperation of their communities on my behalf if you want to keep any semblance of peace in this realm. You will have only one chance."

After a long, hard think, King Rowan nodded. "I will talk with them and urge their cooperation, yet I cannot promise that a stray individual or other might not take matters into his own hands to protect this nation."

"I'll deal with any unexpected outbursts as I must," the wizard replied. "So make your royal words convincing, sir."

"I will try."

The King shot a glance at the kitchen help, an older woman with graying hair who seemed in charge, and two younger boys of about fifteen and seventeen who stood behind her on either side. All wore gray smocks over their clothes, splattered here and there with bits of dried grease and flour. The woman's hair, limp from the ever present humidity rising from steaming kettles in the kitchen quarters, was covered with a yellow kerchief. The boys each wore a dark woven cap over their wavy brown hair.

"Well, look alive and serve us lunch!" the King commanded with a clap of his hands, indicating for the two boys to set their trays on the desk. He raised an eyebrow when making eye contact with them while Vilna stood silently by the King's side, her hand resting on his shoulder, slightly trembling.

Swiftly the kitchen staff went to work ladling beef soup from a large tureen into three earthenware bowls. Fresh goat's milk was poured into metal goblets and hot biscuits with butter were arranged on a plate. The woman respectfully handed King Rowan, Vilna and Caldurian a cloth napkin each, bowing slightly as she backed away, waiting for her two assistants to collect the serving dishes on the trays so they could depart.

"Is there any other meal request before we leave?" the woman asked, not quite sure whether to address the wizard or the King.

"That will be all, Martha," Vilna kindly said, smiling at the woman. "You may leave now and clear the remaining dishes later."

"Yes, ma'am," she replied, signaling for the two boys to follow her out with the trays.

"Wait, boy!" King Rowan shouted as he set his spoon down after tasting the soup. He grabbed the glass vial of rasaweed from the desk and dropped it on one of the cluttered trays. "Toss that in the nearest rubbish pit," he muttered. "I don't care what the physician said, but I refuse to take any of his blasted sleeping medicine. I can't have my senses dulled while Montavia is under siege. Now leave us to enjoy our lunch."

"Yes, sir," the older boy politely replied with a bow.

"And tell the kitchen not to leave the onions out of my soup next time," he muttered with disgust. "They're my favorite part."

"Yes, sir. Sorry, sir," the boy replied apologetically before hurriedly following the others out the door.

NICHOLAS RAVEN AND THE WIZARDS' WEB - VOLUME 1

Caldurian chuckled as he walked to the desk to get his soup. "Kings never make the best patients, do they."

"Nor the best prisoners," King Rowan replied, staring coolly at the wizard as he took a seat. "At least not this one."

CHAPTER 23

Bread and Soup

Martha returned to the busy kitchens several minutes later with the two boys. They weaved their way among the bread bakers and crockery washers to a quieter corner in the large, stone multi-chambered room. Bundles of dried herbs hanging upside down from the rafters pungently perfumed the air. Several brick ovens built into the walls glowed red with beds of hot embers while the constant chatter of workers added to the stifling heat.

"Well, we did it," Martha whispered to her two helpers as they cleaned off the trays, her hands shaking and her heart beating rapidly. "I was so nervous about bringing you with me, but as you insisted, who was I to argue? Anyway, it worked. You saw for yourself that your mother and grandfather are safe."

"For now," the older boy said, glancing around the room. Though none of the enemy soldiers were keeping watch inside the kitchens, two Enâri guards patrolled the corridor outside. "Still, we have to do something!"

"What you have to do is stay safe, Prince Brendan. That is your job now," Martha whispered to the boy whom she thought acted older than his seventeen years. His sea blue eyes stared back at her, coolly burning under waves of brownish hair. "You and your brother must play the part of kitchen workers until this mess is settled. It's what your mother requested of me."

Brendan sighed, grimacing at his younger brother, William. After the attack on Red Lodge at dawn, their mother had hurried to the kitchens with her sons to find Martha, one of the supervisors who often attended to her family's meals. Vilna asked the woman to disguise the boys as kitchen workers for their safety, informing King Rowan about the deception minutes before he was first attacked.

"But my brother and I can't stay here and do nothing while Montavia is under siege," Brendan insisted, pulling off his cap.

"We'll be safe in the kitchens," William said, his large light brown eyes gazing up at his brother. Though he was equally frustrated, he didn't have an alternate plan. "It's what mother wanted us to do."

"But not grandfather." Brendan grabbed the vial of rasaweed lying on the tray. "He was trying to tell me something when he insisted that I get rid of this vial of sleeping medicine. Grandfather never talks to anyone in that sharp tone of voice. And as he despises the taste of onions, why would he request them in his soup? That was just an act to get our attention, to urge us to do something. I saw it in his eyes."

"What was the King trying to tell you?" Martha asked.

"He wants me to escape and get help somehow. Do you recall what he said to that wizard moments after he saw us enter the room? *Word of this outrage will reach King Justin's ear in Morrenwood.* If that wasn't a signal for us to act, then I don't know what is."

"You can't be serious?" Martha said, keeping her gesticulating hands in check so as not to draw the attention of others. She nervously adjusted the yellow kerchief on her head. "How would you ever get out of the compound? There are guards at every gate."

"We could hide in a supply wagon next time it leaves," William suggested.

"The guards are surely to search those both coming and going," Brendan said, staring at the vial of rasaweed before looking up at Martha with a budding grin. "Martha, all the soldiers outdoors will probably take their meals in the garrison kitchens, correct?"

"That's right, gluttons that some of them are. We've been baking extra bread here to send over since there are fewer ovens in that building," she said. "They are terribly understaffed to handle this flood of hungry men, cooking soup and stew nonstop. And goodness knows what those Enâri creatures eat!"

"Then send William and me over there to help in the kitchens. The garrison is closest to the west gate," he explained. "It is but a tiny barred door, merely a side entrance."

"But two or three enemy soldiers will be stationed there nonetheless," she said. "So it might as well be a hundred. How will you get past them?"

"We'll leave at dark. A new shift of guards usually eats before they take to their posts, right?" Martha nodded as the young prince held up the vial of rasaweed. "Perhaps we can add a little extra seasoning to their soup."

"Sleeping medicine?" Martha quickly pushed Brendan's hand down in case a stray eye should see. "What do you suggest?"

"Pour it into a kettle of soup, serve it to the guards and wait," he explained.

William nodded enthusiastically. "Great idea!"

Martha continued to look busy while she talked. "And soon after, all the men guarding the gates will start to slump over in a deep sleep. What kind of attention do you think that'll draw?"

Brendan nodded sheepishly. "Yes, I suppose it would."

"Still, I think you're onto something," she reluctantly said to Prince Brendan's surprise. "But we need a more subtle plan." The two brothers brimmed with curiosity. "My cousin, Clovis, is a cook in the garrison. Perhaps he can help."

"How?" William asked.

"I have something in mind," she said. "But for now, you two go back to washing dishes. In an hour or so I'll take you with me to help deliver the next two basketfuls of bread to the garrison. I'll leave you there to assist Clovis."

"All right," Brendan said, turning with his brother to leave. "We'll do it your way."

"And Brendan," Martha added in a sharp whisper, "keep that vial out of sight."

After the lunch rush subsided and the kitchen staff began preparations for the evening meals, Martha rounded up two large baskets woven from willow switches and filled them with small round loaves of bread to take to the garrison. She walked down the kitchen corridor accompanied by the two young princes, passing a handful of Enâri guards at their various stations, several of whom inspected the baskets and helped themselves to a snack before allowing the workers to pass. When they finally exited Red Lodge through a side entrance, the trio walked across the cobblestone compound to the garrison with Brendan in the center holding onto a handle of each basket while Martha and William grabbed an opposite handle on either side.

Billowy clouds drifted overhead on the cool autumn afternoon, yet the courtyard trees, gardens and cobblestones were sun-splashed and vibrant. A throng of Island soldiers in long brown coats milled about near the various gates as Enâri guards walked along the top of the wall as if in mindless trances. Traces of black and gray smoke rose from the burnt-out hulk of one of the nearby storehouses. Brendan and William kept their eyes cast down and muttered to themselves, trying to subdue the rising anger in their hearts. Each boy wanted to lash out in some manner but knew it could mean their deaths if they did so.

"I sense how you feel," Martha whispered after they walked past two swaggering Island soldiers who each swiped a round of bread while mocking the kitchen workers. "But if our plan works, you'll be able to do more good on the outside rather than making a valiant yet senseless stand inside these walls. Direct your energies to the escape."

Brendan grunted. "I know you're right, Martha, but it's not easy."

"Most important things worth doing in life never are, so..." She indicated the garrison up ahead. Beyond it to the west was a large well and a thicket of trees, and past that was an open space with a clear view of the northwest corner of the surrounding wall. The small west gate built beneath a stone archway was close to the north section. Two soldiers from the Isles stood guard near the gate. An Enâri watchman would occasionally amble by on the wall above while walking his guard.

Those of King Rowan's troops who were stationed at the compound but not housed in Red Lodge itself were quartered in the garrison. Serving behind the King's walls at least once in their military career was a desired goal and a mark of prestige for every soldier. But today the King's domicile had been turned upside down and the garrison overflowed with an invading horde. Martha hurried inside with Brendan, William and the bread, finding her cousin in one of the back kitchens. The man in a greasy white shirt and a towel over his shoulder greeted her with a huge smile, minus a couple of teeth. An unkempt head of thinning gray hair crept down his shoulders. He directed that the baskets of bread be taken away by some of his other helpers.

"Your bakers are doing fine service in this troubled time, Martha," he said, sipping from a wooden cup after raising it to her in good humor. "May I offer you a libation?"

"I'm still on duty, Clovis. And so are you," she replied with a chuckle. "But I'm here to offer you something, cousin."

"Really? What?"

Martha pointed to Brendan and William. "*Them.*"

"Extra help?" he asked, pleasantly surprised. "Well, we won't turn that down, will we, Sadie!" he called out to a woman across the room working one of the ovens.

"No indeed!" she replied with a laugh.

"Welcome to the garrison," Clovis pleasantly said, addressing the two boys. "I'll set you to work right away and…" He suddenly eyed Brendan and William a bit closer, noting a peculiar familiarity. He scanned their features as he scratched his chin. "And what might your names be?" he asked, not allowing them a second to answer. It suddenly hit him where he had seen the two teenagers before. Clovis glanced wide-eyed at his cousin, silently fishing for an explanation.

"You've recognized them correctly," she whispered. "But do not mention their names out loud."

"No, of course not!" he said, slightly taken aback. "But their hair is so…" He looked at them closer. "Is that really…?" He quickly set his drink down. "Oh, pardon me for this," he added, a bit embarrassed. "I was thirsty from the heat and a bottle of plum wine was the nearest beverage. It won't happen again, young sirs."

Brendan grinned. "You needn't worry about it, Clovis. Carry on as always. My brother and I are in your care now as Martha will shortly explain."

"I'll explain quickly," she added. "I have to get back to my station in Red Lodge."

"Then by all means, tell me what is going on," Clovis said, leading them to an open pantry farthest away from any other workers. "To what do I owe the honor of having them in my kitchen? And what can I do to help?"

Martha smiled impishly. "What you can do, cousin, is make a special batch of your delicious potato and bacon soup!"

"I don't understand," William whispered to his older brother later that evening as they washed dishes in a large metal cauldron of hot, soapy water. The clamor of soldiers eating dinner in the front rooms reverberated throughout the garrison. "Why didn't Clovis just pour the whole vial into their food? Wouldn't that have been easier?"

Brendan shook his head as he rinsed a few bowls in a huge kettle of clean water and stacked them to dry. "Like Martha said, if he had done that, all the soldiers in this place would be falling asleep at their posts in another hour and the alarm would be raised. We wouldn't escape under those circumstances. And who knows what harsh measures the wizard would impose afterward." He glanced reassuringly at his brother. "Clovis has the right idea. He'll send his niece out after the guard changes. That's our best chance."

William shrugged. "If you say so. I'm just glad you're in charge and not me." He happened to glance through an archway into another part of the kitchen and saw a young girl about his age speaking to Clovis in private. He assumed they were discussing the plan. "There she is, Brendan. I hope Isabel is a good actress."

"We'll find out shortly," he replied distractedly as he looked longingly into the wash water. "How I'd like to dunk my head into this right about now," he joked, scratching at his cap in annoyance.

William grunted, trying to suppress a grin. "Pretty soon, I hope." He watched the girl depart and saw Clovis return to work as the spark of humor left him. He sighed anxiously, counting down the minutes until their plan was set in motion.

Isabel stepped out a side door of the kitchen an hour after the garrison was emptied of the last group of guards that had sat down for dinner. The petite blond girl, dressed in kitchen garb and a cloak, carried a large bowl of hot potato and bacon soup covered with a plate and a round loaf of bread sitting on top. She glanced about nervously and took a deep breath before walking toward the west gate under the rising Bear Moon. After passing the well and emerging from beneath a clump of trees, the west gate appeared in view in the near distance. From the illumination of a single oil lamp attached above the guard post, Isabel could distinguish two Island soldiers standing near the archway in the wall. The subtle moonlight guided her the rest of the way.

The guards stood at attention and drew their swords when they saw the dark shape approaching, but quickly relaxed when recognizing a young girl in a cloak. The whiskered men grunted at one another and returned the swords to their sheaths.

"If this is the kind of escape attempts we'll have to deal with, then this will be a boring rotation off the Isles," one of them joked.

"You're right," the other soldier said before addressing the girl. "What do you want, little one? Isn't it past your bedtime?"

Isabel smirked. "That's very amusing, even for an Islander. But I was just working in the kitchens and—"

"Say, what's in the bowl?" the first guard asked, cautiously placing his hand back on the hilt of his sword. "Do you have a knife in there? Maybe a rock?"

"It's soup!" Isabel said, raising the plate and bread so the men could see and smell the steaming liquid. "Leftover potato and bacon from dinner." The guards smelled the enticing aroma, recalling the tasty meal they had eaten only a short while ago. "For the last several nights my kitchen supervisor has allowed me to take leftover soup home to my sick uncle not far from here. He's had the chills awfully bad this week, but is starting to come around." She gazed pleadingly at the soldiers, her large green eyes radiating helpless innocence. "I always pass through this gate when visiting my uncle, but tonight—"

"—we're here instead. Is that a problem for you and your uncle, dear?"

Isabel nervously swallowed. "Well, that depends if you'll allow me to pass through or not. I promise to hurry right back. I still have duties in the kitchen."

The first guard glanced at the other, and then nodded understandingly at Isabel. "As touching as your story is, I can't begin to explain the trouble I'd land in if I allowed any of you people to leave the compound without permission from my commander. No matter your promise to come back, it's not going to happen."

Isabel's eyes began to water. "But…"

"However," the other soldier jumped in, "we understand the difficulty your uncle must be going through, being sick and all, and promise to have one of the off-duty men take it personally to your relative. As soon as the Enâr patrolling our section of the wall passes by again, we'll send word with him to have someone hurry back this way to make your delivery. Where does your uncle live?"

"Just across the main road outside this gate, then down the third lane to the right. He's in the very last house with the thatch roof and a chicken coop on the side," she said. "But do you really mean to do this task for me? I want him to get well."

"Consider it done," the soldier said, taking the soup and bread from Isabel and setting it down on a wall ledge. "Now you'd best be off before a less friendly guard finds you wandering about, okay?"

"All right," she replied with a gracious nod. "And thank you so much for understanding."

Both soldiers smiled as Isabel turned around and hurried back to the garrison. When she had disappeared into the distant shadows, the second guard rubbed his whiskers and kept an eye out in her direction to make sure she didn't return. Satisfied, he grabbed the round of bread and ripped it apart, giving half to his friend.

"This post may not be as exciting as the main gate, but it does have its benefits!" he said with a laugh. He removed the plate covering the soup, then greedily dipped his bread into the broth and ate it. "Now how good is this?"

"Just don't let the Enâr see next time he passes by," the other replied with a grunt as he plowed his bread into the soup and voraciously consumed his bonus meal.

Hidden safely behind the well, Isabel watched as the two soldiers devoured the leftover meal meant for her non-existent uncle. She smiled, proud of her acting skills under duress, and then hurried back to the garrison.

Brendan and William were relieved to see Isabel return to the garrison a short while later as they helped wash down the long rows of tables and benches in the dining area. She sent a reassuring wink their way from across the room before disappearing into the kitchen.

"So far, so good," Brendan whispered to his younger brother, encouraged that something was finally happening to counter the attackers from across the sea.

"Our turn is next," William anxiously replied.

Half an hour later, after a quick word of thanks to Clovis in private, the two brothers slipped out the side door into the darkness. Clovis had provided each of them with a heavy coat borrowed from two of his workers and a small sack with some bread, apples, dried beef and a filled water skin. After double checking to see that no one was around, Brendan and William hurried across the compound to the well, crouching down behind it so they could observe the distant west gate. Though well hidden in shadows at this spot, they still felt as if the eyes of every Island soldier were upon them.

"I can only see one of the guards," William whispered as he peered over the rim of the stone well. "He's standing against the wall on the left."

Brendan noted the man as a knot of uneasiness gripped his stomach. Was one of them still awake? Had their plan failed already? He dared to stand up for a closer look, inspecting the dimly lit area near the arch as best he could. A satisfied smile slowly spread across his face. "I see the other one, Will."

"You do?"

"Yes. He's sitting on the ground against the wall, his head dropped to his chest." He glanced at his brother with a grin. "That rasaweed really works."

"Clovis used half the vial just to be sure," William said. "But how come the other guard is still standing up? Do you suppose he didn't eat any of the soup?"

"That could be. I..." As Brendan strained his eyes for a closer look, he suddenly realized something and shook his head. "That guard is sleeping, too. His head is resting against the wall and his arms are limp at his side. He probably tried to prop himself up when he first grew tired. Besides, if he was awake, he certainly wouldn't let his partner laze around on the ground."

"Good point." William looked at his brother, hoping his next words sounded confident, though fearing they might reveal the anxiety welling inside him. "Ready to go? We can't sit here all night."

Brendan patted him encouragingly on the shoulder before grabbing the sack of provisions. "Let's go–but quietly."

They cautiously left their hiding place behind the well, but before slipping out of the security of the surrounding trees, the brothers surveyed the compound one last time to make sure no guards were wandering about. All was clear. After waiting for the Enâri guard patrolling atop the west wall to pass out of sight, they scurried across the final open stretch of the compound in the dim moonlight, making for the archway. When they approached the two guards, each brother privately entertained fears that one or both of them would instantly awake and take them prisoner. But the two men remained still, one sitting and one standing, deeply breathing in the cool night air.

Brendan glanced at his brother, placing a finger to his lips and then pointing at the wooden gate beneath the archway. William nodded and indicated for his brother to lead the way. They passed under the archway and stopped at the two solid gates a few feet ahead. They were locked shut with a thick piece of oak timber wedged across two iron holders bolted to the door. Brendan handed the sack to his brother, and after taking a deep breath, he slowly lifted up the oak bar and set it against the inner archway. He was about to open one of the two gates when they heard the shuffle of steps and the grumblings of the Enâri soldier passing by on the wall above. Though he had no view of either Brendan or William at the moment, the Enâr might easily have seen his two colleagues fast asleep if he happened to glance over the inner edge. But as the wall was quite wide, Brendan thought the chances were good that the Enâr wouldn't notice during his monotonous patrol. The two brothers stared at one another, holding their breaths for what seemed an eternity. Despite the autumn chill, they were flushed with a warm prickling fear. Finally, the Enâri guard passed by overhead and all was again silent.

William exhaled as his brother opened the gate just wide enough to pass through. Without a word, the two young princes slipped out to the other side, seeing the road ahead bathed in gloomy shadows. Before the Enâr had a chance to turn around and head back this way, Brendan and William left the safety of the archway and dashed across the road, taking refuge in another thicket of tall trees just beyond the way. The sweet smell of pine invigorated them, yet they knew they were far from being safe. Brendan pointed at a narrow lane to the south where about a half dozen houses lay sleepily in the night along the edge of a small field to the right. Moonlight filtered down through gauzy clouds forming high in the sky.

"We'll make for that field," Brendan said. "Stay in the shadow of those houses as we head west. There are a few shops after that, but once we pass the smithy, we'll reach farmland. We'll head for the safety of the woods just beyond."

"And then what?" his brother asked.

"Let's get there first, Will, then we'll figure it out."

With no sign of any patrols, they bolted out of the trees and raced to the nearby field, cutting across the tall dried grass and the remains of some vegetable gardens like a swift night wind. A handful of low buildings greeted them adjacent to the opposite end of the field, a bakery and a candle shop among them. Brendan led his brother along the side of the bakery, carefully peering out around the front corner of the building into the adjacent lane. Since it lay dark and deserted, the two brothers assumed the best and scooted down the dirt road until they neared the blacksmith's shop at the end, tasting freedom with every step. But just before they neared the end of that building which ran alongside the plot of farmland, William noted a growing flash of light coming from that very direction. Brendan saw it too, and the brothers dashed to the right, hiding in the shadows on the opposite side of the blacksmith's shop.

They squatted on the ground next to a rain barrel, their backs to the wall and their heads bowed down to their kneecaps. Moments later, the voices of two Enâri soldiers drifted up the lane along with the light from a blazing torch. Brendan glanced to his right and saw the pair ambling up the road, their backs to him now as they talked to each other in gravelly voices on their watch. Though neither of the soldiers glanced in Brendan's direction, he didn't think they would have seen him or his brother from such a distance. When the Enâri were finally out of sight and earshot, the two brothers remained by the rain barrel for several more seconds in case anyone should return.

"I think we're safe," William whispered shortly after. "And my knees are starting to hurt."

"Then by all means, let's leave at once," Brendan replied with a smirk.

He stood up, and deeming the coast clear, indicated for William to follow him around the back of the building to avoid the main road. Moments later, the two princes were dashing across a farm field, the pungent scent of soil invading their noses as the edges of a nearby forest at the foot of the mountains beckoned to them. Several minutes later, a roof of pine, maple, oak and elm branches covered their heads while their footfalls splashed through puddles of dried autumn leaves littering the ground. After half an hour traveling south, they found a stream and stopped along its banks to rest and have a bite to eat. They built a small fire as the Bear Moon drifted overhead in its westward trek.

"I can't believe we did it," William said, giddy with excitement while munching on an apple as he watched the hypnotic snapping of the flames. "But I only wish Mother and Grandfather knew we were safe."

Brendan spoke reassuringly, sitting against a tree. "Martha will get word to them of our departure. Still, a proper goodbye would have been nice." He smiled at his brother. "And I had no doubts that you could do this, Will, despite the fact that you're my twerp of a little brother."

"Very funny, *Not-Quite-King* Brendan."

"Well, at least I can be a prince again," he said, shoving a hand in his pocket and fishing out a silver ring engraved with images of the royal house of King Rowan. Brendan slipped it on a finger. "We don't have to hide who we are for now. Didn't lose yours, did you?" he joked.

William tossed his apple core into the woods and quickly searched through his pockets, pretending he couldn't find the ring symbolizing his royal birth. "Maybe I dropped it down the well," he said lightheartedly before producing the ring and holding it up to the crackling fire. He put it on, staring at the fine etchings upon the metal band and wondering when he would see home again.

Brendan, sensing a trace of melancholy in his brother, jumped up and ripped off his hat and coat before kneeling by the stream. "I think we're safe now. Besides, I can't stand this anymore!"

William looked up hopefully. "You mean we can…?"

"Yep!"

With excited relief, Brendan dunked his head in the cold water several times, massaging his fingers through his hair. William rushed over to the stream, joyously imitating his brother's antics. After several minutes of brisk soaking, washing and splashing, the two siblings sat by the fire to dry off and keep warm. Their heads of hair, mussed up and tangled, were now each a slightly different shade of golden blond, yet both similar in color to their mother's. William draped the hood of his coat over his head after his hair had sufficiently dried.

"I don't know what kitchen ingredients Martha threw together to concoct that dye, but it was starting to itch terribly," he said.

"But it worked," Brendan replied. "The wizard Caldurian never had a reason to suspect who we were. I think even Mother and Grandfather were shocked the first moment they saw us walk into the study with their lunch, though they never let on."

"I wonder when we'll see them again," William whispered, feeling as if he were half a world away from home. "Soon, I hope."

"Then the sooner we get to Morrenwood, the better," his brother said. "We'll rest here until dawn and continue south. It's about a five hour hike to the Fainin Pass in the Keppel Mountains. Beyond that are the Black Hills on the eastern border of Arrondale."

"But we still have to travel all the way to the western part of the kingdom to reach Morrenwood," William said with a click of his tongue. "That'll take forever."

"So stop talking then and get some sleep," Brendan joked as he lay down by the fire. "You're going to need the rest!"

CHAPTER 24

The Swamp

The steady clatter of horse hooves disturbed the darkness. A cart rattled across the wooden bridge two miles east of Kanesbury. Zachary Farnsworth gripped the reins, deep in thought as he passed over a stretch of the Pine River just beyond the Spirit Caves. It had been thirteen days since he met with the wizard Caldurian. Dooley sat next to Farnsworth, gazing at the swampland on their right bathed in the gentle light of the rising Bear Moon still a few days from full. Square copper oil lamps attached to either side of the cart glowed like a pair of demonic eyes, the light wildly flickering behind the slits in the metal facing. The horses trotted along the dirt road in the cool autumn night, enjoying the evening excursion and not particularly bothered by the weight of the three individuals and other items they were transporting.

Dooley glanced over his shoulder at the open cart, noting several sacks filled with dried food, fruit and vegetables lined up on one side. Along the other side was a row of split firewood, seasoned and ready for burning. What caught his attention most was the heap of heavy blankets tossed over a large object sprawled out in the middle of the cart. Though it remained still, he noticed that if he stared at it long enough, he could detect a barely perceptible rise and fall of the blankets at one end of the object from time to time. He turned back around and rubbed his chin as the night wind brushed through his tangles of dirty blond hair.

Farnsworth glanced at him as he lightly snapped the reins. "Having second thoughts, Dooley?"

He looked down at his dirty boots. "Third and fourth ones, too. Let's just get this over with."

Farnsworth nodded, his dark eyes surveying the terrain ahead–acres of farmland on the left, including Barringer's Landing, and a few miles of swampland to the right, teeming with tall grasses, weed stalks and scraggly trees hiding an occasional island of dry land within the dense vegetation. "Remember, it's all part of the deal with Caldurian. We have to pay our dues if we're going to make our marks on Kanesbury."

"Not the most convenient way to do it," he muttered.

Farnsworth raised his coat collar with one hand as the evening chill deepened, brushing aside the long brown hair hanging over his shoulders. "There are other ways to handle these inconveniences. Nobody is stopping you."

Dooley glared at Farnsworth. "You either, Zachary! You're just as capable of–" He turned and spit onto the passing road. "Like I said, let's get this over with."

Farnsworth nodded, though he couldn't help but chuckle to himself. "We're both corrupt, Dooley, but apparently only up to a certain point, I guess. Then again, this drama is just beginning to play out. Who knows what else we might do if forced to act."

"What do you mean?"

"Well, Arthur Weeks was killed by somebody else's hand and that worked to our benefit." Dooley looked up, searching for an explanation. "Now no one can connect his lies about Nicholas Raven to us. But would either of us have had the nerve to wield that knife against Arthur if necessary? If he ever decided to expose us to the authorities?"

"I don't know." Dooley grunted with disgust. "Probably not. Seems neither of us has the stomach to get our hands dirty in that way. By the look of things, we'd most likely have kidnapped Arthur and dragged him to the swamps like this one." He indicated the body in back with his thumb. "Not the most efficient use of our time, so we'd better watch out who else we make as enemies or we'll be hauling away half the population of Kanesbury. Sooner or later it's going to catch up with us unless we find a better plan."

"I think my plan has gotten us far up to this point," he said with a hint of irritation. "Do as you're told and we'll be all right. I helped convince Ned Adams to get you Nicholas' old job, didn't I?" Dooley nodded. "And he said you did just fine taking that recent shipment to Bridgewater County. So trust me to think things through for the both of us. I know what I'm doing."

"I suppose so."

"You'll thank me one of these days after you obtain a more lucrative job and a nicer house to live in," Farnsworth said encouragingly. "And can you honestly tell me that you wouldn't mind frequenting the finer dining establishments in the village, or associating with the more influential citizens of Kanesbury?"

"I wouldn't stick my nose up at the opportunity," he said, folding his arms and leaning back in the wagon seat. "But you already know that."

"Then let me do my job and those things will come your way in time," he promised. "And who knows, your rise in status just might catch the eye of some of the fine ladies in Kanesbury, say, for instance, Miss Katherine Durant."

"Who said anything about–?"

Farnsworth grinned. "You didn't have to say anything, Dooley. It's obvious you have feelings for her. I stop by the Iron Kettle, too. I hear about things you've said in your inebriated states."

"Perhaps it *had* crossed my mind," he said with a sigh, "though I don't think she'd ever want to be seen with the likes of me. But in time, you never know."

"That's the spirit. And that's why I encourage patience. So if we fully cooperate and don't panic, the rewards will eventually come to us. I want control of Kanesbury, and in your dreams, you see yourself with someone like Katherine," he said. "So don't do anything to foul up the possibility of such dreams becoming reality."

Dooley nodded, letting the words sink in. Success seemed obtainable whenever Farnsworth stated matters so finely. But their deeds of late rested on his shoulders like a load of rocks he could never set down, keeping him awake at night. He feared that he might let slip a few words in public that would reveal everything, landing them either in the lockup or at the hands of an angry mob. He sometimes wished he had never stolen that key when he was ten, yearning simply for the warmth and carefree spirit of that sunny day long ago as the horse trotted past the seemingly endless tract of swampland.

He again indicated the body in back of the cart, eager to change the subject. "About the sleeping spell that strange man had cast on him. How long will it last?"

Farnsworth shrugged. "Indefinitely, I suppose. Arileez is his name, by the way, according to the crow. And he's more of a wizard than a regular man. A spooky sort, don't you agree? I'm just glad Arileez suggested a sleeping spell. It makes this kidnapping so much easier than the last one."

Dooley wrinkled his brow. "So why didn't we bring Arileez along to put Adelaide under a spell, too? It'd save us from hauling out food supplies to her every six days."

Farnsworth glared at him through the gloom. "He doesn't know about Adelaide! I don't want him to know. And I don't want word of her getting back to Caldurian either. She is our mistake, Dooley. The wizard was upset enough when we lost the key, so why risk another example of incompetence?"

"All right! I won't mention it again," he fumed. "But why is Arileez in Kanesbury in the first place?"

Farnsworth shook his head, imagining himself pushing Dooley off the cart for posing yet another one of his inane questions. "Are you blind? Don't you know what that being is capable of?"

"I know *that*!" he snapped. "Stop treating me like a fool. I just want to know the reason Arileez is here. How will things unfold?"

"Watch very closely as the days go by. That's all I can say. Caldurian has a plan laid out that will benefit him and us. Just let it play out," he warned. "The less you know right now, the better."

"As usual!"

"I don't make the rules, Dooley, but I have to follow them." Farnsworth snapped the reins as they were nearing their destination. "But there is something you should know. When Gavin contacted me a few days ago and said Arileez was on his way, the crow also told me of some news regarding Morrenwood. King Justin is convening a war council in fourteen days."

Dooley picked at his teeth with a jagged fingernail. "That's interesting, I guess. But why should I care?"

"Because if you correctly time your flour deliveries to the capital for Ned Adams, maybe you can find a way to make yourself an uninvited guest at the council."

"*What*?"

"You heard me. And you knew this was a possibility all along." Farnsworth explained that he had casually spoken to Ned on the street two days after Gavin informed him of the upcoming war council in Morrenwood. "I asked Ned how your training for Nicholas' job was progressing. He happily told me about the success of your recent deliveries to Bridgewater County and how you were learning the bookkeeping quicker than he had hoped. He added that you would be leaving for Morrenwood soon to deliver final shipments for the King's stores."

"And I'm to act as a spy?" Dooley asked, not happy with the prospect.

"I promised Caldurian as much on the night he showed up to collect the key," he said. "We can't back out now, especially after going through all that trouble to frame Nicholas. Imagine the information we could glean from that meeting. Caldurian would find it more valuable than that old key, I'd wager. So you see…"

Dooley spit on the road again. "Yeah, I see. It's up to me, as usual. Like I know anything about being a spy!"

"Did you know anything about kidnapping before Adelaide stumbled upon us in Nicholas' shed? And apparently you already knew how to be a thief at age ten when you swiped the key from that eagle." Farnsworth was pleased with Dooley's silent response, not in the mood to argue further. "Good then. So you understand," he said, gently pulling on the reins as they neared their turnoff.

When Farnsworth noted a large rock half buried just off the right side of the road, he slowed the horse to a gentle gait and pulled off to the grassy side a few moments later. He directed the steed toward the nearby woods bordering one section of the swamp beyond. They passed under the trees along a vague path that paralleled the main road for a short distance before turning right deeper into the woods, heading closer to the swamp. The intermittent calls of frogs and crickets grew louder and sharper as the horse cautiously drew its load farther into the trees, guided only by the light of the two oil lamps and the Bear Moon drifting above. A few dreary minutes later, he brought the horse to a halt at the end of the path only a few yards from the water's edge. There was only enough room for the horse and cart to turn around for the return journey.

"Here we are again," Dooley muttered before hopping off the cart, feeling suffocated by the surroundings. Numerous trees, thin and arthritic, grew out of the swampy waters like fingers groping at the partially hidden sky in search of escape. Strings of watery, leafy vines had wrapped themselves around their trucks over the years and hung from the branches like tangles of rope or a brood of lifeless snakes. Weeds grew in thick bunches, pungently scenting the cold air.

"I'll get the boats out of hiding," Farnsworth said, disappearing into the trees beyond with one of the oil lamps he had unfastened from the cart.

A few minutes later, a dot of light appeared on the water. Farnsworth drifted along the edge of the swamp in a small wooden boat to where Dooley stood, deftly paddling with an oar. The oil lamp was set near the bow. A second boat followed, attached to the first with a rope. When the boat neared, Dooley grabbed a rope that Farnsworth flung to him and guided it to shore. Farnsworth stepped out and dragged the second boat onto dry land beside the first.

"Let's load up," he said, signaling for Dooley to follow him to the cart. "We'll set him in one of the boats and all the firewood and supplies in the other."

Dooley nodded, wavering on the verge of another complaint but knowing it wouldn't do him any good. He and Farnsworth each grabbed two of the sacks and set them in one of the boats, swiftly repeating the process until one vessel was fully loaded with the firewood and food supplies. Then Dooley climbed onto the cart and waited for Farnsworth to walk around to the back. The heaviest burden was yet to follow.

He glanced at Farnsworth over the pile of blankets and tossed them aside, revealing a body in the night still sleeping soundly on the wooden surface. He sighed, grateful he couldn't discern the man's features in the darkness.

"Ready, Zachary?" he asked mechanically.

Farnsworth nodded and grabbed the man from beneath the arms while Dooley lifted the legs, carefully carrying him off the cart and depositing the body into the empty boat. Dooley retrieved the blankets from the cart and threw them on top of the man, shielding him from view. He sighed with relief when the first part of their task was complete and grabbed the other oil lamp.

Moments later, the pair of boats drifted slowly across the swamp toward a small island hidden among the vegetation, the glow of the lamps casting a pale light upon the murky surface of the water. Dooley sat in the boat with the food supplies, surveying the patch of an island just ahead as he repeatedly dipped his oar in the water from side to side. He had only been here one other time, the night he and Farnsworth swiftly and secretly transported a bound and gagged Adelaide Cooper out of Kanesbury in the inky darkness. He felt a knot in his stomach then, wondering if his alliance with Farnsworth and been for the best. But haunting him even more was the image of Arthur Weeks, his dead vacant gaze staring up into nothingness, an image he couldn't yet shake from his mind. Visions of wealth and prestige that had entertained him so often in the past now grew dim as he floated silently upon the water toward the abandoned robbers' hideout that Farnsworth had procured through some of his unsavory connections. But in spite of his guilt and queasy feelings, Dooley knew that it was too late to turn back.

As his boat touched shore, he noticed a faint yellow light emanating through the cracks in the window shutters of a small wooden shack-of-a-house before him. It had been built on a series of low, thick stilts to protect it during heavy rains. The shutters had been nailed closed with a few wood slats on the outside. Curls of smoke rose above the roof, somersaulting in the cold, damp air. Dooley pulled his craft ashore, grabbed the oil lamp and walked over to a spot several yards to the right where Farnsworth had landed. A tiny, windowless shed built of stone and wood lay hidden close by in the weeds and shadows. As Farnsworth pulled his boat in, Dooley pushed open the warped door of the shed, letting utter darkness escape from within.

"Lay those inside," Farnsworth said, tossing a few of the blankets to Dooley who quickly complied with the order.

He hung his lamp on a large, rusty nail sticking out of a wood beam and spread the blankets in one corner of the shed before stepping outside to help Farnsworth lug the body out of the boat. They carried it inside under the filtered moonlight and set it on the blankets, covering it moments later with the remaining blankets that had been left in the boat. The man lying asleep under Arileez' spell breathed slowly but steadily, oblivious to the whirl of events about to spin out of control in his village just a few miles to the west. Dooley and Zachary exited the shed and closed the door, satisfied that at least one of their reluctant charges wouldn't give them any trouble.

"Now we pay her a visit," Farnsworth said as they walked to the other boat. He and Dooley each grabbed two sacks of food and walked up a flight of ten rickety wooden stairs to the front door secured with a large iron padlock. He produced a key and removed the lock, pushing the door open with a muddy boot.

They stepped into the room, warm with the heat from a small stone fireplace. A few candles on a table provided the only other light. As soon as Dooley closed the door, a small figure sprang at him from behind it, clinging to the back of his shoulders and pushing him away from the front entrance.

"Get her off me!" he shouted, dropping the food sacks and swatting his hands as if trying to chase away a wasp.

"Don't think you can keep me locked in here another moment, Dooley Kramer!" Adelaide hung on and squeezed his bony frame as if trying to force every bit of air out of his lungs. "You'll be thrown into Constable Brindle's lockup before this is over."

"And *you'll* be tied up in a chair if you ever do that again!" Farnsworth barked. He grabbed Adelaide from behind and lifted her small frame through the air, setting her on a wooden chair near the fire. He glared at her like a wolf that had cornered its prey.

Adelaide stared back with defiant steel blue eyes. "You don't frighten me, Zachary, nor does your sorry excuse for a helper."

"Oh, really? We're taking the time to bring you food and firewood, and this is how you react? Dooley even bought you a cake of that fine soap you wanted, Adelaide." He pointed a finger at her as he held his breath for a moment, slowly releasing it through clenched teeth. "But we could just as easily forget to come here one of these days, and then where would you be?"

"You can't do that!" she said, her voice a bit softer and her fiery demeanor quickly growing cold. Adelaide tried not to tremble, but Farnsworth's not-so-subtle threat made her reconsider her tactics. "I would go hungry."

"Then don't cause us any more grief," he muttered. He grunted and stood guard near the door. "Dooley is going to bring up the rest of the supplies while I stand here and make sure you behave. Now is there anything else you'd like to say?"

After Dooley left, Adelaide sat back and adjusted a shawl draped over her thin shoulders, her gray hair nearly matching the color of her dress. "How long are you planning to keep me locked up in this dump?"

"As I said before, I'm not sure. But it's not really an awful place to spend some time in, is it? I paid good money to obtain these quarters."

Farnsworth looked about the small room containing the single table, two chairs, bare walls, a straw broom and a dwindling stack of firewood that Dooley had yet to replenish. An adjoining room to the side had a feather mattress tossed on the floor, and beyond that was a tiny privy. Off the main room to the back was a modest kitchen with a single counter and a few decrepit shelves above. In each of the opposite corners stood a water barrel, both filled to capacity from funneled holes in the roof.

"I have a household to take care of, Zachary. You have to let me go soon!" she begged. "Besides, people are looking for me. They *must* be looking for me. You can't keep me her forever."

"Well, they're not looking for you here, so you might as well put any notion of being rescued out of your mind," he said. "You'll leave when we say you can leave."

Adelaide's face puckered up with fear and hatred for the man, wondering why he would do such a thing to her. She needed more answers. "Why were you and Dooley in Nicholas Raven's shed that night?" she quickly followed up, though not expecting an answer as she had asked that question of Farnsworth several times before. He simply shook his head in reply. "Fine. Don't tell me," she continued just as Dooley walked back into the house with two more sacks of vegetables. "Tell me this instead. Whose body did you two just carry onto the island?"

Farnsworth hesitated as Dooley stopped cold, looking up at him for guidance. "Keep unloading the boat, Dooley!" he snapped, before glancing at Adelaide with a feigned casualness. "What are you talking about?"

"Don't deny it. I spied on you through one of the cracks in the shutters. I saw you carry a body out of a boat and into the shed. Who is it?" she demanded. "Is it dead?"

Farnsworth raked a hand through his long locks and grinned, shaking his head as if he were responding to a child's inquiry. But he felt his heart pound a little bit harder when Adelaide broached the subject, silently cursing the woman for her annoying curiosity.

"There is no dead body inside that shed. I give you my word."

"Your word isn't worth a bucket of cow cud," she muttered, straightening out the wrinkles in her dress. "So who is it?" she asked again as Dooley lumbered back inside with an armful of firewood. "What lucky person gets to live in the fancy quarters?"

Dooley couldn't prevent himself from chuckling as he piled the wood near the fireplace. "The fancy quarters! Just be thankful you got it as good as you do, Adelaide. If that wizard Caldurian were looking after you, why, you might be living at the bottom of this swamp, if you get my meaning."

"Dooley!" Farnsworth cried as he stared down his accomplice with fire in his eyes. "Mouth closed! Just get the rest of the wood."

"Sorry, I..."

"Caldurian? I remember when that madman nearly destroyed our village twenty years ago," Adelaide said, having overheard the wizard's name and snippets of other details about Nicholas Raven and a magic key while imprisoned in Farnsworth's cellar. But she never let on out of concern for her own safety, feigning ignorance. "What does Caldurian have to do with all of this?"

"Nothing! Don't listen to that fool," he snapped as Dooley scurried outside for the remaining firewood. "Now enough questions, Adelaide. This conversation is over!" He stepped closer to the door, impatiently waiting for Dooley to complete his task.

"But, Zachary, I want to know–"

"No!" He raised a finger, silencing her. After Dooley finished unloading the boat a few minutes later, the two men turned to depart. Adelaide stood, futilely pleading with them one more time.

"Please let me go."

"We're leaving," Farnsworth softly said, ushering Dooley out the door.

Adelaide nervously fidgeted with her hair. "When will you return?"

"We'll be back here when we're back. You're set for several days," he said, stepping out. But before he closed the door completely, he looked inside, cautioning Adelaide with a cold stare as he spoke. "Remember, you'll only endanger yourself if you try to flee. There are rats and water snakes everywhere, and I wouldn't even want to think about swimming across this swamp." Adelaide flinched at the notion. "And I just posted a handful of men to monitor the roads along the swamplands day and night to make sure nobody gets in or out," he lied, noting the subtle shade of defeat in Adelaide's eyes. "So consider yourself warned, woman."

He pulled the door shut, leaving Adelaide staring at the blank walls with a heavy heart. As she heard the iron padlock being secured, she sat down in the chair again, gazing blankly at the fire, for the moment not knowing what to do or think or feel.

Dooley and Farnsworth hurriedly rowed the boats across the water back to the hiding place, eager to escape the confines of the swamp. With oil lamps in hand, they hiked the short distance through the trees to where their horse and cart waited.

"I hate doing this!" Dooley muttered as he reaffixed the two lamps to the sides of the cart. "Why did she have to find us in Nicholas' shed that night?"

"Bad luck," Farnsworth said, climbing into his seat.

"That's all we seem to have," he replied, hopping aboard moments later. "There's got to be a better way. What if she *does* escape? What if we're followed or caught? Or what if–"

"Dooley!" Farnsworth glared at him, whispering bitterly. "Enough. I need to think."

"Then think fast. I don't have a good feeling about this."

"I don't like it either," he replied as he snapped the reins and turned the cart around, exiting along the narrow path. "But I wouldn't want to do anything drastic before we accomplished our goal or before I obtain any kind of power." He exhaled a ghostly breath and glanced at Dooley. "Let's be patient until then. Perhaps I can arrange a more permanent solution to our troubles afterward."

"Oh? Like what?"

"Leave the details to me, Dooley. You'd only blurt them out, just like you told Adelaide about the wizard."

"Sorry about that, Zachary. I wasn't thinking," he said, bowing his head and staring at his feet with remorse.

"Just one more *sorry* to add to your list, eh?"

"Nothing should come of it, but I'll watch my tongue next time," he replied apologetically. "But like you said, if you can arrange a more permanent solution to our swamp problem, then what I accidentally said about the wizard won't really matter."

Farnsworth nodded. "Right you are, Dooley. Right you are. Just give me time to ponder the situation and I'll come up with a perfect plan to solve all of our irksome little troubles," he said, looking askance at Dooley Kramer as they approached the main dirt road. "*All* of them."

CHAPTER 25

A Change in Leadership

Katherine Durant approached the Water Barrel Inn as crisp autumn twilight gently wrapped itself around the trees and houses of Kanesbury. She kept warm, buried beneath the folds of her cloak. Thin, feathery streaks of purple and orange faded near the horizon, giving way to a field of white stars that dotted vast charcoal skies. The windows of the inn blazed with a friendly yellow glow, the patrons inside moving back and forth in boisterous delight among mugs of ale and below clouds of pipe smoke lazily congregating near the rafters. The murmur of voices rose in volume when she opened the front door and stepped inside. She removed her hood, revealing waves of long brown hair that matched the color of her eyes.

The warmth of a blazing fire and the scent of fresh pine clippings greeted her as she gazed about the large room filled to half its capacity. A woman carrying a tray of roasted pheasant swiftly passed by, heading to a table of hungry patrons. Katherine noted a tall man sitting alone near the fireplace nursing a drink, his face grim and pensive. She waded through the crowd, taking a seat next to the gentleman.

"I heard that you might be here," Katherine said with a calming smile, noting the red flames reflected in the man's eyes. "How are you tonight, Maynard?"

Maynard Kurtz took a sip of his ale, nodding to greet her. "Almost the same as I was last night," he said with a thin smile. He stretched out his legs and leaned back in his chair, his distinctive silvery-black hair falling over his shoulders. He sighed, staring at the mug cradled in his hands. "Just thinking about Nicholas and Adelaide and wondering where they are at the moment." He glanced at Katherine. "I guess I don't think of much else lately."

Katherine attempted another smile as she looked into the man's eyes, noting a faraway expression. The strain from the disappearance of his two closest companions had surely taken its toll upon him. She could only imagine his heartbreak, wishing she could tell him that Nicholas was innocent, but vowing to keep the promise she had made to him in the ice cellar despite that it weighed upon her day and night. And Adelaide's strange disappearance seemed to produce in him a grief nearly equal to that caused by the death of his wife, Tessa. She couldn't bear seeing Maynard dwell in such anguish and hoped her visit would cheer him.

"Pardon my manners, but may I offer you a drink, Katherine? Perhaps some hot cider or a bit of wine on a cold night?"

"Nothing, Maynard, but thank you. Sitting here by the warm fire is soothing enough. I thought I might keep you company."

"I appreciate that," he said, flashing a grin. "Yet I shouldn't wallow in my dark mood as if I'm the only one affected by these unfortunate disappearances. You miss Nicholas and Adelaide, too."

"I do miss them. Nicholas had invited me to the Harvest Festival dance, but that was not meant to be, I suppose. I wonder where he is at this moment, too. Maybe he found his way to Morrenwood to join the King's Guard after all."

"It's possible, yet I feel he's safe. It's Adelaide that I worry about most," he replied. "Constable Brindle and his men have searched to no avail. I fear the worst."

"Have hope," she said. "I don't deny that something horrible may have befallen her, but I just can't bring myself to fully imagine it yet. Perhaps that sounds foolish or childish, Maynard, but my heart won't give up quite as easily as my mind is apt to at times."

"I understand perfectly, Katherine. Hang on to every bit of hope until the last possible moment. And even beyond that, too." He took a slow sip of his drink. "We'll just have to weather this storm as best we can and prepare for the next one."

"I suppose," she replied, staring at the snapping flames for a moment before the weight of Maynard's words hit her. "Prepare for the *next* one? What do you mean? You sound as if something terrible is headed our way."

He glanced at the young girl, noting a hint of fearful concern in her eyes. "Well, Katherine, you're going to find out soon enough, so I might as well tell you now."

"Tell me what, Maynard?"

He drained his ale before sitting up straight in the chair. "There is news about Mayor Nibbs that will most certainly be floating around the village before the night is out."

"Uncle Otto? What about him?" she asked, her heart aflutter.

"The village council is gathering later this evening to discuss some recent events concerning your uncle, events which have been kept secret by design."

"What secret events, Maynard? Tell me what you know," she pleaded.

He gently patted her hand. "I will," he whispered, cautioning her to lower her voice so as not to attract attention. Though the talk and occasional bouts of laughter throughout the inn afforded them privacy from curious ears, Maynard nonetheless took Katherine by the hand and led her to a small table tucked in a corner of the room. They sat opposite each other as a thin candle in a metal holder provided a flicker of illumination.

"Now what of this meeting concerning my uncle?" she asked. "Will he be there? Does he even know of it?"

Maynard shook his head. "No, Otto will not be in attendance because…" He rubbed a calloused hand over his chin, trying to find the right words. "Since you and your mother are his closest relatives, I think you should know before any others as long as you're here. You can inform Sophia when you go home." He contemplated the words he was about to utter to the young girl. "Your uncle received an unusual visitor at his home last night. This morning he left Kanesbury for an urgent meeting to follow up on that strange visit."

Katherine locked gazes with him, attempting to keep her impatience in check. "Who did he meet with?"

"Do you recall any stories from childhood regarding the Enâri invasion of Kanesbury twenty years ago?"

"Of course. That happened three years before I was born. Some of the older children would make up wild yarns about those strange creatures to scare us, saying that some had awakened from their sleep in the Spirit Caves and were hiding out in the woods waiting to attack us in our sleep." Katherine laughed. "I was petrified of such tales when I was four or five, though later in life I found the bizarre affair a little hard to believe. Yet, the Spirit Caves do exist and that dilapidated watch house still stands across the road from the caves, so I suppose it must have been true to an extent."

"Oh, the events were true," he said, drumming his fingers upon the table. "Kanesbury endured a terrible ordeal for a time because of them."

"I recall stories my mother and father had told me years ago. But what do the Enâri have to do with Uncle Otto *now*?" she asked. "And who was this mysterious visitor you spoke of, Maynard? Who visited my uncle last night?"

"There is no easy way to break the news, so I'll just say it. The visitor was one of the Enâri creatures," he replied, his voice sounding distant in the web of shadows. "They've awakened, I'm sorry to say, and once again their attention is focused on our little village."

Katherine said nothing for a moment, trying to absorb his words. "How can that be? Weren't they under a sleeping spell?"

"They were. But whether the spell wore off or was reversed by a more powerful one, I cannot guess. Now the Enâri walk again, or so your uncle has informed us."

Katherine shook her head in disbelief, her face pained with concern for her uncle and the safety of the village. Maynard took her hand in his, and despite the warmth of the room, she noted that it felt cold to her touch.

"Tell me exactly what happened, Maynard. I need to know."

He nodded, leaning back in his chair. "All right. It began late last night before Otto had contacted me and the other four members of the village council, calling an emergency meeting at once and in secret. He first came to my house alone, knocking on my door as if a pack of wolves were after him. The fright in his eyes disturbed me to my core. 'Maynard, you must come to the village hall at once!' Otto said to me, his coat unbuttoned and his hair a frazzled mess. I almost didn't believe that it was your uncle upon my doorstep."

Katherine found it difficult to believe as well since her uncle was always properly groomed and attired when attending to his public duties as a sign of respect for the office he so much revered. She couldn't imagine him leaving the house on official business with his thinning, stringy hair neither combed nor tied up in back with a black band, or with his coat or vest hanging over his slightly paunchy midsection either unbuttoned or in any way in disarray. Aunt Luella, his deceased wife, had always fussed about Otto's public appearance, encouraging him to show the highest regard for his office. As a tribute to her memory, Otto continued to attend to his mayoral obligations in suitable fashion. Katherine suspected that her uncle must have been rattled beyond description to make such a spur-of-the-moment visit to Maynard's farmhouse in the middle of the night.

"What happened at the meeting, Maynard? Did everyone attend?"

"Yes. Len Harold arrived just as I did, but he didn't know what was bothering Otto either. Finally, after the other three council members showed up and Otto shortly thereafter, we all sat down and got to the nub of the matter–your uncle's visit from one of the Enâri creatures."

Katherine leaned forward, enthralled by Maynard's bizarre narrative. "What did it say to my uncle? Was he threatened or harmed or..." She could only imagine the worst at this point, her heart pounding rapidly.

"No, Otto wasn't harmed, but he was given a warning. The creature wanted Otto to return a small metal box that the wizard Frist had created twenty years ago which held a grave threat to the Enâri race," he explained, noting the look of confusion on Katherine's face. "I don't have time to go into the details of all the history, but the point is that Otto claimed he didn't keep the Spirit Box in Kanesbury anymore. He said he had returned it to King Justin in Morrenwood years ago for safekeeping."

"Did the creature believe him?"

"No, and the hooligan threatened to flood our village with a destructive wave of Enâri five hundred strong to avenge their imprisonment in the caves."

"This can't be happening," she whispered, glancing across the room at the men and women who were enjoying food and drinks and a pleasant evening, blissfully unaware of the ruin that might befall them without warning. "What else did my uncle tell you?"

"He bought us some time, Katherine. Your brave uncle bought the village of Kanesbury some time."

"How?"

"At our secret meeting last night, Otto told us that he had struck a deal with the Enâr who had visited him."

Katherine shrugged. "What kind of a deal?"

"Your uncle appeared distraught, wiping the sweat off his brow despite the coolness of the night. 'I convinced that disheveled beast to allow me to meet with all of the Enâri,' your uncle said to us. 'They are hiding out on an abandoned farm on Barringer's Landing, and I plan to confront them there. I'll do anything to keep that horde from setting foot inside the borders of Kanesbury as they had done twenty years ago.'"

"But what good will that do?" she asked, fearing for Otto's life. "How does he expect to defeat such a mob single-handedly?"

"That's exactly what we said, Katherine, but your uncle was convinced that he could buy us a little time to prepare for the worst. 'I will try to convince the Enâri that I will travel to Morrenwood and retrieve the item they covet so dearly. If they allow me to do so, we can bolster our defenses and seek reinforcements from King Justin should an invasion befall us.' A bold plan it was that your uncle proposed, Katherine. And bolder still was the manner in which he intended to carry it out."

"Tell me what he did," she anxiously replied, though a part of her had no desire to hear the answer, fearing the worst.

Maynard leaned across the table. "He rashly insisted on meeting with the Enâri alone. And he did just that, leaving this morning on horseback at the crack of dawn. I'm waiting right now for the bell in the village hall to be rung to call another council meeting to discuss our next step." Maynard's words of foreboding rose to the rafters, fading into the ghostly swirls of pipe smoke. "You see, Katherine…"

"*Yes?*"

He sadly shook his head. "As of sundown, Otto had not yet returned. Though I loathe saying it, I can't help but fear the worst."

"Then why did you let him go?" she asked, her chin quivering. "Or you should at least have sent others with him. I knew it was a foolish plan as soon as you spoke of it."

"I thought so, too, as did all of the council members. But Otto insisted that he do this alone, and he is the mayor, after all." Maynard patted her hand. "We did take one precaution, though I fear we acted too late."

"What, Maynard? Anything to give me a morsel of hope."

"The five of us kept Otto's visit to Barringer's Landing a secret throughout the morning, waiting for his return. But when the sun climbed past the noon position, we told Constable Brindle what had happened and asked him to track down our mayor with one of his deputies." He saw that his words only made Katherine more distressed. She buried her face in her hands. "We're hoping for Clay's return shortly, and then we'll commence with our next meeting."

"I shall be there," she insisted, gently pounding a fist onto the table. "I'm sure a good many people will want to know what's going on."

"Oh, this will be a public meeting. I can promise you that." Maynard grimly laughed. "I don't think we can keep these strange doings a secret anymore, my dear girl."

"I should think not, especially after–"

Suddenly the clear peal of a bell could be heard above the clutter of voices and the snapping flames in the fireplace. Two additional sobering clangs followed. Katherine and Maynard looked at each other, both sensing that a momentous change was about to overwhelm Kanesbury. Several people at the other tables excitedly wondered aloud why the village bell had been rung.

"The meeting is called," Maynard calmly stated. "Constable Brindle is back."

"But is my uncle with him?" Katherine asked, raising a pair of sad eyes.

He stood and offered a courteous hand to Katherine as the candle flame wildly flickered. "Let's go and find out. The news will be intriguing no matter what the constable has to report."

Katherine nodded pessimistically as she accompanied Maynard through the curious crowd and out of the Water Barrel Inn.

They hurried up the nearest lane and soon arrived at the village hall, a modest two-story building of stone and wood. The windows glowed yellow as someone had already lit the oil lamps affixed to the walls inside. A large wooden belfry, painted lemon yellow with white trim, was built on the rooftop, the bell housed within now silent. A crowd had gathered in the dirt road near the front doors, many people carrying oil lamps or holding aloft blazing torches, all wondering whether a meeting of the council had been called or if a prankster had been up to no good. But when four council members were spotted huddled under the bony branches of a nearby maple tree, many suspected that something was afoot.

"And here comes Maynard Kurtz," a voice in the crowd noted when the head of the village council was spotted with Katherine Durant walking toward the building. Maynard whispered a few reassuring words to Katherine before leaving her to join the others.

But what most caught everyone's attention and ignited a wildfire of speculation was seeing Constable Brindle standing by his horse in front of the village lockup next door to the left, quietly talking with one of his deputies. Another horse stood close by munching on some grass, a light brown steed named Chicanery with a few distinctive white spots between its eyes and near the nose. Every local knew that that steed belonged to Otto Nibbs, but no one saw any sign of their mayor and wondered why Chicanery was standing idly by. When Katherine observed the horse without its rider, her heart froze.

"What's going on?" a voice spoke to her from behind. "Why is the council gathering tonight?"

Katherine spun around, facing a tall, lanky individual with an awkward smile, framed by tangles of black hair. "Hello, Lewis," she said to one of Amanda Stewart's employees. "I'm not quite sure what the hubbub is all about, but I think we're going to find out soon," she said while Maynard and the other council members consulted with Constable Brindle underneath the tree.

"I was leaving work at Amanda's house when I heard the bell," Lewis said. "I miss seeing you in the kitchen as much now that the Harvest Festival is over."

"I'm back to my regular number of hours," she explained, sensing that Lewis had feelings for her. "I hope you're enjoying working for her and Oscar."

"It's a job," he said with a grin, "though the Stewarts have enough tasks to keep me busy all nine days of the week if I wanted. I'll be splitting and stacking wood starting tomorrow. It'll be nice getting out of the hot kitchen."

"I'm glad things are working out for you," she said with a smile, noting that the five council members and Constable Brindle were heading for the front steps of the village hall. "Well, here we go, Lewis."

"Say, what's this all about?" someone in the crowd suddenly shouted at Maynard who looked ill at ease in the glow of the firelight. "And where's Mayor Nibbs?"

Maynard held up a hand to prevent a string of inquiries from being launched as the other council members and the constable stood anxiously by. "I'm going to allow everyone inside the council room to hear what we have to discuss tonight since, by the looks on your faces, I know you have many questions to ask. So please proceed inside in an orderly manner and we'll tell you what's happening."

"Where's Otto?" a woman shouted. "Why isn't he here?"

"As I said, proceed inside," he kindly refrained, "and all of your questions will be answered."

"Well they had better be," someone muttered as people filed into the building, some sticking torches in the ground or leaving oil lamps on the front steps before they did so.

After passing through a small entrance hall with a staircase leading up to the second floor offices, the curious citizens of Kanesbury entered the council room which took up the remainder of the first floor. The wide chamber had several rows of oak benches divided by a center aisle. A long bench was attached to the walls on either side of the room. A pine table stood near the back for the council and the mayor to conduct their business. Six chairs were placed around the table, four in the back against the far wall and one on either side so the public could watch the proceedings. On rare occasions, the room was used for public trials with the mayor of Kanesbury serving as facilitator along with a jury of twenty-one locals. Several oil lamps were affixed to the walls and burning brightly, evenly spaced between the rows of high, narrow windows circling the room. A large fireplace against the west wall sputtered and crackled as it gently warmed the hall.

Everyone quickly found a seat, eager for the mysterious meeting to get underway. Katherine sat on one of the side benches at the end farthest from the table. When Lewis asked if he could sit next to her, she somewhat reluctantly, but pleasantly, said yes. Yet when she noticed the empty chair her uncle Otto would normally occupy at the table, she felt comforted that Lewis was beside her. No one in the room could ignore Otto's conspicuous absence either, with some wondering if an illness, or worse, had befallen their beloved mayor. At last Maynard stood up.

"I know you're wondering why we've gathered at this odd hour, so I'll get right to the point," he said, his eyes occasionally downcast and his voice sounding grim. "Mayor Nibbs had a strange visitor at his house last night, someone many of you have heard of in the past. Someone who…" He studied the crowd of concerned faces hanging on his every word. "Someone who had done great harm to this village many years ago." An audible gasp filled the room as whispers spread among the onlookers. "Since there's no easy way to tell you this, I'll just blurt it out. Otto Nibbs was contacted by one of the Enâri creatures that had attacked Kanesbury twenty years ago."

Several men stood up at once amid groans of panic and shouts of disbelief, demanding immediate answers from Maynard and Constable Brindle. But the boisterous crowd had been too rattled by the comment and it took several long moments and calls for order before everyone settled down.

"If we're going to answer questions and leave at a reasonable hour, one voice at a time," Maynard pleaded.

"We'll try," Bob Hawkins shouted, "but how else do you expect us to act when you tell us those Enâri folk are again on the loose? Where'd they come from?"

"Yeah, answer that!" another cried out. "Are these new ones? Or did the others wake up and escape from the Spirit Caves?"

More anxious moments passed before Maynard could again calm the crowd, pounding on the table to recapture their attention. Constable Brindle, sitting off to the side, glanced at him and raised his eyes, knowing it was going to be a long night.

"I promise to answer every question," Maynard said. "But first let me explain what happened to the mayor last night and this morning–*without* interruption. Then after a few words from Clay Brindle, we'll let you have at it. Sound fair?"

After everyone consented, Maynard revealed the details about Otto's late-night Enâri visitor, its request for the Spirit Box bound with a spell by the wizard Frist, and of Otto's brave yet foolish quest to meet with the Enâri creatures at Barringer's Landing earlier that day. All were fascinated with Maynard's urgent yet soothing words and the pictures they created in their minds. Everyone felt alone in the room, as if he were speaking to no other person. When he signaled for Constable Brindle to stand up and tell his part of the story, the mesmerized onlookers snapped to attention at the harshness of the constable's voice in comparison, as if they had been rudely awakened from a peaceful daydream.

"Past noontime today, I rode out to Barringer's Landing with one of my men to look for Mayor Nibbs," the constable said, wiping a handkerchief across his brow under the warm scrutiny of the onlookers. "We found Chicanery wandering near an empty barn and thoroughly searched the area for Otto. We also discovered the remains of a few bonfires. No doubt the Enâri had made a temporary camp there, but as to where they've fled, I can't begin to guess. My deputy and I investigated until the sun nearly set, but sadly turned up nothing else. We returned a while ago with Otto's horse."

"Surely you'll search some more, won't you?" a young woman on the side of the room softly asked.

Clay Brindle turned his head and saw the helpless look in Katherine's eyes, feeling like a failure that his search for her uncle had turned up nothing. "Rest assured, Miss Durant, that we will resume searching first thing in the morning. I can't make you any promises, but we won't give up yet."

"Like you've given up searching for Adelaide Cooper?" someone shouted disapprovingly from the crowd.

"We are still trying to find that dear old woman!" the constable lashed out. "But a limited number of men can only cover so much ground at a time. And by the way, have you ever joined in one of the search parties?" An uneasy moment of silence followed as the constable took several deep breaths, his face red with contempt. "I thought not. So unless you have anything helpful to add, a little less talk will go a long way toward keeping you from looking like a complete ninny."

Maynard quickly jumped in. "Are there any other questions?"

"Just one," an older lady asked after cautiously raising a hand. "If the Enâri are back–and I clearly remember how awful their first visit was twenty years ago–just how did they escape? Is that evil wizard Caldurian again walking among us?"

Rampant fear and speculation once more swept through the room as everyone old enough to remember the first Enâri invasion mentally prepared for another. Maynard pounded his fist on the table to quiet the crowd before nodding at Clay to continue.

"We have no proof that the wizard is back. Otto told the council that only one of the creatures had visited him. He mentioned nothing of the wizard. Isn't that right, Maynard?" he asked, directing the gaze of the onlookers back to him.

"Correct. We have no proof that Caldurian has returned. In fact, we know nothing about how the creatures escaped," he said. "The Enâr who had spoken to Mayor Nibbs told him only to go to Barringer's Landing to meet with the entire group. It wanted information about the Spirit Box and apparently nothing more."

"So are we to assume then that the Enâri just happened to wake up on their own? How believable is that?" someone else piped up. "The wizard must be around!"

Maynard shrugged. "I can only tell you what we know, but if Otto ever returns, perhaps he can tell us more."

"You mean he can tell us what doom awaits us," muttered another.

"Let's not panic," Maynard insisted, waving a finger. "Let's not conjure up a wizard in our village when we have no proof. "

"That's right," a woman in the front row said, turning around in her seat to face those behind her. "No use getting frightened about things that haven't yet happened."

A moment of heavy silence fell as everyone contemplated the flurry of strange events. What did it all mean, and why was it happening now? Slowly, a man with apple red cheeks seated in the middle of the gathering shyly raised a hand. After clearly his throat, he uttered a few startling words.

"I can tell you how those wicked creatures woke up," he said, his voice unsteady. "But I don't think you'll like hearing the truth–or that you'll like *me* after I tell you."

Constable Brindle craned his head forward, searching out the voice in the crowd. He wrinkled his brow. "Exactly what are you babbling about, George Bane? How do you know anything about those creatures?"

George slowly got to his feet, staring at the sea of perplexed faces. "Well, Clay, I think it might have been me who, uh, accidentally woke them up. It was on the first night of the Harvest Festival."

Clay Brindle scratched his head, wondering if George had just come back from downing a few mugs at the Iron Kettle. "What are you trying to tell us, George? How is that even possible?"

"Well, I was celebrating the festival with a few drinks like everybody else that night," he said, noting Gill Meddy, his drinking partner, out of the corners of his eyes. Gill suddenly turned a shade paler as he sat nervously against the side wall, though George had no intention of implicating him. "I'd been drinking alone when this stranger approached with a bottle of gin, a small pouch of money and a ridiculous bet. I think his name was Mune. He wasn't from these parts. Anyway, who was I to turn down a free drink?" He went on to explain how, in a drunken stupor, he had accompanied the man to the Spirit Caves with the intention of exploring them on a dare. "I think I was supposed to make a lot of money on the bet, but only woke up inside the caves with an awful headache and a terrible fright."

"As I recall, you were gone missing the next day for a time," Constable Brindle said. "When you finally showed up, George, you didn't mention anything about those caves. You had said you slept off your rough night in the woods."

"I did say that," he muttered apologetically, "though it was only half true. The sleeping part, that is, but most definitely not the *in the woods* part. I had been in those caves. I think I bumped my head while running away from–" George swallowed hard as fitful memories swirled in his mind. "They were inside the caves with me. And the voices and blue fog and..." He looked up at Maynard and Clay, happy to finally confess the dreaded details that still haunted him. He described a glass sphere he had carried into the caves that glowed blue and grew hot in his hand until he shattered it against one of the walls. He told of faces in the darkness and of the echo of footsteps in the wavering shadows as a blue fog rose about him like death itself. "It *had* to be a wizard's magic," he whispered, suddenly feeling overwhelmed and lightheaded. He plopped down on the bench and buried his face in his hands, wondering how he could ever look at his neighbors again.

For several minutes, those gathered around him coaxed out more details of that mysterious night. None could help but come to the conclusion that the wizard Caldurian had sent an underling named Mune to release the creatures, and that George Bane simply had the misfortune to be recruited in the vile scheme. Most pitied him more than blamed him, figuring that the deed would have been done anyway, whether George had accepted a free bottle of gin or not.

When the commotion died down and Constable Brindle once again vowed to resume his search for Mayor Nibbs in the morning, one of the other council members stood up and called for everybody's attention.

"In light of these developments and according to village bylaws, I think the council should appoint Maynard Kurtz as acting mayor until Otto Nibbs returns. Or is–*recovered*?" he clumsily added.

"Oscar, is that really necessary at this time?" Maynard asked.

"Well, you are the head of the council, Maynard, and village business has to be properly and legally conducted."

"Agreed," Len Harold said, seconding the motion.

With a unanimous show of four hands, Maynard Kurtz was appointed as acting mayor of Kanesbury. There was a round of polite, yet sober applause from the onlookers, though Maynard wore a troubled expression upon his face.

"I thank you for trusting me with this duty, though under the circumstances, I accept it with much regret and hope for the swift return of Otto," he said. "And as we are now one council member short, I would like to offer up the name of Ned Adams to hold my previous spot for as long as necessary." Maynard glanced at Ned who had been sitting in one of the middle rows. "Since business at the gristmill is slowing down for the coming winter, would you object to such an appointment, Ned?"

"I'd be honored," he replied, standing up and offering a brief nod of acceptance.

After Len Harold officially offered Ned's name for the position and Oscar Stewart raised a hand to second it, Ned Adams was unanimously welcomed as a member of the village council. He kissed his wife sitting next to him and then proudly took his seat at the table. He smiled at several people who wished him good luck, including Dooley Kramer who had just entered the building moments before and sat in the last row.

The brief cheerful interlude following the new appointments quickly dissipated when someone called out from the crowd. "So, Mayor Kurtz, just what are we going to do about the situation?"

Everyone knew that the *situation* referred to the missing Otto Nibbs and a mob of Enâri creatures presumably roaming the countryside and planning unspeakable mischief for the village. Most wondered how Kanesbury could ever protect itself from five hundred beings created through mystery and magic in a faraway land called Kargoth. All eyes were fixed on the acting mayor for an answer.

"I have faith in every member of this village and know we can confront any difficulty that arises," he said. "And though I know my words may sound hollow right now, we have to rely on each other to get through this bleak time. That is where our true strength lies. That is where victory will be achieved." Many in the audience nodded, taking comfort in his words and feeling as if a spring breeze had suddenly dispersed the autumn chill. All looked upon Maynard with newfound respect.

"However, a bit of caution and preparation never hurt either." Len Harold spoke up a moment later, jarring everyone back to the reality of that cold night. "If there is no objection from either the mayor or this council, I'd like to volunteer to go to Morrenwood as an official representative of Kanesbury and present our case to the King. I'm sure he would be most interested in learning about these new developments and perhaps offer us protection should we need it. He and Otto are second cousins, so that should work in our favor."

"Good idea, Len!" someone called out. And quickly the population in the village hall unofficially seconded Len Harold's suggestion.

Maynard looked askance at Len, noticing that the other council members and Constable Brindle seemed pleased with the idea. He stood up and quieted the crowd.

"It appears that everyone thinks this suggestion is a good one, so who am I to object?" he said. "Though I believe our village can handle any problems that come our way, I will abide by the council's good sense in this matter and wish Mr. Harold a safe and successful journey."

"I'll leave the day after tomorrow with my eldest son," Len replied.

Maynard then signaled an end to the meeting and dismissed the council. But for the next hour, the residents of Kanesbury lingered in the shadowy street outside the hall, discussing the startling events with one another and questioning the new mayor about the fate of their community. Katherine and Lewis waded through the crowd and congratulated Maynard on his appointment.

"I have complete confidence that your leadership will make us proud," she said, giving him a hug. "Uncle Otto would be quite pleased with his replacement."

"A temporary one, I hope," he graciously replied.

"That goes for me, too," Ned Adams piped up amid the chatter. "I want you to have your old job back as soon as possible so this village can get back to normal."

Maynard smiled. "As do we all."

"Now I must find my wife," Ned added, glancing about the lively crowd. "She's in here somewhere. Oh, and there's Dooley," he said, talking more to himself now than to the others. "I have to tell him about his trip to Morrenwood in the next few days."

As a dozen conversations played out under the starry autumn sky, a man sitting on a horse cart farther down the road in the shadows watched the excited crowd for a few moments, noting the talk and exclamations echoing across the brittle night air. A thin smile formed on Zachary Farnsworth's face when he heard the phrase *Mayor Kurtz* bandied about several times before deciding that it was time to leave. He gently snapped the reins on his horse as he disappeared into the night, sighing with satisfaction that his plans were finally progressing. He happily headed home after the long ride to the swamp.

CHAPTER 26

An Unwitting Accomplice

Dooley Kramer traveled to Morrenwood with his deliveries eight days after the village meeting. He left on a cold, sunny morning, dressed in his best vest and trousers, his boots scrubbed clean and his heavy brown coat mended and washed. After accepting a polite suggestion from his employer, he meticulously combed back his dirty blond hair and tied it with a piece of dark woolen yarn happily donated by Ned's wife.

Dooley led the way to the capital sitting atop a horse-drawn cart filled with food provisions and some tools and supplies for repairing any of the wagons should such an event arise. Following him was a line of twelve other carts, each pulled by a pair of horses and piled high with sacks of wheat and corn flour ground from the surplus grain harvest that had blessed the lands around Kanesbury. Each cart was covered with canvas and tied securely with rope. These would be the last deliveries of the year purchased for the King's storehouses in Morrenwood, though other shipments had been transported during the growing season to the capital city and other royal storehouses throughout Arrondale. Dooley had correctly estimated that it would be a four-day journey if the weather cooperated, smiling broadly when he finally spotted the Blue Citadel in the distance against the dark green backdrop of the Trent Hills. He inhaled a whiff of fresh pine carried upon a light breeze as the caravan steadily progressed along the last miles of King's Road.

Less than an hour later, he was passing through the streets of Morrenwood, the largest city he had ever visited. And though some sections of town didn't look much different from Kanesbury, many offered a comfortable cluster of stone houses and shops, with streets bustling under the tranquil guard of the rolling Trent Hills. He especially delighted with the clip clop of the horses' hooves upon encountering an occasional cobblestone road, an experience that became routine the closer he approached King Justin's residence proudly situated upon the banks of the nearby Edelin River.

After guiding his dozen charges through the iron gates in the stone wall surrounding the Citadel, Dooley felt as if he had entered a new world. The plans he and Farnsworth had hatched in Kanesbury now seemed petty and unambitious. And though he realized this new perspective was probably temporary, a part of him wished he didn't have to return to his hovel of a home. But for now he savored the illusion that life had gotten better through hard work and effort instead of the false path that had really brought him to this place.

As Dooley gazed up at the Blue Citadel while traversing the vast courtyard, he wondered if he truly could have arrived at this position on his own merits rather than having to rely on a stolen key and unscrupulous schemes. He truly wondered it, but only for a brief moment as a swirl of clouds passed across the sun. Deep in his heart, he knew that he couldn't fool himself about the tortuous path in life he had chosen, so there was no point in trying.

The Blue Citadel served as the visual and political focal point of Morrenwood, its speckled granite blocks seeming as natural a part of the landscape as the legions of towering pine trees and the rushing river descending from the Trent Hills. The royal structure rose five stories high, its bluish-gray speckled stonework taking on various hues depending upon the slant of sunlight caressing its walls when either freshly washed by a fragrant spring rain, blown bitterly dry by autumn's crisp breath or freshly dusted with a downy winter snow. A grand archway was built into the main front wall, the rich blue sky reflecting off the long windows soaring up to the slate rooftop. Banners of blue, silver and white flapped proudly in the lively winds.

Several smaller wings with fewer stories connected to the main building, some rounded in construction while others were more square or tower-like. A parapet ran along sections of the Blue Citadel off the main roof, and several turrets of varying sizes punctuated the grand structure, many sometimes draped with cloth banners or natural garlands depending on a particular season or celebration. Thriving trees, fruit orchards and grazing fields hugged the Blue Citadel on either side and behind it along the Edelin River, while the front boasted of colorful gardens, grass spaces and walkways, all of which were carefully tended and always admired by the nearby population and visitors alike.

Dooley was dumbstruck as he approached the vast structure toward its left side, heading down a slightly sloping paved road that led to the Citadel's storage cellars and stables. The grounds were dappled with ever changing spots of sunlight as strands of gray-tinged clouds passed overhead, blown about by a mercurial breeze. Nearby pines gently swayed in the currents, the fingerlike tips of their branches gently touching the air as sporadic waves of dried maple and elm leaves swirled across the ground.

Shortly, the road opened up to a wide area near the cellar entrances on his right. Several immense wooden stables constructed of pine logs dotted the fields down to the left closer to the river. Dooley brought his column of wagons to a halt, signaling for the other drivers to line up at some watering troughs to allow their horses a well-deserved drink. A worker at the storehouses, wearing a blue and white insignia embroidered on his coat, hurriedly approached Dooley and welcomed him to Morrenwood.

"Hope you had a pleasant journey," the man said, shaking Dooley's hand after he hopped off the wagon. "My name is Hennings."

"I made good time, Mr. Hennings," he said with a smile, handing him his credentials and paperwork for the order that Ned Adams had provided. "What an impressive place this is."

"I enjoy working here," the man said, glancing at the thin sheets of parchment scribbled with Ned's meticulous handwriting. "You're not the one who usually delivers here from Kanesbury," he added, looking up and studying Dooley's face. "What happened to that Nicholas fellow?"

"He, uh, recently changed occupations," he replied. "And he was such a good worker, too."

"Well, all the better for you, I suppose." Hennings walked Dooley around the area, showing him where to direct each wagon for unloading when it was his turn. Several other workers busily unloaded food supplies purchased from various parts of the kingdom for use in Morrenwood as well as for storage in times of emergency. "There are lodgings just beyond the stables where your men can supper and spend the night if you wish. They're not the finest quarters in the capital, but our distant suppliers usually appreciate a free night or two of room and board, compliments of the King."

"Thank you," Dooley said. "After four days on the road, we look forward to a meal at any table and a roof over our heads. It'll seem like dining with the King himself."

"If *any* table is all that it takes, then perhaps you wouldn't mind dining with a mere village councilman instead!" a voice called out from behind. Dooley and Hennings turned around as Len Harold approached at a brisk pace. The tall, lanky man with an easy smile extended a hand to Dooley, welcoming a fellow citizen of Kanesbury to the Blue Citadel.

"What a pleasant surprise to see you, Mr. Harold," Dooley replied, presenting himself with charm and confidence just as Ned Adams had instructed him to do while on the job. "I'd forgotten that you and your son had traveled here."

"Yes, though I didn't expect my stay to be so long. There's a special council in two more days and King Justin invited me to attend. But please, Dooley, call me Len. Everybody else in Kanesbury does, so why not you?" he said with a smile.

"Then I'll do just that–Len," he awkwardly replied, accepting Len Harold's invitation to lunch after they had chatted for a bit.

"Maynard Kurtz, or I should now say *Mayor* Kurtz, asked me to look in on you should our paths cross," he informed him. "As a favor to your employer who was kind enough to accept a position on the village council. I hear Ned Adams is quite proud of how you're handling this new job, Dooley. Good for you."

"Trying my best," Dooley said with feigned modesty before instructing his men where and when to unload the flour sacks. After showing them where they could eat, rest and stable the horses,

Dooley excused himself to join Len for a leisurely lunch in one of the dining halls in the Citadel overlooking the fruit orchards.

The stone room contained several rows of pine tables and benches. A series of long narrow windows on one wall allowed a flood of natural light inside. A large fireplace blazed against the opposite wall as the voices of many visiting minor dignitaries floated up to the thick wooden rafters. Dooley and Len each enjoyed a bowl of steaming pumpkin soup to start their meal. Dooley savored each mouthful after his grueling trip, knowing his men were probably not having a similarly elegant lunch, though not feeling terribly guilty about it at the moment.

"My son would have joined us," Len said, "but Owen is having a swell time roaming about the unrestricted areas of the Citadel and exploring the woods by the river with a few of the other bored boys he'd met."

"Then you're stuck with my company," Dooley joked, glancing around at the other diners. "Are all of these people invited to that council you mentioned? It will be a long and dreary affair if each of them is allowed to speak."

Len shook his head and chuckled. "No, Dooley. Many of the people here either work in the Citadel or are some of the lesser aides to the ones who will actually speak at the council. *Those* people are dining elsewhere among themselves or perhaps with King Justin. There will be much talk and preparation before the formal discussions and bickering begin. There's going to be talk of a possible war," he said, lowering his voice. "King Justin thought it might be wise if I informed the other dignitaries about the recent Enâri activity back home. I guess I timed my trip to Morrenwood just right."

"I guess so, though I'd be nervous having to speak in front of all those people."

"I am a little," Len admitted, "but I've already met a few of them and they seem friendly enough. As the sole representative of Kanesbury, I was even provided a room in one of the corridors where some of the visitors are staying."

Dooley looked up, impressed with the news. "That's quite an honor, Len."

"Well, if Otto Nibbs wasn't second cousin to the King, I don't know if anyone from our village would have received such regal treatment after showing up uninvited. I would've been housed in the lower rooms like most of the others, if that," he said with a smirk. "I also have a badge so I can move around many of the corridors with ease," he said, revealing a circular, light brown leather badge embossed with the official seal of the Blue Citadel. "I suppose I ought to attend a few more preliminary meetings for show."

"That might be a good idea," Dooley agreed.

"Perhaps if you have time, I could show you around the place, Dooley. The hours do drag on and there are still two days until the council. I have to keep occupied somehow," he said, a hint of a plea in his voice. "There are wonderful views from the upper towers, a grand library to browse through, and I could even show you where the war council is to be held. You'd do me a favor by keeping me company for a while."

"If that's the case, then I look forward to a tour," he said with an appreciative nod, concealing the bulk of his enthusiasm.

"Excellent!" Len replied.

Though Dooley was expected to act as Caldurian's spy as Farnsworth had instructed, up until now he had no clue how that would even be possible. Did they just expect him to stroll up to the war council chambers, sit down, put his feet up, listen and take notes? He had no idea where the meeting was even going to be held. But now that Len Harold was eager to play tour guide, Dooley felt for the first time that maybe there was a chance he could do some good and rise a notch or two in the wizard's respect.

"Since this is the last delivery of the season, we don't have to rush home," Dooley said. "Some of the men wanted to spend a day or two wandering about Morrenwood to see how the big city folk live, so I'll have plenty of free time."

"Good. There's a reception for some of the guests a few hours before the council. If your schedule permits, I'd like you to attend," Len said. "My son will find an excuse to avoid such a stuffy affair, no doubt."

"Children his age always have better things to do. They don't want to get mixed up in our messes."

"Maybe even I should have minded my own business and stayed in Kanesbury. As Maynard said at the meeting, we have to rely on each other. We can face any challenge and take care of ourselves." Len returned the badge to his pocket before taking a few more spoonfuls of the hot pumpkin soup. "Up to now, most of what's been discussed at the informal sessions deals with trouble in foreign lands. Those are matters too difficult for this simple butcher to fix which is why I was eager to find you and escape for a few hours. I'm only here to request protection for Kanesbury in case the Enâri return to their wicked ways," he explained. "Though I suppose the attendees will be interested to hear that Caldurian, or even Vellan himself, may be on the prowl in our corner of the kingdom again."

"I suppose they would," Dooley said, "though I hope it isn't true. We certainly don't need either of those two troublemakers causing a ruckus in our village." He engineered a look of revulsion. "Just how horrible would that be, Len? Why, I can't bear to think about it."

"Me either," he replied, lifting a cup of goat's milk. "Here's to Kanesbury. May she always be safe, secure and prosperous."

"I couldn't have said it better myself," Dooley replied, likewise raising his cup and drinking, eagerly looking forward to Len's tour of the Blue Citadel. He couldn't have asked for a more eager guide and unwitting accomplice to assist him in his mission.

CHAPTER 27

The War Council

Dooley's heart pounded as he turned the corner on the stone staircase and casually ascended the remaining steps, anxiously facing a long corridor before him. He had said goodbye to Len Harold moments ago at the opening reception in the lower chamber, insisting that he wanted to leave Morrenwood before noon. Len understood and wished him a safe journey back to Kanesbury, watching Dooley wade through a crowd of chattering dignitaries and aides and then slip out the doorway. What Len hadn't seen immediately afterward was Dooley casually making for the staircase leading up to the council chambers instead of exiting the Citadel as he had claimed. The war council would convene in less than two hours.

As Dooley walked down the corridor, two men approached and quickly passed by in whispered conversation. They hardly noticed him as they descended the stairs, fully engaged in talks about several tiny nations tucked away in the Northern Mountains. Dooley politely nodded as they swept by, relieved they had essentially ignored him. He kept his nerves in check as he continued down the corridor lit with flickering oil lamps affixed to the walls by several windows cut high into the stonework on his right.

Behind the long wall to his left was the chamber where King Justin would hold the war council. Len Harold had brought him here two days ago as part of his tour of the Blue Citadel. He acted considerably impressed as Len walked him through the chamber accessible through either of two large oak doors at each end of the corridor. Though this was an unrestricted section of the Citadel, Dooley was told that members of the King's Guard would be stationed outside the doors and in the vicinity while the council was in session.

On the wall to his right, directly below the line of high windows, hung four enormous tapestries suspended by silken cords. Each wall hanging combined to create one vast depiction of the Blue Citadel and the surrounding hills and woodland, the frothy ribbon of the Edelin River cutting a graceful swath through it all. What caught Dooley's attention most was that each tapestry illustrated one season. The brilliant greens and yellows of a fresh spring accented the far end of the hallway, while a languid summer day and vibrant autumn foliage designated the two middle sections. The frosty blue, white and gray hues of a blustery winter stared down upon Dooley to his immediate right, inducing a momentary shiver upon glancing at that chilly quarter of the landscape.

He hurried past the huge display toward the door at the far end of the corridor. He cautiously looked about, weaving back and forth in slow, stealthy arcs to make sure nobody else was around. Hearing neither voices nor footsteps and seeing no approaching shadows, he opened the door with a trembling hand and stepped inside the chamber, now awash with light from a crackling blaze in a huge fireplace against the long back wall across the room. Several elegantly carved oak support posts were scattered about. He knew there wouldn't be much time before this chamber and the adjacent corridor were flooded with people, so he either had to act now and act fast or promptly leave and tell Farnsworth that this ridiculous idea never had a chance. Dooley swallowed hard, determined to prove himself a success once and for all.

He scurried to the far end of the chamber past a long table adorned with candles, drinking glasses and bowls of fresh fruit. A secondary fireplace warmly burned at this end, its hearth and stone edges blackened with soot. Dooley looked up at the web of broad wooden rafters above, hidden among thick shadows and partially obscured by a slew of small tapestries and autumn garland suspended from the high ceiling. He had discreetly examined this hiding spot when Len escorted him through the chamber two days ago, knowing it was the only realistic place he could conceal himself from wandering eyes.

After one last glance, Dooley hoisted himself on top of the fireplace, using some protruding stones as footholds. When he stood on top of the mantel, he glanced down at the long table, soon to be occupied by some of the most influential people in the kingdom and throughout Laparia. He suddenly felt lightheaded, though he couldn't tell whether it was due to the height at which he stood or because of the extraordinary gathering that was about to take place. He cleared his mind and concentrated on a large beam a few feet off one side of the fireplace that extended from the wall to a support post. He inched his way across to the edge of the mantel and made a short leap to reach the wooden beam. He locked his arms around it and hauled himself up to the top, crouching on his knees to keep from hitting his head on another beam slanting down just above him.

But the difficult part was over and Dooley relied on his tree climbing abilities as a young boy to take him farther into the web of rafters. After a short series of acrobatic maneuvers, he wormed his way onto another large beam near one corner of the long back wall, completely out of view of anyone who would be seated at the table. He rested on the wide piece of oak, his back slightly inclined and his legs fully extended. He didn't have any fears about falling off, but extended an arm through one of the open designs carved into an adjoining piece of woodwork to anchor himself just in case. As an added precaution, he flipped the hood of his coat down over his head so that less of his skin would be exposed. The darkness of his clothes blended in seamlessly with the shadows.

For the next hour, Dooley closed his eyes from time to time, happy to rest awhile after sampling some of the rich and varied foods at the reception downstairs. He listened to the snapping flames from the fireplaces below. The rising heat soothed him and he found it easy to keep his heavy eyelids closed for longer stretches of time. At one point he was roused awake when several members of the kitchen staff entered through a small door near the larger fireplace carrying metal pitchers of water, wine and honey ale which they distributed along the table. He could clearly hear the monotonous chatter of the workers, though it soon bored him and he happily closed his eyelids once again, drunk with sleep, telling himself that he would wait for the real talk to begin before actually paying attention.

As the heat and crackle of flames combined with the murmur of voices wafting through the rafters, Dooley easily succumbed to a deep and dreamy sleep, a faint smile forming on his lips as his body relaxed into the wooden beam as if it were a mattress stuffed with feathers and straw. He heard neither the kitchen staff leaving shortly afterward nor the dignitaries later entering the chamber in small groups through both doors along the corridor. They eagerly took their seats and greeted a smiling King Justin who welcomed them to the final stage of the summit.

"We are gathered together at last," King Justin said, sitting at the center chair of the table, his back to the fireplace. He clasped his hands together, a thin smile beneath his ice blue eyes and cropped silvery hair as he looked about the room. He wore a light gray woolen shirt underneath a vest of autumn colors. He glanced past his son, Prince Gregory, seated to his right, and stared at a pair of empty chairs next to him. "Well, *almost* all of us," the King added, referring to the emissaries from Montavia who had not yet arrived, while at the same time thinking about his granddaughter lost somewhere in the wild. He had dispatched a search team to look for Megan after Samuel returned alone, but the princess' trail had disappeared. But to get through this war council, he and Prince Gregory, Megan's father, put her plight temporarily out of mind, a nearly impossible task if ever there was one. But they would have to try as great matters were at stake. "The absence of the Montavian representatives troubles me," King Justin continued. "I sent out scouts yesterday, but no word has returned. We'll proceed and hope they arrive soon."

"In their stead," Prince Gregory said, "I have invited one of the captains from King Rowan's guard." He pointed out a Montavian soldier seated across the table. "He and a company of his men have been training with some of Arrondale's finest." The prince exhibited many of his father's facial features, and though his hair was long and brown, his eyes were as blue as the King's.

The other representatives were dismayed that King Rowan's envoys had been delayed, knowing that Arrondale had a cordial relationship with its neighbor to the east. A gentleman, nearly the same age as King Justin, leaned back in his chair at one end of the table to the King's left, quietly contemplating what the absence might mean. His large frame was wrapped in dark blue robes embroidered with faint designs of silver and white. A pair of deep, dark eyes nearly matched his unruly mess of thick, black hair. He furrowed his brow in deep contemplation.

"Tolapari, you look lost in thought," the King remarked, eyeing his old friend and advisor. "Though that is hardly unusual for a wizard. Is there anything you wish to say?"

"Not quite yet, Justin," he softly said, offering a smile as he lightly tapped a finger to his chin. "In the meantime, shall we proceed with the tale of war and chaos down south that is Rhiál and Maranac? There are some in this room who have not heard the entire story, and it will give your scribes a delightful challenge to record the full account for posterity." He indicated with amusement the two royal scribes seated at the opposite end of the table, dipping quills into ink bottles and scribbling the official documentation of the war council on parchment sheets.

"That's as good a place to start as any," King Justin replied, pouring some wine into a drinking glass in preparation for a long discussion. He glanced at the nearly two dozen emissaries and their aides seated at the table, representatives of the various kingdoms and nations in Laparia. Several minor officials sat on additional benches and chairs placed along the chamber walls.

King Justin then introduced Lamar, an emissary from the kingdom of Rhiál who sat two chairs away on his left. Between them sat a pale, worried looking man named Nedry, one of King Justin's top advisors. Rhiál was tucked away in the lower reaches of the Ridloe Mountains in the southeast and bordered the western shore of Lake LaShear, a long, narrow lake stretching north to south. On the opposite side of the lake lay the kingdom of Maranac, slightly larger and more populated than its neighbor.

Several decades ago the two nations had been one, but a political war had erupted into a bloody affair, splitting the kingdom nearly in half to the present day. And though that particular war had ended long ago, most of its citizens dreamed of a day when the two kingdoms would reunite in peace despite a signed treaty of separation and the forgotten designs of long-dead politicians. But a current war now brewing between the two kingdoms left many on both sides of Lake LaShear yearning for the functional yet soulless peace they had grown used to over the passing years.

"Thank you, King Justin, for inviting me here," Lamar stated graciously, smiling beneath a mop of iron gray hair. "Since Rhiál has been at war for six months with our neighbor, Maranac, I'll speak briefly of the history that preceded this disaster so everyone is clear on the facts. After which, maybe we can devise a solution to end the madness before it spreads. Without assistance, Rhiál might not last into next spring."

"I look forward to your account," said a man sitting directly across the table. He had traveled from Linden, one of several small nations wedged among the towering peaks of the Northern Mountains near Kargoth. "Linden and my neighbors survive under Vellan's iron fist, rebelling against him occasionally, but not yet at war. But how did Rhiál become embroiled in your current conflict?"

Lamar's countenance was grim. "Simple. King Drogin of Maranac attacked us," he said. "Drogin received the royal title ten days into this year before even the first efalia blossoms of spring had a chance to bloom. His brother, King Hamil, had been assassinated seven days earlier, and what a tragic loss it was. Hamil was a good and honorable man, quite unlike his sibling."

"The newly crowned King Drogin invaded your kingdom without provocation?"

"Yes. About a month later," replied Lamar. "The first attacks were near the southern tip of Lake LaShear. That area contains some of our richest farmland. The strikes were designed to disrupt the spring planting and to test our resistance."

"But why would King Drogin do such a thing?" asked a curious Len Harold.

"Because Drogin blames Rhiál for the assassination of his younger brother."

Len furrowed his brow. "*Younger* brother? How did King Hamil earn the crown if he was Drogin's younger sibling?" Others in the room were just as mystified.

"It seems that many here are not familiar with the politics of Maranac," King Justin remarked. "The ascension of Hamil to the throne before Drogin has always intrigued me. Perhaps you can enlighten us with more details."

Lamar helped himself to some red grapes from a nearby fruit bowl, munching on a few as he told his story. "Hamil's coronation before that of his older brother of two years is at the center of the current conflict. You see, Drogin, who was rightfully first in line for the throne, was an ardent supporter of reunification of our two nations. Even throughout his youth, I've been told, he was always curious about the history of Maranac and how it broke apart sixty-five years ago after a dreary, three-year conflict. When the peace treaty was signed that year in 677, our new kingdom on the lake's west side was called Rhiál, borrowing the name of the village where our new monarch had been born.

"King Drogin was a self-taught scholar regarding that war during his youth, curious about its origins, battles and heroes. This would have been admirable in most cases, but Drogin's interest in the war turned into an obsession. Throughout his early adulthood, rumors existed that Drogin's father, King Cerone, was skeptical of the young man's fitness to one day be a leader. A sad thing, I'm sure, for any father to believe about his son."

The two scribes busily recorded Lamar's words as a rapt audience listened in the weighty silence of the chamber, the hush occasionally punctuated by the pop of maple wood burning in the fireplace or the dull clink of a metal pitcher against the rim of a drinking cup. Though the air felt warm and comforting, all in their chairs were wide awake. Even those who were familiar with the recent political history of Maranac paid close attention as if hearing the narrative for the first time.

"How did Drogin's father come to that determination?" asked a guest sitting on one of the benches against the wall. "When did King Cerone decide that his older son should be passed over for the crown in favor of the younger Hamil?"

"Good questions," Lamar said. "And though I only met King Cerone a few times before he died while I was an ambassador to Maranac, the King in no way confided those personal details to me. Only through a series of discreet conversations and private correspondences with lower officials–plus the occasional rumor or two–do diplomats glean much of the information we work with. Such was the case regarding King Cerone's opinion of his two sons."

Lamar pulled another red grape off the stem and popped it into his mouth. "Before King Cerone died three years ago, he signed a royal decree stating that his younger son, Hamil, would ascend to the throne upon his death instead of Drogin. Well, this was not a highly publicized law for obvious reasons, but it raised quite a stir in the royal corridors in Maranac. Drogin, of course, was a volcano of emotions, claiming he had been denied his birthright, but most people in Maranac I've talked to over the years were privately glad that Hamil should rule them one day instead of his older, reckless brother. Though Drogin never settled down nor had the patience to be an administrator of day-to-day tasks, I guess what troubled his father most was the boy's warped desire to take back Rhiál at any cost. The older Drogin grew, the more he talked about the possibility, no doubt envisioning the day when he would finally rule and make his dream a reality. But if that meant another war, then King Cerone wanted nothing to do with it, and so the line of succession was altered.

"Now there are many people in both kingdoms who dream of the day that Rhiál and Maranac become one nation again, myself included," Lamar said wistfully. "Many stories from my childhood and old paintings recount the wonderful days of the great kingdom of Maranac and the constant traffic of colorful ships sailing east and west across the blue waters of Lake LaShear. And though trade routes still exist, they are few and tightly monitored. The free and spontaneous visits between the shores among family and friends have vanished. A deep regret still pains many in their hearts and souls that, because of long dead, self-serving politicians, a once great nation was transformed into a shadow of its former self. Most realize that if the two sides were ever to reunite and heal, a new bond of trust would need to sprout and flourish, though it would take time. And certain decisions would have to be made as well.

"For instance, which leader would rule this new nation—one of *ours* or one of *theirs*? And precisely where? The old capital city of Bellavon, marking the border at the southern tip of Lake LaShear, was divided in two in 677 as part of the peace treaty. Now Melinas and Zaracosa, the current capitals of Rhiál and Maranac, serve as the political centers on either side of the lake. Without answers to these questions, the two kingdoms will never become one." Lamar plucked one more grape from its stem. "Unless, of course, a crazed brother tries to grab the other half by force."

"And that, regretfully, is where we now find ourselves." The wizard Tolapari's quiet but sharp words cut through the subdued chamber. "King Drogin has usurped the throne of Maranac and is blaming Rhiál for the death of his younger brother, Hamil."

"And the death of Hamil's wife, too," Lamar added. "King Hamil and his wife were returning from an engagement early this year. While on the way back to their residence in Zaracosa, their coach was attacked by a band of horsemen. The King, his wife and all their protectors were killed. Earlier that same day, their only child, Melinda, a teacher in the capital city, disappeared, apparently kidnapped or killed. Of course, Drogin accused Rhiál of her disappearance as well."

"You informed me earlier that King Hamil's guardsmen had slain a few of the attackers before it was over," King Justin said.

"That's true," Lamar continued, "but unfortunately King Hamil's men were overwhelmed in the end. After the bodies of the King and his wife were removed from the site, Drogin's officials allowed observers from Rhiál, including me, to visit the area where the tragedy occurred. They claimed they wanted us to see proof of what we supposedly did. It was all a part of Drogin's excuse to start a war."

"What did you see?" someone asked.

"Many dead soldiers," Lamar muttered, keeping a roiling anger in check. "Some had been felled by arrows and others with swords. The few attackers who had been killed were dressed in uniforms of the royal guard of Rhiál. That itself should tell you that the assault was staged. If Rhiál had attacked, why would we so blatantly announce it? But it didn't matter. Everyone suspected that Drogin was behind the affair. Though he still lived in the royal residence at Zaracosa, Drogin was estranged from Hamil and his family. His denial of power constantly gnawed at him. Drogin only wanted an excuse for war to feed to the public, not caring how flimsy the evidence looked to us in Rhiál." Lamar paused for a moment and took a deep drink of wine, feeling emotionally spent at having to recount the sad details once again. All eyes were upon him, eager to here more of the fascinating, yet dreadful tale. "But our suspicion alone wasn't the only evidence to assure us that Drogin was behind King Hamil's murder," he continued. "We had verification of another kind, too."

"Tell us," Len Harold said, leaning forward, his elbows propped up on the table.

"Less than a week after the massacre, a member of King Hamil's guard who had been secretly in league with Drogin, arrived in Melinas, begging for an audience with King Basil of Rhiál. Of course, the man was apprehended at once and questioned, revealing much about the deadly attack and kidnapping," he said. "You see, the young solider had regrets about his involvement with Drogin and the plan to kidnap Princess Melinda as a way for Drogin to gain power from his brother. At least, that is what the soldier had been told was the plan. It was not until a day after the kidnapping that he heard of King Hamil's assassination, learning shortly thereafter that both events had been orchestrated by Drogin. The guard realized that a new king was about to take the throne with blood on his hands, and that knowledge tormented him, especially since he had a part in it, however misguided. The guard fled to Rhiál the first chance he could to confess the plot to King Basil, fearing that war was in the offing."

"Where is Princess Melinda?" asked an emissary from the nation of Harlow. "And who really attacked King Hamil and his wife?"

Lamar shook his head sadly. "Regretfully, there has been no word about the young woman for the last seven months. She has been missing since the third day of New Spring, the day of the attack. Whether King Drogin killed his only niece or had her imprisoned, your guess is as good as mine. According to her grandfather's decree, she would become queen upon the death of Hamil, being the next direct descendent in the bloodline. Drogin needed her out of the way to take the throne for himself. And as to who the men were behind the attack? Well that, too, is a curious matter," he said with an air of mystery.

"How so?" someone asked.

"When I was allowed to travel to Maranac with my observers to visit the murder scene, we closely examined the bodies of the dead guardsmen and their attackers, all still left in place where they had fallen." Lamar recalled that cold, gray spring day along a dirt road near a thin spread of woods. A steady drizzle of rain dampened the new tufts of green grass sprouting along the desolate stretch of highway several miles from Zaracosa. He could still smell the scent of the fresh soil, pine and blood of that solemn afternoon. "And though the attackers had been disguised as soldiers of Rhiál, one of my men closely examined their corpses and later told me something in confidence. He said that a few of the dead attackers had been armed with daggers with peculiar markings upon them. Two of them also wore rings with similar inscriptions. Apparently the items were overlooked by Drogin's men who had arranged the attack."

Len Harold spoke up as he plucked a small apple from the bowl in front of him. "What was so special about those daggers and rings? What were the markings on them?"

"The tiny symbols upon the items were of seafarers and shipbuilders, probably ignored by most who only took a casual glance. But that one officer with me was a man of the seas himself," Lamar said, "and such a thing caught his eye right away."

"I still don't understand," Len continued. "Both Rhiál and Maranac border the vast waters of Lake LaShear. Ships are a way of life for many there. Why should it be surprising that some of the dead men had personal possessions reflecting that?"

"Because those particular items weren't forged in our region of Laparia," he softly stated. "The peculiar markings in question are indigenous to the Northern Isles."

A flurry of whispers enveloped the room as several people consulted one another about the meaning of such a revelation. Tolapari, sensing that many people had the same question upon their lips, received a nod of encouragement from King Justin before raising a hand to settle the crowd.

"It is true," the wizard said, restoring silence to the chamber. "Soldiers from the Northern Isles are in league with King Drogin of Maranac. That is what you are all wondering. But there is more to the relationship. Our belligerent Island neighbors are assisting Drogin in his war, but they are doing so through the manipulative hand of Vellan himself. The resources of Kargoth are supporting the war in the south and have helped to instigate it. King Drogin is Vellan's willing puppet, seeing a chance to expand his power as Vellan pursues his own selfish ends."

A voice in the back piped up. "How do you know this?"

"I will let our friend from Surna speak on that matter," Tolapari replied, indicating a tall, fair-haired man seated across the table from King Justin's aide.

"In private meetings earlier, I had consulted with King Justin and Tolapari about Kargoth's pact with the Northern Isles," the man said. "Situated on the eastern edge of the Northern Mountains, my nation is not far from the Lorren River and its tributaries. As early as last year, our scouts have reported seeing large rafts laden with supplies and soldiers sailing up the Lorren River from time to time, and then going farther up along the Gray River, one of its smaller tributaries. When they disembark, it is a short journey through one of the mountain passes to the Drusala River which flows down into the dominion of Kargoth. On the Drusala, the Islanders don't have to fight the current which take them to the doorstep of Vellan's stronghold in Del Norác."

"So not only does Vellan have the Enâri, which he created over thirty years ago and continues to expand," Tolapari said, "but his forces are also being bolstered by recruits from the Northern Isles. The ambassador from Surna also told us that a group of scouts from his nation had made a secret expedition along the banks of the Lorren River all the way down to where it empties into the Trillium Sea. They reported back that a ship from the Isles was anchored off the shoreline to deposit troops and supplies into the mouth of the Lorren, sailing unchallenged up the river all the way to Kargoth."

"The few communities thriving along the narrow shores of that area are no match for any arrivals from the Islands," King Justin said. "People living around the perimeter of the Dunn Hills are pioneers, accepting the fate of the wilderness. They are good, robust souls but without a single government encompassing the many villages scattered up and down the coast. They have neither army nor king and prefer it that way. If men from the Isles face any resistance, I'm sure it is minimal. They are staunch allies of Vellan."

"And they are not Vellan's only allies," the envoy from Surna continued. "As my associates from Linden and Harlow can attest to–for we all live under the troubling shadow of Kargoth–many of the original inhabitants and their descendants living in the Drusala River valley are also loyal subjects to Vellan. But it is not by choice, as legend has it." The gentleman lowered his voice, wondering if he should utter one of the popular superstitions in the

Northern Mountains. "After Vellan claimed the region of Kargoth as his own, rumors flourished about how the powerful wizard had cast a spell upon the waters of the Drusala. Those who drank from it were instantly enslaved to Vellan, having an unnatural devotion to do his will. Many claim to have fled the valley to one of our nearby nations upon seeing the spell take hold of others. But whether these stories are true or not, I cannot absolutely say."

"True or not, one thing is obvious–Vellan's followers are legion," King Justin said. "He will be a formidable enemy to face. Already he has a stranglehold upon the mountain nations around him. Surna, Linden and Harlow years ago essentially surrendered their sovereignty to him by conducting trade deals, taking bribes and accepting many of his advisors into their governments. Vellan's subtle threats and occasional violent displays had much to do with the ease in which he wielded his power over the years."

"No one agrees more, King Justin, than I," said an emissary from Harlow. "However, we are at peace with Vellan, mostly. Our three nations exist on the map as independent entities. And yes, it is but a fiction, but remember, our populations have been subject to Vellan's whims before I could first speak as a child. Our leaders have tolerated his presence, accommodating his economic overtures until his influence was tightly woven into our lands. Still, I'll say it again–at least we are at peace, which is a good thing."

"At peace? *That* is a fiction!" said another man of about thirty seated on one of the benches against the wall between the main doorways. His tired, leaf green eyes and unshaven face belied a fiery spirit within. "Vellan's troops have made incursions into our trio of nations over the years, terrorizing villages, burning farms and butchering families in order to get local populations to submit to his will. And it has worked because the governments of Linden, Surna and Harlow have allowed his representatives a say in our affairs under threats of more killing. So to prevent war, our leaders have simply submitted like cowards to his demands and declared it peace."

"We have bought time, Eucádus!" the emissary insisted.

"You have given us a slow death. Over the years, many people, me included, have fled Harlow, not willing to live in a society stripped of freedom and littered with politicians who have willingly allowed that freedom to decay. The same can be said of

Linden and Surna, too. Their populations have diminished as well because those people are seeking a better life elsewhere."

"Well, Eucádus, perhaps if you and the others had stayed, we might have taken the fight to Vellan!" the emissary snapped back. "Abandoning their homelands only made matters worse."

"Abandoning our homelands was a last resort!" Eucádus stood and took a deep breath, trying to keep his anger from blunting his message. "When the governments of all three mountain nations claim to fight for their people, yet follow the will of Vellan out of fear or to keep his tainted money flowing into their coffers, then there *is* no hope that a fight will be undertaken. That is why the people must take matters into their own hands or perish."

The emissary from Harlow waved a dismissive hand Eucádus' way. "We have had this discussion before in private. Let us not bore the others with our rancor. There are more important matters to discuss this afternoon."

"What would those matters be, sir?" Eucádus shook his head, rubbing a hand over his whiskers. "Tell me, why are you even here? Do you offer a plan to fight back, or do you simply want to learn what other nations will do before returning home? This way you and other bureaucrats can position yourselves to survive whatever storm is unleashed against Vellan, whether it is successful or not."

"That's what you and your kind are after, Eucádus–a war!" The emissary stood up, pointing a finger at his fellow countryman. "You'd rush to war when other methods might save us. You'd rather plunge the mountain nations into conflict, destroying innocent lives and a sustained peace, all on a hopeless whim."

Eucádus lowered his voice. "Innocent lives have already been ruined, sir, and the peace you live under is but an illusion. Citizens' livelihoods and homes have been usurped or destroyed, food is rationed, men are rotting in Vellan's prisons, and the only people that seem to thrive are those who walk among the halls of government–and that's only because Vellan still allows it. He would obliterate you and your ilk in a heartbeat if it meant saving his own life or those of the Enâri. And one day soon when the borders of Kargoth are too confined to contain his precious creations, they will flood into our lands like Vellan's advisors have already done, displacing or destroying any of our citizens who remain." His words dripped with both sorrow and disdain. "Harlow, Linden and Surna are mere shells of their former selves, and those in charge have long ago abandoned any desire to break the chains that Kargoth has wrapped around us. Sadly, you've grown comfortable with the state of affairs as they are, abandoning generations to a slow, creeping tyranny."

Eucádus sat down on the bench and folded his arms, his gaze still cast upon the ambassador who returned to his seat moments later, his face red with rage. King Justin tiredly rubbed his brow after viewing the spectacle, throwing a glance at his son next to him. Prince Gregory understood and broke the silence.

"Thank you both for your spirited words. I'm sure everyone here will consider them carefully," he said. "But now would be a good time to hear from the representative of Drumaya." Prince Gregory indicated a well dressed man seated across the table from his father, his beard neatly trimmed and his shoulders squared. "Though good fortune planted the Ebrean Forest as a buffer between Drumaya and the Northern Mountains, your kingdom still engages in much trade with that region," the prince pointed out. "Do you have any words to add to what you've just heard, Osial?"

"Several. And they echo the sentiments of King Cedric who instructed me to convey them here today." The representative addressed King Justin directly. "King Cedric knows that your inclinations lean toward assisting Rhiál in ending their war, and that is admirable. But the kingdom of Drumaya would be loath to enter into such a fray with you if that is your objective. We have long suspected Vellan's involvement in the affairs of the east. Our scouts have monitored his soldiers' movements across the Kincarin Plains for months now. We are not naïve. Yet it would be naïve to think that we'd risk Vellan's wrath by protesting his dabbling in foreign affairs."

Tolapari tilted his head, eyeing Osial. "A murdered King and his wife are a few steps above dabbling, don't you think?"

"In Drumaya's defense, I didn't know of Vellan's involvement in the assassination until after I arrived here," he replied. "It is tragic, and upon hearing my report, King Cedric may have a change of heart. But I can only relate to you his last instructions." Osial nervously fingered his shirt collar, momentarily avoiding eye contact.

"We understand," Tolapari said.

"Yes, and you must also understand that Drumaya buys coal and iron from the mines of Kargoth, among other items. Our farmlands sell and trade substantial food and fruit supplies throughout the Northern Mountains where the growing season is not as long or productive as in Drumaya." Osial folded his hands and rested them on the table. "Vellan could easily interrupt or destroy those trade routes, deeply harming our economy. And what he could do to us militarily were we to infuriate him, well, I dare not utter." The ambassador shook his head. He was used to luxuriating in more delicate verbiage, but King Justin's gathering was of a less formal style than what he preferred. "I know my words may sound insensitive and are probably not what you wanted to hear, but they reflect our reality in Drumaya. Vellan has much influence over us, like it or not."

"And he always will," Eucádus said, "as long as people like you never stand up to him."

Osial sighed, not wanting to engage Eucádus in an argument similar to the last one. He posed a question to King Justin to change the direction of the discussion. "Tell us, what would you do to alter the current state of Laparia? Given the freedom to work your will, enlighten us with your plans."

The King accepted Osial's challenge with good humor. With much talk but few specifics, restlessness was settling over the room. Maybe now was as good a time as any to reveal his intentions.

"We all know that Vellan has designs on Arrondale," he said, leaning back in his chair with an easy confidence. "He has for many years. But I see his involvement in the conflict between Rhiál and Maranac as a precursor to some action against this kingdom. Also, recent word from Len Harold, my fellow countryman from the village of Kanesbury, has strengthened my suspicions." The King indicated Len who sat across the table, urging him to tell of the recent Enâri activity in his village. Len promptly did so, narrating the details of their reawakening in the Spirit Caves, the mysterious visit between Mayor Otto Nibbs and one of the Enâri creatures, and of Otto's subsequent visit to meet with all of the Enâri at Barringer's Landing.

"But our mayor never returned, and a search for him proved fruitless," Len explained. "And though King Justin has asked me not to publicly reveal the purpose of the Enâr's visit, the visit itself is nonetheless proof that Vellan, or his apprentice, Caldurian, is up to no good within the borders of Arrondale."

"What did that creature want from your mayor?" someone asked. "Why won't King Justin allow you to speak?"

"I am not forbidding Len to speak," King Justin stated, not thinking it wise to reveal that the Spirit Box was currently located inside the Blue Citadel. Since Vellan had reawakened the Enâri, it seemed probable that he might also be searching for the one source created by the wizard Frist capable of their destruction. "I merely asked Len to keep secret a nugget of sensitive information which he has agreed to do so. Regardless, it is irrelevant to my point–namely, that Vellan is again stretching his tentacles across Laparia and that Arrondale is the prize he desires most." The King leaned forward, his ice blue eyes alive and determined. "But I will not let it happen, I can promise you that."

"And despite any doubts raised in this chamber, I think most would support you in the end," Tolapari assured him. "If Arrondale ever fell, the fate of Laparia would be dark and grim indeed. If anything, Vellan is focused. He will labor tirelessly to achieve his cruel and gluttonous aims. As some of you know, he once trained me for a short while after settling down in the region he dubbed Kargoth. But after a few months, I sized up his devious nature and fled, knowing I couldn't be part of it. Vellan was banished from his native soil fifty years ago because of ambition. Now he infects our homeland, gaining power, biding his time. I received the bulk of my training from others of the race of true wizards who occasionally traveled in our region. I learned much of Vellan's past and surmised why he acts as he does. One day, I believe, he will want revenge upon his race, using our conquered populations to advance his evil deed." Tolapari recalled his years of training, having been both honored and delighted to hone the trace of wizard-like power somehow coursing through his veins. How it disturbed him that the likes of Vellan and Caldurian could misuse such a gift, yet sadly, it didn't surprise him, knowing that corrupt people would always flourish from time to time, whether among the race of common men or wizards.

The ambassador from Drumaya sighed, gazing at King Justin. "Still, you have not answered my question," he said. "Despite elegant words from you, Tolapari and Len Herald, you have not clearly stated your intentions. What do you wish to do, sir?"

"I'll tell you precisely my plan," King Justin said as everyone breathlessly awaited his answer. "We must send an army into Rhiál and assist King Basil in his precarious fight. We must prevent that kingdom from falling into the hands of King Drogin, a false king propped up by Vellan. If Maranac retakes Rhiál by sword, then a true peace between those two nations won't be achieved for generations, if ever."

Tolapari agreed. "And once Drogin cements his power across the lake, I can only imagine that troops of Enâri creatures and men from the Northern Isles will flood into that region, giving Vellan a second foothold in Laparia."

"But we are nearly ready to attack Vellan himself," Eucádus said, standing up again. "And you should join us. My people, who have fled Harlow over the years along with others from Linden and Surna, have raised a small army to launch an assault. We will try to convince King Cedric of Drumaya to join us, but with or without his support, we will march to Del Norác and look Vellan in the eyes, taking the fight to him. Win or lose, we can't allow our last remembrances of freedom to wither away without taking a stand. What is the point of walking and breathing each day if enslavement is our only fate?"

King Justin looked kindly upon Eucádus as a few people in the chamber quietly applauded the young man's words. The King agreed with his sentiments, yet having seen quite a few more years than Eucádus, he had learned to temper his passion for victory with patience. Vellan's defeat, should it ever be realized, would be a careful and arduous process. He could not lend his support to the rash gesture Eucádus was proposing, however grand or sincere. There had to be a better way. He hoped his words would sway Eucádus and the others to his side for the sake of Laparia.

"You are right, Eucádus. We cannot let our freedom wither away," the King said, standing up to address the crowd. "And Vellan must be confronted soon. For too long we have allowed him to flourish unchecked, turning a blind eye to his ambition and iron rule while supporting him with our trade, fooling ourselves that all would be well in the end. But if you attack him alone now, clearly outnumbered even with help from King Cedric, you will be fighting for a glorious defeat. For thirty-five years Vellan has been breeding the Enâri race, growing them to be stronger and live longer as previous generations die off. I can't imagine what their numbers are now. A concentrated force on our part will be the only realistic way to achieve victory."

"What are you suggesting?"

"I think our wisest recourse would be to overwhelm King Drogin and free Rhiál from his grip," the King explained. "The forces from Arrondale and Montavia–for many of their troops have been training with us–will ride to the aid of Rhiál. And Eucádus, if your troops from the three mountain nations join us, our chances for a swift victory over a lesser foe will increase. A victory there will do much for the morale of Laparia and better prepare us for a later strike against Vellan. And if we can convince Drumaya to join us, so much the better. By restoring legitimate rule to Maranac, we are foiling Vellan's plans to expand his base."

"Not to mention severely wounding his pride," Tolapari said with a smirk, eliciting a round of light laughter from the chamber.

"That can only help our cause," the King replied. "Afterward, having time to regroup to full strength over the winter, we can launch a final attack on Kargoth, this time with Rhiál and Maranac at our side. Only then will we have a fighting chance, Eucádus–a realistic chance for a lasting victory."

King Justin took his seat as everyone silently absorbed his words, most convinced that his plan seemed a wise course of action. The King glanced at Tolapari, noting a vague smile upon the wizard's face. He took it as a good sign that his words were both thoughtful and compelling, yet wondered if his idea would ultimately be agreed upon. They were now nearly halfway through the autumn season. With winter soon to be knocking upon their doors, the kingdoms aligned against Vellan had only one realistic chance to make a move against the tyrant before cold and snow gripped Laparia. King Justin lightly drummed his fingers against the side of his chair.

"That went well," whispered Nedry, the King's advisor seated to his left, looking less pale and worried than earlier. Now that a possible strategy appeared imminent, some of the color had returned to Nedry's thin face and the tightness in his facial muscles had lessened. He combed a hand through his long, graying hair, eagerly awaiting the verdict.

Though Nedry had been a loyal advisor for many years, the strain of politics in unsettling times had taken its toll upon him. More and more, he was envisioning a quiet retirement to escape the long hours necessary to perform his job. Being at the beck and call of the King had its allure and privileges, but too many sleepless nights and chronic indigestion had worn him out. He wondered if it was time to relinquish his authority to somebody younger.

"I suppose we'll find out shortly just *how* well," King Justin whispered as he poured himself more wine. A few moments later, Osial cleared his throat to speak as the crowd settled down.

"You have presented a solid argument, King Justin, one that I will bring back to King Cedric," he said. "I cannot guarantee that the kingdom of Drumaya will support you, but in light of the new information I have learned today, I cannot guarantee that it will not support you either."

"Spoken like a true diplomat," Eucádus replied. "But since you have not turned us down completely, I will take that as a good sign. However, speaking on behalf of the populations-in-hiding from Harlow, Linden and Surna, I offer our full support to King Justin's proposal." He nodded respectfully to the monarch. "Your plan makes sense and I am happy to be a part of it." He made eye contact with the ambassador from Harlow with whom he had argued earlier. "And to my fellow countryman, I am not sure what details you'll report of this assembly when you return home, but know that those who have left the mountain nations have not abandoned them. Though we conceal our location until we are ready to fight, remember that it is Harlow, Linden and Surna that we still fight *for*, and may this knowledge provide you hope that better days are yet possible."

"I will let others know what went on here," the ambassador said graciously. "Though Vellan's advisors infest our country, I am still a patriot. I'll communicate our decision on the sly to those who might support a rebellion. Perhaps it's time for those of us who have become comfortable with the way of things to start preparing for the inevitable stampede, for it is coming from what I've heard here today." He flashed an uneasy grin. "Better to get behind it than in front of it, I suppose."

"A wise choice," Tolapari said.

Others in turn offered encouraging comments about King Justin's plan, much to the delight of Lamar, the ambassador from Rhiál. So after twenty minutes of speechifying from a handful of individuals, Lamar finally stood up to thank everyone for their support. But just as he started to speak, a guard in the Blue Citadel quietly entered the chamber through one of the main doors and discreetly caught Nedry's attention. As Lamar continued talking, the King's advisor left the table and hurried to the guard, consulting with him in whispers. As the guard spoke, Nedry's eyes widened in astonishment. A moment later he was standing behind King Justin and speaking softly into his ear.

King Justin was equally surprised upon hearing the news, turning to Nedry. "They're here now?" he whispered, not wanting to interrupt Lamar's speech.

"Yes," Nedry replied. "They returned with our scout who found them hiking along King's Road this morning. Shall I have them brought in?"

"Of course! Right away. This is both curious and troubling at once. I'm sure the council will think so, too."

"And there's one other thing," Nedry added, lowering his voice further as he spoke in hushed, grave tones. King Justin went pale at the news, taking a slow, deep breath.

"Bring them at once," he ordered.

"Right away," Nedry said, hurrying back to the guard who then escorted him out of the chamber to the puzzled looks of many.

Lamar was equally perplexed and turned to King Justin. "Shall I cut short my remarks? You appear otherwise occupied."

"Forgive the interruption, Lamar, but a new wrinkle has just been added to this war council," he cryptically explained. He noted how Tolapari coolly folded his arms and leaned back, contemplating what the fuss was all about. "Yet fear not, for all shall be revealed, well, right now."

The King indicated the opening chamber door that Nedry had exited through moments earlier. Nedry reappeared, followed by two young men in weather-stained traveling clothes, their faces etched with worry. When the captain from Montavia recognized the blond haired brothers, each wearing a silver ring, he immediately stood up and bowed slightly toward them, a look of amazement upon his face.

Nedry ushered them to the pair of empty chairs next to Prince Gregory where they were heartily greeted by him and King Justin. When the new arrivals sat down, the captain from Montavia did likewise as murmurs of wonderment enveloped the room.

"Allow me to introduce our visitors," King Justin said. "These are Princes Brendan and William, grandsons of King Rowan of Montavia. They have journeyed far to get here, and now we'll learn the sad facts about why the emissaries from their kingdom had never arrived. I'll let them speak before we divulge this council's decision."

The two brothers looked at one another, and then Brendan stood to address the crowd. His troubled sea blue eyes scanned the gawking faces before him. "It pains me to report that my homeland of Montavia has been attacked. Soldiers from the Northern Isles have invaded the capital of Triana and some of the larger surrounding villages. They have done so in league with a troop of Enâri creatures led by the wizard Caldurian. I had been told that about five hundred Enâri are in control of my grandfather's residence of Red Lodge. There are about as many Island troops stationed throughout Triana, though some of them also guard Red Lodge. I have no specifics about troop levels in the other villages. My younger brother and I escaped at the urging of our grandfather to seek help from King Justin, and we are here to do just that."

It took no time for Brendan to be peppered with questions regarding the surprise invasion and the safety of King Rowan. He answered each one, particularly pleasing his audience with the story of his and William's daring escape. Len Harold posed a question when one bit of information started to gnaw at him.

"When exactly did the invasion occur?" he politely asked.

"The Islanders and the Enâri launched their attack before dawn fifteen days ago, the twenty-third day of New Autumn."

Len did some quick calculations in his head. "The *twenty-third* day? You're sure of that date?"

Brendan nodded. "Quite sure. Why do you ask?"

Len furrowed his brow as if he were trying to solve a nagging riddle. "Well, because on the *twenty-fourth* day of New Autumn, I had attended a meeting in my village of Kanesbury where we've had our own dealings with the Enâri years ago–and apparently just recently. Not to bore you with all the details, but on the evening of the twenty-third, Mayor Otto Nibbs had supposedly been visited by one of the Enâri creatures. The next morning he left for a place called Barringer's Landing to meet with all of them."

Tolapari tapped a finger on the tabletop. "And your point would be...?"

Len glanced at the wizard. "I shall assume that the five hundred Enâri creatures who attacked Montavia are the very same five hundred who reawakened and escaped from the Spirit Caves outside Kanesbury about a month ago."

"That seems logical," King Justin said.

"If that's the case, how could Mayor Nibbs have met with the creatures outside our village if they were already in Montavia invading King Rowan's city?" Len scratched his head. "That would be impossible, so why would Otto have said it?" he whispered, more to himself than to the others as the thought continued to nag him.

"As interesting a puzzle as that is, we now have a bigger problem to deal with," Tolapari said. "How do we save Montavia? Earlier I was contemplating the war in the south and Vellan's hand in it. He has used Island troops to assist in flaming the tensions between Rhiál and Maranac. And since the two emissaries from Montavia never arrived here, I began to speculate what would happen if Vellan had also encouraged the Northern Isles to invade that kingdom. Now my suspicions have been confirmed. He has done just that, trying to develop a third foothold in Laparia directly on the eastern border of Arrondale." The possibility sent ripples of alarm throughout the gathering. "If Vellan succeeds, he'll have Arrondale in his aim on three different fronts–from the northeast, the southeast and the southwest, with Arrondale's back to the Trillium Sea. It would only be a matter of time before this kingdom fell and Laparia was totally consumed."

"And after that horrible outcome, Vellan will continue to grow and multiply his massive forces, finally sending his deadly plague west across the Tunara Plains to the wizards' valley for his ultimate revenge," King Justin added, reluctantly contemplating such a dark world with Vellan at its helm. "It is a bleak future I portend, but unless we act now, I fear it will become a reality."

He told Brendan and William about the council's decision to send armies from both Arrondale and the trio of small nations in the Northern Mountains to aid Rhiál in its war with Maranac. They readily agreed with the decision, only asking that part of the force from Arrondale be reserved to repel the invasion in their homeland.

"The troops from Montavia that are now training here will be honored to ride alongside any forces you would assign to this mission," Prince Brendan said. "Montavia must be freed before the Northern Isles send reinforcements."

"It goes without saying that Arrondale will aid its neighbor," King Justin replied. "I'll split the army that I was going to send to Rhiál and therefore must raise more recruits before we launch our offensive." He looked across the table at Osial. "It is now even more important that you convince King Cedric to join Eucádus and his troops when they ride east. Drumaya's help is imperative."

"I'll do my best," he promised.

"And should the representative from Drumaya need assistance in convincing his good King of our plight," Eucádus interjected, "I suggest he invite both Prince Brendan and Prince William to speak with King Cedric himself. After all, they now know firsthand of the danger that faces us all."

"Point well taken," Osial returned, "though I can handle the discussion with my King. But thank you for the suggestion."

"You're welcome," Eucádus said with a rebellious gleam in his eyes, noting that both Brendan and William were valiantly trying to conceal their mirth at the exchange.

"Yes, well, very good then," King Justin said, taking back the reins of the meeting. "And after everyone returns to their respective homelands, our messengers will surely be busy in the days ahead as we coordinate strategies. We now stand at the tenth day of Mid Autumn. The winter season begins the month after next. By this time next month, I hope the fortunes of Laparia will look brighter. So on that note, I officially dismiss this council."

King Justin sharply pounded his fist on the table, offering an encouraging smile. At that same moment, the gathering responded with appreciative applause for the King's hospitality and leadership over the last few days. Soon the room was awash with conversation as the bustling crowd arose, some individuals slowly making their way to the exits, eager to partake of a meal or to depart Morrenwood at once, while others lingered about the chamber or in the adjacent corridor to discuss the particulars of what had just transpired. The flames in the two fireplaces snapped in the air like snake tongues,

NICHOLAS RAVEN AND THE WIZARDS' WEB - VOLUME 1

releasing comforting billows of heat that wafted up to the rafters, gently swaying the array of small tapestries and colorful garlands strung across the ceiling.

The sound of applause disturbed his dreams, followed by an incessant chattering that annoyed him to no end. *Can't they just leave me alone and let me sleep?* It had been such an arduous trip across the kingdom and he wanted only a bit of rest and nothing more. *Why are they so noisy?* But the maddening talk continued, so he was determined to say something to quiet them up.

Dooley suddenly opened his eyes, irritated for a moment until his vision focused on a portion of the ceiling nearly pressed to his face. He tried to sit up until he realized his left arm was wedged through a carved hole in an adjoining piece of woodwork next to the large oak beam he was now lying upon. He remembered where he was, realizing he must have dozed off for a moment as the remnants of his dream dissolved. He felt much better now and fully refreshed, eager to listen in on the war council that was beginning below. He glanced to his right, and through the opening in the hood draped over his head, and through the web of rafters and shadows and the parade of tapestries and garland hanging nearby, he could barely make out the movement of bodies as a palette of colors drifted below. He could not discern any of the faces connected to the glimpses of head tops, shoulders and feet meandering about, but he could distinctly hear snippets of conversation that the excellent chamber acoustics provided. Dooley eagerly paid attention, waiting for the preliminaries to conclude so he could absorb the crux of the gathering.

"*It's been an enlightening few days here at the Citadel.*"

"*I can't wait to get back to Linden now, sit down and enjoy a roasted pheasant! Why, it's as if...*"

"*...and I'll be sure to send word that...*"

Dooley wrinkled his brow as he listened to the bits of conversation that appeared to be drifting out of the chamber and into the adjoining corridor where the huge tapestry of Morrenwood hung, splashed in the radiant glory of the four seasons. As the silence in the chamber deepened, except for a few leftover voices, he felt a cold knot form in the pit of his stomach. His heart pounded and his palms began to sweat. Dooley wondered what Farnsworth would say to him when he returned home. He feared what Caldurian would do to him the next time they met. His lips began to quiver. He realized with horror that he had slept through the entire war council.

END OF PART THREE

PART FOUR
PRELUDE TO WAR

CHAPTER 28

One Lit Candle

Monstrous flames crackled wildly in the bitter breezes rolling off the Trillium Sea and across the grasslands. Nicholas glanced up at the stars but found no comfort in them as he sat on a log and warmed his aching body in front of the bonfire. They appeared cold and aloof staring down upon the stony shore, not concerned about the travails that had befallen either of the two men huddled close to the blaze. It had been a couple of hours since the soldiers from the Northern Isles had attacked Nicholas and Leo, leaving them unconscious as they kidnapped Ivy, her desperate screams still echoing in their minds. Nicholas imagined her being hauled off to the ship and sailing away across the cold, cruel waves. Though he shivered and his head burned, he felt more wretched for Ivy's plight than his own. The Trillium Sea was vast and the Northern Isles might as well be on the other side of the world. He thought about how he could possibly reach the Isles, and if he ever did so, how he would locate Ivy.

He recalled their predawn conversation by the fireplace in Castella's kitchen three days ago, though it seemed like weeks had passed since they shared that tender moment. He was overwhelmed by the dizzying sweep of events that had led them from there to here, part of him wondering if he would ever see Ivy again. Hope drained from his heart as he warmed himself by the fire. He glanced at Leo sitting close by, his friend having the worst of the injuries.

"How's your wrist?"

Leo turned his head, making an effort to smirk. "Feels a lot better than the back of my noggin, but I think I'll live. On the bright side, I'll probably get a good sleep tonight."

"Sporadic bouts of unconsciousness will do that for you," Nicholas said, trying to keep the mood light. "And you have your choice of tents, too. No second class accommodations here."

Five abandoned tents, tormented by the wind, lined the edge of the tall grass. The other three bonfires once blazing along shore had burned down to glowing embers. A short distance away, their two horses wandered through the field with the pair of steeds from Madeline and Mune's wagon. They would begin the return trip to Boros in the wagon tomorrow morning, neither having any idea how to break the sad news about Ivy to Castella, her aunt and uncle at the candle shop, or her parents in Laurel Corners whom they had not yet met. A cold and dispiriting journey awaited them.

"Part of me doesn't want to leave, Leo. Maybe if I stayed awhile..."

Leo glanced at his friend and shook his head, guessing that Nicholas blamed himself for Ivy's kidnapping. As he stared back into the fire, he couldn't help feel responsible himself, but knew that wallowing in their regrets wouldn't bring her back. "Nicholas, the ship's not going to return," he flatly stated. "And delaying our return won't accomplish anything except to prolong her family's anguish."

"I suppose."

"And even if there's a chance of rescuing Ivy–and I have no idea where to begin–I know it's not going to be accomplished by sitting here on this miserable beach."

Nicholas took a deep breath. He knew Leo was right but hoped for a miracle anyway. He wished he had had more time to know Ivy and talk with her, smiling as he remembered giving her the scarf he had purchased in Boros. But deep in his heart he knew the two of them wouldn't be enjoying moments like that again any time soon, if ever. He closed his eyes, letting the snapping flames lull him to the verge of fitful slumber.

They awoke at midmorning after several needed hours of uninterrupted sleep. After a brief breakfast under bright sunshine, they hitched up a pair of horses to the cart and tethered the other pair to the back and began the return trip to Boros. With the food supplies that had been left behind in the cart, they didn't have to worry about stretching out the remaining rations Castella had provided. Nicholas spotted a sack of apples and grabbed two, tossing one to Leo.

"Just like old times," he said, recalling their trip north up Orchard Road with Princess Megan. "You must miss her."

"Even more so now after all that's happened," he replied as he guided the horses across the stony terrain. "Megan's going to be very upset. She never cared for the idea of trading identities with Ivy and will probably blame herself."

"Ivy wanted to do it to protect her." Nicholas watched as the stalks of tall grass monotonously passed by on his right, trying to convince himself that she had done the right thing. But maybe they had been foolish, fighting against forces they had no business dealing with. He reminded himself that the fight had been brought to them by the likes of Madeline and Mune, the man who tried to kidnap Megan at the Plum Orchard Inn, and Sims, whom they had paid off with Leo's apple money. Nicholas even threw Dooley Kramer and Arthur Weeks into the mix, realizing that people sometimes had no choice but to act when others were aligned against you. That notion offered him cold comfort as the wagon rattled eastward across the windswept coastline.

The journey back took nearly four and a half days, about a day longer than the forward trip since Nicholas and Leo found themselves oversleeping on several occasions as they recovered from their injuries. A rainstorm during the second day of traveling added to the delay, but in time the grasslands thinned out. Their spirits lifted when they finally saw the western edge of Sage Bay in the distance. Soon they turned south for the village of Cavara Beach where they would pick up the main road leading to Boros. They were certain that Megan and Castella were both racked with anxiety at their delay.

As twilight descended and the first stars peered down from a crisp autumn sky, they passed through the sleepy village of Cavara Beach, the scent of wood smoke and the occasional bark of a dog carried upon a breeze. They traveled the rutty road, anxious to get back to Castella's house and a warm meal. When they were about two miles from Boros, they heard the faint clip clop of hooves upon the road and saw a solitary figure on horseback approaching from the east, the nearly full rising Bear Moon plastered against the skyline behind it.

"Evening," Leo said as the stranger advanced, the moonlight reflecting off his face. The young man on the horse quickly stopped, clutching the reins.

"Is that you, Leo? We've been looking all over for you." He rode up close to the cart, curiously surveying the vehicle. An expression of disappointment suddenly crossed his face. "Isn't Ivy with you? Is she in back?"

Leo recognized the man as Jonathan, one of Uncle Aubrey's two sons. Leo had briefly met him when he had gone to Aubrey's house with word about their plan to pay off Sims. He introduced him to Nicholas before explaining what had happened to his cousin. Jonathan bowed his head, stunned by the unfortunate news.

"I'm sorry," Nicholas said. "We were so close, but…"

"I'm sorry too," Jonathan muttered. "We had been taking turns patrolling these roads at times and searching out the area around Cavara Beach for any sign of you. We never imagined that you had gone so far west. My parents will be disappointed. Ivy's parents will be devastated."

"Let's get home so we can tell them," Leo said. "We'll figure out what to do when there are more minds to consult. Right now Nicholas and I don't know what to think."

"Follow me," Jonathan said as he turned his horse around and trotted back to Boros toward the rising moon.

When they arrived in the village, Nicholas and Leo instructed Jonathan to send word to his father about their return, promising to stop over as soon as possible. First they were eager to see Castella and Megan and let them know they were safe. As Leo guided the wagon up the winding street soon afterward, the sight of Castella's house filled them with joy. Candles flickered in the downstairs windows and the wreath of dried goldenrod and corn husks still decorated the door. After Leo secured the wagon and horses in the shadows on the side of the house, they walked around front, almost reluctant to knock on the door and divulge the bad news. But before they had a chance, the door flew open with Megan standing there, silhouetted against the warm glow of firelight.

"I saw you through the side window," she said excitedly, finding comfort when seeing the faces of her two protectors. When she noticed that Ivy wasn't with them, her heart sank. The despondent looks upon Nicholas and Leo's faces told her everything she needed to know.

"Is Ivy back?" a voice called from within the house. Castella peered over Megan's shoulder a moment later, her spirit equally crushed soon after. "What happened?"

"We failed," Nicholas said with a sudden moody edge to his voice as she quickly ushered everyone inside. When he noticed Ivy's light brown cloak hanging from a wall peg that Megan had brought back from the candle shop, a brief surge of bitterness welled inside him. The plan to switch identities now seemed foolhardy and ill-conceived, and he chided himself for ever going along with it. "We made a terrible mistake. We should have gone to the local authorities for your protection," he said, eyeing Megan as a stream of air escaped his tightly pressed lips. "Instead we just…"

Megan, sensing that Nicholas might be casting some of the blame upon her, held back an urge to lash out at him in his distressed state. "Tell us where Ivy is," she calmly inquired. "Where have you two been all this time?"

"It's a long story," Leo said, reluctant to tell it since he knew Castella's heart would break. But when he saw the pained expression already upon her face and noted her trembling hands, he already guessed that she expected the worst.

"Let's go into the kitchen where it's warmer," she suggested. "You boys look like you could stand a bite to eat." When Castella glanced at Nicholas, noting his sullen mood, her expression hardened. "And if you want to blame anyone, Nicholas, then blame Ivy and me. We were the ones who cooked up this scheme in the first place. So if you have something you want to say, now is the time."

Nicholas, taken aback by her forthrightness, realized that he wasn't the only one hurting by Ivy's absence and regretted his cool demeanor since walking into the house. He shook his head, offering an apologetic smile. "No one is to blame, Castella, especially you. Just attribute my mood to being tired, sore and hungry."

She nodded. "Well, I think I can do something about the latter," she replied, signaling for them to follow her into the kitchen where she was soon serving tea and buttered biscuits at the table to help absorb the awful news she knew was forthcoming.

Nicholas and Leo took turns explaining their chase across the grasslands, expanding upon every detail whenever Megan or Castella insisted. When they mentioned that it was Megan's old nursemaid, Madeline, who was behind the kidnapping, Megan shook her head but didn't appear shocked at the news.

"I guess my grandfather was right," she said. "Ghosts from the past still haunt us. But I never heard of that gentleman named Mune whom Ivy told you about. Just another scoundrel trying to live off the misery of others, no doubt."

"But where would they have taken Ivy on that ship?" Castella asked, feeling as if she had lost her own daughter. "If they sail to the Northern Isles..." She looked at her guests, her face ashen. "How will we ever get her back?"

"Her captors still believe that Ivy is Princess Megan, so that ought to keep her safe," Leo said. "At least I hope so."

As Leo continued to speak, Nicholas looked wistfully at the hearth and relived his and Ivy's short time together, missing her now more than ever. He didn't want to imagine what hardships she might endure because of his failure to save her, wondering if she was sailing across the tumultuous waters of the Trillium Sea while believing she had been abandoned to a life of misery and imprisonment. Her predicament seemed massive and unconquerable compared to his own complications that had caused him to flee Kanesbury. He searched his heart for any possible way to save her.

"Megan, maybe your grandfather can help!" he blurted out, interrupting Leo in mid-sentence. Megan, Leo and Castella looked at him, sympathizing with his anguish. "Sorry, but my mind was wandering. I just..."

"I know what you're thinking," Megan calmly said. "And I intend to do just that. I don't know what kind of assistance my grandfather can provide, but I'll ask him to help us save Ivy when I return to Morrenwood. I can't remain here another day while other people's worlds are falling apart because of me. I'll leave first thing in the morning."

"*We'll* leave first thing in the morning," Leo said, gazing into her eyes. "I intend to go to the capital with you, like it or not. We'll stop at my parents' house first. I'm sure they're worried sick."

"Count me in," Nicholas said, a tinge of hope filling his heart.

"I wouldn't have wanted it any other way," she replied. "I don't know what I'd do without you two bumpkins at my side."

"That settles it," Castella said. "I'll prepare some food for the return trip. It seems this adventure of yours is just getting started."

Later that evening, Nicholas and Leo stopped at Aubrey and Nell's house to explain what had happened. Ivy's father, Frederick, was also there. He had been visiting from Laurel Corners when Jonathan arrived with the bad news about his daughter. Though devastated, Frederick decided that it was useless to tell the local authorities about the situation.

"They won't be able to do anything," he said. "Besides, if whoever has Ivy still believes she's the princess, then that might be her best protection right now. Why risk word getting back to them, however improbable, that Ivy isn't of the royal bloodline."

When Nicholas explained that they would go to Morrenwood to request help from King Justin, the news cheered Ivy's father. He was proud that his daughter had offered to help protect the King's granddaughter, but he knew a perpetual black cloud of doubt and regret would follow him until he held her in his arms once again.

"It feels so discouraging," he whispered. "But if the King can help find my daughter, I suppose I can hang on to that bit of hope."

"Sometimes the tiniest bit of hope is all you need to go on," Nell said. "Just like having one lit candle–and I know a thing or two about candles," she said with an encouraging smile to her brother-in-law. "From a single burning candle you can light another one and then another one still, until..."

"It felt like we were stuck with nothing but wet wicks over the last few days," Nicholas said with a hint of desperation. "How are you supposed to go on like that?"

Nell shrugged. "I didn't say it would be easy, dear, but you have to find a way. Light the first candle–and perhaps your trip to Morrenwood will be just that–and then see if you can light another one with it."

"We'll try," he said, giving a smile of encouragement to Ivy's father.

Aubrey, though, offered one bit of good news when he tossed the pouch of fifty copper pieces on the table that he and his sons had retrieved from Sims.

"That scoundrel will think twice about plying his shady deeds in these parts again!" he said, pleased to return Leo's apple money.

Though Megan had hoped to leave the following morning, a series of treacherous rainstorms rolled in at dawn, battering the region for two days and flooding some of the roads, making travel impossible. Castella, though, was happy for the company and Megan was grateful that Nicholas and Leo could fully rest and recover. They talked often around a warm fire as flashes of lightning ignited the skies and thunder reverberated across the bay, wondering how realistic a chance they had at finding Ivy, yet determined to try.

They remained with Castella for one more day after the skies cleared to allow the soaked lands to dry out. In the meantime, they helped her clean up the storm damage around the house. But when the following dawn broke sunny and cold, Nicholas, Leo and Megan finally made a sad and somber departure. They hugged Castella and promised to get word back to her as soon as possible. They left Boros in Leo's apple wagon, leaving behind Madeline's wagon and horses for her to keep or sell as she saw fit.

They headed south, and by early afternoon they neared the village of Plum Orchard. Megan insisted that they make a brief stop for lunch at their favorite inn. Leo had planned to anyway, and all were happy to greet Ron and Mabel Knott once again, conversing with them over a meal in the back dining room. The trio decided not to reveal Megan's true identity to their friends, though it was more out of concern for Megan's protection and for the safety of Ron, Mabel and their family rather than a lack of trust. Leo hoped one day he could reveal everything to them about the mysterious goings-on which occurred that one fateful night at their lovely establishment.

Several hours later just after sunset, Leo finally neared his parents' farmhouse aglow with yellow light as a stream of wood smoke escaped from the chimney under a moonless sky. He brought the wagon to a halt near the huge willow tree silently standing guard in the murky twilight. He was happy to see the apple red barn and inhale the sweet smell of soil and decaying leaves lingering in the evening air. Leo held Megan's hand and smiled, delighted to be back home but knowing it would only be for a short stay. There was still much hardship the trio had to face in the days ahead, with no one knowing where the long and tiring roads would finally lead them.

CHAPTER 29

The Medallion

Leo's parents sat side by side near the fireplace, gazing wide-eyed at their son and his two friends who had just finished explaining the events of the past several days. Joe Marsh puffed on a pipe, letting trails of bluish-gray smoke rise lazily to the ceiling while his wife crossed her arms, allowing the surreal words to sink in. Henry, Leo's younger brother, sat contentedly on the floor near the hearth eating a piece of apple pie, taking the fascinating narrative in stride.

"So you're an actual princess? And right here in my house," Annabelle calmly remarked, fidgeting with her dress sleeve while gazing at Megan. "I would have served something fancier than beef stew had I known."

"And you're really wanted for murder?" a fascinated Henry asked Nicholas as he downed another forkful of pie.

Nicholas grinned uneasily. "As I said before, Henry, I didn't kill anybody. I was framed for the murder."

"*Still...*" he replied, munching on his dessert.

When Leo announced that he and Nicholas would escort Megan to the capital and request the King's help in rescuing Ivy, his parents fully supported their actions. After they learned about his and Nicholas' trials along the coastline, they felt confident their son could manage a trip to Morrenwood, certain that King Justin's soldiers would handle any dangerous matters regarding Ivy thereafter.

In the meantime, Leo and his friends stayed for three days on the Marsh farm, helping with some pre-winter chores. He also found time to give Megan a tour of the farm and apple orchard, regaling her with his plans for the future.

"No doubt it involves everything related to apples," she said with a chuckle as she and Leo walked hand in hand through the frosted grass alongside the barn.

"And you too, I hope," he said, stopping to look into her eyes as Megan returned his tender gaze. For the first time in the many days they had known each other, they were finally able to enjoy each other's company alone. He thought she looked beautiful wrapped in the elegant folds of her cloak in the brisk autumn chill, though feeling as if it were a fine spring morning. "Would it be forward of me if I..."

"Not at all..." she whispered as she leaned forward to accept his kiss, both bathed in a splash of sunlight filtering through some nearby pines.

"It's not every day that I'm allowed to kiss a princess," Leo remarked with an affectionate smile.

"And it's not every day that I allow it," Megan replied, returning a mischievous grin. "But fortunately for you, my father and grandfather aren't around. They would have thrown you in a dungeon for sure!" She laughed, leading Leo by the hand toward the large willow tree near the front of the house.

"I'll behave myself in Morrenwood," he said as he happily followed Megan wherever she wished to go. "I'd never forgive myself if I got kicked out of the Blue Citadel on my first visit!"

The trip to the capital commenced on a clear morning under sapphire blue skies. Leo didn't know when he would return and promised to send his parents a post to keep them updated. After an exchange of many hugs and goodbyes, Nicholas, Megan and Leo traveled south down the last stretch of Orchard Road in an apple-less cart, the surrounding trees still ablaze in spots with autumn's fiery colors. When they reached River Road and turned west, Nicholas recalled when he and Megan had stood at that very spot on the second day after they had first met. It was here he had agreed to accompany her to Boros to avoid going back to Kanesbury and face his troubles. He glanced at Megan and they smiled, both recalling the conversation.

"And you're *still* not going home," she said with a friendly chuckle. "What you'll do to avoid facing those complications."

"I'm happy that one of us is finally going home," he replied. "I'm looking forward to meeting your father and grandfather and telling them how much trouble you've been. Leo and I should be rewarded handsomely for our efforts, saving royalty and all."

"You'll enjoy a few fine meals compliments of the King's kitchen and consider yourself well compensated." She patted Leo's knee and smiled. "Don't you agree?"

"Wholeheartedly!" he said.

Megan leaned close, giving Leo a quick hug. "Oh, that was the perfect answer. Now I know why I like you so much."

"See that, Leo, you're a quick learner," Nicholas joked. "This should be a much more pleasant trip than the one to Boros."

After everyone laughed, Nicholas settled back into silence, his thoughts automatically drifting to Ivy and where she might be. It didn't seem proper that he should enjoy even a fleeting moment of camaraderie among friends while she silently endured her trials, but he knew that life would go on while he planned a way to find her. Yet a part of him feared to acknowledge that one day he might accept the idea that Ivy was gone forever. As empty as he felt after leaving Kanesbury, he knew that abandoning Ivy in his thoughts and to those who had kidnapped her would be far worse, carving out another piece of his soul that could never be replaced.

They spent the night alongside River Road as it gradually turned southwest, the Pine River flowing silently to their left under a blanket of stars. The Fox Moon, now a mere sliver, had already dipped below the western horizon as they sat around a small fire and talked. Leo asked Megan about life in the Blue Citadel.

"Though my opinion is somewhat prejudiced, you won't find a more magnificent structure in all of Arrondale," she said, honored to have lived there all her life.

"The Blue Citadel is a beautiful place," Nicholas agreed, "though I've only seen it from the outside when I made my deliveries for Ned Adams. However, the storage cellars are first-rate!"

"I look forward to a grand tour," Leo said, noting the smile on Megan's face in the dancing firelight. He was happy that she seemed content and relaxed in his presence and hoped he felt the same when meeting her father and the King.

A gray morning dawned the next day and the smell of rain lingered in the air as they made an early start. By midmorning they turned west onto King's Road, leaving behind River Road that continued southwest to Bridgewater County and the southern border of Arrondale. Small forests of pine grew on each side of King's Road along its first few miles. Nicholas and Megan recognized this as the place where they first met and had shared a campfire in the Darden Wood to their right.

"Who knows where we'd be now if I had continued on to Morrenwood alone while you evaded Samuel in the wilderness," Nicholas said, recalling their distrustful first encounter. "But it seems I'll get to make that journey after all."

"And you'll get to spend more time in these woods again," Leo said, quickly guiding the team of horses through the narrow strip of field on the right leading to the border of the Darden.

In the distance, a swath of dark gray clouds suddenly let loose a pounding rainfall that rapidly sailed eastward. Sheets of cold droplets swept across the area. Nicholas, Megan and Leo had just time enough to seek shelter under the trees before the storm hit with a fury. In time the breezes calmed down, yet the rain steadily fell, halting their progress for several hours. They cheerfully endured the delay, building a fire and enjoying a leisurely lunch under the treetops. Not until mid-afternoon did the rain cease and they once again took to the waterlogged road, slowly making their way westward through an occasional village or passing by a tract of tired farmland. Leo stayed on the road as long as he could to make up for lost time, but as the waning daylight dissolved into shadowy darkness, they were forced to call it a day. They pulled off to the side of King's Road and spent a chilly night under the cover of the low, dreary clouds.

Their glum demeanors disappeared at midmorning the following day when the clouds broke and a freshening wind sweetened the air. Warm and glorious sunshine dried the roads and revived the travelers' spirits, making the next leg of the journey tolerable despite a lingering chill. The sight of deer feeding in nearby fields or a rafter of wild turkeys gobbling and strutting on a grassy hillside served as occasional diversions to the monotony of the long stretch of road. A fleeting shadow of a soaring hawk or crow sped across the dirt road from time to time as Leo held the reins, leading them steadily westward through the passing hours. But what finally caught the trio's attention most was a colorfully painted wagon sitting on the side of the road under a thicket of maple trees up ahead, a nearby campfire sending swirls of blue-gray smoke into the mid-afternoon air. A solitary figure in a hooded cloak stooped over the fire, adding pieces of wood to the blaze.

"I can't believe it!" Megan softly said. "It's *her*."

"Who?" Nicholas asked.

"Slow down, Leo." Megan excitedly patted his wrist as he brought the wagon to a halt near the side of the rode. "I need to speak with her."

"Do you know what she's talking about?" Nicholas asked Leo, who simply returned a shrug and shook his head. Soon the figure by the fire looked up at them, apparently delighted to have some company on the lonely road.

"A pleasant welcome, travelers!" the woman said, bundled in a cloak splashed with colorful swirls, geometric shapes and images of stars, leaves and comets, all bursting in shades of green, yellow, indigo and tangerine. She flipped back the hood to reveal a slightly unkempt head of light blond hair above a set of lively eyes and a contagious smile. She also wore a pair of thin beige gloves that extended partway up her forearms.

Leo hopped off the wagon and assisted Megan down while Nicholas jumped off the other side, finding the woman strangely familiar. When he took a closer look at the large wagon under the maple trees, the back section enclosed with wooden panels and painted as vibrantly as the woman's cloak, he suddenly remembered the story Megan had told them in her room after her attempted kidnapping at the Plum Orchard Inn.

"You must be–"

"*Carmella!*" Megan shouted, walking over to greet the woman who was old enough to be her mother. "It's Megan. Do you remember allowing me and Samuel to spend the night on the road with you about three weeks ago?"

"How could I forget such a pretty face?" she said, giving her a hug. "But where did you disappear to, young lady? And who are these fine gentlemen with you?"

"That's a long story, and I'll be happy to tell you all about it," she said, introducing Leo and Nicholas. "But first I'd like to apologize for sneaking off in the night without thanking you for your hospitality. And second–can you tell me what happened to Samuel?"

Carmella tossed her arms in the air and laughed. "He abandoned me the very next day, all in a panic when he realized that you had left. We had searched for hours looking for you and then gave up, assuming you were long gone in whichever direction you set out. Samuel quit as my driver, leaving me stranded alone in the wild after he decided to return to Morrenwood, assuming you had probably gone that way, too." She offered an impish smile. "Apparently he chose the wrong path, seeing as you're traveling from the opposite direction. Did you ever make it to Boros?"

"I did," Megan replied, "with help from my two friends."

"Reluctantly at first," Nicholas said. "But we've sorted through all that."

"Wonderful! I want to hear every detail." Carmella invited them to sit on some logs near the fire as she chatted away. In short order, she served hot tea and raisin biscuits which everyone eagerly accepted, enjoying the respite from the weary road with a friendly voice and some warm food.

"Carmella, you mentioned that Samuel agreed to be your driver before he left you in the wilderness," Leo said as he munched on a second biscuit.

"That's right. I'd been traveling the back roads searching for my cousin, having heard weeks ago that she passed through those parts," she said, pulling off her long gloves to reveal a pair of pumpkin-colored hands. "Liney did this to me with one of her spells years ago, the wicked girl. And the little magical training that I've had isn't enough to reverse her handiwork. I need to find her to get the counter spell and to give her a piece of my mind. But as I haven't had any success in tracking her down, I'll be heading back home to the village of Red Fern for the winter. But that's another story," she said, putting the gloves back on. "Anyway, Samuel left me and looked for Megan, leaving me without a driver again. And though I drive myself when I absolutely must, I prefer to hire that task out to others so I can concentrate on my magic studies and my pursuit of Liney. I'm a wizard, after all, or nearly one. Or at least on my way to being one–probably closer to the initial steps in that journey rather than the latter. Still, someone of my yet-to-be-attainted status should have her own driver, don't you think?"

"I don't see why not," Nicholas said, concealing a smile. "So, Carmella, how long have you been studying the magic arts?"

"About twenty years," she said matter-of-factly, sipping her tea. "But after my first teacher deserted me, I was left to learn what I could on my own. His loss!"

"How long ago was that?" Leo asked, as amused as Nicholas was by her story but keeping a straight face out of courtesy to Carmella and for fear of upsetting Megan.

"Oh, that'd be about twenty years ago, too," she said, prodding the fire with a large twig. "Minus one month. That's how long my training lasted back home in Red Fern. And for some strange reason, none of the few wandering wizards I've since encountered over the years were eager to take me on as an apprentice after offering me a few lessons. I had to learn most everything on my own with a few spell books I discovered and purchased. In the meantime, I work my small farm in Red Fern to earn a living, going out now and then to sell potions that I brew or tell fortunes for a small fee." She nodded confidently. "I'm pretty good at reading palm lines and face freckles or consulting river pebbles. Would you like to toss a handful? No charge."

"No thank you," Leo politely replied. "I'm happy to let my future unfold as it will. So far I haven't been disappointed," he said, gently nudging Megan who sat next to him.

"Suit yourself. I guess there's something to be said for living life as it comes barreling at you. I guess that's what I'm doing now."

"Carmella, we're on our way to Morrenwood," Megan informed her. "Since it's just a stone's throw from Red Fern, why don't you join us on the road? I'm sure Nicholas wouldn't mind serving as your driver." She leaned forward and glanced at him with a playful gleam in her eyes.

"It'd be my pleasure," Nicholas said. "It's a bit crowded on that other wagon."

"I appreciate the offer," Carmella replied, deeply touched by his kindness. "But at this moment I don't need a driver."

"You enjoy navigating the roads by yourself?" Leo asked. "You seem to have made it back to King's Road without any trouble from wherever you'd been stranded."

Carmella shook her head. "No, it wasn't me, Leo. As I said, I don't need a driver right now because one recently found *me* in the wilderness."

Megan and the others glanced around the campsite. "Really? I don't see anyone."

"He's out gathering firewood," she said, when suddenly they heard a branch snap nearby as if someone had stepped on a fallen tree branch. "Oh wait, here he comes now." Carmella pointed to the edge of the maple trees just beyond her wagon as a short, burly figure in a floppy brown hat and an ill-fitting coat emerged from around the corner, an armload of firewood hiding its face. "There you are," she said, urging him forward. "Come here, Jagga. I have guests I want you to meet."

The Enâr suddenly stopped, lowing his arms just enough so that his dark, suspicious eyes could see over the wood and study the new arrivals. Convinced that they weren't going to attack him, Jagga grunted before setting the pile down near the remaining kindling he had gathered earlier. He sat on the ground several yards away from the crackling flames.

"Why are you sitting way over there?" Carmella asked, signaling him to join her and the others. "Come here where it's warm. These are my friends, Jagga. Nothing to be worried about."

"I am fine here, Carmella," he said with a sharp nod, still eyeing Nicholas, Megan and Leo with lingering trepidation.

Nicholas gazed at him, fascinated by Jagga's roughly hewn shape and tangled strands of hair peeking out beneath the silly looking hat upon his head. Though he had never seen one of his kind before, after all the stories he had heard growing up in Kanesbury, he knew at once that he was looking at a member of the Enâri race that had attacked his village twenty years ago. He stared dumbfounded at Carmella, wondering how she had met and bonded with such a creature out here in the wild.

Minutes after Arthur Weeks had been murdered during the Harvest Festival, Jagga raced through the woods in Kanesbury along the Pine River, his fingers clutching the key he had stolen from Dooley Kramer's house. The Enâr quickly fled the village and the large crowds, heading west. Even though it was his first night awake after a forced twenty-year sleep, Jagga had no desire to celebrate, neither with men nor wizards nor even his own kind. They were all responsible to some extent for killing his freedom, but now he possessed the very key to preserving that freedom forever.

Jagga walked for several hours through the countryside until he felt safe enough to rest beneath some trees in a field. He drank greedily from a stream and then collapsed on the ground and gazed up at the stars, a sight he hadn't seen in twenty years. A large crescent Fox Moon was setting in the west, casting faint silvery light upon the tips of the tall grass and weeds. He held up the stolen key and examined it in the gloom, knowing he must get rid of it or destroy it, though reluctant to part with the object for fear that someone else might discover it. If the key was ever used to open the Spirit Box, his life would be over. The formidable entity growing inside for the last twenty years would consume him with the power of a raging fire and turn him into the rock and soil from which he had been created by Vellan so many years ago.

Jagga couldn't decide his next step. Returning to Vellan was out of the question. He feared that the mighty wizard would condemn him for running away from Caldurian and disobeying the orders he had communicated through the blue fog inside the caves. Yet even if Vellan did accept him back, he knew his loyalty would always be in question. Though the other Enâri may have had their doubts about serving Caldurian because of his past mistakes, they did so out of devotion to Vellan. But Jagga's allegiance had diminished while in hibernation, affording him an awareness of his personal freedom that the others lacked. He wondered if he hadn't been fully asleep during those twenty years which perhaps allowed resentment at being a slave to build up inside him. Or had Vellan created him differently, making a minor mistake he had overlooked? Regardless of the answer, he decided to run until he felt safe.

After a short rest, Jagga continued his westward trek, staying off the main roads whenever possible. He continually thought about the key, wondering what to do with the cold piece of metal. He somberly recalled how he had obtained the item, plunging a knife into the chest of Arthur Weeks. His mind had been on fire then. Now in the cool autumn night, he reconsidered the act he had rashly committed, a seed of regret growing inside him. He wondered if he deserved his freedom now and considered throwing the key into a nearby pond. But Jagga was unwilling to depart with his treasure just yet in case someone else should find it. He walked the next several days and nights with only the key and his muddled thoughts to keep him company.

One evening as the grays and purples of twilight cloaked the surrounding fields and hills, Jagga heard a sharp, metallic clank echo across the landscape. He noted the silhouette of a distant farmhouse, its windows awakening with the soft glow of yellow light. A sagging barn stood nearby next to a few smaller buildings, a flicker of firelight visible through the wide open doorway of one of them. He recognized the repeated striking of hammer upon anvil and was suddenly inspired. He hurried across a small tract of land and cautiously approached the building, peering into the doorway from one side as another hammer blow fell.

Inside, a tall man worked a red hot piece of metal with a hammer, shaping it across a large anvil next to a glowing brick forge. The heat inside the wooden building flowed out into the cool autumn night like a puff of dragon's breath. Jagga, seeing no one else around, took a wary step inside and stared at the man framed by a backdrop of fiery red and orange light. The man glanced up, staring at Jagga in perplexed silence, never having seen an individual so unusual looking. He raised the hot piece of metal with a pair of tongs, causing Jagga to flinch before he plunged it into a barrel of cold rainwater, raising a cloud of hissing steam as the metal cooled.

"Hello, stranger," the man said, lifting the metal out of the water and setting it down upon a wooden workbench. "Something I can help you with?"

Jagga rubbed his brow, wondering how he should handle the situation. He felt apprehensive about being here and wondered if he had made a mistake, yet the man didn't make him fearful in the least as he silently gazed back with curiosity.

"I need help." Jagga held up the key. "I need this thing not to exist."

"*Hmmm*, is that so," the man said as he ambled over to Jagga, holding out his hand. "Let me see it, please." Jagga looked up into the man's eyes and slowly handed him the key which he accepted and briefly examined. "It'll be no trouble melting it down or forming it into something else. What do you want me to do exactly?"

"I want it gone," Jagga said with a shrug, as if his first instructions should have been plain enough.

"Well, I can melt it down and mix it with other metal the next time I make a horseshoe."

"No, no!" he nervously insisted. "I need it gone *now*! Pound it out. Pound it flat. Shape it into something else." He emitted a gravelly sigh. "I want it not a key, but I still want to keep the metal with me. Understand?"

"Perfectly," the man replied, noting Jagga's unease yet deciding for some unknown reason that he needn't fear the creature, whatever it was. He signaled for Jagga to follow him to the forge. "I think I can help you, mister," he said as he secured the tip of the key with a pair of metal tongs and shoved it into the glowing embers. A few minutes later it glowed red and the man lifted it up for Jagga to observe. "Now I will make it *not* a key."

"Good!" he replied with a toothy grin. "Good."

Grabbing a small hammer, the man slowly formed the heated metal into a compact mass, placing it into the embers a few times to reheat and keep it malleable. Soon the former key was shaped into a blob of hot metal which the man pounded flat into a disk, carefully working the edges until it looked like a large coin. After heating it a final time, he grabbed a metal punch and tapped a single hole near the edge as Jagga watched in fascination. The man plunged the object into a water barrel with the tongs for several moments. Rising steam sizzled off the surface as the metal cooled. When it was cold to the touch, he examined it before handing the object to Jagga.

"What do you think?"

"Nice," Jagga said, looking up with a smile. "It is definitely not a key anymore."

"It is not," the man replied. "Given time, I would've been more meticulous and imprinted some designs onto the metal, but I sense you're in a hurry."

Jagga nodded, still looking at the round piece of metal, its edges quite smooth considering the rush job the man had performed under his scrutinous gaze. "Why did you put a hole in it?"

"You said you wanted to keep it, didn't you?"

"Yes," he muttered.

"Well, then, that'll help keep it safe," the man replied as he searched through a messy pile of scrap items on one corner of the bench. Soon he fished out a piece of thin leather cord and cut off an appropriate length before taking back the piece of metal from Jagga. He threaded the cord through the hole and tied the two ends into a tight knot, holding it up. "Now you have yourself a proper medallion to wear around your neck. You won't lose it that way."

Jagga nodded as an appreciative smile spread across his face. He took the medallion from the man and placed the cord over his head, pleased with the effect when he looked down at his chest and saw it gleam in the fiery light from the forge.

"This is good," he said, proudly holding up the man's handiwork.

"You're welcome," the man replied, assuming that that was the closest to a *thank you* he would receive from the stranger. "What do you plan to do with it?"

Jagga shrugged. "I suppose it doesn't matter now, but I'll keep it for a while," he said. Now that the item was destroyed and couldn't open the Spirit Box, he felt that he had achieved a victory over Vellan and Caldurian, deciding to wear the medallion as a trophy of sorts to celebrate his triumph.

"What did that key go to?" the man asked, leaning against the workbench. But when Jagga furrowed his brow with a hint of annoyance, he decided to change the subject. "Well, it's none of my business. I suppose you want to get on your way and not answer a bunch of questions."

"That is best," Jagga said, slipping the medallion underneath his ragged shirt.

"Hold on a moment," the man said, walking toward the entrance and grabbing a weather-stained coat and a floppy brown hat from a row of pegs on the wall. He handed them to Jagga. "It's cold out tonight and these spare clothes are collecting cobwebs. You can have them. The hat will keep the morning sun out of your eyes."

8

Jagga graciously accepted the items and slipped them on. "Perfect fit," the man said. "More or less."

"This is good, too," Jagga replied, smoothing out the material with his hands. "But I have to go."

The farm owner escorted his peculiar visitor out of the forge to the main road underneath a blanket of emerging stars, wondering if he were dreaming this strange sequence of events. He scratched his head as Jagga disappeared down the road under the first quarter Fox Moon, contemplating what to tell his wife when he went inside for dinner, though unsure that she would even believe his story.

For six more days, Jagga kept to the back roads, fields and woods, living off the land and contemplating where in Laparia to go. He even considered wandering to another part of the world altogether, though knowing wherever he went, he would be alone. The only others of his kind were in Kargoth with Vellan or conquering Montavia under Caldurian's command. In neither location would he be free to live his life, a slave always to the political ambitions of others. For a fleeting moment, he wondered if he had made a mistake destroying the key. Perhaps only if it were used would he truly gain his freedom, but now that was too late.

Jagga sniffed the air the following afternoon, the scent of roasting meat riding upon a thin breeze out of the west. He followed it, tramping through a small field toward a thicket of trees alongside a narrow dirt road. He was cautious at first, but as he neared the road and saw a woman cooking dinner over a fire, he grew less afraid. She was wrapped in a colorful cloak and singing joyfully off tune as she tended to her meal. A brightly painted wagon with a wooden enclosure sat nearby, its pair of back doors open wide to reveal sacks and small barrels of food stuff, rows of shelves filled with glass vials of colorful powders and liquids, stacks of old, tattered books and piles of blankets and animal pelts. The woman looked up as Jagga stood gawking, gazing at the curious sight.

"Hungry, mister?" she asked, smiling at him. "I'm warming up a bit of salted beef if you'd like to join me. Say, I like the look of that hat on you." Jagga nodded, knowing that the woman wasn't making fun of him but really meant what she had said. "My name is Carmella. What's yours?"

After polishing off their meal less than an hour later, they both sat by the fire and sipped hot spiced tea, enjoying a long conversation under the cool sunshine that slowly faded in the west. Jagga was pleased to keep the woman's company, not feeling the least bit intimidated by her and certain that she felt the same about him.

"Since you say you have no place to go, Jagga, you could work for me," she suggested. "I'm in desperate need of a driver. Though the trail to my cousin has gone cold, I still need to return home to Red Fern before winter. There you'll be provided with meals and my stellar company. You can even help me tend to the farm."

Jagga accepted her offer. "It is better than wandering. I did enough of that for years with the wizard Caldurian."

"And look where it landed you–sleeping in a cave for twenty years! He's a wicked character," Carmella said. "Or so I've heard," she hastily added.

"I don't fear him anymore. Or Vellan either. They can do nothing to me now."

"Why's that?" she asked, adding wood to the fire.

"Because I took the key to that nasty device I told you about earlier. I destroyed it. It is gone now. I threw it away."

"The key to the Spirit Box?" Carmella sounded skeptical. "How did you get it?"

Jagga explained how he had extracted information about the key's location from Gavin and eventually stole it from a man named Arthur Weeks, careful to leave out the details of Arthur's murder. "Now I am a *free* Enâr, the first of my kind."

"I guess you are," Carmella said as she sipped her tea while glancing at Jagga over the rim of her cup, suspecting that he was only telling her part of the story. Yet she couldn't blame Jagga for wanting to escape the likes of Caldurian at any cost. "My cousin Liney had once worked for–"

"Here!" Jagga excitedly said, removing the medallion from around his neck and handing it to Carmella. "You keep this for being nice to me. It's a gift."

"A gift for me?" She took hold of the leather string and held up the piece of metal to the firelight. "It's quite beautiful in a subtle way. Did you make this?"

"Someone made it for me, but I want you to have it. I don't need it anymore."

"I'm both honored and flattered," she said, wrapping her fingers around the medallion. But the moment her skin touched the metal, a shiver coursed though her body for an instant and was gone. She looked at Jagga with vague suspicion.

"Do you not like it?"

"No," Carmella replied, forcing a smile. "It's quite lovely. I guess I'm not used to receiving fine gifts from strangers." She placed the medallion over her neck. "How does it look on me?"

"Good. Very good. You let me drive and farm, so I give you that new gift."

"New? How long have you had this, Jagga? Maybe you don't want to part with it so soon."

"I'd rather someone else have it. I wish to forget about it forever," he said with a grunt. "You keep that round piece of metal for your kindness, Carmella. Now that it's an object that can't hurt me anymore, I–" Jagga caught himself in mid sentence. "I just don't need it anymore."

Carmella bowed her head as she held the medallion, suspecting that it might be the melted key when she first sensed the electric spark of magic within it. Now it simply felt cold and lifeless. But Jagga's last words confirmed her suspicion and she imagined what unsavory paths the Enâr might have tread to recover the key from Arthur Weeks and destroy it. She wasn't sure if she wanted to know that answer while watching the flames reflect off the medallion, deciding not to pursue the subject further. Had she been foolish to hire him as a driver so quickly? Or was her mind unfairly contemplating the worst about Jagga before he had a chance to prove himself? She was uncertain of either as the firelight glowed brilliantly in the encroaching darkness.

Carmella invited Nicholas, Megan and Leo to stay for dinner, agreeing to ride with them to Morrenwood first thing in the morning. She quietly promised that she would also answer their questions about Jagga after he left to gather more firewood, thinking it impolite to talk about him while he was in earshot. She could tell by her guests' stunned expressions that they had much to ask her. After their meal, Jagga excused himself to search for more wood in the remaining daylight, preferring solitude to the crowded campfire. The others enjoyed another cup of tea with their conversation, listening to Carmella talk about how she had met Jagga and what he had told her about his recent awakening.

"Though he has taken to my company," she said, "Jagga is wary around strangers. After living under Vellan and Caldurian's thumb, I'm not surprised he is so untrusting."

"I can't believe I've actually seen an Enâri creature," Nicholas said, somewhat troubled. "After all this time, they've finally been released from their sleep, but I wonder why now? And how? Even after all the stories I'd heard growing up in Kanesbury, a part of me doubted their existence."

"The Enâri are real," Carmella assured him. "And Caldurian is real, too."

"But how can you trust Jagga?" Megan asked. "Don't you fear he may hurt you? Nicholas told me stories about how they attacked his village twenty years ago."

"Back then, Jagga was part of a group of five hundred under Caldurian's control," she explained. "Now he is free which changes one's perspective on life. But there's something else." Carmella revealed the medallion she wore hidden under her dress, holding it up to the firelight. "He gave me this, his words suggesting that it was once the key to the Spirit Box which could destroy his race if ever opened. You must have heard of that, Nicholas."

He noted that he had, though believing the Spirit Box was just another part of a convoluted legend. "And you think that your medallion was once the key?"

"I felt magic within the metal," she said, putting the medallion back on and concealing it from view. "But since my training is limited, I can't say for sure. A full wizard would have to examine the item to be certain. Still, I believe Jagga told me the truth about the key he stole, what little he told me. There are details he left out. Darker details, I'm sure. If Vellan or Caldurian ever confronted Jagga about this matter, I can't imagine what misery would befall him. Caldurian *can* show a temper," she said.

Leo looked askance at Carmella, for a moment wondering who exactly they had eaten dinner with. "Are you saying that you know Caldurian?"

"Of course I do, Leo," she casually replied. "He was the wizard who trained my cousin Liney and me."

Megan listened in shock. "You've associated with Caldurian?"

Carmella nodded. "Yes, but don't be so quick to judge. It was twenty years ago, Megan, and only for a month. As soon as I learned of his devious undertakings, I was prepared to turn him in to the royal authorities in Morrenwood." She recalled that troubled episode in her youth with sadness and regret. "Unfortunately, Caldurian and Liney fled my farm in Red Fern and escaped east to the Cumberland Forest with five hundred Enâri in tow, causing all sorts of trouble there as I learned many months later."

"Kanesbury lies on the northern tip of the Cumberland," Nicholas said. "All of that trouble landed upon *us*!"

"Carmella, tell us how Caldurian ended up at your home in the first place," Megan said as she nibbled on a biscuit with her tea. "How did you ever meet the wizard?"

"I met him through my cousin. They showed up at my house one autumn day, asking to stay awhile though not offering many specifics about why. I hadn't seen Liney in months and was happy to have her as a guest, though I sensed she was in trouble," she said. "I was suspicious of Caldurian at first, wondering how Liney had met him. But when I found out he was a wizard and had started training my cousin in the magic arts, I asked if he might train me, too. Caldurian agreed, and so for the next month Liney and I learned much, though she was always a better practitioner of magic than I. It must be her excruciatingly serious temperament. I had no idea then that Caldurian was an apprentice to Vellan. And the group of Enâri who were traveling with Caldurian had hid in the wooded hills less than a mile from my farm. I didn't find out about them until just before Caldurian and Liney fled. It was a hectic month near the end."

"I can imagine," Megan said. "But how did your cousin meet the wizard? Had she known him long?"

"Not very," Carmella replied as she waved her thin hands over the crackling flames, savoring the warmth. "Liney worked as a nursemaid in the Blue Citadel, and it was there that she first encountered the wizard, smitten by his hypnotic presence the instant she laid eyes on him. He recruited her for a scheme of his, and when it failed, they retreated to my home, only leaving after I found out what they had been up to."

Upon hearing those words, Megan, Nicholas and Leo stared at Carmella as if all had been struck speechless, not believing what she had just said. She gazed back at the trio, wondering what part of her story had suddenly intrigued them to such an extent.

"Liney was a nursemaid?" Megan asked. "In the Citadel?"

"Yes. She worked for–"

"–Prince Gregory and his wife, taking care of their infant, Princess Megan," Leo said to Carmella's complete surprise.

"How could you know that?" she asked, quickly pulling her pumpkin-colored hands away from the fire. "Are you a mind reader?"

Nicholas chuckled. "None of us are, Carmella. But you'll find out that we're full of interesting facts about your cousin Madeline."

Carmella stood up, hers arms akimbo as she scanned the faces of her guests. "How do you know Liney's real name? I haven't called her Madeline since we were children."

Leo looked at Megan with a crooked grin. "I suppose we should tell her."

"Tell me what?" she asked as she sat back down by the fire, a trace of worry in her voice. "Something about Liney? If you know the whereabouts of my cousin, please tell me. I must find her."

Megan nodded. "Your cousin was involved in a kidnapping plot–"

"–of Princess Megan when she was an infant," Carmella said. "Yes, I learned about that incident years ago. But do you have any recent information about Liney?"

"We do," Megan said, "and it's pretty much the same story. Madeline was involved in a second kidnapping plot of Princess Megan several days ago in the village of Boros, but it failed."

Carmella furrowed her brow, perplexed at what she was hearing. "A second kidnapping? Of the princess? How is that even possible? And if it were true, how do you know that it failed?"

Megan sighed, a slight smile upon her face. "It failed because I am here, Carmella, and not with your cousin."

"I still don't understand," she said. "What does Liney–or her attempted kidnapping of the princess–have to do with you, Megan?

How did all of you even learn about my cousin? And where did…?" Her eyes opened wide when the reality of the situation dawned on her. "Megan. *Megan*?" Carmella leaned back, her mouth agape, wondering how she could have been so blind. "You're *that Megan*?"

Nicholas nodded. "Yes, Carmella. *That* Megan. Though Leo and I couldn't believe she was a princess at first either."

"Oh, I believe it," Carmella replied, gazing at the King's granddaughter sitting in front of the campfire in the middle of nowhere and enjoying some of her homemade biscuits. "I don't know why, but I believe your story completely. After all, I have an Enâri driver, so why should this sudden twist surprise me?"

Carmella listened with hushed astonishment as Nicholas and Leo spoke of Megan's failed abduction at the Plum Orchard Inn, the switching of identities in Boros, and the subsequent attempt to rescue Ivy along the grassy coastline of the Trillium Sea. That Madeline had once again dirtied her hands with kidnapping made Carmella furious, but to learn that her cousin was also plotting with a shipload of lawless thugs from the Northern Isles nearly sent her into fits.

She shook her head in dismay. "I'm ashamed to be related to that woman, but I'm not surprised by her activities. After all, if she could do a deed as despicable as this to her own cousin," she said, holding up her colorful hands for all to see, "then what other fiendish and depraved depths wouldn't she sink to?"

"How did that happen?" Leo asked, indicating her hands.

"Liney was jealous," Carmella replied, folding her arms. "Jealous of the attention that Caldurian showed me as he trained us in the magic arts. Liney was so proud of her abilities and felt that the wizard was wasting his time with me. She was the serious student and I was just a fraud in her eyes, barging in on her interests on a whim. *Humph*! She may be able to manipulate fire and conjure up a sleeping spell better than I, but can she… Can she…?" Carmella silently fumed for a moment. "Well, perhaps there is no comparison between our skills, but I've improved over the years! Still, there was no reason for her to cast a spell upon that pumpkin and hurl it at me."

"Is that what caused…?" Leo raised his eyes. "The hands?"

"Yes," she tiredly admitted. "We had been arguing in my pumpkin patch the day after I discovered that the Enâri and the wizard's messenger eagle were hiding out in the nearby woods. I had secretly followed Liney and Caldurian the night before when they left on one of their mysterious walks to meet with the creatures. Well, Liney finally admitted to me in the garden why she had left the Blue Citadel. When I threatened to turn them in, she exploded in a childish rage, ripped a pumpkin from a vine and threw it at me after casting her spell. As soon as I caught it, the orange color began to seep into my skin, covering my hands and traveling up my wrists before I had sense enough to drop the pumpkin and halt the transformation. Liney stormed off and I was unable to reverse her colorful triumph over me.

"When I confronted her and Caldurian in the house, they were preparing to head east. I hadn't even the chance to say a word when I saw Caldurian raise his hands. The next thing I remembered was waking up on the floor about three days later, with Liney, Caldurian, his eagle Xavier and all the Enâri gone. Apparently the wizard had cast a strong sleeping spell on me to give them enough time to escape before I could contact the authorities." Carmella shrugged. "That was the last time I saw my cousin, though I had come close to finding her a few times over the years. But one of these days..."

"Quite a story," Megan said. "My Grandfather will be interested in hearing it."

"Not that it will do any good," she replied. "However, you need to let him know about Liney's dealings along the seashore with the Islanders. I can't imagine what mischief she's planning, though no doubt Caldurian and Vellan have their fingers in it."

"Don't worry," Nicholas assured her. "We'll let King Justin know everything that's happened. But it might not be a bad idea if you came along with us to the Citadel. After all, you have one of the Enâri with you. Maybe he has information that might be useful."

"Perhaps," she said, "though Jagga has been nothing but helpful and kind to me. I wouldn't want to betray his trust."

"However, there are thousands upon thousands like him in Laparia who probably have less than good intentions," Leo said. "Maybe Jagga might want to help."

"Let her think about it," Megan said, noting that Carmella appeared overwhelmed with mixed emotions. "We can discuss it tomorrow."

"I agree," she replied. "I'm not ready to turn Jagga over to anybody just yet. Still, I feel obligated to show the King this." She again lifted the medallion into the firelight for all to see, certain that it was the former key still brimming with magic. "If you don't mind, I would like to accompany you to the Blue Citadel. I'm sure someone on King Justin's staff might be interested in this little trinket, don't you think?"

CHAPTER 30

A Secret Mission

Two wagons rattled along King's Road early the following morning beneath crisp blue skies painted with feathery strands of gray-tinged clouds. Leo led the way to Morrenwood, holding the reins with Megan and Nicholas beside him. Jagga followed closely behind, proudly playing chauffeur to Carmella who sat next to him cloaked in contentment. The cool air heightened their senses as they drew nearer to the capital, anticipating a stunning view of the Blue Citadel against the abundant evergreens upon the Trent Hills. The travelers swiftly reduced the remaining miles to the capital, taking only a few breaks as they were anxious to end their grueling journey.

"Though Father and Grandfather will be furious with me, I'll be able to endure their admonishments simply by having a warm bed and a roof over my head again," Megan said, wrapped snugly in her cloak. "And a meal at a proper table will do wonders, too!"

"A bowl of stew, warm bread and some fine ale is what I'm craving," Nicholas said, imagining a handful of cooks scurrying about the Citadel kitchens to prepare his culinary request.

"You'll be rewarded with all the stew and ale you can consume," she cheerfully replied. "After all, the King will be pleased when you return his wayward granddaughter."

Leo chuckled uneasily. "But will he be pleased with one particular vagabond who has returned *with* her?"

"We'll find out shortly." She placed a reassuring hand upon his as the wagon continued on, the hills, trees and rivers slowly drifting past. "But I'm confident that you have nothing to worry about, Leo Marsh. I'm sure my family will be as delighted meeting you as I was meeting your folks."

"Still, maybe it'd be best if you just introduced me as a guy who sells apples that happened to give you a ride back home," he suggested as the hills of Morrenwood rose upon the distant horizon. "For starters anyway. I'd rather your father and grandfather got to know me a little bit before you say anything about–*us*?"

"Leo, are you afraid of meeting them?"

"No, Megan. Not afraid exactly. Just a little terrified is all. Or perhaps alarmed? Agitated? Maybe panic stricken?" He gently snapped the reins as he deeply exhaled. "But don't worry. Nothing I can't handle."

"Oh, I can see that," she softly teased, tossing a grin Nicholas' way as Leo kept his eyes nervously fixed upon the road.

They arrived in Morrenwood early that afternoon, the sun-splashed city bustling with crowds of people taking advantage of the ideal autumn weather that in the next few weeks would be but a memory. Leo was astounded by the beauty and grandeur of the Citadel as his wagon passed through the main gate, its bluish-gray speckled stonework warmly inviting them into the courtyard. Megan noted the look of amazement in his eyes, eager to show him around her home.

"Go down that road on the left, Leo, and drive past the cellars," Megan said. "There are tree thickets behind the Citadel close to the river but far enough away from the stables and lodging houses. I think it'd be best if we parked the wagons there for some privacy."

"Who are we hiding from?" Nicholas asked.

"We're not hiding," Megan said, "but I don't think it's wise to advertise Jagga's presence until I talk to my grandfather. He'll be interested in knowing how we became acquainted with one of the Enâri creatures. I'm afraid Jagga would be led off to a prison cell if he was spotted freely wandering through the corridors with us."

After they brought the wagons to a halt under the protective boughs of some large pines, everyone disembarked. In front of them to the south rose the back section of the Blue Citadel, its many windows mutely reflecting the green trees and moody peaks of the Trent Hills to the north. Behind them, the soothing sight and sounds of the frothy Edelin River slowly washed the weariness out of their tired limbs and spirits.

"What a lovely place!" Carmella said, deeply inhaling the fresh pine air drifting down through the hills. "Now you wait for us here, Jagga, until we square away matters inside. There are a lot of people who won't be as accepting of you at first glance as I was. Best if you keep unnoticed for a time, no offense intended."

"I prefer it that way," he said with an agreeable smile. "You people go and talk to those you must. I'll build a fire and eat lunch."

"I guess that settles that," Leo replied, happy that Jagga was so accommodating.

"Then follow me," Megan said, leading them to a back entrance of the Citadel. "Whether happy about it or not, everyone is certain to be surprised at my arrival, so let's get this over with." She held Leo's hand, comforted by his support as they trekked across the grassy stretch behind the Citadel until reaching a colorful stone walkway leading to the main back entrance consisting of a large archway with huge wooden doors decorated with iron work. "I hope Father and Grandfather aren't too busy today. I'd hate to interrupt the King's schedule if he has something important planned."

"What could be more important to them than you?" Leo asked, gently squeezing her hand as they approached the archway.

A half dozen uniformed guards stood outside at various posts and observed the foursome, particularly Carmella who was wrapped in her wildly colorful cloak. A few eyebrows were raised as they greeted the new arrivals. When the captain in charge prepared to question the strangers, he paused for a moment as he gazed at Princess Megan, wondering if his eyes were playing tricks on him.

"Greetings, strangers. I must ask you if..." He couldn't help but stare disbelievingly at Megan, almost certain he was looking at King Justin's granddaughter yet knowing that it couldn't be so.

"Your mind isn't playing tricks on you, Captain Percy. I am who you think I am," she said, removing the hood of her cloak. "I need to see my grandfather right away."

"Yes, of course!" the captain replied, offering a slight bow. "Scouts have been sent to look for you, but how is it that...?" He scratched his head. "Who are these...?"

"These are my friends," she said, "and they know who I am. I can vouch for them all."

"Certainly," Captain Percy replied, studying the faces of her companions. "I'll escort you to the King myself, though it might be a rather inconvenient time."

"Why?" she asked. "What's happening?"

"Please follow me, Princess Megan. I'll explain on the way. The Citadel is a very busy place today," he said as he hurriedly ushered the four visitors inside, wondering what strange chain of events had led the princess of Arrondale to his doorway on such a fine afternoon.

A din of excited voices grew louder as Captain Percy led Megan, Leo, Nicholas and Carmella up a set of stone stairs and into a long corridor. Dozens of people milled about, some talking in loud voices or in whispers while many gesticulated with their hands to get a specific point across. Nicholas wondered what was happening as a few people swept past him down the stairs while others seemed content simply to converse and laugh in the echoing hallway alongside a series of four huge tapestries suspended from the wall on their right.

"What's going on?" he asked Megan. "Is it always this busy here?"

"Goodness no," she replied, perplexed by all the activity. "I've no idea what fuss my grandfather has stirred up today."

"A war council has just concluded," Captain Percy said as he indicated for them to follow him to a large oak door on the left beyond the top of the staircase. Another member of the royal guard stood at the doorway. The captain had a quick word with him before returning to the others. "I am told that King Justin is still lingering within the chamber, Princess Megan. I'll take you inside."

"Thank you," she said before glancing at Leo, her watery brown eyes flooded with apprehension. "Though I'm not a child anymore, I feel like I'm about to receive the scolding of a lifetime," she softly remarked.

446

"Trust me, Megan. Your grandfather will be so happy to see your face that he'll forget to be angry at you for running away."

"I hope so, Leo," she said as they entered the council chamber while a few more people drifted out the door at the same time.

The atmosphere was much quieter inside as only a handful of individuals remained in the room, all gathered at the far end of the long table engrossed in conversation. Several empty benches and chairs lay scattered about, and two fireplaces steadily blazed, sending billows of comforting heat to the rafters. Megan and Carmella followed closely behind Captain Percy as he hurried alongside the table to the opposite end. Nicholas and Leo slowed their pace, glancing warily at one another before stopping at a respectful distance and standing at attention against the wall, their hands behind their backs as if they were awaiting a military inspection. As Captain Percy approached, King Justin looked up from his seat, surprised to see him there.

"Pardon the intrusion, sir, but there are some new arrivals to the Citadel who have requested an audience. I took the liberty of bringing them before you immediately," he said, quickly stepping aside so that Megan was revealed to her grandfather.

"Exactly who wishes to see—" King Justin suddenly went silent, his mouth agape the instant he saw Megan. A beaming smile formed beneath his ice blue eyes as he stood and hurried around the table to greet his granddaughter, hugging her as if he'd never let go. "Just where have you been, young lady?" he asked, looking at her with teary eyes before hugging her once more with joyous laughter. "But I suppose you can give me all of those answers shortly. Oh, I can't believe you're standing here, Megan!"

"And I'm glad to see you, Grandfather," she replied, choked with emotion.

King Justin looked up at Captain Percy. "A wise decision, captain, bringing these guests here at once. Now find Prince Gregory, if you will. He's mingling somewhere out in the hallway. Bring him here at once. Then close these doors so we can have some privacy while we sort though this delightful turn of events."

"At once, sir," the captain replied, bowing his head and exiting the room.

"I really can't believe you're here!" the King said, holding his granddaughter's hand. "I thought I might... Well, never mind that. You're back and that's all that matters now." He beamed with pride as the others he had been talking with looked on. With him were his advisor, Nedry, the wizard Tolapari and Princes Brendan and William from Montavia, from whom he wished to learn more about the recent invasion of their kingdom. The King quickly introduced the two princes to Megan. "You might remember Brendan and William when you traveled with your father to Montavia about five years ago."

"We've grown a bit taller since then," Brendan said with a bashful grin, taken with Megan's attractive looks.

"As have I," Megan replied. "It's delightful to see you again, Brendan. And you too, William."

"Who have you brought with you, Megan?" King Justin asked, staring curiously at Carmella.

Megan turned around expecting to see Leo at her side, but noticed that he and Nicholas had kept their distance. So she first introduced Carmella, explaining how she and Samuel had met her after their wagon had broken down in the wild.

"Carmella was such a dear to offer us her kindness and friendship," Megan said.

"Oh, it was nothing," she replied with a light laugh. "I was tickled just to have some company on the road!"

"Still, I extend my deepest appreciation," King Justin said as he took Carmella's gloved hands in his. "You are an honorable and delightful woman."

"Thank you, your Highness. And pardon me if I'm being forward, but you are by far strikingly more handsome than the accounts I've heard in passing give you credit," she replied, smiling with a sparkle in her eye.

"Well, I thank you for that, Miss Carmella," the King said with a hint of embarrassment and good humor. He then noticed Nicholas and Leo standing farther away, assuming they were in the employ of Carmella. But before King Justin could say another word, Megan signaled for Leo and Nicholas to approach.

"Grandfather, I'd also like you to meet two more friends of mine who were instrumental in escorting me safely back to Morrenwood."

"Certainly, dear. Who are they?"

Megan again waved her hand, urging the two men forward. Slowly, Leo and Nicholas walked toward her and King Justin, slightly intimidated in his presence. Megan affectionately placed her hand upon Leo's shoulder as he stood next to her, delighted to introduce him to her grandfather. Leo looked askance at Megan, frozen in fear that King Justin would look disapprovingly upon them even though it was his granddaughter who had placed her hand upon him.

"Grandfather, this is Leo Marsh from the village of Minago, and Nicholas Raven who comes from Kanesbury, of all places."

"Pleased to meet you both," King Justin said, offering a hearty smile. "If you played a part in returning my granddaughter to me, then I am in your debt and look forward to hearing the details."

"It's an honor to meet you, sir," Leo uttered stiffly, shaking the King's hand while unobtrusively trying to get Megan to remove her own from his shoulder as if attempting to shoo away a fly without drawing attention. The King looked Leo directly in the eyes, though what thoughts were running through his mind, Leo couldn't determine from the man's inscrutable gaze.

"The honor is all mine," King Justin said before turning to Nicholas and shaking his hand as well. "A pleasure to meet you, Nicholas. From Kanesbury, you say?"

"Yes, sir," he replied.

"I've been to your village years ago," the King informed him. "In fact, I have two cousins who live there."

"I'm aware of that, sir. Our mayor, Otto Nibbs, and Sofia Durant both often speak of you, particularly Otto when he talks to outsiders about life in Kanesbury."

"Only good things, I hope," he said with a laugh. "But we are second cousins as my father and their mother were first cousins. Still, I don't begrudge Otto milking the relationship to benefit his village. After all, he helped to prevent the spread of some mischief by that dastardly wizard Caldurian twenty years ago when he wisely contacted me for assistance. Your village had gone through some difficult times back then."

"So I've been told," he said, growing quickly at ease. He was delightfully surprised when King Justin mentioned that Kanesbury was an important supplier of flour to the capital city. Nicholas proudly told him that he had been making the deliveries on behalf of Ned Adams over the last two years.

"As King, I must stay informed about all the details regarding the operation of this realm, including what items are being loaded into the storehouses," he said. "You must have recently delivered the final shipments of the year, correct? It's usually this time of autumn that the last purchased supplies from the far reaches of the kingdom roll into Morrenwood."

"Not exactly, sir." Nicholas swallowed, nervously realizing that he now had to explain to the King of Arrondale why he had recently left his job in Kanesbury. He glanced Megan's way, pleading for help, and she jumped into the conversation.

"Grandfather, forgive me for interrupting, but the reason Nicholas didn't make those last deliveries is related to why he was able to escort me back to Morrenwood. He had to leave Kanesbury because of certain–*complications?*"

Nicholas felt like burying his head in his hands. He wished that Megan hadn't brought up his problems back home just yet, but was certain that his past actions were about to be scrutinized for good or ill. He simply stood in silence, knowing there was nothing he could do or say to stop the inevitable.

King Justin furrowed his brow, curiously eyeing his granddaughter. "I don't understand, Megan. I was simply discussing flour shipments with your friend." He scratched the back of his head, perplexed by Megan's statement and noting the unease on Nicholas' face. "What are *you* talking about?"

Megan sighed. "You'll understand momentarily if you allow us to explain where we've been recently. You see, Grandfather, though I was angry that you sent me away to Boros for my protection in these troubled times, you were correct in a way. Danger *was* lurking out there, though it had found me someplace else."

"Then by all means, let us sit and talk. I look forward to an intriguing tale as soon as your father arrives."

"Trust me, King Justin, you won't be disappointed," Carmella said. "I've heard all the details and even I find some of them hard to believe!"

As everyone took a seat at the far end of the table, Dooley Kramer, still hidden in the rafters at the opposite end of the chamber, anticipated hearing a stunning saga. After the war council had adjourned a short time ago, he expected the chamber to quickly clear out so he could make an escape from his cramped hiding spot. His neck and back ached and he feared that he might fall asleep again above the constant rising of heat from the fireplace below. He grew angry at first upon hearing the voices of the new arrivals, figuring he would never get out of the Citadel if the meeting were to continue. But when he heard the name and voice of Nicholas Raven, he was shocked into paying careful attention once again.

At first Dooley couldn't believe what he was hearing. But when he recognized the words *Kanesbury, flour shipments, Otto Nibbs* and *Caldurian* being uttered, a shiver ran up his back, snapping his mind fully awake. How could Nicholas Raven, of all people, be inside the Blue Citadel speaking with the King of Arrondale? *Impossible*! Dooley shook his head, his mind aflutter. And why was Nicholas with Princess Megan, the King's granddaughter? It simply couldn't be, yet Dooley was listening to the very conversation that confirmed it. He settled down, trying to calm his mind and absorb every word. He knew there was no way he would fall asleep this time, giddily speculating what Farnsworth and Caldurian would say when he delivered his report.

After Prince Gregory returned and greeted his daughter in tearful astonishment, King Justin urged her and the others to tell their story. Megan apologized again for disappearing in the middle of the night, learning that Samuel had returned to Morrenwood after searching for her for several days. King Justin had immediately sent out more scouts, but her trail by then had grown cold.

Prince Gregory expressed gratitude for what Ivy had done to safeguard his daughter, though he was heartbroken that the young girl had been taken from her family. Upon hearing those sentiments, Nicholas thought it the perfect opportunity to make a case for her rescue.

"Forgive me if I'm out of place, King Justin, but I was hoping you might dispatch a company of scouts to find Ivy. I'll join in the search," he pleaded, his eyes filled with sorrow and remorse.

The King offered a heartfelt smile. "I understand your thinking, Nicholas, and the affection you have for Ivy, but where exactly would I send my troops? You said that a ship from the Isles was anchored offshore near the grasslands before it disappeared while you were unconscious. Where did it go?"

Nicholas stared at the table, shaking his head. "I don't know, sir. I just assumed it would return to the Northern Isles."

"I don't know either, and that is unfortunate," the King replied. "But do not think that the fate of this young woman doesn't disturb me, because it does. And if down the road I am able to assist in this matter, I shall."

"Something disturbs me even more," Nedry interjected. The King's advisor, his thin face edged with graying hair, again looked his usual worried self. "Why was that ship near the grasslands in the first place? Prince Brendan informed us that Montavia is under siege by the Northern Isles, so we must assume that a fleet of their ships is stationed well to our east above Montavia's northern shore."

"Nobody doubts that," Tolapari said.

"Nor does anyone doubt the story that the ambassador from Surna regaled us with during the war council," Nedry continued. "He said that several ships from the Isles were anchored at the mouth of the Lorren River well to our west."

"Why is that?" Leo asked.

"Apparently they are sending rafts laden with soldiers and supplies up the river into the Northern Mountains, making their way to Kargoth," Prince Gregory explained. "The Islanders are working with Vellan and fortifying his stronghold at Del Norác."

"And that brings me back to my original question," Nedry said. "With part of the Island fleet anchored offshore to our east and west, why was a solitary ship sitting north of Arrondale near the grasslands? From what Nicholas and Leo told us about Ivy's kidnapping, it appears to have been a spur-of-the-moment undertaking. I doubt the ship was routed to that location simply to pick up the woman who they thought was Princess Megan."

King Justin rubbed a hand across his face, contemplating Nedry's troubling words. "What are you saying, my friend?"

"Two questions come to mind," he stated. "One, what was the purpose of Madeline and Mune's visit with troops from the Northern Isles? And two, if they believe they have Princess Megan, what do they plan to do with her?"

"Very astute questions," King Justin said. "I will send out scouts to patrol the area on the off chance that the Islanders will return in such a blatant manner, but my instincts tell me they will not. If that meeting was part of something more sinister, I don't think they'll show themselves so readily again. And where that ship–and Ivy–is now, well, that is anybody's guess. Still, better to have the information than not."

"If that's the case, Grandfather, then you'll be pleased with our next bit of news," Megan excitedly told him.

"There's more?" he said. "I thought the three of you covered your travels from beginning to end."

"We have," Leo said, "but Carmella has her own story to add to the mix. We felt it best to let her explain the details since we weren't there for most of it."

"Proceed, Carmella," the King replied with a cordial smile. "What else do you bring to this table?"

"One of the Enâri," she responded a bit uncomfortably, fingering the medallion around her neck.

The wizard Tolapari wore a bewildered expression. "How did you learn anything about the Enâri creatures, Carmella? What information do you have?"

"You misunderstood me," she replied. "I don't have information about the Enâri. I actually have one of the Enâri creatures with me. He serves as my driver and is camping outdoors along the river near my wagon. His name is Jagga."

A half dozen individuals stared at Carmella with shocked and curious expressions, each wondering if what he had just heard had been heard accurately. She removed the medallion from around her neck and set it on the table before describing the events concerning her meeting and befriending Jagga. When she explained how Jagga had stolen the key to the Spirit Box in Kanesbury and had it melted down, the incredulousness of those listening only increased.

"And *that* is the key?" King Justin inquired, pointing to the medallion. "Or rather what's left of it?"

Carmella nodded. "I know it's a fanciful story, and I found it difficult to believe myself, but when I first touched the medallion..." She picked up the piece of metal and handed it to Leo, indicating for him to pass it to Tolapari. "Having received training in the magic arts, I sensed something unusual about the object the instant I first touched it, but am no longer able to. My powers are limited. But you, Tolapari, are a fully trained wizard. What is your opinion?"

Tolapari raked a hand through his unruly hair as he suspiciously eyed the medallion that Leo held out, finally taking the object by the leather cord and holding it up in the light to study. The simple, unadorned disk appeared particularly unremarkable yet seized his attention like an unsolvable riddle. Finally, the wizard grasped the object, his eyes widening the instant his skin came in contact with the piece of metal, his lungs filling with an involuntary intake of breath. The tips of his fingers grew warm and cold at the same moment as the magic churning within the item announced its presence. Tolapari set the medallion on the table, silently contemplating the mighty power that the wizard Frist had instilled inside the object twenty years ago.

"You are correct, Carmella. There is a potent force inside that piece of metal, a magic undetectable by ordinary folk. Yet it has been altered somewhat when it was reshaped in the intense heat of the forge, perhaps even diminished." Tolapari continued to stare at the object, recalling some of his past adventures in the world of wizardry. "I was trained by Frist, and during one of our visits many years ago he told me the story about how he created a spirit that would someday be capable of destroying the Enâri race if given enough time to incubate. The spirit was imprisoned in a metal box protected by magic and only able to be opened by a similarly magical key–*that* key," he said as he pointed to the medallion. "The particular spell Frist had cast on the outskirts of Kanesbury drained much of the life out of him, he once told me. His challenge to Vellan's power was the most difficult task he had ever undertaken. Frist thought he might have shortened his lifespan because of it."

"Did he?" Brendan asked. Since his brief encounter with Caldurian, the prince was curious about the power of the wizards who roamed Laparia.

"Fortunately no," Tolapari replied. "Frist recovered from the ordeal over time, indicating what a force he was in his own right. He still lives as far as I know. He was, after all, one of the true wizards like Vellan, hailing from the Valley of the Wizards far in the west." He glanced at the King. "It is a fortunate coincidence that Carmella brought this medallion to the Citadel."

"What Tolapari means is that the Spirit Box Frist created is currently inside this building," King Justin explained. "My cousin, Otto Nibbs, who had possession of the box as mayor of Kanesbury, gave it to me several years ago for safekeeping since he believed the Enâri threat to his village had passed. But according to Len Harold and Princes Brendan and William, the Enâri have reawakened."

"You spoke to Len Harold?" Nicholas asked, surprised that a member of the Kanesbury village council was in Morrenwood. "What did he say?"

"Apparently the recent escape of the Enâri has caused quite an uproar in your village, Nicholas. Though Mister Harold mentioned a few particulars during the council, he spoke to me in private beforehand, filling me in on the smaller details."

Nicholas' face paled, fearing the worst. "Have the Enâri attacked Kanesbury again?"

"No! No! Nothing like that," the King replied, quickly relating what he had learned, including Otto's disappearance and George Bane's excursion into the Spirit Caves after being enticed with gin and money from a stranger named Mune.

At the mention of Mune's name, Nicholas thought about all the strange events he had been embroiled in lately, wondering how or if they were related. It intrigued him that one of Ivy's kidnappers had also been in Kanesbury on the first night of the Harvest Festival, yet he couldn't connect the events. Maybe it was simply a coincidence.

Megan noted the distracted look upon his face, her thoughts paralleling his. "You must be wondering why the man who helped Madeline kidnap Ivy was also in your village arranging for the release of the Enâri."

"I am," he said, ready to explain everything that had happened to him in Kanesbury in front of King Justin and the others. He hoped they would indulge the personal speculations of a commoner and not feel that he was wasting their time. "I find it strange that the Enâri were released on the same night that I was arrested for robbery and that Arthur Weeks was murdered."

King Justin leaned back in his chair in surprise, wondering exactly who his granddaughter had invited into the Blue Citadel. Carmella sat up at the same moment, a chill running through her at the mention of the name Arthur Weeks.

"Don't worry, Grandfather. Nicholas didn't rob anybody," Megan said. "He was framed for that crime and the murder, which is why he fled Kanesbury and eventually met me."

"Your grandfather and I both look forward to hearing the details surrounding that episode," Prince Gregory said with an assumed smirk.

"As do I," Carmella added, turning to Nicholas, her heart beating wildly and her hands quivering as she gripped the armrest of his chair. "Did you just say a man was murdered in your village on the very night the Enâri were reawakened?"

"Yes. His name was Arthur Weeks, and word around town was that I killed him," Nicholas said, still incensed by the accusation. "And since Arthur implicated me in the robbery right to my face, well, apparently most folks found it hard to deny that I was his killer. But like Megan said, I didn't do it. And I have a witness."

"Oh, I believe you," Carmella said, gazing at the medallion lying upon the table. "Because I think I now know who killed the unfortunate Arthur Weeks."

"You do?" he asked in disbelief. "How is that possible?"

"Because of something Jagga had mentioned to me, which up until now I never gave a second thought," she replied. "You see, when he told me he had stolen the key from a man in Kanesbury, he briefly mentioned that his name was Arthur Weeks, but said nothing more about him. I didn't pay much attention to the detail as I was so fascinated that Jagga had stolen the magic key–and it happened around the time you said you had fled Kanesbury."

Tolapari leaned back in his chair, nodding. "If a just awakened Enâr needed an excuse for murder, then I guess securing his freedom was as good an excuse as any. And it makes sense, too. If Jagga had abandoned all allegiance to Caldurian and Vellan, then why would anything stop him from pursuing his own agenda at any cost?"

"Even murder," Nicholas softly said as some of the pieces of his life's puzzle fell into place. When he looked up at the others, an enlightened gleam filled his eyes and his world started to make sense again. "If Arthur was killed because he possessed the key to the Spirit Box, and since he and Dooley Kramer were close friends, then I'm guessing that Dooley knew about the key as well. Arthur was killed inside Dooley's house, after all. And that means–"

"–that Arthur and Dooley were involved in something more sinister," Megan jumped in. "You once told me it didn't make sense that those two would go to all the trouble to frame you for a robbery just to get your old job. But if they had possession of the key when Mune arranged for the release of the Enâri creatures, chances are they were in league with Mune or his associates. Otherwise, how would Jagga have learned that Arthur or Dooley had the key?"

"Meaning what?" Nicholas asked.

"Meaning that they needed you out of the way for some reason other than your job," Megan said. "You were about to be arrested, Nicholas, most likely to languish in the village lockup for who knows how long."

He smiled at Megan. "Perhaps you should have been a constable. But word was around the village that I planned to leave for Morrenwood soon to join up with the King's Guard and..." Nicholas suddenly felt embarrassed for blurting out such words in front of King Justin, now feeling a bit presumptuous to have even imagined that the King would want someone like him in the royal guard. But King Justin put him immediately at ease.

"You would have made a fine addition to my guard," he said, the sincerity evident in his voice.

"I'll take the blame for Nicholas not fulfilling his original intention," Megan said. "Remember, after meeting me on the road, he decided to escort me to Boros."

"Which we are very grateful for," Prince Gregory replied. "In a way, Nicholas was soldiering for the King in an unofficial capacity."

"Precisely," King Justin replied, urging him and Megan to continue with their thoughts.

"My point was," Nicholas said, "that if I was already planning to leave Kanesbury, why would Dooley and Arthur go to all the trouble to make it look like I committed a crime?"

"Maybe they had other motives," Megan said. "But it appears that those two were involved in framing you and were probably associating with people connected to the key, including that Mune fellow. So the big question you need to think about is why they wanted you out of the way? How could your presence interfere with their plans, whatever they are?"

Nicholas shrugged. "I'm not sure. I'm just a bookkeeper in a gristmill, after all, and work part time on Maynard Kurtz's farm. For what possible reason would anyone want me out of their way? I have no power or influence in the village."

"Apparently someone thinks you do," Leo said.

"You know Maynard Kurtz?" King Justin asked. "Len Harold mentioned that man's name to me during our discussions. It seems he was appointed as acting mayor in Otto's absence."

"Is that right?" Nicholas asked. "Maynard's a good man, and the village did a wise thing to select him. I live in a small cottage on his farm. He defended me to Constable Brindle after I was accused of the robbery. He's been like a father to me for much of my life."

"Pardon me for interrupting," Nedry said, an elevated sense of urgency in his voice, "but all this talk of local politics and whatnot in Kanesbury, while interesting to a point, doesn't address the matter of the melted key lying upon this table or the fact that one of Vellan's Enâri creatures is camping on the grounds outside the Blue Citadel."

"Fear not, Nedry. I'll have several guards keep an eye on Jagga from a distance as a precaution," the King said. "But from what Carmella has told us, I'm willing to give him a bit of leeway and not toss him in a prison cell. If he was a danger and up to no good, why would he give Carmella the key in the first place? I think Jagga genuinely desires his freedom from all superiors."

"I agree. Yet possessing the key affords us an opportunity," Tolapari said. "If it could be reforged and used to open the Spirit Box, thus destroying the Enâri race, think of the grievous blow such an act would deliver to Vellan. Kargoth would forever be cleansed of the Enâri's insidious presence."

"As would Montavia," Prince Brendan said. "And if this act was accomplished right before any attempt to retake Red Lodge, it would greatly enhance our efforts since all of Caldurian's Enâri troops are stationed in and around my grandfather's residence."

"Then why not take the medallion to one of the smithies in the Citadel and refashion it into a key as soon as possible?" Leo asked. "I shouldn't think that that would be much of a challenge."

"No indeed," Tolapari said, glancing at the King with a trace of doubt in his troubled eyes. "It would be quite easy to have the piece of metal reforged into a key that would fit the Spirit Box. Having it *open* the box is another matter entirely. I'm afraid the task won't be so easy."

"By the look on your face, I suspected not," King Justin remarked despondently. "Where is the flaw in Leo's suggestion?"

"Reshaping the key is easy. Reshaping the magic spell within it is a whole other matter." Tolapari picked up the medallion again, the tips of his fingers and the marrow in his bones attuned to the magic pulsing within. "As I said earlier, its magic has been altered, or possibly lessened, by the intense heat of the forging process. I sense that the original spell cast by Frist is not whole. Only the wizard himself could reconstitute it to its original potency and purpose."

"Still, it is possible, isn't it?" King Justin asked.

"Yes, very much so," he said, gazing at the medallion before setting it down on the table. "But first you must find him."

"Find him? Where exactly is this wizard?" Carmella asked, contemplating the fate of her gift from Jagga.

"He is spending his final years alone, as do many of the true wizards from the Valley. I guided him to a place of his choosing some time ago," Tolapari said, "a request I was deeply honored to fulfill as one of his earliest apprentices."

"Where is this place?" Megan asked.

"Oh, a guide would never reveal such a piece of information unless under the most dire circumstances," he replied. "And though this situation qualifies, I will only divulge Frist's location in secret and only to those few who absolutely need to know."

"Fair enough," King Justin said. "But you still deem this a viable option?"

"Very much so, assuming that Frist yet lives. The damage we could do to Vellan would greatly improve our chances for victory over Kargoth if we confront him in the future. And as Prince Brendan said, it would give us the upper hand in Montavia, too. So the time we have to take advantage of this opportunity is slim since we cannot put off sending assistance to King Rowan for too long." Tolapari glanced at the nine individuals hanging on his every word. "Because of these intricacies, I recommend that word of this development not be allowed outside this group. We should swear ourselves to secrecy until after the key is reforged and used to open the Spirit Box."

King Justin noted the wisdom of Tolapari's suggestion. He urged everyone to extend a hand forward and touch an edge of the medallion, swearing them all, including himself, to keep the details of their plan a secret unless success should one day shine upon them.

After everyone in unison pledged their solemn agreement, they each sat back in silence for several moments, staring at the medallion and wondering what good or ill would come of Jagga's gift. Finally, King Justin's voice broke the hypotonic silence of the room punctuated only by the crackling flames from both fireplaces.

"I thank you all for taking such an oath. But in doing so, we have backed ourselves into a corner," he said, briefly tossing to both Nicholas and Leo a commanding and beseeching glance. "Though Tolapari hasn't yet revealed where the wizard Frist is living out his last days, the medallion must still be delivered to him. And soon, if it is to do us any good, perhaps saving countless lives among the free people of Laparia should we succeed. But we have yet to appoint any individuals to accept this secret mission."

"I would be the first to volunteer," Tolapari said, "but I feel I must accompany the mission to retake Montavia. I must confront Caldurian once and for all as someone should have done a long time ago. He has grown powerful under his master's tutelage, causing as much trouble throughout Laparia as Vellan himself."

"I was hoping you would offer your services in that capacity," King Justin gratefully replied. "And as I will be leading the troops to battle in Rhiál, I will appoint my son to spearhead the charge to Montavia with Princes Brendan and William riding at Gregory's side to help free their homeland. Your presence, Tolapari, makes me optimistic of the outcome."

"And your words give me hope, King Justin. My brother William and I cannot express our thanks for your assistance," Brendan replied as William echoed his sentiments.

In the meantime, Nicholas and Leo glanced at one another knowingly, each having been mentally calculating who in the room remained to go on such a mission. King Justin had made it perfectly clear that he and his son would each lead troops into battle, with Tolapari, Brendan and William accompanying Prince Gregory to the east, which immediately discounted half the people at the table. And since Nedry was too old, and the King most certainly wouldn't allow Megan or Carmella to undertake such a journey, Nicholas and Leo realized what was expected of them. If the King's imploring gaze just moments ago hadn't put them on the spot, then this not so subtle process of elimination certainly did.

Yet Nicholas also felt a rush of pride, believing that King Justin deemed him worthy of his trust and capable to perform such a vital task. He was again reminded of his desire to join the King's Guard before a whirlwind of intrigue had blown him off course. He glanced at Leo, trying to read his thoughts. When Leo returned a discreet nod, Nicholas knew that his friend was thinking along the same lines. They had guided Megan safely home, after all, and tracked down Ivy after a long and arduous journey with the odds stacked against them. Surely delivering a medallion to a wizard hidden somewhere in the wilderness, and then returning to Morrenwood with a finished key wouldn't prove too difficult a challenge. He realized that it was time for him and Leo to step up with pride and do what they could for the safety of Arrondale. Before a lull in the conversation had formed, he addressed the King, hoping he sounded more steady and confident than he felt.

"With your permission, sir, Leo and I would be honored to embark on this mission," he said.

"We just await your orders, King Justin," Leo added, "should you consider us up to the task."

King Justin nodded, a pleased smile upon his face. "Indeed I do think you are both up to the task. Considering all the obstacles you've overcome to bring Megan safely back here, I have no doubts whatsoever. I happily accept your service."

Nicholas and Leo each nodded to the King as Megan and Carmella proudly showered smiles upon their friends. Everyone else in the room was equally confident that the two young men could accomplish the mission just as well as anyone else with proper guidance and preparation. Yet Nedry had a few lingering doubts and decided to address them now while the moment was appropriate.

"Though I'm satisfied with your choice of these fine individuals to seek out the wizard Frist," he said, "I wonder if we might have acted too swiftly in confining this matter to the ten of us." Nedry realized that the constant stress of the job was causing him to overanalyze situations and worry for no reason, but he was duty bound to speak his thoughts. "Wouldn't it be wiser to send a contingent of soldiers with Nicholas and Leo for their protection and to ensure the safekeeping of the medallion?"

"I briefly considered it," the King replied. "And though I appreciate your concern, Nedry, I think the success of this assignment lies in secrecy and swiftness. We're not engaging in battlefield maneuvers but in a mission of stealth. Drawing attention to it is the last thing I desire. I will let Tolapari instruct our candidates about where to go and the best way to proceed, trusting that good fortune will follow them each step of the journey. The medallion made its way to us in a most inconspicuous manner. I believe that same simplicity will guide Nicholas and Leo in their task while the rest of us prepare to launch the rumbling engines of warfare."

"Then I ask, King Justin, that you allow my brother and me to accompany them on this assignment," Brendan said. "We are happy to contribute to the success of the mission since it will help free Montavia, and frankly, I would hate simply to wait around as a bystander while others do all the work."

"I agree," William added with a bit less confidence than his older brother, yet with equal sincerity.

King Justin swiftly tamped down their noble ambitions. "I understand the many reasons why you two would volunteer for this mission, but chances are that you will be leaving for Montavia before Nicholas and Leo return. You will yet have your part to play in this matter. But rest assured, you will not simply wait around until the army sets out. You will be consulting with Prince Gregory on all aspects of the raising and deploying troops to your kingdom. King Rowan will hardly recognize you both when you return."

Brendan offered a feeble smile. "I realize you're trying to accommodate and protect William and me at the same time, King Justin, and I will obey your veiled request to remain here. But I wish I could offer something more substantial to this effort, moving events instead of waiting for them to direct me."

"We must all play the parts we are destined to," Tolapari said, "no matter how tedious they sometimes seem. Yet you may face grueling challenges before this is all over, whether you wish to or not. So be prepared for the call when you least expect it."

"Wise words for us all," King Justin agreed, glancing at his advisor. "Don't you think so, Nedry?" he asked, wanting to end any further speculation on the matter.

"I do indeed, sir," he replied, his mind preoccupied with a sudden thought. "I do indeed."

"When will Leo and Nicholas leave, Grandfather?" Megan asked, gently squeezing Leo's hand below the table. "Have they no time to rest after their travels?"

"Fear not, Megan," he replied, noting her obvious affection for Leo. "I won't boot them out the door right this minute. There are preparations yet to be made, and Nicholas and Leo have earned a bit of rest. However, if this task is to be completed in order to give us an advantage in Montavia, it must commence soon. Though our armies and supply trains must still be assembled and advance scouting parties dispatched, I think that Gregory should leave for Montavia by the end of next month at the latest, though each day sooner, the better. I most assuredly will be in Rhiál before then, facing whatever threat King Drogin has prepared. Therefore, if Nicholas and Leo depart at dawn on the fourteenth of Mid Autumn, three days from tomorrow morning, that will give them four weeks with possibly a few days to spare to complete the journey." King Justin turned to Tolapari. "Will that be time enough for wherever they're going?"

"Quite sufficient," the wizard said, "assuming there are no unusual delays. But who can ever say what trouble might prowl among the shadows on the road, especially when time and secrecy are of the essence?"

Prince Gregory offered an amused grin. "And on that cheerful note, I think we should all repair shortly to one of the dining rooms and have a proper meal if we are done in here, Father."

King Justin nodded. "I agree. After sitting through both the war council and this impromptu second council, we all need some air and nourishment to clear our heads. There'll be time enough later to attack the details."

The King stood and exited the chamber as the others followed amid small talk and whispers, all eager for a leisurely break and a hot meal. Nicholas and Leo talked among themselves as they left the room last of all, wondering exactly what kind of an expedition they would be facing as they closed the door behind them, leaving the room in utter silence.

Dooley remained in the rafters for several minutes, ecstatic that the pair of meetings had finally ended. His neck and back ached terribly and pangs of hunger gnawed at him until he could barely tolerate it. At last, confident that he had a few minutes to make an undetected escape, he flipped off his hood, crawled among the rafters and clambered down one of the wooden support posts, smiling with relief when his feet finally touched the floor. Spying the bowls of leftover fruit on the table, he grabbed two apples and shoved them in his coat pockets before peering out one of the doors into the main corridor. Everyone had left and the hallway was as empty as when he first arrived. Without delay, he slipped out the door and hurried down the steps to the lower lever, making his way outdoors as stealthily as a midnight cat.

About an hour later as the afternoon wore on, Dooley and his workers were once again on the road, a caravan of thirteen wagons leaving the borders of Morrenwood and starting the long journey back to Kanesbury along King's Road with Dooley at the lead. Less than five minutes outside the city, a large black crow alighted on the seat next to him, cawing once to get his attention, though it was totally unnecessary as Dooley had noted the bird's fleeting shadow and intimidating wingspan before it landed.

"I was told to expect a visit from you," he softly spoke to Gavin before glancing at the wagon behind him. But the driver was far enough behind not to hear or notice Dooley speaking.

"What have you to report?" Gavin asked. "Caldurian awaits my return in Montavia, anxious to hear what information you gleaned from the war council."

Dooley swallowed, prepared to lie to the crow in part to cover up the fact that he had fallen asleep through all of the meeting. Luckily, the mystifying arrival of Nicholas and the others provided him with some useful information to make up for his mistake.

"The war council was short on specifics, Gavin, though King Justin is planning an eventual assault to repel the invasions of Rhiál and Montavia." Dooley felt fortunate that the King had referred to such actions when he was speaking to Nicholas. "Unfortunately, the details will be hashed out at later meetings."

Gavin flapped his wings in disgust. "I flew all the way to Morrenwood to receive such a useless report? Caldurian already suspected that King Justin would try to rally his neighbors for support. We wanted to find out the who, when and where of all of it. The wizard will be hugely disappointed!"

"Don't condemn me so fast," he replied. "I may not have much to report on the council, but I found out some very interesting bit of news afterward."

"Oh?" Gavin asked. "Redeem yourself and tell me at once."

Dooley repeated what he had heard about the medallion and the plan to take it to the wizard Frist and have it reforged, careful not to reveal Nicholas' name. Though Nicholas had arrived in Morrenwood by chance, Dooley felt that Caldurian would blame him nonetheless should he ever find out since he and Farnsworth had been instructed for some mysterious reason to get Nicholas out of the wizard's way. "If they succeed, Vellan's creatures are doomed. King Justin mentioned that he is in possession of the Spirit Box. One turn of the key and it is over for the Enâri. That information alone is worth more than all the words spewed at some tedious war council."

Gavin agreed. "Caldurian will be distressed after he learns about this–and not too pleased having to report it to Vellan either."

"But there may be a way to stop it," Dooley said, grabbing Gavin's attention. "The two men who will be taking the medallion to Frist are leaving at dawn on the fourteenth day of Mid Autumn. Though it wasn't revealed where the pair is going, if you remain at the Blue Citadel until then, you can follow them from the air for a while to get a general idea in which direction they will head. Then report the information to Caldurian at once. He will know how to proceed thereafter."

Gavin congratulated Dooley on this stroke of luck. "Caldurian has stewed for years that the key was stolen from his beloved Xavier who died at the hands of the thief. To get it back will elevate you a few notches in the wizard's mind."

"Only happy to assist. The rewards are irrelevant," Dooley said with feigned indifference. Yet he feared to imagine what might happen to him if Gavin could only read his thoughts and discover that he was the culprit who had thrown the fatal stones at Xavier twenty years ago. Though this new information might absolve part of his childhood crime if the key were returned to Caldurian, he knew that his horrific act would always hang over him for the rest of his life.

"Now I must be off," Gavin said shortly after. "Though it will be a tedious trial waiting around here for a few more days, it must be done. I will do some spying of my own in the meantime, peering through windows and listening in on conversations and such, hoping to glean more specifics about the fate of this medallion."

"If you must," Dooley said, "but try not to arouse suspicion. Your main task is to track the movements of the two who will deliver the medallion. Caldurian can handle the rest."

After Gavin left, Dooley continued home, eager to leave the miles of tired and dreary road behind. All the while he silently fumed, contemplating how Nicholas Raven had escaped the traps that had been set for him in Kanesbury and was once again a detriment to their glorious plans. Farnsworth would be furious that Nicholas had linked Dooley to the robbery, Arthur Weeks' murder and the release of the Enâri, though he would happily report that Farnsworth had not been implicated in any way. It was a minor consolation, but for his own sake, Dooley knew that Nicholas Raven could never be allowed to step foot in Kanesbury again, no matter what the cost.

Chapter 31

Alterations

Nedry pushed open the pale blue stained glass window in his office early the next morning. A cool draft slipped inside, refreshing his already tired body. He sipped a cup of hot tea as he observed the billowy swirl of gray and white clouds lounging above the trees along the Edelin River, mourning the absent sunshine and buoyant atmosphere of the previous day. A murder of crows raised mayhem above the distant pines, their floating forms appearing as tiny black dots against the milky backdrop.

But being into the fifth week of the autumn season, quick changes from delightful sunshine and blue skies to long stretches of ashen clouds and damp spirits was hardly unexpected. Nedry missed the lazy, recuperative walks he would take along the road near the fruit orchards on warm summer days, feeling as if it would be a lifetime before that season would again flourish in the valley. And though he knew there would be glorious days to enjoy in the fall and approaching winter, he assumed that the recent muddying of the political landscape and his nagging desire to retire had magnified his glum disposition. He was considering submitting his resignation to King Justin after matters were settled in Montavia and Rhiál. The King probably suspected as much as Nedry had dropped hints, but as his next meeting was starting shortly, he pushed aside such thoughts and concentrated on the task at hand.

He took another sip of tea and closed the window, turning around to face the tiny room with a single fireplace and a cluttered desk that served as his private office for so many years. But today's meeting would be held in one of King Justin's private chambers to discuss Nicholas and Leo's mission to find the wizard Frist. And though he rarely contradicted the King's judgment and trust in other people, he felt uneasy about sending the medallion off with two strangers into the wild. Despite Princess Megan's faith in the two men and their obvious success in guiding her safely to Morrenwood, he had a nagging suspicion that something could go wrong.

Having suddenly been given a chance to strike a blow at Vellan, Nedry wondered if they might be risking it too casually. Or were old age and obstinacy coloring his views? Nicholas and Leo had demonstrated courage and responsibility in the starkest terms, so perhaps they were the wise choice. If secrecy was at the root of the mission, what better way to cloak it than by recruiting such an inconspicuous pair? He tried to convince himself that that was the way to proceed as he hurried down a flight of stairs to the meeting room. Still, an added layer of precaution couldn't hurt, he mused, racking his brain for a solution.

Tolapari unfolded a large parchment map upon a table in King Justin's upper study, the dull morning light faintly highlighting the black, brown, green and blue images of mountains, trees and rivers in and around Arrondale. He was seated at the table with Nicholas and Leo. The wizard tapped his finger upon a small dot on the western border of the kingdom indicating the capital city of Morrenwood.

"Your journey is quite simple. You'll be traveling from Morrenwood, located here," he said, sliding the tip of his finger in a slight arc to the northwest, "to Wolf Lake in the Dunn Hills right *here*." He pointed to a lake on the eastern edge of the vast mountainous, tree-covered region. "There is a small island upon the lake where the wizard Frist resides. I guided him there myself. He had spent many happy years exploring the wilderness and climbing the mountains in that region in his younger days, deciding it was where he would spend his final years." Nicholas and Leo studied the map as King Justin and Nedry gazed over their shoulders.

"Well, Leo, it looks easy enough on paper," Nicholas joked, scanning the inky terrain before glancing up at the wizard. "Any suggestions on the best path to take?"

"Of course," he replied, again using his finger to trace out a more specific route. "After leaving Morrenwood and crossing the Edelin River here, you'll ride across this grassy region between the two southern stretches of the Trent Hills, approaching the Gliwice Gap on the western edge. Once you pass through that, the Cashua Forest will stand before you in all its glory. It won't be a difficult journey to this point."

"Good to hear," Leo said. "And from there? Do we go around the southern tip of the forest or go through it?"

"Definitely through it," the wizard said. "And for a couple of reasons. First, you will save time, and the quicker this deed is done, the better. Second, if you did go around the southern tip, as you headed back north you'd be traveling for many miles along the banks of the Lorren River in open view of any troops from the Northern Isles. Their rafts are traveling upriver to Kargoth."

"Why risk a possible encounter with them?" King Justin posed. "They may sail on their merry way, but who is to say that they don't have foot soldiers patrolling the banks here and there? Though various communities thrive along the narrow strip of shore bordering the eastern expanse of the Dunn Hills, there is no formal government in those parts. The Northern Isles are probably being shown token resistance, if any. It is best to avoid trouble if you can."

"We'll go through Cashua Forest," Nicholas said, studying the stretch of woodland tucked between the Lorren River and the Trent Hills. "How difficult can it be?"

"After leaving Gliwice Gap, if you bear slightly southwest to the edge of the forest and enter it there, you should come to a narrow ravine a mile or two inside the woods," Tolapari informed them. "It is the remains of a dry river bed. Of course, your horses won't be able to handle that terrain, so you'll have to sell them as you near the woods. Following the ravine will take you almost to the other side of the forest. If you keep to those bearings until you exit, you'll arrive at a point on the Lorren River opposite the village of Woodwater." The wizard pointed out another tiny dot on the map on the west bank of the river. "You'll have to hire a guide in that village to take you through the Dunn Hills to Wolf Lake. Following a ravine through the

Cashua Forest is one thing, but traversing the wilds of the Dunn is a challenge for anybody not intimately familiar with the terrain."

Nicholas nodded as he studied the map, eager to start the journey yet feeling the weight of its purpose. "And Frist will be able to transform the medallion back into the key?"

"If he can't, then your journey is in vain," King Justin said with grim humor.

"Don't say such a thing," Nedry replied, worriedly walking about the room, his chest tightening. He opened a window overlooking the fruit orchards and inhaled the fresh morning air to calm himself, observing the slow passage of clouds. On a nearby ledge he noted a large black crow picking at a sprig of dried berries it had carried from the woods along the river, the chaotic cawing of its fellow crows still audible in the distance. Nedry wondered why this particular bird preferred to remain alone. "I'm anxious enough as it is about this mission," he added, looking back into the room and leaning against the sill with folded arms. "Restoring the key to the Spirit Box is no small matter. I don't think one should joke about its failure."

"You must relax, Nedry," the King said. "Enduring too many late nights pondering over matters of state is not healthy for a man of your years."

"I'm afraid, sir, old habits are hard to break," he replied. "The only way I know how to perform my job is to thoroughly fret over the details. And since the details of this journey are confined to the five of us, I shall delegate none of the preparations to my assistants. I'll personally arrange for the food supplies, transportation and clothing required for our travelers." He approached Nicholas and Leo. "Since the two of you have three days to spare before you leave, I thought some training with the King's troops might do some good."

"Training?" Leo asked.

"One never knows when a bit of sword fighting or outdoor survival skills might come in handy," King Justin said. "Besides, Nicholas had revealed his intentions of joining up with my guard, so I'm offering you an opportunity to briefly train with my best men."

"I'm willing," Nicholas said, accepting the King's offer.

"Then count me in," Leo replied. "Besides, it might be fun learning how to wield a sword, though I don't expect we'll need to use one on our journey."

"Let's hope not," Nedry said, adding another worry to his long list as he closed the window. He noticed the crow still stationed outside, only now it was perched nearer to the study, its ebony eyes appearing to lock gazes with him. The King's advisor felt a chill run through him as he locked the window, unable to shake a sense of unease that suddenly gripped his spirit.

"Still, we'll look quite a sight roaming about armed in such a manner." Nicholas said, suddenly subdued. "If only we had been better prepared along the grasslands, then maybe Ivy might…" He sighed. "Well, you understand."

"With luck, there won't be many people observing your trek," Nedry replied. "You'll be off the main roads for the most part."

"If on any roads at all," King Justin said. "You'll be traveling through mostly unsettled parts of the kingdom and beyond, but that will be to your advantage. It's been some time since I've ridden to the western border of Arrondale. I envy you the adventure ahead."

"You'll have your own adventure when you leave for Rhiál, my friend," Tolapari remarked. "And unlike Nicholas and Leo, no one will be unaware of your departure from the Citadel with an army in tow as you set out."

Nedry nodded as he glanced at the window again, observing that the crow was no longer perched outside. For some reason the bird's presence had upset him, though he couldn't fathom why.

"Then I had better prepare as well," the King said, offering goodbyes to Nicholas and Leo, explaining that he had to meet with his son and top captains. "Remain here with Tolapari as long as you need to plan your route," he added before exiting the room.

"I shall take my leave, too," Nedry said as a shadow of doubt clouded his mind. "I have other matters that need my attention." He slipped out the study door and drifted down the corridor, his thoughts in a whirl.

Despite a chill in the air, Nedry took a walk along his favorite orchard road before lunch to clear his head and ease his heartburn about the upcoming battles and the secret mission to the

Dunn Hills. He knew that he agonized too much about such matters as if he were king himself, wondering how he would ever adjust to retirement.

He paused and leaned against a wooden fence to study a row of apple trees closing down for the approaching winter, feeling just as vulnerable himself in the cooling air and lessening light of each passing day. But before a sense of melancholy overwhelmed him, he heard fluttering in a nearby branch and turned suddenly. There he spotted a lone black crow apparently inspecting the limb for bugs, certain that it was the same crow perched upon the window ledge earlier. Was he being followed? Was the crow a spy, he wondered, trying to recall what words were spoken in King Justin's study while the window was open. But his troubled feelings soon lifted. Nedry chuckled as he walked back to the Citadel, chiding himself for wallowing in paranoia until he noticed the crow flying back to the building as well, sailing aloft upon the currents toward the upper turrets bathed in milky gray light.

Throughout the rest of the day, Nedry attended to his regular duties as well as making sure that horses and adequate food supplies were prepared for Nicholas and Leo's journey, making no mention of the purpose for such requests. Later in the afternoon while on his way to check in with the seamstresses about clothing arrangements, he heard a shuffle of hurried footsteps behind. Just as he turned around, Brendan and William were barreling toward him. Nedry slowed down the two princes with a raised hand, wondering what the fuss was about.

"You're a difficult person to track down," William said, grinning and out of breath.

"Sorry for the intrusion," Brendan added, "but we were hoping for a moment of your time. My brother saw you turn the corner and bolted after you."

"Quite all right," Nedry replied, leading them to a large alcove with two oak benches. A single oil lamp on the wall cast subdued light and flickering shadows upon the surroundings, highlighting a stone sculpture of a horse standing upon its hind legs. Nedry sat down while Brendan and William took a seat on the opposite bench, the younger prince anxiously tapping his feet upon the floor. "Now how may I help you?"

"We didn't think we should bother King Justin with our request," Brendan began, "not wanting to appear ungrateful and all."

"Is there a problem?"

"Not at all," he said. "But William and I were wondering if we might have the King's permission to leave the Citadel for a few days to wander the countryside."

"To explore," William said, his light brown eyes wide and eager.

Brendan sighed, finding his words awkward and ungracious even before they were spoken. "The truth is that–"

"–you're bored to death?" Nedry guessed with a note of amusement.

Brendan nodded, slightly embarrassed. "You might say that, Nedry. And we don't mean to sound ungrateful, but it's going to be a long month before we return to Montavia. And truth be told, though we've already sat in on a meeting with Prince Gregory and informed him of all we know about the invasion of our kingdom, there is really little else for us to do until we ride. He and his captains have everything under control."

"No doubt," he agreed. "Therefore, I shall be happy to present your request to King Justin in the morning. I see no reason why he should object."

"Thank you!" William said. "As much as I like it here, I feel kind of useless doing nothing. I wish we could have gone with the others, wherever they're headed."

"You mean Nicholas and Leo?"

"Yes," Brendan said. "You don't suppose the King would change his mind and let us tag along, do you?"

"No chance, I'm afraid." He lowered his voice and glanced out the alcove, wary of any passersby. "King Justin prefers that that journey be made in secret. The fewer eyes that notice, the better."

"I understand. So I hope we can go on our own journey," William said, "even if it is just tramping around the countryside for a few days. And I don't care who sees us!"

Nedry raised an eyebrow upon hearing those words, a new thought taking hold. "Where would you go?" he asked.

"We want to explore the southern reaches of the kingdom," Brendan said. "Perhaps along the Pine River into Bridgewater

County and a bit beyond. I've been studying maps in the Citadel library."

"Excellent choice," Nedry said, noting to himself that they would be taking a route opposite that of Nicholas and Leo. He rose and shook hands with Brendan and William, apologizing that he must be on his way but assuring them that their request was as good as granted. "But keep this matter between us. I'll let you know the King's decision soon," he promised as the two princes repeatedly thanked him before they departed, leaving the King's advisor alone in the alcove to ponder the matter for a few more minutes before his meeting with the seamstresses.

When Nedry dropped by a short while later, the women were busily tailoring travel clothes and long wool overcoats for Nicholas and Leo's trip, laughing and enjoying tea as they attended to their duties. As Nedry entered the large stone room replete with looms and spinning wheels and shelves crammed with bolts of materials and spools of thread, an older woman in charge greeted him.

"Hello again, Nedry," she said with an eager smile. "It's a rare chance that you ever stop by, and here it is that you visit us twice in two days. Why are we so honored?"

Nedry grinned as a stream of sunlight breaking through the clouds spilled onto a slate floor through a round stained glass window. "I'm flattered that you consider my visit an honor, Miss Alb, but I wanted to see how you were progressing on my request."

"Swimmingly!" she said, gently touching the back of her graying hair and wiping out the wrinkles in her work dress. "Everything will be ready by tomorrow morning."

"Excellent. But I'm wondering if I might make an additional request," he added, "hoping it won't be too much of an inconvenience."

"Certainly not," she said, motioning him to a small table that served as her desk. She sat down, offering Nedry a chair on the opposite side. "Some tea?"

"None at the moment, thank you."

"Then how may I further help you, Nedry, with this mysterious assignment?" Miss Alb asked, brimming with anticipation.

"Well, ma'am, if at all possible, I'd like you and your seamstresses to make two second sets of travel clothes, though not as many are needed in this case. And two more wool overcoats as well." Nedry furrowed his brow as he gazed appreciatively at Miss Alb. "Will that present any problems or delays?"

"As the request comes from you, none that I can foresee. I'll just add a few more workers to get everything completed on time," she replied, happy to be of service. "Then maybe one day over lunch you can tell me what all this sartorial secrecy is about."

Nedry leaned forward and spoke softly. "I'm afraid, Miss Alb, that my job prevents me from disclosing certain details of ongoing operations, despite your valued assistance in such." He stood and courteously bowed his head. "However, having lunch with delightful company is never forbidden. Day after tomorrow if you're free?"

"I look forward to it," Miss Alb replied, blushing.

"I'll pick you up at noon," he said before making his exit.

Moments later, Nedry made his way through the Citadel corridors, awash with flickering torchlight and the crisp scent of autumn whenever he passed by an open window. But his mind was elsewhere as he contemplated the timing of Brendan and William's excursion away from the Citadel and how their little adventure to relieve some chronic boredom might serve his own purposes.

King Justin ordered breakfast brought to his study the following morning so he could eat while scrutinizing several maps of Rhiál and its vicinity before a later meeting with Prince Gregory and his captains. Nedry entered the room after knocking upon the door, apologizing for the interruption.

"Not to worry, Nedry. What can I do for you?" the King asked as he sipped some sweet cider, looking up from his desk.

"I won't take much of your time, sir, but I was contemplating a minor change to Nicholas and Leo's travel itinerary."

"Oh?"

Nedry nodded. "As an added precaution, I thought it might be wiser if they instead left near the midnight hour the day *before* their planned departure at dawn. Let them cross the river in darkness and travel a few miles into the foothills of the Trent," he suggested. "It will be a moonless sky at that hour, after which they can continue on the next morning at their leisure out of sight of curious eyes. Why draw attention to their departure if we don't have to?"

"That makes sense," King Justin said, taking a bite out of a biscuit and glancing at the map in front of him, eager to plot out his journey to Rhiál. "Very well, Nedry. Apprise Nicholas and Leo of the change." He pointed to his plate. "Biscuit? Cook gave me plenty extra this morning."

"Thank you, but I've already breakfasted," he said as he ambled toward the door. Nedry turned around as if something had slipped his mind. "Oh, there is one other minor matter. I talked to Prince Brendan and Prince William yesterday, and needless to say, they are a bit on the restless side having to wait all this time before their return trip to Montavia. Possibly an entire month or more."

"I suppose sitting in on a few strategy sessions will only alleviate their anxiety so much."

"I'm afraid so. They were wondering if they might take a few days to explore the countryside, with your permission. I got the impression they were feeling cooped up like chickens in a pen."

King Justin laughed over his map. "I should say so at their age. Last thing they probably want to do is listen to a bunch of old men prattle on while their country is under siege. They're eager to confront Caldurian *now*. I suppose roaming the hills and fields will help them cope in the meantime and build their confidence." The King swished his hand through the air in the affirmative. "They escaped and traveled here from Montavia with little difficulty, so by all means, fix them up with supplies and horses and let them at it."

"I shall do that," Nedry said. "They'll probably leave the morning after tomorrow, wanting to spend some additional time first with Prince Gregory to discuss the ride to Montavia. I think they'll stick to the southern routes along the Pine River, so no chance of them getting lost or in danger."

"All the better," King Justin replied, hunched over his maps as he ferociously studied them. "All right then. See to it."

"Excellent," Nedry softly said, preparing to slip out the door. "As you wish."

Nicholas and Leo were informed of the change to their departure time after Nedry spotted them walking across an interior courtyard after enduring three hours of instruction in sword fighting.

476

After lunch, they planned a session of rock climbing upon a stone outcropping farther up the river with some of the King's guardsmen.

"I'll be glad to leave earlier," Nicholas said, massaging an aching shoulder. "It'll be more relaxing than what we're going through now."

Leo and Nicholas remained in the Citadel the next day to go over their route one final time with Tolapari. Afterward, Nicholas enjoyed a long nap while Leo walked with Megan through the fruit orchard under a fleet of wispy clouds tipped by the sun's golden light.

"I'll miss you, Leo," she said, her hand in his as they wandered along a trail of decaying leaves. "Return quickly–and safely–from wherever it is you're going."

"I wish I could tell you, Megan, but I'm not allowed."

"I understand," she replied, stopping to kiss him while she clasped his hands.

Leo was lost in the warm touch of her lips, wishing that he didn't have to go. Suddenly he looked up at the Blue Citadel in the near distance. "Maybe we shouldn't..."

"What's the matter, Leo?" she asked, noting his gaze fixed upon the granite fortress. She grinned, understanding his sudden discretion. "I know what you're thinking."

"You do?"

"You're afraid my father or grandfather is right now peering out one of the Citadel windows and monitoring your every move."

"It had crossed my mind."

"Don't worry. They're not," she said. "However, we aren't alone."

Leo looked around. "What do you mean?"

Megan pointed out a man riding a horse in a pasture near the tree line along the river. A second man was hiking through a field across the orchard road in the opposite direction. "Grandfather assigned a few men to keep an eye on me from a distance in light of recent events. I've consented not to argue the point this time."

Leo swallowed nervously. "Are they going to report back everything they see?"

"Of course not! They aren't spies, Leo. They're protectors. There are even a few other men watching Jagga near the river," she said. "*They'll* do a bit of spying on the Enâri creature to be on the safe side. Carmella said she'll spend time here as long as the weather holds out since Tolapari has agreed to give her a few magic lessons in his spare hours. Jagga's moves will be closely watched while they remain on the grounds."

"I feel in good company, being watched just like an Enâr," he joked.

"I'm the one being watched. You just happen to be in the line of sight, Leo. So don't feel too put upon."

He sighed. "I'd feel less anxious if your father and King Justin knew about us. We never told them about our friendship."

"No, we didn't," Megan replied. "But I did."

Leo's eyes widened in panic. "You did? *When?*"

"Yesterday, while you and Nicholas were playing swordsmen. But don't worry," she assured him, taking his hand as they walked again. "My father and the King both suspected that we had affections for one another. They're not blind, after all."

"And neither had any objection?"

"You're not locked in a prison cell, are you?"

"Not yet," he said with a nervous grin. "But I suppose there's still time."

Megan burst out laughing. "You are endearing when you agonize so, Leo. But didn't I tell you there was nothing to worry about? We may be of royal blood, but we're still regular people. Besides, since you're soon to be leaving, I suspect Father and Grandfather decided not to make an issue of our relationship. What their attitude will be when you return though, I cannot say. But I believe they have no qualms at the moment."

Leo sighed. "Still, how am I going to face them next time now that I know you talked about us?" He shot a fearful glance at Megan. "You don't suppose–?"

"Suppose *what?*"

"That King Justin is sending me on this mission just to get rid of me?" Megan rolled her eyes. "It's a possibility."

"Are you sure you didn't fall and bump your head when you climbed those rocks, Leo Marsh?" Megan giggled, playfully taking his arm in hers. "Let's go inside and I'll fix you a cup of tea to quiet your wild imagination. Can't have you running off to save the kingdom all bothered and such," she said as the Citadel shimmered in subtle shades of blue in the stabs of autumn sunlight.

A thick fog lay upon the river the following morning, rolling over the fields behind the Citadel with catlike stealth. But a few hours after the sun's ascension, the swirling white mist dissolved. Soon the capital was alive again with autumn's cool embrace under a clear blue sky. Inside, Nicholas and Leo made final preparations for their journey later that night, packing up the extra clothes that Nedry had provided and reviewing their map.

They enjoyed a last lunch with Megan and Carmella in a private dining room, feeling as if they were about to leave and never return. Megan and Leo noted a vague sadness in each other's eyes, both wishing they had just one more day to spend together. Nicholas then raised a cup to his friends, wondering when or if they would ever be together again.

Shortly before midnight, Nedry escorted Nicholas and Leo through the Citadel and out a minor back gate, not speaking a word to the guards at their post. An hour earlier, they had said their last goodbyes to Megan, King Justin, Prince Gregory and Tolapari, at which point they were given possession of the medallion. Nicholas agreed to carry it, slipping the leather cord over his neck and concealing the object beneath his shirt. Now, bundled in long wool overcoats, the two travelers followed Nedry across the fields beneath a starry black sky to an area beyond the stables and lodge houses. Much farther to their right, neither could see any bonfire near the area where Carmella and Jagga had set up camp, assuming they were asleep for the night.

"Here we are," Nedry whispered, greeted by the gentle snorting of a pair of horses in the cool night air. "The animals have already been laden with your food, clothing, supplies and weaponry, so you are all set to go. Your own horses, Leo, will be cared for in your absence."

"Thanks, but those are my father's horses," he replied, "which he'll be anxious to get back one of these days. I mentioned they were holding up nicely in the short post I wrote yesterday telling them of my delay. My brother will be less than thrilled about the extra chores he'll inherit. I thanked him in advance in my letter," he joked.

"This is quite a jump from selling apples or keeping track of flour sales, isn't it?" Nicholas said, wondering where the next few days would take them.

"Then I suggest that you both keep your eyes to the road and your wits about you. A lot of people are depending on your success," Nedry reminded them.

"We'll try not to disappoint," Leo said as he climbed on his horse, anxious to start their journey. Nicholas did likewise, taking one last glance at the few remaining lights burning inside the Citadel.

"Follow the river to the second bridge and cross there," Nedry advised. "It's only a few miles away. Then find a place to spend the night in the foothills. You can begin your true journey in the morning. Good luck to you both."

"Thanks, Nedry," Nicholas replied. He and Leo nodded a brief goodbye before disappearing into the night.

Nedry watched as darkness devoured the two travelers before returning to the Citadel to finish some work that was piling up. He still had much to do before seeing off his next two travelers the following morning.

Nedry sat hunched over his desk after midnight, finishing a few correspondences. He scribbled upon a sheet of parchment with a quill pen he repeatedly dipped in an ink bottle. When he completed the last note, he carefully folded the parchment twice and slipped it into an envelope before lighting a blue stick of sealing wax. He allowed several drops to fall upon the back flap to fasten it shut. He then affixed the official impression of his office into the wax with a metal seal and sat back in his chair, satisfied that his work for the day was finally finished.

He sighed as a bone-deep weariness crept over him. He gazed out a round window beyond the desk into the inky darkness, too exhausted to move. Candlelight reflected off the window pane and Nedry stared at the hypnotic flickering, his eyelids growing heavy. Two tiny images of the burning candle also appeared lower in the window and close together, from time to time disappearing for an instant before returning. He amusedly watched what he assumed was a trick of his imagination before rousing himself awake, determined to retire to his room for the night. But as he was about to blow out the desk candle, he again noted the two tiny reflections low in the window pane. He studied them for a moment before realizing that they hadn't been conjured up by his imagination. The reflections originated on the *outside* of the glass.

Nedry dashed toward the window, but before he had a chance to throw it open, the tiny pair of reflections disappeared in a swirl of blackness. He unlocked the pane and hastily swung it open, spotting a fleeting ebony shadow and hearing the distinct flutter of wings. He knew that the crow he had noticed earlier in the day had been perched on the ledge, the candle flame reflected in its eyes. His deepest suspicions had been confirmed. A spy of the air had been in their midst and Nedry felt vindicated that he had sent Nicholas and Leo away under the cover of darkness. He hoped his next move tomorrow morning would doubly ensure their safety.

Brendan and William hadn't expected to see Nedry as they finished an early breakfast in the nearly empty dining hall overlooking the fruit orchards. The King's advisor sat down with them, wishing the boys well on their excursion.

"We had said our goodbyes yesterday and planned to slip out at the crack of dawn," Brendan explained. "We didn't want anyone to bother with us another moment as we've imposed on the goodwill of the Blue Citadel quite enough."

"Nonsense," Nedry said. "It's an honor to accommodate the grandsons of King Rowan in any way we can. I figured I would accompany you to the stables and send you off. Besides, I'd like to double check that all the supplies I ordered for you have been loaded onto your horses." He noticed that Brendan and William each had a long wool overcoat draped on the backs of their chairs identical to the ones sewn for Nicholas and Leo. "The royal seamstresses did a fine job on those coats. They'll come in handy as the weather turns."

"Indeed. So thank you again for all your help," William said, finishing up a biscuit with his tea, his eyes filled with the zeal of youth and the prospect of a new and exciting day to explore.

A short time later, Nedry escorted the two princes to the stables under a slowly awakening pale blue sky. Brendan and William climbed on their horses, eager to start their journey south. Nedry walked with them along the road past the Citadel storage cellars until they reached the front cobblestone courtyard and gardens, the clip clop of horse hooves echoing off the stone walls. The King's advisor waved to the two brothers as they continued on alone through the front gates, wishing them well on their journey as they disappeared from his sight.

Nedry walked away from the archway at the main entrance, waving good morning to the guards on duty as he made his way back to the Citadel. He sat on a small bench beneath a tree near a row of hedges along the front, already tired as if he had been awake for hours. He leaned back and gazed up at the sky, waiting for a sign he hoped might not reveal itself. But less than a minute later, a faint shadow drifted across the courtyard as a large crow abandoned its lofty perch near the top of the Citadel and landed upon a stone post near the front iron gates. The sleek black bird craned its head this way and that before taking flight again, riding high upon the autumn currents while keeping its curious eyes fixed upon the two riders who had just departed the courtyard.

Nedry's heart fluttered and his body felt cold when he witnessed the sight, wondering if he had overstepped his authority by manufacturing this diversion. Though he tried to convince himself that everything would turn out fine since Brendan and William would only be gone for a handful of days, he already regretted that he had manipulated the start of their journey for his own purposes. But if a bit of trickery provided Nicholas and Leo some added protection on their mission, it would be well worth it. He stood to return to work, not yet prepared to divulge the details of his maneuver to King Justin. And as there was nothing to do now to affect the outcome, he decided to let events unfold as they may and await the results, hoping his good intentions would pay off.

482

CHAPTER 32

Silent Pursuit

Brendan and William traveled leisurely along King's Road for an hour, bundled in wool coats and with hoods draped over their heads, their white wisps of breath rising in the chilly morning air. In time they passed through a community of farmhouses and small shops slowly awakening beneath a lemon yellow sun. Here a narrow road broke off from the main thoroughfare, heading southeast through a terrain of lush, low hills, vigorous streams and fertile farms. From what Brendan recalled while studying maps in the Citadel library, he estimated that they'd have to traverse a twenty mile stretch before linking up with the southern portion of River Road in Bridgewater County which extended for miles beyond Arrondale's border.

"If we follow the Pine River at that point, it'll take us to the north end of Lake Lasko near the Red Mountains," he told his brother, his sea blue eyes shaded from the morning light by the rim of his hood. "It's a huge lake. An impressive sight, I'm sure."

"After several days of riding, that'll be a good place to camp out for a while before turning back," William said, inhaling the sweet scent of decaying leaves and wood smoke that spiraled up from chimneys on distant rooftops. "I'm glad you asked for permission to leave, or I would have done it myself. I needed to get away from the Citadel. I'd have gone mad wandering the corridors and thinking about Mother and Grandfather all alone in Red Lodge."

"Unfortunately, they're not alone," Brendan reminded him.

"I know. But I'm sure they feel alone, and we can't do anything about it yet." He sighed, flipping off his hood and running a hand through his mop of wavy blond hair. "I want to be in the first group of men when we take back our homeland."

"I don't know if Prince Gregory will allow that, though I understand how you feel," he said as they trotted along the dirt road. "It'll take time to raise enough troops and ready supplies for the march, so be patient. And we're allowing a few extra days for Nicholas and Leo to return with the key. If they open the Spirit Box just as we're approaching Red Lodge, think what an advantage we'll have over Caldurian and the Islanders. With the Enâri troops out of the way, the others won't know what hit them."

"Let's hope they can time it so," William said, glancing at his brother with a slight grimace. "But first let's hope they return with the key."

Brendan nodded. "*Whenever* they open the Spirit Box will be good timing, eliminating five hundred Enâri in one stroke, not counting Vellan's own in Kargoth."

"If only we could be there to see it." William took a drink from a water skin hanging from his saddle. "I could do for a bite to eat. How about you?"

"Are you ever not hungry?" Brendan smirked, pointing to a clump of oak trees a half mile down the road alongside a field of tall grass. "We'll take a short rest near those trees and let the horses graze if your stomach can hold out for a few more minutes."

"I can manage," he said as a slight breeze picked up, pushing along a fleet of low lying clouds from the west.

A short time later they dismounted beneath the partial shade of the nearly leafless oaks and allowed the horses to graze in the grass and drink from a nearby stream. They plopped down against the massive trunks and enjoyed an apple and half a biscuit each with their water, savoring the small morsel and the precious freedom of the open road. Soon after, a large black crow glided through the air and alighted on one of the tree branches, flapping its wings a moment later and landing on a patch of bare ground just outside the ring of shade, searching for bugs in the dirt.

"I think it's after your food," William joked.

"I'm not too poor to share." Brendan ripped off a large crumb from his biscuit and tossed it to the bird who greedily gobbled it up.

"Don't be too generous or it'll follow us all the way to Lake Lasko and back." William chuckled as he munched on his apple. "If that old bird thinks he's getting any of my meals…"

"He wouldn't stand a chance."

Brendan stared at his brother with mixed emotions as they leaned against the tree, an uneasy sigh escaping his lips. William noted his concern and sat up straight, knowing that something was on his brother's mind. He took another bite of his apple, expecting a reply to his unspoken question, but none was forthcoming.

"All right, Brendan, out with it. I know by that oh-so-serious expression on your face that something's afoot. What's going on?"

Brendan couldn't help but smile. "Can't let one slip past you, Will. You're just too old for me to fool anymore."

"For the most part." He tossed his apple core into the grass. "What's on your mind?"

Brendan distractedly traced his finger through the cold soil. "It's about our journey. I think it's going to extend a little bit farther than to Lake Lasko."

"That's fine. How much longer?"

"How does all the way to Grantwick sound?"

"Grantwick? That's the capital of Drumaya," he said. "From Morrenwood, that's over twice the distance to the north tip of the lake."

"Thanks for the geography lesson, Will, but I already know that. Still, that's where I mean to go. Are you with me?"

"Why wouldn't I be?" his brother asked, a bit perplexed.

Suddenly the nearby crow flapped its wings and uttered a mournful caw, ascending into the air like a launched arrow. Gavin had heard enough to confirm where the two travelers were heading. The messenger bird flew to the northeast with lightning speed to inform Caldurian of their destination, knowing the wizard would devise a plan to retrieve the medallion before the pair could deliver it to the wizard Frist. Moments later, Gavin's tiny black shape faded into nothingness against a vast blue backdrop.

"Someone is sure in a hurry to get somewhere," Brendan muttered.

"And not even a *thank you* for the bread crumb," William lightly added. "But back to what you were saying. Why do you want to travel to Grantwick? There might not be enough time to return to the Citadel before the army sets out for Montavia."

"We'll have plenty of time and some to spare. Don't be such a worrywart." He playfully punched his brother on the arm.

"I'm not worried. Just wondering why you want to go all the way to–" Then the reason suddenly hit him. "You're going because of what Eucádus had said at the war council, right?" Brendan nodded. "I don't think King Justin will be too keen about this."

"That's why I muddied the truth about wanting to leave the Citadel for only a few days." Brendan reminded his brother of the heartfelt words Eucádus had spoken to them while the plans for war were being arranged. "I know King Justin didn't want me to involve myself with politics, but what would it hurt if I had a brief conversation with King Cedric? If we tell him everything that happened to us in Montavia, illustrating the real threat posed from Kargoth and the Northern Isles, maybe he'll be willing to join us and help liberate Rhiál. Though it doesn't help Grandfather directly, any strike against Vellan can only assist us in the long run. We've got to try, Will. If we're to govern Montavia some day, then what better training in diplomacy than this?"

William shrugged. "Who am I to argue with my older brother? Besides, you're going to be King before I am, so…"

Brendan laughed. "So it's my reputation on the line?"

"Something like that," he said as he got to his feet and stretched. "Now let's quit lazing around and get moving. You've just more than doubled the miles of road ahead of us, so no time to waste jabbering away beneath a tree. There's work to do."

"As if you even know the meaning of the word." He slapped his brother on the back before they climbed on their horses and continued along the road as distant clouds floated in from the west.

On the sixth day of the journey, they rode along the shores of Lake Lasko, the dark, snowcapped peaks of the Red Mountains looming ominously to their right in the west. Sparkling sunlight reflected off the surface of the vast lake roiling with choppy waves in a gusty breeze, the distant horizon a razor straight line beneath cornflower blue skies. The two princes wore heavy overcoats as they sat around a crackling fire, basking in the warmth as Brendan finished heating up a pan of venison stew he had prepared from their supplies. He dished the meal into two wooden bowls, handing one to his brother. William passed out some biscuits and greedily dipped one into the hot meal.

"Not bad. Picked up a few cooking tips from Clovis?"

"Grandfather said that to be a good leader one should make an effort to know about the livelihood of every person that serves under you," Brendan replied. "Besides, just like you, I love to eat."

"No denying that," he said, greedily consuming the steaming fare. He stared out across the lake for several moments, contemplating all that had happened over the last couple of weeks. He wondered what he might have done during the invasion had he been king, though glad such a fate wasn't his so early in life. "Do you ever think hard about it, Brendan? Being a king, I mean."

"Sure. I have to, Will, being next in line for the throne. Ever since Father died four years ago, well…" Brendan looked at his brother, seeing hints of their father's facial features in the boy. Though they had both inherited their mother's blond locks, the two brothers were similar in most other appearances to their father, Prince Kendrick, including his good-natured temperament. "But I'm in no hurry to exchange my silver ring for the royal one upon Grandfather's hand. He has plenty of good years left in him."

"I know that. I'm just wondering if you think you'll be ready when it's your turn. Since Father will never be king, you were deprived of a chance to be at his side to learn from him and…"

Brendan sighed, sensing his brother's sadness. "I miss him, too, Will. So does Grandfather. And I'm sure he regrets everyday that he sent him to lead that mountain survey in his place. But it was an accident."

"I know."

"But I've learned much at Grandfather's side, too, particularly how much he loves us and would protect us with his very life," he said. "Yet he trusts our abilities as well, which is why he hinted that we escape and seek out Arrondale's help. So if ever one day–" He suddenly stopped, hearing a rustle in a thicket of nearby trees, causing him and his brother to look behind them simultaneously.

A moment later, a large brown deer stepped gingerly out into the light, gazing toward the fire while standing completely still as if studying the two strangers who had intruded upon its territory. Brendan and William smiled at the animal but remained stationary so as not to frighten it away.

"Luckily for it we have plenty of food," William said, "or I'd send you off hunting for that deer."

"We have no bow and arrows, or have you forgotten," Brendan reminded him. "Unless you expected me to chase after him with a knife?"

"Not really," he said, polishing off his stew. "I wonder if it's hungry." William grabbed an apple out of a pouch lying nearby and sliced it in half with a knife. "Let's see."

He stood and gently tossed one of the apple halves toward the deer where it landed a few feet from the animal. The deer flinched and then cautiously approached the piece of fruit, sniffing it out in a patch of tall, withered grass before noisily devouring it. A few moments later, the deer took a few steps closer to the campfire and stopped, staring at William and the other half of the apple in his hand.

"He's expecting it now, Will. Don't tease the animal," Brendan said, observing its formidable antlers and mesmerizing stare that seemed to probe the very depths of his thoughts. He watched as the deer consumed the second piece of apple William had thrown its way, fascinated yet slightly unsettled by the animal's peculiar gaze. There was something about the buck's eyes that bothered him, though he couldn't reason why as the disquieting sensation persisted. He finally told William not to feed the animal anymore when he saw his brother reach for a second apple. "Better save the rest for us, Will. He'll find his own food."

"All right," he said, helping himself to more stew. "There's a little left. Finish it off?"

"No, you go ahead," Brendan muttered, his attention still fixated on the deer. He clapped his hands several times and spooked the animal so that it ran back into the trees. Yet later, after they had doused the campfire with lake water and continued south along the road, he couldn't shake the uneasy feeling that that particular deer was still observing them deep within the dark of the woods.

Twilight slowly enveloped the surroundings as the sun dipped behind the Red Mountains later that day. An orange and purple hue tinted the wispy cloud strands lingering near the western horizon. Brendan and William had passed through several farming communities on their journey, but now approached a larger village nestled in a swath of pine along the lakeshore. Each looked forward to a restful night at an inn, believing that after many days on the road sleeping in woods or abandoned barns, they deserved a small treat. Both were eager for a hot meal and a warm bed as their horses ambled along the road on the outskirts of a village called Parma, but they stopped suddenly near the border when seeing a large shape lying upon the side of the road in the shadows.

William first suggested that it might be a dead animal until they rode closer and saw the shape slowly rise to its feet. Brendan slowed his horse, holding out a hand to caution his brother. But when they were close enough to distinguish a man's face in the fading light, they breathed easier. A middle-aged gentleman, sporting a black coat and gray hat, greeted them with a wave of his hand.

"Hello, gentlemen," he softly spoke, sounding out of breath.

"Are you all right, sir?" Brendan inquired. "We saw you upon the roadside and–"

"Oh, I'm fine now, having had a little time to sit here and recover. It's the other man who tried to rob me that received the worst of it, I think, even though he got away with my horse." The man laughed. "Hit him with a large stick in the kneecap just before he galloped away, I did. Howled like a wolf that stepped on a thorn. Serves him right."

"You're certain you're not hurt?" Brendan asked as he dismounted.

"Still in one piece, thank you. You needn't worry."

"Where'd the other man go?" William asked. "Do you want us to contact the local authorities?"

"No point," he replied. "He fled south through Parma about ten minutes ago and probably disappeared into the foothills. I'll never see him or my horse again. Luckily I kept my money on my person and found a piece of an oak branch to fend him off. He'll think twice before robbing again. The name is Sorli, by the way."

Brendan introduced himself and his brother, offering to escort Sorli into the village. When they mentioned that they were going to look for an inn to spend the night, Sorli recommended an establishment close to the lake and offered to buy the brothers some dinner in exchange for their kindness.

"It's not necessary," Brendan said. "We're happy to help, what little we did."

"Your concern is worth more than you can imagine," he replied. "How many people would assist a total stranger in these troubled times? My heart will break if I must take no for an answer."

"Well, in that case…" William said, his appetite growing.

About twenty minutes later, the trio found an inn named The Silver Trout, a large stone and wood structure built near a group of towering pines close to the lakeshore, its windows aglow with soft yellow light as the sweet scent of chimney smoke permeated the air. Soon Brendan, William and Sorli were dining on fried lake trout and washing it down with fresh apple cider. Amid the low light and competing conversations, they savored the meal while talking over their respective trips south, though Brendan and William avoided any mention of their true identities or the real purpose about traveling to Grantwick. On the sly, Brendan indicted for his brother to remove his silver ring as he had done, just to be on the safe side.

"I have several business interests on the south end of the lake," Sorli explained during the meal, "and I'll have to purchase another horse now or I'll be late for my appointments. When are you two supposed to arrive in Grantwick?"

"We have no appointed time," Brendan said, seated across from Sorli and studying his features in the dim light. The man's full face and sleepy eyes under a mess of brown hair reminded him of no one in particular, yet seemed oddly familiar nonetheless. "We're visiting our elderly aunt and uncle for the winter to help them out on their farm."

"If we like it, we just might stay through the spring!" William said, eager to add to his brother's fabrication. "I mean, what could be more fun than digging in the dirt and milking cows from first light to sunset?" he said while shoveling a forkful of fish into his mouth.

Brendan offered an awkward grin to their dinner host while looking askance at his brother. "Seems Will can hardly wait to start."

"Apparently so," Sorli agreed. "And best of luck to you both, whatever your future holds," he said before polishing off the last of his cider. As he set the cup on the table, he looked at the two brothers as if an idea had just struck him. "Pardon me if I'm imposing, but since our paths are the same for the next day or so, I was wondering if you'd allow me to accompany you until I reach my destination. After my recent encounter with that highway bandit, I'm embarrassed to say that I'm a bit anxious about taking to the road again all alone, especially in the dark hours."

"I don't see why not," William said. "We'd love some company, right, Brendan?"

"Uh, sure," he replied, briefly distracted as he found himself unable to keep from casting furtive glances at Sorli, growing more convinced that he had seen this man somewhere. Had he ever visited Montavia before? Or was it simply his imagination run wild? Brendan was tempted to ask the man if he had ever traveled to Triana but decided he had better not. Still, he could not shake the vexing sensation each time he looked into the man's eyes, feeling as if someone other than this man was staring back at him.

Later, after a final drink and some conversation near the main fire in the crowded common room, Sorli excused himself for the night, prepared to retire to his room. Brendan and William shook his hand, thanking the man for providing them such a wonderful meal.

"I look forward to your company on the road in the morning," Sorli said. "The owner informed me that he will have one of his stable hands find a horse for sale in the village, so I'll be ready to ride directly after breakfast."

"Glad to hear it," William said, wishing him good night. Brendan simply raised his hand goodbye as Sorli disappeared through the doorway. He continued to stare in the same direction for a moment after the man had departed, his mind oblivious to all else.

"That was a nice gesture," William said, flopping back in his chair by the fire. "I'm so stuffed that I couldn't eat another bite. And that's saying something for–" He looked curiously at his brother who stood frozen in place. "What are you looking at, Brendan? Sit down and relax. We won't be stopping at an inn every night."

Brendan turned and looked at his brother, his face pale and taut. "We need to go out and check on our horses, Will. Come on."

"Why?" he asked, contented to sit by the fire. "The stable hands will take good care of the team. No need to worry."

Brendan sat next to William and looked him straight in the eyes, speaking in a low voice so that no one would hear. "Yes, Will, there *is* a need to worry. Just follow me outside as if nothing's the matter and I'll explain everything. You have to believe me."

"You can't be serious, Brendan?" William uttered the comment to his brother about fifteen minutes later as they guided their horses along a rutty dirt path off the main road outside of Parma. A nearly full Fox Moon rose high in the east, casting silvery light upon the countryside and distant tips of the Red Mountains standing guard in the west. "That's the silliest thing I've ever heard!"

Moments earlier when they had abruptly left The Silver Trout, Brendan told his brother not to ask him any questions while they retrieved their horses from the stables and engineered a stealthy escape from the village. After they had turned off the main highway to conceal their whereabouts, planning to keep to minor roads and open fields for the next day or so while still heading south, Brendan finally let William pummel him with questions.

"How could Sorli have actually been that–" William sighed with exasperation, unable to complete the sentence. "Again, you can't be serious!"

Brendan composed himself as they rode quietly through the night, a handful of dimly lit farmhouses scattered across the rolling hills. "Will, I'm being utterly serious, or why would I have rushed us out of there? I don't trust Sorli. He's not who he claims to be. I can't explain it, but he is not what he appears."

"And you saw proof of this in his *eyes*? How come I didn't?"

"Maybe you're too trusting and too young–or were just too consumed with your fish dinner," he replied. "I'm not sure. But like I said, that strange feeling I experienced every time I caught a glimpse of his eyes was the exact same reaction I had when I observed that deer you had fed on the roadside earlier today. It was as if..." Brendan looked up at the moon, wishing his brother had been able to confirm his fears. "It was as if somebody else existed behind those eyes in each case, quietly spying on us. My heart and soul were chilled to the core."

William found it impossible to believe his brother. "So what you're saying is that Sorli and that deer are one and the same? That the deer followed us all the way to Parma and–*turned into Sorli*?" He couldn't keep a straight face when he spoke the words to his brother.

"Something like that," Brendan muttered, finding it difficult not to acknowledge the humor in William's statement. "I know it sounds preposterous, but I can't deny the threat I felt to our safety, Will. Stranger things have happened in this world, and I didn't want to take a chance that harm might come to us, especially to you."

"I appreciate that, Brendan, but still…"

"I know, Will. And you have permission to laugh at me all the way to Grantwick," he replied. "Still, I feel better that we're back on the road and out of sight from curious eyes. After we're south of Lake Lasko, we'll return to the main road. I'll be happy when we get past these mountains and are riding through the Swift River Valley. The sight of the Ebrean Forest will do us both good. But for now, just accept what I did even if you can't believe it. Maybe one day we'll be able to laugh about this over a pint of ale."

"Looking forward to it," William said, grinning at his brother in the moonlight. "Though I've already started on the laughing part!"

They avoided the main thoroughfare for a couple more days as a precaution, traversing little used cart paths, open fields and patches of scrubland before finally returning to the road to speed up their journey. After they had traveled several more miles, the road veered to the east, wrapping around the southern portion of the lake, so the two brothers again left the road and continued west to the Swift River Valley through a gap in the Red Mountains. They passed uneventfully along the valley, crossing various tributaries that fed into the Swift River until they reached the west bank of the main watercourse. From a distance, Brendan pointed out the northern tip of the Ebrean Forest now in view, happy to see the soothing stretch of green beckoning to them like an old friend.

"It won't be long before we sit down to speak with King Cedric," he said, eagerly anticipating the end of their journey.

"I can only imagine what words King Justin will have with Nedry once they realize we're not coming back as soon as we promised." William chuckled. "I hope Nedry isn't scolded for helping to arrange our little expedition."

"Nedry can honestly say he had no idea of our intentions," Brendan replied. "Still, I feel a bit guilty for putting him in that position, but what's done is done. We'll suffer any consequences when we return. In the meantime, we have miles to ride before we reach those woods. Grantwick isn't much farther beyond."

They rode their horses under a blue sky dotted with billowing clouds drifting eastward like massive ships upon a borderless sea. Finally, six days after leaving The Silver Trout in secret, the sibling princes approached the city of Grantwick as cool purple twilight descended upon the sprawling countryside. They guided their steeds along the quiet streets of the outer sections of town under the high Bear Moon a day past first quarter. Brendan, spotting a young couple passing by hand in hand in the opposite direction, stopped to ask which road led to the center of Grantwick. The man tipped his hat, obliging him with a detailed answer.

"But it won't do you any good going there tonight."

"Why's that?" William asked.

"The four gates in the wall surrounding King's Quarters and the adjacent settlements are barred at night. Have been since the end of Old Summer. No one's allowed in until sunrise."

"All because of the war in the east and the troubles in the Northern Mountains," the woman elaborated after Brendan pressed them for more details. "King Cedric is a cautious man, fearing that Vellan's influence over Surna, Linden and Harlow will eventually work its way here. Though we have the Ebrean Forest as a protective shield, Kargoth's cold breath and dogged grasp still reach far."

"Do you think he'll ever invade your lands?" Brendan asked. The couple looked at each other, unsure how to answer. "Well, we've taken up enough of your time. Thank you for your help. My brother and I will find another place to pass the night."

William waved goodbye as he and Brendan sauntered down the road on their horses, soon finding the way to the center of Grantwick from the eastern side. As the coupled had warned them, the main gates were barred and guarded inside and out, so they rode by from a distance, not even bothering to approach the men on duty for information.

"I'd rather enter in the morning without any fuss," Brendan said. "I want as few people to know about our business as possible."

"So in the meantime?" William asked.

"Seeing that it's such a lovely night, I suggest we ride all the way around the wall to the west side facing the forest. It's not far to the eaves of the Ebrean from there," he replied. "We'll camp out under the boughs and practice what we'll say to King Cedric tomorrow before treating ourselves to a good night's sleep."

"I'm not very tired, but a warm fire and a full meal would be just the thing," William said as the line of thick wooden posts of the distant wall drifted slowly past.

Several hours later, Brendan opened his eyes to the glowing embers that remained from last night's fire. The nearly third quarter Fox Moon climbed in the east behind a veil of thin clouds. The Bear Moon had disappeared in the west while they slept. He closed his eyes again, bundled in his coat and hood and wrapped in a blanket, calculating that it was still a few hours until sunrise and eager for more sleep. But a moment later his eyelids snapped open. He sat up and looked around. William was missing.

He searched near the campsite, whispering his brother's name several times, but receiving no reply. He could see no silhouette of an individual wandering near or far in the light of the moon and grew fearful. After waiting by the embers for a few more minutes and hoping that William would return, he decided to walk along the edge of the woods, first in one direction, then in the other while softly calling out William's name. After wandering about five hundred feet to the south while staying parallel to the tree line, Brendan stopped and surveyed the area.

"Will! Where are you?" he called out as loudly as he dared, his fear and frustration mounting. He turned around and headed back north, planning to return to the campsite before walking the same distance in the opposite direction. But he hadn't gone a hundred feet when he caught sight of a stooped shape searching the area around the campfire and near the horses. He shook his head and sighed. "Will!" The startled figure looked up, observing Brendan fast approaching before fleeing into the woods.

When Brendan reached camp, he stood with arms akimbo as he scanned the trees. "Will, enough of this!" he whispered harshly. "Where are you? Come out of the woods at once." But only stony silence followed. Brendan fearfully wondered if it was really William whom he had spotted. He grabbed a dagger from his supply pack and a large stick from the kindling pile and plunged into the woods to follow the stranger, believing he would lead him to his brother.

He searched for almost a half hour, listening for sounds of snapping twigs or rustling leaves, but the tenuous trail had evaporated. He burrowed deeper into the woods, not certain which direction he was going and using faint glimpses of filtered moonlight to guide him. But even that proved useless after a while as more clouds rolled in and darkened the sky. Nearly an hour after entering the Ebrean Forest, Brendan realized that he was lost and would have to wait until dawn before he could find a way out. He walked a few more uncertain steps, blaming himself for the horrible situation that had befallen him and his brother. He was ready to drop down on the forest floor in despair when he noted a dark shape sprawled out at the base of a nearby tree, shifting slightly in the gloom.

Brendan clutched his dagger in one hand and the stick in the other as he inched closer, but the object remained still. When he reached the shadowy mass, he leaned over it and slowly exhaled a sigh of relief. He gently prodded the slumped figure with the toe of his boot, tossing the stick aside and sheathing his dagger.

"Wake up, you lazy troublemaker!" he said to his brother. Brendan's delight upon finding William safe and sound outweighed, for the moment, his urge to scold him.

William opened his eyes. "*Wha...*" He looked around, for a moment disoriented until he recognized his brother in the murky shadows. "Brendan, what are you doing here?" He sat up straight and rubbed an ache in his shoulder. "By the way, where's *here?*"

"We're in the middle of the woods, Will. Lost, I think."

William nodded, his recollection of events returning to him. "I remember now," he said, scowling at Brendan. "Why did you run away after we talked last night? And what were you talking about? You sounded quite mad."

Brendan sat next to his brother. "What are *you* talking about? The last time we spoke was before we fell asleep by the fire."

"Not quite," he said. "We spoke to each other inside the woods when you asked me all those strange questions."

"I did?" Brendan's heart beat faster, certain his brother hadn't been dreaming as he recalled the dark figure who had been spying around the campsite. "Tell me exactly what happened to you, Will. Every detail."

Prince William yawned. "All right. I went for a walk around midnight, I guess. I couldn't sleep well," he said, continuing to massage his sore shoulder. "You were sound asleep. I walked along the edge of the woods for a good distance when I heard a voice calling my name from inside the trees. It sounded like you, Brendan, and as I thought you were playing a trick on me, I went into the woods after you."

"That wasn't me. But what'd you find?"

"*You*, of course, though it took some doing following your voice this way and that through the trees. I'm not quite sure how deep inside I chased you, because as you see, I couldn't find my way back out. I decided to sleep here until the morning light." William gazed curiously at his brother. "Why'd you do that?"

Brendan rolled his eyes. "Will, it wasn't me. I'd been sleeping the whole time until I awoke and saw you missing. I went searching for you." He noted a veil of confusion upon William's face in the vague, predawn light. "Tell me about this conversation with–*me*."

"You asked me if I had it safe."

"Had *what* safe?"

"Had *it* safe. That's what you wanted to know, Brendan. Did I have *it* safe?" William shrugged. "When I said I didn't know what you were talking about, you grew angry and demanded to see it."

Brendan leaned back against the tree, contemplating William's mysterious narrative. "And this person who apparently looked like me didn't give you any clue as to what he was talking about?"

"None at all. After insisting a second time that I let him see it, I replied again that I had no idea what you–or rather *he*–was talking about," William explained. "Then he ran away. I tried to follow but lost the trail. And well, here I am."

"And here I am with you," Brendan remarked before telling his brother about the figure he had spotted looking for something near the campsite and the horses. "I guess we can assume that he was looking for *it* there as well, whatever *it* might be."

William scratched his head. "You're truly saying that it wasn't you who I chased after through the woods and talked to?"

"It wasn't, Will. How many times must I insist?"

"I suppose no more than that," he said, unnerved. "So who did I talk to, Brendan? I wasn't dreaming. And what was he looking for that he apparently thought one of us possessed?"

"I don't know, so we'd best keep our eyes open," he gravely replied. He stood and surveyed the ominous stretch of woods coming alive with a hint of gray. The cool, damp air felt as oppressive to their spirits as did the sudden change in their fortunes. "If somebody out there is after us, I want to find him first."

"Agreed," William said, wearily standing up. "But first we have to find our way out of here. Any suggestions?"

CHAPTER 33

A Cabin in the Woods

William shook his brother awake as he lay curled up on the forest floor, his face pale and cold in the dull morning light.

"*Now* who's being the lazy one?" he said as Brendan slowly sat up and rubbed his eyes. "On your feet. It's getting brighter."

Brendan yawned. "Did we both fall asleep?"

"We needed the rest, though I've been up awhile. From the look of things, I'd say we're lost. I see gray sky above but no sign of light anywhere around us."

"I guess we choose a path and start walking." Brendan stood and worked the aches out of his heavy limbs. He deeply inhaled the pine scented air to revive himself. "I could stand some breakfast, but all our supplies are back at the campsite with the horses."

"Maybe they'll enjoy a pleasant meal," William joked, pointing a finger in one direction. "I think we should go that way."

"Why?"

"It looks like the least menacing section of the forest."

"Not by much," Brendan muttered as he examined the endless prison of towering trees woven together with suffocating shadows. The cold ground was littered with decaying leaves, broken twigs and moss-shrouded limbs that had fallen in years past. "Well your choice is as good as any, so lead on. But if we come out on the other side of the forest with the Northern Mountains looking down on us, I'll have you to blame."

"We'd be that much closer to Kargoth," his brother said lightly. "We could have a sit-down with Vellan and try to talk some sense into him. It'd save King Justin the headache of going to war."

"If only it could be so simple, Will. I fear that Vellan's mind is as stubborn and immovable as the mountain he lives in." He grabbed a branch lying on the ground and snapped part of it off across his knee, using the larger piece as a walking stick. "What possesses him to grasp power just for the sake of exerting it over others, well, I could never quite figure out. He only brings misery to people."

"And Caldurian is a lesser version of him," William said, wondering what mischief the wizard was inflicting upon Montavia.

"But still powerful," his brother reminded him. "We saw it for ourselves and had better not forget it." He rested a hand on William's shoulder, looking bluntly into his eyes. "If either of us is king one day, we must always remember how we felt when we were attacked–when the Islanders, Caldurian and those Enâri creatures stormed Red Lodge and threw our lives into chaos. We must vow never to let that happen again, Will, and be prepared to defend Montavia at all costs."

William nodded, barely able to reply, not used to hearing his brother speak so earnestly. "I promise," he managed to utter, seeing the wisdom in his brother's eyes and feeling for a moment as if he were already king. "I'll remember."

"Good," he said, offering a reassuring smile before they began their trek through the woods. He wondered what Montavia might look like once they returned, certain that his mother and grandfather were enduring the hardship with honor and resolve. He hoped their ordeal would soon be over once Prince Gregory entered Triana with him and William riding at his side. Though he had told his brother not to expect them to be leading the charge, Brendan couldn't help envisioning that scenario nonetheless. His imagination was the only power he could wield at the moment to save their kingdom.

They hiked through the Ebrean Forest for over an hour, feeling as if they were traveling in circles. William uttered aloud that he may have picked the wrong direction. Brendan smiled to himself, thinking the same thing but wanting to give his brother the opportunity to voice that notion first.

"Maybe you should choose another way, Brendan, so we can find our way out. I'm getting hungry."

"What makes you think I'll fare any better?"

William grunted. "Can it get much worse?"

"I suppose not." Brendan pointed to a low rise in the ground several yards away. "Let's hike up that knoll and look for any sign of daylight through the trees. If we see nothing there then we'll head that way," he decided, swinging his arm ninety degrees to the right. "I wish the clouds weren't so thick this morning. I can't tell where the sun is located. Maybe they'll thin out as the day wears on."

"Or before we wear out. I'm so hungry that the tree bark is starting to look good!"

Brendan marched up the knoll as William followed, feeling hungry himself but putting it out of his mind. His first duty was to lead them back to the campsite and then arrange an audience with King Cedric. But if he couldn't accomplish either soon, all his addresses to William about being a good leader would ring hollow. He wondered if their journey to Drumaya had been such an intelligent idea after all, but as he reached the top of the knoll, his spirits lifted. In the hilly stretch of forest before them, the intoxicating sound of splashing water caught their attention.

"A stream!" William shouted, scrambling down the other side of the knoll and racing toward a narrow waterway flowing among moss covered rocks and creating a series of mini waterfalls. The gentle rush of water emitted a hypnotic language of its own that whispered among the trees. The brothers were soon greedily drinking as if the water itself was a fine meal on its own.

"That definitely hit the spot," Brendan said moments later as he stood up, brushing the dirt off his trousers. "Now if only a platter of roasted venison would magically appear for our dining pleasure! You wouldn't turn your nose up at that, would you, Will?" He noticed his brother standing frozen in place, staring off in the distance. "What are you looking at?"

William turned, smiling. "I can't promise you venison, but would a cabin do?"

"What are you talking about?"

"*That!*" William pointed to a cluster of trees beyond the stream. "What does it look like to you?"

Brendan strained his eyes and gazed among the distant shadows, confirming his brother's discovery. "You just made my day, Will. But who could be living out here in the middle of nowhere?"

"Let's find out," he said eagerly. "I've no objection to sampling some middle-of-nowhere food if you aren't."

"If the prince so decrees it, then that's what we'll do," Brendan jovially spoke as he searched out a path of rocks and carefully led them across the noisy stream.

Moments later, he and William emerged through a clump of trees and cautiously approached the two-story cabin built of roughly hewn pine logs in a small clearing. A stone chimney was blackened around its edges, but no swirls of smoke escaped at the moment. Thick wooden shutters sealed any window openings. The front door was closed. Tall grass and weeds, now dried out, had grown messily around the area. Thick clouds passed overhead. Brendan signaled for his brother to follow him around to the side and back, but there the weeds had grown untended among heaps of discarded pine branches. A stack of chopped wood stood piled against the back wall.

"Doesn't look like anyone's around," Brendan said.

"From the appearance of this place, it doesn't seem as if anyone's been here for quite a while. Shall we go inside?"

Brendan nodded. "But let's knock to be sure," he said as they made their way around to the front of the cabin.

A moment later, Brendan rapped his knuckles against the door, though neither expected an answer. He repeated this a second time, and after waiting a few moments in the dense silence of the forest, he decided that the place was temporarily abandoned. He grabbed the handle and pushed the door open, a stale darkness greeting them as they stepped inside.

"Hello," Brendan called out, his words eaten up in the shadows. "*Hello?*"

"Guess nobody's home," William said, his courage growing.

He walked past his brother and pushed open one of the front shutters, allowing more light into the room. A stone fireplace stood against the side wall, a blanket of cold ashes and charred logs piled inside. An old table in the center of the room was surrounded with a half dozen wooden chairs. Several shelves filled with dishes, clay storage jars and other items lined most of the downstairs walls. A ladder constructed from sturdy oak branches that had been stripped of their bark stood against the back wall and extended through a hole in the ceiling to the room above. When William eyed a cloth sack lying on a narrow counter below another unopened window, he scurried over to examine it. He smiled when he peered into the bag, reaching inside and removing an apple. He tossed it to Brendan before pulling out another one for himself.

"Should we?" Brendan asked.

"If we find any parchment and ink, we'll leave a note promising to repay the food," he said with a grimace before taking a bite of the apple. It tasted sweet and crisp, causing him to speculate that perhaps the owner of the cabin had recently been here. "Eat up while we have the opportunity."

"I suppose you're right," Brendan replied, joining his brother in their apple breakfast. As he savored the fruit, he turned around when a rustle of leaves sounded outside the still opened front door. He flinched, startled to see a young deer roaming in the clearing, its nose to the ground searching for a morsel to eat. "I can't believe it," he softly said, indicating for William to take a look. "We seem to attract those animals, don't we?"

William laughed. "If it wasn't a different deer, I might be suspicious and think we were being followed."

"Well we're not feeding it this time," he said as he promptly closed the door. "Let's build a fire and warm up, then we can check the upper room. Until we determine our bearings, there's no point in leaving this place. We might as well make ourselves comfortable."

Less than an hour later, they were sitting in front of a blazing fire, each having finished a second apple and a bit of dry bread they found wrapped in cloth next to the fruit. They stretched their legs, warming the soles of their boots in the soothing billows of heat.

"Though it's early, I feel as if I could doze for hours," William said. "The little sleep I got last night wasn't the restful sort."

"There are mattress rolls and blankets upstairs," Brendan reminded him. "Take a nap if you'd like. We won't leave for an hour or two until the sun's higher. Maybe some of the clouds will have burned off by then and we'll be able to find our way out." He stood and walked across the room. "In the meantime, I'll fill one of the containers in the stream. I'm thirsty." After he spotted a clay pitcher sitting on one of the cluttered shelves, he happened to glance out the window and laughed as a cool draft wafted inside. "Guess who's still keeping an eye on us, Will?"

"What's that?" he asked, craning his head back.

"Our friend is nosing about," Brendan replied, admiring the deer feasting on the vegetation outside. "It must have heard us talking about the apples."

"Feed him from your share," William said. He stood and stretched, feeling tired. "I think I *will* go upstairs and rest. I don't want to nod off if we ever meet with King Cedric."

"Go ahead. I'll be back shortly." He closed the shutters just as the deer raised its head. "Pleasant dreams."

"Thanks," William muttered as he started to climb the ladder to the sleeping loft, his eyelids growing heavier by the moment.

Brendan took the clay pitcher from the shelf and walked to the door, grabbing the handle. "But don't expect to sleep away the entire morning," he amiably warned his brother who was halfway up the ladder. "I'll wake you when I'm ready to leave."

"Don't hurry on my account," he replied with a yawn.

"Lazy heap," Brendan said with a chuckle as he swung open the door.

He immediately jumped in fright, startled to petrified attention as he gazed at the shadowy, grotesque figure looming in the doorway. The pitcher fell from his hand and shattered as he stumbled backward, crying out in terrified disbelief. William, his head nearly through the hole in the ceiling, looked down at the sudden commotion and felt his heart grow cold. The wizard Arileez stood tall in the doorway, the lifeless eyes in his skeletal face locking gazes with Brendan. The wizard's shock of white hair flowing beneath the hood of his battered cloak belied the darkness of thought and purpose coursing through the arteries and nerves of his ancient body. Arileez removed his hood and advanced toward Brendan, the young prince experiencing a strange familiarity emanating from deep within the eyes staring back at him, the exact same eeriness he sensed when looking into the eyes of both Sorli and the buck they had fed along the road. When the initial shock wore off, he found his voice and warned his brother.

"Will, get out of here!" he shouted, scrambling to the fireplace and grabbing a metal poker. He raised it in the air to fend off Arileez, daring him to take another step. "Who are you?"

"Give it to me," Arileez commanded in a voice both rasping and shrill, draining the hope out of all who heard it.

William looked down at the surreal scene as he hung onto the ladder, feeling as if a dreadful dream had wrapped itself around his mind before he had fallen asleep, yet knowing it was all too true. He had to help his brother. "I'm coming, Brendan!" he said despite the tightening of his vocal cords and the pounding of his heart.

"Stay up there, Will! I'll follow if I can!" Brendan shouted.

"Enough!" Arileez sputtered, his patience already spent. "Give it to me now."

"Give you *what*?" Brendan said, fending him off with the metal poker though forced to take another step back.

"Give me the medallion!" he demanded as he grabbed one of the wooden chairs and hurled it at his foe. Brendan jumped out of the way before it exploded into a cascade of splinters against the stone fireplace, the metal poker falling out of his hand.

"*Brendan!*"

"We don't have it!" Brendan shouted, having nearly forgotten about the object as he scrambled to his feet, reaching for the lost weapon. But when he saw Arileez rush toward him, he grabbed a wooden leg from the broken chair and swung it wildly at the wizard, grazing Arileez's arm before he spun out of the way.

"Enough!" he shouted, rushing at the prince as he attempted to retrieve the metal poker.

But as Brendan grabbed the object and started to raise it, Arileez extended his right arm and made a long sweeping movement through the air. Brendan lurched backward and watched the wizard's hand move past his chest in seeming slow motion, his eyes wide with disbelief as the tips of the wizard's fingers liquefied and transformed into a sharp talon of a bird of prey, the pointed, curved weapon quickly enveloping the entire hand. When Arileez brought his arm back to attempt a second swing, Brendan raised the metal poker to keep his attacker at bay, unable to avert his eyes from the fantastical reconfiguration he had witnessed. But in that moment of distraction, Arileez grabbed the fire poker with his left hand and tried to wrench it from Brendan's grip. When Brendan instinctively turned to pull back, Arileez swiped the talon through the air again, striking him squarely in his abdomen, the razor-sharp tip piercing through the prince's garments and skin like the icy blade of a merciless sword.

Brendan stood frozen in place as if a jolt of lightning had struck him. Slowly his right fingers uncurled and the piece of metal fell to the floor. In that same moment, he bowed his head and saw the wizard's talon imbedded in his body, for an instant unable to speak or feel or react, but only watch in muted wonder. Arileez removed the talon with a sudden pull and Brendan collapsed to the floor, his knees buckling under the cold, heavy weight of his body. He lay on his back, hearing William's terrified screams in the background as his fading eyesight observed the wizard's talon transform again into a normal hand, only now the five fingers were stained with his own blood. As he helplessly watched Arileez wipe the blood on the folds of his cloak with cruel satisfaction, the sounds around him swiftly diminished until he could hear only the faint beating of his heart. He blinked a few times as the light grew dim and gray and murky, his mind awash in a flood of vivid memories until the young prince of Montavia closed his eyes and then heard and saw no more.

"Brendan?"

Arileez looked up when he heard the frightened call, seeing William hanging onto the upper rungs of the ladder, overwhelmed with shock and disbelief. He stared at his brother's body, unable to absorb the reality that had just bombarded him. When his gaze locked onto the wizard's vacant eyes, he felt as if a sharp slap to the face had flung him back to reality.

"I will ask you the same question," Arileez said, his voice tinged with a seething undercurrent ready to explode if the boy did not provide the answer he sought. "Where is the medallion you removed from the Blue Citadel?"

"We don't have it!" William said, his eyes burning with tears. "We never did."

Arileez took a step closer as William simultaneously raised himself up another rung. "I don't believe you. I was told–"

"I don't care what you were told. We don't have it!"

"Who does?"

"Why should I tell you?" William snapped. "Who are you and why do you want it?"

"That's not your concern. Tell me what I wish to know or I'll kill you, too."

"Others took the medallion," William replied as he gingerly climbed one more rung of the ladder, his head just below the opening. "That's the truth. I have no idea where they took it. No one else was permitted to know."

"Who has it?" he sputtered.

"Two others," he said, for a moment unable to recall Nicholas and Leo's names, hesitating to mention them for fear they might be tracked. His mind felt on fire as the unyielding pressure from the wizard's gaze held him with an invisible hold. But using every last bit of strength, he resisted his will. "Their names are unimportant. And beyond that, I swear I know nothing more!"

Arileez seethed at the boy's defiance, but ratcheted down his grating tone to place the prince at ease and perhaps gain more information. "I was informed that two individuals are seeking out the wizard Frist to have the key to the Spirit Box remade, but you claim not to be one of them," he replied. "Perhaps I believe you, but I still need to know the location of the wizard whom they seek."

William swallowed, unsure how long he could stall, certain that Arileez would spring at him once he was convinced that this line of questioning was futile. "We weren't told that information. Their mission was kept secret. My brother and I were just roaming the countryside for our enjoyment. I give you my word."

Arileez stroked his chin as he considered his options, believing the boy was telling the truth. Somewhere along the way, the messenger crow had relayed faulty information. "You are sure this is all you know?"

"I swear!" William said.

Arileez shook his head as he looked at the floor, seeming to have made up his mind about what to do. But before the wizard could react, William raced up the final rungs of the ladder and disappeared through the opening into the upper room, fearing he would soon be dead like his brother. The low-ceiling room was dark expect for the outline of pale daylight seeping through cracks around the thick shuttered windows on either end. William rushed to one window and pulled open the shutters, allowing a flood of daylight and cool air into the stuffy room, but the opening was too small to get through. He looked around for anything to use as a weapon or hurl down at the wizard through the floor, but there was nothing except several thin mattress rolls and blankets.

He teetered on the verge of panic as he ran across the floor to the opposite window. As he tore past the opening in the floor, a hand reached up and grabbed him by the ankle. William tumbled face first to the floor and spun around on his back, yanking his foot free from the wizard's grip as he bashed the heel of his other boot into the bony fingers holding him prisoner.

"Let go!" he shouted as the ghostly figure of Arileez ascended slowly through the hole in the floor, a pale gleam of mindless death in his eyes. But as the wizard tried to raise himself higher on the top rungs of the ladder, he inadvertently loosened his grip, allowing William to pull his leg free and scramble to the other end of the room.

William ripped open the shutters, relieved to find a larger window. He glanced over his shoulder. Arileez had pulled himself up into the room and was ready to spring. William looked out the window and saw the piles of discarded pine branches below, knowing they should cushion his fall when he jumped. He heard footsteps. Arileez was heading his way. No time to think. He had to leave now!

"Stay!" the wizard commanded, lunging at William who was teetering on the narrow sill.

Just as he was about to leap down, Arileez pushed William in the back, causing him to lose his balance and tumble out the window in an uncontrolled fall. The wizard heard the boy cry out as his body disappeared, then all went silent. Arileez stuck his head through the opening and peered at the ground, seeing the prince sprawled out upon a pile of pine branches, eyes closed and face to the sky, his body unmoving. Arileez sighed with irritation, wondering if the trip was worth his effort.

Over the next few minutes, the wizard searched the two bodies and every corner of the cabin, but found no sign of the medallion that Gavin had insisted would be traveling south to Grantwick with these two men. But since he had found nothing here or at their campsite which he had searched hours ago, he accepted the fact that he had been gravely misled and followed the wrong people. After one final sweep of the cabin, Arileez stormed outside, leaving Brendan's body alone on the cold floor in the somber silence.

As he briskly trudged across the leafy clearing, the wizard extended his arms. His body suddenly liquefied while reducing its size at the same time. In the next instant, Arileez swiftly transformed into a large, red-tailed hawk. With a few powerful flaps of its wings, the bird shot airborne and was soon flying freely over the vast emerald expanse of the Ebrean Forest. He glided northeast on the shifting currents, disappointed that this mission had failed, yet anxious to get back to the village of Kanesbury and report his findings to Caldurian.

CHAPTER 34

The Clearing

The aroma of simmering soup enticed William to open his eyes. For a moment he thought Martha had left a tray of lunch in his room at Red Lodge. Had he overslept? Had he been sick? The ceiling looked unfamiliar and a cool, damp cloth had been placed behind his head. An uncomfortable throbbing in his neck nudged him fully awake, and soon the imagined images of Martha and Red Lodge were replaced with the horror that had been unleashed.

He whispered his brother's name as he struggled to sit up, his heart pounding, his head swimming. "Brendan!" he called again before going silent, noting three men sitting at the table and staring at him as if he were an exhibit at a village fair. "Who are you?"

A fourth man stooping over the fireplace while stirring a kettle of soup over the crackling flames echoed his question. "Who are *you*?"

The stranger's unshaven face beneath a head of dark brown hair appeared honest enough to William, though he was hesitant to say anything until he learned more. The man joined the others at the table, at which point William realized that he had been lying on the floor on a straw mattress brought down from the loft. He glanced at the area near the fireplace. His brother's body was missing.

"Where's Brendan?" he asked. "Where's my brother?"

The men looked apprehensively at each other before the first one answered. "My name is Ramsey. These are friends of mine. My I have your name?"

William glanced about, wondering who these people were. But as they had apparently tended to his injuries, he decided he could at least trust them with his name. "I'm William." He picked up the cool cloth and held it to the back of his head.

"You had a bump, but no cut," one of the others said. "You knocked yourself out on a chunk of wood wedged under those pine boughs out back."

"I think I'll survive." William again looked at the area where Brendan had fallen. "Please, where is my brother? He collapsed over there after he was..." He took a few uneasy breaths, swallowing hard, wondering if what had occurred a while ago had actually happened. "Where is he?"

Ramsey fixed his uneasy gaze to the floor before looking up at William. "What happened here? We found you unconscious outdoors about two hours ago and your brother inside on the floor. Who did this to you?"

The young prince shook his head. "I don't know. He appeared out of nowhere. He was standing outside the door. When Brendan opened it to get water, he attacked us." William, his spirit distraught, his eyes burning and wet, pleaded again for a simple answer to his question. "Where is my brother?"

William knelt on one knee, alone beneath a pine thicket on the edge of the clearing. His arm rested on a low pile of split logs that had been neatly stacked in a rectangular pile over Brendan's body. This would serve as a temporary grave until he could accompany his brother home to Montavia where he would be properly buried with the honor he so deserved.

Earlier, Ramsey had confirmed what he already knew in his heart–that his brother had perished from the terrible wound inflicted upon him. Ramsey had shown William his brother's body which had been removed from the cabin and brought outdoors after wrapping it in a blanket. William felt cold and disoriented when he removed the covering from Brendan's face, his brother's eyes forever closed, his countenance peaceful and fair. At his request, Ramsey's men dug a shallow grave and placed the wrapped body within, covering it with pine branches before building a cairn of wood over the deceased.

Now, William knelt there in the late morning silence, alone with his brother, alone with his leaden thoughts, wondering how he would ever break this wretched news to his mother and grandfather as a stream of hot tears flowed down his face.

Later, while downing a bowl of hot soup and bread, William cautiously answered some of the questions the men posed to him as they sat around the table. He told them he was a citizen of Montavia who had been visiting the capital of Arrondale with his brother when they decided to journey south for some adventure.

"You travel much for one so young," Ramsey said as he dipped a chunk of bread in his soup, sensing that William wasn't telling him everything yet willing to give the boy leeway considering the trauma he had suffered. "Why are you roaming in these parts, and how did you get lost in the Ebrean?"

William studied the faces of the quartet over the rising steam from his bowl, wanting to trust them to a point but knowing he had taken an oath in the Citadel not to reveal information about the medallion. Though he had spoken of the same to his attacker, he discounted that breach considering the circumstances. But these men who had fed him and tended to his injuries deserved some answers, so he decided to be honest yet vague until he found out more.

"Could you first tell me if I'm far from Drumaya's border? My brother and I only took refuge here to wait until the sun rose higher before we tried to find our way back."

"You are deep in the forest, but not far from the kingdom," Ramsey said. "From where in Drumaya did you enter the woods?"

"We were in Grantwick and then hiked to the Ebrean, camping along the tree line. The gates to the King's Quarters had already been closed for the night." He helped himself to more bread, ripping another piece off a large, round loaf and soaking it with broth. Only now he realized how truly hungry he was.

"Why were you planning to visit the inner city?" another man asked as he leaned back in his chair, picking at his teeth with a sliver of pinewood.

William paused as he raised a bit of bread to his mouth. "We were, uh–sightseeing." He greedily devoured the piece of food and ate another spoonful of soup, momentarily avoiding eye contact.

"There weren't enough interesting sights in Arrondale's capital that you had to travel all the way down here?" Ramsey asked, eliciting a few chuckles from the others. "Or have you had your fill of Morrenwood already?"

"Not exactly," William replied, knowing that they would press him until he supplied a reasonably logical answer. After helping himself to a few more spoonfuls of soup, he looked up warily, debating how much information he should offer. "Well, my brother and I were hoping for an audience with– I mean, hoping to meet with–" He froze, realizing he might have already slipped up. He ate another mouthful of bread as Ramsey looked on curiously. "We were to meet with someone. A friend."

Ramsey smiled. "Does this friend have a name?"

Moments of strained silence followed as the flames snapped in the fireplace. A cool breath of morning air poured in through the open window. William finished the last of his soup, pushed the bowl aside and glanced at Ramsey. "Forgive me if I'm not completely open with you. I appreciate what you've done for me, but... Perhaps if you told me more about yourself, I might be able to say more."

Ramsey grinned, noting that the others were likewise amused. "I think what you're really saying is that if we told you more about ourselves, you might be able to decide if you trusted us or not. Yet here you are in our cabin, eating our food, and with your injuries tended to." William's face turned a light shade of red. "Don't worry. I take no offense at your caution, especially after what you've endured. But since you are an intruder here–though by necessity–you shouldn't be surprised that we don't open up to you simply because you ask. You have to earn our trust, not the other way around."

William locked gazes with his questioner, feeling as if he had unintentionally insulted the man. "I'm sorry. I didn't mean…"

Ramsey dipped the last of his bread into his soup bowl and finished eating. "As I said, I take no offense. Besides, I am the least of your worries. Even if I wanted to answer all your questions, there is someone else who you must report to first before we can allow you to return to Grantwick. You may be silent to us, but he will certainly want to know everything that happened here regardless of your doubts and insecurity." Ramsey walked over to the hearth and threw another log on the fire, stoking the flames with the metal poker.

"*He?*"

"My leader," Ramsey said, glancing at William over his shoulder. "We all report to someone, don't we?"

"I suppose. Could you tell me his name? And is he around here?" he asked, briefly looking about the room.

Ramsey stroked his chin. "Right to the point. I admire that trait in both friend and foe. But I won't reveal his name to you. That is his privilege. But we'll leave shortly and seek him out. It'll be quite a hike deeper into the trees before we reach his residence. You may want some more bread and soup first."

"All right then. Thank you," William said, realizing he would get no more answers at this time while feeling both eager and fearful about what might lie ahead. He briefly debated whether he should make a run for it the first chance that presented itself, risking hunger and being permanently lost. Or would staying close to Ramsey and his men be the wiser alternative? Even though he didn't completely trust them, he realized that he didn't yet fear them and took that as a good sign.

"Be prepared to leave in another hour and expect some brisk hiking. We should arrive by twilight."

"All right." With the interrogation of sorts over, William suddenly felt tired and overwhelmed by the day's events. Though he absorbed with interest all that Ramsey had told him, his thoughts and emotions turned to his brother lying beneath the somber clouds outdoors. "If you don't mind, I'd like to sit with Brendan again for a while. I feel that…"

"Of course," Ramsey said, his voice radiating concern. "We'll stay in here to discuss our journey. Or would you like one of us to accompany you?"

"No thanks. I'd prefer the solitude, if you please," he replied, though in the back of his mind he wondered if Ramsey suspected that he might try to flee. As he stepped outside the cabin in the deepening quiet, William wondered where they would be going and who exactly would be greeting them when they arrived.

They talked little during the first two hours of the hike. Though the trees were thick and shadowy, the gray blanket of clouds had begun to thin, allowing rays of sunshine to stab through the treetops as the early afternoon progressed. The scent of sweet pine mixed with the sharp pungency of decaying leaves being crushed underfoot. William, dressed in his overcoat to ward off a damp chill, breathed in the revitalizing aromas. Ramsey and his men wore hooded jackets of lighter material beneath thick cloth ponchos in shades of russet, umber and fern. The travelers halted occasionally to drink from passing streams and refill their water skins, and later stopped near a large outcropping of rock to eat a brief lunch of dried venison, corn biscuits and apples. The meal tasted like a feast to William after such a strenuous pace. Though he and Brendan had traveled many miles south, they had leisurely ridden on horseback. Only during their escape from Montavia had he moved with such speed and determination.

He recalled the flight to Morrenwood with his brother, and though their mission to seek help from King Justin was both grave and urgent, he had enjoyed their time traveling together, sharing stories and ideas while passing through the mountain valleys and across the roads and fields of Arrondale. Now, he was on a completely different journey with four strangers, yet William felt incredibly alone. Part of him wished that Brendan had survived the attack in the cabin instead of himself, knowing that his brother was far better suited for the burden of leadership should that eventuality ever arise. He vowed to do his best nonetheless, knowing he owed that to Brendan who gave up his life to save him.

Another hour had passed when they began to climb up a gradual rise in the forest floor. Here the trees grew thinner and the light brightly shone. William took pleasure in the rich blue sky as the clouds broke and drifted east. He savored the warm touch of sunlight upon his face as it made its westward trek toward the Northern Mountains.

"We are near one of the outposts," Ramsey said, stopping to allow everyone to catch his breath. "It is little more than an hour's hike from there to our destination. Now rest for a moment."

"Gladly," William said, sitting upon a rock to stretch his aching legs. He drank greedily from a water skin Ramsey had provided as the others quietly discussed the way forward. He realized how foolhardy it would be now to make a run for it, guessing that he would surely remain lost and probably die of cold and starvation. But just as he grew comfortable, briefly closing his eyes and thinking that this respite might last awhile, Ramsey called for everybody to continue. William sighed and reluctantly got to his feet, wondering if the journey would ever end.

They continued on swiftly like a blur of shadows. But less than twenty minutes later as they hiked along a gurgling stream, a half dozen men suddenly stepped out from behind several trees just ahead, all armed with swords or bows at the ready. William stopped with an audible gasp and looked to Ramsey for guidance, expecting the worst. But when he saw a faint smile spread across his face and noticed the armed men lowering their weapons, his rapidly beating heart began to settle as he realized that the men must be from the nearby outpost.

"Tell me that you have a kettle of stew on the fire, Harbus, and I will be in your debt," Ramsey joked as he approached the leader of the group and shook his hand.

"Would you expect anything less?" he replied with good humor, his long dark hair peeking out from beneath a weather-stained hood. "Bread, cheese and ale are on the table, too." He glanced at William. "Who is the boy?"

"Ladle out the stew and I will tell you. But be quick," Ramsey said. "I want to reach the Clearing before sundown."

William shot a curious glance at Ramsey. "The Clearing? What's that?"

"That is our destination," he said.

After the five guests sat down to eat with Harbus and his men at the cabin outpost, Ramsey told how he had found William and his brother's body at the hunting cabin, though unable to explain the terrifying entity who had committed the atrocious murder. William listened in subdued silence as the men talked, not in the mood to rehash the details, though knowing he'd have to explain everything at some mysterious place called the Clearing.

"My condolences for your loss," Harbus said to William.

"Thank you," the prince replied. "Your words are a comfort."

"And your culinary kindness is a blessing," Ramsey added as he finished his meal. "But we cannot tarry much longer if we are to reach the Star Clearing before sunset. I need to make my report and get some rest before the final march back to Grantwick."

"You have information from some of the other Clearings?" Harbus asked.

"There are others?" William piped up, realizing he shouldn't have interrupted as Ramsey cautioned him with a raised hand.

"Two are on the march now, Harbus, and they will already be encamped near Grantwick before we arrive."

"So after all these years of preparation, we're finally on the move," he replied with a mix of satisfaction and unease. "At times I thought we were simply putting down roots like the trees we've lived among, never really intending to make a stand in the end."

"You were always an impatient one," Ramsey said. "But for good or ill, the time has come." He then addressed William, sensing the numerous questions and boundless curiosity bottled up inside him. "And yes, there are other Clearings within the Ebrean. Five in all. From what I've observed of you so far, I think I can trust you with that bit of information."

"That is where you live? In the Clearings?" William asked. "Not in the cabin where you found me?"

Ramsey chuckled. "That cabin where we found you is just one of many small lodges we have built for our hunting parties to use when needed. The four of us were part of a scouting team and stopped there for a meal before returning home to the Star Clearing. We do not permanently man those buildings. However, others do constantly occupy a series of outposts like this one that surround each Clearing. We protect our residences and monitor all who may roam about."

"Brendan and I might have eventually found you somewhere along the way in our lost travels," he said.

Harbus grunted, scratching his whiskered face. "Chances are *they* would have found you first."

William sighed regretfully. "Sadly, they didn't."

Ramsey sensed the crushing grief weighing down upon William, knowing that the best thing right now would be for him to keep moving. He quickly downed the last of his ale and gave his compliments to Harbus. "We can't tarry here any longer. We must continue for the Star Clearing. I'm sure William is as anxious to get there as we are."

William nodded as he rose from the table with Ramsey and the others, quickly gathering their supplies for the final stretch. After wishing Harbus farewell, the five travelers exited the cabin into the cool, crisp air of late afternoon and proceeded northward through the maze of trees, rocks and decaying undergrowth. Flashes of clear sky gazed down from above, its blue richness having deepened as the sun continued to dip slowly in the southwest.

Ramsey and his friends traveled the last few miles to the Star Clearing in record time, propelled by a longing for the journey's end and the anticipation of a leisurely meal among family and friends. William thought that the final stretch was swiftly covered as well, though he was motivated mostly by the desire for answers from someone in charge. He needed to know what the leader of the Star Clearing had in mind for a young prince from Montavia who had lost his way in the woods.

As he contemplated the matter, he hypnotically stared at his boots while treading over the cold ground, hardly noticing that the pace of their hike had lessened. Nor did he hear Ramsey speak aloud to the others as the last brilliant beams of sunlight shot across the emerald treetops in the southwest.

"I said we're *here*," Ramsey repeated, tapping William on the shoulder.

"*Huh?*" he muttered, looking up while shaking his mind free of muddled thoughts. "I was just…" He held his breath for a moment in mid-sentence, astounded by the sight before him.

They had just climbed a slight rise in the forest when they halted and stood before a huge clearing tinged with the golden light of the setting sun. The open space, roughly circular in shape, measured over a half mile in diameter and was surrounded by a wall of living trees. And though William was utterly impressed when seeing a rural, yet vibrant village suddenly appear out of nowhere in the middle of a forest, from a bird's-eye view the Star Clearing would appear as nothing but a tiny speck against the vastness of the Ebrean as a whole. A slight breeze stirred among the thatched rooftops of some of the nearer cabins as the scent of wood smoke wafted through the air. A handful of white stars were discernible in the darkening skies of twilight.

"This has been our home for the last seven years," Ramsey told William with wistful pride. "Yet I would abandon it tomorrow if Harlow, Linden and Surna were free nations once again."

"You and the others once lived in the Northern Mountains?" he asked. Ramsey nodded. "I'm guessing not Kargoth," he added with a slight grin.

"Your questions will be answered soon," he replied. "Enough talk now. Let's conclude this journey. It's been almost a week since any of us have seen our wives and children. I can only hope that they have missed us half as much as we've missed them."

They wandered through the Star Clearing across a patchwork of dirt paths, passing several homes already glowing with firelight. All were ready for the coming colder months as piles of chopped wood had been neatly stacked along the sides of the buildings. Most homes stood beside generous plots of land that had been thriving gardens during the spring and summer, but now lay fallow, awaiting the inevitable snowfall of the winter season. A large stream passed through the middle of the Clearing, though William noted that several homes had wells dug nearby. Near the farthest edges of the circular village along the northern border, a handful of large fields were cultivated to grow corn, hay, apples and other vegetables, while chickens and livestock were raised on a separate farm nearby. William assumed that the other four Clearings were similarly arranged, guessing that Ramsey and his men were involved in some type of protracted struggle against Vellan. Though he terribly missed Montavia after only a thirty-one day absence, he couldn't imagine the heartache that Ramsey and the others felt after being separated from their homes for seven long years.

As they advanced toward the center of the Clearing, one by one, Ramsey's three companions bid him and William farewell and returned to their homes. Since he was in charge of this expedition, it was Ramsey's responsibility to report his findings before he could finally see his own family. Soon after, he escorted William to a sprawling wood cabin of two stories set beneath several tall trees and mottled with the purple and gray shadows of twilight. Burning torches were affixed in metal holders near the main doorway and along the front of the building. Off the cabin's main section were several smaller wings of similar construction built at varying angles to match the flow of an adjacent stream coursing through the gently sloping landscape.

"Is this where your leader lives?" William asked. Though the structure didn't match the scale and elegance of Red Lodge, it was impressive to behold nonetheless.

"He does," Ramsey said, "though other families reside here as well. In fact, we all lived here to begin with when the first few of us moved to the forest. This was the original building we constructed that served as our home. Now it mainly houses our government, so to speak, as the rest of the Star Clearing expanded around it. But many still visit the large common room a few times each week to catch up on the news of the day or to relax during some of their free time."

"Still, your leader must consider himself very lucky to live under such a fine roof. His part of the residence must be vast indeed."

"Quite the contrary," a vaguely familiar voiced called down from a small wooden balcony above, the tall figure wrapped in murky shadows. William couldn't distinguish the man's face, though he recalled hearing his voice recently. "My quarters here are quaint, to put it politely, and my wife wonders why we don't build our own cottage nearby. But I tell her that since I was elected to represent this Clearing, I should remain where I am accessible to everyone." The man noted that Ramsey was grinning at his comment. "And how was your trip to the Fox and Pumpkin Clearings?"

"Productive. The men are already making their way to the border of the Ebrean, but I can provide you the details later. I am just glad to be home," he said. "And I have brought a guest."

"So I see. Hurry inside. We'll meet in the small dining area. We'll have dinner while we talk. I hear there's roasted lamb tonight."

"We'll be right there," Ramsey replied as the man stepped through a small doorway and disappeared inside.

"He seems an affable sort," William said. "And though I look forward to meeting him, his voice is vaguely familiar. But how could that be?"

"Maybe hunger is playing tricks on your mind. As you've never been to these parts before, how could you have ever met our leader?" he asked. "Anyway, the sooner we're inside, the sooner all your questions will be answered." He indicated for William to follow him up a stone path to the front entrance, after which Ramsey opened a sturdy but ornate door constructed of pine wood, allowing the warmth within to greet them. They stepped inside as the flaming torches gently flickered in the evening air.

After passing by the common area occupied by a handful of people, quiet conversation and a crackling fire, Ramsey and William walked down a narrow hallway. They entered a small room with three round tables and a fireplace built into one corner. The table nearest a window had three place settings and a flickering candle. The pine walls, floorboards and ceiling beams had been recently cleaned and polished, and the warmth from the fireplace made William think he had stepped into a fine inn along a well-traveled highway. A moment later, someone entered the room behind them.

"My wife is going to join us for dinner, Ramsey, but we'll have to set an extra plate now that you've brought a guest," said the man who had been on the balcony. "Who do I have the honor of welcoming to the Star Clearing?"

Ramsey and William turned around to greet the man, but before Ramsey could utter words of introduction, he noticed that William and his leader were staring at one another with expressions of vague wonderment as if each were trying to attach a familiar face with a forgotten name. Though they had only briefly encountered one another sixteen days ago, it didn't take long for either of them to recognize the other's face.

"*Eucádus?*" William articulated the gentleman's name with mild shock, remembering that this man from Harlow had asked him and his brother several questions after they arrived unannounced during the war council at the Blue Citadel. The tall man with light brown hair, leaf green eyes and a freshly shaven face appeared less haggard and anxious than he had been at the sometimes boisterous session. "You're the leader of this place?"

"Indeed I am." Eucádus was pleased that the boy had remembered him since he and Brendan had been bombarded with inquiries from so many people during that hectic afternoon in Morrenwood. "And how does a young prince from Montavia find his way deep into the Ebrean Forest to my very doorstep?"

Ramsey stood there agape. "You two know each other?" An awkward grin was plastered across his face until he suddenly processed Eucádus' last few words. "And did you say *prince*?" Eucádus nodded. "Of Montavia?"

"It seems that Ramsey is not aware of your lineage, Prince William. Did you not see it fit to inform him?" he asked with amusement.

"The truth is, we had both kept personal information to a minimum as there were issues of trust," he said. "But had I been informed by name that you were the leader Ramsey had spoken of, I would have felt more at ease to reveal my true heritage." William reached into his pocket, remembering that he and Brendan had removed their silver rings while in the village of Parma. He slipped it on his finger, glad to have a bit of normalcy return to his life. "I suppose it's safe to wear now that I'm among friends."

"You have nothing to fear here, Prince William," Eucádus assured him. "Right, Ramsey?"

"Not a thing, Prince William," he meekly replied, hoping he hadn't inadvertently insulted the boy through his words or actions during the day.

"That's good to hear," he said, "though I would much prefer it if you would both call me William–or even Will–if it wouldn't be too much to ask. Though I'm proud of my title, it tends to wear on me a bit outside of formal occasions."

"Then Will it is," Eucádus said, admiring the boy's good-natured disposition. "And where is your brother? Did you make this unexpected journey to our temporary homeland by yourself?"

"He did not," Ramsey said, uncomfortably clearing his throat.

"So where is Brendan?" Eucádus glanced at William for an answer, noting a sad, faraway look in the boy's eyes now glistening in the firelight. When William and Ramsey stared knowingly at one another with grim expressions, Eucádus sensed that something terrible had transpired. His heart suddenly filled with anguish over words not yet spoken, over words he was dreading to hear.

While eating dinner with Ramsey, Eucádus and his wife, Liana, William explained how he and Brendan had left the Citadel while preparations were made for the marches to Rhiál and

Montavia. Only after they were on the road, he said, did his brother reveal his true intentions of seeking an audience with King Cedric of Drumaya, hoping to convince the monarch to join in the fight for Rhiál's freedom. The others listened with great interest about their encounter with Sorli and of Brendan's suspicions of that man and the deer along the roadside.

"I guess my brother was correct," he said after he recounted in grim detail the attack and astounding transformation of the stranger's hand while in the cabin. Though William described Arileez' appearance in extraordinary detail, no one at the table had ever encountered or heard of the likes of him before.

"A strange species of wizard, perhaps, or some vile sorcerer of the kind the world has never known," guessed Eucádus. "But what troubles me most is how he found you—and why. What was the creature after?"

"I can tell you," William said as he ate a forkful of roasted lamb and washed it down with some apple cider, scanning the three faces watching him in fascination. "Well, to a certain extent."

"Please do, but in your own time," Liana kindly said, offering a motherly smile as she gently touched his arm. She could tell by his strained expression and the tone in his voice that William had suffered deeply. She knew he would never completely recover from the horror he had witnessed.

William nodded gratefully for her concern. "I had taken an oath with others in the Blue Citadel not to reveal what it was that that thing who attacked us was after. However, I could tell you without technically violating my oath that it is something which might serve in our fight against Vellan. If certain people are successful in their mission to locate a particular person in an undisclosed place, well then, Vellan and some others might be in for a surprise."

Eucádus glanced at Liana and Ramsey, trying to gage their reactions to what they had just heard, noting they were as perplexed by William's words as he was. He sat back and rubbed his chin, not even trying to make sense of the particulars. "I would never ask you to violate an oath, Will, and I won't begin now. But how does a mysterious mission to find somebody living who-knows-where tie in with the attack on you and your brother?"

"The man who killed Brendan assumed that we had the object to which I referred, to which I took an oath not to reveal." He tiredly shrugged his shoulders. "Why he assumed that, I don't know. And perhaps I never will."

"A horrible case of mistaken identity," Ramsey said.

"My brother and I were attacked twelve days after we left Morrenwood, so I can only conclude that the individuals whom that strange entity were really after are now far away and safe from his grasp." William wondered where Nicholas, Leo and the medallion were at this moment and if they had yet located the wizard Frist. "At least in that respect, Brendan's death was not in vain."

"From what you told us, your brother fought and died valiantly," Eucádus said. "You should be proud of him. He would have been a fine addition to the fight we are going to take to Vellan."

"So you are going to confront him?" William asked. "I had suspected as much from what little I learned, but Ramsey did not give me many details about the lives or intentions of those in the Five Clearings."

"He was just being cautious, as he should have been. But as you did learn that there are five of these communities," Eucádus said, "Ramsey must have had an inkling that you were on our side."

"Though I had no inkling that you were a prince," he replied with a genial smirk.

"Still, I would like to know more of how the Clearings came into existence if it is not too much to ask," William said.

"I shall be happy to tell you," Eucádus replied as he refilled each of their cups from a wooden pitcher of apple cider. "All of us living here and in the other Clearings are from the three mountain nations currently under the cold shadow of Kargoth. Ramsey hails from Linden, closest of the three to Vellan's border, while Liana and I call Harlow our home. We now all reside inside the protective borders of the Ebrean Forest for these past seven years."

"Why?" William asked.

"It is not because we prefer it," Ramsey said, "but because our lands have been turned into shells of their former, independent selves. Our leaders have allowed this to happen, whether out of fear, greed or outright collaboration with the enemy."

"Vellan essentially commands the destiny of our countries," Eucádus continued, "including our trade, our armies and the very

NICHOLAS RAVEN AND THE WIZARDS' WEB - VOLUME 1

movements of the people themselves. His so-called advisors have been accepted into our governments, willingly or not, after violent attacks had been staged throughout the trio of nations, killing many people and destroying homes, businesses and farms. And though Vellan's Enâri troops cross our borders at will to raise havoc from time to time to achieve his aims, it is only a matter of time before they flood across permanently and take up dwellings where they will."

Ramsey nodded, the distress on his face palpable. "Our informants tell us that Enâri raids are becoming more frequent to ramp up fear among the people."

"You communicate with people back home?" William asked.

"Of course. We have a network of spies. From time to time some of us have even returned to our homes for short periods under cover of darkness to promote our cause and recruit more members, but not without risk."

"Some of those who have spoken out against Vellan's tyranny at home have been killed or disappeared," Eucádus informed him. "But instead of fighting back, those in power have made excuses for the dictator inside his mountain in Del Norác to keep what measly positions and privileges that Vellan allows them." He noted the look of disgust upon William's face. "So years ago, after fruitless efforts to change the situation in the Northern Mountains, a movement slowly took root. Many of our people escaped and regrouped here in the northern Ebrean where we could flourish and grow unbothered. Our Clearing, known to its residents as the Star Clearing, is the oldest and northernmost of the five. The others take the names Oak, Fox, Pumpkin and Haystack."

"And each has its own leader, too?"

"Correct, though we coordinate with one another on decisions affecting all the Clearings. We keep in regular contact as our goals are identical–namely, to defeat Vellan and free our respective homelands."

"When will that push begin?" William asked.

"The day after tomorrow," Eucádus said. "At least that is when our mechanism will be set in motion. But we will not be confronting Vellan directly, though that was our original intent for many years. As you learned at the war council, the political landscape has changed in recent days. We now shall take the fight to Vellan in a more roundabout way."

"By confronting his supporters in Maranac and defeating King Drogin," William said with enthusiasm, recalling King Justin's plan.

"Exactly. You have arrived at a most interesting time, Will. Our troops will leave the Star Clearing at dawn and hike to Drumaya and meet with King Cedric. We'll get his final word on whether or not he'll join our march to Rhiál. If you recall, there was a man at the war council who was King Cedric's representative. I had spoken to Osial before you and your brother arrived."

"I remember the name," William said.

"Anyway, he had promised to speak to King Cedric to convince him to join our cause. I sensed that the ambassador was more with us than against us after we had had our say, though just barely." Eucádus shook his head as he drank from his cup, still plagued with doubts. "We'll find out shortly if we have another ally in the fight. Otherwise, we march alone to Rhiál. We must make a stand with or without Drumaya's assistance."

"You will not be totally alone," William said. "King Justin shall ride to Rhiál, too. He will bring with him a formidable force."

"Indeed he will," he replied with an encouraging smile, "though the numbers that ride with him will be lessened now that Prince Gregory heads to Montavia with part of the army to free your homeland. But since you claim that some mysterious mission is underway that might benefit us all, well, that gives me added hope."

"And to me also," he said, going silent for a moment. William stared uneasily at his plate before looking up. "I suppose it's not much to offer, but I request that you allow me to go with you to Rhiál. I'm not a professional soldier, but I owe it to my brother to have a part in this fight, however small or inconsequential."

Eucádus was impressed by the boy's heartfelt offer. He noted a hint of trepidation in Liana's face, yet knew that he couldn't possibly refuse such a petition after what William had been through. Ramsey nodded his approval as well.

"Will, after we arrive in Drumaya and schedule an audience with King Cedric, I would like you to speak with him about the invasion of Montavia as your brother had originally planned," he suggested. "If the King is made to understand the seriousness of the blight spreading over our lands through your words, then that will be a vital contribution to our cause." But before William could voice any objections, sensing that he was already being forbidden to join the fight, Eucádus held up a hand to silence him. "And after our meeting, regardless of the outcome, if you still wish to accompany us over the Kincarin Plains to Rhiál, I will not object. You deserve to chart your own fate out of respect for your brother."

"Thank you," he said gratefully, his heart welling with mixed emotions. He vowed to do everything he could to train himself to be a capable leader in honor of his brother. As he picked up his fork, he realized that his first test in that arena might be both the greatest and the last one of his short life, but he promised to see it out to the end regardless of the consequences. His road to one day being a king started now.

CHAPTER 35

A Loose Tooth

William, along with most of the adult men in the Star Clearing, started the dawn march to Grantwick two days later. Any other men staying behind with the women and children were either too young to fight or too old for such a long journey. A second contingent also remained to man the outposts and help run the day-to-day operations. But regardless of who stayed back at the Star, Oak, Fox, Pumpkin and Haystack Clearings, all five communities would be rendered somber and lonely in the coming weeks, their remaining inhabitants constantly questioning if loved ones would ever return. Tears flowed and hugs were plentiful before the journey commenced. And when the marchers finally disappeared into the deep shadows of the towering trees, armed with swords, bows and daggers, and weighed down with food and other supplies, family members with anxious hearts and knotted souls looked helplessly on, all wondering if their lives were ending beneath the withering leaves of fall.

William's march back to the forest's border was tiring, tedious and swift. After a while, passing tree after tree and hearing the rhythmic footfalls of his fellow travelers, he grew unaware of the passage of time and felt as if he were drifting along on the edge of a murky dream. They stopped for brief meals and talked little, but as the miles progressed and daylight waned, he grew accustomed to the tempo of the woodland trek and paid more attention to his surroundings. The scent and texture of the trees and the variations in sky color as the sun shifted positions registered more sharply in his mind rather than rushing by in a blur. His eyes soon anticipated the bright green patch of a distant mossy rock and his ears the sound of an approaching stream instead of merely being pleasantly surprised by them. And though William knew he would probably be lost in these woods if he were alone, the young prince, nonetheless, cultivated a higher level of confidence because of this task. He had always relied on Brendan to make most of the decisions whenever they were together, and though Eucádus was in charge, he felt an empowering sense of solitude among the hundreds of men marching alongside him. Perhaps this was just a small part of the process, as Brendan had often told him, of preparing oneself to be a leader. William recognized the growth inside him yet wished with all his heart that his brother could be at his side flinging a wisecrack or playfully punching him in the shoulder.

They stopped a final time a couple hours before twilight, enjoying a bite to eat along a swift stream. While many of the men quenched their thirsts and refilled empty water skins, Eucádus found a moment to speak with William near a large, mossy boulder. The man from Harlow wore a dark green, weather-stained poncho over a brown hooded jacket. With a long sword at his side, boots splattered with mud and a day's growth of beard, he reminded William more of the man he had seen at the war council than of the gentleman he had shared dinner with two nights ago.

"How are you holding up, Will? You've covered many miles these past few days." Eucádus took a drink from his water skin. "Sleep should take hold as soon as your head hits the ground."

"I think you're right," he replied, noting a vague sadness in the man's eyes despite the smile on his face. "And how are *you* holding up?"

"Excuse me?"

"You must miss your wife, though we've only traveled a day."

Eucádus nodded, unable to deny the fact. "Liana is always in my thoughts as I'm sure that the wives and children of all these men are in theirs." He noted a similar emptiness in William's expression.

"I would conclude that Brendan is a part of your mediations as well."

"He is."

"Your brother is on our minds, too, though some of us have not yet found a proper moment to commiserate with you." Eucádus patted William on the shoulder as if he were the boy's father. "But we will one of these days. In the meantime, walk with me the rest of the way to Grantwick. I have spoken enough of military matters to my fellow soldiers during this hike and would prefer a bit of regular conversation. You can tell me about Montavia. I've never been to your kingdom and have many questions."

"You've come to the right person," he said, delighted to tag along. "And you can tell me about Harlow and the other mountain nations, especially Kargoth. I'm embarrassed to say that Brendan was a finer student of history and geography than I ever was."

"Then each of us will commence with our first lesson posthaste," he said as he weaved his way back to the front of the line with William in tow. "There are many wonderful tales I can tell you about Harlow and just as many horrible ones I can spin about Kargoth. Which would you prefer?"

"Choose a cheerful account to start with," William suggested as the lines of soldiers reformed. "I'm in the mood for something easy on the mind, if you understand."

Eucádus let out a pleasant laugh. "We could all stand a little cheer right now amidst the trees and the growing darkness. I promise to do my best," he said before signaling for the troops to move out, eager to reach the forest's edge before the sun set on this last day of Mid Autumn.

They covered the final miles to the border of the Ebrean in record time as all looked forward to breathing the open air and setting up camp. Evening fast approached as William observed the lines of fading daylight through the distant trees. His heart leapt knowing that they had finally reached the end of a long and arduous journey. He glanced at Eucádus, noting the silent look of delight upon his face. But though the first leg of their mission was over, he couldn't imagine where the tumultuous waves of the following days would sweep him.

The men exited the woods about a quarter mile south where William and Brendan had made camp three nights ago. The city of Grantwick lay just to the southeast, splashed in the last rays of golden sun descending behind the Northern Mountains. The Bear Moon, about four days from full, ascended in the eastern sky. Everyone felt as if a massive weight had been lifted from their shoulders when they stepped into the cool open air, their spirits for a moment, untroubled and festive.

"At last," William said as he walked upon a patch of dry grass. "Though I'm miles away from Montavia, I feel as if I have arrived home."

"The Ebrean has not been kind to you, Will, so it is no wonder," said Ramsey who walked up behind him. "May the future look kinder upon the prince of Montavia."

"Upon all of us," Eucádus softly uttered before pointing to the north along the tree line. "Look, our friends await us."

William glanced north, and after a flurry of soldiers parted before him, an amazing sight was revealed. Less than a half mile away, a series of bonfires were spread out across the open field like a scattering of stars. A multitude of small tents of gray, brown and white material had sprung up as several thousand men from the other four Clearings milled about, some eating and telling stories while others attended to the ordering of the enormous encampment. He was impressed to see such a grand display silhouetted against a crisp autumn sky in the deepening twilight where just days ago there had been only grass and quiet.

"I'm dumbfounded," he said as he, Eucádus and Ramsey walked to the encampment. Some followed as others continued to spill out of the forest. "How many are there?"

"Counting the Star Clearing, I estimate we'll have close to four thousand men," Eucádus said. "Though now I think we can call ourselves soldiers, for this is the fate we have willingly accepted."

"But as impressive a gathering as it is, it is still a small force," Ramsey added. "Still, we'll fight hard if it comes to that. And with help from King Justin, we'll have an opportunity to strike a deadly blow at one of Vellan's allies."

"All the better if we can convince King Cedric to join us," Eucádus said. "He must listen to reason."

William chuckled. "Merely by looking over his fence, he's sure to see this astounding sight. Maybe that alone will give him the encouragement your previous pleadings have failed to provide."

"I hope you're right, but with or without the King, we shall leave these parts soon." Eucádus glanced up at the handful of stars winking in the sky, contemplating his dear wife and the beauty of springtime in Harlow, wondering if he would ever return to either one. "It would be of much comfort to have the men of Drumaya accompany us across the plains, but we'll know for sure tomorrow. For now, let us join our brethren and set up camp. I have an appetite in search of a meal, be it only a bowl of soup and a stale biscuit."

"Sounds like a feast to me," William said.

The smell of wood smoke and damp grass stirred William from a deep slumber. He lay upon a thick blanket folded in two while wrapped snugly in another one draped over his coat. He had fallen asleep by one of the bonfires with several soldiers after talking long into the night about their upcoming trek to Rhiál across the vast Kincarin Plains. The sun rose in the southeast while the waning crescent Fox Moon drifted higher like a white gemstone, soon to be obscured in the morning sky by the glare of the fiery yellow orb.

After shaking the lingering sleep from his head and storing the blankets with his other supplies, William grabbed two apples from a sack of food and hurried to visit the two horses he and Brendan rode when they set out from Morrenwood. After having arrived at the encampment last night, William was delighted to see that his horses had been taken care of by the soldiers who had arrived earlier. He even found the spot where he and his brother had made camp, happy to discover their supplies still untouched, including his store of apples. When he offered the two steeds the sweet, crispy treat in the frosty air, they were delighted as they munched on an early breakfast.

"I thought for sure, Will, that we were going to have to wake you up this morning after the paces we put you through yesterday," Eucádus said a short while later, happy to find the young prince in such good spirits.

"I guess I'm getting used to life outdoors," he replied as he stroked the horses, each animal a rich brown color, though William's horse was a shade or two lighter than Brendan's. He looked at

Eucádus, slowly exhaling as his ghostly white breath rose into the awakening blue sky. "As I can only ride one horse, I'll happily give you Chestnut if you require a steed. It was Brendan's horse, though both were lent to us compliments of King Justin."

"I'd be honored." Eucádus smiled, caressing the horse along its nose. "Though men from the Haystack Clearing have been breeding horses on the Ebrean's northern border for just this day, we do not have the numbers to supply an army of our size. There are enough for the leaders, their captains and our scouting parties, and of course some to use for moving supply carts. With Chestnut in the mix, Ramsey can have my horse." He stared at the animal, sensing a quiet pride beneath its genial nature. "Aptly named, too."

"Brendan and I named our horses on the road for something to do to pass the time. I kidded him for picking such an obvious one." The boy rolled his eyes. "*Chestnut*."

"Oh, so what did you name your horse?"

William grunted. "I decided to call him Lester. I figured after I teased Brendan, I had to come up with something a bit unusual. Don't know why that name came to me, but Lester it is. My brother had a good laugh as I expected he would." He continued to run his hand across the horse's silky mane. "It was a great afternoon we spent together that day. Ordinary, but I'll always remember it."

"That is wisdom speaking," Eucádus said as he gently patted his horse. "An appreciation of life's simplicity will help keep you grounded in reality. That is a good trait for any leader to possess."

"I'm far from being a leader yet."

"But it is best that your training begin many years in advance so you're not caught unawares when the time comes." He placed a foot in the stirrup and climbed upon Chestnut. "Now accompany me for a brief ride around the perimeter and then we'll find something to eat. After that, we'll form a small party and ride to Grantwick. The west gate is open by now and I'm sure King Cedric is expecting us. Whether he will be cooperative is another story."

William mounted his horse and stood proudly at Eucádus' side. "Then let's not keep him waiting. But as you said, breakfast first. I always think better on a full stomach."

Eucádus grinned. "There is it again–wisdom!"

The unarmed party set out to Grantwick two hours later to seek an audience with King Cedric. They totaled sixteen–the leaders of each of the Five Clearings, two of their most trusted captains each, and William, prince of Montavia. They rode across the wide expanse of grassland at a leisurely pace to the city and then proceeded through the streets of the capital to the west gate as the sun inched higher in the southeast.

The wooden barricade surrounding the inner city was constructed of a series of narrow tree trunks anchored into the ground and rising eight feet high, each secured to the next one with sturdy pegs and iron spikes. Four main gates were built into the fence facing north, south, east and west. All were attended to by the King's guardsmen around the clock, though people were free to pass coming or going during daylight hours. King Cedric and his family, along with his staff and ministers, resided in a three-story structure of dark stone and wood called King's Quarters. The inner city of Grantwick thrived around it. But even after the enormous fence had been built years ago, Grantwick continued to grow outside the protective barricade, predominately to the south and east. There were a few farms and residences in the north, while the area beyond the west gate and streets all the way to the border of the Ebrean remained an empty field for riding and grazing.

As Eucádus and his party passed through the west gate, some uniformed soldiers on duty smiled and said hello to those men they recognized from previous visits. Some silently hoped to join their military campaign against Vellan. While these soldiers admired King Cedric, many believed their monarch was too cautious a man when dealing with Vellan. Though Drumaya was still free, its citizens could feel the growing threat of the menace in the Northern Mountains.

As the guards watched Eucádus and the others pass by, several thanked them with heartfelt nods, knowing that these exiles from the mountain nations had served as a silent army over the years. Though never needing to call upon them, the people of Drumaya were confident that the men of the forest wouldn't have thought twice about rushing to their aid if a crisis arose. But now that the woodland forces were preparing to march east across the Kincarin Plains, citizens of Drumaya were certain to feel less secure and more vulnerable to Vellan's presence, knowing that the Ebrean Forest had been vacated of their silent and invisible allies.

"May your meeting with our King prove fruitful," one of the guards quietly said to Ramsey who rode in back of the line with a few other captains.

"We'll try our best to make a strong case," he replied in kind.

"Who is the boy?" another asked, indicating William after he and Eucádus had passed by.

"Our secret weapon perhaps?" Ramsey said with a grin to the puzzled amusement of the captain riding next to him.

"Well, good luck with that," the guard muttered to himself, scratching his head while he and his fellow soldiers watched the sixteen men disappear down the lane into the center of town.

"Here we are at last," Eucádus said to no one in particular as he dismounted Chestnut under a line of sprawling oak trees in front of King's Quarters. The others did likewise, tethering the animals to a rail along a line of water troughs. "Let us see if the King will grant us an audience today."

He led the group beneath the shade of the oaks until they reached a stone walkway perpendicular to the line of trees and leading to the front entrance of the building. A second row of oaks continued along on the other side of the stone path. They ascended a set of five granite steps leading to a long porch extending the entire length of the building. A series of small recesses had been craved into the front of the building at regular intervals from one end to the other, each containing a stone carving of a hawk, eagle or falcon native to the region in various poses. Two armed guards stood at attention at the main arched entrance while several people casually strolled across the porch to either of the narrower staircases on each end. One of the guards, having met Eucádus and two of the other Clearing leaders before, cordially greeted them as they approached.

"We wish to inquire about arranging an audience with your King," Eucádus said. "At his convenience, of course, though today if possible."

Before the guard could reply, the front door opened and a tall, stern looking woman with white hair and piercing blue eyes stepped out and glanced at the group of sixteen. A younger man serving as an aide stood behind her. Eucádus politely nodded to the woman, but before he could utter a word, she abruptly held up a hand and sighed.

"No, no, no! This won't do at all. Far too many at one time," she said, scanning the array of faces. "Though King Cedric was expecting another visit from your group after seeing the campfires on the border of our lands, he is not in the mood to host the likes of a celebration. He has already granted you an audience, sir," the woman explained to Eucádus, "but I can only allow the administrator of each Clearing a seat at the table, as it were. The other," and here she began to furiously count, "…eight, nine, ten, *eleven* of you shall be escorted to a waiting area where breakfast shall be provided."

Eucádus couldn't conceal a smile of gratitude and amusement as he placed a hand upon William's shoulder and ushered him to the front of their group. "Minister Nuraboc, I kindly request that you allow this young gentleman to also attend our meeting, for he wishes to speak with the King. It is of the utmost importance."

The Minister looked down upon William with a probing gaze. "And he is…?"

"This is Prince William of Montavia who has much to tell the King," he explained. "He has traveled far and has endured many harrowing ordeals."

Minister Nuraboc noted William's blond hair and the silver ring on his finger, and though she had never met the boy before, she possessed the political acumen to know that those would be two attributes of a royal grandson of King Rowan. "Did you escape your homeland, sir, or had you already departed before the invasion?"

"Escaped, ma'am," William replied. "My brother and I had fled to Morrenwood to seek help from King Justin."

The Minister noted a tinge of sorrow in the boy's eyes and softened her tone considerably, deciding to let any further inquiries be handled by King Cedric. "I am truly sorry for the turmoil visited upon your country, Prince William. Of course you may consult with the King. We are honored by your visit."

William politely nodded. "Thank you, minister. And I am honored to be here."

"As are we all," Eucádus added.

"Then would the sixteen of you please follow me inside to the foyer," she said, signaling the men to accompany her at once through the doorway. Minister Nuraboc introduced her aide and instructed him to escort the ten captains to a nearby dining area for breakfast while the others proceeded down a separate corridor to meet with King Cedric. "Despite any misgivings you may harbor because of your previous meetings, the King is anxious to meet with you, Eucádus," the minister said as she led the remaining six to a reception area adjacent to one of the interior gardens.

"Well, I suppose that's as good a reason as any why I should look forward to this visit more than the others," he replied halfheartedly as they walked swiftly through a second hallway. "But I will let King Cedric speak before my doubts are allayed."

"I wouldn't expect any other answer from the leader of the Star Clearing," she said with a faint smile. They approached the reception room and entered through a small carved archway of rich, polished oak.

The chamber was uncluttered and bright, its white walls trimmed with elegant pine molding and adorned with framed charcoal drawings. Several large leafy plants towered in the corners of the room while a multi-paned arched window overlooked an outdoor garden, allowing in light from the southwest. Wooden chairs were arranged on either side of a large fireplace on the opposite side of the room, while a table covered with white linen stood against the side wall. Members of the kitchen staff had earlier brought out pitchers of cool drinks and platters of various cheeses, breads and fruits and set them upon the table with plates, cups and cloth napkins. A set of blue candles had been lit and displayed on one corner of the elegant arrangement.

"Welcome to my home, gentlemen," said a soft-spoken King Cedric while standing near the window with his wife, Beatrice, and their two young children, a son and a daughter. He was dressed in rather plain clothes–a beige shirt under a plaid vest, brown trousers and a matching pair of boots. The light brown hair growing around the sides of his balding head was flecked with wisps of gray. A pleasant smile beamed from King Cedric's oval shaped face as he approached to shake the hands of his visitors. "I'm delighted to see the five of you again, and all at the same time for a change," he said, firmly grasping Eucádus' hand with whom he was most familiar. He then greeted the other four leaders, namely Ranen, Jeremias, Uland and Torr of the Oak, Fox, Pumpkin and Haystack Clearings, respectively. "This is indeed an honor."

"It is all ours," Eucádus replied.

"Thank you for speaking with us on such short notice," Ranen added, eyeing the food table. "And for your generous reception." He was about the same age as Eucádus, bulky and slightly taller with long, black hair tied up in back with a strip of blood red cloth.

"I was expecting you for a final visit one of these days after the war council in Morrenwood had concluded," the King said. "As soon as my guards saw your encampment forming on the border of the Ebrean, I suspected you would be on your way shortly." He introduced his wife and children to the men of the Clearing. His son, Liam, who was seven years old, smiled proudly when he was introduced, revealing a missing lower tooth which elicited a ripple of affectionate chuckles from the guests.

"Liam lost his tooth two days ago and is very proud of that accomplishment," the King explained as he brushed a hand through his son's hair. "He was a very brave boy." King Cedric then took note of William, observing the silver ring on his finger before glancing up at Minister Nuraboc for an explanation.

"Sir, this is Prince William of Montavia," she said. "He has traveled here with Eucádus and his associates and has need of a word with you."

"Yes, yes. Thank you, Judith." The King shook hands with William. "A prince of Montavia has traveled all this way to see me. You must have a story indeed, young man. My representative, Osial, who had attended the war council, mentioned that you and your brother arrived by surprise at the conclusion of that meeting. Osial would have been here, but he is on another assignment. I look forward to hearing from you and learning more about the invasion of your country. A sad state of affairs indeed."

"I shall answer any of your questions," William said.

"And I all of yours." The King clapped his hands. "But first let us partake of some of the fine food and drink my staff has prepared, then after we can sit by the fire and discuss, well, those matters that we are all here to discuss!"

About twenty minutes later, after eating and lighthearted conversation around the table, King Cedric's wife and two children departed the room, leaving the others to their private deliberations. The King occupied a chair closest to the fire opposite Eucádus, while William, Minister Nuraboc and the other four leaders filled out the remaining seats. King Cedric leaned back and rubbed his chin, noting the steely gaze in Eucádus' eyes.

"Well, I suppose I should reveal my decision forthwith, and then we can take things from there," the King said. "That is why you are here, after all. I'd like to tell you that–"

Eucádus suddenly raised his hand, his tone urgent. "Please, sir, before you say anything, I ask that you indulge me for one moment to speak my piece, and then perhaps hear out Prince William. His story alone is of dire relevance."

"You may both speak for as long as you wish," he kindly replied, "but first let me say that–"

"I do not wish to appear rude," Eucádus again interrupted. "That is not my desire. But I beg that you let us have our say before you render your decision." He leaned forward in his chair, eyeing his four counterparts for moral support before once again addressing the King. "The fate of so many will depend on your pronouncement."

King Cedric seemed slightly taken aback, though not offended in the least. He glanced at Minister Nuraboc who only responded with the slightest tilt of her head. The tension in the room grew as thick as storm clouds as the King folded his arms. For a moment, Eucádus thought he had stepped over the line, trying to present his case for an alliance before King Cedric could shoot him down. But the mood lightened considerably when a thin smile appeared on the monarch's face.

"You seem a man possessed, Eucádus, so I will defer to you," he said with an easy tone. "And I do not find you rude, by the way, so let that not worry you or your colleagues. Speak your mind, and I will listen attentively." He then addressed the four other leaders. "And after that, each of you may also contribute whatever bit you think I should hear. Last of all, Prince William can apprise me of his exploits. Then, and only then, will I have my say in these matters." King Cedric brushed the hair along one side of his head. "By then, of course, I think all of us will be ready for more food and drink regardless of the outcome. Agreed?"

Eucádus nodded. "Agreed."

"Then by all means, my friend, proceed."

"Very well," he replied, taking a slow, deep breath. "As you know from Osial's report of the war council, King Justin is forming two armies, sending one to free Montavia and the other to Rhiál to aid King Basil in his fight against Maranac. That is where our small army will march to also, though precisely when King Justin's troops will arrive there is not known. But we must leave soon, and so it is vital that your army accompany us. We are less than four thousand men from the Clearings, and though a potent force, I fear we are not enough to alter the course of that war alone. But with the men of Drumaya at our side, we would be a power to be reckoned with. The war goes ill for King Basil and Rhiál, such was the word at the council. It is only a matter of time until King Drogin of Maranac achieves control of the region."

"And Drogin's success simply means another foothold for Vellan to occupy in Laparia," Ranen elaborated. "If Drogin achieves victory, soldiers from the Northern Isles and the Enári will have another place to call home. You know this is so, King Cedric."

The King kept silent as he listened to the pleadings of the five leaders and to the warning that, regardless of the outcome of their efforts in Rhiál, they would never return to the Ebrean Forest to live. Should they succeed in Rhiál, they would continue on to a final confrontation with Vellan in Kargoth. But should they lose, that would be the end of their resistance movement, and it would only be a matter of time before Drumaya itself was overrun by Vellan's locust-like army. When Eucádus and his friends had finally exhausted their arguments, King Cedric addressed the young prince, inviting him to contribute to the debate.

"Eucádus asked me to speak about Caldurian's invasion of my country," William said, "though I suspect you already know the particulars after my brother and I spoke at the war council."

"Ambassador Osial's report was detailed," the King replied.

"That is why I will tell you a different story, one concerning my brother," he said. "One of a more recent nature. It is a horrible tale, yet there is an element of hope around its edges."

King Cedric saw a veil lift in front of William's eyes, revealing a wrenching pain within their watery depths. He couldn't imagine what experience this young boy had endured, but his heart chilled and his spirit trembled when he learned of the vicious attack in the hunting cabin and of Brendan's subsequent death. The contemptible hand of Vellan apparently reached into even the most obscure corners of Laparia, creating havoc and death with its touch. King Cedric and Minister Nuraboc were deeply moved by the boy's account, both unable to speak for several moments after he had finished.

"I cannot adequately express my condolences for your loss, Prince William. Your brother's death must be a grievous wound to your heart," the King said.

"Thank you for your understanding," William replied. "But there is more to my story. There was a reason for the attack which I cannot fully reveal because of an oath I have taken, yet something is in motion that might give you hope for our eventual success and alter your outlook about joining our cause."

"Please tell me."

Without alluding to any specifics about the medallion or of Nicholas and Leo's mission, William did his best to paint a picture of their small chance to wound Vellan, perhaps fatally, and possibly soon. King Cedric listened to his cryptic explanation with intrigue, feeling his heart lighten with the possibility of good news.

"Though my brother and I were mistaken for the other two on that secret mission, I can only guess that Brendan's death has bought them valuable time and safe passage," William concluded, gazing up at the King with a sad but determined expression.

"I didn't expect to hear today what I have just heard," King Cedric remarked. "Had I an inkling of what you had been through, William, I would have told you my decision right from the start and spared you from having to relive your horror despite Eucádus' dogged persistence to speak his mind first. But that is how the morning has unfolded."

"What are you saying?" Eucádus asked, his hopes deflating as he locked gazes with the King, his hand gripping the side of his chair.

"What I am saying is that—we are with you."

"But surely, King Cedric, you cannot–!" Eucádus' words flew from his mouth before the King's comment had had a chance to register in his mind. He quietly sat there as still as a tree on a windless day, his eyes open wide, his mouth slightly agape, considering if the words running through his head were indeed the ones King Cedric had actually uttered. He glanced at the other members in his group, all now grinning and in buoyant spirits, before looking again at the King. "Did you just say that–"

"–my troops are with you? Yes," he calmly replied, relishing the dazed expression upon the face of his guest. "Yes, I believe I did, Eucádus. That is what you wanted to hear, wasn't it?"

"I think it was," William said with amusement.

Eucádus nodded, his thoughts aflutter. "Yes, it definitely was, but…" He leaned back in his chair, staring at the King. "You say you had planned to join with us. When did you decide this? And why?"

King Cedric stood to stretch his legs, pacing in front of the large fireplace, a satisfied smile upon his face. "I had planned to tell you right at the start of this meeting, hadn't I, Judith?" he said, eyeing Minister Nuraboc.

"He did indeed," she replied, obviously pleased to have been in the know.

"Yet because you had been so determined to speak first, Eucádus, I decided to let you have at it, even though I needed no further convincing." He shrugged, resting an arm on the edge of the mantelpiece. "But you are younger and more eager than I am, I suppose, so I understand your enthusiasm. Osial told me of the battle of words you had with the ambassador from Harlow at the war council, your fellow countryman. I was prepared for much the same here today. And your lands have been invaded while Drumaya is still free, so the desire for swift results is also in your thinking."

"All you say is true, King Cedric, and I apologize if my presentation appeared brusque now and then," Eucádus said.

"No apology necessary. It is a refreshing trait from time to time."

"But still, I must ask you again–why did you change your mind and decide to join us?" he asked. "When did this transformation take place?"

"Well, I suppose it is now my turn to tell a story," he said, retaking his seat. He thought for a moment as the flames crackled in the background while a flurry of falling leaves, visible through the arched window, swirled in a gentle breeze in the adjacent garden.

"But perhaps I should tell you first about my son. Liam, you remember, lost his tooth about a week ago."

Eucádus furrowed his brow, noting a similar bewildered expression upon William's face when the boy glanced his way. But as this was the King's home, Eucádus felt obligated to hear him out. "I remember," he said. "Please, tell us more."

"It was the most amusing thing, in a sweet sort of way, to watch Liam walk around our home while constantly wiggling that tooth for days on end, hoping it would fall out, yet afraid to give it a good pull." King Cedric uttered a delighted laugh. "I even offered to do the deed for him, but he would have none of that, allowing it to consume his time yet fully aware of the final, inevitable outcome. Then one day he was chewing a pear and bit down on the wrong side and, well…" The King casually waved a hand through the air. "He buried the tooth in one of the gardens and made his wish."

Eucádus nodded at King Cedric, slowly seeing beyond a few of his long held perceptions of the man. He finally understood a little bit more about the ruler of this kingdom. "And I hope his wish is granted, sir."

"So does he," King Cedric said with a smile. "Though I'm not supposed to know, Liam subtly informed his older sister, who then told my wife, Beatrice, who then told me, that he wants a dog. But we shall see." The King studied the shroud of exhausted worry upon Eucádus' face, imagining what he and his demoralized people have been enduring for so many years. "I am not a naïve man, Eucádus. I know how the world operates. But I have always put the security of my people first and have kept them safe. Alone, or even allied with you, we could not have withstood a direct attack on Vellan no matter how much we may have wished it. But when King Justin sent word that a war council was to be held, well, I guess that that was my bite on a pear." Eucádus raised an inquiring eyebrow. "You see, deep in my heart, I knew one day in the near future that Vellan would either be confronted by our free nations or he would consume us all. And though I sent Osial as my representative to the council with instructions for caution, I knew that King Justin was going to act regardless of the prevailing mood. The war council was just for show. Let's be frank–if King Justin determined that Arrondale was threatened, then what other nation in the region could seriously claim itself to be safe?"

"King Justin is a wise man," Eucádus said.

"He is. And so while Osial journeyed to Morrenwood, I quietly began to assemble my troops and volunteers from the middle and southern provinces for the inevitable pulling of the tooth, so to speak. They are gathered with weapons and supplies on the eastern shore of the Swift River across from the village of Wynhall twenty-five miles south of here. I shall join them with the northern forces in three days, alongside yours, if you wish."

"It is very much my wish," Eucádus replied, still astounded at King Cedric's turnaround. He glanced at William, Ranen and the other leaders and noted the tempered enthusiasm upon their faces at such promising news. Yet at the same time, all solemnly recognized the burden and responsibility placed upon their shoulders. Their brief smiles quickly dissipated.

"Then it is settled," the King said with an exhalation of relief. "I had already sent Osial to Morrenwood a few days ago to inform King Justin of my intentions, and only my highest officers in Grantwick yet know of this plan. But that will change swiftly, I am sure. Since we are now combining forces, it will allow King Justin a little more time to gather his two armies since he must fight on dual fronts." The King stood and invited Minister Nuraboc and his guests to refill their drinks at the table before raising his glass to mark the somber occasion. "For good or ill, a spectacular force is about to be released and astounding times are ahead. May safety and good fortune guide us and protect us over green grass and through swift water, under skies deep blue or crying gray, and wherever darkness or swords should descend upon us if it is so ordained." He drank from his cup as did the others, their thoughts swirling with a mix of doubt, confidence, wonderment and fear. And all knew that that would be the case over the days and weeks ahead.

CHAPTER 36

Across the Golden Plains

Three days later, King Cedric's northern army departed Grantwick on a cool morning alongside the troops from the Five Clearings. They traveled south along the Swift River and by the end of the day the two forces had arrived at Wynhall. The soldiers crossed a stone bridge spanning the river and met up with the King's southern troops encamped in a field on the eastern shore. Combined, the assembled armies of Drumaya totaled over six thousand men with less than a quarter upon horseback. Eucádus estimated that the Five Clearings added nearly four thousand more brave souls to the mix.

"We number just over ten thousand altogether," King Cedric remarked in the approaching twilight as he gazed out upon the spread of men, horses, tents and bonfires nestled between the gently flowing river and the southern tip of the Bressan Woods. "Still, it is a formidable force and will be a welcome sight to the men of Rhiál, though what state their army is in, I cannot guess."

"Our scouts will report back. Hopefully the situation won't be as bleak as we fear," Eucádus said, offering an encouraging tone.

The kingdom of Maranac was larger in area and population than Rhiál, and at the war council it was revealed that King Drogin's troops had already taken control of the southern portion of Rhiál which contained that country's most productive farmland. Neither

Eucádus nor King Cedric could make a guess regarding the current state of Rhiál's people or of its available food supply. Was it a population on the brink of starvation and defeat, or were its citizens nobly struggling to fend off the enemy until help arrived? Since the war council had convened twenty-two days ago, Eucádus assumed King Justin had sent word to Rhiál's King Basil about the impending arrival of military assistance. Such a bit of promising news might go a long way toward bolstering the confidence of his beleaguered army. And though confidence wouldn't feed a host of hungry soldiers or help fend off the swift blow of a steel blade, Eucádus hoped it would strengthen their spirits so they could endure for a little while longer.

The journey across the Kincarin Plains commenced at dawn the following morning beneath dreary gray skies of late autumn. Wispy white breaths of men and horses were carried away by thin breezes sweeping across the brittle grass still tinted with a golden summer hue that faded with the vanishing year. The loneliness and desolation of their journey was echoed in the mournful caw of a single crow gliding above the Bressan Woods that steadily disappeared behind them.

"It is an amazing sight," William said to Ramsey later in the day when he trotted his horse alongside him. King Cedric, Eucádus and the other leaders of the Clearings rode in front of the advancing army to discuss strategy. William craned his head back, gazing at the dark curving lines of men, horses and wagons stretching over the plains like a meandering river. "I've never seen such an assembly. It's quite stunning."

"It is indeed," Ramsey replied, taking a glance himself to fully appreciate the collective sacrifice of the many friends and strangers dutifully following their leaders. "Many are not sure what to expect, though have taken up this valiant cause nonetheless. Some wonder if they'll ever return while others envision the freedom that their countrymen will one day enjoy again because of these labors." He sighed. "Still, others contemplate the continued rise of tyranny should we fail."

William nodded reflectively as the reasons for the military gathering overshadowed its dramatic appearance. "And what do you think as we make our journey east?"

Ramsey looked at the young prince and thought for a moment as their horses moved forward with an even gait. "I think of all three, Will, as I assume most men do. After all, in this business there is plenty of time to think between the few harrowing moments that test your spirit. A little introspection is necessary to prepare you for the times when you must act swiftly without having the luxury to think."

William was silent for a time, his eyes fixed to the rider ahead of him as his thoughts drifted. "I suppose if I had been more prepared in that cabin I might have..." For several moments, he couldn't shake the image of Brendan lying on the cabin floor, struggling to claim his final few breaths before darkness found him. "He deserved better from me."

Ramsey caressed the layer of whiskers upon his face as he sought for the right words to allay William's doubt and remorse. "I don't suppose anyone can ever speak the right words to make you feel differently about what happened, Will. Perhaps you don't want them to either. But whatever blame you carry in your heart, also carry the knowledge that the enemy you faced was one nobody could have prepared for. From what you described, you are fortunate to have survived yourself. Even the bravest soldier would have been questioning his actions afterward were he in your place."

William tightly gripped the reins. "I'd like to reply *I suppose* to your explanation, and maybe someday I might allow myself some leniency. But for now all I can do is relive that scene in my mind and trudge ahead with the doubts." The prince of Montavia flashed an appreciative smile. "Still, your words are a great comfort, Ramsey, and will be remembered. I'm grateful for that."

"Glad I could help," he replied as they continued to ride side by side over the lonely gray miles in subdued silence.

They camped under a black sky devoid of stars, some of the troops keeping warm in tents while others took turns tending to the bonfires and catching a few hours of fitful sleep from time to time. Sentries patrolled the perimeter in short shifts, keeping their weary watches throughout the night. One by one the hours gradually passed until the eastern horizon was delicately tinged with the first languid hints of gray. The second day across the Kincarin commenced much like the previous one, with the bleak light of dawn rousing heavy

547

eyelids to open and sore limbs to move. After a brief breakfast, the camps were disassembled and the grand march continued.

They veered slightly to the northeast at one point, making for a stretch of short, straggly trees growing among a swiftly flowing stream which they would follow for a while to the delight of both the men and horses. Here kindling for fires was plentiful and a cold drink of fresh water seemed a kingly delight. But eventually the stream led to a low swampy area which they soon passed, and in time the open plains once again provided the dominant vista for the steadily moving army. In time, the setting sun disappeared behind a bank of clouds moving in from the west, its bulbous edges exploding in lustrous shades of purple, red and orange that elegantly punctuated the end of another day. Soon the watch fires of night flickered in the darkness as restless sleep took hold of the troops, the stony silence occasionally interrupted by the anxious grunting of horses or the rustle of dried grass among a chilly night breeze.

A flurry of fine snow greeted the troops the next morning, providing an amusing distraction to the travelers while painting the landscape in cheerier tones if only for a while. The tiny white flakes thinly covered the ground and dusted the tents, refreshing the air and serving as a brief reminder that the start of winter was just over two weeks away. After everyone had breakfasted amid the whitened landscape, they packed up and proceeded onward. By midmorning, all were grateful to see the clouds break up on a strengthening breeze and the sun reclaim its dominance in a sapphire blue sky. The snow quickly melted and for a time the mood of the travelers grew cheerful and optimistic. When the lines halted in early afternoon so the men could rest and lunch, King Cedric walked among the open grass, looking out to the east and pointing.

"The central tips of the Ridloe Mountains beckon to us," he said, admiring the towering peaks visible in the far distance. "Rhiál lies just beyond the gap in the range."

The long chain that comprised the Ridloe Mountains originated in the north on the shores of the Trillium Sea east of Montavia and stretched far to the south beyond the borders of Laparia, sloping in a gradual line from northeast to southwest. A large gap in the mountain range about halfway down from the northern tip contained the kingdoms of Rhiál and Maranac that were separated by Lake LaShear, an elongated body of water once serving as a binding landmark to the formerly unified nation.

"Bad enough that Vellan has destroyed our own nations in the Northern Mountains, but now he's exporting his twisted ambitions to the far regions of Laparia," Eucádus softly spoke as he gazed eastward. "It's not right."

"We will do our part to stop him," said Jeremias, the leader of the Fox Clearing, pounding a clenched fist into his open hand. "Though a powerful wizard he may be, the people who fight for him in the east are simply men like us. Though his weapons can be marched to Rhiál, his magic cannot."

"I have to agree with you," King Cedric replied, delighted to hear a spirit of optimism stirring among the troops. "Vellan will have his match one of these days, but for now we must attend to Drogin, one of his proxies. He will be a challenge, no doubt, but I feel inspired to victory now that we are assembled and marching toward the mountains. May that spirit linger with us all the way to Rhiál."

"And may King Justin and his men arrive there when we do," William added, eliciting a round of smiles from the gathered leaders.

"Whatever awaits us in Rhiál is what will await us," Eucádus said philosophically. "We shall confront our fates as best we can."

King Cedric nodded, prepared to address that point further when he suddenly grew silent, his attention drawn to the south. Two men on horses quickly advanced, one team of several scout pairs that the King regularly rotated out to reconnoiter the surrounding terrain while the main army moved forward. The horses slowed as the men approached and dismounted to make their report. The King greeted the two soldiers with a nod.

"Edgar. Bornby. What news have you?"

"Sir, Edgar and I spotted a line of tracks about three miles south, heading east and running parallel to us. But the tracks originated from the southwest," Bornby eagerly reported. "I'd guess about twenty to thirty horses in all."

"And when did they pass?" Eucádus inquired.

"I'd estimate about two days ago, more or less," he replied.

King Cedric thought for a moment. "Coming from the southwest, I would guess that a party from Kargoth has been dispatched by Vellan. But whether they are on a mission to Maranac or had been monitoring us remains to be seen." The King praised the scouts for their work and ordered them to get some rest and a meal. He quickly dispatched a replacement team to the south as well as some additional scouts to fan out eastward. "If Vellan ever had any doubts that Drumaya would one day stand up to him, he has them no more," the King quipped. He turned to the others under the warmth of the noonday sun. "Now I think it is time that we had some lunch before moving on, gentlemen. I am quite craving a roast pork dinner and a slice of alaberry pie, but I'm guessing I'll have to settle for a bowl of hot stew and a buttered biscuit instead!"

After the troops had eaten and enjoyed a short rest, everyone marched forward across the plains for several more hours, appreciating their progress yet knowing they still had a long way before reaching their destination. The air had grown calm and cool as the sun drifted toward the western horizon, the thin shadows of the army stretching eastward and moving in unison like a line of silent, gray ghosts. King Cedric constantly scanned the topography ahead which had turned slightly hilly and overgrown with scrub brush, knowing he should have heard from some of his forward scouts by now. Though the atmosphere chilled as evening approached, he undid the upper buttons of his coat and wore no hood for a time, his wariness and focus overriding any notice of the elements.

Shortly before the sun had set, one of the several riders a short distance ahead waved his arm in the air, signaling that he had spotted something. At once, King Cedric, Eucádus, William and several others swiftly approached, soon noticing several shapes lying on the ground covered in the gentle splashes of the fading sun. The King and his men dismounted to investigate. The other riders on horseback arranged their steeds in a semicircle around the area in question. King Cedric felt his heart go cold when seeing three of his scouts dead before him, riddled with stab wounds, their horses apparently stolen. When William saw the pale faces of the dead men and noted their bloodstained garments, be couldn't help but think of his brother and turned away, feeling Brendan's death all over again.

"These men were ambushed," King Cedric remarked, his voice hard and his eyes grim. He looked to his right, noting the folds in the land and a scattering of boulders nearby in the otherwise predominantly barren landscape. How many of the enemy had been hiding here and waiting for their chance to attack, he could not guess.

"Ambushed and outnumbered," Eucádus said as he looked around at the trampling of footprints in the grass and patches of soil.

"Vellan has left us a message," the King softly said, his eyes fixed despondently upon the deceased soldiers. "But he will regret it one day soon if I have any say in the matter." He called to one of his captains. "We will bury these men here. Make arrangements," he said, resting a hand on the man's shoulder as he looked back to address the rest of his army. "If we are victorious, we will return for their bodies and escort them home for a proper burial in Drumaya."

"Yes, sir," the captain replied before leaving to carry out the order.

But before he had left King Cedric's side, several harrowing screams shattered the night air, originating behind the huge boulders embedded in the plains. As the King spun around to pinpoint the source of the commotion, a half dozen dark shapes sprang out from behind the rocks waving drawn swords and rushing across the sloping ground toward them. A group of soldiers jumped in a protective stance in front of King Cedric with arms at the ready while several others, including Eucádus, drew their weapons and sped toward the advancing enemy. But a second before he left, Eucádus saw William draw his own sword, preparing to rush forward with the group.

"It is not yet your time to fight," Eucádus said, locking gazes with the boy and silently conveying to William that he would have other opportunities to avenge his brother's death. He then sprinted to the battle as William watched in awed silence.

A brief clash of swords followed and several arrows flew from some of King Cedric's finest archers. In short order, five of the six attackers were killed and one lay severely wounded upon a patch of dry grass stained with his blood. While a team of soldiers spread out and searched for any more of the enemy among the rocks and knolls, King Cedric knelt down near the wounded man to see if he could still speak. As the man was dressed in clothing and armed with weapons indigenous to the nations of the Northern Mountains, Eucádus assumed he was a native of Kargoth.

"Vellan will be victorious," the young man whispered as he gasped for breath, his eyes wildly alive yet somewhat clouded, unlike those of a normal man.

"But you will not be around to see it if he is!" one of the soldiers standing over him bitterly replied.

King Cedric held up a hand for silence before looking down at the dying man. "Where are the others in your party? Are they riding on to Maranac to assist Drogin?"

"Riding on to victory," he replied with a strange smile, nodding as his breathing grew more erratic. "Just as our leader..." His head suddenly tilted sideways as his final breath left him, his skin turning as cool and pale as the evening.

King Cedric shook his head in disappointment as he got to his feet, but before turning away, he noticed a peculiar thing about the man's face. The haziness within the blue color of his eyes suddenly faded while the tightness in his facial features softened as if a great weight had been lifted from the dead man's mind, if such a thing were possible. King Cedric glanced at Eucádus who stood next to him.

"Did you see that, or is my mind playing tricks?" he asked.

Eucádus nodded, taken aback. "I saw it as well, King Cedric. It was as if lifelessness itself had left the deceased body, making it look more alive though it is yet dead. Does that make sense?"

"Sense or not, I agree with what you say."

"As do I," said another soldier who had been peering over the shoulders of others in front of the body. "If this man was a native of Kargoth and loyal to Vellan, then he may have drunk from the Drusala River. Vellan is rumored to have placed a spell upon that waterway running through Kargoth after he settled down in the area, enchanting those who unknowingly quenched their thirst with its cool liquid. Total devotion to Vellan's will awaits anyone who mistakenly drinks from the Drusala. Death has finally freed this unfortunate man from the spell."

"I have also heard such tales though never fully believed in them," Eucádus said. "I am inclined to believe otherwise right now."

"If that's the case, then I'm sorry to say that perhaps these men are better off in their current state," King Cedric sadly remarked. "But death is a steep price to regain their freedom. Slaves to a master and not even aware of it. We shall bury them, too, near the rocks where they were hiding. May they have genuine rest in their untimely deaths." He turned away in silence to consult with his captains.

"I feel somewhat sorry for them now," William said in an aside to Eucádus. "If Vellan cast a powerful spell over their very will, then what chance did they have to resist?"

"Apparently none," he replied, leading William away from the dead bodies so they could be moved. "Unfortunately, it doesn't bring back any of King Cedric's men. It is a grievous wound he will not soon forget."

After the bodies were buried and words spoken to commemorate the loss of the three soldiers from Drumaya, the army moved onward for a short while, advancing into another purple twilight. As the lustrous light dimmed along the western horizon, fiery white stars popped out in the east one by one. A sliver of the crescent Fox Moon closely trailed the sun, briefly appearing brighter after the glare of sunset had diminished before finally disappearing behind the western horizon as well. Before full darkness had settled upon the landscape, the army set down temporary roots once again, though moods were both somber and bitter as tent stakes were pounded into the hard ground and bonfires crackled fitfully in the cold night air.

CHAPTER 37

A Common Bond

They continued on the next day without incident, reaching the gap in the Ridloe Mountains near sunset. The splash of waning daylight against the dark, looming mountain range softened the stony guardians marking the western border of Rhiál. They still had over a day's journey to reach the capital city of Melinas. Much of the land would be open and unsettled until they reached the interior closer to Lake LaShear. And since Drogin's army currently occupied only the southern portion of Rhiál, neither King Cedric nor Eucádus expected to encounter any of his troops this far north in the kingdom.

By the end of the following day, they had passed through much farmland and several small villages, greeted as heroes by many though they had not yet been challenged in battle. King Cedric sent scouts to the capital city early in the afternoon to inform King Basil of their arrival sometime the next day. After enduring cold weather, deadly attacks and sheer tedium across the plains, the troops were anxious to set down an encampment, see new faces and talk to the people of Rhiál. Though many of the citizens they met along the road spoke eloquently about their troubles, most expressed confidence that victory might now be achieved against Maranac. The one constant in all the stories, however, was that no one could comprehend why such a tragic turn of events had occurred. Though the two lakeside nations were divided, it had been inconceivable that reunification would ever be achieved through war. Most believed the people of Rhiál and Maranac were not enemies, but only separated by time and mismanaged history.

The sun peeked out behind a slew of iron gray clouds late the next morning when the long lines of troops were only a few miles from Melinas. The air blew cool and moist, filled with the fresh scent of evergreen. Soon a contingent of five men on horses advanced from the east, two of the men displaying colorful banners that flapped in the intermittent breezes. One flag contained the emblems of King Basil's royal house against a white and gold background. The other was the flag of Rhiál itself, containing several nautical illustrations in vivid hues matching the surrounding land, water and mountains. In the upper left-hand corner was a small rectangular patch of rich blue color boasting white crested waves and snowcapped mountains bathed in the light of a rising sun. That tiny image was a replica of the original flag of Maranac when it was once a single nation before war divided it decades ago. The current flag of Maranac contained that same image of a glorious past, as if each kingdom quietly held in its heart a faint hope to one day reunite in peace.

When the five horses stopped near King Cedric and Eucádus, one man greeted them. He had fair hair, shortly cropped, and hazel eyes set within a grim but determined face. "Welcome to Rhiál, King Cedric of Drumaya and Eucádus of Harlow. Your scouts have informed us of your approach and King Basil was heartened by the news. I am Captain Silas. I will guide you both to meet with the King along with others of your party whom you choose. But I respectfully ask that you keep their numbers few. The King has been quite ill of late. I will give you details on our ride to the capital."

"I'm sorry to hear that," King Cedric replied.

"It is unfortunate. Still, we are honored by your support."

"We, too, are honored to be here, captain, and are eager to meet with your monarch," the King said. "It has been a long road but our purpose has propelled us swiftly to your borders."

"Thank you," he replied. "Now I will take you to King Basil while my men direct your troops to the encampment near the King's estate on the lake."

King Cedric chose Captain Tiber, one of his most loyal aides, to accompany him and left the others in charge to coordinate with

Captain Silas' men. Eucádus tapped Ranen to ride to the estate along with him and William, leaving Jeremias, Uland and Torr, the leaders of the remaining three Clearings, to assist with the movement of the troops to the campgrounds. Moments later, the six men on horses departed and galloped the remaining miles to Melinas underneath a slew of breaking clouds and amid the heightened tensions of an encroaching war.

King Basil's estate was a modest three-story building of white clay and stone, surrounded by a low wall of colorful round rocks and gray mortar. Several trees dotted the landscape situated less than a quarter mile from the western shore of Lake LaShear. The wooden docks extending from the shoreline were cluttered with dozens of small vessels while several larger sailing ships sat anchored offshore, their vacant masts and wind-tossed rigging appearing skeletal against the cloudy skies.

Captain Silas escorted his guests from the stables where they left their horses to the guarded front doors of the estate. William inhaled a draft off the water, closing his eyes for a moment as they walked across the grassy compound, enjoying the cold quiet of the enormous lake. The distant call of sea gulls and the steady wash of waves upon the shore punctuated the breezy atmosphere. Gentle trails of bluish-gray smoke rose from a series of round, white chimneys along the rooftop. All of the shuttered windows were outlined around their edges with intricate designs in dark blue reminiscent of the background color in Maranac's original flag. A larger copy of Rhiál's current flag was suspended lengthwise from one of the upper windows of the estate, the material gently undulating in the draft. After entering, they ascended a spiral staircase to a second floor room on the northeast corner of the estate. A sentry stood watch at the door and greeted Captain Silas with a nod.

"The minister of finance departed minutes ago, captain, and had said that the King was finishing his lunch while they talked," the guard reported.

"Very good," Captain Silas replied as he knocked before opening the door and leading his guests inside.

The large, shadowy room was dimly lit by streams of dull light flowing in from two windows, one on the east side facing the lake and the other on the north end with a view of the distant hills. Low flames crackled in a fireplace on the west side. A large canopied bed in the corner between the two windows appeared hastily made. King Basil sat in an upholstered chair nearby, his half empty lunch dishes next to him on a small table. The King was dressed in a long, woolen robe over his clothes, and though he appeared frail and his face looked pallid and his eyes tired, he greeted his visitors with a smile as he carefully stood to shake each of their hands. With an effort, he then sat his tall frame down again and sighed.

"Forgive me for appearing as if I had just awakened, but it is not too far from the truth," King Basil replied with a laugh, combing a hand through his unruly graying hair. "I am taking more rest lately than is probably the mark of a good king, but as I instructed Silas to inform you on your ride over, my heart is not that of a young man anymore. And not a particularly good heart for this older man either," he said with a knowing grin. "But my physician says rest, so I rest."

"You should trust your doctor," King Cedric replied with a kind smile.

"I fear that one of these days while I'm at rest, I shall remain at rest–permanently!" King Basil laughed again, offering his counterpart the chair opposite his lunch table. "Please sit."

"Thank you," King Cedric said, taking the seat. King Basil directed the others to pull up the wooden chairs lined along one wall.

"Someone will be here shortly to remove these dishes. I'll have them prepare everyone a proper meal after such a long journey," the King said. "I was overwhelmed with joy when your scouts arrived yesterday with news that aid was coming out of Drumaya and the Northern Mountains. Now I must alter my plans for our next–and most likely final–military move, but that is a good thing. King Justin of Arrondale also sent scouts with word that he is coming, but the timing of his arrival is not fixed."

"He has done much to stir the passions against Vellan, raising two armies at once," King Cedric said. "And though I was loath to follow his lead initially, I now see the wisdom of his actions. But my friends, Eucádus and Ranen, have known the wise path all along."

"I suspected that it was the wise path, King Cedric, but some days I feel as if I know very little," Eucádus replied. "But now we all walk upon this same path and that is all that matters, is it not?"

"Indeed," King Basil replied, clasping his hands together. "We will have a fight ahead of us, and that is what I wish to discuss. There is something in the works, and now with your added numbers, we'll have a better chance for success. I fear this is our last and best opportunity to end the war or be consumed by it." He paused for a moment, his eyes misting. All could see that some draining emotion had suddenly overwhelmed him. "My only two sons have already fallen to the wretchedness of this conflict. Morton, my oldest, was killed in a battle down south about three months ago. My heart nearly gave out then when his body was brought back exactly two months to the day after my other son was reported missing."

"What happened to him, sir?" William softly asked after offering his condolences, seeing the loss of his brother mirrored in the King's words and expression.

"After several minor attacks on our docks one week in New Summer, we responded with a surprise raid on the other side of the lake near Zaracosa, Maranac's capital. Victor, my younger son, led one of the raiding parties. And though we had a partial success in destroying some of the enemy's ships and weapon stores, it came at a heavy price. There were many dead, wounded and missing. Victor was one of the latter, and so for five months I have not known the fate of my son, my only heir should by some miracle he still be alive upon my death." King Basil shrugged, choking up. "Though I try not to despair, I find it difficult not to resign myself to the probability that he is dead and that his body will never be recovered. But such is the price that those who make war must often bear."

"But this war was brought to you, King Basil. It is Drogin who is responsible for all who have perished in the conflict," Eucádus said. "I'll not dignify his abysmal rule by giving him the title of *king*."

"Many do not," King Basil replied, "as they see him as a false king, a usurper."

"But one with power," King Cedric reminded them. "So what are we to do?"

"We make an all-out assault on Maranac before it can bring down a final crushing weight upon us," King Basil said with a sudden gleam in his eyes. He leaned forward, almost whispering. "We are privy to some valuable information from behind enemy lines that we must act upon soon, near dawn, five days from tomorrow."

"How did you come by it?" Eucádus asked. "And is it reliable?"

King Basil nodded confidently. "Very much so. But first you must understand that as powerful as Drogin is, his core support is thin. He may rule Maranac, but he has not earned the devotion of a large majority of his people. Many suspected that he seized power at the beginning of the year and was behind the murder of King Hamil, his younger brother. His desire for absolute power became clearer when he replaced many of his captains and political advisors with men close to him but with little knowledge of military affairs and matters of state. He even recruited men from the Northern Isles to mix in among his troops and lead most of his companies. Their loyalty is to Drogin alone, not to Maranac. And Drogin's loyalty is to himself and the power he can amass."

Eucádus informed King Basil how troops from the Northern Isles had invaded Montavia, telling him of William's escape from the kingdom with his brother. The King was distraught by the news, yet was more saddened still after William recounted Brendan's death. Now more than ever, King Basil was determined to stop Drogin and his allies before they could spread their poison any further.

"After the war started, some men within the Maranac army were distraught by what Drogin was doing," King Basil continued. "They hadn't the power to stop him though, as many were demoted or summarily discharged as Drogin consolidated power. Still, a small cabal managed to get word to us that an opposition group called the Hamilod Resistance was forming, though it was slow going and overly cautious. On two different occasions, word was sent to me through intermediaries about upcoming attacks that Drogin had planned in our southern provinces. I was able to send reinforcements to one engagement just in time. I moved my people to safety on the other occasion as we would have been vastly outnumbered. Those two instances saved many lives and kept Drogin off balance, though our other defeats have been numerous. Still, I have no reason to doubt the new information I received eight days ago from the resistance."

"What does Drogin have planned?" King Cedric asked.

"I'll give you a condensed version before you have a proper meal," King Basil replied, his breathing labored. He paused, taking a sip of water from a metal cup on the table. "Captain Silas will go over the particulars later as we refine our strategy. But according to our sources, Drogin plans to attack us on two separate fronts at dawn, seven days from tomorrow. One part of his army is supposed to storm our docks visible from this window with a fleet sailing across the water. Another band of soldiers will march up the coast to Melinas from Drogin's stronghold in our southern provinces." The King took a second sip of water and leaned back in his chair, visibly tired. "But we plan to beat him to the punch."

"How so?" Eucádus asked. "And when?"

"Silas can tell you," King Basil said with a flick of his fingers, needing to take a break from talking for so long a stretch.

"We will strike before dawn five days from tomorrow," Silas said. "That will be two full days before Drogin plans to attack. With your arrival, we can send a larger force south and confront him before he reaches the capital. Also, we have been in secret talks with the kingdom of Altaga to the north. Their people know the peril we face and fear that if we fall, it is only a matter of time before Drogin and Vellan draw them into their web."

"Are they sending an army?" King Cedric asked.

"Not exactly," Silas continued. "What they are doing is constructing a fleet of rafts on the edge of the forest near the northern tip of the lake. Some of our troops will meet them and sail down the lake along the eastern shore and attack Drogin's fleet at Zaracosa in a predawn raid at the same time we hit him in the south."

"If we cannot defeat Drogin, at least we will badly cripple his forces to keep him at bay well past next spring," King Basil said, feeling better. "That is my hope anyway. I told King Justin's scouts of this secret plan when they were here, and they will relay that information back to him for what it is worth. But as I said before, whether King Justin and his army arrive before we make our move is yet to be seen." King Basil sighed, tiring again. "Enough talk. I grow weary once more and need rest, and all of you could stand a proper meal. I shall have the kitchen staff–"

At that moment there was a knock on the door and the King bid them to enter. Stepping into the room was one of the kitchen cooks, a tall, middle-aged woman with dark hair and eyes that matched, and a thin boy with freckles who was about a year younger than William. They were here to collect the lunch dishes from the King's meal, quickly gathering the plates, bowls, utensils and leftover food on two trays.

"Nyla, please prepare a fine meal for Captain Silas and my guests in the private dining area downstairs across from my study," he kindly requested before introducing the visitors.

"Right away, King Basil," she responded after offering a brief curtsey for the gathered royalty. The young boy named Aaron politely nodded his head in respect.

"You will not be disappointed," King Basil cheerfully remarked to the others. "Nyla has been working in the kitchens for well over a year and can prepare a roasted pheasant that you could weep over."

"You exaggerate, sir," she graciously responded.

"And Aaron, her young helper here, has kindly accompanied me on several walks around the compound when the weather was fairer and my health was more accepting of the challenge. But I fear my days of long walks are over," he said wistfully.

After Nyla and Aaron departed, William noted a distant sadness in King Basil's eyes, believing that the loss of his sons had probably contributed more to his ill health than the physical ailments themselves. "Perhaps by springtime you'll be able to take to the outdoors again," he suggested. "Maybe all this trouble with Drogin will be over by then and you'll start to feel better."

"Anything is possible," the King replied with a smile, though in his heart he knew it was not to be. "But I think I shall have to live with the memories of those walks, just as I must live with…" He emitted a slow, deep sigh born of painful recollections. "The boy, Aaron, reminded me of my sons when they were his age. Morton and Victor always loved to walk along the docks and watch the ships, just as he does. I guess his company gave me hope that maybe Rhiál would turn out all right in the end, but we may be down to our last gambit. Even Aaron has felt the sting of war, having escaped to

Melinas with some of his neighbors from the southern provinces after Drogin invaded. His father remained behind the enemy lines to fight with the local resistance. The boy has had no word from him since late spring." King Basil smiled kindly at William, remembering the words the young prince had said about Brendan. "It seems that no one has gone unscathed by the recent turmoil in Laparia. I regret it had to be this way."

"As do I," William whispered, feeling sorry that King Basil was enduring his heartache alone and in such ill health.

The King sat up and offered his guests a strained smile. "Now is not the time to dwell in melancholy, especially with guests here. Captain Silas, please lead these fine gentlemen to the dining area where you can discuss matters at your leisure. Then early this evening we'll gather with all the captains, spread out our maps and review our final strategy. In the meantime, I am due for another rest. I will feel better by tonight."

With an assisting hand from the King of Drumaya, King Basil stood up and bid his guests goodbye, watching them disappear through the doorway one by one. William, the last to exit the room, closed the door behind him, though not before taking a final glance at the monarch, feeling a bond of shared sorrow with King Basil while knowing that neither could do anything to lessen the other's grief. It was a weight that each would have to endure in his own fashion, and for the most part, alone.

CHAPTER 38

On the Battle's Doorstep

Lunch was served after Captain Silas escorted his guests to a private dining area where they could enjoy a view of the docks with their meal. William sat between King Cedric and Eucádus on one side of a finely set table opposite Ranen, Captain Silas and Captain Tiber. Three helpers from a nearby kitchen, including Aaron, brought out large plates, pitchers and bowls of hot food to serve their visitors.

As swiftly as the trio of kitchen workers flitted around the table, they just as speedily exited the room as Nyla stepped through the doorway. The head cook smiled pleasantly as she approached the table, briefly touching the back of her dark hair which was secured with decorative pins.

"I hope your luncheon will be satisfactory. If there are any other requests, I'll happily attend to them at once," she said, seemingly eager to please.

"You have gone above and beyond, my dear woman!" King Cedric replied with a gracious smile. "Thank you."

"I can only echo the King's sentiments," Captain Silas said.

"In that case, I shall leave you gentlemen to discuss your business in private." Nyla offered a slight bow. "If there is anything you require hereafter, do not hesitate to ring," she added, indicating a small brass bell in the center of the table. "One of my workers will promptly answer. Enjoy your meal."

When she left the room, the hungry travelers attacked their plates with enthusiasm. They ate and conversed spiritedly, describing their journey across the Kincarin Plains to Captain Silas, including the ambush of the three soldiers by zealous servants of Kargoth. Silas was dismayed to hear of their sacrifice even before they had stepped foot in Rhiál, stressing the urgency of defeating Drogin in the next few days.

"If we don't, death and destruction will spread to the capital like wildfire," he warned. "I suspect that Drogin is feeling invincible, but when word reaches his ears that help has arrived on our side, he may be less inclined to look upon us as a crop ready to be mowed down by his army. He will be unpleasantly surprised to see us on the offensive, for up until now, he has been driving this dreadful war."

"Then our march will not have been in vain," Eucádus said with a gladdened heart. "When do you plan to move troops for the dual attacks?"

"By midmorning in four days we will begin our separate marches," the captain replied, tracing the routes with his finger over an imaginary map on the table linen. "One army, after meeting troops from Altaga in the north, will sail down the eastern shore of Lake LaShear and attack the fleet at Zaracosa. The other will march down the western shore to battle forces occupying Rhiál's southern provinces. At dawn, two days after, we strike."

"And we will be victorious," Captain Tiber remarked, the fiery resolve in his steely blue eyes matching the confident tone of his words.

As the discussion continued, William listened with fascination, though contributed few words. His limited knowledge of warfare derived from what he had read in history books, and he now began to feel that he was simply a spectator in matters where he didn't belong. He wondered if he had been allowed a seat at this table merely out of respect and pity, simply because he was a prince and had suffered a grievous loss. Later, after everyone had finished lunch and stepped out onto a stone patio for a breath of the fresh lake air, William took Eucádus aside and addressed him pointblank about his role in the upcoming campaign.

"Who shall I be riding with?" he asked, gazing out at the slew of fine sailing vessels in the distance. "Am I to go north where the rafts are being assembled, or ride south to the battle along the lakeshore?"

"I am not in charge of such decisions," Eucádus said, aware of the young man's state of mind. "That is a matter for King Cedric or King Basil to decide. And though I sense that you feel your presence here is mere ornamentation, you must also recognize that you are of royal lineage."

"How can I forget?" he muttered.

"You shouldn't ever," Eucádus said. "Your brother, once heir to the throne of Montavia, is no longer with us, and the home of your grandfather, King Rowan, is now under siege. His fate is not now known to us. Conceivably, though I do not wish it, you might be the only surviving heir to the throne. So there is more to it than personal pride, Will, as to where your next steps should take you in this war."

He held his breath for a moment, his frustration quickly diffusing as Eucádus' words sunk in. He exhaled the cool lakeside air, feeling like his old self again. "I didn't mean to sound cross and apologize if I seemed so, Eucádus. I guess I never considered the possible consequences of my actions."

He smiled. "No apology required. I was once your age, too, and couldn't wait for the world to catch up with my aspirations. But that is normal. However, when we meet with King Basil this evening, all of these maddening details will be sorted out."

"I suppose so." William suddenly felt deflated and unworthy to think that he should be involved in making such grand plans. "Perhaps the rest of you should decide what is best in the days ahead and my place in it. I've much to learn, it seems."

"Learning never stops, even at my age," Eucádus said.

"I think I'll take a walk later while you sort things out," he decided. "To be honest, I could use some time alone after all that's happened."

"That might not be such a bad idea." Eucádus indicated through the doorway that the three kitchen workers had returned and were clearing away the lunch dishes. "King Basil mentioned that Aaron was fond of walking along the docks. Maybe he could give you a tour of Melinas later on while we discuss military matters. However," he said, "I promise to meet with you tonight, and while we share some buttered biscuits and a pot of tea, I will apprise you of the particulars of our meeting. Agreed?"

"Agreed," William said, shaking his hand. "I'll seek you out after dark."

"Until then," he replied before leaving to have a word with King Cedric who was still engaged in conversation with the others.

William, in the meantime, stepped inside the dining area and called to Aaron just as the boy was leaving the room with a tray of dirty dishes. The two other workers had already departed. Aaron looked up, ill at ease. Though William was only a year older, he was still a prince and Aaron felt slightly intimidated that he had sought him out. Nyla had instructed her staff to show the utmost respect to King Basil's royal guests.

"Yes, Prince William?" he asked, afraid to look him directly in the eyes. "How may I help you, sir? Was there a problem with your meal?"

"Hardly," he casually responded. "It was delicious, especially after dining on cold bread and stew the last several days."

"I'm pleased to hear that, sir. Is there some other matter I can help with?" he asked, his green eyes gazing timidly beneath a head of mussed-up hair.

"First, you can stop calling me *sir*, Aaron. We're nearly the same age, after all."

Aaron was hesitant to respond, looking around to see if anyone else was in the room. "Nyla, my superior, instructed me how to properly address the people we serve. I don't think that she would approve of–"

"Don't worry," William said with a grin. "If she or any of the others are around, you may call me *sir* all you want. But if it's just us, *Will* is preferred."

Aaron nodded. "Yes, Prince William. Uh, I mean..." He furrowed his brow. "Yes, Prince *Will*?"

William laughed. "You'll have to work on that. But in the meantime, I'm free later this afternoon and would love a tour of Melinas. King Basil said you're fond of walking by the docks. Care to show a stranger some of the local sights? I need to clear my head of all this endless talk," he said, pointing to his luncheon companions who were still conversing on the patio.

"I'd be happy to," Aaron said. "I'm off kitchen duty in a few hours." He indicated the pile of heavy dishes on the tray. "I should get back there now, with your permission."

"Oh, sorry," he said, walking with Aaron out of the room. "I'm keeping you from your job. And please, none of that *with your permission* talk either."

"Yes, uh–*Will*," he replied uncomfortably as they walked down a narrow hallway toward the kitchen. "Where shall I meet you?"

Before William could answer, Nyla stepped out of a doorway as Aaron approached with the tray of dishes. She looked down upon the boy with a disapproving stare until she noticed William.

"Prince William, what a pleasant surprise," she politely said. "Is something the matter? Has one of my workers erred in some way?" She glanced at Aaron a second time. "I'd be only too eager to make amends."

"No amends required," he said. "My compliments to you on an excellent meal."

"Thank you."

"I was pestering Aaron for a moment, delaying him from his duties," he said apologetically. "He agreed to walk with me around town later on, perhaps along the docks. I have free time and could use the company. I'm more in the way, I think, than helpful when it comes to discussing military matters."

"Aaron will make an excellent guide then, as he is fond of exploring along the lakeside," Nyla replied, smiling at Aaron.

William agreed to return to the kitchen in a few hours after Aaron's work was finished, eager to wander about and pretend for a time that he didn't have a care in the world, much like he had done with Brendan after they left the Blue Citadel twenty-four long days ago. But right now, all of that seemed part of another lifetime.

The crescent Fox Moon lounged in the western sky after sunset, the horizon streaked with a radiant orange glow. The inky darkness east beyond Lake LaShear was punctuated by a handful of stars above the small boats and anchored ships bobbing on the surface. Lamplighters ambled along the streets, putting a flame to each wick in the many oil lampposts dotting the major lanes of the city. William and Aaron wandered along the main road through town which ran parallel to the sandy lakeshore to the east. Beyond the sand and running along the water's edge was a stone walkway. Wooden docks extended off the walkway into the water, alongside which many small fishing craft were tied up, safe for a few more weeks before winter's grip would retire them for the season. Bonfires burned on the shore near a handful of wooden shanties where a few hardy fishermen worked diligently into the evening repairing their netting and lines. On the west side of the main road were a series of shops, all now closed for the night, their windows tightly shuttered.

"I often stop by and listen to the fishermen tell their stories, especially in summertime," Aaron said, having warmed up to William and feeling as if he were an old friend. "Now there are just as many soldiers around manning the larger ships. I've shared stories with them, too, though many of the tales are not as cheerful."

"King Basil mentioned how you traveled up here from the south," William said, uncertain whether he should mention the boy's missing father. He soon learned that he needn't have worried about broaching the subject.

"Before my village was overrun by King Drogin's men, my father insisted that I travel north to safety with some of our neighbors. He stayed behind with others who banded together to fight," he explained, his voice as distant as his thoughts. "My mother died when I was younger, and now I wonder if I'll ever see my father again. In the meantime, I work in the kitchens."

"Where to you live?" William asked.

"I use the staff quarters in the basement, especially when I must wake before dawn to work the early shift," he explained. "Occasionally I'll stay with my old neighbors. They're not far from here and are like a second family to me. I'll take you there for dinner one of these days if time allows."

"It's good that you have a connection to home, though I'm sorry your life was turned upside down. Unfortunately, that's become the norm for many in Laparia these days." William stopped and gazed over the darkened waters, recalling the time he and Brendan shared a meal near Lake Lasko and fed an apple to that deer. Such a simple action had marked a drastic turning point in their lives. When Aaron asked what he was thinking about, William looked at him with a pained expression, drawn back to the present.

With surprisingly little reluctance, he told his new friend about his brother and their clever escape from Montavia and their harrowing excursion into the Ebrean Forest that changed both of their lives forever.

"And sometimes I think I'm the only one affected by this war," Aaron remarked as they approached the end of the main road and headed down a nearby lane. "Compared to your adventures, I've had an easy life while everyone else around me fights."

"I haven't engaged in an actual battle myself, though I did witness one on the Kincarin Plains," William admitted. "Regardless, everyone plays the part he's supposed to, I guess. Don't go looking for trouble just because you feel you want to get involved. I've been thinking the same way, and you know what?"

"What?" he asked as they passed through a fluttering circle of light cast off from one of the lampposts.

"No matter where I go, trouble seems to find *me!*" William couldn't help but laugh as they wandered through a crowd of passersby blanketed by the night. "So let's not rush to find it any faster, okay?"

They returned to the estate an hour later. William dropped off Aaron near the kitchen quarters just as Nyla was passing by. She inquired of the boys if they had had an enjoyable evening in town.

"Very much so," William replied, recounting all the sights Aaron had shown him. "It felt good to wander about with no place to go, as if I were back home with my brother. We're going to explore the docks tomorrow evening, too."

"If such is your desire," she said. "I prefer sitting by a fire on cool nights such as these and sipping a cup of blackberry tea while catching up on my mending. And that's exactly what I'm going to do now," she said, flashing a pleasant smile. "Goodnight, Prince William. Goodnight, Aaron."

They said goodnight to Nyla before she disappeared down the corridor. William then left Aaron to search for Eucádus and hopefully learn about any developments in the upcoming battle with King Drogin. But when he was informed that Eucádus was still engaged in a meeting, he decided to go to his room on the third floor and lie down, the fresh air from his recent walk and the rigors of the past weeks finally catching up with him. He promptly fell asleep when his head hit the feather pillow, enjoying a dreamless, recuperative rest until the first rays of the rising sun peeked through his window shutters the following morning.

On that same evening, about an hour after she had left William and Aaron near the kitchen quarters and returned to her room, Nyla donned a heavy cloak, draped the hood over her head and stepped quietly out a side entrance of the estate as she had done from time to time on many evenings throughout the year. A guard standing watch greeted her with a smile.

"Evening, Miss Nyla. Out for another walk?"

"Most definitely, Mr. Souder. I feel as if I've been cooped up in that kitchen for a week straight!" she replied with a genial laugh. "I shall stop by and visit my sister as well. Mildred has been a tad under the weather lately."

"Sorry to hear that, ma'am. My best to her," he replied. "Oh, and that bit of roast beef one of your workers sent out earlier was beyond delicious. I thank you for that, as always."

"I'm only too happy to share extras, Mr. Souder. Until later," she said with a pleasant wave before disappearing in the glow of a nearby lamppost lighting the way along the main walk leading into town.

Shortly afterward, Nyla wandered the murky streets of Melinas, occasionally glancing from side to side, though certain nobody passing by could identify her. After walking along the main road past a butcher shop now closed for the night, she slipped around the corner to her right and headed down a dark, narrow alley, her footsteps echoing off the cobblestones. A moment later she stopped at a wooden door, but before knocking, she looked up and down at each entrance to the alley. Seeing no one approaching or passing by, she rapped upon the door, impatiently waiting for a reply. After a second knock, she heard a muffled voice, apparently its owner not in a hurry to open up.

"I'm coming," somebody muttered on the other side. Soon the door was unlocked and opened a crack, a face peering out into the cool darkness. "Who is it?"

"I'm looking for Bosh. Is he here?"

"Who's asking?"

"*I'm* asking," Nyla said sternly, stepping into the faint firelight escaping through the crack and removing her hood. When the man recognized her face, he quickly stepped back and opened the door all the way, inviting her in.

"What are you doing here?" he asked, glancing down both ends of the alleyway. After she entered the room, he closed the door and locked it. "You're not supposed to visit this place, Nyla. You know the procedure."

She sighed, not in the mood to be lectured to. "I helped design the procedure. Now is Bosh here or not? I need to speak with him at once. I have important information that couldn't wait to go through proper channels."

"All right," the man said, appearing tired and disheveled. "He's in the back room discussing things with the others. I'll get him."

"Thank you."

A few moments later, a tall, unshaven man sporting a tangle of dark hair and dressed as if he worked on a fishing boat entered the room, a smile of surprise registering upon his face the instant he saw Nyla. "I can't believe you're here," he said, his voice grave yet exhibiting an affectionate edge as he rushed to her.

"I got tired of standing over steaming kettles and listening to chatty underlings," she joked. She took his hands in hers and kissed him, letting the man hold her in his arms. "How are you, Bosh?"

"Better now," he replied, kissing Nyla on the back of her head as she rested it on his shoulder. "Still, why are you here? What's so important that you ignored procedure?"

She stood back and looked Bosh in the eyes, a thin, knowing smile upon her face. "I may be able to lead you to some valuable information that will help our effort. But I had to be quick about it. We may not have another opportunity."

"Go on," he said, inviting her to sit at a small table against one wall. A candle flickered on the tabletop in the otherwise spartan room. Low flames burned in a nearby fireplace.

"An army from the west has recently arrived, if you haven't already noticed."

"How could anyone miss it?" he said. "Word has already been sent south with the particulars."

Nyla explained about the gathering in King Basil's room earlier that day with King Cedric, Prince William, Eucádus and the others. "Later, they met for lunch to strategize against King Drogin, no doubt, except for King Basil. He is still very ill."

"That's not surprising, Nyla. But unless you were allowed to sit in on those gatherings, how does this help us?"

She smiled. "Because I know exactly where the young prince of Montavia is going to be tomorrow evening, nearly alone and unprotected. Can you imagine what military details he might possess?"

Bosh rubbed his whiskers, suddenly interested in where the conversation was heading. "Tell me how you know this."

Nyla explained that Prince William had struck up a friendship with Aaron, one of her kitchen workers, and told of their planned excursion along the docks on the following evening. "Should you somehow confiscate that young bit of royalty, think of the benefit to our cause, to our leader."

"I'm doing just that," Bosh said, nodding.

"Drogin planted us here months before the war started, and though I'm able to glean a few scraps of information from inside the estate from time to time, it can't compare to anything like this opportunity," she said, brimming with excitement. "What propitious timing too, with Drogin on the verge of an attack."

Bosh reached across the table and held Nyla's hands. "This could be very useful, my dear. Tell me more."

She gave Bosh detailed descriptions of William and Aaron. "If one of your men keeps a lookout of the estate before sunset, you will most certainly see the boys as they leave. You can follow them from there to the docks so there is no mistake."

"There are several vantage points close by, yet still far enough away to remain discreet," he said. "Though I feel confident that this war will end in our victory, I won't turn up my nose at a possible advantage like this."

"I thought not, so I risked the visit," Nyla said. She kissed Bosh's hand still warmly clasped to hers. "But I must leave soon. I'm never out too long on my walks and don't want to arouse anyone's suspicion. I'm visiting my sister again tonight."

Bosh grinned. "You don't have a sister."

"But I've always wanted one."

"When we're back in Zaracosa where we belong, you'll be so happy that you won't even think about such things," he said as he walked Nyla to the door. "We'll have much to do then, helping Drogin rule these lands as they should be. Imagine the rewards he'll send our way if this latest ploy helps our cause."

"I'm imagining," Nyla said. "But even if it doesn't..."

Bosh nodded, a snakelike smile beneath his furrowed brow. "Don't worry. Prince William and his friend won't be returning to the estate. You'll have to hire another worker to wash the crockery, I'm afraid."

"Oh well, the inconveniences of war." She kissed Bosh goodbye, caressing his face with her hand. "Farewell, husband," she said before draping the hood of her cloak over her head.

"Farewell, wife," he replied with a distant smile. "Watch yourself."

"I will," she promised, gazing into his eyes one last time before stepping out the door and back into the cold, black chill of fading autumn.

After a thick, morning fog lingered upon the lake and surrounding area for a time, the next day turned sunny and cool as billowing clouds sailed lazily overhead. King Cedric, Captain Silas, Eucádus and the other captains and Clearing leaders made separate rounds to the various battalions encamped in the fields to the west and south of King Basil's estate. The King himself remained inside, though received regular updates from couriers on the battle preparations. Troop movements to the north to meet up with the raft builders from Altaga, and to the south to directly confront Drogin's main army, were scheduled to begin in three days.

Today, William had the pleasure of accompanying Eucádus and Ramsey as they inspected and consulted with some of the troops stationed on the western field. He proudly rode upon Lester as the trio made their rounds all morning and into the afternoon. On a few occasions, he rode alone to the estate to deliver correspondences directly to King Basil as did other couriers from different locations.

As Eucádus and Ramsey neared one tent to discuss matters with several company leaders, William gazed about at the activity swirling around him, a heightened sense of anticipation enveloping the mass of military might. Some men engaged in training exercises, the clanking of metal swords and the swish of speeding arrows wafting through the air. Others tended to the mundane tasks of stoking the bonfires, washing laundry, mending tents and preparing meals for the sea of soldiers. Sweet smelling wood smoke drifted into the sky and dispersed on a mischievous breeze. He viewed the landscape as a stunning and exhilarating sight, yet knew that when this vast engine of war finally moved forward and the clash of swords drew actual blood, his mind would harbor none of the romantic notions in which he now indulged.

"Such an impressive view never wears off," Ramsey commented to him as they wandered through one company of soldiers near noontime among a sea of colorful flags and banners fluttering in the breeze. "It's amazing how a committed group of men will fight for the freedom of others when they're organized behind great leaders. Yet I'm equally amazed, though in a different way, when I witnessed so many men from my country of Linden tolerating the slow corruption of our nation to Vellan's will. It was as if they simply gave up without a fight, letting him methodically wrap up Linden's cherished way of life in twisted webs of deceit like a gluttonous spider." He shrugged as he looked at William. "I will never understand it to my dying day."

"Nor would I," William said, "though I'm pleased that none in Montavia were happy to see Caldurian and his Island troops attack our kingdom."

"But your land was attacked in front of everyone's eyes. The invasion of Linden, Surna and Harlow was executed subtly at first as too many leaders walking the corridors of power were corrupted one by one, ultimately blinded as to where their loyalties should have lied. Now the mountain nations are on the verge of an Enári invasion to follow the political dismantling of our governments. We must succeed here to have any hope for victory back home."

William slapped Ramsey on the back and offered an encouraging smile. "I'm certain we'll succeed. I admit I was less hopeful when I heard the sad stories about your homeland during the war council. But standing here in the light of day and seeing all this before me, my confidence is renewed."

"Those are heartening words," he replied as he rubbed a hand through his mop of dark brown hair. "Let's hope that sentiment remains when gray clouds gather and darkness falls."

"Always the optimist!" William joked. "But before I ride back to deliver Eucádus' next report to King Basil, let's find a bite to eat. No matter how bad things might appear, a good, hot meal is sure to turn your thinking around."

After a brief lunch with Ramsey and a few other soldiers, William rode back to the estate to deliver his latest report to King Basil. The King was in a fine mood, having finished eating lunch himself after waking up from a short nap. He invited William to stay for tea, eager to speak with the young prince about matters other than war and politics. William was delighted to join him, sitting opposite the monarch in the same chair King Cedric had occupied upon their arrival. A stream of bright sunshine pierced through the partially closed drapes on the lakeside window, scattering the dusky shadows that had gathered inside the room.

"I grow weary of the constancy of this struggle and crave some conversation, however short, about any other subject," the King said as William poured them tea from a steaming kettle. "I used to quiz my sons, Victor and Morton, on the names of the various mountains in the Ridloe chain or the types of industry prevalent in each province of Rhiál and such. They seemed to enjoy it, especially after they grew smart enough to counter my inquiries with questions of their own. When the boys stumped me, they had a fine time announcing their victory to any who would listen!"

William laughed as he imagined those two young princes barreling through the corridors, shouting with joy. "Reminds me of competitions I had with Brendan, but being the older one, he usually won them all whether in athletics or intelligence." He sipped his tea with a heavy heart. "But now they are all gone, your sons and my brother. It is hardly fair, is it?"

"No, it is not, and my heart breaks because of it," King Basil replied, a thick melancholy entwined with his words. "But as short as their time was, my sons had lived full, adventurous lives. I am truly saddened that Brendan had fallen in the prime of his youth. You may never be able to reconcile that fact, William, but always remember your brother when you live out your days. In time, the hurt will diminish some and good memories will take its place, but I will not say that that road shall be easy. It will be as exhausting and painful as, well, this war." The King managed a smile. "And I had mentioned that I didn't want to talk about it."

William nodded. "I'm afraid this war and their deaths swirl about us whether we wish to recognize it or not. I don't suppose we have a choice."

"I guess not," he replied, eyeing the dark corners of the room. He slowly raised his cup to William and offered a toast. "Here's to those who left us, too soon and without warning. May their memories forever linger."

William lifted his cup, and through the rising steam he noted an overwhelming grief set deep within King Basil's eyes, knowing that it mirrored his own and wondering how long it would torment him. The pair silently sipped their drinks, the room awash in streaks of dazzling sunlight amid a swirl of bitter shadows.

William met Aaron bounding down the corridor adjacent to the kitchen a few hours later, both eager to taste the fresh, evening air and feel a cool breeze off Lake LaShear. They exited the main entrance of the estate, sauntered down the front walk as the lampposts were being lit, and passed through the gate in the stone wall to the front road. As they wandered toward the city, pointing at distant ships on the water while chattering away, neither boy was aware of a man watching them from behind a thicket of trees upon a weedy knoll, the stranger's eyes fixed upon their every movement. After William and Aaron entered the main part of town, the man left his post and followed, keeping a safe distance as he blended into the passing crowds and thickening shadows.

"Though he hasn't yet told me directly, I think Eucádus is going to ask me as a favor to stay with King Basil when the army departs," William said, though with none of the disappointment he would have shown just a day earlier. "To keep him company and act as his personal messenger and the like. I don't suppose I'd mind either. I've grown fond of King Basil and we have much in common."

"Didn't you tell me yesterday how anxious you were to wield a sword and avenge your brother's death?" Aaron asked, imagining himself doing the same in honor of his missing father.

"Sometimes I talk without thinking," he replied. "Despite my desire to contribute on the battlefield, I believe my presence at King

Basil's side might help him more than any medicine. And me, too, I must admit. I hope that doesn't sound selfish."

"After what you've been through, it sounds normal." Aaron pointed far down the shore as they wandered along the main road. The wooden docks were crowded with small crafts bobbing upon the water. "I see a fire burning by Jack Grindol's shanty. He must be planning to work late tonight repairing his nets. Chances are he's frying up some fish for his evening meal."

In the light of the Fox Moon, now near first quarter, William noted a look of hungry anticipation upon Aaron's face. "I thought you just ate dinner before I arrived?"

"And your point would be?" He burst out laughing. "My stomach has room for another meal and then some. Besides, Jack always cooks extra. He'll have enough for both of us. He's a great storyteller, too. I'll bet he's never talked to a real prince before."

"Lead the way," he said with a smirk. "But I'm thinking that I'm getting the better deal here."

They continued down the road until the sandy shore widened to their left. Several bonfires crackled in the fading twilight. But just before William and Aaron stepped onto the beach, they heard a faint call farther down the street now vacant of passersby and dimly lit only by the Fox Moon and the light flowing out of nearby windows. William looked up when he heard the voice again.

"Over there," Aaron said, pointing. "I see someone on the ground up ahead."

He and William hurried toward the person, surprised to see a man sitting on the edge of the road with his back against a vacant building. The stranger, unshaven and grimacing, appeared to be in pain as he massaged his right ankle through the side of his boot. He looked up at the boys, grateful that they answered his call.

"What happened, sir?" Aaron asked.

The man laughed, seemingly embarrassed. "Caught my foot in a rut down the road a ways. Twisted it bad, I think." He took a deep breath, continuing to tenderly rub his ankle. "Thanks for stopping."

"Can we help?" William asked, kneeling down on one knee next to him.

"I'd appreciate a hand up," he said. "I don't live far from here. If you could help me hobble back, I'd be most thankful. So would my wife."

"Happy to do so," William said as he assisted the man to stand, allowing him to lean upon a shoulder for support. Aaron helped to guide him from the other side as they walked back in the direction from which they had come.

"I'm Meklas, by the way," the man said, shaking William and Aaron's hands as they introduced themselves. "I live around the next corner near that butcher shop. Sorry to impose upon you like this."

"It's not a problem," Aaron said. "Will and I were looking for something to do."

"Can we find a physician for you?" William offered.

"No, no," Meklas insisted. "I just want to sit by a fire and rest my foot on a chair. If I don't feel better by morning, maybe I'll seek help. Ah, here's my lane."

He pointed to the butcher shop ahead, dimly lit by a nearby lamppost. The trio turned down the darkened, cobblestone street to their left, their footsteps echoing off the walls and consumed by the night. Soon they approached a wooden door that Meklas indicated as they eagerly helped the struggling man to his destination.

"Just a couple more steps and you're home," Aaron said.

"I only hope my wife doesn't scold me," Meklas remarked with a trace of mirth in his voice. "I was supposed to have been home an hour ago. She'll insist that I got my comeuppance for being late to the dinner table again."

"We'll speak in your defense," William promised as Meklas knocked on the door.

"I'll take all the help I can get," he replied as he pounded on the door a second time. "I'm home!"

"Are you sure your wife is home?" Aaron joked as William laughed, neither noticing as two other men entered the lane from the far end. A moment later they were near the doorway.

"Locked out again, Meklas?" one of the two men asked though the shadows with a hearty laugh.

William and Aaron were startled by the new arrivals and glanced at the two strangers, unable to distinguish their faces.

Though Meklas introduced them as two of his friends, William felt a slight wave of apprehension pass over him.

"I hope not," Meklas replied to the man's question.

Suddenly sounds from behind the door were distinctly audible and William felt at ease again. "This must be her now," he said.

Meklas nodded. "And certain to have my skin."

"No doubt!" one of the men replied as the door swung open.

But just as William and Aaron looked inside, expecting to greet either Meklas' disgruntled or overjoyed wife, they were both surprised to see a tall man with tangles of dark hair and a grim smile stuck to his face. "Glad you could make it," Bosh said.

Suddenly, the two men in back grabbed William and Aaron by their collars as Meklas broke away and stepped into the room. Before either of the boys could react, they were pushed inside and heard the door slam behind them. William's heart raced as he attempted to spin around and free himself. But before he uttered a word, a dirty, callused hand was slapped against his mouth and the tip of a knife blade pressed to his throat. William's eyes widened in terror when he saw that Aaron was being similarly held.

"So far, so good," Bosh said, studying the faces of his captives, satisfied that they matched the descriptions of the boys Nyla had provided the previous night. "Am I going to have any trouble from either one of you?" he asked as the two men holding them slowly raised their knife blades in front of William and Aaron's faces. The two boys simultaneously shook their heads. "Wonderful. That was the right answer," he replied. "Now we'll be able to talk like civilized men. That's the reason I brought you here, after all—to talk."

CHAPTER 39

Through the Billowing Fog

William was shoved into a room and stumbled to the floor. All went dark as the door was slammed shut and locked. Dim light flowed beneath the bottom from an adjacent room, the faint glow mixed with the frustrated mutterings of Bosh and his associates. Their voices diminished as the men retreated to another area. William turned over and lay on his back, his head pounding, his body aching. He tasted dried blood on the corner of his mouth where Bosh had slapped him.

"Are you all right?" Aaron whispered from among the inky shadows, feeling responsible for William's injuries.

"Yes," he replied with difficulty. "I just need to rest for a few minutes. I…" He exhaled deeply, never having felt so sore in his life. For a moment he imagined what Brendan might have experienced while he lay dying on the cabin floor.

Bosh had questioned him for an hour, demanding information about King Basil's military plans. When William refused to answer time and time again, Bosh slapped him, telling him that he knew he was a prince from Montavia and had associated with King Cedric and others who had traveled from the west. William didn't deny the claims but revealed nothing more, only enraging the man until he slammed a fist into William's stomach and shoved him against the wall while two other men looked on in amusement.

"Look, this is me going easy on you, *your Highness*," Bosh had said with contempt. "What's to follow won't be as pleasant, so think about it," he added before pushing William into the windowless room and locking the door.

Now, William stared into a black void, wondering who his captors were and how they had discovered his identity. Was there a spy among King Basil or King Cedric's troops? If so, what other information had already been revealed? He shuddered, a nauseating chill in the pit of his stomach as he fully comprehended the peril that had befallen the resistance. He slowly turned his head, and though unable to see Aaron, he knew he was sitting close by, no doubt scared and confused. William vowed to protect the boy just as Brendan had protected *him*, but he feared he had little time.

The stench of warfare was in the air. William knew they had little chance of escape against four men, and should they break him, he figured that he and Aaron would probably be killed. What worried him even more though was what would happen to Eucádus and the others should matters here play out for the worst. He wondered what his brother would have done in this situation, envisioning Brendan's smile in the darkness before he lapsed into fitful sleep.

The rattle of the metal lock shook him from his slumber. William's head swam with remnants of blurred dreams and echoes of sharp voices. It felt like the dead of night, and when the glow of firelight splashed into the room, he realized that he had probably slept only a few hours. Dawn was still a vague hope.

"Ready to talk now?" Bosh said, kicking at William's boot.

He struggled to sit up, his muscles sore and tight, his eyelids heavy. Aaron, who had been sound asleep a few feet away, sat up as well, fearing for the prince's life.

"I said all I have to say," William replied, his voice dry and raspy. "You'll learn nothing more from me."

"Is that so?" Bosh's words were edged with bitterness, his tall frame eerily silhouetted against the sickly glow of firelight.

"He said he won't talk!" Aaron snapped. "Leave him alone."

"Nobody's asking you, kettle scrubber, so mind your own business." Bosh glared at William. "Last chance, prince, before it gets ugly. Are you going to talk?"

William shook his head, his heart pounding with fear despite a small part of him not caring what they'd do. He was growing weary of the whole affair. "I'll sit down with you," he said, "but I won't talk. *Ever.*"

Bosh, his arms akimbo, gazed at him for several icy moments before sharply sighing. "Fine. Then maybe he will!" In a flash, he bent over and grabbed Aaron by the arm, yanking the boy to his feet. His fingers gripped him like a vice.

"Leave him alone!" William cried, jumping up, ready to rush at the man.

But Bosh pulled out a knife and held it to Aaron's throat just as Meklas entered the room similarly armed. William looked at both men and took a step back.

"That's more like it," Bosh said. "If you won't cooperate, then maybe your friend will have sense enough to do so."

"I told you, he doesn't know anything!" William pleaded, seeing the fear in Aaron's eyes as the boy tried to control his erratic breaths. "It's the truth. He hasn't attended meetings nor is he privy to any military matters. Leave him alone. Please."

Bosh pretended to be impressed by William's valiant defense. "Well, if what you say is true, then there really isn't a need for me to question this boy. He might as well go back to the kitchens to wash dishes and bake bread." He snapped his fingers and smirked. "Ah, but then he might turn us all in to the authorities. That wouldn't be good for me and the boys." He raised the tip of his knife so that the firelight reflected off the sharp blade, making it clearly visible to William and Aaron. "If this one really doesn't know anything, I guess we don't need him here taking up valuable space." Bosh shoved the boy at Meklas, who grabbed Aaron behind the collar and waved his knife at him. "Meklas, you and Gelt take him out and get rid of the body. I'm sure there's a nice spot on the bottom of Lake LaShear that will have him."

"I'll find one."

"No!" William cried, advancing a step with terror in his eyes. "Don't hurt him. He won't turn you in. Isn't that right, Aaron?"

Aaron nodded.

"Sorry, prince, but he's got to go," Bosh coldly responded. "Unless..."

William swallowed hard, knowing what his captor was about to say but asking him the question anyway. "Unless *what*?"

"If you tell me what I want to know, your friend will live," he replied matter-of-factly. "We'll have a nice, friendly chat in the next room and he can continue to sleep in here." Bosh cleaned beneath his fingernails with the knife tip, speaking his next words with chilling deliberation. "Therefore, if the next words out of your mouth are anything, and I mean *anything* other than *I'll tell you what you want to know*, then your friend is going to be killed in front of you—right here, right now. Meklas is just itching for a reason to use his dagger, but it's all up to you. So, Prince William of Montavia, anything you want to say?"

Crestfallen, William watched as Meklas positioned his knife near Aaron's throat. He could sense the terror overwhelming his friend and wished that he had never dragged the boy into his world of war, politics and deceit. But now the worst deed would have to be done. William hated himself at the moment, having no desire to ever be king if decisions such as these would be laid upon his lap. But like it or not, he had to decide now. He glanced up at Bosh, gazing into his captor's eyes with boiling disdain.

"I'll tell you what you want to know," he replied.

Eucádus accompanied King Cedric late the following morning as they wandered among the battalions spread out across the field south of the estate. They were to meet shortly with Captain Silas and others to refine their invasion strategy now that the last scouts had returned with updated information about Drogin's troop positions along the southern shores. King Basil was still prepared to move his army in less than two days.

Eucádus entered a large tent with King Cedric where nearly a dozen other men awaited Captain Silas. Several small benches were laid out in a semicircle around a table where officers would present the latest information. The sides of the tent undulated in a gusty breeze as the men took their places. Eucádus spoke to the King in private in back of the tent.

"I have not seen Will today," he said, "and had to recruit another courier to send messages to King Basil at the estate. I instructed him to locate the prince, assuming William had been at the King's side, but King Basil relayed that he had not seen the boy since lunchtime yesterday."

"Nor have I in my wanderings," King Cedric replied. "It's not like William to take his leave so freely."

"Perhaps his wanderlust got the best of him as he explored the lakeside," Eucádus guessed, explaining how William had become good friends with Aaron and that the two had a penchant for exploring the city after sunset. "I thought it would do his spirit good to spend time with someone his own age considering all he had endured."

"A fine idea. Perhaps they wandered too far and passed the night outdoors," the King suggested. "William spent much time on the road with his brother. Maybe his time with Aaron is helping him cope with Brendan's loss."

"Maybe, but it is far too late in the day for him not to have yet returned. I might be worrying needlessly, but Ramsey also mentioned that he saw no sign of William earlier among the western camps." Eucádus furrowed his brow, beginning to worry. "As Captain Silas isn't here yet, I'm going to slip out for a moment and send a few soldiers to the estate to check for William and Aaron one last time. If they're not back, I'll instruct the men to scour the docks and areas nearby." He sighed, looking very much the beleaguered parent. "I hope I'm making more fuss than need be, but…"

"Despite being a prince, William is still a young boy," the King said with a chuckle. "He may feel like he's escaping from his studies for a day. Perhaps being immersed in our stifling routine of endless, dreary meetings has taken its toll on him. Coupled with his brother's death, maybe he just needed to escape from *us*."

Eucádus grinned, feeling better upon hearing such an explanation. "I understand your logic, sir, and am now inclined to believe that that is the case. Still, I'll send some men to ease my mind. I'll only be a moment," he said as he slipped out through the tent flaps into the blustery gray of approaching noon, trying to convince himself that William would show up any minute. He had grown fond of the boy from the moment he arrived at the Star Clearing and would never forgive himself if something happened to him. He hoped his anxiety was unjustified.

But several hours later, anxiety turned to fear. Eucádus received word from the estate that Aaron had never shown up for work in the kitchens that morning. Apparently Nyla had nervously reported him missing after a search of the estate proved unsuccessful. A scout even visited the nearby home of Aaron's former neighbor where he occasionally spent the night, though he was not there either. As the sun sank beneath the western horizon, Eucádus gazed east across the cold, black waters of Lake LaShear as he stood by the walls of the estate, awaiting the arrival of a second group of men sent into Melinas to search for William and Aaron. His chest tightened as his mind juggled several disquieting thoughts regarding their disappearance, blaming himself for whatever fate might have in store as war was about to break out, wondering if he would ever see either of them again.

After William had been questioned by Bosh, he and Aaron slept uneasily for a few hours before being awakened again near dawn. They were ushered outdoors into cold darkness at knifepoint and ordered to climb on back of a horse-drawn wagon, guarded under the watchful eyes of Meklas and Gelt. Bosh drove the wagon to a small farmhouse several miles outside the city. The fourth man remained back at their quarters in Melinas.

"Where are you taking us?" William asked as the sky grew milky gray along the eastern horizon. "I told you what you wanted to know." Meklas glanced at him coldly, making him feel as if the man were staring directly through him. No one spoke another word until they arrived at the farmhouse.

When the wagon stopped, William and Aaron jumped off the back at Meklas' command and were led to a barn near a one-story clay house with a thatched roof. The surrounding area was beset with dried weeds left over from warmer days. The boys were shoved inside the abandoned structure which smelled of stale hay and soil.

"Now keep quiet or we'll tie and gag you," Bosh ordered. "Understand?"

"We understand," Aaron muttered with an air of defeat.

"Why aren't you letting us go?" William asked. "We had a deal."

Bosh grinned. "A deal? The deal was that you talked and I let *him* live," he explained, pointing a finger at Aaron. "I never said anything about letting you go."

"What do you plan to do with us?"

"That is yet to be determined," he replied. "First I must learn the value of the information you provided us last night. For both your sakes, I hope you weren't lying about King Basil's intentions. Now no more questions! If you behave, perhaps Meklas will bring you breakfast." With that, Bosh closed the pair of doors and barred them securely with a thick piece of oak wood lying on the ground. He signaled for Meklas and Gelt to follow him to the farmhouse.

"How long do we have to keep them?" Meklas inquired, not looking forward to the tedious task.

"Until they cease to be assets," he said. "The one is a prince, and though I don't expect Drogin's offensive to fail, he'd make quite a nice bargaining piece if it does."

"What about the other one?" Gelt asked. "He's not royalty."

"But the boy's safety is of great concern to the prince, so that allows us control over him," Bosh explained. "We'll get rid of them only when we're absolutely sure we don't need them. Until then, they'll remain here under your supervision. Now let's have breakfast before Gelt and I take to the road. We have important news to spread to our contacts, compliments of the prince of Montavia."

"Well, we're not dead yet, so I guess that's a good thing," William softly said, his words swallowed up in the suffocating gloom. The first hint of daylight was visible through cracks in the barn walls. A pair of small windows located high up near opposite ends of the roof revealed the drab gray morning.

"Seems the only way out is the way we came in," Aaron said as he pushed against the pair of double doors. They held fast against his weight.

"When it gets lighter, we'll see where we stand. Maybe there's another way out," William said, plopping down on the ground. He sniffed the air a few times, grimacing. "Don't know if I have an appetite for breakfast anymore. All I smell is rotten straw and," he sniffed the air once more, "the delightful lingering aroma of cow. I suppose we could have had worse accommodations."

He sighed and leaned back against a wooden post, recalling the talk he had had with Bosh a few hours ago that saved Aaron's life. He felt cold, wondering if he made the correct decision, assessing the consequences that might befall this kingdom because of his words. Should he have sacrificed both their lives for the sake of Rhiál? He thought he could have resisted Bosh to the very end if it had been only his life at stake, or so he imagined, gladly willing to die so that King Basil could achieve victory. But William realized he hadn't the heart to sacrifice an innocent boy for the cause and wondered if he could ever lead a nation if such were the choices he'd be forced to make from time to time. He sadly shook his head, not fully convinced that a right choice even existed.

Aaron sat across from William in the gloom, barely able to discern his outline. He rested his arms on bent knees, avoiding looking at the prince even through a veil of darkness. He realized the conflicted feelings William was probably battling right now and felt guilty that he was the cause of it.

"I want to thank you for..." He sighed, looking at his friend. "Will, you shouldn't have had to choose between my life and..."

"You don't have to say anything, Aaron. I did what I did and now it's over. Maybe I should have let them kill us both."

"Maybe, but that's easier said now than when you had no time to think about it."

"I suppose," he replied. "But I feel rotten. I feel like I betrayed everybody. How do I live with that on my conscience?"

"You can fret later. First we have to find a way out of here and warn everybody about what the enemy knows," Aaron replied. "By the way, what *do* they know?"

"I told Bosh everything, so I don't see why you shouldn't know either. King Basil is going to move his armies the day after tomorrow to counter an attack by Drogin's troops planned several days from now." William quickly explained the particulars to Aaron. "But if Drogin finds out, Eucádus and the others will be marching into a trap–and it's all my fault."

"I'll share the blame," Aaron said. "If I hadn't taken you into town, none of this would be happening."

"But it was my idea to accompany you there, and all because I was bored." William was disappointed with himself all over again. "If I had stayed in Montavia we wouldn't be in this mess." He thought hard for a moment, considering exactly how they had landed in their curious predicament. "I was wondering earlier about who identified me to Bosh and the others. Someone at the estate or among the armies must have let them know that I was a prince and what I looked like. How would Meklas have spotted us along the main road otherwise?"

"I was thinking about that before I fell asleep," Aaron said. "But I'm sure a lot of people both inside and outside the estate are aware that you're a prince."

"True, but Bosh also knew that you worked in the kitchens. He called you a kettle scrubber, didn't he?"

Aaron grunted. "Yeah, just before he put a knife to my throat. But many people know you're a prince and that I work in the kitchens. It doesn't narrow down the list much."

"Not really. I think that–"

Suddenly William heard voices outside and jumped up. He ran to the doors, and though they were securely barred from the outside, he could still push them open just a crack to allow him to peer outdoors into the unfolding morning. Aaron stood beside him, anxiously awaiting a report.

"What do you see, Will?"

"Looks like Bosh and Gelt are unhitching the horses from the wagon," he said, one eye pressed to the narrow slit between the doors. "Meklas and two other men are talking to them. That other pair must have been living at the farmhouse already." He glanced at Aaron. "It seems that Drogin planted his spies all over Rhiál before he started this war. How are we supposed to know who to trust?"

"Let me take a look," Aaron said as William stepped aside. A moment later the boy watched as Bosh and Gelt snapped the reins of their horses and galloped down the dirt road, disappearing beyond a thicket of trees in the gloomy morning. "There they go, ready to send word about King Basil's plan." He turned his head, glancing anxiously at William. "What do we do now?"

William shrugged, searching for an answer.

Aaron heard the shuffle of footsteps about an hour later and raced to the doors, staring through the space between them. "Meklas is coming with one of the other men." He glanced at William who was now visible in the morning light seeping through the upper windows. "I think it's breakfast time."

Moments later, the wooden bar was removed and the barn doors were opened. Meklas stood with a small cloth sack and a bucket of water. The other man, armed with a knife, stood silently in the background. Meklas tossed the sack to William.

"Bosh said I had to feed you, so eat up," he snickered. He set the bucket of water inside the doorway. "Enjoy your beverage, too."

As he turned to leave, William called out. "Where did Bosh and Gelt ride off to? They seemed in a hurry," he said with a peculiar grin that caught Meklas' attention.

"Were you spying on us? You might be a prince, but that doesn't count for much here."

"I was just wondering where they went. I assume to pass along that *valuable* information I provided," he said with apparent delight, glancing at Aaron with a grin. Aaron, who appeared baffled by William's relaxed demeanor, nodded as if in the know.

"That's exactly where they went," Meklas said, annoyed at William's show of bravado and slightly unnerved that the prince seemed less than concerned that King Basil's war plans were being revealed to the enemy.

"Glad to hear it," William said with a pleasant smile. "Now leave us so Aaron and I can enjoy our meal, sparse though it is."

"You do that, prince," Meklas muttered as he began to close the doors.

William laughed. "Not *quite* a prince, but I suppose it doesn't matter now that Bosh has left."

Meklas exhaled through clenched teeth as he slammed the doors shut, aggravated that he had to watch these two. Yet something about William's sudden change in attitude bothered him. He glanced at the man with the knife standing behind him, silently seeking his opinion before he yanked open the doors once again. He glared at William.

"What do you mean *not quite a prince*?" Meklas asked. "Are you taunting me? Bosh said I wasn't to kill you, but he said nothing about teaching either of you a lesson."

William raised a hand to calm Meklas. "All I'm saying is that I'm not who you think I am. I'm neither a prince of Montavia nor a prince from anywhere, for that matter."

"Oh? And why should I believe that?"

William fished out a piece of bread from the sack and tossed it to Aaron while helping himself to some as well. "I don't really care if you believe it," he said while eating. "All I needed was for Bosh to believe it so he'd deliver the false information I gave him. Worked like a charm!"

"You were a good actor," Aaron said, playing along with William's ruse though not quite sure where his friend was going with the act.

Meklas swallowed hard, unable to determine if William was lying or not. "What do you think?" he said, referring to the man behind him. "This one here wants us to believe he's not a prince." He glared at William. "You think I'm falling for some scam that you tricked us into delivering bad information? Do I look that stupid?"

"No comment," he muttered.

"Well I'm *not* falling for it! You're stuck here," Meklas replied, "at least until Bosh returns."

"*If* he returns. He's doing exactly what he was set up to do," William said. "Aaron and I are here because our contact wanted you to find us along the docks. This was all a scheme to infiltrate your group."

Meklas breathed heavily as William's words raced through his mind. The man behind him appeared uncomfortable, wondering what to believe.

"You think he could be telling the truth?" he whispered.

"Of course not!" Meklas sputtered. "It's a ploy to escape."

"It's no ploy," William assured them. "I'm guessing that Aaron and I are dead regardless of what happens, so I just wanted the pleasure of knowing that *you* know you've been duped by our contact. Your befuddled expression makes it all worth while. And when King Basil's men either arrest you or slay you, why, that will be sweeter still."

Meklas was about to slam the doors shut, knowing William was purposely provoking him, when the tightness in his facial muscles suddenly softened as he figured out the prince's subtle line of attack. "Ha! Your contact, as you say, couldn't possibly be your contact, and therefore I now know your story is false. Nice try, prince."

The armed man started to laugh. "Yeah, Nyla is one of us, so how could she be a spy for you?"

"Quiet!" Meklas snapped.

"Maybe we turned her allegiance to us," Aaron responded matter-of-factly. "Everybody has a price." The expression upon his face didn't reveal a flicker of surprise at the mention of Nyla's name. Inside, however, he felt cold and angry, learning that the woman he had worked next to for several months in the King's kitchen was a conspirator.

"Like that would ever happen," the man continued. "Bosh's wife would never–"

"Would you please shut up?" Meklas said, spinning around and locking gazes with him. "They already got the information they wanted as soon as you opened your big mouth the first time! Why give them any more?"

"*What?*"

Meklas shook his head and sighed. "I'll explain it later." He looked up at William and Aaron, surprisingly calm. "Well, I suppose it doesn't matter that you know about Nyla's identity, because as you said, the both of you will probably end up dead. So enjoy that bit of knowledge in the time you have left, for all the good it'll do you." He offered a cold smile before slamming the doors and barring them shut. He walked back to the farmhouse with the other man.

Inside the barn, William noted a look of shock and disgust upon Aaron's face, sensing the betrayal the boy was feeling. "At least we now know who arranged our abduction, though it doesn't bring us any closer to getting out of here."

"No, it doesn't," Aaron replied, his mind elsewhere. He wandered over to one corner of the barn and dropped down on a pile of hay, tossing his piece of bread aside. "I can't believe Nyla is a spy." He glanced at William. "That was a fine bit of deception against Meklas, though I must confess that I'm disappointed with the results. To think I was rather fond of that woman despite her stern manner."

"Nyla apparently fooled a lot of people, including King Basil," William said as he looked about the barn in the growing light and sighed. Aside from several piles of hay, there were three empty horse stalls and little else inside. And even if one of them could somehow scale the walls to reach one of the windows, both openings were too small for either one to fit through.

"We have to get back to the estate and warn the King."

"Warn him about Nyla and his compromised plans," William replied, taking a seat next to Aaron. "Bosh won't keep us around the moment he realizes we're no longer of any use, so we'll have to make a run for it the first chance we get. I'd rather die escaping than just sit here waiting for them to finish us off at their leisure."

"Agreed," he said with a determined nod, hoping that William didn't detect a wave of fear and dread washing over him.

William hoped that Aaron couldn't sense similar feelings tormenting him as well as they faced the slow march of hours ahead.

The shadows had deepened when William and Aaron woke from a deep sleep sometime before sunset. They noticed that another sack of food and more water had been placed on the ground inside the doors. William smirked.

"I guess we were both so tired that we didn't hear Meklas," he said, wandering over to see what provisions their captors had provided. "More bread, some apples and something that looks like a piece of dried meat. I suppose it could be worse."

"It will be if we don't get out of here," Aaron said. "That means we have to pay attention. No more sleeping the hours away."

"I don't think we could help taking that last nap," he replied, tossing Aaron an apple. "It sneaked up on both of us. We desperately needed rest. But now that we're refreshed, let's think logically about our predicament. We haven't much time–and neither do our friends." William sat down and munched on an apple himself. "So, any ideas?"

"I was hoping you might start the discussion," Aaron replied.

"Very well," he said as a stream of air escaped his lips followed by a protracted and anxious silence. "I have a feeling it's going to be a long and dreary night."

Meklas trudged to the barn the following morning beneath a cold, gray sky, carrying a sack of food and muttering under his breath. Another man from the house followed him with a wooden pail filled with water, equally irritated with their task.

"Bosh better send word today about what to do with these two urchins or I'll start taking matters into my own hands," Meklas said as he approached the barn doors. "Are you with me, Hank?"

The man behind him shrugged. "I don't know. If swords are about to be unleashed near the capital, I think we'll be safer here until it's all over one way or another."

Meklas scowled, disappointed by his associate's attitude. "I'm dying of boredom on this farm. I'll take my chances back in Melinas. You can sit here and rot for all I care." He removed the wooden bar from the doors and opened one of them wide enough to let in some daylight, dropping the food sack on the ground. "I want to see what all our hard work has been building to over this last year or so."

"I just want to be paid," Hank bitterly replied.

"That's all you ever think about. I…" Meklas paused as he scanned the interior. He opened both doors as wide as he could, allowing the full light of day to flood inside. His heart pounded when he saw neither one of his charges. "*What?*"

"What's wrong?" Hank asked, stepping up beside him. When he saw no sign of either boy and noticed that two long boards from the horse stalls had been pulled apart and were leaning against a wall below one of the windows, he expected nothing good to come of it.

Both men rushed in, fearing that William and Aaron had escaped through the window during the night. Meklas held up a hand, signaling Hank to be quiet. "Those openings are too small even for them," he said, studying the boards placed against the wall. "And even if they had managed to shinny up those planks, they still couldn't have reached the window." He smiled like a snake. "They're still in here."

As Hank surveyed one side of the barn, Meklas scouted out the opposite end, quickly drawn to a large pile of hay near one of the busted stalls. As he cautiously approached, he noted a small, dark patch protruding from the hay, guessing it was the tip of a boot. He snapped his fingers to get Hank's attention while at the same time leaning in closer, his hand reaching for a dagger at his side. But before he grabbed his weapon, a narrow length of board suddenly shot out from underneath the hay like a fist and hit Meklas squarely in the jaw, sailing him backward onto the hard ground where he wailed and writhed in pain. William jumped up from beneath the hay and brandished the piece of wood like a sword as Hank stormed at him with his dagger unsheathed.

"I'll fix you!" he cried, his face contorted in anger as he prepared to lunge at William.

"That's what I was hoping for," William said with quiet confidence, raising the piece of wood as if ready to strike.

But just as Hank was about to leap onto the hay, Aaron burst out from beneath another pile behind him, wielding a piece of wood from the horse stall. With all his strength, he slammed it against Hank's upper back, causing the man to stand up straight as if an electric shock had surged through his spine. William didn't miss a beat and heaved the end of his weapon into Hank's stomach like a battering ram an instant later, collapsing him to the floor.

"Let's get out of here!" William cried, swiping Hank's dagger. He leaped off the pile of hay and grabbed Aaron by the arm and headed for the doors, taking the sack of food with them on the way out.

They slammed the barn doors shut and barred them closed with the heavy piece of wood, the cries and groans from Meklas and Hank fading in the background. Without a word, William signaled for Aaron to follow him into the nearby woods where they ran through the trees and undergrowth for several minutes before stopping for a brief rest.

"Why didn't we grab their horses?" Aaron asked when he caught his breath.

"Thought about it," William replied, wiping beads of sweat off his forehead. "But I didn't want to risk getting the attention of that other man still inside the house. We'll be safer in the trees until we put a few miles between us and them. If they don't know which direction we went in, it'll be impossible for them to track us down."

"Do you know which direction we're going in?"

He looked around and shook his head. "Not really. Do you?"

Aaron offered the same answer. "Still, we're better off lost than imprisoned."

"Absolutely. Now we have to get *unlost*," William said encouragingly, "and find our way back to Melinas. We have to warn King Basil that the enemy will strike first. Let's go!"

Like a pair of jackrabbits, the two young men raced through the woods, hoping that time and good fortune were on their side.

Eucádus and King Cedric met with King Basil on the night before the combined armies were to set out north and south. If everything went according to plan, they would engage Drogin's troops two days from dawn tomorrow in surprise attacks. The trio went over the particulars one last time as they enjoyed a light dinner in King Basil's room. The monarch was highly alert and acutely aware of the details regarding the upcoming maneuvers, yet an air of distraction hung over him. Eucádus and King Cedric empathized with his state of mind for they were experiencing it as well.

"No word on either of them?" King Basil asked after they finished discussing military matters.

"Nothing," Eucádus said. "Another scout returned and made a report less than an hour ago. There are no signs of William or Aaron anywhere in Melinas."

"It has been two full days since they left for their walk," King Cedric added. "Dozens of people have been questioned in the streets and along the shore, and though a few knew who Aaron was, none reported seeing him or William on the night of their disappearance. It is most troubling. Are they hurt, lost or abducted?" He paused, not wanting to vocalize the one thought on everyone's mind. "Or dead?"

"If that should be the case..." King Basil rubbed a quivering hand across his face, unable to continue.

"We all feel responsible," Eucádus replied, sensing his fragile state.

King Basil nodded, regaining his composure. "Yes, but maybe tomorrow will bring better news when the morning sun is high. I have no choice but to believe that."

Eucádus watched silently as the King took a sip of tea, noting to himself how old the man appeared. He locked gazes with King Cedric, each realizing that the other had no idea if William or Aaron would ever return.

Dawn broke cold, gray and foggy the following day. A thick, swirling mist covered the lake and shoreline as it had for the past several mornings, seemingly freezing time itself in Melinas and on the adjacent fields until the sun could rise high enough to burn off the ghostly white vapor. Eucádus stepped out of the estate into the grim silence, the damp mist caressing his face upon a soft breeze. In the east, he could barely discern the outlines of the masts on the tallest ships, their tips protruding through the fog only to greet dreary, overcast skies. To his south, he noted the eerie flicker of bonfires in a sea of thick, white mist among the troops. It seemed as if hundreds of eyes were staring back, tormenting him from deep inside a restless dream from which he could not wake. Forgoing a meal inside the estate, he decided to wander among the soldiers and have breakfast with some of them, sensing an anxious expectation pervading the ranks. Everyone would be on edge today, awaiting King Basil's order to move out and confront an uncertain fate in this most mercurial time in their history.

He found Ramsey in the midst of conversation with a group of men keeping warm by a fire. A few soldiers still slept in nearby tents, but many were waking with the change of the guard, unable to find restful sleep. Ramsey handed Eucádus a cup of hot cider and a beef biscuit, inviting him to join the discussion. The two of them would be leading one of the armies south with Captain Silas.

"Some of the men were wondering where we might expect to encounter Drogin's troops," Ramsey said. He warmed his hands over the flames as wisps of fog evaporated in the gush of heat.

"And will King Justin get here in time to aid us?" a voice asked among the crowd.

Eucádus heard the apprehension in that voice which matched the uncertainty reflected in many of the soldiers' faces. He wished he had the right words to bolster their spirits and calm any lingering fears, but commanding an army was a new experience for him. Though he and others in the Clearings had prepared for this moment for years, now that it was upon him, he wondered if he could live up to others' expectations.

"I will not pretend that I know fully what to expect in combat, nor can I foresee the time of King Justin's arrival," he said in a calm, steady voice. "But after meeting and talking with so many of you these last few days, I'm confident that we can face and defeat any challenge Drogin sends our way. We fight for freedom, both for your people in Rhiál and for my countrymen in the Northern Mountains. And because we know this cause is just, and because we know this fight was brought to us by tyrants, we shall seize unwavering strength from that knowledge to use in battle against even the most determined foe." Eucádus scanned the brave faces gathered around him. "I believe such strength is inside each and every one of you gathered on this field, and it will allow our forces to hold their ground when the time comes. And mark my words– when the enemy senses your resolve, they will realize only too late that we fight from a position of power and with a sense of honor that they will never experience nor understand. So in the end, they will never defeat us. It will be you who shall stand atop the hill of victory when the day is finally done, and all of Laparia will know of your triumph."

In the still of a gray morning shrouded in mist, the small group of men gathered around the crackling fire spoke not a word after Eucádus had finished, as if the faint echo of his words still lingering in their minds was too precious to dispel with a boisterous cheer or some clumsy remarks. Several men gathered around the other bonfires nearby also looked on, having heard his stirring address. By their appreciative expressions, Eucádus guessed he had found the right words to provide them at least a bit of hope and courage to face the long march ahead. He gently slapped Ramsey on the shoulder as he walked past, disappearing through the fog to seek out a moment of solitude as the men whispered among themselves.

Eucádus stopped at several other fires over the next hour to speak with more soldiers as the sun climbed above the lake behind a veil of iron gray clouds. But as the early morning wore on and the landscape grew lighter, the fog began to burn off, revealing the faded greens and browns of a dying autumn landscape. All across the south and west fields near King Basil's estate, the gathered troops were acutely aware that the march to the great battle was about to begin. On a strengthening breeze, tiny patches of blue peeked out from the cloud masses above. The billowing fog upon Lake LaShear and blanketing the adjacent lands began to disperse like a frosty breath in wintertime air.

When most first heard the chorus of voices rippling across the field, they assumed that the gathered companies were eager to begin their marches north and south as this had been a moment long waited for. But when a forest of tall ship masts was suddenly revealed upon the lake in the fading mist, each one boldly flying the flag of Maranac, a temporary, leaden hush gripped the gathered armies. And to the south upon a distant ridge and across the grassy field before it, a horde of stony faces awaited silent and still, thousands upon thousands of the enemy clearly revealed as the last wisps of fog were swept away by the awakening breeze or melted in the morning light. It was as if King Drogin's vast army had sprung up from the ground during the night like a field of mushrooms after a pounding rain. Upon cooling lake waters and across the hardened land, the opposition had arrived at King Basil's doorstep. The enemy was prepared to end this bitter conflict and reabsorb the kingdom of Rhiál, whether by force or by surrender, into its turbulent dominion beyond the distant shore.

END OF PART FOUR

NICHOLAS RAVEN

AND THE

WIZARDS' WEB

is continued in

VOLUME 2

~ CHAPTERS 40 - 85 ~

and is concluded in

VOLUME 3

~ CHAPTERS 86 - 120 ~

~ Books by Thomas J. Prestopnik ~

Nicholas Raven and the Wizards' Web
an epic fantasy in three volumes

A Christmas Castle
a novella

The Endora Trilogy
a fantasy-adventure series for pre-teens & adults

The Timedoor - Book I
The Sword and the Crown - Book II
The Saving Light - Book III

Gabriel's Journey
an adventure novel for pre-teens & adults

Visit Thomas J. Prestopnik's official website
www.TomPresto.com

Made in the USA
Middletown, DE
12 June 2022

66826604R10334